Albion Park

Daniel Peppé

Clink
Street

To Charlotte

Chapter 1

June 2014

Owen grabbed a large holdall and one of his guitars from the sleeper bus. His was the last stop. The rest of the band had got off in West London. He slammed the door shut and waved goodbye. As the bus drove off, Chalky leaned out of the window.

'You can breathe out now, you fat git.'

Their tour manager liked to accuse Owen of sucking in his stomach whenever he was around Stuart, the much thinner – and much younger – lead singer from Run for the Shadows.

Once the bus was out of sight, Owen dropped his bag on the pavement and rolled himself a cigarette. Shielding his eyes from the early summer sun, he looked up at Keynes House. Like the other two blocks which comprised the Bevan Estate, the unremarkable low-rise flats needed refurbishment. Age, wear and neglect had left them looking unloved and unlovely. When he was a kid, the shared balconies used to be filled with plants and flowers. These days satellite dishes emerged from the facade like different types of fungi. Balconies were spilling over with bicycles, pushchairs and laundry. No longer testament to the pride of its tenants, the outward appearance of the estate betrayed the transitory nature of so many of its residents.

A man wearing a sleeveless high-vis jacket and an ill-fitting hard hat stood in front of the flats. He was peering through a device attached to a tripod. A colleague wearing a similar coat was standing about thirty feet away, clutching a staff. Owen sucked on his cigarette and watched as the man wandered around. Occasionally he would stop and hold the bar vertical to the ground while his colleague looked through a lens. Owen took a final drag from his cigarette, flicked it to the floor and picked up his stuff.

Owen's flat was one of three on the top floor of the block, the only split-level apartments in the building. He had lived there for the entirety of his forty-one years. After his mum's death, he had taken over the tenancy. He and Jacquie sometimes fantasised about moving to the country or perhaps exerting their right to buy. But these ideas were never close to being financially viable. The best they could hope for was a flat swap. So far, they hadn't seen anything worth relinquishing their flat in Albion Park for.

'Oh… it's you.' Jacquie said, opening the door. 'Where's your key?'

'Were you expecting someone else?'

'I didn't think you were due back until tomorrow.'

Jacquie stepped aside as Owen walked in. He leaned towards her and attempted a kiss, but she was already making her way back into the flat. Owen followed her into the front room.

'How was it?' Jacquie said, sitting down on the sofa.

Owen puffed out his cheeks and nodded his head. 'Yeah, you know. Tiring.'

'Nice to be away, though, right? I wouldn't mind a holiday.'

'It was hardly a holiday.' Owen clenched his jaw; the muscles at the side of his face pulsed with irritation. 'Where are the boys?'

'Harley's out. Dexter's in his room.'

Owen stood at the bottom of the stairs and called out for his son. Dexter soon emerged from his room, smiling. At least someone looked pleased to see him. Sometimes when he was away on tour, Owen would envisage his return home. He would imagine himself walking through the front door holding a bag full of gifts. Delighted to be reunited with her partner, Jacquie would greet him with open arms. Meanwhile the kids, giddy with excitement at their father's return, would be eager to see what presents he had bought them. Jacquie would get them both a drink and, together, the family would sit down for a meal at the mini dining table. Excited at being together once more, everyone would be chattering over each other.

It was rarely, if ever, like this. At least this time, though, Owen had remembered to get the boys a present.

'I've got something for you.'

Owen crouched down and opened the zip on his holdall. After rummaging around for a few seconds, he pulled out a scrunched-up replica Bayern Munich top. He threw the gift at Dexter as he came down the stairs. The boy held the shirt in front of him. He seemed happy. Owen kissed the top of his son's head and ruffled his hair.

'I've got a new game. Do you want to come and see?'

'I'll come up in a bit.'

'Have you got to go away again?'

'No, not for a while.'

Dexter hugged his dad and scampered back up the stairs.

Owen walked into the kitchen. The room was stifling and airless. He grabbed a beer from the fridge and joined Jacquie in the front room.

'Do you want one?' he said, holding up the bottle. Jacquie shook her head and turned on the television.

The front room led out onto a small balcony. Beer in hand, Owen leaned against the balustrade and looked out over the nearly five acres of private park which sprawled out beneath him. The stink from the bins snaked up from below. It was a smell every resident of the small estate was familiar with. During hot weather, it was always that much worse. In mid-summer, the stench would sometimes become unbearable. Occupants of the flats were left with the unenviable option of either opening their windows and allowing in the fetid air or keeping them shut and overheating in their apartments.

Down below, Owen could see Georgi laying gravel out over the path. When he was younger, Owen's mum, confident of knowing where her son would be, used to stand on the same balcony and ring a bell whenever she wanted him to come home. Wherever he was in the park, Owen would always hear the sound. A couple of neighbours began to employ a similar tactic. Initially it confused the children, but they soon learned to recognise the characteristic timbre of each respective bell.

In those days, everyone was allowed access to the park. It didn't matter whether you were one of the lucky home-owners whose house backed onto it or whether you lived in one of the flats on the Bevan Estate. No one cared. Not like now. Anyone who currently lived around Albion Park was left in no doubt of its status as a privately owned and managed park. Several digitally printed aluminium safety signs were screwed to trees facing the flats. Each one warned potential trespassers that they would be prosecuted if caught encroaching upon the land. Not that it made much difference. Not for the kids anyway. If anything, the prospect of getting caught made incursions into the park that much more exciting.

Owen turned around and faced Jacquie, who was still sitting on the sofa.

'There were some workmen outside the flat when I came in just now.'

'Chartered surveyors,' Jacquie replied without turning her head away from the TV. 'They've been there for the last few days.'

'I don't even know what they do.' Owen took a swig of his beer. 'What's the camera for?'

'Apparently, it measures the rise and fall of the land.'

'Why do they need to do that?'

'I don't know. Why don't you go and ask them?'

Jacquie got up from the sofa. Owen followed her into the kitchen. As she reached into a cupboard, he tentatively put his arms around her waist. It felt intrusive, but he wanted to break the ice with an affectionate gesture. It seemed easier if she wasn't looking at him. Leaning forward, he kissed her on the neck. Jacquie continued to rummage through the open cupboard as if oblivious to the other person forlornly clinging to her.

'Are you hungry?' she asked.

Letting go of her waist, Owen stepped back and leaned against the counter.

'No, I ate not so long ago.'

He pulled himself up and sat on the worktop, his legs dangling over the front of the dishwasher.

'Where did you get those shoes?'

Owen looked down admiringly at his white Converse trainers, customised with an embroidered Hokusai wave.

'Amsterdam. Pretty cool, aren't they?'

Jacquie's nose crinkled with disapproval. 'Bit old for shoes like that, aren't you?'

Owen looked down at his feet again. 'I like them.' He took a swig of his beer. Jacquie watched his Adam's apple move rhythmically up and down as he swallowed.

'I bet they were expensive…'

'I didn't have to pay for them.' Owen rubbed at the corner of his mouth with his fingers. The shoes had cost £175. 'We all got a pair.'

He jumped down off the kitchen top and grabbed another beer from the fridge.

'I'm going to need some money,' Jacquie said.

Owen breathed in deeply. 'How much?'

Having reeled off a list of things the boys required, Jacquie proceeded to run through all the stuff they needed for the house. This included a new hoover and a new dishwasher. Owen's heart sank. That was the thing he liked most about being on tour: the suspension of the quotidian. Yes, there was a routine, but you were in a different place every day, with different people. And no one bothered you about faulty household appliances.

'I've paid for the summer clubs, the last two months' council tax… electricity. I also had to buy Harley a new—'

'OK, OK. It's not a competition. I was just asking how much.'

'Six hundred pounds… make it seven.'

'I'll sort something out tomorrow.' Owen shook his head and sighed.

'What?' Jacquie said, taken aback. 'Would you rather I didn't ask for money?'

'Give me a break. I've just walked through the door.'

'Give *you* a break?' Jacquie stared at Owen, her expression stern and unyielding.

'I'm going upstairs to see Dexter.'

Owen's younger son was sitting cross-legged on the floor of the room he shared with his older brother. Owen poked his head around the side of the door.

'Hey, mate. Is it OK if I come in? Is this your new game?'

'Yeah, *Minecraft*. Shall I show you?'

While Dexter explained to his dad the concept of creative mode, the need for shelter and the health bar's importance, Owen looked around the bedroom. It was the same room he had slept in as a kid. The flat had seemed huge then. He was the only one of his friends on the estate who lived in a split-level flat. They all used to marvel at the space and the posh open-tread stairs with gaps in-between. Now it felt as if the walls were closing in on him. The lack of space made him feel anxious. Lots of things made him feel anxious these days. Perhaps it was depression. He wasn't entirely sure what the difference was.

'Basically, there are two different dimensions,' Dexter said. 'The end is the hardest place, like ever, because you must defeat the Ender Dragon, which can be respawned if you put crystals by the exit portal. Dad! Are you listening?'

The door slammed downstairs.

'That's probably Harley,' Owen said.

Dexter looked up at his dad as he walked out of the room. 'Don't you want to watch me build a furnace?'

'You can show me in a bit.'

Harley was standing by the front door talking to his mum in urgent hushed tones. He looked up to see Owen standing on the landing outside Dexter's bedroom. He acknowledged his dad's presence with a swift upward nod of his head.

'Is that it?' Owen said. 'I've barely seen you for the last couple of months. Come here.'

Owen gave his elder son a crushing hug and stepped back to look at him. Harley's tightly curled hazel blonde hair and green eyes revealed little of his Jamaican heritage. Owen was light-skinned himself, but nothing like Harley, who looked like a white boy. He reminded Owen of his mum; he had the same aquiline nose and pronounced jawline. Dexter looked more like him. Or at least Owen liked to think he did. It amazed him that within just three generations his grandparents' shared ethnicity was almost undetectable in his eldest son. Harley had grown since he last saw him. His shoulders were squared off; he looked more thickset. A previously emerging surliness had now settled into his face.

'What have you been up to?' Owen asked. 'You're all sweaty.'

'Not much.' Harley glowered at the floor.

Owen looked down at his son's trousers; there was a large rip in the fabric above his knee. On closer inspection, he noticed a ruddy graze on the side of his wrist.

'Have you been in a fight?'

Harley shook his head.

'We got chased in the park, innit.'

'Who by?' Jacquie said.

Reluctantly, Harley explained how he and a couple of friends had been messing about in the new playground when one of the residents appeared from nowhere and began to shout at them.

'What was he saying?'

'Not much.'

'Care to elaborate?'

Harley frowned at Owen.

'A bit more information please.'

'He said that he was going to call the police and that we had no right to be there.'

'You don't have any right to be in there.'

Jacquie stared at Owen intensely.

'What?' Owen said. 'Harley knows the risks of going in there. It's half the fun.'

'How did you rip your jeans?' Jacquie took Harley's hand and looked at his wrist. 'And this?'

'The man started chasing us.' A hint of a smile appeared on Harley's face. 'He was vexed. I slipped, coming back over the wall. He grabbed Jack by his jacket. Me and Dom did a runner.'

'Did he put his hands on you?' Jacquie asked.

'Nah.'

Harley didn't seem too distressed by the incident.

'Is Jack alright?'

'Yeah, he's fine. He wriggled free.'

Owen looked at Jacquie and raised an eyebrow. 'Not a lot we can do, really.'

'Are you OK with this?'

'The park is privately owned. The residents can do what they like.'

'They can't go around grabbing kids.'

'It doesn't sound like he did. He didn't even touch Harley.' Owen asked his son if he had ever seen the man before.

'Yeah, he lives in the big house next door to the chef.'

'Has he got a moustache?'

Harley nodded. 'Can I go now?'

Owen watched his eldest son take off his shoes and begin to make his way upstairs.

'Where are you off to?'

'My room.'

'I've just got back. Have you not got anything to tell me? What's going on at school?'

Harley looked at his mum.

'He's tired,' Jacquie said. 'It's been a long week.'

As he watched his son shuffling up the stairs, Owen was struck with a profound feeling of loss. He felt the acute sadness of moments never to be repeated. Was it his inability to slow things down or change what had already happened which was at the root of his disquiet? Sometimes it felt like everything around him was accelerating while he remained at the centre, still and unmoving. Harley was growing up so quickly. So much had happened in such a short period. But rather than embrace these changes, Owen could only reflect on how they highlighted his own inertia.

The crack was undoubtedly bigger. In less than a month, the large horizontal fracture had more than doubled in size. Parallel sets of smaller fissures had now established themselves on either side of the primary rupture. They spread outwards across the wall like blood vessels in search of a heart. An online search had informed Kitty that one could estimate the severity of a crack by holding the edge of a pound coin against it. If you could fit one of these coins inside the gap, it was safe to assume you were dealing with something other than cosmetic damage. It didn't say what type of damage one could infer from the width of three-pound coins.

Kitty placed one hand on the wall and the other on a nearby chair and pulled herself up from the floor. Shaking her head in disappointment at the restrictions imposed by an ageing body, she stood up and straightened her back. A ground vibration surged through the basement. Boxed bottles of wine rattled while bits of rubble tumbled from the cracks. Kitty's phone rang.

'Hello? Owen? I can barely hear you. The noise coming from next door makes it almost impossible. What? Look, why don't you just come over? I'll be here for the next hour or so.'

Kitty stomped upstairs towards the boot room, angrily muttering to herself. The door handle was stiff and offered more resistance than usual. She barged it with her shoulder. The door dragged across the floor like a stylus on glass. Kitty walked out into the garden, followed by her two spaniels, Echo and Hermes. The magnolia tree, which Kitty planted the day she moved into Albion Park, was covered in dirt and ash. Next to the tree, a spread of building detritus had obscured the petals of some blood-red peonies. Kitty faced her neighbour's Victorian mini-mansion.

'How many more rooms do you people need?' she yelled.

The Rijkens had lived next door to Kitty for nearly five years. They moved to London from New York soon after the financial crash. Kitty had taken an immediate dislike to Nicholas Rijkens. Within a couple of months of moving into Albion Park, he had ingratiated himself with the park committee through a series of donations. His promise to pay for two new ride-on lawnmowers and a set of carbon steel Japanese gardening tools ensured members of the committee chose to look the other way when his own gardener ripped out a lilac tree, a well-established dog rose bush and a large fig tree. In their place, he planted an avenue of bamboo. The hollow-stemmed plants formed a corridor from his garden gate to the gravel path surrounding the park. Jennifer, Nicholas' American wife, told Kitty that the bamboo was intended to provide continuity. At the bottom of their garden, they had created a miniature replica of the koi pond which Monet built at his house in Giverny. Jennifer told Kitty the ageing painter had also planted a bamboo grove surrounding the pond. Any complaints about the invasiveness of the plant and its potential to colonise had fallen on deaf ears.

When it came to garden planning, there was a time when residents deferred to Kitty's superior knowledge. With the help of a gardener, who was on a retainer from the park committee, she had wanted to create an organic park free from pesticides and unnecessary chemicals. Any deference, however, ground to a halt soon after the arrival of Nicholas Rijkens and his family. The uprooting of the trees was quickly followed by the sacking of the gardener, widespread use of weedkiller and a proliferation of topiary.

As she turned to go back inside, Kitty spotted Owen

coming down the path which ran along the side of the house.

'I thought once you hit forty you had to be on holiday to get away with wearing shorts like that.'

'Not you as well. Jacquie had a go at me yesterday about my shoes.' Owen looked down at his legs. 'They are a bit Italia 90, though, aren't they? It's too hot to wear jeans.' He wiped his hand across his mouth and spat on the floor. 'Urgh. What is that?'

'It's all the filth coming from next door. Look at all this crap that's landed in my garden.' Kitty lifted the large leaves of a plant.

'The noise has been so bad this week, I haven't been able to concentrate. I've still got so much to do for this exhibition. Look at this.' Kitty pushed at the newly resistant boot room door. 'It opened just fine yesterday. The doorframe must have shifted.'

She stepped back and looked up at her house. 'These houses are built on shallow foundations. They don't go down as far as the depth of a double basement. The Georgians and Victorians knew about building on clay; they knew how to avoid subsidence. As soon you dig deeper... well, that's when the problems start.'

'Why's it all taking so long?' Owen asked.

'I heard they had suffered from groundwater inflow. But what do you expect? What was once London's second largest river runs directly underneath us, for God's sake.'

Although Kitty was convinced that one of the two streams which eventually merged around Camden Town and formed the River Fleet ran directly underneath Albion Park, others had a different opinion. Some believed the two streams ran either side of the park, while others argued that both had been encased in sewer pipes. Kitty would always point to the groundwater flooding that was sometimes visible around the park as evidence of high water levels caused by the lost river.

'I did warn them,' Kitty continued. 'You know, when Erin Pearson bought that house, there was a sitting tenant who had the top two floors. The whole family used to sleep in the basement. Every time it rained, a side wall would open up in the basement, and a stream of water would run across the floor, past the children's beds and out the opposite side.'

Owen and Kitty walked back into the house. Because of the noise and showers of dust being pumped from the neighbours' side of the wall Kitty had felt it necessary to keep the French windows shut. Up until just a few days ago, when the hot weather was announced, the Aga had still been on. The residue of warmth which still lingered only added to the heat. Kitty sat down in one of the chairs which surrounded a large oak refectory table.

'There's a pitcher of lemonade in the fridge. Be a darling and bring it over here, please.'

Owen walked into the larder on the other side of the kitchen. He opened the fridge door.

'Do you mind if I have a beer?' he asked, a bottle of lager already in his hand.

The kitchen table was covered in all sorts of crap. Books, magazines and recipes competed for space with kitchen utensils and jars of home-made chutney. Owen placed the jug on the table and sat down next to Kitty. Another subterranean rumble growled up from underneath the kitchen floor. The pitcher of lemonade wobbled. Various items on the dresser began to shake. A few postcards and private view invitations fell to the floor, followed by a plate commemorating the 1984 miners' strike, which smashed to pieces when it hit the ground.

Kitty got up from her seat and walked over to where the

pieces of broken ceramic lay scattered on the floor. She shut her eyes and steeled herself.

'I loved that plate,' she said.

She explained to Owen how a NUM representative had given it to Hugh, her late husband, after doing a piece on the Battle of Orgreave for the BBC. Kitty picked up one of the larger pieces and repeatedly turned it over in her hand.

'Would you get me a dustpan and brush from the utility room?'

When Owen walked back into the kitchen, Kitty was still crouched on the floor, fingering the broken bits of plate.

'I thought the council were supposed to be clamping down on all these basement extensions?'

'It seems everything and anything can be bypassed once you've accrued enough wealth.'

'I hope you're keeping tabs on all the stuff that's been damaged?'

'Don't worry about that.' Kitty put her hand out for Owen to help her up off the floor. 'I'm in regular contact with my lawyer. It's a sorry state of affairs when a planning system favours some schlub's vanity development over the quality of life of their neighbours.'

She sat back down on one of the chairs. 'When did you get back?'

'Yesterday.'

'Is that it now?' Kitty asked. 'Are you all done?'

'For the time being.'

Owen pulled a pouch of tobacco from his pocket. Holding up the packet, he looked towards Kitty for approval. Although she had stopped smoking nearly twenty-five years ago, Kitty didn't object to Owen having the occasional cigarette in the house. She liked the smell of the tobacco while it was still in the packet. The damp, woody aroma reminded her of Hugh.

'It feels like you've been away for ages. I bet the boys were pleased to see you.'

Owen picked at the label on the beer bottle. 'Dexter was. It's hard to get much out of Harley these days.'

'I'm sure it's just his age. You were the same once. Sometimes you barely said a word. It could be quite disconcerting.'

On the wall next to the French windows was a painting of a boat in a harbour. It had been hanging there since Owen was a kid. The artist was an old friend of Kitty's. When Owen was younger, he would stare at the painting for minutes on end but could never work out what was going on. The paint had been applied in thick, gnarly layers. It was rugged and abstract. He always thought the irregular forms were supposed to be a landscape. The idea that it might have been a boat had never occurred to him.

'There was a bit of an incident in the park last night.'

Kitty sighed. 'Oh, what now?'

Owen explained how Harley and his mates had been chased by Simon Landes.

'Apparently they were just fooling around in the play-ground when he turned up out of nowhere and started shouting at them.'

Owen got up from his seat and looked out onto the garden. It was a joyous explosion of colours, rambling yet organised in its chaos. Through spring and summer, an array of different hues was carefully orchestrated by Kitty's accomplished touch, the considered positioning of each flower and plant reflecting her innate understanding of colour.

'What was he saying?' Kitty asked.

'You know, the normal stuff about the park being private property and how they had no right to be there.'

'I wouldn't be surprised if he was hiding in one of the bushes, waiting for trespassers,' Kitty said. 'The man is obsessed.'

'With what?'

'Trying to ensure the gilded cage remains impregnable.'

'He's not doing a very good job of it.'

'And therein lies the problem. You wouldn't believe some of the ideas that get bandied about at the residents' meetings these days. Simon's solution is to build an extra high wall between the flat and the park. That seems to be the most popular idea. The Italian and his husband suggested a barbed wire fence and guard patrols. Can you believe it? Anyone would have thought Simon would be happy the playground was being used at all. I never see anyone out there. Honestly, the amount of money spent on it. It makes me so angry. You know they don't even refer to it as a playground?'

'What else can you call it?'

'A "learning environment".' Kitty showed her distaste for such a phrase by grimacing and enacting a fake shiver.

Owen finished his beer and placed the empty bottle on the table. He looked as if he was about to say something. Instead, he finally lit the cigarette which he had rolled earlier.

'I wanted to ask you a favour.' Owen tapped the cigarette a couple of times on the edge of the ashtray, even though there was no ash to flick. 'Could I possibly borrow a bit of money? I'm sorry to ask.'

'Haven't you just made lots of money?'

'It's just cash flow,' he said. 'I haven't even submitted an invoice yet.'

There was a brief pause. 'OK.' Kitty sounded uncertain. 'Are you sure?'

'Yes… it's fine. But I will need it back this time.'

Owen slapped his forehead with the palm of his hand. 'Shit. I'd completely forgotten about that.' He dragged his hand down over his face. 'I'm sorry, Kitty. I'll pay everything back as soon as I get paid… I promise. OK?'

Kitty peered out over the top of her glasses. She resembled a disapproving teacher.

Owen picked up a letter from the table and waved it at Kitty. 'New pen pal?' he said, changing the subject.

Kitty could tell Owen was worried that she might start asking questions about his finances again. The last time he asked to borrow money, Kitty had enquired whether an alternative career had ever been considered. Owen had become visibly uncomfortable when the conversation then moved onto pensions and financial plans. But as long he continued to ask for money, Kitty believed she was entitled to pry.

'The trust put me on to him.'

'Isn't Belmarsh Category A?'

'It is. Nabeel has been incarcerated for terrorism-related offences.'

'Jesus, Kitty.'

'He was wrongly convicted. I saw a letter from his solicitor. Whatever he was charged for, it didn't amount to terrorism. It seems he was arrested simply for having spent time in Syria. The poor man has been deeply traumatised. I know you disapprove.'

'I don't understand why you can't support a charity that's a bit less… challenging. Maybe one that looks after sick kids… or the homeless.'

'Everyone else is doing that. How will anything ever improve if you don't look after the most difficult parts of society? You should try it. It might make you feel better about yourself.'

Owen looked at the time on his phone. 'I better be going,' he said. 'I've got to pick Dexter up from school.'

'Shall I transfer the money into your account?'

'That would be great. Thanks again, Kitty.'

Owen muttered to himself as he left Kitty's house. He had hoped she might have forgotten about the outstanding loan. He hated asking her for money. It made his calf and neck muscles tense up. Owen walked out onto the street. The sun was beating down on his neck; perspiration trickled from his armpits. He squeezed the sweat-saturated material of his T-shirt and sniffed his fingers. Looking up, he noticed two girls on the other side of the road staring at him. He hadn't gone far before they crossed over and walked towards him. Owen pushed his chest out and flattened his stomach.

'Hey, you're that guy from Run for the Shadows, aren't you?'

Owen smiled enigmatically and carried on walking. The girls walked with him.

'We saw you at the gig in Brighton. Is that where you live?' one of them said, looking at Kitty's house. 'We're practically neighbours. My parents live in that house over there.'

Owen could see his face reflected in the sunglasses of the girl who was doing the talking. The house she pointed to belonged to Max Crossley, the celebrity chef.

'What's your name?'

'Daisy. And this is Ziggy. She was at the concert too.'

'Is Max Crossley your dad?' Owen didn't recognise Daisy. He knew who her dad was, though. Everyone knew Max Crossley.

'Might be.' Daisy tilted her head to one side and lifted her sunglasses. A strand of blonde hair straggled seductively around the edge of her face. Some poppy-red lipstick augmented her natural pout.

'I'm Owen. Has anyone ever told you that you look like Debbie Harry?'

'Who?' Daisy laughed and looked over at her friend, who so far hadn't said anything, and shrugged her shoulders.

'Doesn't matter.' Owen wanted to make a joke but didn't

know what to say. A release of adrenaline produced a fluttery sensation in his stomach. He felt strangely intimidated. He wondered whether such an encounter would have made him nervous when he was younger.

'How long have you lived in that house?' Daisy asked. 'My parents will be pleased. They hated the woman that lived there before.'

'It's not my place,' Owen said. 'And Kitty still lives there. She's a good friend of mine.'

Ziggy tried to suppress her laughter.

'I live in the flats over there.' Owen gestured towards the Bevan Estate. He thought he detected a look of disappointment on Daisy's face. 'How come I've never seen you around here before?'

'I'm not here that much,' Daisy said, with a nonchalant shrug. 'I spend most of my time in LA.'

'Do you work out there?'

'Her dad's got restaurants in California,' Ziggy said. 'She goes out there in the school holidays.'

Daisy elbowed her friend. 'Don't listen to her.'

'School holidays? How old are you?'

'How old do you think we are?'

Daisy raised her eyebrows and smiled at Owen. It was hard to tell how old she was. Her poise and self-assurance were not that of a schoolgirl. She was evidently in possession of a type of knowledge that eludes the young. Her knowing smirk suggested she understood the weakness of men and the power she possessed.

Owen blithely shook his head. It was a convincing expression of indifference.

'Well, it was nice meeting you, Daisy.' He turned to her friend and nodded courteously. 'And you, Ziggy.'

'I'm twenty-three', Daisy said, as Owen turned around and walked away.

Owen stood naked in the bathroom. He looked at himself in the mirror. Like an expectant mother, he held his stomach with both hands. He stood sideways and observed his body from a different angle. If he pushed his belly out as far as it would go, he looked like Mr Greedy. Moving in closer to the mirror, he spotted grey hairs sprouting on his chest like emerging seedlings. He could see them in his stubble too. It wouldn't be long before his hair started to go grey, he thought. Stripped of his standard uniform of jeans, Converse and vintage band T-shirt, Owen was starting to look his age. For so long, his youthful looks and studied cool had belied his advancing years. He had always effortlessly fitted in with whoever he was hired by. But as he got older, the bands and artists he worked with were seemingly getting younger. He was fifteen years older than the drummer from Run for the Shadows. As he considered his naked body, Owen thought how if he were dressed in cords, brogues and a crew neck jumper with a shirt collar underneath, he would look like a teacher. Or any other professional of his age.

A tepid shower provided some respite from the heat of the flat. After weeks of showering in grotty backstage bathrooms, it was a pleasure to be washing in his own bathroom again. Even though the shower head was at chin height, and there was little room to manoeuvre.

After a few minutes, he got out, put on a towelling robe and went downstairs. Jacquie was at work. The kids were at school. He was on his own for the first time in ten weeks. Owen sat down on the sofa in the front room and rolled himself a joint. The early afternoon sun poured in through the windows. The hazy beams of light highlighted the sloughed-off skin cells and fibres, which swirled around the room. He picked up his phone, put on the new Beck album and scrolled through his messages. Conrad had sent him an old picture of the band they used to be in. It was from the front cover of a French magazine: *Attention. Ici vient The Rubber Band.*

Owen replied to the message.

– *Where did you find that? I've not seen it before*
– *Packing up the flat…moving next week. Found loads of stuff. More to come.*

Conrad sent through another photo. This one was of Owen onstage at a European festival. The picture had been taken from behind the drummer. Owen was topless and facing the camera. It was the biggest crowd they had ever played in front of. Owen enlarged the photo on the screen and admired the pose he had adopted for the photographer. His legs were apart, his back was arched. He was leaning back slightly, his fingers splayed high up on the fretboard. The stance was ironic, a parody of a guitar hero. But he looked good. A patina of sweat emphasised the contours of his physique. The veins on his biceps were visible. Owen saved the picture to his phone and then uploaded it to his Instagram account with various obligatory hashtags.

#tbt #therubberband #timeflies and the caption: *me when I could still get away with going on stage topless.*

He always felt ashamed after posting pictures of himself. It was all so transparently needy. But the comments which landed soon after always gave him a lift. For his previous Throwback Thursday post, Owen had uploaded a still from an old promo he had once been an extra in. He clicked on the photo to see who had liked it. Daisy Crossley had started following him. He clicked on her profile and spent the next thirty minutes hovering over photos of her in various stages of undress. A strategically placed sheet or improvised sticker ensured not everything was revealed. But it left little to the imagination. When one of her twenty-eight thousand followers left a comment underneath a picture of Daisy and her friend Ziggy locked in a topless embrace, expressing his desire – to be the meat in that sandwich – he was excoriated by Ziggy for even looking in the first place.

In a different photo, Daisy was sitting with her back to the camera, looking over her shoulder. Her arse was close to the lens. A pair of thong-like bikini bottoms were lost in her bum crack. Someone had written:

– y u always posing like u askin to be banged???

The question provoked an onslaught of outraged followers furiously leaping to Daisy's defence.

– the fact that ur even associating a photo of the female body to 'asking for it' mate ur cancelled.

Another follower or friend had written:

– wtf u taking the way she sits as asking for it??? fuck off w ur rapist mentality.

Many of Daisy's posts triggered a conversation about whether she was a feminist or a slut. Daisy mostly seemed to stay out of the arguments which raged underneath her pictures. Although one time when she wrote:

– U may not like my version of empowerment but don't hate on me for it

Someone else replied:

– ur just a porn star but without the paycheck loool.

Later that afternoon, Jacquie returned home early from work. Even though the balcony windows were open, she immediately recognised the distinctive smell of Owen's preferred type of hash. She hated him smoking around the house. Her concern was that the boys, particularly Harley, might one day interpret their father's refusal to quit smoking pot as a justification for their own use.

Jacquie walked into the front room. Owen was fast asleep on the sofa. His open bathrobe revealed a slightly sagging gut that had flopped inelegantly to one side. On the floor next to him was a dirty ashtray, a half-smoked spliff resting on the side. Jacquie called out his name a few times, each exhortation louder than the previous one. Finally, he woke up.

'It's nearly three-thirty,' she said. 'Have you been lying there all day?'

Looking bewildered, Owen closed his bathrobe and sat up on the sofa. 'So what if I have?' he said. 'I'm knackered. I haven't slept properly for ages.'

The way she looked at him, Owen recognised that Jacquie perceived him as something separate from herself. While she had been at work, he had been lying around smoking dope. It meant little to her that he had been away working for the last ten weeks. She had never considered touring as work. As far as she was concerned, Owen's vocation was part of an extended adolescence.

It hadn't always been that way. When they first met, Jacquie had been impressed by his band's appearance in the magazines she read. But, as she often cruelly reminded him, his career had since followed a reverse arc of progress. He had been moderately successful at the beginning, but an accumulation of experience and expertise had, counterintuitively, been coupled with diminishing returns. Run for the Shadows were doing well. But Owen was a stand-in replacement for Jonny, their founding member and guitarist who had been rehabilitating for the last year after a skiing accident.

Jacquie bent over and picked up the ashtray. Owen noticed the small muscles around her left eye twitching. The skin at the corner looked thin and had collapsed into folds, creating tiny heaps of excess skin. He thought about the picture of Daisy looking over her shoulder at the camera. Owen got up from the sofa and stretched.

'Those bins stink,' he said.

'Don't leave the windows open then.'

Jacquie walked into the kitchen to empty the ashtray. Owen followed her in and poured himself a glass of water.

'The surveyors are outside again,' Jacquie said. 'There are some builders with them today. They were digging around the wall next to the park.'

'Maybe they've finally agreed to build that community centre.'

Jacquie reached into the cupboard for some Nurofen. Owen could tell his presence in the flat irritated her. No doubt she had been looking forward to having some time on her own before the boys came home. She seemed rattled by the sight of him sleeping in the middle of the day. He wondered how she would react if he tried to instigate sex. What would happen if he told her: I'm going to fuck you now? That's what he used to do. He could almost make her come simply by telling her what he intended to do.

There was no way he would try something like that now. Owen wasn't prepared to risk the humiliation an attempt at spontaneous passion would no doubt incur. He could just imagine the look of disgust on Jacquie's face as unannounced he pressed his mouth close to her head and started to whisper filth into her ear. She would probably spit on him. Or call the police.

Chapter 2

July 2014

Nicholas Rijkens sat in his home office, his hands covering his face. Barely able to bring himself to look at the figures, he peered at his monitor through a gap in his fingers. Only ten months ago he had stood on a stage at the Chedi Hotel in Andermatt and revealed his top investment ideas for the coming year. Nicholas told the audience of industry peers and investors about a company that manufactured liquid crystal polymers. According to him, M&T Technologies not only possessed a low risk of negative movement but also the potential for double-digit appreciation.

Ever since the depths of the financial crisis, when he had achieved an eleven per cent positive return for Westbourne Investment Partners, Nicholas had been earmarked as a rising star. Someone who had the potential to become one of the leading event-driven investment managers. When he decided to launch his own flagship fund, observers were surprised by the speed at which he reached over two hundred million in assets. Always on the search for potentially market-moving insights, investors began to listen out for his pronouncements. Increasingly he found himself being invited to talk at investment seminars. He had a reputation as the fund manager who had managed to keep his head while others around him were losing theirs.

Confidence in his latest investment recommendation had been sky-high. Ever since M&T Technologies agreed on a takeover offer from the Minton Corporation, the plastics sector had rallied dramatically. This meant that the Minton Corp would have to increase its bid. If they didn't, M&T Technologies would remain independent but bolstered by the response of the industry. Aside from Nicholas, who bet a large proportion of Delta's fund, several other funds also invested heavily in M&T Technologies. When Nicholas stood on the stage and predicted huge returns for investors, shares were trading above the Minton Corp offer price. By March of this year, they had increased their takeover offer. The deal was now worth nearly fifteen billion dollars.

Recently, though, things had taken a turn for the worse. Having cleared the necessary global regulatory jurisdictions, there were fears that to promote domestic industrial policy (specifically Huawei's control of the new 5G technology) the Chinese Ministry of Commerce might hold out on the deal. Suddenly, shares in M&T were being offloaded. From a high of one hundred and eighteen dollars in March, shares had dropped by nearly fifteen per cent. Nicholas knew he would have to offload his entire position before the deal collapsed completely. This would mean significant losses for his fund. And a black mark against his reputation.

'Would you like some of this pomegranate juice? It's yummy.'

Jennifer, Nicholas' wife, was standing at the door of his office holding two glasses. She was wearing cropped leggings and a matching vest.

'No, I'm OK, thank you.'

'You should try some, it's so good for you. It's full of anti-oxidants and vitamin C. I just made it.' Jennifer walked towards Nicholas and handed him a glass of juice. 'You haven't forgotten that you're looking after the kids this afternoon, have you?'

Nicholas threw his head back and groaned.

'Oh, Nick! It won't be for long. All you've got to do is organise some food and maybe entertain them for a couple of hours.' Jennifer's thick Rhode Island accent emphasised each quick-fire syllable.

'A couple of hours?' Nicholas said. 'How long is your yoga session?'

'One hour. But then Tanya and I are going out for lunch. We won't be long. I did tell you all of this.'

'I know, I know. I just don't understand why you had to give Lovely and Agrippina a day off on the same day.'

'Apart from Christmas, it's the only day of the year they both take off together. It's a big deal, this Barrio Fiesta. Lovely told me it's the largest gathering of Filipinos anywhere outside of the Philippines.'

'What time does Camille's Mandarin lesson finish?'

'Twelve thirty. I'll be back before music lessons start.'

'What shall I give them for lunch?

'I don't know. Jeez. Take them out if you want. Anyone would think you've never looked after your own kids before.'

Nicholas looked wounded. Jennifer perched herself on the desk in front of her husband, her legs slightly spread. Nicholas could perceive the mound of her pubis through the fabric of her leggings.

'What's wrong?' Jennifer placed a finger underneath his chin and lifted his head, so his eyes met hers. 'You know it will get better. There's always blue sky after a storm. You've just got to get through this bit.'

'It's all my fault,' Nicholas said, pulling his head away. 'I should have seen it coming. Or at least got out earlier. CJ warned me.'

Jennifer leaned forward, her hands resting on her knees. 'Would a blowy make you feel better?'

Before he could respond, Jennifer had crouched down in front of him and was wrestling with his belt buckle. One of her nails caught the flesh around his hips as she tried to pull his jeans down.

'Ow!' Nicholas exaggeratedly rubbed the affected area.

'Help me out here. You need to lift your ass off the seat.'

Nicholas sighed extravagantly. His reaction was more like that of someone at the cinema who had an end-of-aisle seat and had to keep on standing up to let other ticket holders through. He tightly grasped the arms of his seat as Jennifer tried to rouse his cock. The sight of his wife attempting to elicit a reaction made his toes curl. Nicholas dug his nails further into the leather-bound arms of his chair while Jennifer placed his timorous penis in her mouth. After a while, she looked up from between his legs.

'You need to relax,' she said. Nicholas threw his head back while Jennifer continued to toil determinedly below. 'I'm not having much luck here, am I?'

Nicholas looked down; Jennifer was holding him between her thumb and forefinger.

'I'm still full from breakfast,' he said.

'I'm worried about you, honey. This keeps on happening.' Jennifer remained on the floor, her legs curled up underneath her. 'You know, I recently read that this sort of thing can sometimes stem from—'

Nicholas cleared his throat, usually a signal that he no longer wished to proceed with the conversation.

'Maybe you should talk to someone?' Jennifer stood up, took her ponytail out of its hairband and re-did it.

'I don't need to talk to anyone,' Nicholas snapped. 'I'm

stressed out about work. I can't concentrate.' He tucked his shirt into his trousers. 'Shouldn't you be getting on? Your friend will be here soon.'

'Wow – what a gorgeous house. How long have you guys been here?'

'About five years now,' Jennifer said.

'I love what you've done to it. It looks so...' Tanya scrunched up her face as she searched for the right word. '... contemporary.'

Internally the Rijkens' house offered few clues to its Victorian past. Apart from the front facade, its nineteenth-century heritage was mostly eschewed and replaced with an ultra-modern architect's showpiece. A formal sitting room and dining room off the front foyer of the house was a nod to its background, as was the odd chandelier and bit of crown moulding. But mainly the house consisted of open areas and multi-levels occupied by different living spaces.

'How's the basement coming on?' Tanya asked.

'Don't ask. It's taking so much longer than we'd hoped.'

Jennifer had met Tanya Hardman at the last park committee meeting; she and her husband Gary had recently bought one of the townhouses in the new development on the other side of the park. Christened New Park Villas by the developers, they were built on the site of a block of flats that had previously been used as a hostel for ex-servicemen and women. Modelled on the classical architecture of Nash's Regent's Park villas, all five houses had been granted access to the park. The developers paid the other keyholders eight thousand pounds each for the privilege. To avoid any capital gains issues, this money was then placed in a fund to finance the future upkeep of the park. Overriding the veto of a couple of members, the park committee decided to withdraw twenty-two-thousand pounds from the fund to pay for a new playground.

Failing to introduce himself, Nicholas walked into the room and made himself a coffee.

'You must excuse my husband,' Jennifer said. 'Just because *he's* having a bad day, he wants everyone else to as well.'

Tanya was dressed in a loose-fitting vest and a small pair of tight white training shorts. As he leaned in for an introductory peck on the cheek, Nicholas caught a glimpse of the top of her breasts. They appeared rock solid and immovable, as if hewn from granite. Tanya smiled at Nicholas. The skin on her face was taut and devoid of wrinkles, her eyes an ultra-vivid green. Everything looked slightly unnatural but not glaringly so. It was more about the cumulative effect various procedures had had on her face. Nicholas wondered when the tipping point occurred. At what moment did cosmetic surgery cross the threshold from being a confidence boost, a minor alteration here and there, to something more akin to self-mutilation. Something which alludes to deeper psychological issues. Tanya wasn't at that point yet, she was still attractive, but it wouldn't take many more procedures to deliver her to the cusp.

Nicholas leaned against one of the kitchen units. 'How are you and your husband enjoying life in the park?'

'I tell you what, we absolutely adore it. I used to live just around the corner. When we saw the prospectus for the development, it became our mission in life to grab one of these places. It's a dream come true.' Tanya barely paused for breath, her whirlwind sentences often punctuated with nervous laughter.

'I thought everyone might be a bit up themselves,' she continued. 'Do you know what I mean? But we've been made to feel so welcome. I was just saying to Jen how gorgeous your house is.' Tanya rested her hand on Jennifer's shoulder. 'You've done it up so nice. All the houses around here are beautiful. We feel blessed.'

'I haven't been inside any of the new places,' Nicholas said. 'But I would say that it's one of the best-looking new developments I've seen. Such a massive improvement on what was there before.'

'We're hosting the next residents' meeting at our house,' Tanya said. 'I can give you a tour then if you like?'

Jennifer handed Tanya a glass of juice. 'Shall we get started?'

Before walking out of the room with Jennifer, Tanya turned to Nicholas. 'Lovely to have finally met you,' she said, smiling.

Nicholas returned the sentiment before asking Jennifer what time Georgi was due to clean the koi pond.

'About four o clock, I think. We'll be finished way before then.'

Nicholas watched with disdain as Luc and Camille stripped their pizzas of the toppings and placed clumps of cheese and onion on a plate next to them. Luc had a look of disgust on his face as he shook the cheese from his fingers. It was as if they were covered in shit rather than mozzarella. Once they had got rid of the bits which engendered such displeasure, all that was left were two sorry-looking bits of dough with a derisory smear of sauce on top.

'I thought you both wanted pizza?' Nicholas asked.

Camille wrinkled her nose. 'It's got too much stuff on it.'

'That's what a pizza is.' Nicholas said. 'A flat round base of dough with a load of stuff on top.'

Aware of the hypocrisy inherent in his type of parenting, Nicholas wasn't prepared to labour the point. He often berated Jennifer for being lax and letting the kids get away

31

with too much. If his wife had been at the table, he probably would have kicked off about Luc and Camille's reluctance to eat their food. Jennifer and the two nannies were left in no doubt as to how Nicholas expected his children to be raised. On those rare occasions when he looked after them on his own he was not nearly as strict.

Camille pushed her plate away and began counting in Mandarin. As she raced from one to thirty, she kept one eye on her dad, vainly hoping he would acknowledge her efforts. Nicholas, however, was much more interested in his device. He had just received an email from Jay Brandon. Jay was responsible for compiling the Luxury Investment Index for one of the big banks. He often sent Nicholas emails containing investment suggestions or the names of artists Nicholas should follow.

Desperate to get his attention, Camille began to bark demands at her father in Dutch. Both children were bilingual, their accents perfect in both English and Dutch. Nicholas' accent, on the other hand, was unplaceable, an indeterminate Dutch/American hybrid with a hint of received pronunciation thrown in for good measure. Even as a schoolboy in Amsterdam, his accent had possessed an East Coast intonation. A reflection of a childhood obsession with all things American.

'Sorry, sweetie,' Nicholas responded in Dutch. 'I'm in the middle of some work.'

Nicholas carried on reading his email. This time Jay had sent him photographs of the work of a young artist called Melt, whose prices, he advised, were about to soar. Nicholas studied the photographs. Each picture contained nothing more than the painted outline of a dancing figure. Drips of paint poured from the figure's hands and feet and collected in pools at the bottom of the canvas. The only difference between the various paintings was that each figure was rendered in a different pose and colour.

Jay reported that the artist had brands and fashion labels tripping over themselves to work with him. He had already designed some trainers for Louis Vuitton and more recently collaborated with Ace Hotels on a collectable cutlery set. Each item in the collection featured one of his trademark figures engraved into the handles. Nicholas replied to the email. He was interested in learning more about Melt and asked Jay if he could find out about prices.

'Right, you two.' Nicholas finally looked up from his phone. 'Shall we go out to the playground?'

Resistant to his father's suggestion, Luc asked if he could stay home and practise his cello.

'No, come on, Luc. It's a beautiful day. You can practise later.'

'My tummy hurts,' Luc said, wincing. 'I don't feel like going to the park.'

The feigned stomach ache was a common avoidance tactic of Luc's. He wouldn't have even tried such an overused strategy with his mum. But the boy sensed there was still some mileage in the ploy where his father was concerned.

'Let's go, Luc. A bit of fresh air will do you some good. Your tummy ache can't be that bad; you didn't even mention it during lunch.'

'There's nothing to do in the park,' Luc said.

Camille was also reluctant but less inclined than her elder brother to create a fuss. Nicholas was just keen to get them outside. If they stayed indoors, he would inevitably have to play with Camille while Luc practised his cello. There were too many builders' tools in the garden to let them play out there on their own. If they went to the park, Nicholas could sit on one of the benches and do some work while the kids entertained themselves in the playground.

'Will you play hide and seek with us, Papa?' Camille asked her father.

'I will in a bit.'

'No! Now. We're bored.'

Nicholas raised his eyes from his screen and shook his head in disbelief.

'You've got this incredible new playground all to yourself. You possess vivid imaginations. Go and play… make up a game. Do whatever it is children are supposed to do.'

Luc stood at the bottom of a rope ladder and made a desultory attempt to climb it. It was only seven rungs high, but having got to the third one he decided that was high enough and started to come back down. Cautiously he tried to place his left foot on the rung beneath him but couldn't secure a foothold. He dangled his leg, hoping the ladder might miraculously attach itself to his foot and assist his descent without any further effort on his behalf. Meanwhile, his little sister tried to walk across a balance beam about ten inches off the ground. She kept calling out for her dad to come and hold her hand as she attempted to walk across it.

'Do it on your own, sweetie. Nothing will happen if you fall off.'

Camille stretched out her arms and, with considerable uncertainty, placed her left foot on the beam while her right foot remained on the platform. Before moving any further, she looked over her shoulder to ensure her father was watching. Tentatively, she placed her right foot on the beam and slowly moved her left foot a little further forward. 'Papa, Papa. Look at me. Look at me.'

Nicholas looked at his daughter, wobbling precariously. She had progressed about fifteen inches and didn't seem likely to recover her balance.

'I'm watching,' Nicholas said, sounding deliberately disinterested. He didn't want to convey the impression that he was proud of his daughter's attempts to cross the beam. The theory was that, if he appeared unmoved by his children's efforts, they might push themselves further.

After his younger brother's accident, Nicholas' own parents virtually ignored him and his elder sister for the remainder of their childhood. And while Nicholas had no intention of ever being as cruelly negligent as his own parents had been to him, he did believe their indifference to his achievements had spurred him on to do even better. Nicholas had understood that for the foreseeable future his little brother would be the sole focus of his parents' attention. They were mentally, physically and financially consumed by the demands of looking after a quadriplegic child. His mum, embittered and resentful at her new role as a round-the-clock carer and terrified by the family's now compromised financial status, was determined not to let Nicholas forget that he and his sister were supposed to have been keeping an eye on Thomas when the accident happened. Nicholas had hoped his status as a high achiever might have helped re-focus some of that lost attention. His children, however, didn't seem to possess a shred of that determination. Nicholas almost resented Luc and Camille for the ease with which they capitulated to even the most benign of challenges.

Luc had moved on to the new sensory gardens by now and was trying to play 'Für Elise' on the outdoor xylophone.

Meanwhile, Camille had also given up on the balancing beam and sat cross-legged on the ground, making a daisy chain. Finally, the two children seemed to be occupying themselves, granting Nicholas the opportunity to send some emails.

Jay Brandon had replied to his message. He had already contacted Melt's gallery for an accurate breakdown of prices. If he moved quickly, Jay believed that Nicholas could pick up an original painting for £150,000. In a year, he promised, the same painting would be worth maybe five times as much. Nicholas looked again at the photos. They seemed familiar. He wondered whether he had seen them at Art Basel. Last year, a Swiss investor had flown him out and introduced him to the art fair director. Nicholas had been fortunate enough to receive a tour before the feeding frenzy began. Following the director's advice, Nicholas had bought three works of art, including a large piece made of found lettering which just said 'Motherfucker'. Having only lost her own mother the previous month, Jennifer couldn't believe the insensitivity of her husband's purchase. Nicholas sold the piece at an auction in London, making a tidy £70,000 profit in the process.

A scream followed by a succession of howls ripped through the tranquillity of the park. Immediately Nicholas knew it was Luc. He jumped up from the bench, grabbed Camille and ran towards the screams. Luc was lying next to the Bug Hotel writhing on the floor, his blood-soaked hands covering his face.

'Oh my God.' Nicholas dropped Camille on the floor and sprinted to his son. 'Luc. Luc. Are you OK?'

Shocked and obviously in pain, Luc couldn't stop shrieking. Nicholas began to prise his hands away from his face. The boy started to hyperventilate. There was a gash above his left eye, which was bleeding heavily.

Nicholas roughly pulled Camille's T-shirt over her head and used it to stem the blood.

'What happened?'

Luc was too shocked to explain anything. Meanwhile, Camille had also started to cry and was trying to run back to the house.

'I want my mummy,' she sobbed.

Nicholas instructed Luc to hold the T-shirt to his head and ran off to grab Camille.

'Camille,' he shouted, 'you are not bloody helping.' Nicholas firmly put his daughter back down on the floor and warned her not to move.

'Let me have a look.' Luc permitted his father to inspect the wound. Thankfully the shirt had absorbed most of the blood. Although nasty, the cut didn't look too serious. The panic which had overwhelmed Nicholas when he spotted Luc lying on the floor began to dissipate. The thought of something happening to his son under his watch was too awful to contemplate. Even after all these years, the horror of his brother's accident still intruded on his mind. The traumas of that day were so readily accessible. It didn't take much for Nicholas to convince himself it was all about to happen again.

Luc lay on the sofa while Jennifer and Tanya cleaned up his face and attempted to calm him down. Jennifer held his hand, trying to elicit information, while Tanya mopped his brow with a damp flannel.

'It will be one of those little shits from the flats,' Nicholas said, fetching a glass of water from the fridge. 'And that bloody woman from next door has the temerity to suggest they should be allowed access to the park.'

Jennifer flashed Nicholas a look which suggested his comments were not helping anyone.

'Try and talk us through what happened,' Jennifer said to Luc, her voice calm and compassionate.

'I was playing....' Luc repeated the words a couple of times before finally composing himself. 'I was playing on the xylophone... something hit me on the head. It was a stone... or a rock. It hurt so much... I couldn't....' He started sobbing again, his words, lost in a torrent of tears and snot, rendered unintelligible.

'You poor thing.' Tanya ran her fingers through Luc's hair.

'Did you see you anyone who might have thrown something?' Jennifer smiled lovingly at her son.

Luc shook his head. Jennifer looked at Nicholas and shrugged her shoulders.

'This was obviously done on purpose,' Nicholas said.

'How do you know that?'

'Oh, come on.'

'Where are you going?' Jennifer asked. Nicholas had started to make his way towards the back door.

'I'm going to find the person who did this.'

'Shouldn't we just call the police?' Not wishing to upset Luc any further, Jennifer's voice remained measured.

'By the time they arrive,' Nicholas said, 'whoever did this will be long gone.'

'They'll be gone anyway,' Jennifer said. 'Even if you did find the culprit, what are you going to do? It was probably children. It might have been an accident or a game that went wrong.'

'No way was this an accident.'

Chapter 3

'It was strange seeing those pieces again. After all this time, I had almost forgotten what they looked like. They're so different to nearly everything I've done since.'

'The paintings you did after Hugh died were guided by raw emotion. They were instinctive. Your more recent work requires so much planning.'

Kitty was sitting in the front room of her house talking to her old friend Ed. Ed had been looking after the dogs overnight while Kitty went to Cornwall to attend the opening of a group exhibition. 'Aftermath' was a show exploring *the consequences of death and its impact on the artist.* It featured three of Kitty's paintings.

'They're too derivative,' Kitty said. 'They look like Clyfford Still knock-offs.'

'And what's wrong with that?' Ed said. 'People like them.'

'Yes, they seem to. I just wish people always responded in that way. I can always tell when someone is genuinely moved. They tend not to say much. Often, they simply stand in front of the piece and... well, absorb it. Equally, when someone is unaffected, they're prone to over-enthuse. They'll often waffle on about how the work made them feel or what it reminded them of. People start searching for lofty comparisons or revert to that unintelligible artspeak you're so fond of spouting.'

Ed raised his hands as if they were claws and made a hissing sound.

'Speaking of which,' Kitty said. 'What the hell is cut-and-paste culture?'

She was referring to a piece Ed had recently written for the online arts magazine he edited. In it, he had described Kitty's recent work as being *a paean to days gone by but with a nod to contemporary cut-and-paste culture.*

'It's the world we live in,' Ed said, as if repeating some ancient lore.

'Aah, I see. So that explains it then.'

'Look, jokes aside, I think you've really hit on something with these collage films. Whether you realise it or not, you've managed to make an interesting comment on our relationship with contemporary culture.'

'Is that just because I refuse to use a computer?'

'Partly,' Ed smiled. 'But also, I think by sticking to these more traditional mediums, you allow accidents to occur. The unexpected can still intervene. This doesn't happen in the digital realm.'

Kitty laughed and shook her head disbelievingly.

'You may laugh,' Ed continued, 'but I would argue your latest work represents our new reality.'

'Oh, you've completely lost me now.'

'You see, our brains have to absorb so much information these days. So much more than we ever used to. Consequently, we've developed new methods to help us process all this knowledge. We cut out the bits we find useful and discard the rest. In a way, we're creating our very own bespoke collages.'

'What was it I was saying about unintelligible artspeak? I've always said critics can make sense of anything.'

'Oh, piss off.'

'Look, it's kind of you to say these things.' Kitty rested

her hand on Ed's. 'But I'm not sure if anyone else would agree. I wish I could say it was all part of a master plan. But the truth is, my intentions are so much more prosaic. I simply find editing with a splicer easier than using some bit of fancy software that will take me years to learn. Life is too short. I have a finite number of days left on this planet. I don't intend to waste them staring at a computer screen.'

'Instead, you intend to spend them wrapped up in endless reels of 16-millimetre film?'

Known in those days as The Rev, Ed and his sometime boyfriend, The Judge, befriended Kitty soon after she and Hugh moved into Albion Park. The two of them were members of Circle of Shame, a music and performance art collective that occupied one of the many squats surrounding the park. In those days, no one with money or options wanted to live around Albion Park. The middle classes had all upped sticks and left for the suburbs. The inner city was the preserve of either those without a choice or those hankering after an alternative lifestyle. Still struggling to find its post-war identity amid a landscape of gloom and industrial chaos, London was a city in decline. Kitty, however, believed she had found her spiritual home among the misfits of Albion Park. Functional families lived alongside musicians, students, anarchists, poets and avant-garde communes. Everyone was allowed access to the park, regardless of whether you were a keyholder or not.

Kitty asked Ed if he had time to come up to her studio and look at some of her recent work. 'I would be interested to see what you think.'

'Do you know what?' Ed said coyly. 'I snuck up there last night and had a peek. I couldn't help myself.'

'I thought you might. Well... what do you think?'

Aside from the collage films, Kitty had also been working on a series of boxed assemblages for an upcoming exhibition. For a while now, these boxes had become her preferred medium. The move from painting to three-dimensional collage and film had reinvigorated a previously flagging career.

'I honestly think they're lovely.'

'Lovely?' Kitty couldn't help but sound disappointed.

'Yes, they're so poetic. I love the piece you're currently working on. You know, I think I might have been there that day.'

The boxed assemblage Ed was referring to depicted one of the impromptu and bizarre performances that sometimes used to occur around the park. A young man, dressed only in a harness and cheered on by onlookers, had climbed out onto a window ledge on the fourth floor of one of the houses. In big white letters on the front of the building, he had painted the slogan: 'It's Going to Get Worse.' Kitty was working from some photographs she had taken that day. She had cut out the man and the slogan from the photo and glued them to an old oil painting of hers. The picture depicted one of the picnics which used to take place in the park. As long you bought a dish, everyone was welcome. Around the base of the box, Kitty had placed various found objects, including the inside of an old Edwardian pocket barometer she had once dug up in one of the flower beds.

'I worry they're too decorative,' Kitty said. 'Too crafty. Do you know what I mean? I want them to be challenging and political. Not lovely and poetic.'

'Perhaps it's hard to be challenging within this medium.' Ed paused for a moment. He had a habit of twitching his nose in-between sentences. 'But I would definitely say they are political,' he continued. 'These pieces tell the story of the people who used to live around here. Looking at it now, who would believe it was once full of anarchists and scumbags?'

'Exactly,' Kitty said. 'I wanted to remind people that

places like Albion Park weren't always populated by arrivistes and hedge funders.'

'Speaking of arrivistes, I bumped into one of your lovely neighbours while I was out walking the dogs.'

'Oh, really?' Kitty made a face as if she was expecting Ed to tell her something awful.

'Very tall American woman. She's got one of those revolting Pomeranian dogs. It looks like a puffed-up loo brush with bulging eyes. The little shit wouldn't stop barking at me.'

'That's....' Kitty clicked her fingers as she tried to remember her name. 'I know it perfectly well. Her husband is quite a well-known plastic surgeon. He specialises in penile implants, would you believe.'

'You're kidding?'

'No, really. Apparently, he invented a type of prosthesis that simulates an erection. What is their name?'

'Don't worry,' Ed said. 'It will come. Whatever her name was, she asked me if I lived around the park. When I told her—'

'Christine and Seth Pritzker,' Kitty interjected loudly. 'Sorry, please continue.'

'When I told her that I was a dog walker, she said non-residents were obliged to keep their dogs on leads.'

'So, what did you say?'

'I told her that I had been walking dogs in the park for years. And in all that time, I had never heard of such a rule. More to the point, I asked her if she intended to pick up the turd which her dog had just curled out on the lawn.'

Kitty gasped and put her hand over her mouth.

'Do you know what she said?' Ed continued. 'She said it was none of my business and that I was speaking above my pay grade.'

Once Ed had gone home, Kitty tried to get some work done in her studio. The noise coming from next door made it difficult to concentrate. At weekends the builders were supposed to stop before 1pm at the latest. For the last two Saturdays, though, they had carried on working until well after three. Kitty had already left a message for her lawyer. The two of them had now compiled a list of grievances. These included structural concerns, noise pollution, week-end working, lack of communication and general damage to property. More recently, Kitty had noticed an increased amount of vermin in the garden. There was also evidence of rats in the basement. Or at least something had been sharpening its incisors by gnawing on the pipework. Georgi had her told that building work often resulted in the dis-placement of the local rodent population. It was another complaint to add to an ever-growing list. Unable to work, Kitty decided to take the dogs for a walk.

So as not to have to look at the crowded mass of bamboo planted outside the Rijkens' house, Kitty took a right turn outside her own gate and began walking anticlockwise around the perimeter of the park. Apart from the occasional opening, the park's outer edge was almost entirely enclosed by tunnels of leaning trees and bushes. Kitty walked past the Bevan Estate; its ruinous appearance was the source of much disconcertion among residents of the park. The sprawling ground cover of herbs on the flower bed directly beneath the wall, which separated the park from the flats, was flattened and trodden down: a crushed patch of comfrey providing evidence of repeated incursions from the flats.

All around the park, a sequence of paths criss-crossed from one side to the other, each one passing through a dif-ferent secluded glade. Kitty carried on along the circular path. The sound of hosepipes watering walled-off lawns competed with the noise of aeroplanes, nearby traffic and a colony of feral parakeets. Residents were fond of reciting various outlandish theories as to why these birds were so visible in London parks. Some said it was attributable to a pair that escaped from the set of *The African Queen*. Others preferred to imagine the plague of green birds were the progeny of Adam and Eve, two parakeets released by Jimi Hendrix as a symbol of freedom.

Every twenty feet or so, a signposted door reminded one that twenty-four-hour CCTV recording was in progress. Beyond the reinforced gates ubiquitous glass boxes and jazzed-up extensions glistened in the sun. From the front, most of the houses surrounding the park looked distinct from one another, each property designed by a different architect for a competition held just before the Great Exhibition. From behind, though, the houses were increasingly starting to look the same. Each household aping the aspirations of its neighbour.

Kitty cut across one of the lawns, past an avenue of beech trees. Above her head, slender branches curved upwards and inwards, attaching themselves to the encroaching limbs of neighbouring trees. A magnificent, almost ecclesiastical canopy spread out from the trees over the lawn. The ceiling was so dense that even on a sun-drenched afternoon, the area underneath was shrouded in a spectral half-light. Distracted by a curious beating sound, Kitty stopped for a moment. It was hard to work out where the noise was coming from. Small changes in the pitch gave the impression the source was moving. The noise possessed an agitated urgency. It sounded panicked and desperate. Unsettled, Kitty quickly proceeded along the path.

Relieved to be away from the sound, she stopped once again. A mass of scented white osmanthus was growing in the dappled shade of an oak tree. She closed her eyes and breathed in the flower's fruity aroma. The creamy tubular-shaped flowers appeared trusting and guileless. They reminded Kitty of an Amish bonnet.

Up ahead, Kitty noticed that an unusual amount of yellow light had penetrated the tree foliage. It splashed across the lawn, creating a spread of unfamiliar shadows. An unexpected gap had appeared, exposing two of the houses on the new development.

Kitty had been enjoying daily walks in the park for nearly forty years. Intense familiarity meant she was sensitive to every change and alteration which occurred. Each feature of the park was scored upon her memory. The trees, especially, had always been important. She was aware of the leaf arrangement, branching pattern and health of nearly every one of them. After the storm of '87, Kitty had assumed responsibility for overseeing the replanting and regeneration of the trees. Knowing that deadwood provided habitats for insects and wildlife, she persuaded residents to leave felled trees rather than clear away the debris. In many cases, the trees continued to grow. Elsewhere Kitty saw the storm's aftermath as an opportunity to replace some of the lost coniferous trees with deciduous trees. She could often be spotted talking to one of these trees. It wasn't an affectation. She truly believed they could speak and that one day humans would crack the code of their language. If anyone cared to listen, she would tell them how humans and trees didn't just share similar functionalities like growing, breathing, reproducing and dying; they also shared DNA.

As if locked, Kitty's jaw dropped and remained open. In the spot where, only a couple of days before, a thirty-metre ash had stood, there was now nothing but a freshly sawn stump. She looked around, her eyes darting from side to side as if hoping to spot someone running away with a chainsaw tucked under their arm. Kneeling beside the freshly severed base, Kitty wiped a film of sawdust from its surface. The perfectly formed age-defining rings neatly arranged in concentric circles made her feel giddy. Each one of the hoops presented a slice of recent history and perhaps a glimpse into the future. She could think of no reason why it should be cut down.

'You poor thing,' she said.

For a while, as if consoling a dying animal, Kitty remained on her knees stroking the stump. Eventually, she pulled out her phone and called Ed. He had seen two tree technicians working in the park the previous day. Ed told her that the area around the tree had been encircled with barricade tape. He had walked past while one of the technicians, suspended from some rigging, sawed off branches.

With one hand on her hip and the other hand clutching the back of her neck, Kitty stared at the trunk. There was only one person, she decided, who could have been responsible for the felling of this tree.

'Simon fucking Landes,' she muttered angrily.

The gate to Simon Landes' garden was open. Georgi was on his knees, changing the lock.

'What happened here?' Kitty asked.

Georgi stood up and wiped his hands on his overalls. 'Someone super glue lock… and that's not all.'

He pulled the gate towards him. Someone had painted a big, blue, ejaculating penis on the front panel. Scrawled underneath were the words *posh cock fucko*.

Kitty took a sharp intake of breath. 'Oh my!' She placed her hand over her mouth.

Georgi signalled to keep the noise down and then said in his singsong broken English accent: 'Mr Landes is here… he not happy.'

'Serves him right.' Kitty laughed at the badly painted phallus. 'Where is he? I need to speak to him.' Georgi gestured towards the house.

Apart from Kitty, Simon Landes and his wife Rachel had lived in Albion Park longer than anyone. Their house, which was on the other side of the park to Kitty's, had previously been a residential home for people with mental disabilities. It was one of the first institutions in the UK closed as part of the government's plans to transfer residents back into the community. The house was an extravagant red-brick Victorian Gothic villa with parapeted gables and trefoil windows on the ground floor.

The centrepiece of the garden was a cast stone replica of the Farnese Hercules. It stood proudly in the middle of the lawn on a concrete dais. The garden was immaculate. The unnatural brilliance of the artificial grass produced a dazzling glare in the afternoon sun. Kitty could see Simon speaking on the phone in his conservatory. He finished his conversation and walked out to greet Kitty with a smile that disappeared as quickly as it had arrived.

'I assume you had something to do with the tree that's been pulled down?'

'Hello, Kitty', Simon said breezily. 'How lovely to see you.'

Simon was wearing a pair of white Borg-era Fila shorts and a Penn State University T-shirt. With a luxuriant wedge of grey hair, thick moustache and leathery tan, he resembled an ageing Magnum PI.

'Well?' Kitty snapped. She hadn't planned to be so instantly confrontational, but Simon often brought out the worst in her. He raised his hands in a calming gesture. 'Oh Simon, how could you?'

'Before you start jumping to conclusions, will you let me—'

'There was absolutely nothing wrong with that tree.'

'Kitty, will you please give me a chance to—'

'Have you forgotten? They're protected by preservation orders.'

'Are you going to let me bloody talk?'

Kitty looked around to see if she could spot Rachel anywhere. She hadn't seen her for months. Tabitha Fraser told Kitty that Rachel had left Simon for another woman and now spent most of her time at their house on Santorini.

'For your information, Kitty.' Simon blinked. His eyelids remained closed longer than one would expect. They fluttered slightly as he spoke. 'I went through all of the correct channels.'

Kitty looked incredulous. 'You mean to tell me that you got permission from the council?'

Simon announced triumphantly that he would go and get his computer. 'You can see for yourself,' he said.

'What possible reason could there be for taking it down? The ash trees were checked for dieback only three months ago. They all got a clean bill of health. The arboriculturist told me what to look out for. I regularly check for signs.'

'I can't remember off the top of my head. I'll have to refer to my notes. Why all the fuss anyway? It's one tree…' Simon looked over Kitty's shoulder towards the gate. Georgi was still on his knees, scrubbing at the graffiti. Kitty turned around to see what was distracting Simon.

'Have you seen what they did to my door?'

'I don't want to talk about your door. What about this tree? Why wasn't I consulted?'

Simon sat down on a bench and rubbed his eyes with the palms of his hands. Kitty had never understood what Rachel ever saw in him. She was far too good for him. As far as she knew Simon had hardly worked a day in the last thirty years. Conversely, Rachel had earned a fortune from a cosmetics company that only seemed to get bigger. Kitty imagined that Simon's obsequiousness, obsession with money (even though he didn't earn any of his own) and determination to exert absolute control over the park committee was a serious turn-off. No wonder she ran off with a woman, Kitty thought.

'Yevgeny has donated nearly eight thousand pounds to pay for—'

Kitty raised her hand, a signal for Simon to stop talking. 'Who the hell is Yevgeny?'

'Yevgeny Orloff... from the Villas. I'm sure you've met him. In fact, I know you have... I was there. He's Lada Orloff's father.'

Kitty made a face that suggested she had no idea who Simon was referring to.

'She's a very successful model,' he added.

Simon resembled a proud parent when he announced that a supermodel was living in Albion Park.

'And he asked you to chop down the tree, did he?'

'The Orloffs are paying for hundreds, if not thousands, of new trees to be planted in the borough.'

Kitty bit the inside of her cheek, her mouth screwed over to one side. It all made sense now. The tree had previously been blocking a view of the park from two of the new houses. She looked down at her feet and nodded her head as she processed the information. She couldn't bear looking at Simon. She wanted to slap him around the face. He was like a child, easily impressed and eager to please.

'I suppose it was just a matter time before an oligarch bought one of these houses.'

Simon rolled his eyes. 'Oligarch? What are you talking about, Kitty? You seem to oppose everything out of some kind of misguided rebel code of conduct. I know you hanker after the days when Albion Park was full of dossers and drug dealers. But, thank God, those days are long gone. Move forward, Kitty. The past is a foreign country and all that... embrace the changes.'

'Don't be so ridiculous,' Kitty replied. 'I'm not averse

to change. I just resent what you, and the likes of Yves…
Euge… whatever his name is, are doing to the park. You're
ruining it.'

'Ruining it? We're re-colonising it. Who do you think
these houses were built for in the first place? I don't understand you, Kitty. Because one thing's for sure, you certainly
benefit from someone like Lada Orloff buying property
here. Anyway, it makes it more interesting. All these people
from various parts of the world… living here.'

'They're too rich to be interesting,' Kitty said.

Simon laughed.

'What's so funny?'

'I do wonder about you sometimes, Kitty. I recently heard
someone described as a man with a fork living in a world of
soup. It reminded me of you. Forever angry. Forever tilting
at imaginary foes.'

Georgi approached them and told Simon that he had
fixed the lock. 'But the graffiti not,' he said. 'I'll need to
paint again.'

'Bloody vandals.' Simon gave Kitty a pointed stare as if
somehow she was responsible.

Unable to conceal her glee, Kitty smiled broadly. 'Don't
say I didn't warn you.'

'You warned me? About what, exactly?'

'About going after those kids. I heard about the incident
in the park the other night. Why can't you just leave them
alone? What harm are they doing?'

'Have you seen my door?'

'Yes, I did. Very poetic. What was it again, "posh fucking
idiot"?'

'"Posh cock fucko", actually.' Simon pulled at the hairs of
his moustache. 'It doesn't even make sense.'

'At least that stupid new playground is getting used,'
Kitty said.

'The only reason the playground isn't being used by kids who are allowed access is that they're too bloody scared to go out there. We're not going to put up with it any longer.'

'We?'

'Everyone's had enough. I don't want to have this discussion with you right now. Any grievances can be aired at the residents' meeting.'

Chapter 4

The evening sunlight was dancing among the trees of Albion Park. Georgi peeled away a final layer of paint. The door's solid timber was now completely exposed, the woodwork restored to its natural state of beauty, and the big blue penis expunged.

Without stopping to eat, Georgi had been working on the door all day. Simon had offered him some homemade hummus and potato latke, but Georgi had declined the offer. Residents from around the park admired Georgi's work ethic and can-do attitude. Nothing was ever too much for him. When he first came to England, he was told that many English workmen were militant clock watchers, often downing tools at bang on 4pm, regardless of where they were at with the job. Georgi always made sure that he stayed until the job was finished.

With a heavy heart he stared at Simon's door. He couldn't quite believe this was where he had landed. When he arrived in England nearly five years ago, he had hoped to pick up where he left off in Bulgaria. He looked around at the domestic fortresses which surrounded the park. He could easily have been living in a house similar to the properties in Albion Park. Before the crash, Georgi and Mariya were looking to upgrade their rented three-bedroom apartment in Lozenets for a two-storey house in Boyana with a guest-house in the garden. Once upon a time, he too could have rubbed shoulders with the businessmen, government officials and lawyers who congregated in the prestigious neighbourhoods on the outskirts of Vitosha. He, too, could have lived among distinguished members of Sofian society as an equal. As opposed to being a subordinate odd-job man, reduced to cleaning graffiti off garden gates.

'I think maybe we should leave it like that.' Simon stepped back, tilted his head and looked at the door through squinted eyes. 'It looks pretty good to me.'

'You don't want me to paint now?'

'No, let's leave it as is,' Simon said. 'I can always get you back if I change my mind. Besides, it's getting late. Will you join me for a beer?'

'Thank you, no, Mr Landes. I go home now.'

Georgi had a gentle voice. It belied his muscular frame and distinctive Southern Slavic looks. His accent was strong, and although he spoke English reasonably well, Simon frequently felt compelled to correct his mispronunciations.

'Georgi, I insist. You do drink beer?' Georgi gave Simon a look as if he had asked him if he knew how to change a plug. 'Then have a drink with me. You've been hard at it all day.'

Simon passed Georgi a bottle of beer. The two men sat down on a bench near the gate, which opened out onto the park. Georgi lifted a thick, hairy arm and wiped his brow. A guff of body odour escaped his saturated armpits: the heavy, ammonia-tinged smell drifted into Simon's orbit.

'It really is a gorgeous evening,' Simon said. An involuntary look of distaste appeared on his face as he tried not to breathe in. Georgi took a sip of his beer and shuffled uncomfortably in his seat, unsure how to proceed with the conversation. 'I'm sorry about the incident with Kitty earlier on,' Simon said. 'She's a bit of a character... if you know what I mean.'

'She has no husband, so she is doing what she likes.'

'Quite,' Simon laughed. 'She does have some jolly funny ideas.'

An awkward silence lingered. Georgi stared at the floor and took another sip of his drink.

'How long have you been in the UK for now?'

'Almost the six years.'

Simon nodded his head sagely. 'And were you in a similar line of business back in Poland?'

'Bulgaria,' Georgi said.

'I'm sorry. Of course, Bulgaria. What did you do back home?'

Georgi proceeded to tell Simon how, before his business went under, he had been the boss of a successful construction company. His firm had built a series of houses that were part of a settlement situated at the foot of Vitosha Mountain, about ten kilometres south-east of Sofia. The homes were modern, well-built, and appealed to aspirational Sofians, like himself and Mariya.

'So, what happened?' Simon asked.

'The crash ruin everything. I was working project for Irish businessmen. They leave. Like that.' Georgi blew into his fingers and mimicked a puff of smoke. 'I can't pay staff or bills. Everything collapse.'

'That's terrible.' Simon assumed a look of exaggerated concern. 'What is the situation there now? Any better?'

Georgi told him how friends back home reported that things were on the up once more. Especially in construction. EU funds had invested heavily in infrastructure. It was anticipated the economy would soon reach its 2007 level again.

'Will you go back?'

'I don't know. Perhaps. I would like one day.'

'You don't need to pronounce the k in know,' Simon said. 'Imagine it's not there. Like *no*, as opposed to *kerno*.'

Georgi grunted and took a swig of beer.

'Are you busy?' Nicholas Rijkens was standing at the garden gate.

'No, no, Nicholas, please come in,' Simon said. 'Georgi and I were just sharing a beer.'

Nicholas gave Georgi a puzzled look. 'Where were you today?'

'I've been working for Mr Landes.' Georgi looked towards Simon.

'He's been here all day.'

Nicholas sat down on the bench next to Georgi. 'Weren't you supposed to be cleaning my pond this afternoon?'

'No,' Georgi said. 'This is next week.'

Nicholas sniffed at the air before getting up from the bench and moving to a low wall opposite Simon.

'I think it was today,' he said, glancing at the underside of his shoe.

'I show you.' Georgi stood up and reached into his back pocket for his notebook.

'Put it away,' Nicholas said, with a condescending wave of his hand. 'It doesn't matter.' He paused before adding: 'Having said that, if you arrange to do some work for someone, it's usually a good idea to actually turn up.'

Georgi disliked Nicholas. He had done ever since the man had dismantled an automated feeder which Kitty had commissioned Georgi to make. At the time, Kitty had become attached to some foxes who used to loiter near her gate. Georgi devised a contraption that provided food for the foxes at regular times. The prototype was built out of MDF with a battery backed-up internal clock and LCD backlit display. Having learned BASIC coding on his cousin's Pravetz microcomputer, Georgi was able to complete the necessary programming.

Although it was ingenious, Nicholas was furious about the feeder. He argued that the box would attract more foxes to the park. There had already been one scare when a neighbour caught a fox looking at their child through the kitchen window. Although the incident didn't sound particularly serious, the response from some of the residents suggested otherwise. Dino Sarti and his husband Tambah had reacted as if there was a bear on the loose. After Kitty had refused to move the feeder, Nicholas dismantled it himself. Kitty threatened him with a civil claim for damage to her property but ultimately decided not to pursue any course of action.

Georgi could tell that Nicholas' manner made Simon feel uncomfortable.

'To what do I owe this pleasure?' Simon said, changing the conversation.

'There was an incident in the park today.'

'What? What kind of incident?'

'Luc was attacked.'

'Attacked?' Simon shrieked. 'What do you mean attacked?'

'Someone threw a rock… or perhaps a stone while Luc and Camille were playing in the new learning environment.'

'And it hit Luc? Is he OK?'

Georgi continued to stare at the floor while Nicholas and Simon discussed what had happened.

'He's OK now… I think. But he's got a nasty cut on his forehead. I don't suppose either of you saw anything?'

'I've been in the house all day. Georgi, you've been by the gate. Did you see anything?'

Georgi looked up. He shook his head without speaking.

'Who would do such a thing?' Simon said. 'It's bound

to be one of the yobbos from the flats. Have you seen what they did to my door?'

Nicholas looked towards Simon's gate.

'It's gone now,' Simon said, 'but it was vandalised last night. Have you called the police?'

'Jennifer did. I'm surprised they haven't been here. I saw them outside Kitty's soon after they left my house. I presume they went to the flats too.'

'And?'

'So far nothing...'

'This is outrageous,' Simon said, blinking furiously. 'Something must be done. We've been procrastinating for too long. We need to propose a motion for the next meeting.'

Nicholas sniffed at the air again. 'What *is* that smell?'

Turning to Simon, Georgi announced that it was time for him to go. 'Thank you for beer,' he said. 'Please, let me know if you want to paint door.' Georgi turned to Nicholas and asked if he still wanted him to work the following Saturday.

'I wanted you to work this Saturday... Look, I don't know. I'll see what Jen thinks.'

Simon accompanied Georgi as he walked through the garden towards a large gate leading to the street. He draped his arm around Georgi's shoulder. 'It's so awful about Nicholas' boy.' From the corner of his eye, Georgi could see Simon's hand resting conspicuously on the side of his arm. 'Perhaps you could listen out for any info that... you know... might help us catch the perps.' Simon handed Georgi an envelope full of cash. 'There's a bit extra in there. Just a token of my appreciation. I'm sorry if I got you into trouble.'

Once Simon had gone back into the house, Georgi spat on the floor and muttered to himself in Bulgarian. Friends back home wouldn't believe the way he allowed Nicholas

Rijkens to talk to him. No one there would have dared be so disrespectful. Georgi kicked out at a stone. It ricocheted off his foot and slammed into the side of a white Land Rover Discovery parked outside the Crossleys' house. The noise of the impact made him flinch. Luckily no one was around to witness his act of minor vandalism. There was never anyone around. Automated gates would occasionally open, and oversized cars with tinted windows would glide in and out of properties. The only people one ever saw walking down the street were residents from the flats and the occasional police foot patrol. One never saw police on the beat anywhere else in the borough.

Kitty was watering plants in front of her house. She called out to Georgi as he walked past. Georgi, however, was still muttering to himself and didn't hear her calling. She turned off her hose and tried again. Finally, Georgi turned around.

'Georgi, I'm so glad I ran into you. Can I have a quick word?' Kitty signalled for him to come into the secluded driveway of her house. 'Did you hear about what happened in the park earlier?'

'With Rijkens boy? Yes, I heard about this.'

'It's probably nothing,' Kitty said. 'And I hope you don't mind me telling you. But when I was looking out of my studio window earlier, I saw your son and another boy running from the park. It was around the same time as the incident.'

'Are you sure was Dominik?'

'Yes, I'm sure it was him. I didn't see who the other boy was.'

'Did police come?'

Kitty nodded. Georgi slapped his hand against his forehead and swore loudly in Bulgarian.

'Don't worry,' Kitty continued, 'I didn't say anything.'

Georgi could already smell Mariya's bob chorba from the top of the stairwell. The scent of spearmint and pork blended revoltingly with the putrid aroma coming from the bin bags dumped outside his neighbour's door. One of the refuse sacks on the landing had split. A chicken carcass was half hanging out, along with some eggshells, rotten vegetables and bits of soiled tissue.

'Filthy, lazy pigs', Georgi said to himself as he passed his neighbours' house. Whenever he complained to the woman who lived next door about her lack of hygiene, she would just stare back at him. The woman had lived in London for as long as him, but still hardly spoke a word of English. Her son had once threatened to stab Georgi after he threw one of the bags of rubbish through their door. The boy was only about fifteen. His jutting lower jaw and provocative glare made Georgi's muscles tense up. He expected respect from someone so young. After all, what did this boy know about life? If Owen hadn't been there, Georgi might have held the boy over the balcony by his ankles. Teach him a lesson. Owen told him that the gang the boy knocked about it with were dangerous. Apparently, one of them had been convicted for the attempted murder of a local schoolboy. His reputation meant little to Georgi. But it did bother him that Dominik had to live next door to someone like that.

Georgi walked into the flat. Mariya was cooking at the stove. He gave her a kiss on the back of her neck and put his arms around her waist. He asked her in Bulgarian if everything was OK.

'Everything is fine.'

'Sure?'

'Yes, of course. Why wouldn't it be?' Relieved that the police had obviously not been to the flat, Georgi leaned over his wife and grabbed a piece of bread. He dunked it in the soup before Mariya could slap his hand away.

'Where's the boy?' Georgi put the piece of bread dripping with liquid into his mouth. It was scalding hot and burned his tongue. Georgi opened his mouth and let the offending item, replete with viscid threads of saliva, flop out of his mouth onto the chopping board. Mariya looked on with disgust.

'It serves you right, you greedy pig. You have no manners.' Mariya pushed her husband out of the way.

Georgi drank a glass of water that was on the kitchen top. He pulled Mariya towards him.

'You stink. Go take a shower.'

'It's the smell of a working man. You like it, really. It turns you on,' Georgi said, resisting Mariya's attempt to escape his clutches.

'No, it bloody doesn't. It makes me feel sick. Doesn't anyone at work say anything?'

'No, of course not.' Georgi looked offended. 'It's not that bad… is it?' He sniffed one of his armpits and shrugged his shoulders.

'Believe me, it is. Go and wash before we eat. Dominik is in his room, playing his soccer game.'

'That boy will never become a person,' Georgi said. 'Always in front of his screen.'

'Leave him alone. I'll call you when the food is ready.'

Georgi went to the toilet to wash. There was barely any room in the basin to squeeze in his shovel-like hands. The room was so short of space, he had to stay on the spot as he turned around. His flat in Sofia had two bathrooms, with plenty of room and sturdy ceramic basins, toilets and baths. When he sat on the toilet in this flat, the end of his penis would either dip into the water or rub against the side of the pan. He felt as if he was sitting on a child's toilet. Through the walls, he could hear the bass-heavy rumble of Dominik's game. Apart from the kitchen, the swampy drone permeated almost every part of the flat. Dominik could mindlessly play the game for hours on end. Georgi objected to his son's devotion to staring at screens. But equally, he was happy Dominik spent so much time in the flat. The more time his son spent at home, the less potential there was for him to get into trouble.

Georgi stood outside Dominik's bedroom and knocked on the door. The knock was unnecessary, but Georgi could remember what it was like to be thirteen years old. He had no desire to catch his son in an act of self-gratification. After about thirty seconds, he walked into the bedroom and in Bulgarian told Dominik to put the game down.

'Hold on. I've nearly finished.' Without waiting for a response or even looking up Dominik continued to feverishly pound away at the handset. Georgi walked up to the beanbag his son was slumped in and yanked the handset out of his hand.

'Dad!'

Tossing the game controller to one side, Georgi bent over his son and hauled him up by his ear. The boy howled and scrambled to stand up. Georgi gave him a cuff around the side of his head. The boy yelled once more and covered his ear with his hand. Georgi immediately slapped him around the other side of his head. Dominik was now in tears.

'Dad... please. Stop... what's wrong with you?'

'What did I tell you? What did I bloody tell you?' Georgi said, wagging a hairy finger in his son's face.

'I don't know, I don't know. What have I done?'

'Do not shit where you eat. If I've told you once...'

Dominik had wriggled free from Georgi and was backing away across the room. 'I don't know what you're talking about, Dad.'

'Don't bullshit me, boy.' Georgi slowly moved towards Dominik. 'I know what happened in the park today.'

Hoping his mum would come to the rescue, Dominik raised his voice. 'Dad, please...' Georgi slapped his son around the top of his head, then raised his hand as if to strike him again.

'Dad... Please. Stop.'

Mariya came into the bedroom and looked at Georgi. 'What the hell is going on?'

'Tell her,' Georgi said.

'Tell me what?' Dominik sat on his bed and rubbed his ear. He looked at his dad with hate-filled eyes.

'Will someone please tell me what is going on?' Mariya pleaded.

Georgi told his wife what he knew about the incident in the park earlier. Mariya's attention, however, was solely focused on her son. Sitting on the bed next to him, she turned Dominik's head towards her and inspected his face for marks. Regardless of whatever he said, Georgi knew Mariya would somehow manage to concoct a defence of Dominik's actions. When Georgi had finished explaining what had happened to the Rijkens boy, Mariya turned to Dominik and said: 'Do you know anything about this, sunshine?'

Dominik shook his head imploringly. 'No, Mum. I swear I didn't do anything.'

'Do you promise that you weren't in the park this afternoon?' Mariya asked.

'I swear on Baba's life.'

Mariya looked at Georgi as if to say – I don't think he's lying. Maybe you've let your temper get the better of you again.

Georgi believed Mariya did the boy no favours. She always succeeded in exculpating him from any accusations of wrongdoing. There had been an ongoing battle of wills between the two parents ever since Georgi was kicked out of the matrimonial bed. At the time, Dominik was suffering from respiratory problems. But Georgi had understood the precedent which it had set. As a dad, he felt he needed to provide discipline and counsel. He wanted his son to grow up with the same code of masculine values instilled in him as a boy. Mariya, however, enviably eyed the deconstructed men and stay-at-home fathers so visible in their part of North London. She wanted Dominik to grow up to be a modern man. To eschew the old-fashioned values of his father.

'How will the boy ever become a man?' Georgi said.

'A boy learns masculinity from his father,' Mariya barked. 'What sort of man do you want him to be? Like your father… like you?'

'I hope I'm not anything like you,' Dominik said, emboldened by his mum's presence.

Georgi walked over to his son's gaming console and picked it up. 'See this,' he said, shaking the console at his son. 'This was paid for with money I earn from working in the park. And these…' Georgi picked up one of Dominik's trainers. He then picked up a hoodie off the floor and flung it across the room. 'And this. Do you understand what I'm saying?'

Dominik stared at his father, his face dark with defiance.

'The police would have come here if he was a suspect,' Mariya said. 'Why don't you believe him?'

'Because he was seen running from the park.'

'But he just promised me that he wasn't in the park this afternoon.' Dominik offered his mother a wounded smile. 'Even if he was spotted,' Mariya continued, 'that doesn't mean he did it. It sounds like the boy is OK. It could have been an accident.'

Ignoring Mariya's excuses, Georgi walked over to his son. With his index finger under the boy's chin, he lifted Dominik's bowed head.

'Stay out of the park. I mean it. If I hear you've been in there, you will be in big trouble. Do you understand me?'

Dominik screwed up his face. His cheeks heaved excessively as he tried to control his breathing. Sometimes when Georgi looked at him, it felt as if he was looking at himself. He remembered trying to hold back tears as his own father reprimanded him.

Georgi's father had been a distant figure, slow to show affection but quick to chastise. Just as Dominik did now, he had sought out his mother for comfort whenever his father vented his frustrations on him. Georgi had spent a lifetime resenting his old man's temper. He had never felt comfortable in his presence. His father's aggression had alienated him. Now, as a parent himself, he knew that he was free to choose behaviours that supported Dominik rather than repeating old patterns. He wasn't destined to replicate the mistakes of his father. So why did he continually do so?

Georgi stomped out of Dominik's bedroom and slammed the door behind him. Ignoring the stench from the various bins and discarded bags of rubbish, he stood in the corridor outside his flat and looked out over the park. To his left, he could see the eaves of Kitty's house. He could hear music coming from her studio. During the summer, she would often play music in the early evening, her windows left wide open while she worked. The piece she was listening to reminded Georgi of his flat in Sofia, which overlooked the front room of a pianist's apartment. Every day, for two to three hours, often with his windows open, the man practised in his front room. The pianist's flat was one floor lower than Georgi's. As he ran through his exercises and repeated patterns of movement, all Georgi could see were the hands of the musician and the keys of the piano. He never saw his face. He wasn't even sure who he was. Georgi used to sit outside the café opposite, drinking coffee and watching people coming in and out of the building, trying to guess who the pianist might be.

The music coming from Kitty's was calming. Georgi shut his eyes and listened as the plaintive melody, combined with the evening birdsong, momentarily transported him. The stacked notes cascaded into one another and floated above the trees and flowers. A group of people were eating outside in one of the gardens. The occasional distant laugh would blend with the music, fading in and out, inadvertently providing a counterpoint to the endlessly varied phrases of the birdsong. For a moment, peace reigned as a turbulent day was bid farewell by the dreamlike layers of harmony which mirrored the sound of the birds twittering below.

Chapter 5

Kitty stood in front of the New Park Villas and stared down at the sawn trunk of the ash tree. She reached into the battered old leather messenger bag slung over her shoulder and pulled out a hacksaw. Like a surgeon inspecting a patient, Kitty crouched over the stump. Slowly, she began to saw off pieces of the tree and place them in her bag. She wanted to collect as much wood as possible before the tree technicians came back with their grinders. After the altercation with Simon Landes, Kitty had decided to create one of her assemblages based on the chopping down of the tree. Kitty was still angry that the tree's cycle of seasons had been prematurely terminated to improve Yevgeny Orloff's view of the park.

'What are you doing?'

In front of her, Kitty could see a pair of slender, sockless, bronzed legs emerging from a garishly patterned set of running shoes.

'It looks a bit weird now with that big hole in the trees.'

Without looking up, Kitty acknowledged the sentiment with a mumble of agreement.

'It's Kitty, isn't it? We've met before.'

Kitty finally looked up and squinted at the person standing in front of her. 'I'm sorry. I don't remember.' Kitty put her hacksaw away, took a camera out of her bag and began taking photos of the stump. The woman stepped back to give her room, but it didn't seem as if she was about to leave. Kitty bristled at her presumptuousness.

'My name's Tanya. I live in one of the new villas.' The addition of an upward inflexion at the end of every sentence ensured each of Tanya's statements landed like a question. 'I wonder how old it was?' Kitty looked at Tanya quizzically. 'The tree? I wonder how old the tree was.'

Kitty turned her head back and continued to look through the viewfinder. 'It was nearly twenty-seven years old,' she said. 'I planted this tree just after the storm of 1987.'

'I remember when that happened,' Tanya said. 'I lived just down the road at the time. I had a friend who lived in the flats here.'

'Really? What was your friend's name?'

'Gail McDonald…. she had red hair. We were in the same class at school. I used to love playing here. There were always tons of kids hanging about. We used to climb on the trees which were blown over. Someone once told me the flats were built on top of an old bomb factory blown up during the war. Do you know if that's true?'

'I don't think they would have built an ammunition factory in such a built-up area. Do you?'

Kitty tried to get up but struggled to stand from a crouching position. With one hand on her back and the other on the tree stump, she tried again.

'Here, let me help you.' Tanya stretched out her hand. Ashamed that she required assistance to get up and disappointed that she wasn't young any more, Kitty reluctantly grabbed Tanya's hand. Like a raging river, each moment of her life had rushed by. It seemed like only yesterday she and Hugh had moved into Albion Park. Yet here she was, all these years later, a widow in the latter third of her life requiring assistance from a stranger. Would her younger self have even recognised the person she had become? No doubt she would have found herself to be petty and interminably bourgeois as she worried about invasive plants and the ethics of her neighbours.

'The estate was built on top of an old bomb site,' Kitty said. 'At the time they were beacons of hope, built on top of all that destruction. The flats that were pulled down to make way for your house, they were built on a bomb site too.'

'Is that right?'

'Three houses obliterated by a direct hit. It's funny to think those buildings have already been replaced.'

The two women moved towards the outskirts of one of the many secluded parts of the park. A thick evergreen hedge, which had been trimmed and perfectly shaped, surrounded the lawn. In the middle was a round cast stone two-tier fountain.

'What did you say your friend's name was again?'

'Gail McDonald.'

Kitty shook her head. 'The name doesn't ring a bell. Are you still in touch?'

'I haven't seen her for years,' Tanya said. 'Her parents bought their flat and then sold it as soon as they could. I think they moved out to Welwyn Garden City.'

Kitty noticed Tanya's fingernails, which were bitten down to the quick. The cuticles were raw and flaky, a surprising imperfection amongst a host of cosmetically maintained features.

'Is it strange being back here?' Kitty asked.

'Not really. Everything has changed so much since then.'

'More's the pity,' Kitty said.

'Why would you say that?'

'Look at what they've done to this garden. It's so… so

municipal. Too many straight lines. There's nothing natural about a straight line.'

'Oh no. I think you're wrong. It's lovely here. It used to be a bit of a dump. The whole area was. When I was growing up, if someone had shown me where I would end up living, I'd never have believed it.'

Kitty wanted to tell Tanya how she believed globalisation was responsible for transforming Albion Park from a once open, diverse community into a closed-off, gated fortress populated by a wealthy elite who cared little for the community at large. She wanted to explain how the acquisitive tendencies of her neighbours had created a hostile environment for everyone else. She wanted to express how sad she was at the growing disconnect between the homeowners around the park and the residents of the Bevan Estate. But why should she burden this woman with her grievances? Why should she trash the achievements Tanya was entitled to feel proud of?

'If you were a child living around here now,' Kitty said, 'you wouldn't be allowed anywhere near the park.'

'It's different now, though, isn't it? I mean, everywhere is so much rougher. The people around here... they just want to protect their kids. I was at Jennifer's house when their son was hurt. It was horrible.'

'I just don't think incidents like that would happen if the residents were a bit more inclusive. Excluding people always creates more problems than it solves.'

'How do you mean?'

'Resentments build among those who are denied access. Meanwhile, everyone around the park becomes more and more paranoid about this imaginary threat from beyond the walls.' Kitty bent down and rubbed her fingers on the bud of a lavender bush. 'I just think we all need to take a bit more responsibility for the community we live in.' She inhaled the scented aroma from her fingers.

'Well, I've got no problem with keeping people out,' Tanya said. 'I worry about crime and intruders too. Everyone just wants to feel safe, don't they?'

'Did you know rates of burglary are lowest in wealthy areas?'

'Really?'

'Of course. Everyone has CCTV cameras and sophisticated alarm systems.'

'You should see our front door,' Tanya said proudly. 'No one's ever going to get through that.'

'If security is such a concern,' Kitty continued, 'did you not consider moving to one of those high-end towers that are popping up all over the place? They all have extra security.'

'They don't have the space. Not like this.' Tanya gestured with her hand to the park. 'Anyway, why do you live around here if you dislike it so much?'

'If some of the residents had their way, I wouldn't,' Kitty laughed.

Suddenly spooked by something, the dogs began barking in unison. Kitty looked up to see Tambah and his son Bruno emerge from behind a hedge. The two dogs were running around, bumping into each other as they barked at Tambah. Kitty called them, but they ignored her instruction. With a look of terror on his face, Tambah picked up his son and tried to shoo the dogs away.

'Don't worry,' Kitty said, frowning at Tambah's s response, 'they're completely harmless. Poor old Echo is a bit short-sighted. As soon she starts barking, it sets the other one off.'

'They should be on a lead,' Tambah said. He was shielding Bruno as if at any moment one of the spaniels might leap up and snatch his son. 'Could you pull them away, please?'

Echo was still barking aimlessly as if she didn't know

how to stop. Hermes, meanwhile, had lost interest and wandered off somewhere.

'You really don't have to worry,' Kitty said, smiling. 'They've never hurt anyone.' She attached one of the dogs to a lead and called for the other. Hermes eventually emerged from a bush with a leaf stuck to his head. Kitty put a lead on him too.

'We should be able to enjoy the park without the fear of being attacked by dogs,' Tambah said. 'It's totally *unsozial*. In Switzerland, we have fines if you let your dog off the lead. Owners have to go on courses.'

'Look, I'm sorry my dogs barked at you. But I can assure you, they are completely harmless. See, Echo is being nice now.'

Still cradling his seven-year-old in his arms, Tambah slowly backed off. He glowered at the dogs as he retreated.

The moment he was out of earshot, Kitty turned to Tanya. 'Honestly. The way that man and his husband carry on. I pity the poor child.'

Kitty told Tanya about an email Tambah had sent out to residents the previous Halloween. Concerned that Bruno might have an intolerance, he requested that only gluten-free sweets be given to their son if he came to their door trick-or-treating. In the email, Tambah included a list of sweets he deemed safe. *Do let us know if you don't have time to go to the shops,* he had written. *Either Dino or me can pop round in the afternoon and leave you with some gluten-free treats.* Dino signed off the email with one further request. *Bruno is so excited about his costume; it would be fabulous if you could all pretend to be super scared when you answer the door. Happy Halloween, everyone! T&D xxx*

'That does seem a bit over the top,' Tanya said.

'Right, I'd better be off,' Kitty said. 'It was nice to meet you.'

'Do you not go to the residents' meetings?' Tanya asked.

'Not always. Why do you ask?'

'I didn't see you at the last one. We're hosting the next one at our house.'

'Of course. I should have made the connection. I saw your name on the memo. I'll make sure I'm there this time.'

Kitty walked back through the park towards her house. Once again, she heard the strange flapping sound that had bothered her so much the previous day. She looked around but still couldn't establish where the noise was coming from. Although it lacked the urgency of the day before, it still sounded desperate and unnerving. Kitty looked up and scanned the various trees which crowded over her. Directly above her head, she spotted a raven hanging from a piece of string wrapped around a branch. She immediately recognised the string as the leftover from a kite that got stuck in the tree a few years ago. The remainder of it had blown away over time. The raven was hanging upside down, a single eye focused on Kitty. The bird's piercing dark pupil and white iris looked human. Possibly believing a rescue was imminent, it wasn't struggling. However, the branch seemed too high up for a ladder. Kitty was unsure how she would be able to help the creature.

She decided to phone the fire brigade, but the receptionist on the switchboard complained that they were overstretched and under-resourced. As much as she would like to help, she simply couldn't allocate any firefighters for something so trivial. Kitty phoned Georgi, who came down to look at the bird. He also told her that nothing could be done. The bird was too high up. Georgi was perplexed as to why Kitty should be so concerned about it in the first place. 'It dead soon. Why you care so much?'

When Georgi left, the bird, seemingly cognisant that

help was not on its way, began to violently flap its wings. Its body jerked and twisted as it dangled from the string. After a flurry of exertion, it swung like a pendulum from side to side before another frenzied struggle ensued. As the bird writhed, it continued to look at Kitty, its previously beseeching stare replaced by one of menace. Kitty was reminded of an illustration she once saw. It was of a human body with a crow's head attacking a woman. The sinister birdman, dressed like a nineteenth-century dandy, was pulling a semi-naked woman over the corpse of a man. Unable to tolerate being near the bird any longer, she began to walk away. As if cursing Kitty's ineffectiveness, the bird started to screech.

When she got home, Val, her new cleaner, was just finishing up in the kitchen.

'What's wrong with you?' Val said. 'You look like you've seen a ghost.'

Kitty sat down at the kitchen table and told her what had just happened in the park.

'Why do you let it affect you so much?' Val said. 'It's not your fault.'

'It's another living being,' Kitty said. 'I could feel its pain.'

'What can you do?' Val shrugged her shoulders and continued dusting the shelves.

Kitty picked up her phone and dialled the RSPCA. No one was overly concerned about the plight of the animal, though. Especially once she explained how high up it was.

Kitty opened her bag and placed the cuttings from the tree on a worktable. She then went over to some shelves, bowed under the weight of materials. Magazines, records, films, books, fabrics, pots of clay, paintbrushes, tubes of paint, rolls of cotton thread, boxes of photographs, jars of linseed oil, bottles of turpentine, dossiers on her favourite subjects crammed with cuttings, all competed for space on the wall-to-ceiling shelves which covered two sides of her studio. Finally, after rooting around for a few minutes, she retrieved a wooden frame-like box about the size of two shoeboxes. She liked the idea of these new pieces being contained in small spaces. It was as if she was partitioning her grievances.

Kitty placed the box on the worktable and began arranging the various bits of wood. Most of it would need to be cut down to fit inside the box. The plan was to create a solid wooden base and then add other elements as ideas revealed themselves. A few hours were spent shaping the wood from the tree and considering how different textures might be added. On some pieces, she intended to gouge grooves into the surface, while on others she could dye the wood or perhaps age it. She wanted the elements to resemble mysterious ancient artefacts.

Most importantly, though, any wood she used must come from this tree. In her mind, it had assumed a totemic quality. Its felling emblematic of the changes which had taken place around her.

After some time, Kitty's thoughts returned to the bird and its attempts to escape the inevitable. She went back downstairs. The dogs were both lying on the floor of her kitchen. The chronometric precision of their body clocks knew it wasn't time for their late afternoon walk. Neither of them even bothered to open their eyes until they heard the trigger sound of keys jangling in the boot room door.

The dogs ran off ahead as Kitty began her first circuit of the park. Instead of continuing past the tree where the bird was hanging, Kitty cut across the park and walked towards the tennis court. The Crossley girl and a friend were sitting on the grass near the court. They were about thirty yards away from Kitty. Even from there, she could smell the heavy aroma of whatever it was they were smoking. She remembered sitting in the same spot with Hugh and some others from around the park, a few of them stoned on (no doubt much less potent) hash. Hugh had recently started a new post at the BBC as a foreign affairs correspondent. Since moving to Albion Park, the previous year, he had been out of the country much of the time. Initially covering the fall of Saigon and then more recently a spate of incidents in Northern Ireland. He was always a bundle of nerves whenever he came back from Belfast.

Kitty didn't want to disturb the Crossley girl and her young friend, so she headed back towards the Bevan Estate. She approached the area where the bird had been with trepidation. It was still there, suspended from the tree, its short leg tightly wrapped around the string of a child's former plaything. Exhausted and probably dying of thirst, it seemed to have accepted its fate. The bird was no longer struggling, but its eye was still open. It looked so different from earlier that day when its panic had managed to scare Kitty. Now it hung limply, waiting for death to release it, the blue sheen of its crown visible from below.

'I'm so sorry,' Kitty said. 'Please forgive me.' A tear ran down her shadowy face. She stared up at the bird. Having rejected her amends, it closed its eye and tucked its head under one of its wings. Distraught by her powerlessness and inability to alter events, Kitty looked down at her feet. On the floor next to her trainers, she spotted a single faded black feather. She bent over and picked it up. Without looking at the bird again, Kitty walked back towards the house.

Chapter 6

The studio revealed nothing of the fine weather outside.
There were no windows. That is, there were no windows
that let in any natural light. At the back of the room, two
sheets of quarter-inch laminated glass looked out onto
another studio. A blind had been placed over it. Owen's
room was an old live room. It had been separated from the
larger studio, which the window looked onto. The studios
were in a complex underneath a railway arch in Hackney.

Since he'd got back from being on tour, Owen had spent
much of his time in the studio milling around the edges
of doing something. He had installed some new software,
tidied up his computer and rewired some equipment.
But it was all a diversion from the task of making music.
This Monday, however, Owen had arrived at work with a
renewed vigour. Over the weekend, a DJ friend had forwarded him a link to an unreleased album. Owen knew of
the artist, but up until now he had never paid him much
attention. Having drunk a bottle of red wine, he put on his
headphones and listened to the whole record. It wasn't that
the music was unlike anything he had ever heard before. Far
from it. But Owen was seduced by the intimacy of what he
heard. The production was warm and textured. He loved
the simplicity and familiarity of the synth sounds. He liked

the naivety of the imperfect vocals and the thread of melancholy which ran throughout. It sounded like the music he would make himself. Owen thought he could use the record as a starting point for his own music. A lack of direction had recently stymied creativity. But now, he had a sound in his head to pursue, something he could use as a memory reference point. He opened another bottle of wine and resolved to go into the studio after the weekend and make some new music. Something he hadn't managed to do for a while.

Owen played the album back once more. It was hard to recreate the enthusiasm he had felt on Saturday night. Alcohol attenuated the voices of negativity that buzzed around his head; Monday mornings amplified them. Owen possessed a solipsism born of feelings of inadequacy. Although outwardly confident as a young man, any self-assurance had, paradoxically, always been laced with intense self-doubt. Moderate success had provided him with tools to contain this defect. But, like a retreating wave revealing permanent rocks, with age the confidence had ebbed away. All that remained was unsparing self-criticism. These days he wasn't even sure who he was supposed to be making music for. Did he have an audience any more? Probably not. Owen would go to the studio to make music because that's what he had always done. He didn't know what else to do.

Still, all he needed to get started was a sound to cling onto: something to try and emulate. Eventually, whatever he did would become his own. After about an hour of messing around, he had created a simple loop that sounded OK. The chord progression was playing through a string machine patch. The clipped staccato pulse reminded him of something by Steve Reich. Underneath, Owen had looped some percussion that wobbled and hissed in time with the music. He closed his eyes and tried to imagine a melody. Although he had never claimed to be a singer, the untutored vocals on the record he'd been listening to had provided the confidence to try it himself.

He was interrupted by a knock at the door. Tony, the studio manager, was standing in the doorway. Owen was three months late with the rent.

'I'm sorry, O,' he said. 'If you don't pay me by the end of the month, I'm going to have to ask you to leave. Business rates are crippling me. I've got a waiting list as long as my arm for these studios. I can't afford to carry anyone... even you.'

Owen had previously promised Tony that he would clear all outstanding debts as soon as he got back from touring. Once again, he offered various guarantees that the end-of-month deadline would be met.

'The moment I get paid, I'll settle up... I promise. You know I'm good for it.' Owen was unsure how he was going to manage this. Apart from some shows with Run for the Shadows the following month, he had nothing on for the foreseeable future. Three months of touring and promo had finished. He had little to show for it. Nearly everything he'd earned had simply paid off loans and debts accumulated before the tour. He was loath to go down that route again.

Once Tony had left the studio, Owen wasn't really in the mood to continue working on his nascent idea. He pressed play and listened back to what he had done. It all seemed utterly pointless. How could he justify working on new music? He needed to come up with a plan to earn some money quickly. He stared at the profusion of winking lights, the illuminated meters which flashed and sparkled. The cryptic spray of knobs and dials teeming with numbers and rune-like symbols. He had always been captivated by the idea of the artist, surrounded by technology, working tirelessly through the night. Now he was looking at these once-beloved bits of equipment and considering what he could sell. He could keep a few choice items. But the rest would raise some much-needed cash.

Owen decided to call Joe Sayles, his old publisher. Although no longer in possession of a publishing deal, he and Joe had remained on good terms. They had previously discussed the possibility of Owen going into the studio with one of Joe's young artists. Owen had gone off the idea after Joe had sent him some demos. They were awful. Or at least they bore no relation to the sort of music Owen wanted to make. After vacantly staring at the phone for a while, Owen finally called Joe. The two of them arranged to meet for a drink later that day.

Scrapping the idea of pursuing a new track, Owen scoured his various drives for anything he could present to Joe. There was an abundance of abandoned projects, half-formed ideas and finished songs which had never seen the light of day. Nearly everything he listened to deserved better than to be languishing on a dusty hard drive. There were a couple of tracks that he couldn't remember doing. He wasn't even sure if they were his. A lot of the music he uncovered, though, had been binned on an impulse. Owen could recall his thinking at the time. Several tracks had been discarded simply because they sounded like something else or because he had heard another record that sounded better.

After a couple of hours of compiling ideas, Owen took a break and looked at his social media accounts. First, he checked his Instagram account for likes and comments. He then scrolled through a few favourite accounts, including one which consisted exclusively of people getting hit by things and falling off things while in the process of taking selfies. Owen then browsed through Stuart from Run for the Shadows account before looking at Conrad's.

All this activity, however, was just a precursor to the main event. Namely, spending time poring over Daisy Crossley's profile. Two new pictures had been uploaded since the previous night. One of the photos depicted Daisy lying on her back wearing a bright blue neoprene bikini. The photo had been taken from directly above. Owen enlarged the picture. The horizontal outline of a bar nipple piercing was visible through the fabric of her bikini top. This everyday accessory confirmed a sexual adventurousness. Owen got a thrill from knowing Daisy had been willing to endure pain to enhance pleasure. The other photo was a close-up of Daisy applying some mascara to her eyelashes. Her tongue was touching the top of her upper lip as she leered at the camera.

Owen pressed 'Like' on the picture of Daisy in her bikini. He then got flustered and immediately unliked it. Annoyed with himself, he closed the window and moved over to her Facebook page. Here a far more wholesome image was being presented to the world. There were old photos of her at boarding school, photos of extravagant family holidays. There were group pictures populated by friends who appeared equally privileged and likely to succeed in life. Owen scrolled down the page, fascinated by photos of this girl who might have lived less than fifty yards away from him but seemingly inhabited a different world altogether. Daisy had it all: she was young, rich and beautiful. Owen wondered whether aspiration and ability would ever dictate individual progress. He thought about the careers advisor at school who suggested probation officer as a possible vocation for him. When Owen replied that he wanted to be a dancer or a musician, he was asked to leave. The careers advisor told him that if he wasn't going to take it seriously, they might as well terminate the meeting.

Unlike Daisy, whose life had been cushioned by privilege, Owen had experienced a society determined to impose limitations upon him. He had lived within a system whose structures expressed contempt for who he was yet still expected him to prove that he belonged. He could remember bananas being thrown at Justin Fashanu and John Barnes. The gollywogs on the side of jam jars were still fresh in his memory. Owen was born in a decade where popular culture featured characters complaining about the nig nogs next door, blacking up was commonplace, and kids drew NF signs on schoolbooks as if they were the initials of a top forty act. He still believed that most white people held a negative opinion of him. Not every white person was racist, though. Or at least some were much less prejudiced than others. These were the people he had tried to seek out. Owen hoped they could understand his struggle and perhaps ease his passage. After all, their heritage belonged to him too.

The bedroom reeked of excess alcohol, which an overworked liver had failed to remove. The remaining toxins had escaped through Owen's pores and breath. It smelt awful. Jacquie stood at the entrance of the bedroom door, shaking her head in both pity and disgust. It was Tuesday morning; she had to be at work in forty-five minutes. Owen was supposed to be looking after the kids, but who knows what time he had got home.

With his mouth wide open, Owen rolled onto his back. For a moment, Jacquie considered squirting shampoo into his mouth. It was no more than he deserved. At around five o clock the previous afternoon, Owen had called to say he had a meeting with Joe Sayles. Apparently, Joe had contacted him about a young singer/songwriter he wanted him to produce. Owen had promised Jacquie he wouldn't be late and that he would only have a couple of drinks. The last time the two of them had met up, Owen had gone AWOL for two days. Afterwards, he claimed someone had spiked his drink with a drug that made him lose track of time. She was so bored of it. She didn't understand how he wasn't bored of it by now too.

Owen's naked body was stretched out on the bed. It looked like he had just fallen out of the sky. Jacquie shuddered at the unsightly spectacle. For a while, she simply stared as if Owen was an installation in a museum. He reminded her of one of those hyper-realistic sculptures where every pore and hair follicle appeared amplified.

'Wake up. I've got to go.'

Owen growled as he rolled over onto his front. Jacquie watched his buttocks tense and rise as he farted.

'Disgusting pig.' She walked out of the room to see if Dexter was awake. He was sitting up in bed reading a Hawkeye comic.

'Am I doing football club this afternoon?'

Jacquie crouched down and picked some dirty clothes up off the floor.

'Yes, you are. And afterwards, you are going to Tariq's house.'

Dexter put down his magazine and sighed loudly.

'Why the sighs?' Jacquie asked.

'I don't like Biffy.'

'Who's Biffy?'

'The cat. It scratches.' Dexter stuck a finger up his nose. 'And his bum hole smells of mini cheddars.'

'What are you doing going near his bum hole?'

'I didn't. Tariq told me.' Dexter picked up the magazine and started reading again. 'I love Hawkeye,' he said. 'Some say he's the weakest Avenger. I think Black Widow is. What do you think?'

Jacquie went into the bathroom and put the dirty clothes in the washing machine. Owen entered with a towel wrapped around his waist. He started rummaging through the cabinet above the sink.

'Where are the painkillers?'

Ignoring the question, Jacquie put the washing machine on. Owen followed her as she left the bathroom and went downstairs. His face was puffy, the skin around his eyes bloated and shadowy. He looked like a boxer the day after a fight. Owen went into the kitchen and poured himself some water. Harley walked in with an empty cereal bowl; his face crinkled as he caught a whiff of his dad's odour. Owen waited for Harley to leave before trying to talk to Jacquie.

'Why are you ignoring me?'

'The kids have got football at two o'clock. Dexter is going home with Tariq afterwards. Harley will probably hang out with Jack. They will need some lunch before they go.' Jacquie picked up her handbag and put on a jacket. 'Do you think you can manage that?'

'Why are you being like this?' Owen asked.

Jacquie turned around and began to walk out of the flat. She called out to the boys and said goodbye.

'What have I done wrong?'

Jacquie shut the door behind her. As she walked down the corridor, she could hear the muffled sound of Owen's risible exculpation.

'It was a work thing!' he shouted.

She laughed as she thought how often the same excuse had been utilised. As if this proclamation legitimised lousy behaviour. Jacquie noticed how she didn't even get angry any more. That probably wasn't a good sign, though. She wondered how one knows for sure when a relationship is over. The two of them had weathered numerous rocky patches. Yet, somehow, they always managed to blunder on.

Her friend Nova had suggested that Jacquie speak to her astrologer. Jacquie thought it hilarious that someone should have their own astrologer. And even though she presumed it was all bollocks, Nova still convinced her to have a consultation. After Jacquie introduced herself via email, Tiffany quickly responded with an explanation of what services she offered. The astrologer was at pains to point out that she was not a psychic and did not practise anything which was not explicable by natural laws.

When Jacquie asked how she would know when the time was right to separate from her partner, Tiffany replied that it was the right time to move on if Jacquie imagined the future and her partner was not involved. Jacquie couldn't remember the last time Owen *had* been a part of any visons of her future. When she asked where she would be living in ten years, Tiffany answered that such predictions were beyond her remit. Even so, through the anatomy of the cosmos and her understanding of planetary influences, she managed to confidently tell Jacquie that her eyesight would remain good. That she would manage to avoid schizophrenia and would also enjoy sex well into old age. Sex, Jacquie thought, may have been scarce as she entered middle age, but at least she had some geriatric nooky to look forward to.

Jacquie looked at the time on her phone; there was a missed call from her boss. Something must be up. Dorota never called before work. Nothing was usually so vital that it couldn't wait until she got into the office. There had recently been talk of merging the charity or possibly going into partnership with someone else. There were several organisations out there covering similar territory. But while demand for their services was going up, they were all experiencing reduced donations. Like all charities, The Well-Being Foundation relied on individual philanthropy and public funding from local government. The perfect storm of recession and spending cuts was always going to wreak havoc.

Jacquie had been at the charity for nearly ten years. She

loved it there. After years of working in nightclubs, wrestling with the perceived vacuity of her job, the Foundation provided her professional life with a significance and value previously missing. Everyone wants to feel significant. Everyone wants to think that what they do with their time somehow makes a difference. Jacquie was convinced that feelings of lack of self-worth were what made everyone so horrible to each other. She envisaged this only getting worse as more jobs were rendered obsolete by automation and people felt increasingly redundant. She had recently read somewhere that increased use of artificial intelligence in the workplace would lead to a new renaissance. Once people had been freed from the tyranny of the daily grind, they would have more time to engage with loftier pursuits. Jacquie thought this sounded unlikely. She imagined a future where people, deprived of a reason to get up in the morning or relegated to lower-skilled jobs, spent much of their time trolling others on social media.

She bit down on her lip as she considered the possibility of no longer working at the Foundation. Although she understood why they might want to seek new partners, she was worried what that could mean for her job. Whatever organisation the charity ultimately partnered or merged with, presumably they would have their own events organiser.

After three packed buses failed to stop, Jacquie eventually got on the 24. It was the same every time she went to work. The underground was even worse. She had given up trying to get on the tube in the morning. Life was too short. Jacquie sat on the top deck and stared out of the window as the bus went past the site where Harley and Dexter's nursery used to be. The council had closed it down the year before, along with the youth centre, which Harley had only recently joined. It was one of only two centres in the borough rated outstanding. They were already building a new block of flats in its place. Jacquie remembered how difficult it had been getting the boys a place. All the local mums were desperate to get their kids in there. Jacquie had been taken aback by the ferocity of some of the parents' determination. She even fell out with one girl who she had become friends with at antenatal classes. Harley got a place at the nursery, but her kid didn't. Consumed by the injustice of it all, the girl couldn't bring herself to speak to Jacquie again. She lived closer to the nursery than Jacquie and was convinced that subterfuge must have won Harley a place. Parents who thought a secured place assured safe passage through a series of good local schools discovered a murderously competitive edge they had previously been unaware of. It was the fear their child might suffer a disadvantage that kept them awake at night. The same worries sometimes tipped parents into pits of irrational resentment. Mothers developed strange facial tics whenever schools or nursery places were discussed. Their whole demeanour would change the moment the subject was raised. The kids were only three.

In the end, Harley didn't get a place at the primary school. He didn't get a place at his second, third or fourth choice school either. Albion Park was just out of the catchment area of three primary schools, all designated outstanding by Ofsted. Even though it wasn't really feasible, Jacquie wanted to send Harley to a private school. At that point, Owen was still earning relatively well, and Jacquie had started working at the charity. It was beyond their means, but Jacquie was convinced a private education would bestow upon Harley all the things she and Owen had missed out on. She had zero experience of the independent school system and was unaware that, like any other institution, there were good private schools and there were bad ones. Naively she believed private equalled superior. Although she chose to ignore the politics or any issues of perpetuating inequalities,

Owen was adamant that no child of his would ever go to a private school. He thought she was out of her mind for even considering it. If for no other reason than financial.

Harley and Jack were sitting in the front room playing on the Xbox when Jacquie returned from work later that day.

'Where's your dad?'

'Upstairs.'

'Is he sleeping?'

Harley shrugged his shoulders and continued playing the game.

There were many things about Owen Jacquie had once found attractive. Unfortunately, she now resented him for many of those things. When they first met, Owen had seemed oblivious to the financial arrangements one must put in place to receive essential utilities. He was often sent warnings for non-payment of council tax or unpaid electricity bills. His mobile phone number was frequently changing because he would forget to pay his bills. It wasn't that he didn't have the money. His mind was just elsewhere. Jacquie liked the idea of Owen as a creative outlier. If anything, she encouraged it. He was consumed by music and didn't allow himself to be impeded by the minutiae of quotidian life. Jacquie bought into his personal myth and enjoyed perpetuating it. The introduction of children, however, pissed all over this dynamic. The mental and physical exhaustion gradually made Jacquie less and less tolerant of Owen's idiosyncrasies. Almost overnight, the nature of their relationship was booted from a self-serving flight of fancy into a puke-stained, sleep-deprived reality.

At first, while Owen's star still threatened ascendancy, Jacquie remained supportive of his ambitions. But as the prospect of success waned, so did her tolerance. Now, his inability to function as a normal adult seemed unformed.

Jacquie no longer perceived Owen as a nonconformist or a maverick. In her opinion, he was just lazy. She interpreted his dogged pursuit of success as a desperate attempt to cling to his youth. She believed that he wouldn't know what to do with himself or even who he was any more once he eventually let go. Meanwhile, she had to live with a man who slept in the afternoons because he had stayed up all night drinking.

When Jacquie walked into the bedroom, instead of finding Owen crashed out on the bed, she discovered him putting clothes away.

'What are you doing?'

'What does it look like?'

A basket next to the unmade bed was full of ironed clothes. Jacquie sat down on the bed; it was warm and smelt of bodies.

'Dorota has decided to merge with another charity,' she said.

'Why would she do that?'

'I guess she thinks it's the only way the charity has any chance of surviving.'

'What would that mean for you?'

'Who knows.'

Owen had a worried look in his eyes as he considered the implications of Jacquie losing her job. 'Shit,' he said, still deep in thought. 'That sucks.'

A sardonic half-smile twitched on Jacquie's face. It was an expression Owen was familiar with.

'What's that look for?' he asked.

Jacquie shook her head wearily. She was about to point out that Owen would be expected to support her until something else turned up if she did lose her job. 'Doesn't matter,' she said. She looked around the room and sighed. The paint in the corner of the ceiling was cracked and flaking.

'Joe said he might have a bit of work for me. That should bring some money in.'

Jacquie offered a disinterested nod and asked Owen if he had spoken to Tariq's mum. There was a knock at the door downstairs.

'That will probably be her now,' Owen said.

Jacquie answered the door. Val, Jack's mum, was standing in the doorway. 'You've got that crackling sound as well,' she said. 'You can hear it everywhere in my block. It must be the wires, right?'

Jacquie looked up at the ceiling above the corridor. 'Yeah. It started last year after we had those leaks.'

'Has anyone been to look at it?' Val asked.

'What do you think?'

'Same here. They're useless. It must be a fire hazard. Will the council do anything about it, though?'

Val had lived on the estate for nearly ten years. She had three kids. Jack was the same age as Harley. The twins, Katie, and Lucy were twenty-one. Val was tall and skinny with deep-set sullen eyes and tightly pulled back hair. She was wearing lipstick, which bought attention to the thinness of her top lip. 'Is Jack here?'

Jacquie stepped aside and ushered Val in. 'They're in there,' she said, gesturing towards the front room.

Val stuck her head around the door and said hello to Jack. As she bent forwards, her hitched T-shirt revealed a bouquet of flowers tattooed on her lower back. The spray of pastel-coloured petals contrasted against her waxen skin. It reminded Jacquie of a coffin tribute. Although the two of them had always got on reasonably well, Jacquie had always been wary of Val. She used to work at a casino in Soho. Her boss was a Chinese gangster who laundered money by lending it to punters on a losing streak. Inevitably a vig was added on top of the loan, and violence promised if payments were missed. Val used to be one of the cash carriers, always looking out for potential loanees. She possessed an easiness around criminality. She knew how to get hold of things, how to get rid of things. Most of the villains in the area seemed to be a cousin or a nephew. One of her uncles hosted guided tours of East End gangland haunts. For a while, Val used to help him out.

'Have you got time for a cuppa?' Val followed Jacquie into the kitchen and sat down at the small dining table. She picked up a copy of Dexter's school photo, which had arrived in the post that morning.

'He's looking more and more like his dad, isn't he? He's going to be a proper heartbreaker when he grows up.' Val continued to study the photo. 'He doesn't look much like Harley, though, does he? Is there something you're not telling me?'

'Ha! I wish,' Jacquie said.'

'Oh, like that, is it?'

'Hmmm… How's the job with Kitty going?' Jacquie said, changing the subject.

'Yeah, alright, I suppose.' Val shrugged her shoulders. 'It's only a cleaning job, isn't it? Kitty seems nice enough, though. She gave me a bonus this week. I've only just started.'

'That sounds about right,' Jacquie said. 'Hit her with a few hard-luck stories. She'll give you a bonus every week. She's a sucker for a victim that one.'

'It's funny. She usually runs out of the house the moment I start cleaning. I think she likes to think the elves do it while she's out.'

Jacquie laughed.

'Did you hear about what happened in the park last week?' Val proceeded to tell Jacquie about the incident involving Luc Rijkens. 'Kitty reckons she saw Dominik doing a runner soon after it was supposed to have happened,' Val continued. 'She told me that at least one other kiddy was with him but couldn't see who it was. It's going to be one of our two, isn't it… or both.'

'I heard the police visited a few flats,' Jacquie said, spooning some sugar into one of the cups. 'I didn't know what it was about, though. How badly was the boy hurt?'

'It wasn't even that bad.' Val chewed at some skin around her thumb. 'Something like this was always going to happen. I'm just glad it wasn't anything worse.'

'Have you spoken to Jack about it?'

'What's the point?' Val said. 'He's not going to own up to anything. You can hardly blame them, can you? The way the residents carry on. They're asking for trouble. Spaces like the park shouldn't be allowed to be private. My Jack can see the new playground from his bedroom.'

'It reminds me of this bloke Owen used to work with.' Jacquie passed Val a cup of tea. 'He collected toys, *Star Wars*, *Planet of the Apes*. All that stuff you should have grown out of by the time you hit your teens. He had tons of it, all in its original packaging. He kept the toys in a room, just out of reach. When his son, who was only about seven at the time, used to stay with him at weekends, he would have to sleep in this room, staring at all these fantastic toys. They were close enough to see, but the kid wasn't allowed to touch any of them.'

'It's like some weird kind of punishment, isn't it,' Val said, blowing on her cup of tea. 'That's exactly how Jack feels. No wonder our lot are getting narked.'

Chapter 7

August 2014

The room resembled one of the pictures of Whitney Houston's bathroom taken soon after her death. The basin resembled a giant ashtray, the area around it littered with old lighters and empty fast-food cartons. The distressed antique mirror panels framed in gold gilt were decorated with kissed lipstick smudges. Mercifully the mirror was unable to reflect the chaos that was the bathroom floor. Crouched over the toilet bowl, Daisy Crossley knelt with her head almost at a right angle. Two fingers of one hand explored the further reaches of her oesophagus, while the other hand held her phone. Somehow Daisy was managing to read a message while at the same time vomiting up the remnants of whatever she had recently eaten. Her body had been trained to purge itself of the nutrients it needed whenever prompted to do so. It was a far cry from the early days when sometimes it could take up to an hour for anything to come out. When it did, the shock of the movement often caught her body by surprise, frequently causing Daisy to piss herself. These days she was more than capable of multi-tasking while puking.

Having successfully obliterated any nourishment, Daisy wiped her mouth on a nearby towel, flushed the chain a couple of times, brushed her teeth and gargled some mouth-wash. Once she had masked any potential smell from the vomit with perfume and deodorant, she applied some eye drops to alleviate any redness from the strain. Finally, before she went downstairs to face her mum, Daisy checked her teeth in the mirror. The acidity from regular bouts of binge purging had started to erode the enamel in places. They were looking glassy and weirdly free from stains or lines. Daisy was reluctant to go back to the dentist who had called her out during her last appointment. He had rec-ognised the symptoms straight away.

Even though comparisons between Daisy's fluctuating weight and Emma's self-professed inability to put on weight were more than likely at the root of Daisy's problems, Emma Crossley acted as if oblivious to her daughter's disorders.

'You can blame your dad,' Emma once said. 'You're just like him. He only has to look at an eclair and you can see the pounds piling on. When I was modelling, I used to eat whatever I wanted and never put on weight. I was so skinny, but with big tits. Just lucky, I guess.'

Such unhelpful pronouncements weren't just reserved for her daughter. When Daisy's friend Leila insisted on only eating a single piece of the lobster and langoustine ravioli Max had especially made them, Emma said, while pinch-ing her hips, *Sometimes I wish I was anorexic.* When Ziggy, having hosted a protozoan parasite for the better part of three months, returned from the USA looking like a stick insect and suffering from epithelial ulcerations, the first thing Emma said to her was, *Look at you. You are so thin. You look fab.*

Max frequently warned Emma about referring to her-self as fat in front of Daisy. It had been going on for years. Like his wife, Max was unaware of any latent disorders. Still, common sense dictated that complaining about non-existent weight issues in front of one's impressionable young daughter probably wasn't the best idea.

'You complaining about being fat,' Max had once said to Emma, 'is like me complaining about being too skinny. It's absurd.'

An enormous portrait of Max and Emma dominated one end of the Crossleys' industrial-style kitchen. The painting was strangely artless. The faces of Max and Emma possessed a Victorian sentimentality. Both were staring back at the artist with soppy doe eyes. There was no suggestion of the painter trying to get beneath the skin of the sitters. Rather than a work of art, the painting resembled one of the queasy portraits of the couple which occasionally appeared in soft-focus, celebrity-obsessed magazines.

Emma was sitting at the table with her laptop open. Next to her was a pile of unopened packages.

'Are any of those for me?' Daisy asked.

'They're all for you.'

Daisy poured herself a large black coffee. Caffeine combined with cigarettes suppressed the hunger pangs which inevitably arrived after a purge. The combination managed to keep her engine ticking over once she had dumped the fuel.

'Oh, that's fantastic.' Emma clapped her hands together. 'That is such good news.'

'What are you so happy about?'

'*Wallpaper* is going to write a piece on us.'

'Is that good?'

'Is that good?' Emma sneered at her daughter's ignorance. 'Are you joking? I've been making home furnishings for just over three years. *Wallpaper* is probably the most influential design magazine in the world. I would say that's pretty good going. Wouldn't you?'

Daisy sat down opposite her mum and began opening one of the packages. Inside was a fluorescent pink swimsuit. Daisy held it up to her chest.

'Why do you keep getting sent swimwear?' Emma asked.

'What's it to you?'

'Do you have to be quite so hostile?' Emma began typing into her laptop keyboard. After she had replied to her publicist, she looked at Daisy again. 'Well, are you going to answer me?'

'Brands ask me to wear their stuff.'

'Brands ask you to wear their stuff.' Emma gave a look of overemphasised puzzlement. 'Why?'

'Why not?' Daisy opened another one of the parcels.

Emma mimicked Daisy's surly reply.

'Look, I've got about forty-five thousand followers on Instagram. Every one of my posts gets over fifteen thousand likes. Brands want their stuff to be seen.'

'How much would you get for wearing that cheap-looking swimming costume?' Emma said, prodding her finger at the garment.

'I'm not being paid anything yet. I get free product.'

'You're not even getting paid?' Emma laughed.

'You're so fucking condescending.'

'Well, I would be surprised if any reputable brand would... you know.'

'No, I don't know. You don't finish any of your sentences. Everything you say is an implication.'

'Well, I just think some of the stuff you post is so degrading. I saw that picture of you in that revolting green bikini. It was so high cut. If you had a single pube you would have seen it.'

Daisy shook her head and mumbled, 'Don't look if you dislike it so much.'

'I mean,' Emma continued, 'it's like feminism never happened.'

'Ha! That's rich coming from you. Are you talking about

the type of feminism that lets an eighties rock star put you on a leash and keep you in a cage?'

'That video was directed by Tony Kaye.'

'I couldn't care if it was directed by Christopher Nolan. It's one of the most demeaning things I've ever seen. I'm demonstrating what it means to live inside an autonomous body. Which is the opposite of what you were doing.'

'No, you're not. You're posing in your underwear.'

'What's the difference between that and being plastered over billboards in a lingerie ad?'

'You have control,' Emma said. 'You could present yourself any way you like. Why choose to promote this image? Surely you can do better than taking your clothes off. I mean, who are you trying to impress?'

'You had control too,' Daisy said. 'No one forced you to be a model.'

'I didn't have control of how I was represented.' Emma pursed her lips with annoyance. 'But at least I got paid properly for the loss of that privilege.'

Daisy folded her arms and snorted derisively. 'You were reinforcing stereotypes,' she said. 'You were a slave to the gaze. I'm reclaiming my body from its objectification in a patriarchal culture.'

Emma put her hand over her mouth and started to laugh. 'Oh, darling, don't kid yourself. What you're doing does not signify female empowerment. You're just giving men what they want. It's slutty.'

Daisy recoiled from Emma's comment. 'Why can't you ever say anything nice? I mean, literally every time you open your mouth, you say the wrong thing.'

'I don't mean to,' Emma said. She reached out her hand and placed it on top of Daisy's. 'I'm just worried about you, that's all. You've always been such a bright girl. I don't want to see you waste your talents.'

Daisy pulled her hand away. 'How does taking off my clothes detract from any talent I supposedly have?'

'I just don't think it chimes with this idea you have of yourself as a feminist.'

'I'm trying to make some money. It's no different from what you did.'

'Darling, but I made proper money. You're being sent fast fashion and shitty make-up that's bad for your skin.'

Jamie, the younger of Daisy's two brothers, walked into the kitchen. Without saying a word to either Daisy or his mum, he opened the fridge door and grabbed a Pyrex bowl full of pasta. His complexion bared scant relation to the seasons. London had recently been blessed with glorious weather, yet Daisy's brother looked like someone who was suffering from an allergy to daylight. His skin tone possessed a greenish hue. His hair was lank and greasy. Jamie stood in front of the microwave, transfixed by the rotating platter inside. Meanwhile, Emma, glad to escape the conversation she had been having with Daisy, began typing noisily on her keyboard.

'Hey, Jamie.' No reply. 'What have been you up to?'

With his back facing her, Jamie continued to ignore his sister.

'I haven't seen you for a while.'

Jamie's head fell back onto his slumped shoulders. He sighed loudly as Daisy attempted to instigate a conversation.

'Have you not got any pre-season training this year?' Daisy looked at Emma, hoping she might have registered Jamie's refusal to engage. Emma was consumed by whatever email she was reading now.

'Jamie. Jamie!' Daisy waited for a reply. 'Why are you being so fucking rude?' The ping of the microwave announced the food was ready. 'What is wrong with you?' Daisy said as her brother scurried past with his bowl of food. 'Freak.' Daisy resembled a carp as her mouth fell open in outrage. She looked at her mum incredulously. 'And you say you're worried about me?'

'He's just been a bit down since he split up with Pink.'

'A bit down? Mum, he's like a zombie. He never leaves his room. He wasn't even with her for that long. It seems like a bit of an overreaction.'

'I don't think it's anything to worry about.' Emma picked up her phone and started tapping out a message.

'Hector's worried,' Daisy said. 'He told me that when Jamie's not playing on his console, he spends most of his time clicking from porn site to porn site.'

'That's perfectly normal for a boy of his age.'

Daisy put her head in her hands. 'It's not normal. Hector tried to speak to him about it. He said Jamie got angry and defensive. I think you should talk to Daddy about it.'

'I'm not going to bother him right now. He's got more than enough on his plate.'

'What could be more important than his son's mental health?'

'Now that's not fair. You know he cares.'

'No, I don't.'

'Your dad is very stressed right now. The first episode of the new series is on tonight.'

'Great,' Daisy said under her breath. 'More humiliation.'

'What's that supposed to mean?' The skin on the bridge of Emma's nose folded into a series of neat creases as she spoke.

'I don't know why he has to be such an arsehole. ITV2 are repeating the first series. I watched an episode the other night. It was horrible. At one point, he poured the sous chef's velouté all over her shoes. I'm amazed someone doesn't sue him... or stab him.'

'Your father has high expectations. He just wants people to perform at their peak.'

'And if they don't, he humiliates them?'

'Oh, come off it, it's just a bit of fun.'

'You call being bullied in front of millions fun? I don't think anyone even gives a shit about the cooking part of the show. Especially in America. Viewers just want to hear Daddy call one of the contestants a twat or a wanker. *I said cardamom, not cinnamon, you bell-end.*'

Emma sniggered at Daisy's impression of her father. 'It's showbiz. No one believes he's like that. If he was all lovely and cuddly, the show wouldn't have an audience. Besides, the new series reveals a different side to him. It's the real him.'

Daisy laughed. 'Why does every person on TV believe there's a demand for them to reveal their *real selves*?'

'Do you know what?' Emma said, irritated. 'We should all just be grateful that we got another series commissioned.'

For the first two series of *The Competitive Chef,* Max Crossley was presented as an irascible, no-nonsense cook who took no prisoners in the kitchen. He was notorious for his weight, his volatility and the amount he sweated while cooking. Each week Max was joined in the kitchen by an unknown professional chef. Together they competed against another celebrity chef and their assistant. The two kitchens would prepare the same meal and present it to a panel of food critics, who declared a winner. The total number of viewers for each episode of the second series averaged around 2.1 million. Max became a personality the US public loved to hate.

'It's going to be even more embarrassing than the first series. It's not exactly compelling TV, is it?' Daisy adopted the voice of a trailer voiceover. '*Will Max manage to lose eight stone in one year, or will he just stay fat...* who cares?'

'It was five stone. And FYI, the viewing figures suggest that millions of people care. The new series has topped the network's ratings for non-scripted shows. It's a hit... no thanks to you.'

'Here we go,' Daisy said.

'Well, the least you could do is agree to participate.'

Daisy's eyes hardened. 'Do we have to talk about this again?'

'After everything your dad has done for this family, I think a bit of gratitude wouldn't go amiss. The boys get it.'

'The boys get what?'

'They understand the need for everyone to do their bit.'

'They didn't have a choice.'

Around the same time the second series of *The Competitive Chef* went on air, a programme featuring a similarly abrasive (this time French) chef was broadcast on a different channel. With nearly five million viewers *Le Chef*, featuring Serge Berbizier, was The Fox network's second highest-ranked unscripted TV series. Serge looked more like a matinee idol than a TV chef. Each episode of *Le Chef* invariably included some kind of mishap, resulting in Serge taking off his top. Hordes of lustful men and women would tune in especially for this moment. The highly stylised and tightly choreographed unveiling of Serge's ripped physique proved so popular it was immortalised in a meme. It had even featured in an episode of *The Simpsons*.

'Do you know what? You should be thanking me,' Emma snapped. 'If I hadn't suggested a change of direction, ABC would have cancelled the show.'

Daisy couldn't help but question her mum's motives for suggesting the new series should focus more on Max's home life. Sales at her interior design company had improved exponentially. Prior to the series being aired in the US, Temple & Jenks had received zero Stateside exposure. Now they were receiving requests from upmarket design magazines and selling their products in Grade and De Sousa Hughes.

Daisy had also noticed sparkles of glee in her mother's eye every time one of the US magazines referred to her as 'Lady E'. Emma was the show's breakout star. Her affected Home Counties accent, long face, symmetrical features and polished aristocratic looks gratified Americans' fascination with the British upper class (although Emma was from High Wycombe and distinctly lower middle class).

'Personally,' Emma continued, 'I thought the subplot about Max's attempt to lose weight was a stroke of genius. Not only did I save the show, but I probably saved his life too.'

'I just think it's all so… so beggy,' Daisy said.

'Beggy?'

'Yeah… you're exploiting your family's private life for financial gain. It's revolting.'

The shadow of a smile passed across Emma's face. 'Admittedly, appearing on a prime time TV show isn't quite as virtuous as spreading your legs for free swimwear.'

'Fuck you!' Daisy snapped.

'You really have no self-awareness, do you?' Emma adjusted her laptop screen and began typing into her keyboard again. 'Don't worry though, darling. It does come with age.'

Chapter 8

The train pulled out of the station. Slowly it began its journey south towards the coast. Jacquie threw her head back and emitted a long-drawn-out sigh of relief. She wanted to escape. London was hot and oppressive; tempers were beginning to fray. An edgy undercurrent had descended upon the city. Earlier that day, she had gone to Dalston to drop the boys off at her parents' house. As she and the kids walked past Dalston Kingsland station, Jacquie had accidentally barged her holdall into a man. With zero concern for the kids, the man turned around and screamed in Jacquie's face. *Watch where the fuck you're going, you silly bitch.* The man held his stare and glowered menacingly at Jacquie, willing her to engage. Thick flecks of spittle were splattered across his chin. His wide-eyed stare and wonky eyes made him look demented and dangerous.

Too concerned for their own safety to intervene, people passed by, inured to scenes of such aggression. Desperate to get away, Harley pulled at his mum's arm. The three of them crossed the Kingsland Road and made their way down Ridley Road Market. A police cordon at the beginning of the market prevented them from going any further. Forensic officers clad in hooded overalls, latex gloves and face masks scoured the immediate vicinity for evidence. An innocuous-looking white tent signified something dark and tragic had taken place. The three of them turned around and went back onto the Kingsland Road. A woman was arguing with someone in front of a hardware shop. As the row escalated, the woman began kicking over a display of large plastic containers and crappy pots and pans. Meanwhile, ignoring the tumult, everyone else went about their business, determined not to let the antics of a few nutters impinge upon their day. Passers-by kept their heads down, hoping not to be noticed or picked on by the next person who decided to cause a scene.

Jacquie was raised on these streets, and although the area had been considerably poorer then, it had felt connected. Familiarity, togetherness and mutual respect had been the glue that united a community. Jacquie now found herself feeling increasingly dislocated from the city she had grown up in. Rejected by a place she had pledged a lifetime's allegiance to. She had never wanted to live anywhere else. London had always felt like the epicentre of everything that mattered, and she an essential part of its fabric. But her loyalty had not been reciprocated. Those in charge had collectively conspired to flog the integrity of the city to the highest bidder. In the process, they ignored the people who were the very essence of the place. All over the city, neighbourhoods were being violated and fractured. Jacquie wasn't so naive that she didn't realise gentrification had always existed in some form or another. But the current climate felt different. It wasn't just a case of middle-class incomers populating edgy inner-city areas; this was vast swathes of London being transformed almost overnight. Local economies were affected, high streets diminished and community spaces shut down to facilitate the construction of more and more luxury housing. Much of which would remain empty. The city was awash with soulless steel and glass edifices – financial assets dressed up as aspirational urban dwellings.

But realistically, affordable housing for those who had been displaced had virtually disappeared. Jacquie obviously wasn't the only one who felt this way. A feeling of disaffection was palpable. People had become alienated in their environments and were lashing out at each other. Where the odd incident in the street would once have been attributable to London's edgy vivacity, Jacquie now detected a dysfunction that was poisoning the well.

Owen's failure, yet again, to return home before sunrise had compounded her desire to get away. He hadn't responded to any of her calls the previous evening but was now inundating her with messages. Each ping of her phone represented another plea for forgiveness. Jacquie turned the phone to silent and sent Caroline a text.

I'm on the train. will you meet me at the station x?

She couldn't be arsed to read any of Owen's messages. There was an awful familiarity with how these episodes unfolded. She knew the messages would be full of hollow promises. She was unsure as to why this occasion was worse than previous ones. It just was. She no longer cared enough to respond. Owen had been drinking heavily since he got back from being on tour. He was probably depressed. But Jacquie found it hard to be sympathetic while he continued to stay out most of the night.

Further down the carriage, Jacquie spotted a young dad and his daughter. She briefly felt guilty for not bringing the boys with her. They would have enjoyed a weekend away. But Jacquie needed some space and time to talk to Caroline. The dad was combing his daughter's hair. His clumsy attempts to make a bun made Jacquie laugh. There was a large overnight bag on the luggage rack above their heads. Jacquie imagined the man was a single father taking his young daughter away for the weekend. The girl was probably about the same age as Harley. The dad looked like he was in his mid-thirties. He was well presented with closely cropped hair and a beard. On his wrist was an oversized watch. Jacquie wondered what he did for a living, what kind of place he lived in, and how many women he had slept with since he split up with his partner.

Having already decided he was definitely a single father, Jacquie contemplated what might have happened to the girl's mother. Why did she allow this man to get away? Maybe she was dead? Of course: that's why he and the girl had this incredible bond. It was the two of them against the world. The thought added an exciting new dimension to the backstory Jacquie was concocting.

The girl said something to her father that made him laugh. His smile revealed a gap in his front teeth. He seemed so confident and relaxed. The guy looked up and caught Jacquie laughing to herself as she enjoyed his unsuccessful attempts to hold his daughter's hair in place. He smiled at Jacquie and held out the hairband and brush.

'Typical man,' Jacquie said as she walked towards them. 'Absolutely useless.' She took the hairbrush from the dad and sat down opposite his daughter. 'How would you like it done, darling?'

The girl asked if she could have 'one of those messy, twisted bun things'. The dad passed Jacquie a tin of hairbands and pins. His hand lingered for a millisecond longer than she'd anticipated. The thrill of skin contact made her shiver. Jacquie began to gather the young girl's hair. She pulled it into a high ponytail and pinned down the bun before loosening some of the shorter strands.

'Look at you,' the dad said. 'You look so pretty.'

Jacquie thought about how rarely she enjoyed this type of routine intimacy with Owen and the boys. The role of a family, primarily, should be about bringing up children. Supporting and protecting them and enabling them to grow into well-adjusted adults who can do the same for their children. This insignificant moment with a stranger compounded a feeling that had been eating away at Jacquie for some time: she was failing her children.

'My name's Spencer,' the girl's father said. 'Where are you off to?'

Jacquie introduced herself and said that she was going to Hastings.

'On your own?'

She hesitated before smiling. 'I'm meeting my husband there.'

Jacquie got up from where she was sitting and said goodbye to the young girl and her dad. She shimmied back down the carriage with a renewed swagger. The brief exchange had provided her with a welcome fillip. And although she had no intention of responding to the attention of any old person, the lingering hand, the sustained gaze, had provided an insight into what being single could be like. For too long, her life had been devoid of romance; her desires subsumed by her role as a virtual single mother. For years she and Owen had tolerated a serviceable sex life. It was infrequent, functional and without passion. Essentially the two of them had tacitly consented to remain in a loveless relationship for the sake of their kids. Knowing all about errant fathers himself, Jacquie was confident Owen was determined his children should not endure a similar fate. But at what cost? His intentions were laudable, but he did little to ensure it wouldn't happen. Owen wasn't sticking around because he genuinely believed it was best for the kids. How could it be? No, if Owen was honest with himself, he would realise the only reason he was prepared to endure the status quo was that he didn't want to be separated from the boys. Ultimately it was a selfish decision and one which would increasingly affect Harley and Dexter.

Jacquie inhaled a lungful of the salty air so redolent of British seaside towns. The distinctive tang immediately conjured images of burnt-out piers, noisy arcades and fleet-footed junkies. The lunatic cawing of nearby gulls made the scene even more vivid.

'I can see why people like it down here,' Caroline said. 'My sister loves it. But she's been here a while now.'

Jacquie looked out towards the beach, which was immediately adjacent to the road. The heat coming off the pavement made everything flutter and wobble. The beach was busy with revellers, benches facing the sea crammed full of pensioners. The promenade bustled with skateboarders, cyclists and groups of kids in bikinis and shorts. The reflection coming off the sea was so bright, Jacquie had to shade her eyes as she looked out towards the distance. She wondered why the light which flickers and shimmies when sunlight reflects from the water was so seductive. It made her want to run into the sea.

'It seems pretty good to me,' she said. 'Everyone looks so happy.'

The two of them walked down Carlisle Parade, past the crappy hotels and once-glamorous facades of numerous Regency apartments, towards Caroline's flat, which was a stone's throw from the sea.

'What an incredible view.' Jacquie looked out from the sitting room bay windows over the tiny strip of water which separates the UK from mainland Europe. 'Can you see France from here?'

'I wouldn't have thought so. At least I've never seen it.'

'When you fly over, it looks like we're practically touching. Funny to think that from just over there, you could drive to India or China.' Jacquie was quiet for a moment as she continued to stare out of the window. 'This place is lovely,' she said.' It must soften the blow a bit after everything that happened?'

Without missing a beat, Caroline confirmed that this was not the case. It was the first time Jacquie had seen her since she left London. The intervening period had not been kind to her. She looked thinner; her hair was greyer than she remembered. Caroline was about ten years older than Jacquie, but she had never looked it. The stress of the last few years had left its mark.

While Caroline went to the kitchen to make coffee, Jacquie sat down on a black faux leather tub chair next to the window. She looked around the flat. There was barely anything in it. Caroline's old flat used to be full of possessions and bits of tat. Much of the furniture would be draped in exotic silks and fabrics, while the shelves were packed with Central Asian trinkets and books on spiritual guidance.

They had met when Jacquie was in the throes of severe postpartum back pain. She had been sleeping terribly. This, coupled with the strains of looking after a small baby, had nearly sent her over the edge. A friend recommended Caroline, who specialised in manipulative therapy and postural guidance. Jacquie became a regular client. She used to spend hours prostrate on her couch with her face sticking through a breathing hole, staring at the weave on an old Afghan prayer rug. None of this stuff was evident in the new flat, which was utilitarian where the other had been homely.

Caroline walked back into the room and handed her a coffee. Jacquie was about to ask if most of her stuff was in storage but, concerned that she might be pouring salt on an already livid wound, thought better of it.

'What's the sea like?' Jacquie asked.

'I don't go in. It's too cold. Besides, it's filthy with sewage and whatever else is pumped into it.'

'It can't be that bad.' Still in possession of a childlike fascination with the sea, Jacquie gazed longingly out of the window. It seemed like a world far removed from the one she inhabited.

'Stupidly, I didn't bring a swimming costume. Have you got anything I could use?'

'Are you serious?'

'I can't be this close and not go in. We can catch up properly when I get back.'

Caroline went to her bedroom and soon returned with a couple of swimming costumes and one of her daughter's bikinis.

'Do you have a full-length mirror anywhere?' Jacquie asked, eyeing Martha's skimpy bikini with concern.

Caroline showed Jacquie to her bedroom. Apart from a colourful bedspread and a bedside table with a framed photo of Martha, the room was as austere as the rest of the flat. Jacquie leaned over to take a closer look at the photograph. Next to the picture, she noticed a pack of antidepressants and some tranquillisers. Caroline had always been an evangelist for herbalism and alternative methods for treating what she referred to as cultural illnesses. She believed modern living manufactured depression and could be combatted without resorting to prescription medicines. When Jacquie became depressed after the birth of Dexter, Caroline advised against standard medicinal solutions and recommended a series of coping skills. This included exercise, healthy eating and St John's Wort. Jacquie was shocked by the blister pack of pills hanging out of an open box of venlafaxine.

Jacquie sat down on the edge of the bed, took off her shoes and trousers and then stood up and removed the rest of her clothes. She caught a glimpse of herself in a large mirror that was leaning against the wall. Her immediate reaction was to bend forward and cover her breasts with her right hand and forearm. She walked over to the mirror. There was so much she disliked about herself. She particularly hated the crumpled mesh of skin that encircled her belly button. Although serving as a reminder of the two children she had once carried within her, the way the skin slumped and folded made her tummy look aged.

Having endured body issues during her adolescence and early adulthood, Jacquie had bloomed during her two pregnancies. She had revelled in her changing shape and the role her body was fulfilling. She had marvelled at her enormous breasts and the way Owen responded to them. Since having Dexter, though, her body had once again become the source of any number of self-esteem issues.

Jacquie chided herself for holding up parts of her body, even though no one else was there. Jesus, she thought, I've produced two enormous children who have fed off me and clung to me until my body virtually gave up. Two children who denied me years of sleep and rest. And yet here I am, berating myself for my appearance.

Jacquie turned her back to the mirror and craned her neck to get a glimpse of her bum. The prospect of walking across the beach in a bikini filled her with dread. She may as well have been contemplating walking across it naked.

On the rare occasions since she gave birth to Dexter that she Owen had sex, Jacquie always insisted on turning the lights off. She could tell Owen had been shocked by the extra weight she carried. She felt betrayed by the man whose children she bore and sacrificed her body for. Who was she kidding on the train earlier? For a moment, she had felt desirable. But as she stood naked in Caroline's unfriendly bedroom, the thought of sleeping with a stranger terrified her.

What was the point of it all? In a futile attempt to reclaim her pre-childbirth figure, Jacquie persisted with various diets and fitness regimes. She had not only given birth to two children, but nearly a decade had elapsed. Nature had proceeded as expected. Everyone experiences the inexorable decline of their bodies. Why couldn't she be kinder to herself?

Jacquie tossed aside the bikini; she wasn't even going to bother trying it on. The other two costumes looked too frumpy. She wondered why she was even going through with this palaver. However, she wasn't about to allow a moment of spontaneity to be hijacked by a bout of self-loathing. With a renewed resolve, she decided on the less dowdy of the two costumes.

'Wow, look at you,' Caroline said, a smile finally breaking through her frown. 'You look great.' She passed Jacquie a bathrobe and told her to leave her stuff at the flat. 'Just go down to the beach in your costume.'

Jacquie looked horrified at Caroline's suggestion. The voice inside her head, which told her that everyone would be gawping at her, became louder. They would all be pointing at her shapeless arse, shocked at how she had let herself go. She hated that she allowed herself to be bullied by such chatter, which fed back on a constant loop.

'Fuck it,' Jacquie said as she tightened the bathrobe cord around her waist. 'I'm going to do it.'

Jacquie walked across the road which separated the flat from the promenade. The sun was beating down hard. The tarmac felt spongy and cushioned. On the pavement, an old man in a wheelchair was letting his dog crap on the floor. The dog's quivering hind legs made her feel sick as she walked past. The beach was packed with people not doing much. The tide was high, and there was no available sand for the kids to play in. Jacquie found a spot on the beach, kicked off the flip-flops she had borrowed from Caroline, and let her robe fall to the floor. She hobbled inelegantly over the pebbles and stones towards the sea.

Without testing the water or allowing herself to be deterred by the green slime on the stones or the bubbly film of scum that lapped against the shore, Jacquie waded in. Once the sea was above her knees, she dived under. The shock of the cold water sent her heart racing. She gasped for air, swallowing a mouthful of seawater in the process. For a moment, it felt as if she had forgotten how to swim. Jacquie flapped her arms like an idiot as she thrashed around in the water, trying to find her stroke. With a spasmodic and graceless breaststroke, she eventually began to swim, knowing that she needed to move to stay warm.

Earlier that day, when the sea, with the sun glistening on its surface, had appeared so enticing, Jacquie had naively imagined herself swimming in fresh, clear water. Perhaps floating on her back as she gazed at the sky above. Instead, she received a rude awakening when she dived under the surface, only to be greeted by a murky green vortex of swirling sand and poor visibility.

Although she had not swum very far, the beach already seemed some distance away. The buildings on the promenade resembled architectural miniatures. Jacquie swam out further. The only sounds she could hear were the lapping of the water and the squawk of a couple of gulls circling above. One of the birds swooped down and landed near her. It looked huge from up close. Its beady brown eye swivelled around mechanically and stared directly at her. Unconcerned by Jacquie's proximity, the bird craned its neck, drank some seawater and began dipping for food. Jacquie swam away from the gull and looked out towards the sharp lines of the horizon. For a while she trod water. There was nothing in front of her. No other swimmers. No boats. Nothing. It looked beautiful. Gazing out towards the distance, she realised how much she craved open space. To look out onto unchanging landscapes which revealed nothing about the society she lived in.

Later that evening, after Jacquie had showered and slept (all the energy her body expended earlier trying to keep warm had bought on a sudden fatigue when she returned to the flat), the two women sat by an open window in the front room, sharing a bottle of wine. Jacquie was basking in a glow of contentment. She couldn't remember the last time she had felt so relaxed. As the sun began to set, even the noise of the gulls became less irritating. With each sip of wine, Caroline also became less brittle. The two women sat on opposite chairs, with their legs curled up underneath them, talking candidly to one another, just as they used to when Caroline lived in London.

'You haven't mentioned Owen once since you've been here.'

Jacquie looked out of the window towards the peaceful desolation of the horizon. A solitary kayaker, cutting an elegant swathe through the water, glided inside her line of vision.

'There's not much to say,' Jacquie said.

'Is it that bad?'

'We're forever going around in circles.'

'You could always try stepping out of the circle.'

Jacquie continued to watch the kayaker move purposefully through the gently undulating water. 'Owen's stuck in a mindset which he's occupied since I first met him. It's like he refuses to change… or to grow up. I don't know. I guess we've just diverged and want different things now.'

'You know, he might never grow up,' Caroline said. 'Lots of men don't.' She poured the remnants of the bottle into Jacquie's glass.

'It's terrible. I'm starting to hate him for it. Just the sight of him makes me angry.'

'What will you do?'

'I don't know. It's complicated. It's Owen's flat. But I can't afford to move out. The problem is, he can't either.'

'Really?' Caroline sounded surprised. 'Is he not working much these days?'

'Yeah, he's working,' Jacquie said. 'But he's a hired hand. The band he's currently playing with are doing well, but he gets paid a fee per gig. You'd be surprised how little he earns.'

'Ask him to leave,' Caroline said emphatically. 'Don't waste time battling to save a relationship that's doomed. What's the point? Move on while you're still turning heads.'

'Turning heads? I wish. That doesn't happen any more. I feel invisible these days.'

'Rubbish. I saw you getting checked out on the beach.'

'Anyone under fifty?'

'I mean it,' Caroline continued. 'Tell him to leave.'

'I can't do that' Jacquie said. 'Owen grew up in that flat. His mum died there. It should be me leaving.'

'I thought you said you couldn't afford to. Don't forget, the boys are his responsibility too. If it has become untenable, then he's got to go. It's simple as that.' Caroline got up and went into the kitchen to fetch another bottle of wine.

An otherworldly glow lit up the horizon as the sun began to disappear behind the headland.

'What are those cliffs over there?' Jacquie asked.

'The Seven Sisters.'

'It's so beautiful with the sun setting behind it.'

'That's where Beachy Head is... you know, the place where people go to kill themselves.'

Jacquie thought about all the people who had thrown themselves off the cliffs. It looked benign and peaceful, a place of comfort instead of somewhere which had witnessed so much tragedy. Caroline held the bottle towards Jacquie, who gestured that she only wanted a little bit.

'I know you've been seduced by the sea and the view,' Caroline said as she poured some wine into Jacquie's glass. 'And on a day like today, it is like being on holiday. But how often do we get days like this? I never wanted to leave London. All my friends are there, my clients. I feel like I've lost everything.'

Jacquie thought how she wouldn't mind swapping places with Caroline. She was sure that she could be happy if she lived in a place overlooking the sea. It was so calming.

'When I finally managed to buy my flat,' Caroline continued, 'I thought I would be there forever. And then, at least if anything happened to me, I had an asset to pass on to Martha. The council promised I would be able to stay on the estate.'

'How much did they give you in the end for your place?' Jacquie asked.

'I was robbed.' Caroline rubbed at her eyes. 'They gave me one hundred and eighty thousand. Two-bedroom flats in the replacement scheme were selling for over four hundred thousand.'

Jacquie shook her head in disbelief. 'I don't understand how they can get away with it.'

'The developers said the financial crash forced them to reconsider their original pledges.' Caroline threw her head back and finished off her glass of wine. 'Honestly, it makes me want to cry.'

Chapter 9

Jennifer hadn't even rung the doorbell yet, but Nicholas already looked bored. With his hands clasped behind his back, he rocked onto the slender heels of his calfskin loafers. Jennifer straightened out her dress and looked at her husband.

'What are you waiting for?' he asked.

'I know you hate these things,' she said. 'But please don't make it quite so obvious.'

Finally, Jennifer rang the doorbell. A full-toned chime replete with twinkling harmonics reverberated around the property.

The tri-monthly park committee meeting was not due to start for another half hour. But Tanya, eager to show off her dream home, had arranged for Nicholas and Jennifer to arrive early. Gary answered the front door and ushered his guests into the marble-floored hallway. Nicholas extended his arm and the two men shook hands. Gary's grip was crushing, as if trying to squeeze the marrow from the bones of Nicholas' hand. As he handed Gary a bottle of wine, Nicholas noticed a snotty smear of powder around the rim of his nostril. Gary leaned towards Jennifer and kissed her cheek.

'Lovely to see you again, Jen. You're looking gorgeous as usual.'

The three of them walked through the hall into the kitchen. The echoes of their footsteps ricocheted off the bare white walls. Tanya was in the kitchen, standing beneath one of two five-tier crystal chandeliers. They looked like wedding cakes, suspended from a coffered white ceiling. Hanging on the wall on one side of the kitchen was an enormous black and white photograph of Kate Moss by Mario Testino. The far end of the kitchen featured bifold glass doors, which opened onto a terrace. All the worktops were made of white marble. Everything was spotless, as if nothing had ever been cooked in there before.

Gary held up the bottle and inspected the label. 'This a good one, is it? Côte Chatillon,' he said, making no attempt to pronounce the French correctly. 'Let's open it and see, shall we?'

Tanya was wearing a tight black sleeveless dress that clung to every cosmetically enhanced curve. Nicholas watched Gary proudly ogle his wife as he plunged a corkscrew into the bottle. Gary was shaven-headed and barrel-chested. Although smaller than Nicholas, he had an imposing physical presence. His movements were languid, but his face was stern and combative. He resembled an ex-fighter who had lost the inclination but not the ability.

'This is the first time I've been to one of these new houses,' Nicholas said, looking around the kitchen. 'It's very impressive.'

'We like it.' Gary poured the wine evenly into four glasses. 'At nearly five mill it would be a shame if we didn't, wouldn't it?'

'The others will be here soon,' Tanya said. She looked at Nicholas. 'Would you like a quick tour before they arrive?'

Nicholas picked up his glass and followed Tanya through the kitchen, back into the hallway and up a curved staircase with chrome balustrade and leather-wrapped handrail.

'Shall we start at the top?'

Tanya's tour was a breathy parade of large white rooms with little in them. Nicholas counted five bedrooms on the top two floors. Apart from the master bedroom, all the rooms were empty. The house appeared to be devoid of intimacy. Nothing looked used or lived in. There weren't even curtains or blinds on the windows in most of the rooms.

Nicholas scanned Tanya and Gary's bedroom for clues, hoping for an insight into their lives. Next to the bed was a table with a pile of neatly stacked magazines on top. Above the upholstered headboard was a photograph of Gary and Tanya on holiday. They were lying side by side on sun loungers. Nicholas squinted his eyes. The two of them were naked. Their bronzed bodies glistened under a spread of oil. They looked like cooked sausages as they held cocktails up towards the photographer.

'Mai Khao beach,' Tanya said wistfully.

'Is that Thailand?' Nicholas knew where it was. He just didn't know what else to say. He could feel the warm spread of a blush appear upon his face.

'Phuket,' Tanya said, wrapping her mouth around the first syllable. 'We try and go every year. We love it there.'

Tanya continued to look at the photo as if inviting Nicholas to study it further.

'Very nice,' he said, glancing briefly at the image.

Eventually, Tanya moved away from the picture. She smiled teasingly at Nicholas before indicating that he should follow her out of the bedroom.

A series of discreet floor-to-ceiling wardrobes lined the corridor outside the bedroom. Tanya opened one of the doors. Aside from a couple of sealed boxes, there was nothing else in there.

'Have you not moved all your things in yet?' Nicholas asked.

'We don't have much stuff,' Tanya said. 'We're minimals.'

'Minimals?'

'Gary says that you don't need external things to be happy. He likes to know that, if need be, he could fit all of his stuff into a couple of suitcases.'

'Presumably that doesn't include the two crystal chandeliers in the kitchen?'

Tanya laughed and placed her hand on Nicholas' forearm.

'They came with the house, silly.'

When Tanya and Nicholas returned to the kitchen, Gary and Jennifer were standing at either end of a vast marble island with a waterfall countertop. The whole thing nearly spanned the width of the room. Other than as a place to congregate, it seemed to serve no functional purpose. Tanya had previously told Jennifer that it established visual continuity, but it was too big and unwieldy. It rose out of the plane of the kitchen like a pagan place of worship.

'We like to call this room the family room.' Tanya walked up to her husband and draped an arm around his muscle-bound frame. 'Apart from the bedroom, it's where we spend most of our time. Isn't that right, Gal?' Tanya looked at Jennifer and winked.

Nicholas thought it strange to refer to the kitchen as a family room. There was no indication anywhere in the house that Tanya and Gary had children. Nicholas presumed this wasn't for want of trying. He imagined Tanya as someone who would have been desperate to have kids. She had been brilliant with Luc after the incident in the park. Perhaps they were unable to conceive? No doubt Jennifer would say that it explained her predilection for cosmetic surgery. Having spent time on the couch while working at Citigroup, Jennifer was familiar with many of the concepts and the jargon used by therapists. She loved to analyse the behaviour of others. She would probably interpret Tanya's penchant for altering her appearance as evidence of a psychological crisis. An inward expression of the guilt she felt at her failure to fulfil her expected role within the relationship.

'You left this here the other day.' Tanya's hand lingered as she passed Jennifer a rose gold chain bracelet.

Jennifer looked sheepishly at Nicholas. The bracelet had been a gift after she gave birth to Camille. 'I didn't even realise it was missing. I can't believe I didn't notice.' She placed the jewellery in her handbag. 'I love that bracelet.'

'That was hard work the other night.' Gary winced as he rubbed his side. 'My hip has been giving me gyp ever since.'

'That's not unusual,' Jennifer said. 'But you need to be careful with your hips; the cartilage can become inflamed if you don't watch it. I'll show you how to contract your muscles as you stretch.'

'He did well though, didn't he?' Tanya said. 'He's very supple considering how muscly he is.'

'Your shoulder stand pose was excellent. For someone who says they haven't done much yoga you look like a natural. You're obviously very fit.'

'Do you like yoga, Nick?' Tanya moved away from Gary and poured some more wine into Jennifer's glass.

'It's not really my thing.' Nicholas hated yoga. He hated the egotistical instructors who believed extreme suppleness equated to heightened spirituality. He hated the way people bowed and said *namaste* at the end of each session. When Nicholas challenged one of Jennifer's friends on this, without any irony, she claimed that the use of Sanskrit contributed to her mental and physical health.

'Nicholas isn't a very spiritual person,' Jennifer said, laughing. 'Spiritual capitalist. It's a bit of an oxymoron, isn't it?'

'Oxy what?' Gary said.

'You should join us sometime,' Tanya said. 'It would be fun. The more, the merrier.'

Jennifer was helping Tanya carry plates of food into the dining room. Gary and Nicholas had moved out onto the terrace and were looking out over the park.

'Are you prepared for the descending of the hordes? With everything that's been going on recently, tonight's meeting might be a heated one.'

'Bring it on,' Gary said. 'I love a good ruck.' Gary turned to look at Nicholas. His left eye was sunken, the ridge above the socket slightly bulged.

'Tanya told me about your boy. How's he doing?'

'He's OK now. The wound has left a bit of a mark, but it should disappear eventually.'

Nicholas waited for Gary to say something else. But instead, he just nodded his head a few times as if responding to an inner dialogue.

'What do you do?' Nicholas asked.

'Not much these days. A bit of this... a bit of that. You know?'

Nicholas didn't know what to say next. Gary seemed fine with prolonged gaps in the conversation, but Nicholas found it excruciating. He was delighted when he heard the elaborate sound of the doorbell signalling new arrivals. Nicholas and Gary were soon joined on the terrace by Simon Landes and Emma Crossley, who apologised profusely for Max's absence. They were quickly followed by the Frasers, Yevgeny Orloff and Ajoy Kohli, a property developer from Mumbai who had recently bought the last remaining house in the new development.

Other residents, including Seth Pritzker, his wife Christine, Dino Sarti and his husband Tambah, were gathering in the kitchen.

'I'm so glad you could both make it,' Simon said to Yevgeny and Ajoy. 'Our meetings often suffer on account of the jet-set lifestyle enjoyed by so many of our residents. But

I think we might have a good turnout tonight.' Simon spotted Nat and Tabitha Fraser and motioned for them to join him. 'Yevgeny, Ajoy, let me introduce you to the Frasers. Nat and Tabitha have lived at number twenty for... how long is it now?'

Simon looked at Nat, who said, 'It will be fifteen years this Christmas.'

'Nat is a senior partner at a rather prestigious and very profitable international law firm.' Simon leaned into Yevgeny and Ajoy. 'His firm is a member of the magic circle of elite British law firms. A jolly good person to know,' he said, tapping his nose and winking.

Around the room and on the terrace, residents had gathered in groups and were chatting with each other. Tanya had gone into the dining room to make sure everything was ready for the meeting, while Nicholas had moved into the kitchen and was speaking to Emma Crossley. Jennifer and Gary were talking on the terrace. Gary whispered something into Jennifer's ear. Whatever he said caused Jennifer to cover her mouth in mock horror and then playfully shove him on the side of his shoulder.

Simon looked at his watch and turned to the congregated group. 'Is everyone here now? We should probably get cracking.'

'Is Kitty here?' Nat asked. 'I haven't seen her. She is supposed to be coming.'

'*Quelle surprise*,' Simon said, turning to Nicholas. 'It's so unlike Kitty to make a dramatic late entrance.'

The meeting was held in the dining room, where Tanya had arranged some chairs around a long deco-style dining table. On top of a matching oak sideboard with mirrored central doors, there was a selection of canapés, dips and bowls of sliced vegetables. Finally, the residents started filing into the dining room.

'We can't start without Kitty,' Nat said. 'I wouldn't have turned up if I thought she wasn't coming. The last meeting was *so* boring without her.'

'OK,' Simon said wearily. 'But if she's not here in five minutes, we will have to start.'

There were sixteen chairs around the table, ten of which Tanya had borrowed from Jennifer. Thirteen of them were occupied. Tanya was busy filling glasses and offering around trays of canapés, while Simon positioned himself at the head of one end of the table. He opened his briefcase, put on a pair of glasses and organised various papers related to the meeting. After two minutes, Simon looked at his watch again. 'Right,' he said. 'We can't wait all night. Let's get started.'

'Hopefully that will be Kitty now,' Nat said as the doorbell echoed around the house. Tanya put down the tray she was holding and hurried out of the dining room. Kitty was standing at the front door holding a jar of home-made jam.

'Have I missed much?' Kitty handed Tanya the jar.

'No, they're waiting for you. I think Si's getting a bit impatient, though.'

'Good,' Kitty said.

'Good of you to finally join us, Kitty,' Simon said. 'We missed you at the last meeting.'

Nat Fraser stood up and pulled out a chair for Kitty to sit on. Kitty smiled at Nat before leaning over and kissing Tabitha on the cheek while Simon introduced her to the group.

'OK,' Simon said, clapping his hands together. 'Shall we begin? He handed Emma Crossley a pile of papers and sat back down in his chair.

'Jolly good,' Emma said. 'As the vice chair of the park committee, I notify everyone present that this month's meeting has officially begun.'

Nat whooped and pulled his chair up to the table. Emma stood up and went around the room, handing out sheets of paper.

Once the attendance sheets had been signed and handed back, Emma Crossley sat back down in her chair. 'Good evening, everyone. I will quickly run through the main points of our last meeting, which was hosted by myself and my husband.'

'Best grub we've ever had,' Nat called out, his hand cupping his mouth.

'Thank you, Nat. Although I think we would all like to thank Tanya and Gary for tonight's magnificent spread.'

'Oh absolutely,' Nat said. 'No offence meant to any of our other marvellous hosts. But you know, Max Crossley... you would expect it to be pretty good.'

Emma proceeded to read a summary of the last meeting. This had included a proposal to install Georgi Markov as the new permanent part-time gardener, a discussion about the annual summer party and a presentation of the final invoice for the new 'learning environment'.

'All members agreed on the amount,' Emma said, reading from her notes. 'The committee instructed our treasurer to settle the bill with Playscapes Ltd.'

'Well, that was an appalling waste of money.'

'Here we go,' Nat said cheerily, rubbing his hands together. 'Good to have you back, Kitty.'

'Honestly,' Kitty continued. 'They must have thought all their Christmases had come at once. We probably paid about twenty thousand pounds over the odds for that playground. It's already falling apart. Which is no mean feat, considering hardly anyone ever uses it.'

'OK, now Kitty, that is simply not true,' Dino replied in typically dramatic fashion. 'Our little Bruno simply *adooores* the new playground. He's just scared of all the rough boys.'

Dino was a native Neapolitan and the creative director of a luxury couture brand. Meanwhile, Tambah, his half Congolese husband, hailed from Zurich and was the founder of Xier, an ethical genderless fashion label.

'Bruno plays with Camille and Luc in the playground all the time,' Tambah said. 'Isn't that right?' Tambah looked at Nicholas, who unenthusiastically nodded in agreement. 'But after the attack on poor Luc,' Tambah continued, 'there is no way we will let him out there any more.'

An agitated murmur rippled around the table. 'That's so sad,' Christine Pritzker said.

'Can everyone quieten down a bit,' Simon said. 'We will discuss the appalling incident with Luc in due course. But meanwhile can we let Emma finish please?'

'Finally, the issue of access to the park was discussed,' Emma said, continuing with the minutes. 'It was felt that there were not enough members present to take a vote on Simon's proposal, which is to build a higher wall between the Bevan Estate and the Park.'

'Dear Lord,' Kitty muttered loudly.

After thanking Emma for her summary, Simon announced that next on the agenda was members' reports.

'For those of you who have never attended one of our meetings, this section allows committee members to report on the progress of any park-related activities they've been involved in.'

Tabitha Fraser informed the meeting that she had recently spotted a family of toads near the shed. She asked the residents to tell their children to be very careful when cycling in the park. 'They are the sweetest little things,' she said. 'Tallulah and I have built a little grotto for them to live in. Unfortunately, their numbers are declining rapidly. So, do come and see them while you can.'

'Toads?' Dino said, a look of alarm on his face. 'Aren't

they very dangerous? My assistant's dog was poisoned after licking a toad. What about the safety of the children?'

'Darling.' Tabitha adopted a tone of exaggerated concern. 'I suggest that everyone instructs their precious little munchkins not to go around licking toads. If they can do that, then I'm sure everything will be hunky-dory. The frogs are fine to lick, though. In fact, they taste quite nice.'

'How do you tell the difference between a frog and a toad?' Dino asked.

'You could always give it a kiss and see what happens,' Tabitha answered.

'It's supposed to be a princess who kisses the frog,' Kitty said. 'Not a queen.'

'Very funny.' The open and closed vowels of Dino's Italian accent accompanied by constant hand gestures lent everything he said a theatricality. 'While we are on the subject of poisonous things,' he continued, 'the other day Bruno suffered a terrible reaction to one of the plants in the park. I cannot remember its name… it grows everywhere. It has yellow flowers and emits this… sticky white fluid.'

'It sounds like euphorbia,' Kitty said.

'Yes, euphoria, that is it.' Dino pointed his finger at Kitty. 'Bruno got some of the liquid near his eyes.'

'It was so scary,' Tambah added. 'Bruno's eyes swelled up. He couldn't see anything.'

'That sounds terrible,' Christine Pritzker said. 'Was he OK?'

'We had to go to the eye hospital. Luckily the doctor knew straight away what was wrong.'

'Everyone knows about the sap from euphorbia,' Kitty said. 'You should have warned him.'

'We should tell the new gardener to get rid of it,' Dino said.

'What do you mean?' Kitty said.

'Dig it up. *Tutto*.'

'Don't be so ridiculous,' Kitty said. 'By that logic, we might as well dig everything up. We could concrete over the entire place, if you like? Then there will be nowhere for any scary animals to make their home, and everyone will have a perfect view of the park.'

'Now you are just being facetious,' Christine said.

'Can't you just tell your son to be a bit more careful in future?' Tabitha asked.

Dino and Tambah looked at each other in disbelief. 'Bruno is a tactile and curious boy,' Dino said. 'He's very sensory led. He likes to explore the physicality of things.'

Kitty turned to Nat. 'God help us. We're surrounded by idiots.'

'Before we move on to Old Business,' Simon said, 'I would like to tell you all about a very generous gift from the Orloffs. They have kindly offered to pay for the tennis court to be refurbished. This will include a new surface, a new net and all the mesh fencing replaced with new polythene netting. They've also offered to pay for a new clubhouse to be built. It's been a while since anyone used the court, but I expect everyone will get a huge amount of pleasure from it.'

'Just like the playground,' Kitty muttered under her breath.

'Once the clubhouse has been built, there will be a book inside where anyone wishing to use the court will be able to reserve a time slot. Seth suggested we might organise an Albion Park tennis tournament. I think that could be a lot of fun.' Simon raised his glass towards Yevgeny. 'On behalf of us all, I would like to say a big thank you for your generous offer. We're so very fortunate that you chose Albion Park as your London residence.'

Yevgeny gave a broad smile and acknowledged the appreciative comments.

'When it's all ready,' Tabitha said, 'perhaps we could allocate a day or an afternoon each week where we allow kids from the flats to use the court?'

'That's a great idea,' Kitty said.

Frustrated by Tabitha's unwanted suggestion, Simon looked pleadingly towards Nat.

'Don't look at me,' Nat said.

'How many potential tennis stars are currently sitting at this table?' Tabitha continued.

'I used to play a lot of tennis in Mumbai,' Ajoy said.

Kitty looked puzzled as she tried to fathom the relevance of his comment.

'There are kids in those flats who might never get the opportunity to play tennis,' Tabitha said. 'Even if they have a God-given talent, they might never find out. That's a terrible thought.'

'If any of them are fortunate enough to possess a God-given talent,' Nicholas said, 'it's not our duty to make sure it doesn't go to waste.'

Kitty turned around to Nat. 'When will that man take some responsibility for someone other than himself?'

'OK, OK,' Simon said. 'We take your point, Tabitha, and I'm sure everyone admires the sentiment. However, the likelihood of us discovering the next Serena Williams is highly unlikely. Whereas I would say the chances of the court getting vandalised are extremely likely.'

'Give the kids from the flats a stake in the court, and I bet you they will look after it,' Kitty said. 'Alienate them even more and yes, it might get vandalised. There's not even that many of them, for heaven's sakes.'

'Do or be damned. I'm not entirely convinced by that argument, I'm afraid,' Simon said.

'I think it's a good idea,' Nat put in.

'This is a discussion probably best suited for another

meeting,' Simon said evasively. 'Work hasn't even started on the court yet. We've got a lot to get through still.'

Nat looked at Tabitha and rolled his eyes.

'Well, I would like to propose it as a motion for the next meeting,' Tabitha said. 'Emma, could you make a note of that, please?'

Kitty considered the Frasers to be something of an enigma. She was never sure where their loyalties lay. Tabitha often helped Kitty around the park. They both shared a love of gardening and had similar views on how the park should be looked after. Like Kitty, Tabitha was also concerned that the residents, if left to their own devices, would happily allow Albion Park to transition into a faux reality where any evidence of diversity, or anyone less fortunate than themselves, would be virtually eradicated. On the other hand, the Frasers were occasional guests at Simon's house. Tabitha also once let it slip that Delta Capital Management had invested in the behavioural insights company that she was a director of.

Emma made a note of Tabitha's proposal for the next meeting. 'Anybody else, before we move onto Old Business?'

Dino proceeded to list the reasons why he believed dogs should be banned from the park. Apart from the clear and present danger they so obviously represented, Dino was also disgusted at *tutta la merda di cane*.

'It's nothing to do with Zsa Zsa,' Christine interrupted. 'I always pick up her mess.' She stared meaningfully at Kitty.

'Oh no you don't.' Kitty wagged her finger at Christine. 'Don't try and pin this one on me. I always pick up after my dogs. And any others that I find, come to think of it.'

'Dino has taken photos of all the turds he sees,' Tambah said. 'We think they all look like they were done by the same dog. Or perhaps the same breed,' he said, looking at Kitty.

Kitty choked on the mouthful of water she was just about to swallow. 'You did what?' she exclaimed.

Tambah gave an indignant shrug. 'Why should Bruno be expected to play where dogs do their business?'

'Oh, don't be such a prick,' Kitty said.

A sharp collective intake of breath hissed around the room. Tambah placed his hand over his heart. His pained expression suggested he might find it hard to ever recover from such a terrible insult. Jennifer placed her hand on Tambah's shoulder and asked him if he was OK.

'Kitty, we can't abide language like that,' Simon said. 'You will have to leave if you continue to insult other members.'

Dino insisted that Kitty should apologise before the meeting went any further. Kitty took off her glasses and rubbed her eyes.

'Tambah, I'm sorry the word prick causes you such distress. But this is not Switzerland. This country is famously a nation of dog lovers. And I don't appreciate, having lived here for a little over three years, your attempts to bend the rules of the park to your will.'

'That wasn't a very good apology,' Dino said.

'Well, it's the best you're going to get.'

Dino brushed his hand under his chin in a forward, flicking motion towards Kitty. Simon shook his head wearily and took a deep breath.

'Right, let's move on to Old Business,' he said. 'Specifically, the issue of non-keyholders using the park without permission. At the last meeting, there was overwhelming support for introducing more stringent measures to prohibit trespassing. However, as Emma mentioned earlier, more members needed to be present before a meaningful vote could take place. In light of recent events, this issue has become more pressing than ever. Over the years, there have been a few isolated incidents, but recently we have all detected a new hostility. The most recent example being the appalling attack on Luc.'

Christine Pritzker looked towards Nicholas, offered a sympathetic smile, and mouthed: 'How is he?'

Nicholas nodded his head as if to suggest 'He's OK thanks, but it was pretty bad.'

'Don't get me wrong,' Kitty said. 'I'm not making excuses for what happened—'

'I should hope not,' Jennifer interjected.'

'But don't you see?' Kitty continued. 'As long as we keep on excluding people from the flats, incidents like this will continue to happen. It's so divisive. I don't understand what you're all so scared of.'

'What are we scared of?' Nicholas said. 'Hmmm, let me think. I mean, imagine, God forbid, if something happened to one of our kids while they were playing in the park?'

'I can't believe we're still having this conversation,' Seth Pritzker said. 'The incident involving Nicholas' son is evidence enough that we need to tackle this issue. We've been talking about it for the last few years. Something needs to be done. Now.'

'Segregation is not the way forward,' Kitty said. 'You're all deluded if you think it will make the park any safer. On the contrary, it cuts us off even more from the surrounding community. If anything, it makes us more of a target.'

'We'll just have to see about that, won't we?' Simon avoided Kitty's gaze and smiled nervously at the Pritzkers.

'Kitty's right,' Tabitha said. 'There's enough room for everyone here. Most of us have large gardens anyway.'

'We don't have a big garden,' said Gary. 'One of the reasons we bought this place was because of the park. I might have had second thoughts if it had been a public space.'

'See!' Simon brandished a hand towards Gary. 'It has always been this way. You know that, Kitty. The flats have never had authorised access. I applaud your efforts to be inclusive and your desire to help local kids. But the fact of the matter is, if you let a few of them in, you will have to let everyone in.'

'That's right,' Gary said. 'Why should we pay for everyone else?'

'But it wouldn't be open to the public,' Tabitha said. 'It would just be residents from the flats.'

'Let's take a vote on it,' Simon said. 'Who in this room agrees with the proposal that we should build a higher wall?'

'Have it your way then, Simon,' Kitty said. 'Build a wall of apartheid.'

Simon stared pointedly at Kitty and shook his head in disbelief. He took a sip of water and cleared his throat. 'A wall of apartheid?' he said. 'Why would you say that?'

Nat emitted an uncomfortable cough while Emma Crossley told Kitty she had overstepped the mark with her previous comment. Tanya looked at Gary, hoping he might be able to explain what had just happened.

Simon noticed Tanya's look of bewilderment. 'For those of you who don't know,' he announced to the group, 'Kitty believes her left-wing credentials exempt her from any accusations of prejudice. Apparently, raising a few pro-Palestinian placards in Parliament Square gives her the right to question the ethics of others.'

Tanya turned to Yevgeny, who was sitting next to her. 'What did she say?'

Yevgeny put his finger over his mouth. 'Shhh.'

'Why is everyone so angry?' Tanya said to no one in particular.

'What?' Kitty looked around the table. 'I was merely pointing out that Simon's idea for a wall reminds me of another barrier of cultural oppression.'

'This is not the place to voice your toxic opinions.' Simon

began twisting the hairs of his moustache. 'No one wants to hear them.'

'Simon, I think you are overreact—'

'The sad thing is, I don't think you even understand what anti-Semitism means.'

'Oh, please. Are we not allowed to criticise Israel without being labelled anti-Semitic?'

'I think we should move on now,' Nat said, interrupting. 'We're going wildly off brief. We didn't come here tonight to listen to you two squabbling.'

'I don't know about that,' Gary said. 'I'm quite enjoying this.'

The Pritzkers both gave Gary a withering look. As did Tabitha and Emma.

'Of course Israel can be criticised. There's plenty to criticise,' Simon said, ignoring Nat's effort to ameliorate the situation. 'However, it is possible to believe in the state of Israel and oppose its government's policies. It is possible to be a Zionist and support Palestinian statehood. But I think you and your friends would like to deny the right of Israel to even exist.' Simon ran a hand through his thick mop of hair, displacing a couple of tufts that remained sticking out.

'Simon, leave it,' Nat said sternly.

'Well,' Simon said. 'It's not as if it's the first time.'

The previous year Simon had confronted Kitty in the street while she was on her way to a demonstration for Palestine. She was walking with a younger male friend who was wearing a Free Palestine T-shirt. Simon accused Kitty and her friend of being terrorist sympathisers. He told them that their support for organisations like Hamas and Hezbollah was not only offensive to Jews but also paradoxical to their supposedly liberal values. Kitty's friend had rounded on Simon and called him an imperialist. He told Simon that Israel was both a racist and a colonial enterprise and compared Israel's treatment of the Palestinians to the Nazis' treatment of the Jews. Kitty later apologised to Simon for the vehemence of her friend's retort, but the incident inevitably further soured relations between the two of them.

'Are you OK?' Emma said, resting a hand on Simon's shoulder.

'Yes, yes. Sorry… Where were we?'

'We were discussing access to the flats… we were about to take a vote.'

'Right,' Simon said, trying to regain his composure. He took another sip of water before continuing. 'Shall we have a show of hands then? Those in support of raising the height of the existing wall raise their right arm.'

Nearly everyone in the room, apart from Kitty and Tabitha, raised their hands. For a moment it looked as if Nat was about to raise his arm, until a rebuking stare from his wife apparently changed his mind.

'I declare the motion carried,' Simon said.

'Building a wall will not solve a thing,' Kitty said. 'History has shown that if you create two separate societies that are so unequal, forced redistribution of wealth is inevitable.'

'Oh, this is ridiculous,' Nicholas said loudly. 'It's like being back at university.'

Simon sniggered as he wiped something from his eye. 'Overthrowing the state of Israel? Revolution on the streets of London? You're going to be a busy lady, Kitty. Watch out everyone, the Bollinger Bolsheviks are coming.'

An eruption of laughter broke out around the room. Even Nat and Tabitha were giggling.

'Ignore them, Kitty,' Nat said. 'I hardly think you're the only champagne socialist sitting around this table.'

'I'm not a champagne socialist,' Kitty said.

'No,' Nicholas said, 'there's no hypocrisy inherent in your type of politics at all.'

'In Switzerland, we call them *Cüpli-Sozialisten*,' Tambah said, still laughing at Simon's joke.

'Or cashmere communists,' Dino added. 'Much more chic.'

'Would anyone like some more canapés?' Tanya asked nervously. Simon's joke had lifted the mood and eased the tension. Residents began talking among themselves while Tanya walked over to the sideboard and grabbed a tray of blinis. Both Yevgeny and Tabitha poured themselves drinks; meanwhile, Nicholas walked over to Simon and gave him a mollifying pat on the back.

'What's next?' Simon asked Emma, who was still busy writing notes.

'New Business.'

Simon allowed everyone to carry on talking for a bit before announcing the next topic. Energy levels had dipped. There was little appetite among other residents to carry on with the meeting. When Emma reminded Simon that they still needed to agree over Georgi's proposed role as a part-time gardener, Simon replied, 'Oh God, I forgot about that. I think it might call for a bit of unilateral decision-making. Don't you?'

A few people had left the room. Jennifer, Gary and Tanya had gone into the kitchen. Those that remained were paying little attention to Simon and Emma.

'Shall we skip Announcements and go straight to the Adjournment?' Simon asked Emma. 'I know we haven't covered everything, but it looks like people have lost interest.'

In the kitchen, Gary had lined up three shot glasses and began pouring tequila into them. 'Let's have a proper drink, shall we? Babe?'

'I'll have one if Jen does.'

'Not for me, thanks,' Jennifer said.

'Oh, go on,' Tanya said. 'We deserve one after sitting through that.'

Gary handed Tanya and Jennifer a glass. 'Chin chin.'

The three of them downed their shots in one gulp. Jennifer grimaced and gritted her teeth in response to the potency of the liquid.

'Are the meetings often like that?' Tanya said. 'The last one was a bit more civilised.'

'They're hardly ever that bad-tempered. It's whenever Kitty's there. She's a pain in the ass.'

'I quite like her,' Tanya said. 'She's very friendly.'

'Are you joking?' Gary poured another shot of tequila into his glass. 'She's a right old battleaxe. I bet she's a dyke.' He knocked back his drink and dragged his wrist across his mouth.

'She used to be married,' Tanya said.

'So? That doesn't mean anything.' Gary put his arm around Tanya's waist. 'We should hang out more.' he said, looking at Jen. 'You know, the three of us. You'd like that, wouldn't you, babe?'

'We definitely should.' Tanya winked at Jennifer.

'Another one?' Gary said, holding up the bottle.

'We should probably be getting back to the meeting.' Jennifer got up from the stool. 'Hopefully things will have calmed down a bit.'

In the other room, the residents' meeting had fizzled out. Kitty was in the hallway speaking to Tabitha while Simon, Seth Pritzker and Nicholas were still sitting at the dining table.

'To build a bigger wall, we'll have to pull the old one down,' Seth said. 'It could be quite expensive. Maybe we should just put a fence on top of the existing wall?'

Simon slowly nodded his head in half agreement. His normally well-coiffured hair was still looking ruffled. 'That would solve the problem of trespassers coming into the park while the wall is down.'

'No. The flats look bad enough as it is,' Nicholas added. 'With fencing on top, it will look even worse. It will get pulled down.'

'Whatever we do decide,' Simon said, 'we're going to need to get permission.'

'Why?' Seth said.

'It's a conservation area. Plus the council own the wall.'

'As long as we pay for it,' Nicholas said, 'I wouldn't have thought there would be any objections.'

Chapter 10

A wave of guilt washed over Jacquie every time she walked past Julius' flat. That was a lot of guilt to contend with. His home was on the ground floor of Attlee House. Although the front door was on the other side of the building to the main entrance, Jacquie walked past it several times a week. Part of the window which looked into his kitchen was broken and boarded up with cardboard. The yard in front was littered with bits of old furniture, which the landlord couldn't be bothered to remove.

It was shocking how little time it had taken for the property to deteriorate. Before Julius moved in, the front patio had resembled a demonstration of gardening ingenuity. The previous tenants had won a council In Bloom award for their balcony garden. Having lived on the estate for thirty-five years, Viv and Alf found themselves in the fortunate position of being able to buy their flat off the council. Within a couple of months, they had flipped it, and the flat became part of a private landlord's portfolio. Within another three months, the council themselves were renting back the same property at market rates. Not only had they missed out on any profits and lost a potential social rented home, but they were also spending any income from the sale on housing benefits. It was a warped system that defied reasonable logic. A stroke of vote-winning genius for the Conservative Party, an attempt to democratise homeownership, had become another business opportunity. It made Jacquie so angry. She didn't resent Viv and Alf, or, for that matter, anyone else who managed to buy their own place. More than anything, she wished to be a homeowner too. What made her angry was that it was done at the expense of other people in need. Any social ambitions supposedly inherent within the policy had been negated by the market. The system had opened the door to rogue landlords who couldn't care less about tenants or their neighbours. On top of all of that, any profit-seeking by the landlord had been guaranteed by the council. None of it made sense any more.

Jacquie hadn't been around to see Julius for a while. She used to try to visit him at least once a week. But what with the kids, and taking on more hours at the charity, it was hard to create time for Julius too. That was the narrative she assuaged her guilt with, anyway. Whenever she tried to help Julius, Jacquie always felt overwhelmed by the amount that needed to be done. His existence seemed so miserable. Sometimes she wondered about one's purpose after reaching old age. Could you be anything useful? She hated to think of the denouement of her life resembling anything like Julius. The prospect of having nothing to look forward to but being burdened with the awful wisdom of knowing how one's life had played out terrified her. There would be no more dreams to follow. There would only be regrets to contemplate and perhaps a fading recollection of anything good that might once have happened.

As long as Jacquie didn't see or hear Julius, she found it easy to scurry past his flat and rationalise her avoidance with thoughts of systemic failures. This time, however, the sound of him coughing in the kitchen stopped her in her tracks. She walked up to his flat and knocked on the front door and braced herself.

'Who is it?'

'It's Jacquie.'

'Hold on, hold on.'

Jacquie could hear Julius swearing about something or other. She leaned over and peered through the partially covered kitchen window. A single exposed lightbulb was hanging from the ceiling; the worktop was crowded with bulging bin liners and a plastic washing-up bowl. She could hear the old man shuffling along the corridor, wheezing as he walked. Julius opened the door, turned around and walked back into the flat. The smell was intense. The rank, pissy odour hit Jacquie like the thud of heat one feels when stepping off an aeroplane in a hot climate. Jacquie covered her face and followed Julius into the front room. Even in midsummer the flat felt damp and mouldy. Jacquie could see drifts of black fungus migrating from the corner of the walls across the ceiling.

'Sorry I haven't been around for a while. I've had a lot on at work.'

Julius looked harrowed. Jacquie imagined that he must have felt abandoned by her. Apparently he had a son and a daughter who didn't live too far away, but Jacquie had never seen them.

'Is there anything you need doing?'

Julius said something, but it was hard to understand what he said. It was like his tongue was too fat for his mouth. It disrupted his speech and gave him a lisp. That, combined with a heavy Grenadian accent, sometimes made their exchanges hard to follow.

'What was that?'

Julius told Jacquie that he was going to have to move out of the flat. When Jacquie asked him why he explained that the boiler wasn't working, and that the landlord had informed him he would have to vacate the premises while it was being replaced.

'That doesn't sound right,' Jacquie said. 'There's no reason why you should have to move out. How long has it not been working for?'

'Some guy come to fix it. But it stop working almost straight away.'

Julius started coughing. It sounded like he was about to choke. He held up an empty glass. Although he was wearing shoes, Jacquie noticed he had no socks on. His ankles looked swollen and full of fluid. The skin on his legs was stretched and scaly. Jacquie took the glass from him and went to the kitchen to get some water. Jacquie wanted to help, but she also wanted to get the hell out of there. The kitchen was in a pitiful state of disrepair. Two cupboard doors were hanging off their hinges. Meanwhile, where there used to be a cooker there was now a gaping hole. The linoleum on the floor underneath had been ripped, revealing rotten floorboards and exposed pipes.

Jacquie looked around to see what was being used for cooking in the absence of an oven. But she couldn't see anything. Walking back into the living room, she handed Julius a glass of water.

'How do you prepare food?' she asked.

'I bought a hob from Argos.'

Julius pointed to a double electric ring on top of a sideboard.

'You cook in here?'

When Jacquie had once discovered that Julius was sleeping on a single mattress on the floor, she had helped him buy a new bed. When only one tap in the flat produced water, she had arranged for a plumber to come around. In the past Jacquie had organised food deliveries and doctor's appointments, and paid bills. But she always felt hopeless when confronted with the squalor of Julius' life. Nothing she was prepared to do would ever change anything. A couple of minor errands were never going to make enough of a difference. Sometimes she thought Julius would be better off without her. Her occasional appearance raised hopes, only then to be dashed by her subsequent disappearance.

'Give me the number of your landlord. I'm going to call him. You shouldn't have to live like this.'

Previous attempts to secure a visit from the local environmental health officer had come to nothing. One of the most successful deficit reduction programmes ever imposed had ensured that local councils could no longer run essential services efficiently. Julius told Jacquie the council had sent his landlord a warning letter. But no legal notice had been issued. Far from having the desired effect, the warning seemed to provoke the landlord into further extremes of neglect.

A couple of other leaseholders had recently sold their homes too. Jacquie assumed they had been sold back to the council, as the properties were now occupied by emergency tenants. Apart from Julius' flat and one other family, all the flats on the bottom two floors of Attlee House now housed temporary tenants. Over the years, the demographic on the estate often reflected the state of global geopolitics at any one moment. There had been an influx of Kurds after the Iraq War. Sudanese following the war in Darfur. Somalis on a second migration fleeing Dutch Islamophobia. Poles and Rumanians after EU accession and Syrians escaping the civil war.

There were hardly any secure tenants left now. Those who hadn't managed to buy their own flats had been offered places on home purchase schemes. This effectively involved the council buying back secure tenancies from long-term tenants. This money could then only be used in the purchase of a non-council-owned property. Unless the tenant had personal savings, it was unlikely to be enough to secure a deposit on a place in London. A few recipients, however, had moved out of the city. With so many temporary tenants and freeholders, there weren't many people left on the estate invested in its appearance. It had never looked worse than it did now.

Owen sat on the balcony, his feet resting on the railings, an open packet of tobacco on his lap. Jacquie pulled up a chair and sat down next to him.

'Can I have one of those?'

'Someone's had a bad day.' Owen finished rolling a cigarette and passed it to Jacquie.

'I've just been at Julius'. I think the landlord might be trying to get rid of him.'

'Why do you say that?'

'Julius has been told that he has to move out while the landlord fixes his boiler.'

Owen shrugged his shoulders. 'What's the problem?'

'I don't think he'll let him back in. I wouldn't be surprised if his landlord sells the flat back to the council. Everyone else seems to be doing it.'

Owen leaned towards Jacquie and lit her cigarette. You could tell she was a non-smoker by the way she held the fag. Her fingers were always too far away from the butt. She also puffed her lips out before exhaling. And when she did finally breathe out, instead of a thin stream a great cloud of smoke gushed from her open mouth. Owen noticed it the very first time they met. He had never understood why she bothered. It never looked particularly enjoyable.

'I thought the council were supposed to be skint?' he said. 'They've got enough money to buy back all of these flats, but they can't afford to fix the lights on our landing.'

'None of it makes sense,' Jacquie said, her eyes squinting against the stinging smoke.

Owen got up and walked to the kitchen. He soon came back holding a bottle and two glasses. 'I don't understand why Julius isn't in a home.' He poured some wine into a glass and passed it to Jacquie.

'Who's going to pay for that?' Jacquie took a sip of her drink. She could feel the cold liquid spread through her chest. 'He's got no money. God knows where he'll go if he has to move out. It's all so unfair. It hurts my head thinking about it.'

She got up from where she was sitting and leaned against the railings. Jacquie had been the first person in her family to go to university. In her second year of studying Sociology and Politics at Goldsmiths, she completed a module on 'Fiscal Sociology and the Transformation of Capitalism.' Looking out over the park, she was reminded of a phrase that an American economist used to describe a society where privately owned resources were clean and efficient; meanwhile, public spaces remained unsafe and overcrowded. He described it as private affluence and public squalor. For Jacquie, Albion Park represented the embodiment of these inequalities. 'God, I'm fed up with staring at everyone else's good fortune,' she said.

Here we go, Owen thought. The pulsing of the muscles around Jacquie's jawbone was often a signal for others to steer clear. Owen was off to Germany the following day. He had some gigs with RFTS before returning to London for a show at the Roundhouse and had been hoping they could enjoy a reconciliatory drink before he left. Relations had been glacial for a while now. He felt like Jacquie had given up on him. Her disappointment was palpable; he could feel it every time she walked into the room. Having said that, she was always in a bad mood after visiting Julius.

'It could be so much worse.' Owen got up and stood next to Jacquie. 'Have you seen those flats they've built looking out over the rubbish dump? I wouldn't fancy living there. We've got it pretty sweet if you ask me. Lots of greenery. Nice houses…'

'I'm just tired of feeling like a second-class citizen. I'll never have their kind of money.' Jacquie gestured towards the houses surrounding the park. 'But I want something better than this dump.' She put her empty glass down on the floor. 'I need to piss.'

While Jacquie went upstairs to the bathroom, Owen picked up his phone and clicked on Instagram. His recent monitoring of Daisy Crossley's account was verging on obsessive. At least a couple of times an hour he would find himself mindlessly scrolling through her profile. Random uploads ensured he received enough dopamine hits to keep him coming back for more. Owen's compulsive surveillance was finally rewarded with a new upload. Daisy had posted a photograph of herself, dressed only in a Blondie T-shirt, blowing a kiss at the camera. She had also sent him a private message.

Any chance of tix for the RFTS gig?xcx

A more judicious person than Owen would have ignored the message. Apart from a bit of cachet among some people nearly half his age, what good could possibly be gained by giving Daisy tickets? However, he also reasoned that a bit of starry-eyed adulation (that only someone as young as Daisy would be prepared to offer a stand-in guitarist) might be just what he needed. No one he knew cared about the artists he played with any more. Those days, unfortunately, were long gone.

The sound of the toilet flushing upstairs prompted Owen

to put his phone back in his pocket. Jacquie came back out onto the balcony and topped up her glass. Within a couple of minutes she had polished it off and was pouring herself another one. Down below, the early evening sun had managed to force its way through the branches and bushes and cast elongated silhouettes across the flower beds. The occasional break in the canopy revealed roses tumbling down brick walls into wide borders crowded with snapdragons and catmint. Owen could see Kitty going for her early evening walk with the dogs. For as long as he could remember he had been watching her perform this daily routine. Sometimes, as a child, he would hop over the wall and join her. Together they would walk around the park. Owen would ask Kitty about her work or whatever news story Hugh was currently involved in. In those days, Kitty had a highly strung Dalmatian who used to jump up at anyone approaching them. During the summer months, the park was nearly always full of people, all of whom would give the dog a wide berth as Kitty went for her afternoon walk.

'How much do you reckon she's worth?' Jacquie said, looking down at Kitty.

Ignoring the question, Owen continued to stare out over the park.

'The house alone must be worth at least five, six, maybe seven million. And then there's all the family money…'

'Look, I really don't care', Owen said, with an irritated twitch of his head.

Having grown up around Kitty, he had never possessed the fascination with her finances Jacquie seemed to have. He had never even thought of her as being rich until Jacquie told him that she was. Kitty had never lived anything resembling an affluent lifestyle. She lived modestly and considered outward displays of wealth vulgar. Apart from the size of her house, there were no other indications of her being particularly well-off. She and Hugh had bought the house in the early seventies. Owen seemed to remember Kitty once telling him they only paid sixteen thousand pounds for it. She might have been re-mortgaged up to the hilt. He had no concept of how much or how little she was worth. He had always been aware there was a successful family business lurking somewhere in the past. But Kitty was the black sheep of her family. As far as Owen knew, she hadn't spoken to either of her brothers for over twenty years.

'You don't care?' The skin around Jacquie's eyes crumpled into crow's feet as she scrunched up her face. 'I don't believe you.' She poured herself some more wine. There was a brief pause in the conversation before she added, 'Imagine if she left you the house…'

Owen watched as Jacquie drifted off into a reverie. 'Are you envisaging Kitty's death as the answer to our problems?'

Jacquie turned away and looked longingly towards Kitty's house. 'It's probably the only way you're ever going to make any proper money…'

'Is that all you think about? Money, property… who's got what.'

'What's wrong with that? Maybe you should start thinking about it a bit more. Or perhaps you've forgotten that you've got a family to support?'

Jacquie looked at Owen, her copper-flecked eyes challenging him to respond.

'Listen to yourself,' Owen said. 'Things might have slowed down for me, but I still earn more than you do. I always have done. You're the one with the degree. You go and earn some decent money for once.'

The argument quickly escalated. There they stood on the balcony, effortlessly retrieving historical resentments which they used as weapons to batter each other with. It had been like this for a while now. Like many relationships which slowly fall apart, the deterioration began with an intangible feeling – a malaise. Neither of them was able to identify what that feeling was, but both knew something was wrong. Like a faulty computer that stutters and whirrs during start-up, the signals are often overlooked. Something must be causing the machine to make these noises. Any doubts, however, are discarded because, ostensibly, it still works. Gradually though, other more obvious things start to go wrong, until finally the computer breaks down and can no longer function. All the warning signs were ignored until, suddenly, it was too late.

'I don't have to put up with this,' Owen said. 'I thought we could have a nice drink together before I go away. But everything always turns into an argument with you.' He walked into the front room and picked up his wallet off the coffee table.

'Where are you going?'

'Out.'

Owen opened the front door and walked out into the corridor which connected the flats on his floor. A couple of mangy-looking pigeons with deformed feet and unkempt feathers patrolled the landing by the stairwell. Owen shooed them away and descended the concrete steps, which hadn't been cleaned for God knows how long. He hurried out of the block as quickly as he could. Once outside, he reached for his phone.

Hey Daisy. I'll put you +1 on the door
Message me if you have any probs.

Chapter 11

Nicholas dropped his head and gritted his teeth. 'Come on!' he shouted. The exercise bike wobbled from side to side as he lifted his bum from the saddle and pedalled even harder. Salty beads of sweat cascaded down his forehead and dripped into his eyes. Searching for a personal best, he glanced down at the power meter to check his stats. He was averaging over two hundred and eighty watts, which seemed unusually high. The programme was an emulation of the final stage of the Tour de France. Eager to see the faces of the cheering crowds on the screen as he raced down the Champs-Élysées, Nicholas lifted his arm and wiped the sweat from his eyes. He had never been at the front of the peloton at this stage of the workout before. To his left, the front wheel of another rider came into view as it moved to overtake him. Worried he might have started his sprint prematurely, Nicholas screamed as he pedalled harder. A rush of adrenaline propelled him forward. The cyclist to his left no longer seemed to be a threat and the finish line was now in sight. Once more, Nicholas bowed his head and tried to push through the pain in his thighs. He could feel his legs beginning to cramp. It was no good; he had peaked too early. With about forty yards to go, two cyclists appeared on his right shoulder and overtook him. While his burning leg muscles capitulated under the stress, more riders raced past. Nicholas eventually came tenth. Two seconds off his personal best.

The offices of Delta Capital Management occupied the top four floors of a five-storey, Grade II listed townhouse on the north-eastern side of Berkeley Square. Once predominantly residential, most of the houses surrounding the square were now occupied by hedge funds, asset management firms and headhunters. The Neo-Renaissance facade of DCM's offices made it one of the more distinctive buildings in the area. Visitors always commented on the three-foot-high stone-carved putti carved into the arch above the doorway. Through the trees surrounding the square, Nicholas could just about see the Pre-Raphaelite sculpture of a vase-carrying, semi-clad nymph. Someone told him that one of the thick plane trees in the square was the most valuable street tree in Britain. There were at least thirty of these trees planted around the enclosed space. He failed to see what qualities one might possess which made it more valuable than the others. They all looked the same to him.

While recovering from his workout, Nicholas looked out over the mass of workers enjoying the sun. Surrounded by motorbikes and cars, people jostled for space, imbibing toxic fumes as they escaped the heat of their non-air-conditioned offices. Nicholas looked on bemused. He failed to see what kind of pleasure could be gained from sitting in an overcrowded square in central London on a hot day. In a city, wealth affords privacy and peace, he thought. Only the well-off can remove themselves from the noises and proximity of others. Money buys space when one lives in an environment where others do not have any. This was nothing new, though. Regardless of the type of economic system, inequality within densely packed cities had always existed. Plato recognised this over two thousand years ago when he wrote that all cities were divided into two: one the city of the poor, the other of the rich. With different life experiences, different educations, different value systems, different habits, these two sections of society have always occupied different realities. Plato, however, argued that excessive individual wealth harmed society. Whereas Nicholas believed it created incentive. Inequality was essential to encourage risk-taking. Without the prospect of substantial rewards, what other initiatives could be used to incentivise entrepreneurs? A nation of individuals endeavouring to get rich inevitably leads to economic growth, which subsequently leads to social and political progress. That's what Nicholas admired so much about Americans. They weren't hung up over divisions in society. They just wanted to get rich.

Outside the locker room Carla, Nicholas' Spanish PA, reminded him that he had a six-o'clock meeting with Mark Delaney from the Hand & Hyle Property Group, a development firm Delta had recently acquired a stake in. She also told him that CJ, Delta's Managing Director was back and clear for the next hour or so.

'Can you ask him to come to my office? Say, fifteen minutes.'

Delta was reeling from the Minton Corp takeover debacle. Although Nicholas had written an open letter to clients apologising for investing so much of the fund in M&T Technologies, he was still feeling pressure from several investors who wanted to redeem their investments. He and CJ needed to come up with some concessions to mollify worried clients.

Nicholas quickly showered and made his way down the three flights of stairs to his office, where CJ was waiting for him.

'Did you see the headline?' Nicholas chucked CJ a copy

of *City A.M.* 'From Hero to fucking Zero. It's the same guy who used to call me Nicky Midas. Can you believe it?'

'Don't worry about it.' Without bothering to look at the story, CJ tossed the newspaper to one side. 'It's tomorrow's fish and chip paper. You'll be the golden boy again soon enough.'

'I wouldn't be so sure. Look what happened to that friend of yours. Only twenty-five per cent knocked off the value of his fund. He recouped all his losses within a year. But his reputation has never recovered.'

'He had nothing like your track record. There's nothing we can do about the stories that are out there. But we can practise a bit of damage limitation.'

'What do you suggest?'

'You're not going to like this,' CJ said. 'But I say we cut our performance fees and—'

'And what?' Nicholas had a feeling he knew what was coming next. CJ had alluded to it once before as a possible solution when envisaging worst-case scenarios.

'Maybe we should allow those investors who want to leave to take what is left of their money.'

'It will ruin us. I can't believe you still see that as a solution.'

'It will quash any feelings of discontent. We have a stable base. I think you'll be surprised how supportive most of our clients are. Get rid of the malcontents and get on with recouping our losses.'

'There'll be an exodus. People are angry that I didn't anticipate problems with the Chinese.' Nicholas sat down behind his desk with his fingers intertwined. His knuckles were white from the strength of his clutch. 'How about we sell our stake in Tetra Systems?' Nicholas looked at CJ, who appeared unimpressed. 'And cut our management fees... in exchange for a larger cut of performance should we outperform.'

'I just don't think that's enough. Remember, we're not just trying to prevent clients from redeeming; we also need to attract new business. I say we cut our management fees by thirty beeps, lower performance fees to sixteen per cent and sell our shares in Tetra. We can put some of that money towards the residential fund.'

Nicholas whistled. 'That's brutal.' For a while he stared at two aeroplanes crossing in the sky. He tried to imagine all the different lives contained within those two slabs of aluminium. Everyone breathing the same air. He thought about every other plane that would fly over the city that day and every other city in the world, every desert, every expanse of ocean and every sparsely populated bit of countryside. Millions and millions of people, thinking their own thoughts and worrying about their own lives. Finally, he turned to CJ and added, 'If we're going to reduce our fees, let's at least lock them in for longer. Can we agree to that?'

CJ inclined his head and nodded slowly.

'OK,' Nicholas said. 'I'll prepare a letter after my meeting.'

It's a five-minute walk from Berkeley Square to the hotel on Park Lane where he'd arranged to meet Mark Delaney. A journey Nicholas was more than familiar with. Usually, he would cut across the square and come out opposite Annabel's. Today, however, the square was still heaving with sun worshippers who, in fear of the vicissitudes of a standard British summer, were determined to stay out while the good weather lasted. Instead, Nicholas walked around the perimeter of the east and south side of the square and headed up Charles Street past Mark's Club. When he got to the Chesterfield, Nicholas took a left down Queen Street, past Murano, before crossing over Curzon Street and cutting through Shepherd Market. This warren of exclusive clubs, Michelin-starred restaurants and foreign embassies was the London he loved. A virtual state of its own that somehow managed to maintain a separateness from the rest of the city. It was as if there was an invisible barrier keeping out those who didn't deserve to be there. The grand Regency architecture and abundance of blue plaques paid homage to the area's rich history. But for Nicholas, this playground of the elite felt new, dynamic, and awash with kindred spirits from all parts of the globe. Go-getters whose collective efforts had transformed London into the capital of the world. He continued up Market Mews, on to Pitt's Head Mews, past the old stables which at one time would have provided servants accommodation, and out on to Park Lane to the hotel.

Jennifer called just as Nicholas was about to enter the hotel. Adam, the project manager overseeing the basement extension, had just informed her that they might have to re-think the number of access routes. 'He says that, because of the size of the basement, one extra access point won't be enough.'

'Are you serious?' Nicholas said. 'And this has only just come to their attention?'

'It seems that way.'

'Where are they suggesting it should go?'

'Well, Adam thinks the best solution will be a doorway from the gallery to the garden. It means we will have to put in outside stairs.'

Nicholas had been the last person in the park to submit an application for his basement extension. The design had been so extravagant he was surprised when it got green-lit. At nearly five hundred pounds a square foot and covering almost two thousand square feet altogether, the former coal cellar included a ten-seater cinema room, state-of-the-art gym, vertical wine cellar and a twenty-five-metre swimming pool. However, the feature Nicholas was most excited about was a fifty-foot-long gallery with walk-on roof lights being built underneath his garden.

Nicholas walked across the inlaid marble floor of the lobby and made his way to the top of the hotel. Although he ate there at least twice a month, the view never failed to stir him. Beneath the restaurant, London presented herself supine and submissive, her infinite glories offered to anyone who could afford them. Nicholas spotted Mark Delaney at a table by the window, looking out over Hyde Park and Knightsbridge. The glistening flicker of the Serpentine and the endless blue sky was more redolent of the Mediterranean than central London. The smoggy fumes rising from Park Lane provided a hazy filter, adding a dreamy layer to the vista.

It was early evening and the restaurant was quiet. Only a couple of tables were occupied. At one of the tables, two men were having a heated conversation in Russian. One of the men sat with his back towards Nicholas. The other was seemingly attempting to pass himself off as much younger than he really was. Nicholas wondered at what point in the history of western culture older generations began to emulate the young instead of the other way around. The man was probably in his late fifties; his laser-bleached teeth clashed aggressively with a richly bronzed tan. He was wearing a T-shirt emblazoned with the meaningless slogan 'The Wild Love West'. The two men stopped talking as Nicholas walked towards them. Eyeing Nicholas suspiciously, the man in possession of the ultra-white teeth made use of the break in the conversation to childishly suck on a straw. He immediately resumed talking once Nicholas had passed.

Mark Delaney stood up and greeted him. Like a political leader trying to impose himself upon a foreign dignitary of equal stature, he placed his left hand on Nicholas' shoulder as they shook hands. His right-hand grip was overly firm.

For a while the two men remained standing as Delaney guided the conversation through introductory small talk. Within a couple of minutes, they had touched on the weather, Angel Di Maria's transfer fee and the defection of Douglas Carswell.

'What's going on with his face?' Delaney said as he sat back down in his chair, unfolded his napkin and placed it across his lap. 'He looks like he's had a stroke.'

'His defection's a blow for the government, that's for sure.' Nicholas sat down opposite Delaney and opened the wine list. 'I think Carswell reckons he can single-handedly rebrand UKIP. He wants to make it more palatable to middle England. The Tory Eurosceptics know that if Farage carries on the way he's going, he'll damage any chances they might have of winning a referendum. They need Farage. But they also need him to appeal to a broader selection of the electorate. I wouldn't be surprised if other Tory MPs are ready to follow.'

'You're carrying on as if a referendum is a done deal.'

'I don't see Merkel compromising on freedom of movement. Do you? People are freaked out by the migration figures. How the hell is Cameron going to get the numbers down? Membership of the EU's no longer just an issue for a small group of Tory idealogues.'

'Well, I guess we'll just have to wait and see, won't we?'

'What do you feel like drinking?' Nicholas said, studying the wine list.

'You're the expert. Whatever you recommend. As long as it's white. I don't fancy red on a day like today. Oh, and nothing too sweet either.'

Nicholas called the waiter over and ordered a bottle of Puligny-Montrachet.

'How's business?' he asked.

'You know what? It's pretty bloody good. We finally

submitted our proposals for the scheme in Peckham. The development in Reading is finished. That's already been nominated for an Inside Housing Award... which was a nice surprise. We're currently looking at overseeing the construction of nearly three thousand new homes in London and the South-west.' Delaney sat back in his chair and smiled. 'Business, as they say, is booming.'

The waiter arrived with a bottle of wine; he showed Nicholas the label and offered him the cork, which he chose not to inspect. He then poured a small amount into his glass for approval. Nicholas checked the colour against the white tablecloth. While keeping the glass on the table, he swirled it a few times to release the aromas. He then sniffed the drink, took a sip, and rolled it around his mouth before turning to the waiter and acknowledging his approval.

'How's everything with you?' Deep frown lines appeared on Delaney's forehead as he assumed an appropriate look of concern.

'I'll assume you've heard all about our recent investment mishap.'

Delaney confirmed that he had read about it.

'Unfortunately, these things happen,' Nicholas continued. 'I wish they didn't. But it comes with the territory. The important thing is how one recovers from a setback like this. We're already adapting and looking at ways to evolve. One thing I can say for sure is this won't have any effect on our residential strategy. If anything, we're looking to take on more staff to push the fund.'

'That's good to hear,' Delaney said. 'Because there are some exciting opportunities currently knocking about.'

The restaurant was getting busier, with customers eager to take their perch high above the city. A large Persian-looking woman was sitting alongside a pretty, much younger woman at one of the tables. Preoccupied with her phone, the older woman was paying no attention to the younger woman, who acknowledged Nicholas' presence with a coquettish smile. While Nicholas blankly stared back, Delaney continued to tell him about two estates in North London due to be regenerated. The first was a seven-hundred home development in Wembley.

'I think we're in with an excellent chance of winning this tender.' Delaney went on to tell Nicholas that the brother-in-law of Hand & Hyle's finance director was a partner at the law firm that was helping Monarch Housing Association form a joint venture company to redevelop the estate. Nicholas, however, was too busy thinking about the pros and cons of testosterone replacement therapy to properly absorb anything Delaney was saying. Talk of affordable rent tenures and district heating networks remained unprocessed while Nicholas considered the side effects of this kind of therapy. Jennifer was keen that he should explore all potential remedies. She had even suggested possibly talking to Seth Pritzker about penile implants. Nicholas was furious at this suggestion and made Jennifer promise that she wouldn't pursue this unilaterally. As a concession, he told her that he would consider hormone replacement therapy. But did he really want to embark on a treatment that carried possible risks like breast swelling and smaller bollocks? He was certain lack of testosterone was not the issue.

While Nicholas was mulling this over, Delaney was still telling him about the incredible opportunities that had recently presented themselves. Another scheme he was *mega excited* about was the Bevan Estate in Albion Park.

'Did you say Albion Park?'

'Yeah. It's a lovely part of the city.'

'I live there.'

'Really? I always thought you lived in Highgate. Don't know why.'

Delaney explained that the local council regarded the Bevan Estate as the jewel in the crown of their housing portfolio. 'Their repair bill alone is about three hundred and fifty million. They need to raise capital. They've lost all their funding, and obviously there's a limit to how much they can borrow. Outside of W1, parts of W8, and I suppose SW10, Albion Park is one of the most desired addresses in London right now. I don't need to tell you the sort of money that could be made from selling three hundred and fifty new homes.'

'Would it all be private?' Nicholas asked excitedly.

'Not completely, no. Some existing tenants will get moved over to the new development. There will be an allocation of affordable housing; there has to be. But the council have been smart. A lot of the secure tenants have already gone. They've all been replaced with short-termers. These people have no historical ties to the community. They don't care where they live. They're just grateful to have a roof over their heads. Most of them will be moved on elsewhere. There will be a few unhappy bunnies; there always are. But it shouldn't involve too much displacement. Hundreds of people would have to lose their homes to make this sort of money from some of the council's other stock. They've been left with no choice. They have to sell their assets.'

Nicholas looked stunned.

'Are you OK with this?' Delaney asked.

'Am I OK with it? It's probably the best news I've had in months.' Nicholas took a sip of wine and patted his lips with a napkin. 'The estate is an eyesore,' he said. 'It depresses me just looking at it.'

'The tenants will be crying out for it to be redeveloped.'

'How do we make this happen?' Nicholas asked. 'Who are we up against?'

'You're not going to believe this,' Delaney said, smiling.

'The council won't even be putting this project out to tender. We were nominated as preferred bidders the moment plans for the development were discussed.'

'How the hell did you manage that?'

'The chairman of the borough planning committee is…' Delaney tapped his fingers rhythmically on the table. 'Put it this way: he's been the beneficiary of my largesse on several occasions. Boy, could I tell you some stories about him…'

'That is very good news.' Nicholas clapped his hands together and laughed. 'Look, whatever you need,' he said, 'it's there. Just tell me what we have to do.'

'All you need to do is hold on to your stakeholders and ensure the fund doesn't collapse. We're going to need access to a substantial war chest if we're going to deliver this pipeline.'

Chapter 12

September 2014

As the final notes of 'I Go to Pieces' rang out, Owen bent down and manually increased the feedback intensity on his effects pedal. The multiple echoes rapidly regenerated, crashing into one another as delay times were cranked up. By keeping the pedal depressed, Owen ensured the increased motor speeds and feedback level became a monstrous slab of noise. Gradually he mixed in some more distortion and faded out the dry signal entirely. Happy with the effect, he held the settings for a while before dropping his guitar to the floor. A shrieking wash of feedback and modulation enveloped the auditorium. Owen bent over and grabbed a beer from the cluster of bottles gathered around his amp. Then, without acknowledging the crowd's applause, he sauntered offstage and made his way to the dressing room, where he was greeted by the tour manager.

'Why do you always rush off the stage like that?' Chalky asked.

The cramped dressing room was dominated by a large Hollywood-style make-up mirror. Owen took a towel from the table, removed his shirt and began to pat himself down.

'It's not my band. The crowd don't care about me. They

want to see Stuart and the others. I leave the limelight for them.'

'It looks like you're embarrassed to be up there,' Chalky said.

'Embarrassed to be on stage? Me? Nah.'

Owen finished off his beer and grabbed a bottle of Jack Daniel's from the fridge as the rest of the band bundled into the dressing room. Stuart, the ninety-per-cent-cheekbone singer with an overextended fringe and an alpine sense of entitlement, sat down in the chair next to him.

'What was all that about at the end?' Stuart leaned forwards and inspected his face in the mirror.

'What do you mean?' Owen poured some Coke into his glass of whiskey.

'You know, chucking your guitar on the floor. It's a bit of a cliché, isn't it? A bit rock 'n' roll.'

'The strap on my guitar came undone. I just dropped it on the floor. No big deal.'

'It might have been alright to do that sort of thing in your day.' Stuart picked up a cotton wool pad and began to remove eyeliner from his face. 'I just think it looks a bit naff, that's all.'

Chalky looked at Owen and rolled his eyes.

'While we're at it,' Stuart continued, 'I nearly tripped over those bottles by your amp as I came off stage. I could have broken my neck.'

Unable to hide his irritation at this reproach from the singer, Owen took a gulp of his drink and kissed his teeth. He stared at Stuart's reflection in the mirror. 'Anything else?'

Stuart avoided Owen's glare and continued to remove his make-up before muttering, 'The amount you drink, I don't know how you remember the songs.'

From their first rehearsal together, Stuart had constantly

been niggling at Owen. If he wasn't finding fault with his onstage habits, he was criticising his clothes (Stuart had forbidden him from wearing an old Peter Tosh T-shirt at a gig in Cologne) or else the way he played a particular sequence or voiced his chords. No one else in the band highlighted the same issues, not even Jonny, who had sat in on rehearsals to help Owen learn the songs. When Jonny was hospitalised a few weeks before the tour was due to start, Stuart had been vehemently opposed to hiring Owen. 'He's too old,' he said. 'It won't work.' At the time, though, there weren't many people available who both the management and the record company believed could learn the parts quickly. Yes, Owen was older than the rest of the band, they argued, but he was a safe bet. He still looked good. Most importantly, though, he wasn't too expensive.

Owen finished his drink. He held out a plastic cup towards Chalky, who was going around the dressing room with a magnum of Prosecco, a gift from the record company.

'Has anyone got any names they want to add to the list for the after-party?' Chalky looked at Owen. 'O? You haven't given me any names yet.'

'Do you know what? I'm probably going to get off,' Owen said.

The band had only got back from Germany that morning. Owen hadn't even had time to go home yet. The following day was Jacquie's mum's seventieth. She had already texted Owen, reminding him that her brother had booked a table for lunch at a pub in Stoke Newington. Owen had phoned her back and tried to wriggle out of it, but Jacquie had been adamant. She accused Owen of only thinking of himself before making him promise that he wouldn't *go out and get fucked up after the show.*

'Come on, Owen,' Chalky implored. 'We've got no more gigs for a while. I'm off on tour again next week. Who knows when we'll see each other next? Let's go out and celebrate. We'll have a hoot.'

Disinclined to sit at the back of the tour bus and play computer games with the rest of the band, Owen spent most of the travel time on tour seated at the front of the bus with Chalky playing backgammon and watching John Cassavetes films. Chalky had a couple of kids roughly the same age as Harley and Dexter. Unlike Owen, though, he was separated from his partner. He told Owen it was impossible to be away as much as he was and maintain a relationship. Chalky was devoted to his job and life on the road. While belts were tightened to the point of suffocation and budgets disappeared into the ether, he was a record company's dream. He was organised enough to work as a tour manager, sufficiently tech-savvy to strip and install a studio and scary enough to occasionally double up as security. He never had to worry about where the next job was coming from.

Owen felt his phone vibrate in his pocket. It was a text from Daisy.

gig was banging wots going on now. P.s u looked fat on stage xxx

Taken aback by Daisy's comment, Owen put his hand on his belly. Did he really look fat? Surely his guitar would have covered up his paunch. He re-read the message before putting on a clean T-shirt.

'Come out with us,' Chalky pleaded once more. He leaned over and whispered in Owen's ear. 'There will be loads of birds. Plus it's a good opportunity to do a bit of schmoozing. You might get some work.' Chalky pulled out a plastic baggie from his pocket and waved it in front of Owen's face. 'Would a bit of hurry-up help convince you?'

Owen sheepishly extended his hand and took the bag.

'Good boy...' Chalky said.

Owen looked at the time. It was just gone eleven. He promised himself he would leave the party at one-thirty. Besides, Chalky was right; he needed another job. Record company parties were often a good place to do a bit of networking.

Additionally, the thought of Daisy Crossley turning up had piqued his interest. Even though he knew he should steer well clear. And even though she had called him fat.

Owen opened the toilet door and pulled down the sticky plastic loo seat with his foot. The prospect of sniffing the drugs had given him butterflies, which subsequently mutated into an urgent need to poo. As he sat on the toilet, Owen texted Daisy:

After party @ The Underground. You +1 on the door. Maybe see you their x

Why did he put a kiss at the end of the message? He had purposefully avoided signing off with a kiss when he messaged her the other day. Fuck. Owen reached for the baggie; with the corner of a credit card, he managed to scoop out a mound of the powder, which he then carefully placed under his left nostril. He felt a stinging sensation just beneath his ears as he began to salivate. The combined smell of the cocaine and effluents made him feel queasy. Owen took a deep sniff from the card, repeated the action once more, using his other nostril, and put the baggie away. A little lump of compressed powder fell from his nose and landed in a fold of his jeans. Owen picked it up with the tip of his freshly licked little finger and pushed it back in. He sniffed vigorously. His mouth twisted at the bitter combination of diluents and adulterants. Immediately he felt a numbness at the back of his throat.

'Better now?' Chalky said with a wink as Owen walked back into the dressing room.

'All good,' Owen said. He asked Chalky if he could put Daisy's name plus one on the list.

'Done.'

Owen could feel every agitated thud of his heart as it motored beneath the surface of his skin. He placed his hand on his sternum and pressed down. The manic flutters of the besieged organ whirred just beneath his fingers. The normally metronomic pulse felt erratic and arrhythmic. Owen had recently read an article about a guy in his early forties who suffered from an aortic dissection after a coke binge. The man described experiencing excruciating pain as blood travelling under high pressure tore apart the layers of his aortic wall. Sitting in the back of the car with Chalky, Owen worried he was about to suffer a similar fate. Slowly he began to enact circles with the palm of his hand. It felt pacifying as each circular motion impeded the force of the rush. Like a parent soothing a baby, Owen comforted himself with an audible shush. Chalky looked at him suspiciously and laughed.

The two men were in a cab heading to the after-party. It was nearly eleven-thirty, and the traffic on the Holloway Road had ground to a halt.

'This journey's doing my head in,' Owen said. 'Shall we just get out and walk?'

'Forget that. It will take forever.' Chalky suggested that they take a left through Drayton Park and carry on towards Dalston via Highbury Fields. 'Cheer up,' Chalky said. 'I'd have left with the others if I'd known you were going to be such a miserable git.'

Although the traffic eased up once they had left the Holloway Road, the car was still moving too slowly to accommodate the buzz. Owen was desperate to get to the venue and have a drink. Without alcohol, the effects of the cocaine were too edgy and unsettling.

'I'll be alright once I get a drink in me.'

Too charged to talk, Owen continued to stare out of the window. Row upon row of grand Georgian houses passed by. He wondered how so many people could afford to own one of these places. When he was younger, he remembered thinking perhaps only a handful of millionaires existed somewhere in the world. A million was such an unobtainable figure, the preserve of superstars, scions and royalty. As a designation it no longer held any potency. London was a city full of millionaires and billionaires. Owen tried to think of new definitions which could accommodate the different degrees of wealth which now existed. He wondered what percentage of black households even owned their own home. Let alone houses like the ones he was looking at, which were obviously worth millions. How does anyone manage to pass on wealth if they don't own a home?

'Most people can't stop talking after doing a bit of gak. What's got into you?'

'I'm OK,' Owen said. 'Just thinking.'

'That's the problem with you. You overthink things.' With his heavily tattooed arms resting on the back of the passenger seat, Chalky leaned forward and suggested a route to the driver. He looked at Owen and shook his head. 'He hasn't got a scooby where he's going.' Instead of doing a right towards Balls Pond Road, the cabbie indicated left to go up Mildmay Park Road. 'You're going the wrong fucking way, mate...'

Chalky pulled out a plastic baggie from his pocket and held it between his legs. He expertly dipped a Yale key into the powder and suggested Owen take a sniff from just above his lap.

'Not for me,' Owen said.

Chalky looked at him as if he had turned down the offer of free money. Then, without attempting to conceal his actions, he raised the key towards his own face. The taxi driver watched him through his rear-view mirror. Having ingested the small heap, he threw his head back, squeezed the bridge of his nose and groaned loudly.

'I don't get you sometimes.' Chalky turned to face Owen. 'What do you mean?'

'Nothing seems to make you happy. I know people who would give their left nut to be doing what you're doing. You're playing in one of the biggest bands in the country. Every gig is sold out. Yet you've always got a face like a slapped arse.'

'It's not my band, is it? No one's coming to listen to my music. Even though it's better than anything this lot are doing. Chances are, I'll never play with them again. I should have smashed Stuart's head against the mirror. Talentless little prick.'

'Hmmm. And thereby make sure that no one else hires you again… ever.'

'Do you know what? It feels like the last twenty years of my life have been for nothing – all my experience and expertise. In any other industry, you'd be looking forward to yet another promotion or perhaps an even bigger bonus. Instead, the tour's over, and I'm back at square one, looking for work again. You would have thought I'd be used to it by now. But I tell you, it's got harder as I've got older. I hate not working.'

The alcohol immediately had the desired effect and smoothed out the spikes of the cocaine high. Without bothering to leave the bar, Owen finished his drink and ordered another double JD and coke. Chalky had vanished as soon as they entered the club. Owen assumed he was keen to get away after their rather sombre cab journey.

The venue was a series of brick arches leading from a cavernous main space packed with punters. Owen wandered around the club, sipping his drink. Occasionally he would stop for a chat with someone he vaguely knew, but no sooner had the conversation started than he would look for an excuse to extricate himself. A few people came up to him, patted him on the back and congratulated him on his performance earlier, but not as many as he would have liked. It was London; no one was going to get too excited about a stand-in guitarist.

Owen continued to mooch about the club, briefly stopping to listen to a DJ or watch people dancing. He didn't stay anywhere for too long just in case anyone might think he was at the party on his own. Having done a circuit of the venue, he found himself back at the bar, where he noticed Stuart and Jonny surrounded by a throng of people. Stuart was revelling in the attention of a couple of wide-eyed fans. Jonny looked over to where Owen was standing and gestured for him to come over.

Owen loitered uneasily on the edge of the group. Instead of feeling garrulous, the coke made him feel overwrought. He could feel his facial muscles convulsing. While Jonny and Stuart fended off the curious and the starry-eyed, Owen was left feeling like a spare part, painfully aware of others' disinterest in him. When he received a message from Jacquie stating – *if you're not home before 12.30 don't bother coming home at all* – he decided to say his goodbyes and head off. It was 12.25am. He would miss the curfew but believed he could justify coming home at one o'clock.

'Wait, wait, don't go just yet,' Jonny said. 'I wanted to talk to you about something.'

Jonny finished the conversation he was engaged in and draped an arm around Owen's shoulder.

'You were amazing tonight,' he said. 'Pure fucking magic.'

Jonny was sweaty, effusive and way too touchy-feely. He pressed his mouth against Owen's ear as he spoke. Owen could feel the patter of spit landing on his neck as Jonny tried to make his voice heard above the music. The proximity of his lips combined with his slurred Aberdeenshire accent made it hard to understand much of what he said.

'That shit you did at the end. Blew my fucking mind. It was… like… yeah. Yeah! Fucking h-e-a-v-y. Know what I mean?' Jonny was unsteady on his feet. He leaned into Owen and pressed down on his shoulder. Some drink slopped out of his glass and landed on Owen's shoes. 'How you been feeling about the gigs?' He pulled away. His eyes were wonky. A white scum had gathered at the corners of his mouth.

'Yeah, they've been good.' Owen bristled at the arm around the shoulder. He liked Jonny, but the quasi mentor/protégé dynamic made him uncomfortable. Jonny was at least ten years younger than him.

'I love what've you been doing with my parts. It's given me pure ideas. Some of the looped stuff you did on "Violent Light"… it sounded awesome.'

'Thanks, man. They're great songs. I think… if you had two guitarists on stage, you could do a lot more. It would free you up a bit.'

Jonny suggested the two of them go and get a drink. As they walked to the bar, every few feet a different fan stopped them, asking when Jonny intended to return to the live set-up. A boy in a black RFTS hoodie told him that the band didn't sound nearly as good without him. Jonny looked at Owen and winked.

At the bar, Jonny ordered drinks. 'What you was saying just then about, you know, two guitarists…' He swayed from side to side as he spoke. 'It's funny you should say that because ah… well, I was wondering if you would be up for joining the band on a… you know… more permanent basis.'

'Really?'

'Aye. Why do you sound so surprised?'

'I don't know. I wasn't expecting it. Are the rest of the band in agreement?'

'They will be. I've got to finish the next record like. I got a wee bit done while I was rehabilitating, you know, but I could do with someone to bounce ideas off. There's heaps to do.'

'What about Stuart?'

'Mate, Stuey sings the songs. He doesn't fucking write them.'

'Does that mean I would be involved in writing?'

Jonny stuck his finger in his ear and wiggled it around. 'Most of the songs are done,' he said. 'But we could defo work on production together. I'll check with my manager, but maybe we'll be able to put you on some kind of retainer.'

'Wow. OK.' Owen finally managed a smile that felt natural. 'That sounds great.'

'Brilliant.' As the two men hugged, Jonny leaned into Owen's ear again. 'Maybe don't say anything to Stuart or the others just yet. It's probably best if it comes from me. Know what I mean?' Jonny held out an open wrap in his hand. 'Shall we celebrate?'

'What is it?'

'A bit of dizz.'

Owen licked his finger and placed it in the paper envelope. The glassy crushed crystals congregated around the tip of his finger, which he then put in his mouth.

'Hey, you. I saw that.'

Owen looked up to see Daisy Crossley standing in front of him. Daisy was wearing a red bomber jacket, a pair of worn-out tight Levi's and suede-heeled ankle boots. She was standing with her hands in her back pockets. Owen tried to say hello, but the words got caught in his mouth and emerged in the form of an unintelligible squeak. Daisy looked at her friend and sniggered.

'Can we have some of that?' Daisy pointed to the wrap. Jonny looked puzzled; he glanced at Owen, hoping for guidance.

'Are you not going to introduce us?' Daisy asked.

Owen cleared his throat. 'Sorry. Jonny, this is Daisy. Daisy, meet Jonny.' He turned to Daisy's friend, 'I know we've met before, but... I'm sorry, I've forgotten your name...'

Daisy rolled her eyes and introduced Ziggy to Jonny herself.

Daisy's entrance had been a demonstration of youthful self-assurance. Like a dazzling light, she radiated an energy that made those in her vicinity cower. Eclipsed by her friend, Ziggy stood a step back from Daisy. Jonny, meanwhile, meekly held out his hand and offered the girls a dab. Daisy licked her teeth and grimaced at the bitter synthetic taste. She reached out for Owen's drink which he duly passed her. Having taken a swig, she gave the drink to Ziggy.

Jonny asked the girls if he could get them a drink. He pulled out a wad of drinks tickets which he promptly dropped on the floor. Needing a moment to compose himself, Owen offered to go to the bar himself. Daisy had caught him off-guard. After weeks of lusting over her online persona, her appearance in the flesh had unsettled him. That, combined with a twitching cokey dissonance, had left him feeling awkward and out of place. He wondered if he preferred the thought of Daisy rather than the reality. Someone like her demanded excitement and attention. He wasn't sure whether he could access those resources any more.

While waiting at the bar, Owen noticed that Stuart had joined Jonny and the girls. The two barmen seemed to be serving everyone but him. Out of frustration, Owen flashed the laminated AAA pass hung around his neck. Embarrassingly, this failed to provoke the desired response. Owen turned around to check on the others. It looked as if Stuart had focused his attentions on Daisy. The two of them were taking it in turns to talk into each other's ears, both laughing at whatever the other was saying.

'Here he is,' Stuart exclaimed as Owen finally returned to the group. 'I thought you might have wandered off again.'

Owen handed drinks to Jonny, Daisy and Ziggy. 'He made a habit of doing that on tour,' Stuart continued. 'He would leave the party early but get back to the bus after everyone else.' Although Stuart was addressing the group, he looked into Owen's eyes as he spoke. 'It was all very mysterious,' he continued. 'What, no drink for me?'

Owen's vision blurred as he stared at the singer. Whatever he had taken had sped up his body systems. He felt like he needed to do another shit.

'Our friend is DJing at the moment,' Stuart said. 'Do you want to come and check him out?' The invitation was aimed at Daisy. With a flick of his floppy fringe, Stuart gestured towards Jonny and Ziggy, walking off towards the main room. 'Your friend is coming,' he added. Owen interpreted this as the cue for him to leave. He should have gone home earlier. But here he was, hanging around a nightclub taking drugs and competing with a pop star for the attention of a much younger girl. What the hell was he doing? He was an intruder, an interloper. When he was younger, he remembered seeing older men in clubs. He always wondered what they were doing there. They appeared both incongruous and tragic. Their presence in a place dedicated to the celebration of youth made them look pathetic. Owen was probably older now than those men who once attracted his pity.

'Maybe; I'll catch up with you in a bit,' Daisy said.

Unused to such rebuffs, Stuart appeared wounded.

'He loves himself a bit, doesn't he?' Daisy said as Stuart sloped off. 'That's enough about me. Let's talk about you. What do you think about me?'

Owen laughed at her reaction.

'He is very good-looking, though,' Daisy said.

'Not fat like me, eh?'

'What are you talking about? You're not fat.'

'What was that message about then?'

'Huh?'

Owen pulled out his phone and showed Daisy the message she had sent earlier. Daisy put her hand over her mouth and laughed. 'Oh my God,' she said. 'It's a typo. I meant to say you looked fit... not fat.'

A sequence of rushes surged through Owen. His head rocked backwards. As if shy of breathing too loudly, he emitted a small gasp of air.

'Shit, this stuff is quite strong,' he said. 'I think I need to sit down.'

The sound of Daisy getting out of bed woke Owen up. He rolled onto his side and watched as she walked naked to the adjoining bathroom, her unblemished behind betraying barely a ripple as she moved. For a while, Owen lay motionless as he tried to assess where he was, how he got there and why he felt so unbelievably bad. Daisy shut the bathroom door behind her and turned on the shower. Like a recovering patient, Owen carefully sat up and scoured the room for his trousers. He spotted them, discarded and scrunched up, lying on the floor.

Daisy's bedroom was a mess. There was an overflowing

ashtray on the floor next to an empty wine bottle and a half-full bottle of vodka. Next to that, Daisy's bag was lying open, its contents spewed onto the floor. Hoping to retrieve his phone from his trousers, Owen slowly stood up, only to be forced back down again by an intense dizziness. He put his head in his hands and massaged his brow. 'Jesus Christ,' he muttered as he tried to steady his breathing. His lips were splitting, and his mouth was dry. It was nearly twenty-four hours since he had last eaten.

Owen got back into bed the moment he heard the shower stop. Daisy soon emerged from the bathroom looking more refreshed than she had any right to, the previous night's exploits absent from her face.

'Hey.' Daisy began to towel down her hair. Owen willed his face to form a smile. 'What's wrong?' she said. 'You look worried.'

'Is anyone else in the house?' He took a deep intake of breath. His breathing felt irregular and shallow. A prickling sensation crept up his arm as he concentrated on his next breath.

'My dad is downstairs,' she said. 'Get dressed, and we'll go down and see him.'

'Are you serious?'

'Of course he's not. He's never here. It's chill.'

'What about anyone else?'

'No, I told you last night, they've all gone away. Don't you remember?'

'I don't remember much, to be honest.' Owen rolled on to his side. He propped his head up with his hand. 'What was that stuff you gave me?'

'Ket.'

'Ketamine? Bloody hell.' Owen lay back down. Beads of sweat sparkled on his brow like a stellar scintillation.

Daisy asked him if he was feeling OK. 'You've gone quite pale,' she said.

'I'm fine. I... I just get low blood sugar levels. I don't suppose you've got any fizzy drinks in the house.'

Once Daisy had left the room, Owen got out of bed and made his way to the bathroom. He grabbed his phone from the pocket of his jeans. A pair of white boxer shorts lay next to the trousers, a clearly visible skid mark compounding his humiliation. He pushed the shorts into his trouser leg and hurried into the bathroom, bolting the door behind him. The bathroom, like the bedroom, was an unholy mess, the floor scattered with dirty laundry and discarded bottles of beauty products. Owen sat on the toilet and stared at the phone, frightened at what it was about to reveal. On the floor next to the loo he noticed a large brown paper bag. Inside were the remnants of a fast-food takeout, which he emptied into the bin. Ensuring that both his nose and mouth were covered, Owen placed the bag over his face. Slowly he began to breathe in and out, counting to ten between each tremulous breath. It was something he had done many times before. At one point in his life, he had even slept with a paper bag underneath his bed. The process mitigated his anxiety and restored some much-needed carbon dioxide. Gradually his breathing became more regular.

Finally, he resolved to look at his phone. There were over ten missed calls and a load of messages from Jacquie. Owen pulled at his face as if it was a prosthetic mask and emitted a fearful whimper. Too scared to read all the messages, he could only bring himself to read the last one.

You're a cunt. Im going away for a few days – grab your stuff and don't come back.

The phone was dropped, and the paper bag once again planted on his face. As he breathed into it, Owen tried to recall events from the previous night. It was a blur of snatched moments and snippets of garbled conversation. He could remember sitting in the club with Daisy; she talked about her family, particularly her dad. He could recall her giving him some more rancid-tasting powder to dab and Chalky asking him if he wanted to stay with the band at their hotel. But, apart from a fleeting mental image of Daisy taking her jacket off and the two of them kissing by a pool table, whatever happened after the club was a blank. He closed his eyes and wracked his brains. He couldn't even remember if they had had sex.

Owen opened the bathroom door and got back into Daisy's bed. Propped against the pillows, he looked around the room at the band posters and endless photographs of friends. Daisy soon came back in holding a tray of drinks. She handed Owen a cold can of Coke. Like an addict receiving a belated fix, he opened the drink and took a desperate swig.

'Better?' Daisy said.

Owen wiped his hand across his mouth. 'A bit. Yeah.'

Standing in front of Owen, Daisy fixed her stare onto his before allowing her bathrobe to fall to the floor. Owen was allowed enough time to absorb her nakedness before Daisy climbed into bed next to him. The sun was streaming in through the bedroom window; it drenched the room in a brutal light. Owen caught a glimpse of his filthy nicotine-stained fingers, wrapped in over a day's worth of grime. He dreaded to think how the rest of him must have looked or how his breath smelt.

'What happened after the club last night?' he asked tentatively.

'Do you not remember anything?'

'Bits.' Owen rolled onto his back. There was a stain on the ceiling, which looked like spilt coffee. He wondered how it got there. 'I remember talking to you in the club.

And I remember you giving me some of that stuff. But after that… it's mostly blank.'

'You don't remember what happened once we got back here?'

'Not really.'

'That's probably for the best.'

Owen felt a rising tide of shame. There he was, lying naked in bed alongside the star of his recent fantasies; all he could think about was getting out of there. 'Did we… you know?'

'Fuck?'

'Yeah.'

'You weren't capable of doing much.'

Owen covered his face with his hands.

'It's my fault,' Daisy said. 'I shouldn't have given you any more of that stuff.'

Daisy sat up and leaned over Owen. She started to stroke his chest, moving her hand lower with each circular movement. Her body felt slight and delicate next to his. As she moved in closer, the side of her breast touched the top of Owen's hand. He could feel the unobtrusive weight of her bosom press down on his forefinger.

'We could always try again?' Daisy lay back on the bed. Her hipbones jutted out above her pelvis like handlebars. Her breasts virtually disappeared as she lay on her back. 'Be gentle,' she said, smiling. 'I've never been with a black guy before.'

With one ill-considered remark, Daisy had gifted Owen the excuse he was looking for. If ever he was going to have sex with Daisy he would rather it was without the spectre of another panic attack looming large.

'What did you just say?'

The smile faded from Daisy's face as she detected the shift in Owen's mood.

'Be gentle?' Owen shook his head and snorted.

'It was a joke.'

'Not a very funny one.'

Owen sat on the edge of the bed, unsure if he could even muster the energy to stand up and put his clothes on. He heaved his hand across his forehead and wiped away the sweat. His head felt cold and clammy.

'Is this just about fulfilling some type of fantasy?' he asked.

Daisy sat up. She pulled the sheet up over her naked body. 'What do you mean?'

Owen ran his hand through his hair. The side of his head felt numb. It was as if there was an additional layer of skull between his fingers and his nerves. 'Did one of your mates tell you that once you've tried black, you won't go back?'

Owen got out of bed and began to gather his clothes.

'What! Why would you say that?' Daisy stared at Owen open-mouthed. 'Please don't go,' she said. 'I'm sorry if I offended you. I'm so not a racist.'

Owen's breathing had become fast and shallow again. His mouth was so dry, it was as if his salivary glands had stopped working altogether. He felt anxious and frightened. The only thing he could think about was getting out of the house.

'I'm getting out of here,' Owen said, stumbling on his words. 'Do you need to let me out?'

'The door is on the latch.' Daisy looked bewildered.

Without saying goodbye or even looking at Daisy again, Owen hitched up his trousers and rushed out of the door. For a moment he stood on the landing outside her bedroom. He felt himself list as he peered down the five flights of stairs to the bottom floor. He leaned forward with both hands holding onto the banister.

'Are you sure you're OK?' Daisy had followed him out of the room.

Without answering, Owen stood up and made his way down the stairs. Daisy stood on the landing, watching his ignominious retreat.

Chapter 13

'**The crack goes from the basement all the way up the side of the house.** If you stand in front of it for long enough, you can almost watch it get bigger in real time.'

Ed sat down at the kitchen table and picked up a newspaper. Kitty walked into the larder and continued to talk. 'God knows the damage they've done to the foundations. I've tried to warn them. The water table on this side of the park is high enough as it is. Installing a double basement which runs the full length of his garden is only going to make it worse.'

Bad weather the previous day had caused a small amount of flooding in Kitty's basement. This happened occasionally. After the last water ingress, Kitty had paid five thousand pounds to have her basement tanked. Most of the other houses around the park had installed more sophisticated drainage systems. But up until the day before, Kitty hadn't experienced any further problems.

'It might not be anything to do with your neighbour,' Ed said.

Kitty emerged from the larder carrying a plate full of cheese. 'Oh, please. It's a bit of a coincidence, don't you think? All of these things happening at once.'

'What's that smell?' Ed asked. 'Is something burning?'

'I can't smell anything.'

'No, something is definitely burning.'

Ed stood up, and dog-like sniffed the air. He walked around the kitchen, trying to locate the smell. When he opened one of the doors on the oven, a mass of smoke billowed out. 'Jesus Christ!' Ed flapped his arms manically as he tried to disperse the smoke. One of the alarms in the kitchen went off, and the dogs started to bark. Kitty covered her ears while Ed stood on a chair and turned the alarm off.

Once the smoke had cleared, Ed put on a pair of oven gloves and extracted a blackened loaf of bread from the oven. Kitty stared at the burned object, looking horrified.

'I completely forgot I had put that in.'

For a moment, Ed thought she was about to cry. 'It's OK,' he said. 'It's easily done.'

'It's happened a few times recently.'

'What, burning bread?'

'No. Silly mistakes like that. Forgetting things.' Kitty sat down at the table.

'Join the club.' Ed pulled up a chair next to her. 'It's our age. These things happen.'

Out of the corner of her eye, Kitty caught a glimpse of Ed's ageing hands. The skin was loose, bunched up and wrinkled like an ill-fitting glove. His joints were gnarled and swollen. A lifetime's dedication to nicotine and red wine had done him no favours. But when Kitty looked at Ed, she still saw his youthful, full-lipped beauty. Rather than seeing the hairless liver-spotted pate, which he liked to hide under a grey felt fedora, Kitty still recalled the long dark curly hair which tumbled down his neck and caressed the sides of his face. Hugh used to say that Ed reminded him of an angel from a Pasolini film. Men and women would both swoon in his presence, though women would curse his avowed homosexuality. Both promiscuous and debauched, Ed was lucky to survive an era that claimed so many of his friends, including The Judge.

'Do you remember when we first met?' Kitty took her glasses off and wiped them on her shirt.

'How could I forget?' Ed smiled. 'We were sitting on the lawn next to the sundial.'

'You were a wreck. You looked like you hadn't slept for two days.'

Ed shivered at the memory. 'Urgh – don't remind me. No doubt it was that hideous bathtub speed. I'm amazed my septum survived my dalliance with that stuff.'

'I remember The Judge looked demented. I didn't want to sit down with either of you. Hugh had got to know one of those young Irish boys who lived in your building. I think one of them must have invited us to come and join you.'

'Padraig and Gatsby,' Ed said. 'Who knows what happened to those two. Something awful, I fear. Padraig knew some distinctly dodgy characters.'

'I seem to remember it was my birthday,' Kitty continued. 'Hugh had very sweetly bought me a bottle of fizz. I had already removed the foil. I was looking forward to having a drink with him on my own. As soon as I saw you and The Judge, I hid the bottle in my bag.'

'You didn't hide it well enough, though, did you?' Ed gave Kitty a reproving glance.

'Well, I didn't think for a moment that one of you would reach over and help yourself.'

Ed threw his head back and laughed. 'I'll never forget the look on The Judge's face when that cork hit him on the head. I know it's very childish, but still, to this day, it's one of the funniest things I've ever seen.'

'God knows why the bottle popped of its own accord. Hugh had brought it back from somewhere. I think he thought it might have had something to do with the pressure from the aeroplane. The Judge was lucky. It could have taken his eye out.'

For a moment, Kitty and Ed retreated into their thoughts. Both smiled wistfully as they enjoyed their own personal reminisces.

'It's cruel, isn't it?' Ed said.

'What is?'

'Time. I wasted time, and now doth time waste me. Before you know it, life has passed you by. And it's only then you realise how little you understood about it. But it's too late. And one's left with all this knowledge… and you can't do anything with it. It's no good to us any more.'

'Ignorance is bliss, I suppose,' Kitty said. 'How else would you ever manage to navigate your way through life? The young are destined to ignore the advice of the more experienced. And that's the way it should be.'

'I suppose otherwise everyone would give up before they'd even started.'

Kitty picked up a business card from the table and began twirling it between her fingers. 'Do you worry about getting older?'

'Not really.' Ed rubbed the back of his neck. 'To be honest, I try not to think about it too much.'

'You don't think about what would happen if you got very ill?'

'No. Why, do you?'

'Well, neither of us have children or partners to look after us.'

Kitty looked down at the business card, which she continued to turn over and over in her hand. The card belonged to Lady Abigail Vaughan, the CEO of the Bowen Trust. Ever since Kitty had organised an art auction to raise money for the trust, Lady Abigail had considered her part of the fundraising team, albeit an unpaid member. She had visited Kitty the week before to see if she could persuade her to organise another auction. The previous one had raised nearly one hundred thousand pounds; the trust was now rehabilitating more prisoners than ever. Money was needed, particularly to help with accommodation support.

'I tell you what,' Ed said. Kitty continued to stare at the card. 'Oi. Are you listening?'

'Sorry.' Kitty came to with a shake of her head. 'What were you saying?'

'I was going to say, let's make a pact. If either one of us ever gets so ill that life has become unbearable, the other one will help... you know.' Ed dragged a finger across his throat. 'Agreed?'

Kitty laughed at Ed. 'Isn't it illegal to help someone die?'

'Not in some places it isn't. Do you remember Sergei, that ex-ballet dancer I saw for a bit?'

'How could I forget?'

'He organised for his mother to go to one of those places that take care of everything.'

'What was wrong with her?'

'Motor neurone disease. Poor thing.'

'Was he with her at the end?'

Ed nodded his head. The two of them were quiet for a moment. 'This is all getting a bit maudlin,' he said. 'Shall we talk about something else?'

'We didn't make the pact.'

'Consider it done.'

Over on the other side of the kitchen, Ed noticed one of Kitty's assemblage boxes lying on top of the dresser. He looked at Kitty and smiled conspiratorially. 'May I?'

'Be my guest.'

Ed walked over to the dresser and placed a pair of semi-rimmed glasses on the end of his nose. With his hands clasped behind his back, he leaned over the box and closely studied the contents of Kitty's latest piece. Kitty was always amazed at how long Ed could stare at a single artwork. On the few occasions she agreed to visit an exhibition with him, he would often not have moved beyond the first room when Kitty had absorbed the whole show. She found his insistence on forensically examining every artwork he encountered both stultifying and unnecessary.

Eventually, Ed took off his glasses and placed the temple tip of one arm in his mouth.

'What's the relevance of the raven?' he asked.

Kitty told him the story about the raven in the park and how she had picked up one of the bird's feathers. 'I've always been fascinated by folklore,' she said, 'and the way these stories shape our culture. I wanted somehow to link the death of this bird with an ancient legend. Have you ever heard of Bran the Blessed?' Ed shrugged his shoulders. 'In Celtic folklore, he's considered to be the guardian of this country. Some legends even claim that he brought Christianity to England.'

'I was always told that was Joseph of Arimathea.'

'I think we can safely assume it was neither of them. However…' Kitty paused for a moment. 'Now, you've made me forget where I was.'

'Bran the Blessed… the raven?'

'That's right. Well, Bran the Blessed is always represented as a raven. I think his name even means raven in Welsh or Irish. After being wounded in battle, he ordered his own head to be cut off and buried at Tower Hill. They say that as long as his head remains buried then—'

A loud knock on the front door interrupted the conversation.

'Are you expecting someone?' Ed asked.

Kitty shook her head and walked to the front door. Peering through the peephole, she saw Owen standing in the doorway. He was carrying a large holdall. Kitty opened the door and ushered him in.

'What's with the bag?' Kitty asked.

'Jacquie has thrown me out.'

'Oh, Owen.'

'Could I possibly stay here tonight?'

'Of course you can. I'll make the bed up in the flat. I warn you, though, we had a bit of a water situation last night. None of it went into the flat, but it might feel a bit dank down there.'

'That's no problem,' Owen said before following Kitty into the kitchen. Having acknowledged Ed, he sat down at the table. No sooner had he done so than he stood back up again and announced that he needed to go to the toilet.

'He stinks,' Ed said once Owen had left the room.

'What of? I didn't notice.'

'Booze. He reeks of it. Can you not smell it?'

'I couldn't smell anything,' Kitty said.

'What's going on with your sense of smell?' Ed said. 'You didn't smell the bread burning earlier either. Maybe you're anosmic.' Ed picked up his hat and, with a flourish, placed it on his head.

'Oh, don't say that.'

Ed frowned at Kitty. 'I'm only joking,' he said, laughing. 'No need to look so hurt.'

When Owen walked back into the room, Ed got up from the table. He winked at Kitty. 'I'm going to get off,' he said. 'I have a commitment at a seven o'clock meeting. Let's talk tomorrow, and you can tell me the rest of the story.'

Owen smirked at Ed's mention of a meeting. The two of them had spoken before about Ed's sobriety. Like many excessive drinkers, Owen was always intrigued to learn how someone else had managed to stop. Although he had no intention of giving up himself, he admired the resolve in others.

'I hope you're looking after yourself, young man,' Ed said, turning to Owen. 'You know where to find me if you ever need a chat.' Owen didn't say anything but just smiled sardonically.

'I'll see you out,' Kitty said.

Owen could hear urgent whispers as Kitty and Ed conferred at the front door. They could have been talking about anything, but Owen assumed they were talking about him. He wished that he had never asked Ed how he gave up drinking. Ever since their conversation, he always felt guilty whenever he saw him. Ed was one of those recovering alcoholics who liked to diagnose everyone else as a problem drinker. After a couple of minutes, Kitty returned to the kitchen and offered Owen a cup of tea.

'Would you mind if I went straight to bed?'

'I'll need to make the bed up first. Would you like something to eat?'

Owen shook his head. While Kitty went downstairs to the basement flat, he checked his phone to see if Jacquie had responded to any of his messages. She had only sent one more message since calling him a cunt. And that was simply to reiterate how much she didn't want him to be at the flat when she got back that evening. He had considered ignoring the message but decided a full night's uninterrupted sleep was needed before an inevitable confrontation with Jacquie.

Owen had often used Kitty's house as a place of refuge. His mum had encouraged the relationship, especially after she became ill. At the time, Janet's enthusiasm to nurture a friendship between the two of them had seemed like a betrayal. Owen felt rejected. More than ever, he had wanted to cling to his mother to make sure she was OK. He was too young to comprehend her actions. Janet didn't want her young son to see how unwell she really was.

Consequently, during his mum's first bout of cancer, Owen had spent a lot of time at Kitty's house. There was no one else to help out. Janet's mother was dead, and although Owen's dad was long gone by then, her father was still unable to reconcile himself with the fact his daughter had a baby out of wedlock with a black man.

The cellar underneath Kitty's house was huge. There were three spacious storerooms full of canvases, wine, storage freezers, gardening equipment, bits of furniture, the contents of Hugh's parents' house, defunct household appliances, bicycles with one wheel, decrepit old grandfather clocks, boxes of *Paris Match*, boxes of *National Geographic* and endless bits of indiscernible junk. A door opened from one of the storerooms into a subterranean one-bedroom flat. The flat had its own entrance at the side of the house. The only natural light came in through a single frosted vertical sidelight next to the external door. The flat was dark, the ceiling was low and the flagstone floor was cold, but it was homely and welcoming.

Owen lay on the bed. He was exhausted but felt as if he had forgotten how to sleep. Whenever he closed his eyes, fractal-like patterns appeared before him. They danced in pulsations of time. Their motions made him feel nauseous. Owen twitched around the mattress, hoping to find a position that might encourage the onset of sleep. Nothing worked. The more he tried to force it, the less likely it was to arrive. Deciding that a drink might help, Owen got out of bed and went to the storerooms. On the floor, next to an old Power Plate machine, he spotted several boxes of red and white wine.

Owen sat slumped on the sofa for the next two hours, smoking and watching *Mamma Mia* on the movie channel.

He had never seen the film before. It made him feel happy, but at the same time terribly sad because he knew he wasn't happy at all. He was sure he could be if he too lived on a Greek island. So why didn't he live there? Why, of all the places in the world, did he still live in Albion Park? When Meryl Streep's character launched into the pre-chorus breakdown of the title song, Owen started to cry. She was climbing up a ladder next to the side of a house. The tears began to flow when she got to the top and the song kicked back in.

'What the hell is wrong with me?' Owen said, wiping tears from his eyes. He paused the film. He couldn't remember the last time he had cried. His eyes had welled up during the birth of his kids. And once, when he was watching *Superman* with Dexter, he shed a tear during the scene when young Clark Kent lifts his parents' truck and a hint of John Williams' theme plays in the background. As Benny Andersson himself pointed out, Abba had always possessed a melancholy inherent in many artists who hail from places above the fifty-ninth parallel. But Owen's unhinged emotions were representative of something else. These were songs he rarely ever heard. He realised, though, they were deeply connected to his childhood. The songs belonged to a time when his mum was still alive and his dad's absence was not yet a hex on his psyche. When the world was there to be conquered rather than to be defeated by. And potential was still to be fulfilled rather than wasted.

Owen restarted the film only to break down again during 'Our Last Summer'. It was at the moment Pierce Brosnan and Colin Firth shared the lines 'We had a fear of flying, of growing old, a fear of slowly dying.' It wasn't even an Abba classic, nowhere near the quality of 'Dancing Queen', 'SOS' or 'The Visitors'. The three men, vying to be the recognised father of the girl protagonist, made Owen think about how useless his dad was and how ill-equipped to be a parent he had been. He thought about his mum's protracted illness, his own mortality, and the now distant pleasures of youth's golden gleam. He would never be young again. He would probably never get to live next to the Aegean. Or in a house as beautiful and as white as the ones in the film.

Owen poured the last bit of wine into his glass; he had no idea what time it was. He looked at his phone; it was only nine-thirty. There was a long message from Daisy. She wanted him to know that she was so, so sorry. It was a stupid joke and one she wished she had never made. She hoped that he didn't have the wrong opinion of her. She then apologised for perpetuating a tired racial stereotype. Race, she said, was a social construct without biological meaning. Skin colour was the only difference between people, and she was colourblind.

It made Owen laugh when anyone claimed not to see colour. Kitty once told him that race didn't exist. Even his mum used to say that, as a concept, it was meaningless. She said that all humans were part of the same species, but, like cats, we had different outward appearances. Owen used to think that race may not have been important to them, but it patently was to other people. How else could you explain why, as a young man, he was stopped and searched more times than he could remember? Most of his white friends had never once experienced this particular humiliation. Or why he was sometimes not let into the same shops as them. Or why Millwall fans would chase him off the train, but not his friends. It seemed that only those who had never struggled with issues around identity were eager to declare that race no longer mattered. Someone like Daisy knew precisely who she was, where she came from and where she belonged. Owen had never enjoyed that kind of privilege. Identity for him meant confusion. His dad's absence ensured there was never anyone to provide the guidance he needed and craved. He had black mates at school, and there were some families on the estate, but no one he knew was as light-skinned as he was. Some of his friends used to refer to him as whitey or Mother's Pride. Occasionally they even questioned the legitimacy of his blackness. He knew that they were joking for the most part, but there was an inherent irony that he understood. That even if he wanted to, he would never be allowed to identify as white. Even though he was brought up by a white parent, who had grown up inculcated in white lower-middle-class values. Through his mum and Kitty, Owen learned how to navigate the spaces of the white world. They taught him how to appear non-threatening and not stand out any more than he already did. They taught him how to be acceptable to white society. Even though society would never accept him as that. Owen was always either too black or not black enough.

Another message from Daisy appeared on his phone.

Can I see you again?

Owen switched it off and went to the bedroom. He got into bed and turned off the lights. This time, instead of coloured geometric shapes swooping in front of his eyes, a vision of Daisy's naked body appeared before him. She hovered over him, just as she had done earlier that day. He pictured her teasing smile as she watched him drink in her nakedness. With his cock in his hand, he re-imagined the events of that morning. Except this time, instead of shirking the challenge, Owen harnessed his experience and produced a masterful display of lovemaking. Instead of being intimidated by her youth and beauty, Owen overwhelmed her with his sexual prowess. He visualised her lying on her back, writhing in paroxysms of pleasure as he slowly entered her. Daisy took a sharp intake of breath as he gave an initial thrust, her eyes widening as he proceeded. Imagining the point where their bodies coalesced, Owen took pleasure at the sight of his penis, exaggerated in size by the slightness of her body. From then on, like dancers performing a *pas de deux*, Owen effortlessly manoeuvred Daisy from position to position. With his eyes still firmly shut, Owen arched his back as he brought himself to a climax. Unable to prevent himself from spoiling the crisp, fresh sheets which Kitty had recently made the bed with, Owen rolled over into his mess and finally went to sleep.

Chapter 14

Jacquie rarely lamented Owen's absence. On the contrary, she had been shocked how easy the transition from long-term partner to single mum had been. The fact their separation had caused so little distress allayed any doubts that splitting up had been the right thing to do. Although the suddenness of her decision had taken Owen and the boys by surprise, Harley and Dexter had quickly adjusted to their new reality. Owen was only around the corner. If anything, the split had made him a more attentive father. Plus, it had gifted Jacquie time for herself. Something she hadn't enjoyed since before she had kids. The boys would sometimes stay with Owen at the flat underneath Kitty's house. There wasn't much room, and they had to share a sofa bed in the living room. But they enjoyed spending some alone time with their dad. Although he still occasionally went missing, Owen was generally more available than he had ever been.

Harley and Dexter had probably seen more of him in the last six months than they had in the preceding two years. No, the only time Jacquie ever really missed Owen was when something heavy needed to be lifted or if one of the boys needed to be disciplined. Plus, he made an excellent tom kha kai. And his pasta sauces were much better than hers. She missed his cooking. She'd give him that. Although one was supposed to feel miserable after separation of this magnitude, Jacquie felt excited. She had mourned the end of their relationship while they were still together. She had zero inclination to dwell on it any more.

Soon after kicking him out of the flat, Jacquie had asked Owen if he would consider transferring the tenancy of the flat into her name. Owen had been taken aback by the suggestion.

'Jesus, you've got some front,' he said. 'You throw me out of my own flat and then ask me to give it to you?'

'Me and the boys need some security,' Jacquie had replied. 'I need to know that we're not going to end up homeless.'

'I would never let that happen.'

Jacquie made a face that suggested Owen was powerless to affect the outcome of anything. Two weeks later, she broached the subject once more.

'Why don't we just put your name on the tenancy,' Owen had said. 'We could go down to the council and get it done tomorrow. We were supposed to do it ages ago.'

'It's not enough.'

'Well, what then?'

'I think you should give the flat to us.'

'Us?'

'Me and the boys.'

Owen was no longer a participant in Jacquie's pronouns. They were separate entities now. Us and him. Them and me. If Owen had been in doubt about whether Jacquie was serious about separation, her proposition dashed any lingering dubiety. Up to that point, Owen had been behaving as if it was a decision *he* had yet to make. As if he could go back to the flat whenever *he* was ready.

'What if you hooked up with someone else?' he argued. 'You could buy the flat, sell it and make a load of money. Where would that leave me? Why can't you just stay here for the foreseeable? You know, while the kids are growing up.'

'And hand it back once I've fulfilled my maternal duties? Besides, we can't separate and both have our names on the tenancy.'

'Why not?'

'If your name stays on the tenancy, you're entitled to move back in whenever you want. I can't live like that.'

'It's all I've got, Jacquie. You'll leave me with nothing.'

'Apart from providing a home and a bit of security for your kids. Is that not enough?'

'This was my mum's home.'

'You don't think I know that?'

Jacquie was fed up with living amongst the ornaments of Janet's life. Photographs of Owen and his mum were still dotted around the flat. They served as a constant reminder that the property did not belong to her. It was a strange situation, she thought, to be living in the childhood home of her ex-partner, surrounded by his deceased mother's belongings.

While she waited for Owen to decide, Jacquie had chosen to make some changes to the flat.

'Where have you put that picture of me and my mum?' Owen had come to the flat to drop off an old guitar for Harley. After he noticed the absence of the photograph, he began to realise other items had also been moved. 'Hold on. You've moved the Buddha as well, and the marbles... and the cuckoo clock. What's going on?'

'I can't hear you...' Jacquie was in the bedroom. Owen walked out of the room and stood at the foot of the stairs.

'Where's everything gone?'

Coming down the stairs, Jacquie looked bemused by Owen's agitated state. 'I've put a few bits in a box for you.'

'Why? They belong here. The Buddha's head has always been on those shelves. That's where it goes.'

'It's so cluttered,' Jacquie said. 'Besides, I never liked that head. It's a bit naff.'

Owen looked distraught.

'I thought you might like it for your flat.'

The Buddha head, the cuckoo clock, the bowl of marbles, the Beatrix Potter figures, the various jubilee mugs. It was all sentimental clutter. The legacy of a thousand car boot sales, most of it utterly unremarkable. Over the years, however, many of these objects had assumed almost sacrosanct status. They had in Owen's mind anyway. Items would be moved around the flat but never put away, even though Jacquie often hinted they should be. She complained that the front room resembled a shrine – a shabby memorial to the life of Owen's late mother.

Janet used to love car boot sales. Every other Sunday was spent rifling through mountains of cast-offs and piles of tat. Most of the time, she and Owen would potter around South London and the East End looking for bargains, occasionally venturing further afield to places like Chigwell and Isleworth. Janet was no expert, but she did have a good eye and sometimes discovered the odd gem. Unbelievably, she once paid a tenner for a frosted glass Lalique Nemours bowl. The interior of the dish was ever so slightly worn. The maker's mark meant nothing to her, but the exquisite flower pattern that covered the bowl was so deeply moulded and finely crafted that she knew it was something special the moment she held it. When Kitty swooned over her discovery, Janet was so proud of herself. She had always been in awe of Kitty's cultivation. To own something which Kitty unashamedly coveted gave her a thrill. Kitty's friend Ed thought the bowl could be worth as much as a thousand pounds. Janet never wanted to get it valued, though. Not until she was impelled by circumstances. When she became very ill, and money was scarce, she reluctantly asked Ed to sell the bowl for her. She never told Owen how much she got for it. He knew it was a decent amount, though. Some years later, he saw a similar bowl being sold online for over sixteen hundred quid.

'Let me get this straight.' Owen closed his eyes and pinched the bridge of his nose. 'You're getting rid of the stuff you don't like. Right?'

Jacquie mumbled something to herself and began to walk away. Owen followed her into the front room. Dexter was on the floor, making a Lego model. He was wholly absorbed in the task he had set himself. Owen loved the way his son wrapped his tongue over his top lip when concentrating. He used to do the same thing when he was younger. He still did it sometimes when playing the guitar. It would usually be during a solo, or perhaps when playing certain voiced chords which would mean having to stretch his fingers.

'I notice you haven't taken down the painting Kitty gave me,' Owen continued. 'Or the Miles Davis print. I suppose you want to keep those. Yeah? I tell you what' – Owen's voice was steadily rising – 'why don't you give me a shout once you've finished. Let me know the bits you don't want, and I'll get them out of your way.'

There was a long pause followed by a groan from Jacquie. 'Owen, please calm down. You can take everything for all I care. To be honest, I wish you would.'

One Friday morning, after Owen had stormed out of the flat following yet another row about the tenancy, there was a knock on the front door. A young girl holding a clip-board and wearing a hi-vis pullover vest was standing on the shared landing outside the flat. She greeted Jacquie like an old friend.

'Hi, my name is Tawiah. This is Oli. I was wondering whether you might be able to spare a few minutes.'

Jacquie stuck her head out of the door. Standing further down the landing was a slightly older boy with ginger hair. He waved at Jacquie. 'Sup?'

'Sorry, who are you?'

'We're from We Hear You. We're a specialist consultation company that does fieldwork in the built environment.'

'The built environment?'

'You know, cities, buildings, that kind of thing.'

'Who do you consult on behalf of?'

'We mainly work for local authorities and other clients who want to listen to the opinions of people in a specific community.'

The girl looked young; she was probably in her early twenties. She was enthusiastic, unlike the boy, who so far had kept quiet. He appeared to be there for support only. They seemed to be nice kids, though. Probably students earning a bit of extra money during the holidays.

'Why are you here?' Jacquie asked.

'All residents of the Bevan Estate should have recently received a letter from Lisa McFarlane—'

'Lisa McFarlane?'

'She's the council's regeneration officer.'

'I haven't had a letter from anyone of that name.'

'It should have arrived a couple of weeks ago.' Tawiah smiled at Jacquie. She seemed devoid of bitterness or cynicism, her face as yet unmarked by life's inevitable disappointments. Jacquie went back inside the flat and looked through a small pile of letters next to the front door. 'There's nothing here.'

Oli, Tawiah's colleague, leaned over the balcony,

marvelling at the green expanse that spread out beneath him. 'Yo. You have access to that?'

Jacquie shook her head.

'Woah. That's long,' the boy said. 'I bet the youngers just jump over the wall, innit.'

Tawiah looked down at her clipboard and scribbled something on her notes. 'A few of the other residents said they haven't received a letter either,' she said. 'I apologise for that. I don't understand why that would have happened.'

Jacquie asked the girl what the letter was about.

'It's about the council's regeneration scheme.' Tawiah reached into her bag, pulled out a copy of the document and handed it to Jacquie.

Dear resident

My name is Lisa McFarlane. I am writing to introduce myself as your local Regeneration Officer. Together with our partners – the Hand & Hyle Property Group – we would like to speak to all residents of the Bevan Estate about the council's regeneration plans.

Unfortunately, there are currently not enough homes in the borough to meet the needs of the people who live here. The population is constantly growing, placing increasing pressure on our housing stock. We have therefore committed to delivering 3,000 additional homes at council rent levels for our residents. To help reach this target, the council must make good use of its available resources. Consequently, we have included the Bevan Estate in our regeneration programme. This programme provides us with the opportunity to increase the provision of new homes on selected estates and invest in the borough's future. Our ambition is to guarantee that every resident has the opportunity to live in a good-quality, affordable home. We aim to do this whilst also contributing towards alleviating the current housing shortage.

Over the coming months, a series of community consultation events will be held to help us gather feedback from current tenants and leaseholders. Rest assured that we will be seeking the opinion of the residents throughout every part of the process. All proposals moving forward will be subject to full consultation. The first step of this engagement process will be a short questionnaire. This will be delivered by hand within the next three weeks by We Hear You, a community consultant company.

Meanwhile, we will continue to identify how best to redevelop the Bevan Estate alongside our design and development management team.

Should you have any further questions or if you would like to discuss the above in more detail, please do not hesitate to contact me.

Yours sincerely
Lisa McFarlane

Jacquie handed the letter back to Tawiah. 'That's for you to keep,' the girl said. 'I'm sorry you didn't receive it when you were supposed to.'

Jacquie appeared distracted as she tried to process everything she had just read. 'Do you have a copy of the questionnaire?'

Tawiah handed Jacquie one of the sheets. 'Would you like me to go through it with you, or would you rather self-complete?'

'It's fine,' Jacquie said. 'I'll do it myself.'

Unsure as to what emotion she should be feeling, Jacquie sat down on the sofa in the front room. Should she be happy or worried at the prospect of redevelopment? On the one hand, no one could deny the estate was in desperate need of an overhaul. However, Jacquie's status was parlous. Without her name on the tenancy, she almost definitely didn't have any legal rights. Owen could probably throw her out with zero recourse. She wondered whether she could take him to court, force him to assign the tenancy to her. Presumably, having children would bolster any case. She was going to need legal advice, but hiring a solicitor was beyond her means. Unless domestic violence was involved, she knew from her work at the charity that legal aid no longer covered family law. Jacquie rubbed her eyes with her fingers; they felt achy and fatigued. She didn't even like the flat. However, a brand new place on a redeveloped estate was a different proposition altogether. God knows how much one of those would be worth. It would be like winning the lottery.

She picked up the questionnaire. *What three things do you like best about living on the Bevan Estate? What three things do you dislike about living on the Bevan Estate? What would you change about living here?* The questions seemed fairly innocuous. Although technically they weren't even hers to answer. She decided to call Owen and tell him what had happened but was interrupted by another knock on the door.

'Did you know about this?' Val was standing on the shared landing outside the flat, waving the letter from Lisa McFarlane.

'No, I never got it.'

'Me neither. What the fuck's all that about? I reckon they didn't even send it.' Val followed Jacquie back into the flat.

'Why would they pretend to send a letter?'

'Search me.' Val sat down at the small table in the kitchen. 'It's all a bit sudden, though, don't you think?' Val unfolded the letter and pointed to a section of it. 'Look, it says here that they will consult us during every part of the process.'

'Yeah. So?'

'Well, where were we when they decided that the estate needed to be regenerated in the first place? They got a design team involved before they spoke to any of us.'

Val was wearing a black shearling aviator jacket. She took it off and slung it over the back of a chair.

'I like your jacket.' Jacquie rubbed the leather and sniffed her fingers. 'It's so soft. It's gorgeous.'

Val looked proudly at her coat. She stroked it as if it were a darling pet.

'It looks expensive. It must have set you back a bit?' Jacquie poured some water into the kettle. 'How much? If you don't mind me asking.'

'I got it off my nephew. I only paid about a hundred and fifty quid. It's worth nearly two grand.' Jacquie whistled in appreciation. 'I'll give you a shout if you want, next time they've got some clobber to sell.'

Val's nephew lived in Hoxton. He was only nineteen years old and had already served two terms in juvenile prison. He knocked about with a group of boys who regularly went on smash and grab raids on their mopeds. After one of their West End excursions, they would come back to their estate with bags of looted gear which they offloaded at knock-down prices before they could get caught in possession.

'You know they'll tear this place down, don't you?' Val continued.

'Not necessarily.'

'You wait and see if they don't.'

'Would that be such a bad thing?'

'It will be if we have to move out. Imagine the disruption that would cause.'

'Who knows what's going to happen,' Jacquie said, pouring hot water from the kettle into two mugs.

'It all makes sense now, though,' Val said. 'I mean, how hard has it been to get the council to do anything around here? They've been useless for ages. They obviously didn't want to spend any money. They knew all along it was going to get redeveloped. All that stuff about consulting us at every stage of the process. It's bollocks. They must have been planning this for years.'

Chapter 15

April 2015

The motorised glass door retracted with the sleek purr of an expensive engine. Nicholas lovingly stroked the leather treads on each stair as he descended the spiral staircase of his new four-and-a-half-metre-deep wine cellar. Finally, all his wines were in one place. He intended to spend the afternoon organising his bottles. Ever since he was a child, Nicholas had received a particular pleasure from arranging and organising his various collections. It had started with Action Man and toy soldiers and progressed to Tonka Toys and Meccano. He never used to play with his toys in the traditional sense. What he loved to do was to line them up and admire the collection. As an adult, this desire to collect and organise manifested itself in more expensive pursuits, namely investment-grade wines and art. Even the offices and staff of DCM were a type of collection. Something Nicholas enjoyed taking a step back from and relishing the status it conferred, and the sense of achievement it provided.

Nicholas began to move bottles around the newly installed vertical underground cylinder. The bespoke cabinets which lined the staircase had been set at the optimum temperature and humidity. There was enough room to house his collection of over two thousand bottles. Whenever he drank one, he immediately replaced it. He hated to see the collection diminished. Ivor, the therapist Jennifer had finally persuaded Nicholas to start seeing, believed his constant craving for new acquisitions was an attempt to restore previous deprivations. He suggested that Nicholas was continually searching for things to replace the parental love he was robbed of when his brother was injured. Unfortunately, it was a craving that couldn't be satisfied. The acquisition never provided the compensations Nicholas sought. Ivor had convinced Nicholas his hobbies had evolved to overcome various deficiencies within his character. His constant need to collect was a guarantee against the loneliness and despair he had felt as a child. His habit of collecting luxury items may have enabled an escape route to a private domain, but it could never replace the human relationships he found difficult to maintain.

Nicholas opened his laptop and began to refer to the online portfolio management platform he had created. It combined all the available information about each wine, including tasting notes, market analysis and place of purchase. He would spend hours poring over the annual percentage change and the overall gain (rarely loss) of each bottle. The new cellar would be organised by colour, grape and value, with superior vintages stored on the lower shelves. All Nicholas had to do was enter a specific criterion and the platform listed all his wines in terms of value. Although his most valuable bottles were a Burgundian Pinot Noir and a 1945 Chateau Mouton Rothschild, Nicholas decided to organise his sparkling wines first. He could spend hours and hours indulging in this pursuit.

Once he had located whatever bottle the management platform recommended, Nicholas would first hold it adoringly in his hands, as if making eye contact with a newborn for the first time. He would then rub any dust from the bottle and check the notes on the platform, perhaps adding newly acquired bits of info or data. After he had placed the bottle in its allocated space, he would proudly sit and stare at it for a moment as the bottle took its rightful place among the other fine wines.

As ever, Jennifer had felt compelled to chime in with her opinion about Nicholas' desire to collect expensive items – or treasure assets as Ivor liked to refer to them. She told him that it revealed both a need for approval and an attempt to assert himself. Jennifer believed that Nicholas needed to demonstrate that not only was he deserving of the extravagant objects he collected, but he was also somehow exceptional for possessing them. She said that his collections were motivated by profit and status rather than pleasure.

That afternoon, however, he was enjoying himself too much. He had no desire to dwell on any attempts to explain his adult life through the prism of his childhood. For a while, he was able to forget the tribulations of the last twelve months. Having bounced back after the M&T Technologies disaster, Nicholas was once again in deep water. His acquisition of a stake in US biotech company LVP Pharma, which went public in 2013, was being investigated for alleged market fraud. If Delta were found guilty of having participated in a trading securities fraud linked to their stake in LVP, then Nicholas was facing the prospect of a substantial fine. Delta would be able to absorb any sanctions, but it was another black mark against him. The spectre of negative press and more grumbles of discontent from investors weighed heavily on him. Things weren't any better between him and Jennifer either. They had managed to have full penetrative sex in the last year – with Nicholas capable of maintaining an erection from beginning to end – on only two occasions. Both of those occasions were in the same week that Nicholas sold his stock in a Qatari telecoms company. A deal that had received widespread acclaim for bringing Delta back from the brink.

As if that wasn't enough to contend with, the basement's completion had been accompanied by two letters. The first letter was from Kitty's insurers, who intended to sue Nicholas for three hundred thousand pounds to cover the cost of repairs to her house. The letter described how a crack going up a major flank wall had affected the house's stability and caused the roof to open up. As a result, the insurers claimed that not only did the house need to be underpinned, but it also needed an entire new roof and extensive essential structural repairs. The second letter was from Kitty's lawyer, who sought damages for failure to exercise reasonable care and disruption caused by excessive noise and vibration. The lawyer suggested that Nicholas could avoid all legal costs by making *a fair and reasonable offer.* This was considered to be in the region of about one hundred and eighty thousand pounds, including costs.

Sometimes, Nicholas wished he had never agreed to have the basement installed. It felt as if they were living on top of a colossal money pit. However, this afternoon, while he gazed lovingly at his wine and studiously added notes to his management platform, all these stressors briefly dissipated.

'You've been down there for ages.' Jennifer was standing at the edge of the spiral cellar. She looked down at Nicholas. 'Are you going to be much longer?'

Nicholas put down the bottle he was holding and ascended the steep staircase. 'I've only managed to do the first few cabinets. There's lots more to do.'

'It's nearly five-thirty.' Jennifer tapped an imaginary watch on her wrist.

'Yes, OK,' Nicholas said begrudgingly. 'What time are they coming.'

'Around eight. Perhaps you could choose some wine?'

'Sure. I'll try and find something with lots of residual sugar. Nothing too sophisticated.'

'Sorry, what was that?'

'Forget it. I was being facetious.'

'Are you complaining about Tanya and Gary again?'

'I just don't see what you see in them. She's thick as mince. And he doesn't say anything. Hardly ideal dinner party guests.'

'He's a man of few words.'

'More like he's a man who only knows a few words.'

The previous week Gary had joined Jennifer and Tanya for a spin class in their new basement gym. When Nicholas came home from work, he was surprised to find Gary sitting topless in the kitchen, enjoying one of Jennifer's chia seed lemonades. Gary greeted Nicholas with a single up-down eyebrow flash and simply said, 'Alright.' Not even bothering to get up, he remained seated, his legs stretched out in front of him. He was wearing a pair of tight-fit Lycra shorts. The outline of his penis, which tracked down the inside of his thigh, was visible through the figure-hugging material. Gary noticed Nicholas' gaze lingering for a moment too long. Then, without adding to his perfunctory greeting, he finished his drink, stood up and said: 'See you later.' And went back to the gym.

'He's like an early incarnation of man,' Nicholas continued. 'He's anatomically identifiable as human, obviously good at hunting, but the cerebellum has yet to expand. Speech and cognition, unfortunately, are still a problem. But you clearly see something in them. You've been spending a lot of time over there recently. Do you even know where their money comes from?'

'He used to own a chain of discount warehouses. They sold the business a few years ago.'

Nicholas frowned. 'Do you remember the name of the shops?'

Jennifer reached out for Nicholas' hand; she gently stroked his knuckles with her thumb.

'Ah, baby. Does the big strong man scare you?'

Jennifer placed her other hand on Nicholas' lower chest. She began to slowly rub his midriff. Nicholas looked down at his wife's hand and watched it roam around his torso. Jennifer pressed her face into her husband's neck and bit his earlobe.

'Ow!' Nicholas jerked his head away and rubbed the bitten lobe between his thumb and forefinger.

'Oh, I give up.'

'I'm sorry. It bloody hurt.' Nicholas continued to massage his ear.

'I'm going back up to the house,' Jennifer said. 'Don't forget to bring up some wine.'

While Lovely cleared away the plates and empty bottles of wine, Jennifer suggested the group retire downstairs to the new basement.

'Nick, why don't we show Gary and Tanya the gallery?'

Nicholas made a face. 'I haven't started hanging yet,' he said. 'Everything's still leaning against the wall.'

'Oh, we would love to see it. Wouldn't we, Gal? I tried to have a look the other day after our spin class, but the door was locked.'

'Another time,' Nicholas said.

'Are we allowed into the bar, sir?' Jennifer knocked back her drink, got up from her chair and instructed Gary and Tanya to follow her.

Entry to the new basement was via a free-floating staircase which led down to an open-plan entrance hall. Tinted glass doors at one end of the hall led to the gym and swimming pool. At the other end, oak double doors opened onto a bar and lounge area.

Jennifer held the door open for her guests. Although large, the room was moody and cocooning. The walls, ceiling and woodwork were all painted a deep dark blue. Several compact green velvet Chesterfield armchairs were arranged around two black glass-top coffee tables. The main feature of the room was an illuminated granite bar with a curved, mirrored back wall. Bottles of spirits were stacked on glass shelves lit up by LED lighting.

'Oh my God, this is unbelievable.' Tanya looked around the room in childlike wonder. 'How come you didn't show me before?'

'I wanted to surprise you,' Jennifer said proudly. 'Isn't it fab?'

'It's amazing,' Tanya said. 'It's like your own private members' club. Rijkens House.'

Jennifer watched Tanya run her hand admiringly over one of the armchairs. 'Everything is so lovely,' she said. 'You've got such great taste.'

Once she had exhausted her supply of superlatives to describe how much she loved the room, Tanya eventually sat down in one of the armchairs and took her shoes off. 'My feet are killing me,' she said.

Gary had walked over to the bar and opened the door of a wall-recessed wine cooler. He pulled out a bottle of champagne and removed the foil and muselet. The cork was already being coaxed out before Gary asked if it was OK to open a bottle.

'Please do,' Nicholas said, before asking Tanya what she would like to drink.

'I'm feeling a bit tipsy. Maybe I should have something non-alcoholic?'

'No!' Jennifer interjected. 'The night is young. Get her a glass of champagne. I'll have one too.'

Nicholas walked to the bar to get some glasses and another bottle of champagne; Gary had already poured himself a drink and was leaning against the bar. Nicholas smiled at him awkwardly.

'Your missus was telling me the other day that your company is expanding into property.'

'Kind of,' Nicholas said. 'We have a stake in a development company.'

'Is that building and selling?'

'It's mainly large residential schemes,' Nicholas said. 'Estate regeneration, that type of thing.' Nicholas opened the bottle of champagne which he was holding. A curl of smoke escaped as the cold gas hit the ambient air. 'As a matter of fact, the company we have a stake in recently won the tender to redevelop the Bevan Estate.'

Gary looked at Nicholas open-mouthed. 'Fucking hell.'

Nicholas took a tray of drinks over to the table where Jennifer and Tanya were sitting. Tanya was wearing a long, dark cherry-red dress with a plunging neckline; the high slit of the dress revealed the entirety of her leg. Nicholas noticed some italicised text tattooed on the side of her foot.

'What does your tattoo say?'

'It says "Love to Love You Baby".' Tanya took a sip of the drink Nicholas had just handed her. 'It's my favourite song... ever.'

'I'm not sure I know it. Who is it by?'

'Donna Summer.'

'Good grief,' Jennifer scoffed. 'Everyone knows that song... "Ooo, love to love you, baby."' Nicholas shrugged his shoulders. 'The one with the orgasm?' Jennifer frowned disbelievingly at her husband. She looked at Tanya. 'I saw a documentary once about Donna Summer's producer,' she continued, 'I've forgotten his name... Italian-sounding. He said the first version of that song was, like, only five minutes long or something. But after hearing it, the record label boss told them to extend it so he could play it during one of his orgies.'

Gary looked at Tanya, a smirk on his face.

'That makes total sense,' Tanya said. 'It's got to be the sexiest song ever made. Can we put it on?' Tanya tried to get up from where she was sitting but fell forwards into the coffee table, knocking over one of the bottles of champagne. Jennifer started to laugh.

'Oh shit. I'm so sorry.' Tanya dropped to her knees and tried to mop up the spilt liquid with her hands.

'I think you need a straightener, babe,' Gary said.

'Please don't worry about it.' Jennifer was still giggling. She got up from her seat and walked to the bar to get a cloth. 'Nick, can we put some music on, please?'

'I haven't got my phone on me.'

'Can we not use mine?'

'Have you got the Sonos app on yours? I don't think you have. I'll get mine. I won't be long.'

Once Nicholas had left the room, Gary moved over to one of the other tables. He pulled a bag of powder out of his jacket pocket and emptied an amount onto the tabletop.

Jennifer had returned to the table. She placed a towel on the rug where the champagne had been spilt.

'Here, let me do that.' Tanya crouched down next to Jennifer.

'It's OK. It won't stain.'

'But the rug is brand new.'

'Stop worrying.'

Jennifer looked up to see Gary sitting at the table sculpting lines from a heaped pile of narcotics. His movements were well practised and precise, his expression one of dissolute intent. It could have been anyone sitting with her in the bar, she thought. As much as she liked Tanya, really, she was just glad of the company. Glad to finally be using a room that had been designed explicitly with nights like this in mind. But with Nicholas as a husband, occasions like this were rare. Friends for him were tools of expedience. They served a purpose. They helped him get somewhere quicker. Unless Nicholas could detect potential usefulness, he just wasn't that interested in people. Socialising wasn't a method of relaxation; it was a necessary part of business. It was nearly always done during working hours and hardly ever with his wife. It was chauvinistic, purposeful, and boring.

'Does anyone want one of these?' Gary rolled up a twenty-pound note and snorted one of the lines himself. 'Babe, you definitely could do with some.'

'You go first,' Tanya said to Jennifer.

Jennifer looked towards the door. 'No, you go. Please.'

Tanya walked over to where Gary was sitting and leaned over the table. Her husband held onto her hair so it wouldn't disturb the drugs. Once she had ingested the line, Tanya tossed her head back, squeezed the end of her nose and whinnied like a horse.

'That's better,' she said.

'Jen. Do you want one of these?'

Nicholas had never seen his wife take Class As before. The two of them had smoked pot together on a few occasions, but he had never witnessed her try anything stronger. When they first got together, Jennifer told Nicholas that she had dabbled with Ecstasy while living in Hong Kong. She told him about the party crowd she had fallen in with while working at Citigroup. They used to call themselves the Hit Squad. The group of friends included a bunch of Hong Kongers who worked in boutiques on the Canton Road, a couple of expat bankers, an English DJ, a French fashion designer and a member of a Taiwanese pop band. After they had been together for a while, Jennifer told Nicholas about the all-night parties and the clubs of Lan Kwai Fong, which the Hit Squad regularly attended. Nicholas was a control freak; drugs were never going to be his vice. Knowing this, Jennifer was careful about which aspects of (what Nicholas called) her *experimental phase* she chose to reveal to her husband. She never told him about the trips to Taipei and the weekends holed up in the Shangri-La Hotel. She never told him about the crystal meth they used to smuggle in their pants, regardless of the warnings at Taoyuan Airport that declared drug trafficking was punishable by death. Wherever the Hit Squad went in Taipei, a clique of photographers would follow them around, always trying to get a snap of their pop star friend. Chung Chi, however, would always wear a big pair of Versace sunglasses. He was paranoid about his eyes, which resembled the Cookie Monster's once he had smoked a bit of ice. Although Nicholas was ignorant of Jennifer's druggy exploits in HK, he knew all about her relationship with Natty, the French fashion designer. Jennifer told Nicholas how much she used to enjoy being filmed while having sex. But she never said that it was Chung Chi behind the camera. She also decided not to divulge how Chung Chi used to share those films with the other members of OK Bang.

'Oh my God…' Jennifer dropped the rolled-up note and began clawing at her face.

'You didn't finish your line. Here, have some more.' Gary picked up the improvised tube and offered it again to Jennifer.

'What the hell is that?'

'It's MDMA mixed with a secret ingredient of mine. It's a bit harsh when you sniff it. But it's a lovely high.'

Nicholas stood in the doorway and watched Jennifer furiously rub her nose. Rather than being appalled, for some reason he felt relieved.

'What was the name of that song you wanted to listen to?' he asked.

Jennifer quickly moved away from Gary and sat back down at the table with Tanya.

'Music!' Tanya exclaimed. She stood up and began to shuffle to an imaginary tune.

'Donna Summer…' Jennifer paused. She scrunched up her eyes and swallowed. With one hand holding onto the table, she remained motionless for a moment. Nicholas thought she was about to be sick. Finally, she opened her eyes. 'Love to…' she swallowed again. 'Love to Love You Baby.'

Tanya whooped at the mention of the song. Then, like a fatigued flamenco dancer, she raised her arms and started clicking her fingers. The moment the swinging high-hat pattern and the carnal insistence of Donna Summer's libidinous coo started to play, Tanya placed her hands on either side of her waist and began to slowly gyrate her hips.

Still looking stunned, Jennifer remained sitting at the table.

'Do you want one of these?' Gary waved the rolled-up banknote in the air.

Nicholas half raised his hand in a polite gesture of refusal.

'Come on, Jen.' Tanya held her hands out towards Jennifer.

Nicholas looked at his watch. He had hoped his guests would leave soon after supper. Jennifer knew her husband usually liked to end the evening with a coffee followed by a digestif. However, this time she had suggested shots of tequila. The appetite for more drinks and the refusal of coffee indicated neither Jennifer nor their guests intended to end the night soon. Now that they were all high on whatever Gary had given them, he wasn't prepared to stick around much longer.

By now, Tanya had pulled Jennifer up from where she was sitting. The two women were dancing in front of each other. Tanya accompanied each lustful moan of the song with a two-handed caress of her own figure. She dragged her extended fingers over her groin, up over her tummy and around her breasts. Jennifer, meanwhile, swayed her shoulders from side to side, giggling at Tanya's antics. At least Jennifer seemed to be enjoying herself. Nicholas knew that he curtailed her natural impulses. She had always been a pleasure seeker. And although it's not unusual to shed such compulsions once the responsibilities of family life take over, Jennifer seemed diminished by the expectancy that she should mirror Nicholas' abstemious inclinations.

After fifteen minutes of dancing to the same song, the two women continued to sway in front of each other. Gary remained seated, tapping his feet while studying the performance. Meanwhile, Nicholas had been replying to an email from CJ.

The eventual fade-out of the song ushered in an awkwardness. Eager to occupy the space the absence of music had provided, Nicholas picked up the bottle of champagne and filled up everyone's glasses. Gary's jaw had gone slack. He looked up at Nicholas open-mouthed. His eyes were blank and glassy. Nicholas felt he should say something but couldn't think of anything to talk about. Fortunately, up until that point, the loudness of the music had made conversation difficult. He was relieved when Tanya and Jennifer returned to the table. The second song on the album had started to play. It was a dreary piano-led ballad.

'Urgh. Put something else on, please.' Tanya's nose wrinkled, and her upper lip curled disdainfully.

'I wouldn't know what to play,' Nicholas said. 'You choose something.' He handed his phone to Tanya.

Jennifer sat down next to Nicholas. 'Are you OK?' she said, smiling hopefully.

Nicholas could tell Jennifer wanted him to reciprocate with an expression that suggested he wouldn't hold anything against her. For a while, Nicholas remained stony-faced as he contemplated his wife. She looked vulnerable and childlike. Her brow was covered in a twinkling film of sweat; her eyes were wide and pleading. Marriage was a ridiculous institution, he thought. The concept that two people should sign a contract stipulating that they are obliged to remain forever romantically involved was both preposterous and illogical. Marriage constricts, thwarts, erodes and ultimately destroys anything that was once life-affirming and joyous. The once sharp arrows of desire always become blunted and eventually break. Nicholas felt sorry for Jennifer. Sorry that he could not fulfil her expectations, and sorry that he had led her to a place where taking drugs with Gary and Tanya was an exciting prospect.

'I'm fine,' he said, finally returning the smile.

Jennifer closed her eyes. She pursed her lips and exhaled slowly; her chest heaved with each breath.

'We should go for a swim,' Tanya said. 'Do you have music in there too?'

Nicholas nodded his head. 'The music is linked to every room.' He looked at Jennifer. 'Do we have any spare costumes?'

Tanya laughed loudly. She placed her hand on the inside of Nicholas' thigh. 'You're funny,' she said, leering towards him.

Nicholas wondered whether Tanya's breast implants would add buoyancy in the water. Presumably saline implants wouldn't make any difference, he thought. And if anything, silicone being denser than water would make it more difficult to float.

'Come on.' Tanya stood up. 'Who's up for a swim?' Her latest music choice started playing.

'Tuuuune.' Gary got up as well. With one arm raised, he started punching the air and shuffling on the spot. He looked like he was malfunctioning. Although drunk on champagne, drugged out of his gourd and in the presence of friends, a cloud of menace still lingered. Nicholas failed to see what his wife saw in this couple. They were uncouth, uninteresting and unintelligent.

Nicholas leaned over towards Jennifer. 'I think I might call it a night.'

'Don't you want to come for a swim with us?' Jennifer looked up at her husband quizzically. Every time she blinked, Nicholas thought her eyes might stay shut. 'It will be fun.'

'No, I don't think so. I'm tired.'

Jennifer reached out her hand, which Nicholas held in his.

'Swimming might not be such a good idea,' he said. 'You're all quite out of it. Promise me you'll be careful.'

Jennifer's eyes looked like they were just about to roll into the back of her head. She didn't look good. 'I promise,' she said.

Nicholas turned the music down and announced to Tanya and Gary that he was going to bed. 'Help yourself to drinks. And please be careful around the pool.'

Gary smirked at Nicholas' advice. Tanya, however, appeared troubled by the announcement. 'You can't go to bed. It's only twelve thirty.'

'I've got a lot on tomorrow.'

'But it's Sunday. Who works on a Sunday?'

'He does,' Jennifer said, swaying in her seat.

Tanya gave Jennifer a look, hoping she might be able to persuade her husband to stay. Gary remained at the bar and, without turning around to say goodnight to Nicholas, started to make himself another drink.

Nicholas hadn't been in bed for more than thirty minutes when he heard the pad of footsteps on the landing outside his room. Camille and Luc were asleep in the annexe with Lovely and Agrippina. The footsteps possessed too much weight to belong to either of the kids. Neither of the nannies would ever come to that part of the house at night unannounced. It was too early for Jennifer to be coming to bed. Or perhaps she had become as bored with their guests as he had been. Strange that he hadn't heard them leave, though. He rolled over and pretended to be asleep. Jennifer was high. He had no desire to participate in a tedious debrief where she psychoanalysed everyone's behaviour from the evening. Ever since she persuaded Nicholas to start seeing Ivor, Jennifer had been flexing her inner therapist even more than usual. The footsteps sounded apprehensive as they entered the room.

'Nick. Nick. Are you asleep yet?'

Rather than the rounded vowels of Jennifer's New England accent, Nicholas was shocked to hear the glottal stops and dropped t's of Tanya's estuary twang.

'What are you doing?' Nicholas rolled on his back and turned the bedside light on.

'Oh God, I'm sorry. Did I wake you up?' Tanya started to laugh. 'Jen sent me up. You walked off with your phone. We can't play any music. I said not to bother you, but... well, you know what she's like.' Tanya sat down on the edge of the bed. She was trying not to laugh.

Nicholas sat up. He was only wearing a pair of pyjama bottoms. As Tanya's gaze landed on his torso, he sucked his tummy in.

'The Sonos app is on the family iPad. Tell Jen she can use that.'

'Does she know where it is?'

'I think it's in the upstairs sitting room. I'm sorry, but why didn't Jen come up herself?'

'She can't stop dancing. Even without music.' Tanya put her hand over her mouth and laughed again. 'Why don't you come back downstairs and play with us?'

'I'm tired,' Nicholas said.

'Oh, go on.' Looking like a digitally altered Minnie Mouse, Tanya held her hands together and fluttered her eyelashes.

'Like I said…'

Although she was smiling, the rest of Tanya's face seemed unable to respond in an expected way. It was as if her features refused to acknowledge the emotions her brain had instructed them to convey. Her hand drifted across the bed towards Nicholas. An image of his wife being fucked next to the swimming pool flashed into his head. It was like a bit of subliminal messaging. He imagined her lying on her back on one of the chaises longues with her legs in the air, her blue high heels rattling with each workmanlike pump administered by Gary. Nicholas wondered whether he and Jennifer could ever fashion a committed relationship with no inviolable link between sex and love.

And now, here was Tanya in his bedroom. Perhaps this had all been planned. Maybe it was a desperate ploy by Jennifer to try and reawaken her husband's dormant libido. Tanya's presence on the bed, however, failed to induce even a twinge of arousal. If anything, the low lighting combined with the way her features blocked regular emotional expression made him feel queasy.

'Oh, please come downstairs with us.'

'No,' Nicholas said sternly. 'I need to get some sleep.'

Chapter 16

May 2015

Next to the three boards of plans, the artist's impression depicted a paradisal vision of the new development. The drawings were in technicolour. They transported the drab and the utilitarian into the realm of prestige and aspiration. A usually litter-strewn car park had been replaced with an open green space populated by flourishing trees and wisteria growing up the side of buildings. Smart young professionals could be seen riding bikes in pairs while others lounged on benches deep in meaningful discussion. Some residents were depicted standing on their balconies interacting with neighbours. Down below, carefree children skipped around on one of the lawns which separated the blocks.

In the picture, six medium-sized six-storey blocks enclosed a shared podium courtyard. Residents socialising in the courtyards were illuminated by beams of sunlight that flooded through the buildings' gaps. Resting against the wall of one of the blocks were two unlocked bikes.

Val, Jacquie and a dozen or so other tenants were in the crypt of St Luke's Church for an open evening arranged by BRP, short for Bevan Estate Regeneration Partners, the name for the joint venture company set up by the local council, the Hand & Hyle Property Group, Oak Grove Housing and We Hear You. (Understandably they decided to omit the E for estate from the acronym.) The night had been billed as a Community Consultation Event, which would provide residents with an opportunity to get the first glimpse of initial designs for the Bevan Estate.

'I can't believe how quickly they've got all of this organised,' Jacquie said. 'When did they send out those questionnaires?'

'It was only at the beginning of the year,' Val said. 'See, all that nonsense about including us at every stage. I told you it was a load of bollocks.'

'Looks pretty nice though, right?' Jacquie said, taking a closer at the picture. 'I wouldn't mind living in one of these places.'

'I don't know.' Val shrugged her shoulders. 'It all seems a bit unreal to me. Do you know what I mean? It bears no relation to where we live now.'

'But that's the whole point,' Jacquie said. 'They're going to do it up.'

'Why would anyone suddenly choose to upgrade our lives? The council don't care about us. If they cared, the flats wouldn't look the way they do. This is all they care about.' Val tapped her finger against one of the boards. 'The stuff they can sell.'

Out of the six blocks depicted in the drawing that Jacquie and Val currently stood in front of, three had two-storey glass penthouses. 'The only thing that matters here,' Val continued, 'is how much money can be made.'

'What I want to know' – Randall joined Jacquie and Val in front of the boards – 'is where have all the black people gone? Do you see any?'

Val looked closely at the boards. 'I can see one.'

'Where?'

'There. See?' Val pointed to a single cyclist pedalling in the background of the drawing. Randall kissed his teeth. 'Look,' Val said, 'and there's a black woman sitting on that bench over there.'

Randall looked closely at the picture. 'Yeah, I see her. Sitting with her three white mates. OK, that's two black faces. And one of them has just stolen a bike.'

Randall had a flat on the third floor of Attlee House. He was the only leaseholder in the block who didn't rent out their property.

Jacquie turned to him. 'What do you make of all of this?'

'It's fuckeries, isn't it.'

'Why, what have you heard?'

'It's not what I've heard. It's what I've just read. It's all in here.' Randall held up a pamphlet entitled *A Guide for Leaseholders.*

'Where did you get that?' Val asked. Randall gestured to a table on the other side of the crypt.

'What does it say?' Jacquie asked.

While Val walked over to the far end of the room to get one of the booklets, Randall opened the pamphlet and read a section to Jacquie. It stated that if residents expressed a preference for a regeneration programme, then BRP would be working to acquire all the leasehold interests within the Bevan Estate. 'Our aim', Randall read from the pamphlet, 'is to acquire all residential leaseholds at an agreed market value.' Randall started shaking his head. 'Market value? They've run this place into the ground. How much is my flat going to be worth now?'

'Can I have a look at that?' Randall handed over the booklet. Jacquie muttered to herself as she scoured the pages.

'This is exactly what happened to a friend of mine. She was living on that big estate near Elephant. Southwark Council used compulsory purchase orders to buy back flats from tenants.'

'What happened to her?'

'She wasn't able to stay in London. The money she received from the council wasn't enough to buy a like-for-like property. And then she couldn't get another mortgage because she was considered too old.'

'Where is she now?'

'Hastings.'

'Nothing against Hastings. But fuck that,' Randall said.

As Jacquie read the pamphlet, she and Randall were approached by one of BRP's representatives.

'Hi. Alex Burnett.' He stuck out his hand for Jacquie to shake. 'I'm the liaison manager.'

Alex was wearing an air force blue suit with notched lapels and a light blue open-necked shirt. Although he was unshaven, Jacquie noticed stubble around the depression between his throat and collarbone. He looked as if he was probably around the same age as her. His cologne smelt leathery and expensive. Jacquie had to resist the urge to waft more of the odour towards her face. She wondered if he was gay. Alex turned to Randall and held out his hand.

'If you have any queries, you can either ask one of my colleagues or me. There are five of us here tonight. Between us, we should be able to answer any questions you might have.'

'I've got a question,' Jacquie said. 'How many new homes will be built?'

Val had now returned to the group, holding a copy of the leaseholders' guide and another pamphlet entitled *Information for Secure Tenants*.

'That depends on which redevelopment option is chosen. But it will probably be somewhere between three hundred and fifty and four hundred.'

'How many of those will be social rented?' Val asked.

'There will be more affordable housing and the same amount of social housing as there currently is.'

'If you're not creating any new social housing,' Val said, 'what's the point?'

'Through making proper use of the available space,' Alex said, 'we're increasing both housing capacity and supply.'

'What percentage overall will be affordable housing?' Jacquie asked.

'Hopefully, somewhere between twenty and forty per cent.'

'That's a bit vague,' Val said.

'Look, these are just the initial plans. Until we have agreed on a master plan, we won't know what the overall costs will be.'

'And will the rest of the flats be sold privately?' Randall asked.

'That's right.'

Randall gave a long, low whistle of astonishment.

'The three blocks facing the park will be sold at market value. The three blocks opposite are a mixture of shared equity, affordable rent and social tenants.'

'The flats with a view of the park will be private?' Jacquie asked. Alex nodded his head. 'Will they get access to the park?'

'A small selection of properties will come with a key.'

'But no other flats will get access?'

'Who needs the park?' Alex rubbed at the four-day stubble around his chin. Jacquie wondered why beards had evolved. What evolutionary purpose did they serve?

'Look at the plans,' he continued. 'There are some wonderful communal areas. We don't believe a lack of access to the park will restrict the enjoyment of the development in any way whatsoever. Access brings hefty additional service charges. There are also lots of hidden costs. It would be beyond the means of most of the tenants.'

'What about this area here?' Val pointed to a water

feature surrounded by benches and an open green area. 'It looks like it's blocked off from these flats...'

Jacquie looked closely at the plan and followed the line of a hedge with her finger. 'Oh, I get it,' she said. 'This is for people rich enough to buy one of the flats overlooking the park. But not rich enough to buy a penthouse. Isn't that a bit segregationist?'

'Without these types of concessions, nothing will ever get built. It's the money that can be generated which makes these types of projects feasible.'

'Apart from that blocked-off area' – Val moved her head closer to the plans – 'I can't see any other open spaces. There're loads in the drawings. It's a bit misleading, isn't it?'

'You're just looking at the plans for one option. If you look at option two, you will see there is a large communal area.'

'They all look the same to me. You've just highlighted the buildings with different colours.'

Randall took the *Guide for Leaseholders* pamphlet from Jacquie. 'It says here' – he pointed to a section on the second page – 'that if residents *choose* a regeneration programme.'

'Yes.'

'Well... if we don't choose regeneration, presumably we will have opted for something else. What else is there?'

'Look, our objective is to build more homes. The most effective way of doing this is by completely redeveloping the estate. That means replacing what is currently sub-standard housing with high-quality, contemporary homes while improving the environment.' Alex slapped a finger against the palm of his hand and began to enumerate with his fingers. With each new noun, he added another finger. 'Amenities, infrastructure—'

'Is there an alternative?' Val interrupted.

'... or we can look at an infill option. This focuses on

what's already there. We look for gaps around the existing footprint where new buildings could go. I'll show you the plans.'

On the other side of the room, away from the redevelopment options, was another less colourful presentation. Where the first three boards were presented front and centre of the exhibition space, these two boards had the appearance of an afterthought. None of the design effort so evident in the redevelopment plans was present in the infill option. Instead of dreamy utopian artists' impressions, the boards contained site plans, functional architects' drawings and highlighted area maps.

'In these plans,' Alex said, 'most or all of the existing buildings on the estate stay as they are. Any new homes will be built in spaces that are currently used for a different purpose. This would mean the loss of existing open spaces. It would also result in the removal of all the parking spaces.'

'Why?' Val asked.

'To create space for new homes.'

Jacquie puffed out her cheeks and emitted a dispirited sigh.

'Why do you have to build so many new homes?' Randall said. 'Why can't you just do up the estate? God knows it needs it.'

'This borough has a severe housing shortage,' Alex said. 'We *need* to build more homes.'

Jacquie looked at the boards. 'Would the flats be refurbished?'

'If infill appears to be a popular option, then we will test the viability of the option. The extent to which we can modernise, though, will rely on our ability to raise money to pay for refurbishment.'

'Hang on,' Jacquie said. 'If you don't have to demolish the estate and buy all the leaseholds, surely there will be more money to spend? Can't you refurbish the existing flats with what's left over?'

'It doesn't work like that,' Alex said. 'A lot of the money invested on redevelopment would be recouped from market sales.'

Kitty had now joined the group and was studying the plans.

'But with the infill option' – Randall pointed at the boards – 'everyone gets to keep their homes, right?'

'Everyone can keep their homes with both options.'

'That's not what it says here.' Randall waved the pamphlet at Alex Burnett.

'All leaseholders will be offered shared ownership opportunities in the new development. Alternatively, they can transfer their equity into another council social rented unit.'

Randall shook his head and started to gnaw at the skin around his thumbnail. 'You're downgrading me,' Randall said. 'I'm a homeowner. This will make me a tenant again. What about if I wanted to rent my flat out?'

'You will be able to swap the value of your existing home and the home loss payment which you will receive into a new property on the development. Obviously, you would have to make an additional payment to cover what's left over.'

'Are you joking?' The vein on Randall's forehead bulged. Its path from just above his eyebrow until it disappeared into his hairline was clearly traceable. 'Do you know long it took me to save for my flat? You can't do this.'

'There are other options,' Alex said.

'Fuck this.' Randall tossed the *Guide for Leaseholders* to the floor and stormed off.

Val looked at Jacquie and shook her head gravely.

'What about this space here?' Kitty pointed to an unused space on the site plans. 'Why wouldn't you be able to build more flats there and leave the communal spaces as they are?' Kitty was indicating a space between Beveridge House and the wall that separated the estate from the park. Although relatively large, the area served no particular purpose. Half of the space was concreted over. There was a wheelchair ramp with a meandering handrail which didn't seem to lead anywhere. The only people who ever used it were a bunch of local skateboarders. The other half of the space was overrun with a collection of tatty bushes. For years residents had campaigned to have a community hall built on the area.

'Hmmm.' Alex looked at the boards. 'Let me call someone over who will be better qualified to answer your question. After all, I'm just a lowly liaison officer.' He gestured for one of his colleagues to come over. 'This lady just asked why there are no plans to build extra housing on this area here.'

'It's a large area,' Kitty added. 'Surely an extra block of flats here would bring you closer to the quota you're aiming for. Then you wouldn't have to build over the car park.'

'It's a fair point. Firstly, let me introduce myself. My name is Deepak Shah, and I'm head of residential development for this project.'

A couple of other residents had now joined the group congregated around the infill option boards.

'Unfortunately, we are unable to build upon this particular bit of land,' Deepak continued.

'Why?' Kitty asked.

'Believe it or not, but an old hidden river runs underneath this very spot. It has eroded the soil, making it impossible to build upon.'

'Are you referring to the River Fleet?'

'Yes, that's right. Once upon a time it was a major London river. During the Roman period—'

'Yes, thank you.' Kitty pushed her glasses up the bridge of her nose. 'We know all about the history of the river.'

Val turned to Jacquie. 'I don't.'

'I was led to believe', Kitty continued, 'that the river's route runs underneath the other side of the park. About one hundred metres from here.'

'No, no, no.' Deepak's voice rose in pitch as he spoke. 'I think you've got that wrong.'

'Are you sure about that?' Kitty said. 'A few years ago, during a street dig in front of my property, sewer workers hit running water which they informed me was the River Fleet. They showed me a water and drainage map. It goes nowhere near—'

'I'm very sorry,' Deepak said, 'but would you excuse me? The person I was speaking to before you has just come back. Could we possibly continue this conversation in a bit?'

'If you ask me they have no intention of pursuing the infill option,' Kitty said. 'Regardless of anything either one of them just said, all you have to do is look at the money and effort which has gone into the redevelopment plans. And then look at the other plans. They're ticking boxes.'

Kitty, Val and Jacquie were standing near the entrance to the crypt having a cup of tea. There were about seventy other people in the room now. Alex Burnett and his colleagues were moving from group to group, answering questions.

'They just want to build loads of private flats,' Val said, 'sell them off and make a ton of money.'

Kitty nodded her head in agreement. 'I'm sure they are planning to demolish the whole estate,' she continued. 'Imagine how much a brand new three-bedroom flat around here is going to be worth. It's in their interest to underestimate the number of new homes they could build via the infill option. Look at...'

Kitty stopped talking in mid-sentence. The pause was unexpectedly long. As she searched for the words, Kitty agitatedly clicked her fingers. Jacquie raised her eyebrows as she waited for the sentence to be completed.

'I'm sorry.' Kitty laughed nervously. 'I've completely forgotten what we were talking about.' She rested her hand over her mouth and tapped her fingers on her lips.

Val said, 'You were saying how it's in their interest to underestimate the number of homes.'

Kitty furrowed her eyebrows and pursed her lips. She looked at Jacquie and frowned.

'It will come back,' Jacquie said, before turning to Val. 'Is it really so bad if they do demolish the whole place?'

'Imagine the disruption when we have to move out,' Val said.

'Who says we'll have to move out?'

'It says so here.' Val pointed to a section in the booklet. 'See.'

'Shit. I didn't see that.'

'Also, what about all the leaseholders?' Val said. 'They're going to lose their flats.'

'Most of them are landlords anyway,' Jacquie said.

'What about Randall? Or the likes of Georgi and Mariya; they live in a rented place. What will happen to them?'

Jacquie ran her fingers through her hair. She looked over at Kitty. 'Are you OK?'

'I'm fine. I just feel a bit dizzy. I think I need some fresh air.'

'Do you want me to come with you?'

'I'll be fine. Thanks.'

As Kitty walked away, Alex Burnett approached the two women holding up some paperwork.

'What's this?' Jacquie asked.

'Feedback forms.' Alex handed them both a sheet of paper. 'If you could fill them out and return them by the end of the month, that would be great.' Alex looked around to see if he could see Kitty. 'Where's the lady who was with you earlier?'

'She popped out for some fresh air.'

'Will she be coming back?'

Val shrugged her shoulders. 'I can take one for her if you like. I'll make sure she gets it.'

Alex gave Val another form. 'I hope you don't mind me asking, but do you both live on the estate?'

'I live in Attlee House,' Val said. 'She lives in Keynes House.'

'And your friend?'

'Kitty!' Val laughed. 'Are you joking? She doesn't live on the estate. She lives in one of those big old houses that back onto the park.'

'Ah. I see.' Alex nodded his head. 'She seems very invested in what happens to the estate.'

'Kitty has lived around Albion Park longer than anyone. She remembers what it was like before all the wankers moved in.'

Chapter 17

Unsure if he was even in the right place, Owen picked up his macchiato and sat down at one of the tables next to the window. Chalky had arranged to meet him in the new coffee shop between the hairdressers and the estate agent. When he arrived, Owen discovered two new coffee shops and three estate agents, all within thirty yards of each other. He tried to call Chalky, but there was no answer. Owen thought that if he sat by the window and kept an eye on the street, he would probably see him walking past. His flat was just around the corner. He reasoned that if Chalky were heading to the other coffee shop, he would have to walk past the window at some point.

He sipped his coffee and stared at the flow of humanity which streamed past the window. There were so many people – a mass of individuals, each one more important than the other. Like pre-programmed worker ants pursuing an innate instruction, everyone was in such a hurry, desperate to get somewhere fast. Faces were purposeful and determined. Humourless and intolerant. God help the person stupid enough to accidentally get in someone else's way and possibly add an extra ten seconds to their journey. Surely not all these people were going to be late. What was the worst that could happen if they were? It seemed to Owen that you had to pretend to be in a rush even if you weren't.

Owen had been thinking a lot about work recently and how one's identity is so inextricably linked to it. It had become the realm within which people define themselves. If your job didn't define you, then what were you defined by? Everyone wants to be perceived by their peers as being successful. Everyone wants to appear to be living a life of significance. A way of ensuring this is to pretend that you are busy all the time. Because if you weren't busy, then you weren't achieving. Lack of time had somehow become correlated with success. It was used as a misguided gauge of how well you were doing. Complaining about having no free time for anything other than work was bandied around like a badge of honour. Lack of time and lack of sleep conferred social status. The dedication of all of one's time and energy to a business, more than likely owned by someone else, was somehow considered a marker of success.

Owen took another sip of his drink. A young guy wearing a blue cotton French worker jacket walked past the window. He had dark hair with a side parting and a long fringe. The boy looked like Stuart from Run for the Shadows. He kept jerking his head to one side and self-consciously flicking his fringe with his hand to keep it in place. The boy reminded Owen of a dream he'd had the previous night. He was on stage with RFTS but was unable to play his guitar. His left hand couldn't manage any of the chord shapes. As he fumbled around the fretboard, the guitar began to shrink. Chalky had walked on stage and handed him a new guitar, but it kept going out of tune. As he knelt on the floor, wrestling with a tuner, Owen looked up and saw Daisy pointing at him and laughing.

'Earth calling Owen... come in, Owen. Earth calling Owen... can you read me?'

Startled, Owen looked up and saw Chalky standing next to him. 'Sorry, I was miles away.'

'You don't say. I was waiting in the place a few doors down. You didn't even notice me when I walked past the window. You were probably looking straight at me.'

'I tried to call you.'

'Yeah, my phone is out of juice. I forgot this place had even opened.' Chalky looked around the coffee shop. 'They all look the same, don't they.' He pointed at Owen's cup. 'You want another one of those?'

Chalky placed a tray of hot drinks and food on the table and sat down next to Owen.

'Want some?' he said, gesturing to an oversized almond croissant. Owen shook his head and watched as Chalky picked up the pastry and ripped into it. Within seconds he had a smear of icing sugar on his cheek. A small globule of custard had slopped down onto his T-shirt.

Chalky asked Owen what he had been doing since he last saw him. A shower of sugary dust emerged from his mouth as he spoke.

Owen couldn't bring himself to talk about the sessions he had been doing. His old publisher had put him in the studio with a couple of his artists. The money was terrible, and the music vapid. Joe's roster seemed to consist exclusively of aspiring singer-songwriters whose ambition extended no further than providing the soundtrack for the next John Lewis ad. Joe had signed Amelie (the artist Owen had most recently been working with) after her acoustic version of 'Paradise City' was used in a car commercial. Although sappy renditions of well-known songs were ubiquitous, Amelie's insipid interpretation of the Guns N' Roses song was particularly loathsome. Instead of singing the original words, Amelie had sung 'where the air is clean and everyone is pretty'. Before Owen had even met the singer or knew he would be working with her, the song had provoked an outpouring of invective every time he heard it on the TV.

Amelie had arrived at the studio with three equally drippy songs, which Owen was supposed to help her finesse. With Owen unable to hide his indignation at being presented with such songs, however, the session couldn't have gone much worse. After Owen opined that he couldn't polish one turd, let alone three, a tearful Amelie had run out of the studio to call her manager. The session was cancelled, payment withheld, and the arrangement between Joe and Owen was terminated.

'Yeah, I've... er. I've been quite busy.'

'Doing what?'

'Erm... you know, just working on some new music.'

'That's great. I heard some of that stuff you did with Jonny.' As he spoke, Chalky's open mouth revealed a half-chewed spread of pulped croissant. 'It sounded good.'

'You've seen Jonny?'

'Yeah, I've been doing some work for him. He bought a new console. I've been helping him set that up.'

A woman with two young children walked into the coffee shop. Apparently unconcerned about eyeing up a mother with her children, Chalky's head followed the woman all the way from the door to the counter.

Although doing his best to appear nonchalant, internally Owen felt panicked. Eager for news, he wanted to assault Chalky with questions. He hadn't heard from Jonny since going into the studio with him earlier in the year. The promises made that night at the after-party had failed to materialise. Having waited for over four months for Jonny to ask him to the studio, when the invitation finally arrived Owen was frustrated to discover that just some guitar and synthesiser work was required. He had been hoping the sessions would represent the advent of his new status within the band. Based on what the two of them had discussed that night, Owen had expected his new role to include additional production and writing duties.

There had been no talk about Owen's proposed permanent position. Then, one night, after a few drinks had bolstered his confidence, Owen messaged Jonny – *are you still up for me joining the band on a more permanent basis...like we talked about?*

Jonny had replied that he was *defo still up for it.* But *the suits as usual* were *holding everything up.* He suggested Owen contact Martin, the band's manager. Martin told him that it was the record company that was holding everything up. Owen messaged Jonny again, but this time no reply was forthcoming. Reluctant to keep badgering him, Owen hoped Chalky might provide a bit of clarity.

'What desk did he get?' Owen asked.

'A Trident. Series 70.'

'Series 70?'

'Yeah. It's nearly identical to the 80. Same mic pre's, same EQs. It's got sixteen busses rather than twenty-four.'

'Nice. How much did that set him back?'

'A fair bit.' Chalky stuffed the last bit of croissant into his mouth. 'He's bought loads of new gear.'

'So much for there not being any money in music any more,' Owen said.

'Sales may have dried up, but there's still big money flying around. The band got around two hundred and fifty grand for that Audi spot.'

Owen tensed up. Big advances, hefty sync fees, he had been so close to landing them all. Somehow though, the life-changing payday had managed to remain elusive. Always just out of reach. Always happening to someone else. Chalky noticed the blob of custard on his T-shirt and wiped it off.

'Has Jonny said anything to you about me?' Owen asked.

Chalky licked his finger and scrubbed at the custard stain. 'What do you mean?'

'About the deal?'

'I don't know what you're talking about.'

'With the band.'

'Run for the Shadows?'

'Yeah, of course. Who do you think I mean?' Chalky looked puzzled. 'Don't you remember?' Owen continued. 'Jonny said he wanted to make me a permanent member. He wanted me to get involved with the new record.'

'Right. OK.' Chalky sounded uncertain. He picked up his coffee. Owen noticed the hair on top of his head was thinning, the newly applied bleach an attempt to distract others from the impending baldness. 'Have you tried speaking to Jonny or Martin about this?'

'I have, yeah. But they've been giving me the runaround. I thought you might... you know.'

Chalky cleared his throat a couple of times and looked down at his coffee. He rubbed his hand on the back of his neck.

Suddenly Owen wished he wasn't there. He wished he hadn't broached the subject. Chalky's palpable discomfort suggested this was not going to end well. Finally Chalky looked up.

'No mate, no one has said anything to me.'

Relieved to hear that Chalky hadn't heard anything, Owen's eyebrows lifted.

'But if I were you,' Chalky added, 'I wouldn't go getting my hopes up.'

'Why do you say that?'

Chalky took a deep breath. 'They've got some gigs coming up. I've been booking flights, hotels, all that stuff... Your name wasn't on the list of personnel.'

Owen felt any residual optimism squeezed out of him. Outside the window, the rush of people continued unabated. He wished he possessed the certainty of knowing where he was needed today, tomorrow, the day after that, the following week, month, year. So much had hinged on this deal. It had been something for him to cling onto. A branch in hostile waters. Although doubts had recently dominated his thoughts, until Owen was informed of the contrary he was determined to cling to any frayed vestiges of hope. No more, though. Chalky's pronouncement had sounded the death knell for any wishful thinking. Trying not to appear crushed, Owen asked Chalky if he knew why he hadn't been included.

'Does it matter?' Chalky looked over towards the woman with the two small children. One of the kids caught his eye. He smiled at the child. Unnerved by this slyly smiling stranger, the kid quickly turned his head away and said something to his mum.

'Just tell me.'

'Look, Stuart will have got into Jonny's head,' Chalky said.

'Why, what's he been saying?'

'If you must know, he thinks you're too old.'

'Too old?' Owen shook his head.

'And that you drink too much.'

'What?' Owen exclaimed loudly. He looked around the coffee shop and then lowered his voice. 'I drink too much? Are you fucking joking?' Owen fell back in his chair and stared up at the ceiling. 'I can't believe it… Sacked from a rock 'n' roll band for drinking too much.'

'And for being too old…' Chalky gave a roguish smile. The silver cap on one of his canines was exposed. He looked like a wolf, Owen thought.

'Oh, yeah… thanks. I forgot about that bit.' Owen

slapped his hand against his forehead. 'I can't believe it,' he muttered to himself. 'Was I even drinking that much? Did you think I was?'

'No more than usual. But it's different now.' Chalky jabbed at his gums with a makeshift toothpick. 'The younger lot… they're more professional. More careerist.'

'More professional, my arse. Fucking hypocrites. I saw Stuart doing bumps of fucking ketamine. And Jonny is always pissed.'

Chalky looked over Owen's shoulder as the mother and two kids left the coffee shop. He waved at one of the children as he looked up. 'You'll sort something else out. To be honest, I didn't think you would be that bothered. You spent most of the time on tour complaining.'

'I don't understand why Jonny couldn't tell me himself.'

'He probably feels embarrassed,' Chalky said. 'He does rate you. I know that much. I don't think the age thing even bothered him. Jonny only cares about the music. He's a proper head.'

'Why's he dropped me then?'

'Why do you think? Stuart.'

'Fuck.' Owen kicked the table. 'It's all I need.' He leaned forward and put his head in his hands.

Chalky looked around the coffee shop while Owen had a moment to himself. Eventually, he said: 'Have you ever thought about teaching?'

Owen looked perplexed. 'What?'

'Teaching. This geezer I know runs a music college in Paddington.'

'Teaching? What are you going on about?'

'They offer diplomas in sound engineering, production, songwriting. You know the sort of thing. They're always looking for people with good experience. I just thought if money's a problem, I could—'

'A diploma in songwriting? Do me a favour. Failed musicians preparing kids for jobs that don't exist. I would rather never pick up a guitar again than teach in one of those places.'

'Alright, alright.' Chalky playfully gestured for Owen to calm down. 'Forget I even mentioned it.'

'I can't believe it,' Owen mumbled. 'I-can-not-fucking-believe-it.'

'Do you fancy getting a drink somewhere?' Chalky asked.

'When was all this decided?' Owen said, ignoring Chalky's question.

'I don't know. Look, for all I know, it might change. I wouldn't be surprised if Jonny gets in touch. He likes you.'

'Yeah, whatever.'

'Come on, let's go and get a drink.'

Owen was still staring out of the window, shaking his head in disbelief. He finally turned around and faced Chalky. 'Nah. I'm going to get off,' he said.

'Oh… OK.'

'Another time.'

'Sure.' The corners of Chalky's mouth turned down slightly. 'I'll see you soon, though, yeah?'

'I'll give you a call,' Owen stood up. 'And… thanks for trying to help. I appreciate it.'

Owen bumped fists with Chalky, turned around and hurried out of the coffee shop. He walked down the road to the bus stop mumbling to himself and rehearsing his riposte to Stuart. Although his vanity had been injured, Owen was able to extract a small slice of solace from the humiliation of being rejected: no longer would he have to tussle with the mental dilemma playing the guitar for RFTS posed. The band were right: he was too old. He had pretended that any age difference between himself and the rest of them was inconsequential. But it had bothered him. He didn't want to be the old man in the club any more.

There was a time when friends of his and Jacquie's used to joke that Owen must have made a Faustian pact to ensure his youthful looks never deserted him. Even Kitty once gleefully announced that one day Jacquie would discover, rotting in a cupboard somewhere, a grotesque ageing portrait of Owen. Time had rushed past, indelibly affecting everything else, yet somehow he had managed to appear outwardly untarnished. Far from paying heed to diets or fitness regimes, Owen had overindulged and pursued a life of excess. At thirty-seven years old, he had hardly looked any different to his twenty-one-year-old self. More recently, though, the inexorable tug of middle age had begun to exert its forces. The strains it inflicted not only revealed themselves physically but psychically too. The ticking clock that we all live with was getting louder; meanwhile, everyone around him seemed to be getting younger.

Owen sat down at the bus stop and rolled a cigarette. While he waited, he pulled out his phone and looked at the photos Conrad had sent him the previous year. There was one photo of The Rubber Band backstage at The Water Rats. It was one of the first gigs they ever played together. Owen had recently returned to this picture as if it might provide a clue to some of the questions he continually asked himself. Who was I then? What was I thinking? How did I get so old? What happened to me on the way? He enlarged the photo on the screen and zoomed in on their faces. They all looked so young, so good-looking. But everyone looks beautiful when they are young – especially when compared with the disrepair of their older faces. Even the ugly ones looked beautiful. The boring people looked interesting. The thick ones looked like they once knew it all. To stare at the ghosts of one's past is to look at the projection of a personality conveniently moulded over time. Everyone imbues the younger version of themselves with heightened powers. Yet we all mourn the myriad of options we failed to pursue. As if all of us could have been anything we wanted to be, if only we had realised it then. But to convince yourself that greatness was once possible is to ease the burden of failure. *If only I could do it all again.* The truth is you would probably end up in the same place.

Their previous FaceTime call had culminated with Owen jizzing all over his laptop keyboard. The conversation had started innocently enough. Daisy had been in LA for the last six weeks and told Owen how fed up she was and how much she missed London. Almost out of boredom, she had finally agreed to participate in her dad's TV show. The first day of filming had started at 8am. By midday, following a screaming row with her Mum, Daisy was back at her parents' house in West Hollywood packing up her things. Daisy and Owen had started talking again after Daisy, while out of her mind at a party, sent Owen a message.

Dnt know why you got in a such a huff. I saw yr dick & it's huuuuge. Any chance of a pic??

Owen chose not to accede to Daisy's request, but the unexpected message made him laugh. The two of them hadn't spoken since September. Knowing how mortified Daisy would be once she read her sent messages, Owen had waited for the inevitable penitent follow-up before replying.

'Do you want a tour of the house?'

Having been kicked out of the family home, Daisy was now staying with the brother of an old school friend in Santa Monica.

From the little Owen could see of the house, he was already feeling self-conscious about making a FaceTime call from Kitty's basement. Where his room was dark, low-ceil-inged and boxed in, Daisy's room was airy, lucent and expansive. While the basement was oppressive and dispir-iting, wherever Daisy was looked stimulating and alluring.

'Wait there one sec. I'm just gonna get a ciggy.' Daisy placed her laptop down on a table.

She was wearing nothing but a large, loose-fitting LA Lakers vest. She looked even thinner than Owen remem-bered. Her cheeks were scooped out, her face less fleshy. Watching Daisy saunter to the other side of the room reminded him of that morning lying in her bed, watching her naked body slink away from him. The humiliation still weighed heavy. Daisy picked up the laptop and gave Owen a three-hundred-and-sixty-degree view of the space. The room was big and white with wide plank oak floors. A small partition wall with a built-in fireplace divided the space into two halves.

'This is the upstairs living room. There's like an open-plan kitchen living area downstairs too. As much as I don't like LA, I do love this house. It's so vibey. I needed some-where to chill after the stress of being with my parents.'

Daisy continued to wander around the room. She pointed the camera at a framed *Mean Streets* poster and then moved towards some sliding doors which opened onto a terrace. Daisy turned the camera back towards herself.

'I'll introduce you to Danny.'

'Who's Danny?'

'It's Danny's yard,' she said. 'You'd really get on with him. He's a producer too. You might have heard of him. Danny Diamond?'

'Wait...'

Before Owen could tell Daisy that he would rather not be introduced to anyone, she had already turned the computer around and was marching across the room. All Owen could see was a white wood slatted ceiling, which suddenly transformed into a cloudless blue sky.

He opened another can of Guinness. Looking down from a balcony, Daisy tipped the laptop screen towards whoever was sitting below.

'Oi, Danny.'

A guy in a pair of shorts and wearing dark sunglasses looked up towards Daisy. He was sitting in a chair next to a lap pool, typing into a computer.

'Yo Dee!'

'Say hello to my friend Owen in London.'

'Hey, Owen in London,' Danny said, adopting an embarrassing London accent.

'Owen's the guy I was telling you about. You know... from Run for the Shadows.'

'Oh yeah, cool.' The guy lifted his sunglasses. 'Hey man, I love your band. Fucking awesome. When are you coming to LA again? I missed that show you guys did at Shrine. I heard nothing but good reports, though.'

'Thanks.' Owen sounded sheepish. He hadn't even been playing with RFTS at that point. 'Not sure when we'll be back in the US. Soon... touch wood.'

'What did he say?' Danny looked towards Daisy.

'He said he's not sure when the band will be in LA again.'

'OK. Well... hit me up when you're here, dude. We'll hang out. Make some music.'

From what Owen could discern, Danny looked more like a bodybuilder than a musician. He was buff and broad-shouldered. The proliferation of muscle around his neck made his head look small. When he turned to look up at Daisy, his movement was deliberate and robotic. His left arm, pushed out at an angle by oversized lats, was swathed in a colourful sleeve tattoo that stretched from his wrist to his shoulder. Looking at Danny sitting by his lap pool, Owen experienced a rush of envy, similar to how he felt as a kid when watching American films. The mystical grainy glow created by early digital movie cameras represented a place so alien from the one he inhabited: the wide suburban streets, the verdant front lawns, the well-stocked double-fronted fridge freezer, bedrooms which resembled toyshops. It was all so otherworldly and unobtainable.

Daisy walked back into the house with the laptop facing her.

'Do you want to see the studio?'

The first thing Owen noticed when Daisy walked into the studio was a section dedicated to synthesisers. Amongst the banks of keyboards and modules, he immediately spotted two rare and expensive synths. There was a Yamaha CS-80, like the one Vangelis used on *Blade Runner.* There was also an EMS VCS3, the same one Brian Eno used on stage with Roxy Music. The room had been acoustically treated. Bespoke sound absorber and diffuser panels were situated in all the appropriate spots. A large wall-mounted TV monitor framed by a pair of top-end speakers occupied most of the front wall space. The back wall was covered in hard reflective panelling and wooden slats. Serious money had been spent designing this workspace. It was the kind of room Owen had once dreamed of owning.

'What did you say that bloke's name was again?'

'Who?'

'Matey outside.'

'Danny Diamond.'

Owen had never heard of the guy before. He didn't look much older than Daisy. How the hell was he able to afford such an incredible-looking place?

'He said he wants to get me into the studio,' Daisy said.

'I bet he does,' Owen smirked.

'What's that supposed to mean?'

'More like he wants to get into your pants.'

'Hey! Fuck you. He says I've got a good voice.'

'Sure.'

'Anyway, he would have his work cut out getting into my pants.'

'What do you mean?'

'Because I'm not wearing any.' Daisy held the camera in front of her groin and lifted her vest. Placing her laptop on the studio floor, she bestrode the computer like the Colossus of Rhodes. With one foot planted firmly on either side of the screen, she slipped her searching fingers between her legs.

Three days later, when he received another FaceTime request from Daisy, Owen excitedly answered the call. This time, however, instead of wishing to engage in further acts of mutual masturbation, Daisy wanted to tell Owen about a discovery she had made. The day after their wank-fest, Daisy had gone back to the family home in West Hollywood. She knew nobody would be in as they were out filming all day at one of Max's restaurants. Daisy had needed to collect some underwear and some other bits which she had forgotten to pack. She should have grabbed her stuff and got out of there, but the temptation to log into Max's unattended iPad had proved irresistible. Unbeknown to her dad, Daisy knew the password. She was curious to find out what her parents had been saying about the row she had with her mum.

'I think my dad's having an affair.'

'Hmmm.' Owen did his best to discourage further elaboration.

While nosing around her dad's WhatsApp account, Daisy had noticed an empty conversation with someone called Karl at the top of his chats list. The chat had only recently been deleted, as it was dated from earlier that day. Daisy thought little of it and continued to read a conversation thread between Max and Emma. Instead of revealing her parents' innermost thoughts, the messages were exclusively about work. This compounded what Daisy had always suspected. Nothing was more important to her parents than their careers. While reading how much Emma's company had been offered to redesign the saloon at a private members club in London, a message arrived from Karl. Daisy clicked on it and was greeted with a photograph of a young naked woman lying on her back. On top of the picture, someone had inserted the dedication 'Kimberley Loves Max' and outlined the image with throbbing love hearts.

'There you go,' Owen said.

'What's that supposed to mean?'

'Well... That's what you get for snooping. It serves you right, I suppose.'

Daisy recoiled from Owen's assertion. She had half expected his response to be commensurate with the levels of dread she was currently experiencing. But, instead, she was presented with the weary face of a cynic – someone who understood too well the frailties of grown-up relationships.

'My dad says it's some lunatic fan.'

'Why would he have their name in his address book?'

'He doesn't,' Daisy said. 'He has someone called Karl in his address book.' Owen made a disbelieving face. 'I know, it sounds unlikely. He told me that Karl works for Utopia.'

'Utopia?'

'Daddy – my dad's management. I mean... it's possible. There are lots of people in the office. I looked around online...'

'And?'

'I couldn't find any mention of someone called Karl working there.' Daisy covered her face with her hands and shook her head. 'I can't believe my dad would do this to us. Do you think I should speak to my mum about it?'

'Jesus. Don't ask me, Daisy. I'm not exactly the go-to person for marriage guidance.'

Unlike their previous conversation, this time there was no happy ending. Once Owen realised Daisy was too distracted to pursue amatory exploits, he made his excuses and finished the call. He opened a bottle of wine and continued the online sleuthing he had started a few days earlier. The words 'Danny Diamond music producer' provided scant evidence of how Daisy's roomy had managed to afford such an incredible studio. There was more about his love of weightlifting than there were about any musical achievements. Even in interviews ostensibly about his music, he managed to talk more about slamming energy drinks and how his fitness regime enabled him to withstand marathon DJ sets. When he finally spoke about making music, he pretentiously described himself as an 'audio sculptor'. Having listened to some of his music on Spotify, Owen would have described Danny as an average dance music producer. He had around eighty thousand monthly listeners on Spotify. The Rubber Band had two hundred and forty-nine thousand five hundred and twenty-six. Run for the Shadows had over five million.

Owen took a sip of his drink. At some point, he would have to think about replacing all the wine he had taken from Kitty's cellar. Nothing had been said. But what had once appeared to be an inexhaustible supply was now looking limited. He clicked on a link for a record label called Work Out Records. Apart from Danny himself, the website showcased several other artists. Owen listened to some of the tracks embedded on the home page. They all sounded the same. Further down the page, there was a Recent News section which announced:

Work Out records are super hyped to announce that label boss Danny Diamond has scored the upcoming HBO drama 'Yellow Dog'. This follows on from Danny's recent score for the Netflix film 'The Garden of Love'.

Owen quickly typed 'garden of love composer' into his search engine. The revelation that DJ and audio sculptor Danny Diamond, aka Dan Bucholz, was also a successful TV and film composer landed like a punch to the solar plexus. Owen emitted a growling murmur of discontent. Inexplicably he felt devastated. Up to that point, he had consoled himself with the presumption that Danny, like Daisy, was a dilettante beneficiary of parental funds. Eighty thousand monthly listeners on Spotify wouldn't cover the costs of a software modelled version of the Yamaha CS-80. It probably wouldn't even afford one to buy a sample CD of the sounds it made. How someone that young and seemingly inexperienced landed a gig composing the music for Netflix films and HBO shows baffled Owen. He listened closely to the *Garden of Love* score, hoping the answer might lie within the layers of electronic sounds. It all sounded proficient, if not generic. But it was nothing he was not capable of doing himself. If anything, he was convinced he would be able to do better.

Owen loaded up some of his own music. It was something he often did when drunk but never sober. He played 'Move the Needle' by The Rubber Band. Even coming out of his computer's crappy internal speakers, the energy of the music was irrefutable. It sounded so good. He finished off his glass of wine and sat back on the sofa. With his eyes closed, he listened to more songs from their first album. It was easy to recall how he felt when those tracks were finished. At the time, he couldn't believe how good they were. It was so exciting. The album might have ended up sounding too polished and overproduced, but when he was in the studio listening back to the finished mixes for the first time, every single track had seemed like a potential hit. How could the band not be successful? Everyone was in agreement. Success was inevitable – the awards, the accolades, the fame. All of it had been within touching distance. It was the closest he had ever got. He had been trying to emulate that opportunity ever since. Even though listening to those songs filled him with regret and a desperate longing to go back and do things differently, it still felt good to remind himself that he had talent. Maybe not enough talent, but there had been something there.

Chapter 18

At the beginning of the week, Jacquie received a call from Alex Burnett, the liaison manager at the Hand & Hyle Property Group. He wanted to know if Jacquie could come to his office in Shoreditch for a meeting.

'Why do you want to see me?'

'It's OK,' Alex laughed. 'No need to sound so worried. I just wanted to have a chat with you about the flats.'

'Can't we do it on the phone?'

'We could. But I think it makes more sense to meet in person.'

'OK,' Jacquie sounded hesitant. 'Who else will be coming?'

'For the moment, it will just be you. We will be asking other tenants to come in at a later date.'

Jacquie had already arranged to meet a couple of friends later in the week the following night at a pub near Spitalfields. Owen had agreed to look after the kids.

'I could come after work on Thursday,' Jacquie said. 'Around sixish?'

'Perfect.'

Hand & Hyle's offices were on Epworth Street, between the City Road and Great Eastern Street. Jacquie walked down Leonard Street onto Paul Street, looking through the windows of smart young companies advertising services she didn't really understand. There were lots of two-word tag lines: people-inspired, growth-driven, verbal-identity, hyper-personalised. Offices packed with designer furniture and an overwhelming amount of street art suggested money was being made. But it wasn't clear to Jacquie what they did. What were offline engagement tools? What was multi-dimensional communication? Growth hacking? Slolomo? Geofencing marketing?

Jacquie knew the area around Shoreditch and Old Street well. For a short time, she had rented a room in a warehouse on Holywell Lane. But like so many parts of the city, it was now teeming with people much younger than her. They spoke a language she wasn't familiar with. It felt like only yesterday that she was gallivanting around the same streets. Hard to believe now, but the place felt abandoned then. The litter-strewn streets between Old Street roundabout and Kingsland Road offered nothing to anyone. There was one pub, one gay bar, one strip joint and one garage. It was bleak, forsaken and unsightly – but it was also edgy and exhilarating. At the time, most Londoners would have struggled to even tell you where Shoreditch was. They knew it only as part of a couplet from an eighteenth-century folksong about who knows what. Nobody would have predicted that the area would soon be so intensely gentrified and ultimately corporatised.

Having announced her arrival, Jacquie was asked by the receptionist to take a seat. She sat down on a sky-blue modular sofa that spanned two large walls of the reception area. No one else was waiting. There were several colourful Patrick Caulfield-style paintings depicting tower blocks, power stations and gas holders on the reception area walls. There were lots of flat blocks of bold colours, thick black outlines and glossy surfaces. How strange, Jacquie thought, that Hand & Hyle should be celebrating the very buildings they so evidently enjoyed knocking down. Several thickly bound magazines were artfully spread out on a table in front of the sofa. Jacquie picked up a copy of an interior design magazine and began flicking through the pages. The featured houses looked like hotels. Sitting rooms resembled foyers. While bedrooms with oversized beds, wall-to-ceiling velvets and no sign of natural light reminded Jacquie of an upmarket knocking shop. There was an article on one property that had floor space of over six thousand square feet. The owners were determined that nothing in the house should look like anything anyone had ever seen before. Jacquie chucked the magazine back down onto the table. It landed next to another magazine that claimed to cover all aspects of the ultra-affluent lifestyle.

The receptionist asked Jacquie if she would like anything to drink while she waited. Jacquie checked the time on her phone and reminded the girl that she had arranged to meet Alex at six pm. It was now nearly six twenty. After another ten minutes of mindlessly flicking through *Global Living*, Hand & Hyle's liaison manager finally made an appearance. He smiled warmly at Jacquie, apologised for keeping her waiting and ushered her into his office.

'Thanks for taking the time to come in today.' Alex motioned for Jacquie to join him on his side of the table.

Spread out across his desk was a copy of the regeneration plans for the Bevan Estate. Alex stood for a moment contemplating the drawings.

'Who wouldn't want to live here?' he said proudly. 'It will be such a huge improvement on what is currently there.'

'Nearly anything would be,' Jacquie said.

Alex asked Jacquie if she had children. When she told him that she did, Alex embarked on a sales pitch about how vital the environment was for children's mental welfare.

'It's well established,' Alex said, 'that social disadvantage is associated with poor mental health. When coming up with these plans, our design team took a holistic approach, taking particular care over creating a sense of well-being and security. Very important for children, I'm sure you'd agree.'

'Of course,' Jacquie said, emphasising that Alex was stating the bleeding obvious.

'But do you know what the biggest challenge is with a project like this one?'

'Making sure your shareholders make enough money?'

'Ha! Very good… No, the biggest challenge is finding a way of keeping everyone happy. With so many conflicting interests, it can be hard to strike a balance. You see, the council has no money. And they can't borrow any either. With no money, how are they supposed to maintain their housing stock? The fact is they can't. And now the flats are in a terrible… well, you would know. To be honest, I think they might be beyond repair.'

'I'm sorry, but who else do you need to keep happy, apart from the people who live on the estate?'

'Don't get me wrong, the expectations of the community are paramount. However, we have to compromise between what works for the residents and also what's commercially viable. Because to improve the existing housing stock while also managing to create new and affordable homes, the council rely on private entrepreneurs. And as I'm sure you know, once the private sector gets involved, profits are demanded. If the council were able to fund projects like this on their own, then perhaps there wouldn't be quite so many—'

'Unaffordable homes?'

'I wouldn't put it quite like that.'

'Look, why are you telling me all this?'

'We're sensing resistance from some of the residents.'

'What do you expect? You're asking people to pack up their stuff and move out while their homes are demolished.'

Alex sat down on the edge of his desk. He crossed his legs, so his left ankle was resting on his right knee.

'There is no simple solution to the housing crisis.'

Jacquie laughed. 'What do you want me to do about it?'

'We want you to help us sell in our vision to the other residents.'

'What?'

'No need to look so alarmed. It's nothing, really. We just want everything to run smoothly. And we don't want the process to be hijacked by campaign groups and activists who believe we're trying to wage some kind of class war. We think you might be able to help us deliver this.'

Jacquie chewed the inside of her cheek as she continued to stare at the plans.

'Why would I want to do that? What would I get out of it?'

Alex walked over to the water cooler and poured himself a drink. 'The council are our partners on this project. Board membership is 50/50.'

'So?'

'Well, that means we have a say in *all* decisions.' Jacquie looked confused. 'We can help you navigate the perilous process of getting rehoused.'

'Why would it be perilous? Surely anyone with a secure tenancy will be rehoused in the new development?'

'But your name isn't on the tenancy.' Alex took a sip of water and placed the cup on his desk.

'At the moment it isn't,' Jacquie said, 'but my ex is about to sign it over.'

Alex was now sitting in his chair, his elbows resting on the arms. He clasped his hands in front of his chest. There was a protracted pause.

'What?' Jacquie said.

'Correct me if I'm wrong, but didn't your partner—'

'He's not my partner.'

'Sorry. Your ex. Wasn't the tenancy passed on after his mother died?'

'In the end, it was,' Jacquie said. 'After a ten-month battle with the council. What's your point?'

Alex tapped his fingers on his thigh a few times before speaking.

'We will be creating a consortium with a housing association. The council will eventually pass control of their portfolio onto them. Oak Grove Homes has its own policies regarding tenancy transfers and allocation. It's all on their website. I'm afraid they stipulate that a tenancy can be passed on just the once.'

'But we're still with the council.' Jacquie sounded rattled. 'If I get my name on it now—'

'They won't fall for that,' Alex said. 'If your name wasn't on the tenancy as of, I think, five years ago, you won't be eligible to transfer it to the new development. However...'

'Yes.'

'If you can get the tenancy signed over to your name, then there's a chance, in this case, we'll be able to persuade Oak Grove to make an exception.'

Jacquie felt as if her blood pressure had suddenly dropped. She slumped into the chair on the other side of the desk as she imagined being rehoused on the fringes of London. The idea of living at the end of a tube line, swallowed by the suburbs, looking out over retail parks and congested arterial routes terrified her. She had lived in central London all her life. As far as she was concerned, the city stopped at the edges of Zone 2.

'I think you're overestimating the influence I have around the flats.'

'Not at all. We think you would be perfect.'

'What would I have to do?'

'We want you to be part of a residents' steering committee. You'll be responsible for representing the tenants of the estate during the redevelopment process. But we will expect you to promote an agenda that's friendly to us. We will also recommend an independent advisor with whom you will work closely.'

Jacquie put her head in her hands. 'I don't know about this. You're asking me to betray the community.'

'Community? There is no community. It was dismantled a long time ago. Listen,' Alex said. 'This land is worth too much money. There's just no way the council can afford not to realise the value of its assets.'

Jacquie looked out of the office window. Everything was about money, she thought. It informed every decision, every policy, every blind eye that was turned and every light that went green. Money was the reason why she and everyone else on the Bevan Estate might potentially lose their homes. London was a city that welcomed anyone with money, no matter from where it came, and spurned anyone without. Money was the answer to every question you cared to ask. It was the key to every lock.

'If it's a done deal' – Jacquie finally turned her head away from the window – 'why do you need me?'

'We want this redevelopment to happen. We believe it will be advantageous for everyone. Residents of the flats included. Anything that can help us achieve this is worth pursuing.'

Jacquie stood on the balcony of Spencer's flat and looked out over the dense carpet of lights which spread out in front of her. The city air was thick with the exertions of millions of people. She was only a couple of miles from where she grew up, but the city that bore her was barely recognisable from that height. Down below, heavy traffic snaked along the City Road while all around illuminated towers sprung out from the shimmering glow beneath them. As she leaned over the glass balustrade, Jacquie felt touched by the seductive hand of success. For a moment, she understood the arrogance of wealth. It must be hard not to feel innately superior when always looking down on others from a vantage point of such luxury. The city possessed a savage duality. It was a place of two distinct halves being pushed further and further apart. Jacquie would often hear people talking about a trickle-down effect, the benefits of being a global financial centre, and what it brought to everyone else. But she saw no evidence of it. If anything, the opposite was true. The idea that tax cuts and economic policies, which were created to assist the wealthy, would somehow benefit the less well-off made no sense. How could someone argue that the rich needed more help?

To the east, the flashing beacon of Canary Wharf winked from a distance. It reminded Jacquie of when she and her mates used to cycle down to the Docklands and walk among the newly built skyscrapers and office blocks. In those days, the aircraft warning light looked disconsolate. One Canada Square had been completed, but Canary Wharf had been placed into administration following the collapse of the property market. The area was deserted and ghostly. A seemingly abandoned metropolis encircled by wastelands and derelict warehouses. Thatcher's conceptualisation of the future was struggling to break free from the surrounding environment that itself symbolised Britain's decline. The whole enterprise appeared to be a staggering act of hubris. To Jacquie and her friends, it seemed entirely out of place. It was as if Manhattan had been emptied and relocated to the hinterlands of East London.

Jacquie's adolescent brain could never have imagined the changes this development would usher in, the role these buildings would play as guardians of London's newfound place in the world. She and her friends simply relished the opportunity to walk around a deserted city, struggling to comprehend how it had ended up on their doorstep. Jacquie thought about how Canary Wharf had come to symbolise so much of what had happened to London. Its influence had seeped into the rest of the city like spilt ink on blotting paper. No longer a symbol of egregious corporate failure, the familiar flashing light now proudly bestrode one of the most powerful financial centres on earth. How could the likes of her, or anyone else, resist the irresistible? The indefatigable march of progress was ruthless and would never allow itself to be hindered by the unfortunate souls it displaced. The exclusion of those who couldn't afford to keep up was the price of success.

As she rested her arms on the balustrade, Jacquie thought about what Alex Burnett had said earlier. He was right. It was pointless clinging onto the vestiges of a concept of community; there wasn't one any more. Albion Park was too desirable an area, the land too valuable. All decisions were being driven by commercial interests. Concessions for council tenants and the need for properly affordable housing were all an impediment to enterprise. Jacquie desperately wanted one of those flats. She had no compunction about being loyal. Everyone else could look after themselves. The selfish and greedy get rewarded; she had learned that much. It was a truism life in London compounded. Every day one was beaten around the head with it. Greed, apparently, was good. The spirit of envy spurred people on.

After her meeting with Alex Burnett, Jacquie had met her friends Nova and Lucy at The Golden Heart. Thursdays were always busy in London. For many, it was the best night to go out on, in order to avoid the stag dos, hen parties and out-of-towners who descended upon the city at weekends. The three women stood outside the pub with the smokers and others unable to get a table inside. After a couple of drinks, Lucy suggested they go to a nearby cocktail bar that had recently opened.

'Why did she bring us here?' Jacquie asked Nova as she sipped the remnants of her drink.

The basement bar was even busier than the pub. The crowd waiting to get served was nearly three deep, and there was nowhere to sit.

'She's having it off with the bar manager.' Nova held up her Moscow Mule and rattled the ice cubes in the glass. 'Hence the free drinks.'

A young guy in an open-necked white shirt, his tie hanging out of his trouser pocket, barged into Jacquie.

'Jesus.' Jacquie narrowed her eyes and scowled at the culprit. 'It's full of wankers,' she said. 'And unless we're getting free drinks all night, I would rather not have to buy a round. Have you seen the price of a cocktail?'

'Shall we get out of here?' Nova said.

'What about her?' Jacquie gestured towards Lucy, who was by the bar, deep in conversation with the manager. Standing next to her was a tall, bearded man in a slim-fit white cotton shirt. He turned around and noticed Jacquie looking straight at him. The moment of recognition made her look away. Then, embarrassed by her reaction, she hurried to the toilets.

As she looked into the mirror, a tremor travelled up through her body and escaped through her neck. The flush of nerves made her shudder. Her eyes looked tired. She pulled a stick of concealer out of her bag and applied some cream before adding an extra bit of eyeliner. Jacquie laughed at her reflection and then wiped her clammy hands on some tissue paper. She took a deep breath and opened the door.

'You look like you're a million miles away.' Spencer appeared on the balcony holding a bottle of fizzy wine and two long-stemmed glasses.

Her face turned to his. 'I was just thinking how much the city has changed,' she said. 'I grew up not far from here. The City Road was a dump in those days. It was literally a road to nowhere.' Hoping he would notice the way her silk camisole clung to the contours of her breasts, Jacquie leaned against the balcony and pushed her chest out.

'It's getting a bit cold out here,' Spencer said. 'Shall we go inside?'

'No, I like it.' Jacquie said. 'The view is incredible.'

He poured some drink into their glasses. Jacquie looked down at the tiny beads of air that gleefully bubbled up to the surface, only to disappear without a trace once they neared their destination.

'Here's to serendipity.' Spencer raised his glass and fixed his gaze upon Jacquie. Instead of nervously looking away, like she had in the bar earlier on, Jacquie held his stare this time. Apart from Owen, she hadn't had sex with anyone else for nearly fifteen years. Monogamy had denied others the pleasures of her younger body, while age had presented her with a truckload of insecurities. Yet here she was, emboldened by booze, staring into the eyes of a virtual stranger, who she was about to let fuck her.

'I can't believe we bumped into each other again.' Spencer stared purposefully into Jacquie's eyes. 'You know, I couldn't stop thinking about you after I met you on the train that time.'

'Really?' Jacquie scrunched up her nose and raised an eyebrow.

'Yeah. Why the face? I'm not joking. I think you're beautiful. God knows how someone as sexy as you has managed to stay single.'

'Oh my God!' Jacquie said with a derisive laugh. 'I can't believe you just said that.'

She may have protested, but Jacquie loved the attention. It was a feeling she had missed. Spencer's unabashed interest made her feel anxious. But it also made her feel excited and girlish. Even though some of what he said made her cringe – *here's to serendipity* – his wanton gaze was energising. It made her feel alive.

When Jacquie was younger, excessive male attention used to bother her. She was often accused of being rude or hostile, when in fact she was just fed up with having to fend off the advances of libidinous men. Little did she know, one day she would mourn the loss of that power. Having believed it had deserted her forever, and age rendered her invisible, it felt good to have a taste of it again. Sex, she had convinced herself, was overrated. She believed that she could live without it. She believed that the dramas and emotional baggage which would inevitably accompany a new relationship were too much of a turn-off. To persuade herself of this, Jacquie had chosen to forget about the shiver-inducing thrill of sexual attraction and the all-consuming throb of desire. Who wouldn't want to feel this way, she thought? The way Spencer's eyes tunnelled into her reminded Jacquie that she wasn't so old, that she still looked good. And maybe she wasn't invisible after all.

'What?' Spencer said. 'It's a fair question. Your ex must have been crazy to let you get away.'

'Yeah, well… he didn't have much choice in the end.'

Bored of talking, Jacquie wondered whether she should just go ahead and kiss the face that loomed in front of her. She took another sip of her drink. Slowly, she felt her inhibitions slip away as if they had never existed in the first place.

'Are you going to kiss me?' she asked.

Spencer leaned towards Jacquie, open-mouthed. Their tongues immediately began to frenetically probe each other's mouths. Spencer wrapped his arms around Jacquie and pulled her towards him. His hands began to roam freely over her back, hips and waist. Occasionally he allowed his fingers to breach the waistband of Jacquie's knickers. Each moan Jacquie emitted encouraged him to go further. Eventually, she prised her mouth away.

'Turn off the lights in the flat,' she said. 'I want to look out from the darkness.'

While Spencer went inside, Jacquie leaned against the balustrade. Still transfixed, she looked out over the carnival of lights that danced and sparkled below.

'Now, where was I?' he said, as he eagerly resumed where he had left off.

Jacquie could feel the urgent pressure of an erection pressing against her arse. Spencer leaned into her and began to kiss her neck and breathe heavily into her ear. Keen to feel the weight of her tits, he put his left hand under her blouse. Jacquie quickly diverted his hand away from her stomach and chest and towards her crotch. Spencer proceeded to unbutton Jacquie's trousers, which she duly stepped out of.

'Shall we go to the bedroom?' Spencer asked.

'No,' Jacquie said, refusing to turn around. 'I want to stay here.'

Chapter 19

June 2015

Owen handed his studio keys over to Tony, who reciprocated with an envelope full of cash. He thumbed through
the wad of well-worn twenties. Five hundred quid was all
that was left after he had paid back the money owed in
rent. There had been a couple of items he had not been
able to part with, particularly his cherished 1973 Martin
Acoustic, which he bought as a present to himself after he
signed his first record deal. Connoisseurs were often suspicious about the quality of Martin guitars built during that
era. Received wisdom claimed quality control had been
affected by increased productivity. But Owen's D-35 was
the most beautiful acoustic guitar he had ever played. He
was proud to own it. It was solid and robust; the sound
was clean with rich overtones. Then there was his Olympic
white Fender Jag. He loved that guitar too. He loved the
sound it produced when strummed from just behind the
bridge. There were also a couple of synths, his MRK-2 drum
machine, just like the one Sly Stone used on *There's a Riot
Goin' On*, and his 1965 Fender Deluxe guitar amp, which
he had owned for over twenty years.

'I'll give you two grand for the rest,' Tony said.

'Yeah, right.'

'I can do a BACS right now.'

'Get out of here. It's worth about three times that. At least.'

Owen put the envelope of cash into his back pocket and picked up his two guitars.

'I'll see you around, Tony.'

Georgi was waiting outside the studio in his van; they had already packed everything else. Owen stood on the pavement and looked up at the building. It was a relief to have paid off his debts. The prospect of no longer having to pay rent would make life easier. But apart from that, Owen felt beaten. Without a band, without the imminent release of a record, and most pertinently without somewhere to work, could he even claim to be a professional musician any more? Was he even worthy of the denominations he so proudly used to describe himself? Musician, music producer, composer. It was not only how he defined himself, but it was also how others perceived him. It was all he had ever wanted to be.

The previous week Owen had gone for a drink with Conrad. The two of them had known each other since their early twenties. A couple of years older, Conrad had always been someone Owen looked up to. When they were younger, he was the more accomplished musician of the two. He was a multi-instrumentalist, knew his way around a studio and could engineer a record by himself. Unlike Owen, he had never been enamoured with the lifestyle often associated with being in a band. He hated the amount of time wasted on tour. He also objected to having to play the same songs over and over again. Conversely, Owen had always possessed a fanboy infatuation with what he perceived to be the rock 'n' roll way of life. Conrad had been no angel when they were away on tour, but he possessed a more enlightened viewpoint regarding the industry. Owen was thrilled just to be living the life – getting paid to play music in front of an audience was to enact his adolescent fantasies. If he had to sit around all day in a venue or spend most of his time on a tour bus, so be it. It was part of the package. He loved every moment of it: the photoshoots, the interviews, the travelling, the attention. Conrad, on the other hand, was permanently dissatisfied. He enjoyed playing and creating music but couldn't tolerate all the other stuff.

As he looked at Conrad from across the table, Owen had realised just how much he envied his old friend. Conrad had always possessed a certainty and self-assurance. Unlike Owen, he had recognised what they were doing with the band simply wasn't good enough. Plaudits and the opinions of others had meant little to him. Even though they were quickly offered a new deal after they were dropped, Conrad had possessed the foresight and depth of understanding to realise the likelihood of their band ever transcending the ordinary was slim. The way Conrad saw it, he had given it a go; it hadn't worked out, he was prepared to move on. Now that he was head of English at a secondary school in Epping, he had a career arc to follow. A clear path had been laid out in front of him. The lack of this metaphorical path in his own life deeply unsettled Owen. Conrad appeared relaxed and at ease with himself. He was forward-looking and optimistic; he had things to aim for. The future scared Owen. He didn't like to think about it. The disappointments he had experienced and the bitterness he felt had resulted in a jaundiced outlook in which he now perceived everything as defective. It felt like his life had unravelled so quickly. Like the dog crossing the field, following its nose, Owen had haphazardly pursued his own ends in a manner that would make no sense to the onlooker. The dog invariably finds what it's looking for. Whereas Owen had been endlessly searching, forever criss-crossing imaginary fields, but with nothing to show for it at the end.

'Where to?' Georgi asked as Owen climbed into the van next to him.

'Back to the park.' Owen looked at the time on the dashboard. 'We'd better get a move on. The meeting starts in three-quarters of an hour.'

'I'm not going.' Georgi sneered as he spoke.

'Why not?'

'Whatever happens, we lose flat.'

'How do you work that one out?'

'We rent flat from Chinese landlord.'

'So?' Owen laughed.

Georgi turned to Owen and rubbed his thumb over the tip of his index and forefinger.

'Money?'

Georgi nodded his head judiciously as if his passenger had fully understood the implication of his gesture.

Owen rested his head against the window and stared out of the van as it made its way through Dalston.

'If you want,' Georgi said, 'you can work some days with me. I have much work in park.'

Owen tried his best not to sound too deflated. 'OK, yeah. Thanks, Georgi.'

The van pulled up next to a West African restaurant. A man wearing a white embroidered agbada, white trousers and holding a gold-tipped walking cane was standing outside the restaurant talking into his phone. Owen was reminded of something Conrad had said to him the other night. When Owen asked why Conrad had given up music so early, Conrad replied that life had been more challenging for him; therefore he needed the stability a regular job could provide. Conrad believed the darker shade of his skin and Nigerian surname ensured fewer opportunities would present themselves. He believed Owen had been conditioned to feel comfortable pursuing the precarious life of a creative. According to Conrad, Owen had grown up among white middle-class North London aspirations. Things had been expected of him. Conrad believed that even if you do not fulfil those hopes, the expectancy others have for you carries you along.

Owen continued to stare out of the window and think about what Conrad had said. Without even being aware of the finer details, he had been astute in his analysis. When he was growing up, Kitty had always told Owen that he could be an artist one day. She raved about his natural ability and would often bring out his drawings to show her artist friends. Together they would critique his childish doodlings as if analysing a masterpiece. Kitty and her friends would breathlessly comment on every botched line and wonky feature. Looking at some of those drawings now, they seemed no better than what any other nine-year-old would do. But the way Kitty and her friends used to proclaim his *precocious ability* and *innate understanding of form and composition*, anyone would have thought they were talking about a young Picasso.

His mum may not have fitted into Conrad's middle-class designation, but, like Kitty, she had enthusiastically encouraged the idea of a life dedicated to art. Even though she knew Owen's real interests lay elsewhere, Janet had always wanted her son to be a dancer. She had tried to persuade him to audition for Rambert, and although he might well have been successful, music always came first.

Conrad was right, therefore. Owen had grown up inculcated with a value system that might not have necessarily reflected his circumstances. He disagreed, however, that his life had been so much easier than his friend's. At least Conrad had grown up with little doubt of where he belonged. Little Lagos, naturally, was a home from home for the Nigerian diaspora. Growing up among the African hair salons, Ghanaian grocers and church groups of Peckham Rye left zero room in Conrad's burgeoning brain for any uncertainty regarding the nature of his heritage. Whereas Owen had never been anything but confused about where he really belonged. Wherever he went, he had always felt like an outsider. His dad once told Owen that he was more like a white boy than a black boy. Sometimes he had wished that he was white. Life would have been much less confusing.

Owen turned the radio on. They were playing 'I Go to Pieces' by Run for the Shadows. 'That's the last thing I need.' He leaned forward and switched to another station. A female journalist was doing a piece on the immigration crisis in Europe. She described how the German government expected three-quarters of a million asylum seekers by the end of the year. Wave upon wave of migrants escaping conflicts was pouring out of the Middle East. Attacks on those who had made it into Europe had risen sharply. An English politician was being interviewed. He explained how migrants posed a threat to the EU's standard of living. He mentioned threats to the welfare system, cultural threats, threats to the social structure. Everything was in peril. It was as if the demise of Europe was being reported on. Like the barbarian hordes were at the gates, ready to swarm in and overcome a meek and defenceless continent. The reporting was febrile and incendiary. No wonder the public was so anxious. No wonder citizens perceived migrants as a threat rather than a possible benefit to the society which hosted them.

'In Bulgaria, they put very cut wire on border with Turkey.' Owen continued to stare out of the window. 'If anyone come through,' Georgi continued, 'then police use dog.'

'That sounds brutal,' Owen said.

'It works.' Georgi nonchalantly shrugged his shoulders.

'You think that's a good thing?'

'Compare to Germany, Austria... Italy. Bulgaria has' – Georgi made a tiny gesture with his forefinger and thumb – 'very small problem.'

The news programme was now reporting that Islamic State fighters had executed at least one hundred and sixty innocent people in an attack on a Syrian town. The news said that armed ISIS militants deliberately targeted civilians. Apparently, to gain their confidence, the fighters wore uniforms similar to those worn by the Kurdish forces fighting against them.

'Oh my God, this is too depressing,' Owen said. He reached over and changed the station back to 6 Music. They were playing a track from *Endtroducing*; the music reminded Owen of a more innocent, prelapsarian world. Of a time that was pre-9/11, pre-homegrown terrorist, pre-collective narcissism, pre-mass obesity, pre-teen depression, pre-personal branding, pre-mass shooting, pre-like and subscribe, pre-financial meltdown, pre-austerity, pre-Afghanistan, pre-Iraq, pre-Syria, pre-trolling, pre-porn ubiquity, pre-cataclysmic future. A moment in time that seemed like an extended economic boom. When the internet had lofty goals, and world leaders could look to the future and, with a straight face, declare that the next millennium would usher in a period of greater peace, prosperity and freedom. A time when the doomsday clock was closer to eleven forty-five than it was to midnight.

After he had dropped his equipment off in the basement flat, Owen walked around to the front of the house. Kitty was standing on the stairs which led up to the front door. She was saying goodbye to a woman who looked about the same age as her. The two women shook hands. Owen noticed that Kitty used her left hand; her right arm was in a sling. As the woman turned around and walked down the stairs, Kitty spotted Owen standing to the side of the house.

'What happened to your arm?'

'Oh, it's nothing,' Kitty said. 'I had a bit of a fall the other day.'

'Here?' Owen asked. Kitty nodded her head. 'Why didn't you call me?'

'I was with Ed. It really wasn't a drama. It was just me being clumsy.'

The two of them walked through the house to the kitchen. Owen sat down while Kitty began to clear the table.

'Sit down,' Owen said, standing straight back up. 'I'll do that.'

He tried to wrest a teapot from Kitty, but she pulled it away. 'I'm fine,' she snapped.

'OK, I'm just trying to help.'

'Sorry,' Kitty said. 'I've not been feeling myself the last few days.'

'Who was that woman at the door?' Owen asked.

'Abigail Vaughan. She works for the Trust.'

Owen asked Kitty if she intended to organise another auction. 'It was good fun, the last one.'

'Good fun?' Kitty's expression hardened. 'It wasn't supposed to be good fun. Do you have any idea how difficult it is for some of these people to reintegrate?'

'OK. I'm sorry.' Owen half laughed and raised his hands in a pacifying gesture. 'It wasn't fun at all.'

'I don't remember you contributing any money.'

Owen sighed heavily. 'Why don't you sit down?'

'I haven't got time,' Kitty said. 'Everyone will be here soon.'

'How can I help? Shall I make some tea?'

'No. I'll do that in a bit.'

Owen suggested they cancel that afternoon's get-to-gether. He didn't understand why Kitty had taken it upon herself to host a meeting about the proposed regeneration of the estate.

'I can't cancel now; it's too late', Kitty said. 'Anyway, I promised Val.'

Kitty walked out of the kitchen and went to the adjoining larder. Propped up against a vase on the table, Owen spotted an invitation to a party. *Max & Emma request the pleasure of your company at their summer party on Saturday, August 29th.'* This would be the third year the Crossleys had hosted a summer party. In previous years residents of the estate with a view of the park had watched events from their balconies. Each whoop emanating from the open-air dance floor was countered with a succession of jeers and the occasional hurled bottle of water. Last year Jacquie and the kids had been kept up most of the night; the incessant four-to-the-floor beat infiltrated every part of their flat.

Owen picked the invitation up and used the corner to pick out some dirt from behind his thumbnail.

'Do you mind not doing that, please?' Kitty walked back into the kitchen, holding a plate of biscuits.

Owen placed the invite back down on the table. 'Are you going to go this year?'

'What do you think?'

'Apparently, it was quite lively last year… I bet the food is good.'

'Who cares? I wouldn't be seen dead at one of those things.'

There was a knock at Kitty's front door. 'Shit. People are starting to arrive.' Kitty sounded flustered. 'Where's the tea?'

'When they talk about a right to return,' Kitty said, 'it means nothing more than the rights of those who can afford the new rents. The council and developers will refer to affordable housing, but who can afford it? No one on a low income, that's for sure. I read an article about a recently renovated estate in Westminster. To afford the rent in one of the new flats, you would... you would need...'

Kitty faltered. Her sentence trailed off into silence. Jacquie looked over at Owen, who shrugged his shoulders.

'Are you OK, Kitty?' Val said.

Kitty looked worried as she turned to face Val. For a while now, she had sensed something wasn't right – the burned bread, the forgotten names. The recent fall, in particular, had unsettled her. It happened outside the house. Kitty was sure that she must have tripped over a broken paving stone, but when she went back to confirm this, she couldn't see anything which might have caused a fall. Enough incidents had occurred, though, to warrant a trip to the GP. Her doctor simply confirmed what Ed had been insisting all along. Episodes such as the fall, forgotten names and dates, they were all part of the ageing process. It was mostly unavoidable. Kitty, however, was sure something wasn't right. She couldn't corral the words to adequately describe how she felt. She was just aware of a fug that sometimes descended and obscured lucid thoughts.

The day after she visited the doctor, Kitty had been shopping in Hampstead, an area she knew well. She was walking down the high street checking the details of a receipt, but when she looked up she didn't recognise her surroundings. It was like she had been transported to another city. Nothing was familiar. She looked around for a landmark which she might recognise, but everything looked alien. Feeling panicked and scared, Kitty walked into a café and sat down at one of the tables.

A map of ancient Greece hung on the wall of the café. Instead of looking outside, Kitty concentrated on the map. She recited the names of places she recognised. For a minute or so, Kitty stared intently at the map and tried to remember stories associated with these regions. There was Sparta and the legend of child abandonment. Kitty remembered crying as a child when she first learned how infants perceived as not strong enough to be of use to the state were left in the wild to die. She recalled Samos as the place where Epicurus was born. As a student, she remembered liking the idea that Epicureanism was not about excess or physical pleasure but about achieving freedom from fear and anxiety by pursuing modest pleasures. There was Corinth, Lampsacus, Delphi; Kitty managed to retrieve stories and legends associated with all these places. The exercise re-focused her mind. When she finally looked out of the window, the buildings had once again assumed their familiar appearance. Any confusion had been lifted and replaced with a clarity of thought which felt normal. Everything came sharply back into focus. When Kitty told Ed about her misgivings, he upbraided her for going against the evidence. 'Your blood test was clear,' he said. 'The doctor told you it was nothing to worry about.'

'Have you all seen this?' Val held up a computer print-out. 'It says here that the council will be transferring all of their stock to Oak Grove Homes.' Val passed the printout to Estelle from the Beveridge flats. 'You know what that means, don't you?' Val continued. She looked at the faces around the kitchen table. Jacquie stared at her hands, which were gripping a cup of tea. 'It means,' Val continued, 'that we will lose all the protections that are baked into our current agreements.'

'Like what?' Owen asked.

'For starters, our tenancies will go from being secure to

assured. That means we'll have fewer rights; they'll be able to evict us more easily. Our rent might increase. It could also mean that we might lose any rights to pass on our flats to our kids. Will we still have a right to buy? I don't know. Anything could happen.'

'It says here,' Estelle said, 'that if tenants don't want a housing association flat in the new development, they will be given the option of being rehoused in a council-owned property elsewhere.'

'They want to get rid of all the secure tenants,' Val said. 'Think about it. Suppose our tenancy agreement does remain the same; we could move into one of the new flats and buy it under the right to buy. That's profit they're missing out on.'

'What do we do?'

Val looked over at Kitty, who gave an encouraging smile. Whatever had struck her earlier seemed to have passed. Like the other day in Hampstead, any feelings of bewilderment disappeared as quickly they had arrived.

'We need to form an independent residents' group,' Val said. 'Get everyone involved. These people are snakes, trust me. We can't believe a word they say. Have a look at the article.' Estelle passed the printout to Randall. 'Read that bit.' Val pointed to a section highlighted with a neon marker pen.

The piece included an interview with Lisa McFarlane, the council's regeneration officer. In the article, she described how two of the buildings on the Bevan Estate had *profound structural flaws* and would need to be demolished.

'What the... they didn't say anything at the open evening about structural problems.' Randall passed the article back to Estelle.

'See what I mean?' Val said. 'We can't trust them. Kitty, tell them about that bloke you've been chatting to.'

Kitty explained how a friend of hers had introduced her to an architect called Lucian Morrow. Lucian had recently been advising a campaign group from Brent, who opposed the demolition of their estate.

'He has helped them produce design options,' Kitty said, 'and ways of subsidising them. Lucian has lots of experience. He knows what to look out for and understands all the jargon.'

'I think we need to get someone like this involved,' Val interrupted Kitty. 'Someone who has nothing to do with the council.'

Kitty was impressed by Val's knowledge and her natural leadership skills. She seemed to have effortlessly taken on the role of spokesperson for residents of the estate. Kitty thought Jacquie might have assumed this mantle. Surprisingly, though, she didn't seem to be as motivated as Val, who had been galvanised into action by the threat of the flats being demolished. Kitty mostly liked to make herself scarce when Val came to clean. But, increasingly, the two of them would discuss the council's plans for regeneration once Val had finished work. Val had evidently been researching the subject and would bombard Kitty with facts and statistics regarding the impact of estate renewal, population displacement or the history of council housing.

'If we don't get busy,' Val continued, 'we're all going to end up getting rehoused somewhere at the end of the Edgware Road.'

'She won't,' Randall whispered to Estelle, motioning towards Kitty.

'That's right,' Kitty said, before adding, 'I also recently discovered that one of the Hand & Hyle Property Group's principal shareholders is Delta Capital Management. The CIO of Delta is Nicholas Rijkens.'

'You're kidding?' Owen said.

'Who is Nicholas... whatever his name is?' Jacquie asked.

'He lives in the house next door,' Owen said, looking at Jacquie. There was a small, bruised lump just above her left eye.

'No way.' Val spat as she spoke.

'I couldn't believe it either,' Kitty said. 'But I checked on Hand & Hyle's website, and it's true. The man is a devouring worm.'

'We need to get organised,' Val said. 'I'll start speaking to other residents. I don't think half of them have got a clue what's going on.'

'I'll speak to Lucian Morrow,' Kitty said, 'and we can arrange an independent meeting somewhere.'

'Why do you care so much?' Randall leaned back in his chair and looked towards Kitty. 'What difference does any of this make to you?'

'I care about inequality,' Kitty said. 'Something as important as housing shouldn't be left to the market. The market doesn't care about tenants and residents. It doesn't want to deliver properly affordable housing, and it will do everything it can to avoid doing so.'

'You're a socialist?' Randall said.

'Yes. I am.'

Randall looked around the room and laughed. 'You don't look much like a socialist.'

'Who says you can't live in a big house and have opinions about social justice?'

'It just seems a bit... hypocritical,' Randall said. 'You're obviously minted.'

'All I want to do is help,' Kitty said. 'As long as private capital is given free rein, the housing crisis is only going to get worse. I think it's important to make a stand.'

'Have you noticed how everything is in a crisis?' Val said. 'The refugee crisis, the NHS crisis, the crisis in our schools… the financial crisis. I think scaring the shit out of everyone is just a way of pushing through unpopular laws.'

'To be honest,' Jacquie said, 'I think we all sound a bit paranoid. It's impossible that every developer and council official is crooked. There must be untold examples of successful redevelopment projects. What was that mate of yours called?' Jacquie looked at Owen. 'I forget his name. Lives on that estate off the Essex Road.'

'Do you mean Fabio?'

'Yeah. Look what happened to him. His block was knocked down because of safety concerns. The developers built new properties before knocking down the old ones. No one had to leave the estate. And no one lost their flat. Owen's pal ended up with a bigger place than he had before… and a view of the canal to boot.'

'Good for him.' Val pursed her lips as she eyed Jacquie. 'Thing is, we've already been told that we'll have to move out while they renovate.'

After the meeting had finished, Jacquie took Owen to one side.

'Listen, I need some money. You haven't given me anything for nearly a month.'

Owen reached into his pocket and pulled out the envelope of cash Tony had given him. He counted out three hundred and forty pounds and handed it to Jacquie.

'Here, take this. I'll give you some more after the weekend.'

'OK… thanks.' Jacquie put the money into her pocket. 'But you can't keep being so sporadic with payments. It's not fair. I had to tell Harley that he couldn't carry on with his kung fu.'

'Can't you pay it out of what I just gave you?'

'I will now. But how was I supposed to know you were going to give me money this afternoon?'

'I'm sorry,' Owen said, running his fingers through his hair.

'Any more thoughts about the flat?'

Owen clasped the bridge of his nose between his thumb and forefinger and shut his eyes.

'Jesus, Owen,' Jacquie said, 'you can't keep on burying your head in the sand.'

'I'll make a decision soon. I promise. I've had a bad day. Can we talk about this after the weekend?'

'OK. But we need to get this sorted.'

Owen turned around and forlornly started to walk back down the path that ran by the side of Kitty's house.

Jacquie called after him. 'Hey. I didn't say thanks for looking after the kids the other night.'

'Yeah, no problem,' Owen said. 'I meant to ask you, what happened to your head?'

Jacquie instinctively raised her hand to a lump on her brow ridge. She winced as she pressed the protrusion with her finger. 'I dropped my phone in the toilets. I smacked my head on a door handle as I bent down to pick it up.'

Jacquie tried not to smile as she recalled banging her head against the steel balustrade of the balcony while Spencer fucked her from behind. She had felt transported as she looked out over the city. Absolved of all cynicism, guilt and regret, the pursuit of pleasure became paramount. Just for a moment, she had wished to exist in a purely physical realm and pay no heed to any psychological process. She wanted to attain a state where her brain's only function was to flood her senses with dopamine. She didn't care who Spencer was, what he did or what he said. She had just wanted to use his physicality. Jacquie didn't even know if it was possible to feel that way about someone you shared your life with. It certainly hadn't been with Owen. Although, at some point in the distant past, it must have once been like that. After all, there was a time, before kids, before shared bills, before compromise, before total and utter familiarity, when they couldn't keep their hands off each other. It was primal. Like animals, they would do it anywhere and everywhere. But this phase hadn't lasted long. They subsequently spent the rest of their relationship mourning its disappearance and blaming each other for anything and everything.

Owen never forgave Jacquie for not remaining besotted with him. She never forgave him for refusing to change. Owen hated how much Jacquie had changed. Jacquie resented Owen for being so unambitious. Owen hated it that she would give him a hard time for having a good time in Reykjavik, Ibiza, Amsterdam, Melbourne or anywhere else his work had taken him. Jacquie had never forgiven Owen for peeing in her wardrobe while drunk. Owen had never been able to forget the moment Jacquie did a shit while giving birth. He thought about it every time they tried to have sex. Ultimately, they both resented each other for duping the other into remaining in a loveless relationship. Both had expected one thing, but they both got another.

Chapter 20

July 2015

'Has anyone seen Daisy?' Max asked. He continued to look in the mirror as a make-up assistant fussed with his hair.

'You've got more hope of winning an Emmy than you have of persuading Daisy to participate.' Emma was sitting in a chair behind Max, looking into his mirror.

'That's a weird analogy.' Max glowered at his wife. 'We got nominated for the last series.'

Emma rolled her eyes. 'Exactly. You're in with a chance. But it's slim.'

Hector put his head around the door. He asked Emma if she knew what time he would be needed.

'Hector, Hector,' Max called to his son. 'Could you do me a favour, please?'

Hector sighed elaborately. 'What?'

'Could you go upstairs and see if you can find Daisy.'

'Do I have to?'

'I wouldn't have asked otherwise.'

'I'll send her a message.'

'No. Put your flipping iPad down for one minute and go and see if your sister is upstairs.'

'She's probably with her boyfriend,' Jamie said, without looking up from his phone.

'Boyfriend?'

'Yeah. I heard Daisy and Ziggy talking about him the other day.'

'Did you know anything about this?'

Emma looked up from the magazine she was reading. 'Know about what?'

'Daisy's new boyfriend.' Max shut his eyes as the assistant sprayed his hair.

'Why would I know?' Emma said. 'No one tells me anything.'

'I think he's much older than her too,' Jamie said, still looking down at his phone.

'Really?' Emma said. 'That's good. Maybe she'll grow up a bit.'

'Hi, Max. Yeah. So… I thought it might be good if we make this section, like, really organic. You know? It will just be about you guys chilling at home, kicking around some ideas for the party. Perhaps you could have a chat about the menu or the music. Whatever takes your fancy. Have some fun with it. Let's give the viewers an insight into the real you. Sound cool?'

Max distractedly nodded at Scooter, the director of his TV show. Having shot a few episodes in California the previous month, the crew had arrived in England the day before. Although the Crossleys' summer get-together was not for a couple of months, the current episodes were being shot as if they were happening the week of the party.

While everyone prepared for the next shot, Max and Emma took their coffees into the garden.

'Have you noticed how Jamie seems out of sorts again?' Emma said.

'He seems OK to me.'

'Maybe we should organise some online sessions with his therapist. It might do him good to speak to someone.'

When Max flew back to London at the end of the previous year, he finally got around to talking to Jamie about his online proclivities. He had no idea how bad Jamie's X-rated obsession had become. Max had hoped a bit of laddish banter, some candid admissions about his own teenage sexual exploits and an empathetic ruffle of his son's hair would set him straight. He was unprepared for the revelations which followed. Jamie wasn't just addicted to pornography; he particularly liked violent pornography. Humiliation, strangulation, coercion; all nouns which regularly featured in Jamie's search history. Max was out of his depth. He had no idea how to respond as Jamie unleashed a slew of disturbing revelations. His relationship with Pink had fallen apart because he found it hard to perform unless she agreed to enact violent scenes from the films he felt compelled to watch. Max was shocked as Jamie explained how he wanted to choke his girlfriend during sex. He agitatedly bit the skin around his nails until they were bleeding while Jamie described how he became aroused when his girlfriend resisted his advances. Max couldn't believe it as Jamie charted his progress from what he described as vanilla porn to increasingly more hardcore films.

'Why didn't you tell me this earlier?' Max said.

Jamie shrugged his shoulders and looked down at the floor. 'Do you think I'm weird?'

Max rubbed his eyes with his fingers. 'Umm, look… It's… well, put it this way. It's not normal.'

Looking bloodless and ashen-faced, Max returned to the kitchen. 'How did it go?' Emma said. For a while, Max couldn't speak. Finally, he sat down opposite his wife but remained silent. The silence probably only lasted for about thirty seconds, but the drama of the hiatus ensured Emma braced herself for the bad news.

'Jesus Christ,' Max said, still slowly shaking his head. 'Our son has got some weird shit going on his head.'

'What do you mean?'

'He sounds like an aspiring Ted Bundy.'

When Max flew back out to LA, Jamie went with him. Regular sessions with a Beverley Hills therapist seemed to lift his spirits. But now they were back in London, his mood had slumped once again.

Back in the house, Daisy finally came downstairs. She was wearing a pair of Wayfarers, baggy grey tracksuit bottoms and a long pink T-shirt that read *If you don't want to fuck me baby, then baby fuck off.* Laurie, Max's assistant, greeted her in the hallway.

'Hi Daisy, I'm glad you could make it.' Daisy gave Laurie a crooked smile, her eyes glowing with disdain. 'Daisy, this is Scooter, the director. Can you spare a couple of minutes? Scooter would like to have a chat with you about this afternoon's shoot.'

Daisy wrinkled her nose. 'Scooter? Is that your real name?'

'It's a pseudonym. I use it for work.'

'You have a stage name for directing cookery programmes?'

'I do lots of other stuff too.'

'Like what?'

'I've done some cool ads, promos. A few music vids. This kind of thing is my bread and butter. Keeps the wolf from the door.'

'Is there such a thing as a cool ad?' Daisy said. 'Have you done any films?'

'No features yet. But I'm working on a script.'

Daisy poured herself a coffee and looked around the room as she took a first, tentative sip.

'What's it about?'

'It's erm… It's about a rent boy who gets caught up in an organ theft ring. It's like a comedy slash crime caper.'

Hiding behind the barrier of her dark glasses, Daisy seemed unimpressed. Scooter laughed nervously. Daisy liked the effect she was having on him. She enjoyed the way he stumbled and stuttered in his attempts to impress her. She had encountered it before with men of a certain age. Emma once told Daisy that being young and beautiful provided one with a premature insight into men's inherent and eternal weakness. 'They never grow up,' she said. 'And they always think with their pricks. For years the world has been run by little boys who just got older.'

Daisy started picking at some grapes in the fruit bowl. 'What did you want to talk to me about?'

'Yeah. So, this afternoon I want to shoot, like, a happy family scene. You know, with you, your brothers—'

'Are you joking? Happy families?' Daisy tossed a grape into her mouth.

Scooter looked apprehensive. 'I think we'll probably start in your dad's kitchen. See how that goes. I was wondering whether—'

'I'm not doing it.'

'Sorry?'

'I said… I'm not doing it.'

'But your dad said—'

'I couldn't give a toss what my dad said.'

Scooter looked confused. He opened his mouth to say something but thought better of it. 'Are you OK to wait here for one minute?'

Daisy shrugged her shoulders as Scooter went over to the other side of the room and talked to Laurie. She knew Laurie would try and persuade her to participate in whatever pathetic show of family unity her dad had conjured up.

Daisy gave Laurie a little wave when she looked up. She was relishing the prospect of refusing her entreaties. Through the window, Daisy spotted Max and Emma talking in the garden.

Daisy was able to gauge just how annoyed Laurie was by the speed with which she scuttled over.

'Scooter just told me that you don't want to take part in this afternoon's shoot.'

'I don't,' Daisy said.

'No one here will see it if that's what you're worried about. It's only going to be aired in the US. A bit of exposure like this could really open a few doors for you. We could set up some meetings. Right now, everyone loves celebrity offspring.'

'Is that right?' Daisy said.

'Yeah, of course. Are you crazy?'

'Well, since you put it like that…'

'Really? Oh, Daisy, you're a star. Phew!' Laurie jokingly wiped the sweat from her forehead. 'So, you'll do it, yeah?'

'No chance.' And with that, Daisy turned her back on Laurie and sauntered out of the room.

'Do you think my beard makes me look less chubby?' Max held a mirror up to his face and checked both sides of his profile. 'Ali from the network thinks I need to lose a bit more weight.'

'Oh, for Christ's sake,' Emma said. 'Don't lose any more weight. You look weird enough as it is with those teeth.'

'What's wrong with them?'

'They're luminous. I imagine they glow in the dark.'

'They don't look weird.' Max opened his mouth and looked at his teeth in the mirror. 'It's only when you get back here anyone ever mentions them. It's because everyone else's teeth are such a mess.' Max hated the way Emma tried to make him feel bad for showing an interest in his appearance. She didn't think it was very manly.

'You didn't say whether you liked my beard or not. What do you think?' Max jutted out his chin and rubbed both hands along either side of his jaw. 'I think it makes me look quite dignified.'

'Hmmm. I don't think you can be dignified and vain at the same time.'

'Oh, fuck off. You're so English.' Max turned around to see what was going on in the house.

'Look, there's Daisy.' Daisy was standing by the back door, talking to Hector. Max gestured for her to come and join them. Daisy looked up, sneered at her father, and continued talking to Hector.

'Give up,' Emma said. 'She's not going to do it.'

Max closed his eyes while one of the make-up girls sprayed extra foundation onto his face. 'Maybe if you and she hadn't had that—'

'Don't you dare.' Emma gave Max a reproving glare. 'Daisy's refusal to participate has nothing to do with our argument. The two of us made up. This latest debacle is entirely of your own making.'

Max shooed the make-up assistant away and wiped his eyes with a bit of tissue.

'Listen,' he hissed. 'I'm under a lot of pressure. The network never used to care. But ever since le fucking chef's pneumatic niece started working in his kitchen, they've been hassling me to get Daisy involved.'

'Well, I'm afraid it's your own stupid fault. If Daisy hadn't uncovered your latest tawdry affair, she probably would have agreed to be filmed. She was coming round to the idea.'

Max urgently pressed his finger to his lips. 'Could you lower your bloody voice, please? Do you want everyone to know?'

'They will do anyway when fuck face decides to sell her story.'

'She's not going to sell her story. She promised me she won't.'

'Oh great. She promised, did she? That makes me feel so much better.'

After Daisy discovered the naked photo of someone called Kimberley on her dad's phone, Max managed to convince his daughter that Karl was, in fact, a nickname of Fred, one of the assistant managers at Utopia. Fred was from Vermont and a committed supporter of senator Bernie Sanders. He was known around the office as Red Fred or Karl because, somewhat tenuously, Friedrich Engels co-authored *The Communist Manifesto* with Karl Marx. Max's justification was so far-fetched that Daisy felt compelled to give him the benefit of the doubt. She checked Fred's Facebook page, and although there was no mention of his various soubriquets, he was definitely excited at the prospect of Bernie Sanders running for president.

Finally, a candidate with a real progressive agenda he had written.

Max told Daisy that Karl (Fred) had forwarded the photo of Kimberley after some looney fan sent it into the office. He also confessed that both he and Fred thought the girl was quite attractive. Max believed this admission of his own fallibility might lend a veneer of credence to the bullshit.

'There's really no need to tell your mum,' he said, '… or the boys for that matter.'

Max's deceit was too fragile to last very long. While searching IMDb for the name of the music supervisor for the second series of *The Competitive Chef* (Danny Diamond thought it might have been someone he had once worked with), Daisy noticed someone called Kimberley Kidron credited as a make-up artist. With minimal effort, she managed to unearth a photograph of Kimberley online: Max's mendacity was revealed. Daisy told her Mum everything she knew about Kimberley and Max's elaborate excuse. Emma's phlegmatic reaction, however, horrified Daisy nearly as much as the discovery of her dad's affair.

She decided not to tell Hector and Jamie about their father's philandering and their mother's complicity. But, like a Damoclean sword, she suspended the threat over the heads of her parents.

'Alright, alright,' Max said. 'You've made your point.' He reached into a bowl and grabbed a handful of nuts and dried fruit, which he angrily stuffed into his mouth. 'What's all this Jamie was saying about an older man? Do you know anything about this?'

'As if she's going to tell me.'

While looking over at Daisy, who was still talking to Hector, Max reached for his phone and loaded Daisy's Instagram page. 'Keep an eye on her, will you.'

'What are you doing?'

'I'm going to see if I can find a picture of this guy.'

Max began to scroll through Daisy's photos. 'Blimey. Have you seen how many followers she's got? At least she seems to have stopped posting all that soft porn stuff. That's one thing, I suppose. I never did understand why she felt the need to constantly take off her clothes. It was so demeaning.'

'I think she would have argued the opposite,' Emma said. 'She saw it as being empowering and assertive.'

'Empowering and assertive my arse. More like self-absorbed and needy.'

Max stopped at a photograph of Daisy sitting cross-legged on her bed. She was holding up a T-shirt. On the floor next to the bed, Max spotted a pair of white patterned Converse. He enlarged the photo so he could read the slogan on the shirt.

'What does RFTS mean?' Max held the phone up to Emma. Emma squinted her eyes and moved Max's hand out of the way.

'I haven't a clue. It must be some kind of acronym.'

'What about those trainers? Have you ever seen her wear those?'

'They're not hers,' Emma said. 'Look at the size of them.'

'I've never seen a design like that on a pair of shoes before. I quite like them,' Max said. 'Maybe they belong to this mysterious older man.'

'The only *older man* I know who would wear shoes like that... is you.'

Max saw Daisy coming towards them and quickly pulled his phone away from Emma and put it in his pocket.

'You wanted to see me?' Daisy sat down next to her mum. She was still wearing her sunglasses and was holding an unlit cigarette.

'Did I see you speaking to Scoobie just now?' Emma asked.

'Do you mean Scooter?'

'Scoobie, Scooter, whatever. I knew it was something stupid.'

'So?' Max said. 'Will you do it?'

Daisy laughed. 'No.'

'The network really wants you involved.' Like an adolescent boy whose voice was in the middle of breaking, Max occasionally oscillated between high-pitched and a standard register when anxious. 'I honestly think... you know that they might be considering some kind of... spin-off show.'

'For me?'

'Yes... possibly.'

Emma turned her head towards Max and stared at him, open-mouthed.

'The answer is still no.' Daisy sucked the tip of her thumb.

It was sore from rubbing the flint barrel of her Clipper. She shook the lighter and tried again; a steady flame finally appeared. Daisy lit her cigarette. She pulled a bit of tobacco from her tongue and spat it on the floor next to her dad.

'Daisy, please. Do it for me.'

'Why would I do anything for you?' Daisy took a scornful drag of her cigarette and blew out an insistent stream of smoke.

'Oh, stop being so bloody high and mighty,' Emma said. 'You're a bit of eye candy. Play the game, for God's sake. All you've got to do is smile and look slightly interested. And I'll tell you why you should do this: because this TV show enables you to swan around like the Queen of fucking Sheba. I mean, honestly, who the hell do you think you are?'

'I can't believe you.' Daisy looked stunned by Emma's outburst. 'How the hell are you OK with all of this? You're such a fraud.'

'I'm not a fraud, Daisy. I'm a pragmatist.'

Daisy muttered under her breath. 'Yeah, business has been booming since you joined the show.'

'Excuse me?' Emma said. 'I didn't quite catch that.'

'Can we all calm down a bit, please?' Max looked over his shoulder to make sure no one else was listening.

'Hold on, Max.' Emma raised her hand in a halting gesture. 'What did you mean by that last comment, Daisy?'

'Forget it.' Emma was notoriously combative if anyone dared suggest her business success was in any way attributable to Max.

'Spit it out, Daisy.'

Ignoring her mum's demands, Daisy looked off into the distance. As she puffed on her cigarette, she repeatedly tapped her foot on the floor.

'Now you listen to me, you sanctimonious little cow. I've worked bloody hard to build up my business. If there are any freeloaders in this family, it's you.'

'Do we have to do this now?' Max said, trying hard to keep his voice down. Emma and Daisy were sitting on either side of him. He grabbed both of their hands. 'We shouldn't be arguing amongst each other. We need to stick together. Protect the brand.'

'Oh my God. You're serious, aren't you?' Daisy pulled her hand away from Max's. She began to back away from her dad as if he was a poisonous snake. 'That's how you see us now, isn't it? We're a brand – a neat little package to help your career along. You make me sick. There is no brand, and as much as you wish we were, we're not the fucking Beckhams.'

Her head rattling with rage, Daisy stormed out of the house and ran into the street. Making sure no one else was nearby, she removed her sunglasses and wiped tears from her eyes. Terrified that, once she started crying, she wouldn't be able to stop, Daisy took a moment to compose herself. She hated the thought of anyone else seeing her that upset. Once she had calmed down she tried calling Ziggy, but there was no answer. Daisy leaned against the wall outside the Pritzkers' house and called Leila. Leila was useless, though. She only ever wanted to talk about herself, which she managed to do for a couple of minutes before Daisy was able to get a word in. Once she realised Daisy was upset, Leila made her excuses and quickly got off the phone. She had just walked into Agent Provocateur. It was her and her boyfriend's first sexiversary, and she wanted to buy some underwear for that evening. Daisy was annoyed with herself for even bothering to call her. Leila was good fun, but as a friend? Someone to rely on? She was hopeless.

Daisy rolled another cigarette and walked towards Kitty's house. Her bashed-up old Peugeot 406, which was nearly always caked in impossible-to-remove splats of parakeet shit, wasn't parked in the driveway. Daisy proceeded down the path which ran by the side of the house. Owen had told her never to come to the flat unannounced. She stood in front of the battered door of the basement flat, deciding whether to knock or not. Inside, she could hear a drumbeat looping around and around. She raised her hand to the door but then stopped herself from knocking. All she wanted to do was talk to someone. Would Owen want to listen, though? He always appeared irritated whenever discussions between the two of them veered into the intimate. If Daisy did try and voice personal worries, Owen would trivialise her concerns. He was always at pains to emphasise that her stresses couldn't possibly compete with anything he was going through. 'Just wait till you've got kids, debts and a failed relationship behind you,' he would say. 'Then you'll know what stress is.'

Daisy lifted her glasses and wiped her eyes again. Bracing herself, she took a deep breath and knocked hard on the door.

'Daisy! What are you doing here?' Dressed only in a pair of baggy grey shorts, Owen emerged squinting from the dark of the basement. His shorts were hanging low over his hips. The paunch which revealed itself whenever he sat down or wore jeans was less noticeable.

'Kitty's car isn't outside. I thought I'd surprise you. You don't seem to be very pleased to see me.'

Owen looked back into the flat: 'I'm kind of busy...'

'Too busy for a booty call?'

Owen looked back up the path to make sure no one had seen her come in. 'OK, then.' He stood to one side and held the door open.

'Don't sound too excited.'

Daisy had never been to Kitty's house before. She looked

around the room with a disapproving grimace. Owen rushed to the sofa and picked up some dirty clothes and a half-empty bottle of rum.

'Can I get you a drink?'

'What have you got?'

'Beer, water, coffee…' Owen looked at the bottle he was holding. 'Rum? There are some bottles of wine in the room next door.'

'I'm OK, thanks.' Daisy sat upright on the edge of the sofa, her hands resting on her knees. Owen watched her apprehensively as she looked around the room.

'Sorry, I've been swamped. I haven't had a chance to tidy up.' He walked over to the galley kitchen and grabbed himself a beer.

'It's very dark.'

'Maybe take your glasses off…'

Daisy removed her sunglasses and wiped the corner of her left eye with her wrist.

'Not that it makes much difference,' she said.

'Have you been crying?' Owen asked as he pulled up a chair opposite where Daisy was sitting.

'It's hay fever. I always get it this time of year.' Daisy noticed Owen's open laptop. 'What are you working on?'

Owen took a long swig of his drink. 'Just some ideas.'

'For RFTS? Can I hear?'

Owen coughed. 'There's nothing to hear yet,' he mumbled.

'You can do it in here? Don't you need to be somewhere a bit more…' Daisy searched for the right word. 'Professional?'

With a heavy heart, Owen glanced over at his open laptop. He was supposed to be working on a remix. The three horizontal lines of different-coloured blocks arranged on the screen were testament to the small amount of progress he had made. The same tired old drumbeat had been looping around for the last couple of hours. He felt totally uninspired. He didn't even like the track he was remixing. Apart from a vocal wash, like the banks of multi-layered voices in 'I'm Not In Love' and a synth arpeggio, he could not find any redeeming elements to work with. The process was tormenting him. There wasn't even a guaranteed fee. He was doing it on spec. Something he would never have done in the past. When he started out, he would sometimes get paid as much as five thousand pounds for a remix. He would often complete several of these a year. No one would have had the audacity to ask him to work for free. The industry just didn't work like that. And yet now, whether it was a remix for a major label or a pitch for a TV commercial, it was something he was frequently asked to do. Just the previous week, a production company had asked to license one of his tracks for nothing. The promise was always a favour for a favour. But favours were never reciprocated. The moment someone had a decent budget they chose the expensive option. Rarely the person they owed a favour to.

It had taken Owen a lifetime to learn the skills of his trade. Skills that were beyond anything any of these commissioners possessed. He found it all so unbelievably depressing. Was there any other industry where people would ask someone with a CV like his to work for free? Imagine asking a roofer if he could mend your roof for nothing? Or promising a dentist that if he fixed a tooth for free this time, you would use him again at an indeterminate point in the future when you finally had some money. Imagine asking any of these people who asked him to work for free to forego even one day's wages themselves. They would think you had lost your mind.

'When are you going to get your own place?' Daisy asked.

For a while it had been entirely plausible that Owen

should be staying at Kitty's *just until I get my shit together*. But he had been there for some time now.

'What's got into you? I thought you came around here to have sex.'

Although he still didn't want anyone to know about their relationship, the age difference no longer freaked him out. He wasn't doing anything wrong. Owen reasoned that, at his age, he might not have many more chances to have sex with someone like Daisy. Only a fool would turn down such an opportunity.

Daisy took her T-shirt off and sat back on the sofa. She wasn't wearing a bra. Her breasts were pert and cone-like with tips like a dunce's cap. Her nipples jutted out sharply. They reminded Owen of the jelly cola bottles he used to stuff his pockets with as a kid, their length almost exceeding the height of her breasts. Once Owen had removed Daisy's tracksuit bottoms, he slowly pulled down her pants, allowing himself plenty of time to absorb the image her slightly parted legs revealed. After all these years, he had still not managed to abandon the mindset of his adolescent self, the murderously horny young boy who would spend hours staring at photographs of naked women with legs akimbo. That boy could only have dreamed that one day he would be granted the privilege of sitting so close to the ultimate of destinations. Owen wished he could send a message back to his younger self. It would have prevented so much turmoil and despair. Even now, he would look on with wonder at the crumpled folds of flesh expertly concealing access to an array of glistening erogenous zones. Sometimes he just wanted to stare, to devotedly study each quarter and crevice.

'I am here, you know?' Daisy pulled Owen towards her and ran her fingers through his hair. 'It creeps me out when you just stare.'

Owen looked into Daisy's eyes. He could tell she was

searching for clarification – a signal of some sort. Something which would assure her that what they were about to do was not entirely devoid of meaning.

Daisy pulled herself up and kissed Owen on the lips. The tenderness of the kiss made him feel guilty. Since she had got back from LA, their relationship had consisted of a series of furtive moments. Snatched quickies at Daisy's house and rushed blow jobs in the park. They hadn't been anywhere or done anything together. Daisy hadn't received even a glimpse of the world she might have expected to enter when she first pursued Owen.

Owen kicked off his shorts and grabbed a condom from his wallet. Daisy tried to pull him towards her again. 'Hold on, hold on,' Owen said. 'It's not on yet.'

'Forget about it,' Daisy said.

'Really? Are you sure?'

'I don't mean that.' Daisy sounded flustered.

'Huh?'

'Can you just hold me for a bit?' Daisy's eyes were welling up with tears.

'Are you OK?' Owen asked.

'It's nothing. It's just the hay fever making my eyes water.'

'Have I done something wrong?'

'It doesn't matter.' Daisy pulled away from Owen and reached for her T-shirt. The clearly visible vertebrae of her spine protruded like crenellations as she twisted on the sofa. She put on her shirt and looked around on the floor for her knickers.

'Daisy, I'm confused. What's going on?' Daisy lay back on the sofa and pulled her pants up over her hips. Owen ruefully watched the little pubic strip she had allowed to grow back disappear behind the white cotton.

'I'm going to go.'

'Huh?' Owen quickly put his shorts on. Facing Daisy,

he placed his hands on her shoulders and crouched down slightly so he could look into her eyes.

'Look, I'm sorry if I did anything to upset you. I thought it was what you wanted.'

'It was. It is… Oh, I don't know.' In an effort to thwart the tears, Daisy had bitten her bottom lip so hard it was bleeding. She turned away from Owen and put her face in her hands. Behind her back, he shook his head despairingly.

Although he tried not to, he knew he sounded irritated as he said, 'What's got into you?' She didn't answer. 'Daisy…' More forcefully. 'Daisy!'

Owen grabbed Daisy by the shoulders as she put her hand on the latch and spun her around. With her hands still covering her face, she lurched towards him and buried her head beneath his collarbone. Her bony shoulders heaved as she began to cry. Like someone holding a baby for the first time, Owen nervously put one hand behind Daisy's head and tentatively patted her back with the other as she bawled into his chest. Sudden sharp intakes of breath and eerie pauses were followed by throaty sobs and rasping inhalations, some of which were so long and drawn out it sounded as if she might not catch her breath at all. This went on for at least three minutes. During that time, Owen, surprised by the ferocity of her outburst, did not attempt to speak, but just continued to gingerly rub Daisy's back. After a while, the wails of despair began to subside. Once again, he asked, 'What's going on?'

Daisy finally looked up. Her eyes were swollen and even puffier than before. Large salty tears mixed with snot had coalesced into rivulets of fluid that trickled down her face. Through the strands of saliva that hung from the corners of her mouth, Daisy blurted out: 'I fucking hate my parents.'

Owen gave a weary sigh. Apart from Harley, he tried to remember the last time anyone had told him they *fucking hate their parents.*

'I didn't tell you before, but my dad has definitely been having an affair. My mum knows about it, but she just…' Daisy sat back down on the sofa. She wiped her face on a tea towel that Owen handed her. She was still snivelling and sniffing. It seemed that at any moment she might start sobbing again. 'He doesn't care about us…' Sniff. Wipe of the nose, wipe of the eyes. 'The only thing he cares about is his career…' More sniffs. More wipes. 'Everyone fawns all over him…' A big, loud, honking blow of the nose. 'But he's just a fucking arsehole.'

Owen's mind began to wander as Daisy continued to offload. Sometimes he liked to think about how he would answer questions from an imaginary interview. While Daisy protested that *the bitch doesn't look much older than me* Owen envisaged a scenario. His new album has just come out, and he must do the rounds of press and promo.

'Owen, you've said in previous interviews how much you love David Bowie. Out of all his albums, could you pick a favourite one?'

'Wow, that's hard. It's a bit like asking a parent which child is their favourite. I like every record he made between Hunky Dory *and* Scary Monsters. *The first album I remember listening to was* Aladdin Sane. *My mum used to always have it on. By the time I was seven years old, I knew the lyrics to every song on that album. Even as a kid, I knew that it didn't sound like anything else. I couldn't put my finger on it at the time, but I was right. It's got such a dirty, decadent sound. I think Mike Garson's piano solo on the title track is one of my favourite moments in the history of recorded music.'*

'… at first, I felt sorry for my mum. But she seems to be OK with everything. I just don't get it. I could never be like that.'

'But if I had to pick a favourite album, it would be between Young Americans *and* Station to Station. *Either one of them*

could be my favourite record of all time by any artist. Young Americans *is so soulful, sexy and full of yearning. It nails that lush Philly sound; it sounds so authentic. Even though Bowie referred to it as the definitive plastic soul record, I think it's the real deal. I mean, just listen to Luther Vandross and Ava Cherry on BV's. You could hardly call that plastic soul. And to think most of those tracks were recorded only a few months after he had completed* Diamond Dogs. *It's such a departure from the sound of that album. I've always thought Bowie liked to place one song on each record which gave a glimpse of the direction he was heading in next. Like a signifier of what's to come. 'Queen Bitch' on* Hunky Dory *is an excellent example of that. It could easily be mistaken for a cut from* Ziggy Stardust. *On* Diamond Dogs *'1984' could probably have made it on to* Young Americans. *These songs almost provide the listener with a preview of the next album.*

'And now he expects us to smile for the camera and pretend nothing is wrong.'

But where Young Americans *is in thrall to the US,* Station to Station *ditches all of that. It's all about the European canon. It dispenses with anything that is rooted in the blues. It's about Neu! and Kraftwerk, Aleister Crowley and guitars that sound like trains. The DAM trio sounds like no one else on that album. I think that would probably be my—'*

'Are you even listening?'

'Yeah, of course I am. Look, I'm sorry your dad has been having an affair and all that. But it's not like he's the first person to play away from home. Maybe your mum's been having a bit on the side too. That would explain why she's OK with everything.'

Daisy's cheeks started to go red, and her jaw visibly tightened. 'Who knows what goes on in a marriage?' Owen continued. 'Not the kids, that's for sure. Long-term relationships are complicated. Besides, I don't think I'm able to judge someone else for sleeping with someone younger than him. Do you?'

With a splutter and a strange kind of bay, which sounded almost operatic, Daisy started to cry again.

Owen was angry that this drama of Wagnerian pitch had been about Daisy's parents. It was all very adolescent. Daisy was so undamaged it annoyed him. He couldn't be bothered to offer a consoling hug. He didn't even feel capable of pretending to care now.

'Come on, Daisy, stop crying. I'm sorry if what I said upset you. But, you know, you're a big girl now. It's the way of the world. People lie and cheat; they screw the wrong people. It's the way it goes. Everyone's at it. Now you know your parents are no different from anybody else. That must be hard, I suppose. I grew up knowing my old man was a cunt. And my kids will probably grow up thinking the same of me. Each new generation drips with the poison of the last.'

'Your kids won't hate you,' Daisy said, gasping between sobs.

'We all find a way of resenting our parents. Even if they've done nothing wrong.'

Daisy blew her nose into the tea towel, emitting the final few inelegant splutters of an emotional outburst. She looked terrible. Owen got up and poured her a glass of water.

'What are we doing?' Daisy said, finally composing herself.

'What do you mean? Now? I don't know. What do you want to do?'

'No. I mean us. What are we doing? What is… this?'

If Owen had been wondering why Daisy continued to hang around him, her performance that afternoon confirmed his suspicions. Daisy had Daddy issues. That much was certain. She was craving someone to fill the void her dad's emotional absence had created. Somewhat shamefully,

Owen concluded, therefore, that he must be a surrogate father figure. He understood this kind of psychology in some women who were attracted to older men. Often, they are attracted to successful men who are either a replacement for a beloved deceased father or, alternatively, a projection of an idealised version of the father they never had. Owen didn't think he ticked any of these boxes. He was hardly a fantasy father figure either. Perhaps none of these reasons was pertinent? Perhaps Daisy was simply attempting to get her own back on her dad for screwing a younger woman?

'What are we doing?' Owen repeated the question again as he searched for an answer. 'Well... it is what it is, I suppose. I like you, Daisy, but... I mean, you're half my age. You don't want to be wasting your time with someone like me. You're far too young and pretty for that.' Through tears and smudged tentacles of make-up, Daisy offered a forlorn smile. She looked like a prettier version of Courtney Love in her smack-addled nineties heyday.

'Do you want to end it?' She rubbed her nose with the back of her hand.

'I'm happy if you're happy.'

'Is that all you can say?'

'For fuck's sake, Daisy. What do you want me to say? I said I'm happy if you're happy.' His patience tested to the limit, Owen's eyes widened. 'If you've had enough, well... that's fine too. I told you not to expect anything from me. It's harsh, but I've got enough on my plate. You'll understand when you're a bit older.'

Daisy took a deep breath and patted her hair down. 'I should be going.'

'You don't have to.' Selfishly, Owen thought sex might still be a possibility.

'I'm sorry about all of that. I'm just feeling quite emotional. My dad's presence brings out the worst in me.'

'It's OK. I understand.'

Daisy laughed forlornly and looked at Owen as if to say, *really?*

'I'll see you around,' she said.

As she closed the door behind her, Owen stood hands on hips, shaking his head in disbelief.

'Not if I see you first,' he muttered, impotently. A toothless retort heard by no one but himself.

Chapter 21

Nicholas looked out of the window over St James's Square Garden. He was sitting in the members' lounge of his favourite club, waiting for Mark Delaney. The club claimed to be the world's first private members' wine club; it was filled with investors, hedge fund types and city boys who had taken time off from running their trading floors. There wasn't a pair of trainers in sight. A few of the more relaxed members had taken off their ties, but there was no need here for financiers to pretend that they were members of the creative industries.

Nicholas took a sip of his drink. He briefly shut his eyes and savoured the complex flavours of the Rioja as it caressed his tongue and eased down his throat. He couldn't remember the last time he had enjoyed a glass of wine without a sense of looming disaster. The previous year had been a stressful one. Although market turmoil had punished every type of strategy, events-driven funds in particular had been struggling to keep losses in check. Increasingly Nicholas had been looking at new opportunities, especially in distressed markets. This shift in focus had already made a difference. He had just posted his best bi-monthly return since February 2012.

A couple walked into the lounge and sat at a table on the far side of the room. The man looked over at Nicholas and smiled as the woman rummaged through her hand-bag. Nicholas smiled back. The man looked like he might be half Japanese; he had a youthful round face and dark eyes. For a moment, the two men held each other's gaze while the woman continued to pull various items out of her bag. Suddenly embarrassed that his look had lingered for too long, Nicholas turned away. It reminded him of an incident from the night before. He had woken up from a dream spooning his wife. He couldn't remember what he had been dreaming about but was in possession of a fierce erection which Jennifer could feel pressing into her back. Excitedly she had turned to face her husband, her hand gripping his penis so tightly it felt like she might snap it off. She whispered something in Nicholas' ear, but he had pretended to be asleep. 'Well, at least we know it's not a medical condition,' she had said. Thankfully nothing was mentioned the following morning. Having spent much of the previous year blaming his diminished libido on shrinking assets and failed acquisitions, he currently had no excuse as to why he was still incapable of satiating his wife's desires.

'I'm sorry I'm late. The traffic near Waterloo Bridge was appalling.' Delaney sat down at the table and picked up the bottle of wine. 'What's all this then? Afternoon drinking. Are you feeling OK?'

'I've had a good few weeks.'

'That makes a change.' Delaney poured some wine for himself. He sniffed the drink and nodded his head appreciatively before raising his glass towards Nicholas. 'What merger are we celebrating today then?'

'It's a failing French insurance company, actually.'

'Let the bad times roll... at least in France, anyway.' Delaney sat back in his upholstered armchair and crossed his legs. Nicholas noticed he was wearing pink mono-grammed cashmere socks.

'This wine is delicious,' Delaney said, holding the glass up to his nose. 'Am I right in thinking I can smell... strawberries?'

Nicholas nodded his head. 'Yes, well done. It's quite common with a traditional Rioja.'

Delaney took another sip of wine and placed his glass on the table. 'We finally got permission to demolish that old school in Parsons Green.'

'That's good,' Nicholas said. 'Why did it take so long?'

'It's the same old story. Local activists getting het up about the lack of affordable housing.'

'What percentage did you agree on in the end?'

'Zero. Not a single unit. It was completely untenable.'

Nicholas made a disbelieving face. 'No, really, it was,' Delaney continued. 'The objectors bought an action for a judicial review. They argued that the decision to proceed with the development was unlawful because we hadn't publicly disclosed the viability assessment.'

'But it was dismissed?'

'Yes. But this whole viability assessment thing is becoming something of a cause célèbre. The press has jumped on it. Look at the amount of negative coverage that development in Stratford got. They were under a hell of a lot of pressure to publish the VA. The council issued a redacted version, but they forced the developers to publish the whole thing in the end.'

'Surely there's a breach of trust there?'

'You would have thought so, but apparently there's no breach of trust when a public authority fulfils its statutory obligations. But it sets a dangerous precedent. Take the Albion Park development. Initially, the council were looking at a target of thirty-five per cent affordable housing. That was never going to work for us. But if the tribunals start taking a view on a case-by-case basis, any objectors could start making life very difficult for us. And that goes for all these projects. We're not doing anything illegal; everyone is at it. But once the media gets involved…'

'No, I can see that.' Nicholas glanced over at the man at the other table. He was deep in conversation with the woman. 'How's everything going there?'

'With Albion Park? We're experiencing a few difficulties. But nothing out of the ordinary. Luckily for us, so many of the residents have short-term tenancies. Still, it takes more than a couple of meetings to convince people to give up their homes. But we've got a couple of residents helping us out now. It's always good to have a people's champion – someone the residents trust. There'll also be plenty of meetings, forms to fill out, lots of opportunities for residents to feel like their opinions matter. At this stage, the objectors are a minority. Most of the residents can't wait for the flats to be demolished. Having said that, one of your neighbours is causing a bit of trouble.'

'Really?'

'She's an older woman, lives in one of the houses. Alex told me her name…'

Nicholas sat back in his chair. He pursed his lips and blew a silent whistle. 'Let me guess,' he said. 'Is her name Katherine Hutton? Calls herself Kitty.'

'Yes, that's it.' Delaney said. 'Kitty. I take it she has a bit of form?'

'She's a professional pain in the arse. Kitty has lived around the park longer than anyone. She rails against change of any kind. She's one of those people who blames everything on gentrification. As if it's something new.'

'Could she be a problem?'

'Possibly. She hates me enough, that's for certain.'

'Does she even know you're involved?'

'I didn't think so. But word has got out. A couple of days

ago, someone painted a snake on our front gate. Well, I presume it was a snake. Jennifer thought it looked more like a worm.'

'A snake? That's not too bad. I've been called much worse. To be a developer is to be second only to bankers on the righteous left's list of evildoers.'

'As soon as we had the snake removed,' Nicholas continued, 'some other moron came along and graffitied on the gates.'

'What was it this time?'

'Fuck the developers – Money kills culture.'

Delaney gave a scornful laugh and repeated the slogan. 'Idiots,' he said. 'What's culture without money? Could any cultural institution survive without wealthy benefactors? They don't survive through government funding, that's for sure.'

'It wouldn't surprise me if Kitty was somehow behind it. She's full of platitudes about how the rich are destroying the soul of their communities. She believes the influx of money into Albion Park has ruined the area.'

'These people make me laugh,' Delaney said. 'They carry on as if it's a new thing. The lack of awareness is staggering. These changes don't happen overnight. It's a long process. And one that people like her are partly responsible for instigating. The people who used to live around the park would have said the same things about her. But we're going to have to think of a way of muzzling her before people start listening. Any ideas?'

'Believe me,' Nicholas said, 'if I knew how to shut Kitty up, I would have done so already.'

The Star pub had allowed the #savethebevanestate campaign group to use their upstairs room free of charge. Kathy from the Keynes flats knew the landlord and had asked for a favour. The turnout for the first meeting wasn't great. But there weren't that many tenants left who could be considered stakeholders. Over the last couple of weeks, Val and Estelle had been canvassing support among residents. Although many of them seemed receptive to the idea of the estate being redeveloped, there was a growing feeling that tenants were not being consulted on important issues.

Val got up from her seat and stood in front of the group. She began the meeting by reading out the results of a survey she and Estelle had carried out.

'Out of sixty-three residents we spoke to,' Val said, 'forty-two of them felt that current proposals are confusing and vague. While over thirty households said they were worried about housing becoming unaffordable.'

Val began reading from a sheet of paper containing notes she had prepared earlier with Kitty. 'Currently, there is no clarity regarding housing allocations, how tenants will be prioritised for rehousing or the types of tenancies on offer. We were not consulted before they commissioned designs. To me, this suggests that they're just going through the motions. We should be fully involved in all aspects of the process. We have the right to be key players in any decisions which affect our future.'

Randall was sitting behind Jacquie. As Val continued to address the group, he leaned forward and whispered in Jacquie's ear, 'Who's the bloke sitting with Kitty?'

'I think he's probably that architect Kitty mentioned at the last meeting,' Jacquie said.

After Val had finished her opening speech, Kitty stood up and introduced Lucian Morrow to the group. 'Lucian's firm,' Kitty continued, 'offer advice to residents, like all of you, who are being ignored by local councils during the regeneration process. Lucian has kindly come here tonight to provide us with some expertise and much-needed insider knowledge.'

Just as Lucian Morrow began to address the group, the meeting was interrupted by the arrival of Alex Burnett and Deepak Shah.

'I'm sorry we're late.' Alex Burnett raised his hand towards Lucian Morrow. 'Please carry on.' He and Deepak sat down at the edge of the room on two empty chairs.

Lucian Morrow continued his address: 'I believe that increasing housing capacity—'

'Sorry, Lucian,' Kitty said, 'do you mind holding it there for a moment?' She looked over towards Alex Burnett and Deepak Shah. 'This is a closed meeting.'

'Is it a problem if we just sit here and listen?' Alex asked.

'Yes, it is.' Val's default tone of voice was confrontational. 'If we wanted you here, we would have asked you to come.'

'There will be other opportunities,' Kitty said, sounding more conciliatory. 'But there is a reason we didn't invite any BRP representatives.'

Alex tried to convince Kitty and Val of the advantages of letting him and Deepak sit in on the meeting. 'There's really no need for us to be at loggerheads here,' he said.

'Another time,' Kitty said.

'Don't you think it's important that we try and work together? Now that we're here, it could be a good opportunity for us to answer any questions some of you might have.'

Alex looked out towards the group. He caught Jacquie's eye, but she quickly looked away. She already felt guilty for having told him about the meeting in the first place.

'We understand that some of you may feel concerned,' Alex continued. 'But I can assure you, nothing is going to happen without extensive and meaningful consultation. We want to make sure that all of you play your part in helping shape the proposals for the regeneration of the flats.'

One of the residents sitting at the back of the room spoke

up: 'Whose proposals will we be helping to shape? Ours or yours?'

'Ours.' Alex gestured to the room. 'All of ours. We want to work with you. We want to hear your feedback.'

With her hand cupped over her mouth, Val spoke into Kitty's ear. 'How the fuck did they know we were here?'

'Search me,' Kitty said.

Randall asked Alex, 'What's all this about Attlee and Beveridge House not being fit for purpose?'

'I don't think anyone actually said they weren't fit for purpose. But the buildings are beyond repair.'

'Same difference, isn't it?'

Alex looked towards his colleague to help him out.

'The repair bills for all three blocks', Deepak said, picking up where Alex had left off, 'have become so high that it makes no sense to refurbish them. It's easier and cheaper to demolish and rebuild.'

Lucian Morrow raised a hand and introduced himself. 'I'm afraid I don't believe anything is structurally wrong with any of the buildings. I've advised residents that in my opinion an independent surveyor would confirm existing problems are due to negligence and lack of maintenance.'

'That's simply not true,' Deepak said. 'We've had two structural surveys done. There are major issues involved here.'

'Such as?' Lucian asked.

'Apart from crumbling walls due to subsidence, a defective shared heating system and loose bricks in the hallways, the buildings are badly designed. They are environmentally unsustainable and poorly insulated.'

'You haven't really highlighted anything which could be considered a major structural issue,' Lucian said.

'You don't think crumbling walls are a major structural issue?' Alex tried to appear aggrieved on behalf of the tenants. 'Because I certainly do.'

'The loose bricks are mostly due to the high-powered water jets the council use when they occasionally decide to clean the buildings. It can easily be fixed.'

'What about exposed electrical wires? You don't think they're an accident waiting to happen?'

'Again, easy to fix,' Lucian said. 'Any existing danger, I believe, is simply due to negligence. Everything you have mentioned could be resolved through refurbishment. And as for any arguments around sustainability, it's common knowledge that demolition creates more environmental problems than it solves. If the aim is to create good-quality homes, rather than maximising profits, then refurbishment should be the starting point. I've studied all three blocks of flats and come up with some preliminary sketches.' Lucian opened his bag and pulled out a red cardboard folder.

Kitty rested her hand on his arm. 'Do we need to show them this yet?' she asked quietly. 'Why don't we carry on as planned and present our ideas to the residents first.'

Kitty turned around to Alex Burnett and Deepak Shah and asked them to leave. 'This is a meeting for residents,' she said. 'Neither of you was invited.'

'Remind me again how long you've lived on the estate for?' Alex said.

'I've lived in the area for over forty years,' Kitty replied.

'In the area? Does that mean you're not an actual stakeholder in the flats?'

'What does it matter whether she's a stakeholder or not?' Val asked. 'Kitty's a valuable member of our community.'

'We would like to get on with our meeting now,' Kitty said. 'I think you two should go.'

'Let them stay,' someone called out from the back. 'Let's hear what they've got to say.'

'I just think we need to decide on a plan of action… as a group.' Kitty looked towards Val. 'What do you think?'

'I agree. Let's carry on as planned. We can contact this lot when we're ready.'

'No, let them stay,' someone else shouted. This was followed by a small chorus of agreement coming from the back of the room.

A man stood up and asked Alex and Deepak if they could tell them where they would be rehoused while building work took place. 'And how long will it take?' he added.

'We are committed to helping all residents who will be decanted during regeneration,' Deepak said. 'Hopefully, everyone will be able to stay in the borough.'

'What do you mean, hopefully?'

The meeting carried on like this for a while; random voices unleashed a volley of questions and accusations. Who will pay our removal costs? Why can't we have a ballot? How much will a two-bedroom flat cost? You only care about shareholder value.

Georgi's wife, Mariya and another private rental tenant complained that no allowances were being made for people like them. 'Our kids are at the local school,' Mariya said. 'If we have to move out of the area, it will disrupt their education. All of their friends live around here.'

Jacquie thought about Julius. She wondered where he had gone or if he was even still alive. The flat was boarded up now. She dug her nails into the inside of her thigh. The shame made her feel nauseous. He had been bullied into leaving his flat because the landlord wanted to sell, and she hadn't done anything about it. Or at least she hadn't done enough. When the landlord said he would raise the rent if forced to make any changes, Jacquie had contacted Citizens Advice. Apparently, nothing he was doing was illegal. She tried speaking to environmental health services again, but they refused to intervene. Instead of pressing harder, Jacquie had relented. Where had Julius' children been? Why should he have become her responsibility?

'Of course we all want to live on a better estate.' Kathy from the Keynes flats got up from her seat. 'But at the moment, it feels like you're trying to hoodwink us with fancy brochures and hollow promises. You keep saying that you will listen to us, but you've made no real guarantees.'

'And that's exactly why we have set up a steering committee,' Alex said. 'To guarantee that all residents are fully engaged in decision making.'

Val and Kitty looked at each other, stunned by Alex's announcement. 'What's a steering committee?' Val asked.

'It's a formal group that works with the council and other stakeholders to ensure that residents' views are being heard.'

'And who's on this committee?' Val's lips compressed until they were barely visible.

'It's a mixture of residents and independent consultants. The group will be chaired by a resident from the Beveridge flats.'

'Who?'

'His name is Jason Carling. He will be responsible for representing residents at all council meetings.'

'I've never even heard of him,' Val said, looking over at Randall, who made a face suggesting the name was unfamiliar to him too. 'Who else is in this group?'

Jacquie felt her ears go hot. She looked over at Alex pleadingly, hoping that he might spare her the humiliation of announcing her role in the group.

'Jacquie Turner will be the secretary. She will oversee maintaining and organising any legal documents.'

Val looked at Jacquie and mouthed the words 'What the fuck?'

Randall leaned forward and whispered in Jacquie's ear, 'You kept that one quiet.'

'When was all this decided?' Estelle said.

'Anyone can put their name forward,' Alex said.

'How come none of us knew about it?' Estelle looked around at the other residents.

'It was organised by the Housing Department Team,' Deepak said. 'They have been advertising vacancies for a while. The group is looking for more members. There's currently an opening for a vice-chair and a media officer.'

'Media officer?' Val exclaimed.

'Who are the other members?' Estelle asked.

Alex proceeded to list the other five members of the group. This included two other residents, an architect who was also a member of the council's design review panel, a legal advisor who had worked with several local authorities on community-led development projects and someone called Alison Trigg, a principal consultant at We Hear You.

While Alex and Deepak continued to answer questions, Lucian Morrow leaned towards Kitty. 'I've had dealings with We Hear You before,' he said. 'They're notorious for helping councils sway public opinion. Their job is to convince tenants of the benefits of regeneration.'

Kitty looked at Lucian as if she had no idea who he was.

'This steering committee thing,' Lucian continued; 'it's a council-led vehicle. You must proceed with your own group...'

Kitty's eyes glazed over as she stared blankly at Lucian. It was as if all thoughts had been sucked from her mind. Val came and sat down next to Lucian. He repeated what he had just told Kitty.

'Kitty, did you hear that?' Val said.

'She seems a bit under the weather,' Lucian whispered to Val.

'Kitty, are you OK?' Val put her hand on Kitty's shoulder.

'I'm fine,' Kitty said. She was now leaning forwards with her head in her hands. 'Please, just give me a minute.'

While all of this was going on, Alex and Deepak were still answering questions about the steering committee.

'Can there be more than one steering group?' someone asked.

'Technically, there can be as many as you like,' Alex said. 'This meeting today is a group in its own right. So, already there is a residents' steering group and a campaign group. However, the Bevan Estate Regeneration Partners will only recognise the steering committee as a formal consultation group. If you really want to work with the council to help shape plans for the estate, this committee will be the best agency. I promise you that we are committed to working collaboratively with residents to ensure that you are at the heart of all decisions. One thing I would say though,' Alex continued. 'Please be wary of activists and campaigners who accuse the likes of Deepak and me of profiteering and ignoring the rights of residents. There is an ideological agenda at play here. And one that does not have your best interests at heart.'

Chapter 22

August 2015

As we get older and progress through life, we leave versions of ourselves behind. For Owen, many of these earlier incarnations of himself were scattered around Albion Park. They hung from trees and clung to walls like earthbound spirits stuck between planes of existence. As he walked through the park, Owen could spot his infant self, lying on a rug, having his nappy changed by his mum. On the lawn opposite the entrance to Kitty's garden, he could see himself as a toddler learning to walk, each step greeted with a round of applause by a host of onlookers. On the incline which leads down from the rose garden to the tennis court, Owen imagined his ten-year-old self riding a bike with his eyes shut, seeing how far he could go without opening them. Walking past a maple tree, he relived the moment his bike hit one of the exposed roots, and he was catapulted over the handlebars; the impact of the landing pushed one of his central lower teeth through the flesh underneath his bottom lip. The enormous, towering piece of timber – which Owen forgot was called a tree when tripping on acid for the first time – still stood unwavering and proud. The park was a repository of memories; everywhere he looked, a different version of himself existed. And now, as he sat on the same bench that Gail McDonald had wanked him off on all those years ago, he watched as Dominik and Harley played the same games in the same places where he used to play.

For once, the park was a hive of activity. Georgi and a couple of other workmen were getting everything ready for the summer party. A large marquee had been erected, and smaller tents and yurts were scattered around the various lawns. Georgi spotted Owen sitting on the bench, watching the boys play football. He called out, but Owen was too preoccupied thinking about wasted opportunities. It wasn't until Dominik noticed his dad walking towards them that Owen emerged from his trance. Georgi sat down next to Owen and nudged him with his elbow.

'I thought musician like you would have good hearing.'

'What are you talking about?'

'I call you. Many times.'

'Sorry, I was miles away. What's up?'

'Do you want to do work for me?'

'Doing what?'

'Helping with party.'

Owen put his hands up to his face, and kept them there for a while before slowly dragging them back down. Georgi could see the lining inside his eyelids. They were pale pink and surrounded by swollen blood vessels.

'Three days' work,' Georgi said. 'Five hundred and fifty quids.'

'Five hundred and fifty?'

Owen needed the money, but he didn't know if he could face working for Georgi. It wasn't the prospect of doing manual work; that didn't bother him. It was just the thought of working as a subordinate for anyone around Albion Park.

'Cash,' Georgi said.

'What will I have to do?'

Georgi explained to Owen that his duties would involve helping to set up and dismantle the party. Owen scratched at his face. From where he was sitting, he could see the balcony of his flat. He remembered standing there one morning with Conrad watching the sun come up. They had been up all night celebrating their appearance on the cover of the *NME*. Quoting a line from the song by the Spinners, a caption below the photograph read '*You're bound to lose control when The Rubber Band start to jam*'. *Illmatic* was playing in the background. Owen could recall listening to the words of 'The World is Yours' and experiencing a rush of excitement as he anticipated the joys life was about to bestow on him. And now here he was, bereft of life's rewards, contemplating an offer to work as an odd-job man in the park. The same park he once couldn't wait to escape from.

'We have deal?'

'Yeah, I suppose so,' Owen said regretfully. 'When do you want me to start?'

'Tomorrow morning. Nine o'clock.'

Thankfully Daisy was in Majorca until the following week. She hadn't told Owen that she was going away. Relations between them had cooled since the episode in the basement. Owen had read an exchange between Daisy and a friend on Instagram. There was no way he would have agreed to work with Georgi if she had been in London.

'Come on, Dad. Get up. You go in goal, me and Dom will play one on one. I'm Arsenal.'

'Barcelona,' Dominik said.

Owen struggled to raise himself from the bench. He threw his sweatshirt down on top of Harley's hoodie, which was doubling up as a goalpost.

'Come on then, you two,' Owen said, trying to muster some enthusiasm. 'A pound for the first person to get it past me. We better hurry, though.' He breathed in deeply. The fresh scent of ozone hinted at the storm which was about to arrive. 'It looks like it's going to rain.'

Owen picked up the ball and threw it out to the two boys who were jostling for position. The ball rolled past Harley's left side. The two of them quickly turned and ran shoulder to shoulder, trying to barge each other out of the way. Harley was too fast and got to the ball first. Dominik quickly caught up with him and positioned himself between the ball and the goal. Harley tried to dazzle his opponent with a series of elaborate shimmies and step-overs. As he accelerated, Harley attempted to execute a Ronaldo chop, whereby the player in possession jumps at speed and changes direction by flicking the ball with the heel of his non-dominant foot. After he had jumped, instead of landing on the ground, Harley landed on top of the ball. The ball squirted out from underneath and threw Harley backwards with such force Owen could hear his son's head slam against the ground from twenty yards away. Dominik fell to his knees, laughing. Emulating the melodrama of the footballers he idolised, Harley convulsed and flipped like a suffocating fish. Once he realised his son was OK, Owen was also unable to contain his laughter.

'I think that trick needs a bit of finessing, don't you?' he said, in-between bouts of laughter.

'What the fuck are you laughing at, blood?' Harley snapped at Dominik.

'Oi, none of that,' Owen said, lifting Harley from the floor.

'Charming.'

Owen looked up to see Nicholas Rijkens emerge from between two bushes that straddled the path. He pointed at a small sign on the edge of the lawn which stipulated that no ball games were allowed. Owen brushed the grass off

Harley's back. He placed both hands on his son's shoulders and looked him in the eye. 'Are you OK?' Harley nodded and smiled at his dad.

'This is a private park,' Nicholas said. 'I'm going to have to ask you to leave.'

Ignoring the request, Owen retrieved the ball and walked back to the makeshift goalmouth.

'I'm sorry, did you hear what I said?'

Owen pulled a key out of his back pocket and waved it at Nicholas. Then, under his breath but loud enough for him to hear, Owen called Nicholas a wanker.

'Lovely. I see where the boy gets it from.'

'Excuse me?'

'Well, you know what they say. Manners only become important to children if they are important to their parents.'

Although Owen had never met Nicholas before, he knew who he was. He was Kitty's nemesis. *The morally derelict plutocrat*, as she once described him. Her *rapaciously acquisitive* neighbour who wanted to *privatise and displace*. Far from appearing to be the embodiment of a despicable wealthy elite, Owen was surprised at how unimposing Nicholas was. The way Kitty enjoyed describing him, he expected to at least be aware that he was in the presence of someone diabolical.

Nicholas cowered slightly as Owen narrowed his eyes and turned towards him. Then, with a dismissive kiss of his teeth, he turned to face Harley and Dominik.

'Right, you two.' Owen kicked the ball high into the air. 'Neither one of you has got it past me yet.'

Harley retrieved the ball and slowly dribbled it towards the goal. Every time Dominik tried to tackle him, he would deftly manoeuvre the ball just out of reach with the underside of his foot. He was a far more skilful player than his friend and enjoyed teasing him with an array of tricks, preferring to torment his opponent rather than attempt any meaningful shots on goal. Increasingly irritated by his tactics, Dominik finally dispossessed Harley with a lunging tackle. The follow-through of his foot pushed the ball about fifteen feet away from the two players. Dominik shoved Harley out of the way as they both scrambled for the ball. Then, without attempting to beat his opponent, Dominik hit a sizzler with his left foot. The ball eluded Owen's outstretched hand, whizzed over the path behind the goal, and landed in a bed of hydrangeas.

'Oh, well done.' Nicholas slowly clapped his hands. 'And that's exactly why we don't allow ball games on this lawn.'

'Are you still here?' Owen walked over to the flower bed. The ball had landed in the middle of the flowers and crushed some stems. Owen tried to lean far enough forward so he could retrieve the ball without causing any more damage.

'Look what you've done.' Nicholas was standing directly behind Owen as he attempted to reach the ball.

Owen leaned as far forward as he could go. One hand was placed on the soil between several flowers; the other hand reached into the flower bed. He looked like he was trying to pull off an extreme callisthenics manoeuvre as he extended his fingers even further. It was no use. He was going to have to walk on the flowers if he wanted to get the ball back.

'What the hell are you doing?' Nicholas remained standing immediately behind Owen.

Owen stood up and faced him. 'Could you just fuck off, please?' The insult was accompanied by a fit of giggles from the two boys. An imperceptible fleck of spit flew from Owen's mouth and landed somewhere on Nicholas' face. Attempting to amplify the incident, Nicholas slowly dragged the palm of his hand across his cheek and flicked away the imaginary globule of spit.

An eerie light had descended upon the park as clouds blocked out the sun. Like a canopy of bruises, the sky was swollen and purplish. A bloated drop of rain burst on Nicholas' forehead and dripped into his eye.

'Come on, Dad, let's go.' The raindrops became more insistent.

'Yes, off you go,' Nicholas said, with a dismissive flourish of his hand.

Owen visualised himself punching Nicholas in the face. He felt a quiver of excitement as he imagined Nicholas howling in pain as the force of his punch smashed the cartilage in his nose. He pictured blood seeping through the gaps in his fingers as Nicholas buried his injured face in his hands. God, he wanted to do it. Owen swallowed hard as he contemplated hitting him. He opened his fist and stretched out his fingers.

'Dad,' Harley said.

Owen barged into Nicholas, his shoulder slamming into his clavicle. 'Get out of my way.' Nicholas exaggeratedly clutched his shoulder as Owen stomped across the flower bed, crushing the hydrangeas and the begonias planted next to them.

'Dad.' Harley was running backwards, looking at his dad. 'Come *on*.' Owen picked up the ball and ran after his son.

'What do you think you're doing? You can't just let yourself in.'

'Sorry,' Owen said. 'I didn't think you'd be here.'

Owen and Harley had just walked into the flat, their clothes sagging from the rain. Jacquie hadn't been awake for long. She was standing in the kitchen dressed only in a pair of pants and a kimono-inspired silk robe. Owen felt a nostalgic spasm of lust. A backlight irradiated Jacquie's naked figure, her curves visible through the flimsy fabric of her robe. Her tits had got bigger with age, Owen thought. They used to be so much smaller. Jacquie, repulsed by her ex's lecherous stare, covered her mid-section and turned away.

'Wait there. I'll go and put some clothes on.' Jacquie walked out of the room and went upstairs.

'How come you're not at work?' Owen called out after her.

Jacquie had taken the afternoon off. The ongoing saga with the flats was stressing her out. Earlier that week, the steering committee had convened for their first proper meeting. The lack of representatives from the estate had been shocking. Jacquie wasn't surprised when she received a text from Val after the meeting accusing her of being a *traitor & a wrong 'un*. The only thing that did surprise her was that she hadn't got a message from Kitty as well, perhaps denouncing her as a quisling. As if all of that wasn't enough, Alex Burnett had been in contact. He wanted Jacquie to know that it would be hard to convince Oak Grove Housing to allocate her a flat if she didn't hurry up and get her name on the tenancy.

While Harley went upstairs to get changed, Owen grabbed a towel from the laundry basket and dried himself off. He walked into the front room and looked out at the premature twilight. Water was leaking through the window frames. It had gathered in elongated puddles on the interior windowsill and was dripping onto the floor. Owen got on his knees and began mopping up the water with the towel. He noticed a dent at the base of the wall next to the window. The legacy of a tantrum thrown by an angry and confused young man.

It was soon after his mum had first been diagnosed with cancer. She was just about to start treatment and had reached out to Owen's dad, hoping that he might help with their son.

At the time, Owen was probably only a bit younger than Harley was now. He was furious that his mum had contacted Godfrey. Owen was adamant that he didn't want to see his dad. One night, after overhearing his parents arguing on the phone, he had gone into the front room and, in a fit of rage, smashed up a coffee table and made a hole in the wall. He hadn't seen his dad for nearly a year and a half. The last time they had seen each other, Godfrey had been drunk. In front of Owen and his new girlfriend (who Owen had never met before and who was probably only about twenty-four), Godfrey had criticised Janet for allowing his son to become what he referred to as a *maama man*. When Owen burst into tears, his dad told him to *stop being such a sissy*. Ashleigh, Godfrey's young girlfriend, defended Owen, only to have a bowl of cabbage salad emptied over her head. After she witnessed her son's reaction, Janet promised she would never contact his dad again. The next time Owen saw him was at his mum's funeral. He never saw him again after that.

Watching everyone else becoming so vexed over discussions about the potential redevelopment of the estate, Owen had wondered why he remained so indifferent to the plans. While others became increasingly rattled at the prospect of demolition, he had been puzzled by his own lack of concern. As he sat on the floor, his hand rubbing the contours of the dent, all he could think about was how much he hated the place. Let them build luxury flats, he thought. He hoped they annihilated the whole fucking estate.

Jacquie walked back into the room. 'Are those windows leaking again?'

'Yeah. Could you get a bowl to catch the water?'

Jacquie went to the kitchen and got a large mixing bowl.

'You know, last time it started dripping through the floorboards and into the flat below. It beats me how anyone can argue that these flats don't need repairing.'

'Does anyone argue that?' Owen asked.

'Kitty's architect pal does. Speaking of Kitty, have you seen her recently? She's gone very quiet.'

'I saw her yesterday. She's acting weird at the moment.'

'What do you mean?'

'I don't know. She seems irritated by me most of the time.'

'You can hardly blame her. You have kind of outstayed your welcome.'

Owen got up from the floor and wiped his hands on his jeans. 'I've made a decision about the flat.'

'And?'

'I'll sign it over.'

'Really?' Jacquie clapped her hands together. She stood for a moment with her eyes closed, her hands cupped over her mouth. 'Oh, that's so good of you, O,' Jacquie said, finally pulling her hands away from her face.'

Owen couldn't remember the last time she had called him O. Touched by his own generosity, he could feel the pressure of tears beginning to form in his eyes.

'Thank you,' Jacquie said, smiling. 'Thank you so much.' She walked over to Owen and patted his shoulder with her hand.

Owen wasn't exactly sure how he had expected her to respond, but Jacquie's reaction, after the initial surprise, had seemed routine. It was like he was returning a long overdue favour. He thought perhaps a more physical response would have been appropriate. If Jacquie had prostrated herself like a Persian courtier and maybe kissed his feet, then he might have been happy. But the limp hand on his shoulder was a distinct anticlimax.

'I'll phone up the council tomorrow,' Owen said. 'Find out what needs to done. No point waiting around, I suppose.'

'You need to ask them for an assignment. Then we all have to sign a deed. After that, there shouldn't be any problems getting permission.'

'OK.' With his mouth turned down at the corners and his bottom lip jutting out, Owen slowly nodded his head. 'You've really looked into this, haven't you?'

'What did you expect me to do?' Jacquie said. 'I had to find out where we stood, didn't I?'

We. Why couldn't she just say I? Even after an act of such magnanimity, Jacquie insisted on using language which emphasised Owen's separateness from his own kids. Very quickly, the fuzzy feeling of benevolence gave way to anxious flutters of uncertainty.

Chapter 23

Simon Landes stood at the entrance of one of the large yurts designated as a chill-out area. He looked out despairingly from underneath the canvas. Parts of the roof were sagging under the weight of the rain. Pools of water had begun to gather around the edges.

Georgi was running between the marquee and the yurts, trying to keep everything from getting wet.

'Do we have any heavy-duty bags for the speakers?' Simon asked.

'Please. Let me do this. Then I go look at speakers.'

'Where's the guy that was helping you? What's his name again?'

'He's name is Owen. He's taking care of PA.'

Georgi was wearing a green waterproof army poncho and a pair of jungle combat boots. Streaks of mud were splattered across his face. Earlier on, he had slipped over while trying to secure a Delta Capital Management sign to the champagne bar.

'This is going to be a complete washout,' Simon said to no one in particular. 'Georgi, maybe your chap should move the PA to the marquee. Max's guys can set up in the big yurt. Do you know if his assistant has been onto the hire company? Where is Max anyway?'

'He is inside making film.' Georgi strained and groaned as he struggled under the weight of a fridge.

'The man is constantly being filmed,' Simon said. 'It must be exhausting.'

The walls of the yurt were covered in embroidered banners and handwoven kilim carpets. Lanterns and candles were dotted around the room. There was even a wood burner with a pile of logs stacked next to it. 'It looks like that wall rug is wet,' Simon said. 'There must be water coming in from the roof.'

Georgi walked over and patted the offending rug with his hand. He followed a trail of dampness up towards the roof, then got on a chair to take a closer look.

'The canvas has leak,' he said.

Simon stabbed at his eyes with his fingers. 'Is there anything you can do about it?'

'No. I have too much. You must phone hire company.'

'Laurie was supposed to have done that. Where the hell is she? I suppose I'll have to go and find her.'

Simon picked up his umbrella and ran towards the marquee; a collection of kidney-shaped puddles had formed on the gravel path alongside the tennis court. Without noticing them, Simon ran through one of the larger puddles. A pool of water splashed all over his trousers.

'There you are,' Simon said, entering the marquee. He shook his leg and angrily wiped at a damp patch around his groin. Laurie pointed at her handset, indicating that she was in the middle of a phone call.

While Laurie continued to talk on the phone, Simon inspected the tent to see if he could spot any more leaks. Strictly speaking, it wasn't even his party, but Simon had taken the prospect of poor weather personally. He didn't want guests to spend their entire evening crammed inside damp yurts, which looked like they belonged to a tribal leader from the Tatar confederation. The summer party was an opportunity to show off the community to outsiders. The park was the star. So many people were not even aware of its existence. Guests were invariably ultra-impressed when arriving for the first time. Simon received immense pleasure from watching guests milling about, marvelling at the array of hidden lawns, and jealously eyeing up the surrounding houses. He believed the park was one of London's best-kept secrets. Albeit a secret he loved to share with others.

'Sorry about that, Simon.' Laurie put her phone in her back pocket. 'We were trying to work out the logistics of release forms for tomorrow night.'

'Release forms? Oh, please don't tell me you intend to film it.'

'Yes, of course we are. It's going to be the highlight of the season finale.'

'What if it's raining?' Simon tugged at the hairs of his moustache. 'It will look dreadful.'

'Far from it. I think the prospect of the party perhaps being a total washout adds a bit of… jeopardy. You know, will the guests turn up? Is Max going to blow his top and start shouting at everyone?'

'Sounds like bloody awful TV to me.'

'Shall we leave that to Max and the producers to worry about?'

There was a pause in the conversation as Simon reflected on what Laurie had just told him. 'I'm a bit concerned that if it is a washout, we'll all be made to look rather foolish.'

Laurie emitted a huff of impatience. 'Max is not going to let that happen.' She reached for her phone and began typing out a message. 'Anyway, Simon, what can I do for you?'

'One of the yurts has a leaky roof. Someone needs to phone the hire company and get them to come and fix it. Also, if the weather stays like this, we'll need another two large tents. There simply won't be enough room for everyone.'

'Max has put up another marquee in his garden. There's also plenty of room in the house. I think we'll be fine. Now, if that's everything?'

'What about the leaky roof?'

Laurie had already started to make another call. She put her hand over the mouthpiece. 'Can you make sure that gets sorted?' Without waiting for an answer, Laurie returned to her call.

It was all so chaotic. Simon sensed arrangements for the party were playing second fiddle to Max's filming obligations. Admittedly, the weather had not been a problem in previous years, but generally everything had run a lot more smoothly. Emma had been in control of proceedings, whereas Laurie seemed to have been left in charge this year. Simon couldn't help feeling responsible for events in the park. As chairman of the park committee, an unsuccessful party would reflect poorly on him. He wondered whether he should go up to the Crossleys' house and speak with Max and Emma. He knew they were filming, but he couldn't just stand by and watch everything go wrong. He poked his head out of the marquee; the rain hadn't abated. Huge puddles had now formed on the grass. The lawns were looking oversaturated.

Just as he was about to make his way to the Crossleys', Simon's phone rang. It was Emma wanting to know if Georgi had any plumbing experience. She sounded panicked.

'I'm not sure,' Simon said. 'I think he can turn his hand to pretty much anything. Why. what's wrong?'

Emma explained that their basement was flooding. She told Simon that an emergency plumber had been called but was hoping Georgi might be able to stem the flow.

'OK. Let me go and find Georgi. I'll see what I can do.'

Simon opened his umbrella and made his way to the yurt where he last saw Georgi. 'Fucking hell,' he spat as he raced through the puddles and the water splashed up his leg again.

He had never seen rain as bad as this before in London. It had already been going on solidly for over twenty hours. Perhaps the party would have to be cancelled? Surely the Crossleys wouldn't want guests in the house if the basement was full of water. They'd better not be bloody filming, Simon thought. Something like this could affect house prices.

Georgi was no longer in the chill-out yurt. Simon rushed between a few of the other tents. Finally, he spotted him up a ladder, trying to secure lighting to one of the trees. The ladder had sunk into the earth and was leaning to one side. Georgi was standing on a single foot as he tried to reach the branches. The ladder started to tip even more. Georgi, however, seemed remarkably unconcerned at the prospect of falling from the ladder, which was at least eight feet high. The first time Georgi did any work for Simon, he fixed a leak on his roof. He had climbed up an unsupported ladder onto the roof of Simon's four-storey house in the pouring rain. Simon had seen him lean out of windows, hang off awnings, walk along window ledges. Most of the time, he couldn't bring himself to watch whatever it was Georgi was doing. Simon would turn away and pray that he wouldn't have to stand over his broken body.

'Can I have a word, please, Georgi?' Simon said as Georgi descended the ladder.

Georgi nodded his head, and the two of them ran for shelter in one of the yurts. 'I think the Crossleys have a bit of an emergency going on up at the house. I don't suppose you know much about plumbing, do you? I told Emma you probably did, considering you seem to know how to do most things.'

Georgi wiped some water from his brow and offered Simon a twitch of his head. Yes, he did have some plumbing experience. 'I believe the Crossleys' basement is starting to flood,' Simon continued. 'Would you be able to pop up there and see if you can help out?'

'Perhaps they need to pay for proper plumber,' Georgi said, his mouth becoming entangled in the alliteration.

Simon had to suppress a giggle. 'I think Emma has called one. They were hoping you could help out until he arrives.'

'Could you turn that bloody camera off for one second?'

A cameraman was standing at the top of the stairs filming Emma as she came up from the basement. 'I can see water pouring through the holes in the mortar,' Emma said, walking into the kitchen. 'Look how deep it is.' She pointed to the watermark on her wellies, which was about an inch or so above her ankles.

'This is an absolute disaster. Where's the fucking plumber?' Max said, spitting as he swore.

'She said she would get here as soon as she can. All the other plumbers I called were busy. We're probably not the only ones around here with a flooded basement.'

'What about Simon's guy? Where the hell is he?' Max slammed his foot against the door, cracking a panel in the process. 'Why does shit like this always happen to me?'

'Because you deserve it,' Daisy said, jumping down from the stool she had been sitting on.

'Excuse me?'

'You heard me.'

'How is that supposed to help, huh? Huh?'

Daisy held her middle finger aloft and walked out of the kitchen. Max followed her out of the room and screamed, 'I wish you'd stayed in Majorca, you, you… selfish bitch.'

'I think you need to calm down, Max,' Emma said. 'The

veins at the side of your head look like they're about to pop.'

Ashamed that the crew should be privy to the wretched state of his relationship with his daughter, Max sat down on the stool Daisy had just vacated. They used to be so close. Before he started spending most of his time in LA, Daisy had been a self-professed Daddy's girl. Although Max would never admit it, she had always been his favourite child. He couldn't bear the way she looked at him now. Her face betrayed a thousand shattered illusions. Disdain and contempt had taken the place of unbounded devotion.

Jamie walked into the kitchen, his thumbs twitching furiously as he played a game on his device. Capable of navigating his way around the house without taking his eyes off the screen, he felt no need to look up. 'There's someone at the back door for you, Mum.'

'That's probably Simon's guy. Could you let him in, please? Jamie. Jamie…'

'He can't hear you,' Max said, 'he's wearing his bloody headphones.'

'I think ground is so wet it moves much. Maybe falling rocks or soils break pipes. Look…' Georgi bent over, put his hand in the water and picked up bits of debris. 'See,' he said.

'What am I supposed to be looking at?' Emma asked.

'This' – Georgi pointed to some grit in his hand – 'is dirt from broken pipe.'

'Is that bad? How do we stop more water coming in?'

Georgi rolled his eyes. Every question and request landed with the weight of an unwelcome demand. 'First, we need to turn off water and flush toilets. Where is main valve?' Emma looked baffled. 'OK, no problem. I find it. Please, go flush toilets.'

The Crossleys' basement consisted of a bathroom, a

neglected games room, a utility room and a cellar full of all the crap a family accumulates over time. The point of entry appeared to be in the games room, but water was now spreading throughout the basement. While Georgi looked in the cellar for the main water valve to turn off, Emma went into the basement toilet to pull the chain.

'Oh my God! Fuck! Help! Oh shit…' The sight of black water pouring out of the toilet bowl, combined with the stench which accompanied it, caused Emma to instantaneously throw up. Instinctively she placed her hand over her mouth but could not contain the vomit, which forced its way through her fingers. Splats of faecal waste were being deposited on the toilet seat as the malignant liquid spilt onto the floor.

'Jesus Christ,' Emma said, gasping for air. Like a shapeless demon, more of the black water emerged from the plughole in the bath. A pressurised squealing sound could be heard coming from behind the wall.

Georgi stood at the entrance of the bathroom, his arm wrapped around his face. 'Leave,' he said to Emma. 'Get out here. Is dangerous.'

The potency of the stench made Emma feel dizzy. She stumbled and fell against the wall as she tried to leave the bathroom. Georgi grabbed her arm and pulled her out of the room. The moment Georgi shut the bathroom behind them, she promptly vomited once again.

'Oh my God,' Emma said, wiping her forearm across her mouth. 'That's so disgusting.' With a guttural heaving sound, Emma retched again. She leaned against the wall and spat onto the floor.

'Is very dangerous. Very toxic,' Georgi said.

Max opened the door at the top of the stairs. He was just about to ask what all the commotion was about before he recoiled at the stench, gagged and hurried back into the kitchen.

'We need trained plumber.' Georgi, as ever, remained unflustered.

Emma pulled her T-shirt over her face and asked Georgi to help her carry a mattress from the cellar. 'We might be able to stop the water from spreading elsewhere.' The two of them placed the mattress sideways on the ground next to the bathroom door. 'I don't understand how this could be happening,' Emma said.

'We need to leave now,' Georgi said. 'There is bad disease here.'

'We still haven't turned off the water.'

'Maybe main valve is outside. I go look.'

'Do you think they'll have to cancel the party?' Gary started to undo one of the dressing gown cords tying Jennifer's wrists to the bed frame.

'I'm not sure. Perhaps.' Jennifer winced as Gary struggled with a knot. 'The weather looks bad. If it carries on like this, it will be a total washout.'

Tanya emerged from the en-suite bathroom. She sat down on the bed next to Jennifer and began untying her other arm. Once released, Jennifer sat up and inspected the ligature marks on her wrist. They were brownish in colour and accompanied by a light red band on either side. 'That was too tight this time,' Jennifer said, massaging her wrist. 'My arm started to go numb. That can't be a good sign.'

'Yeah, sorry about that.' Gary looked sheepish as he examined the cord. 'I'll use a different knot next time.'

'Could you pass me that towel, please?' Tanya picked up a towel from the floor and handed it to Jennifer. 'I don't like this oil either,' Jennifer said, wiping her stomach. 'It stains the sheets.' Gary had now got up and was rummaging through the drawers of a glass-fronted haberdashery cabinet.

'How many ties does one man need?' he asked. 'And all these socks…' Gary opened the door to a built-in wardrobe. He pulled a boxed pair of trainers down from the top shelf, removed the lid and smelled the contents. He then placed the box back on the shelf and reached for another pair. 'These are all box-fresh,' Gary said. 'Never been worn.'

'What can I say?' Jennifer looked perplexed by Gary's interest in Nicholas' wardrobe. 'He loves trainers.'

Jennifer enjoyed watching Gary's naked body move around her bedroom. Unlike Nicholas, he was proud of his physique and completely un-self-conscious. His back was unusually broad. His lats were clearly defined and protruded from the surrounding muscle like retracted wings.

'Aye, aye,' Gary said, opening one of the drawers inside the cupboard. 'Ulysse Nardin. Nice. This must be worth about…' Gary studied the watch closely. 'I would say at least twenty-five bags.' He took the black and gold watch out of its case and draped it over his wrist. 'Lovely,' he said, nodding his head in admiration.

'What do you think he would say if he walked through the door?' Tanya asked.

'Who, Nick? He's not going to walk through the door. I told you, he's in Frankfurt. He won't be back until tomorrow.'

'Yes, but what if he did?'

'I don't know. He wouldn't be too happy to see Gary's big swinging dick so close to one of his watches.'

'Seriously though,' Tanya said. 'What would he do?'

'Honestly?' Jennifer was still massaging her wrist with her thumb. 'I don't think he would care. I'm sure he knows all about us. Don't get me wrong, he would be pissed that we're doing it here. Apart from that… I don't think he would be too concerned.' Jennifer scrunched up her mouth and lowered her eyebrows over the bridge of her nose. 'I don't know what goes on in his head any more.'

Tanya put her hand on Jennifer's thigh and offered a sympathetic smile. 'I'm sorry, babe,' she said.

'Don't be,' Jennifer said. 'It was Nick who suggested I come to your house the other night. He never gets back from work before twelve these days. I guess he thinks that if I'm with you, I'm less likely to complain about him never being at home.'

'Rubbing his nose in it a bit, aren't you?' Gary said.

'How do you mean?'

'Well, you know, by us being here.' Gary held the watch up in front of his face before putting it back in its box. 'We could have stayed at ours.'

'Maybe you want him to walk in?' Tanya said. 'Have you ever thought about that?'

Tanya got up from the bed and draped herself around Gary. The two of them stood in front of the cupboard with their backs facing Jennifer. Where Gary's body consisted of natural contours and ripples of muscle, Jennifer's physique was one of unnatural stillness and gravity-defying curves.

'Ooh, this is gorgeous.' Tanya turned around and splayed her fingers towards Jennifer, showing off the diamond and emerald ring she had just placed on her middle digit. 'The colour goes with my eyes. Don't you think?'

'Come on, get out of there, you two,' Jennifer said. 'Nicholas will notice if anything is out of place. Let's go and have a swim.'

Jennifer stood up. The crusty trail of dried semen which spread across her newly shorn pubic patch caught the light of a bedside lamp. Like the trail of a slug shimmering on a moonlit path, it emitted a muted glisten. It was mid-afternoon at the end of August, but barely any natural light had entered the room. Jennifer put on a dressing gown which was lying discarded on the floor. She walked into the bathroom and grabbed a couple of robes for Gary and Tanya.

Jennifer's dressing gown cord was still tied around the headboard of the bed. But that was fine; she enjoyed walking around the house with the gown open. It felt decadent and somehow sexier than walking around naked. Jennifer delighted in Gary and Tanya's awe of the physical form. Unlike Nicholas, who she sometimes felt was scrutinising her, logging her every blemish and imperfection. Gary, especially, was no body fascist; he celebrated it in all its various forms. Instead of being disappointed by the marks a life lived had left on Jennifer's body, Gary ran his fingers over them. With an almost sorrowful wonder, he stared longingly at her stretches and blemishes as if lamenting the absence of such marks on his wife's body. Gary would often compliment Jennifer on aspects of her physique which had previously been a source of consternation. She had always wished her legs were longer, her bum was a different shape or that she had fewer moles on her back.

Just like Gary, Tanya was equally as generous with her compliments. She would notice if Jennifer wore a new scent or painted her nails a different colour. Her response would always be a positive one – unlike Nicholas, who would never notice any changes unless Jennifer drew his attention to something. Even then, his reaction would often be one of indifference.

'Aren't the au pairs around?' Tanya asked.

'Don't worry about them.' Jennifer checked the time on her phone. 'They're picking the kids up from school and then taking them to their fencing lesson.'

The three of them made their way downstairs towards the swimming pool.

'Can you smell something?' Tanya said.

Like an animal searching the air for a scent, Gary lifted

his head and sniffed a few times. 'It does pen a bit,' he said. 'It smells of bad drains. Reminds me of where I used to live on the Costa del Sol. The whole place smelled of shit.'

Gary held open the door to the basement. He ushered Jennifer and Tanya through, goosing both women as they walked past.

'Oh dear,' Tanya said, clasping her nose. 'It absolutely stinks in here.'

The simple instruction 'naked men' produced reams of homoerotic imagery. Endless pages of explicit content presented themselves in response to this relatively innocuous search. In a way, it was guilt-free porn. There had been no need to enter a nefarious website laden with malware or compromise one's search history with anything too filthy. It didn't feel especially furtive; no rabbit holes had been descended. It was all reasonably innocent. Although, worryingly, if a child entered the same routine words into a search engine, they too would be exposed to these images. Naked women presumably would produce much the same results. Just less gay. By clicking on any one of the pictures, an array of related images popped up. Within less than a minute, Nicholas had explored hairy Arabs, Latinos jerking off into socks, Indian bears, an Ivy League graduate presenting his penis in a frying pan and perhaps the bendiest cock he had ever seen. It looked like a shepherd's crook. With a no-nonsense, businesslike expression, Nicholas scrolled through the pages as if analysing currency data. He even nodded gravely as he stumbled across 'rough straight man'. Anyone looking on would be excused for thinking Nicholas had just discovered his prediction for the Yen eking out gains against the Dollar had come to fruition. A knock at the door disturbed his seemingly joyless exploration of gay porn.

'Sorry to bother you,' Lovely said. 'Mr Landes is here to see you.'

'Thank you, Lovely. Send him through.' Unhurried, Nicholas closed the page he had been looking at and opened something more appropriate. The Bloomberg trading platform always looked good. The data fields and columns of brightly coloured symbols representing real-time global market figures looked sexy against the black background. Non-professionals were consistently impressed by the density of information displayed on the screen. Pretending to be so absorbed by his work that he wouldn't notice Simon enter the room, Nicholas started tapping away at his keyboard.

'Is this a bad time?' Simon said, poking his head around the door.

Nicholas looked up from his computer. 'No, no. Come in, come in,' he said. 'Pull up a chair.' Apart from the one Nicholas was sitting in, the only other chair was an oversized industrial-style swivel chair with a solid steel circular base. It looked heavy.

'This one?' Simon said apprehensively. Nicholas nodded and continued to type into his keyboard. Scared he might scuff the highly polished hardwood floor, Simon carefully pushed the chair towards Nicholas' desk.

Once he'd sat down, Simon was at a lower level than the desk. He looked childlike as he sat in front of Nicholas. He gestured towards one of the monitors on Nicholas' desktop. 'Do you understand all that data?'

'It's not as complicated as it looks.'

'Really?' Simon said, peering at the screen. 'I generally find most things are more complicated than they look.' Simon noticed Nicholas' passport with a boarding card inside it. 'Off somewhere?'

'No, I just got back.' Nicholas typed a final command into his computer and looked up at Simon. 'I've been in Frankfurt.'

'Business?' Simon asked.

'Well, it certainly wasn't pleasure. Have you ever been there? Weirdly it's being discussed as a potential destination for relocation should the UK leave the EU. A lot of funds are looking to set up offices there.'

'Really, Frankfurt?'

'Frankfurt, Paris, Dublin… Luxembourg.'

'I can't really see a bunch of young traders wanting to live in Frankfurt. Even less so Luxembourg. It's hardly London, is it? Even Paris is comparatively dull.'

'They might not have a choice,' Nicholas said.

'I know you think it's a fait accompli, but I just can't see it myself. Do you know a single person who thinks leaving would be a good idea?'

'The UK is historically Eurosceptic. It always has been. Any campaign to remain will be battling against decades of anti-Europe propaganda. Combine that with uncontrolled immigration and an electorate keen to give the establishment a bloody nose; I envisage millions of people voting to leave.

'I wouldn't be so sure,' Simon said. 'Cameron's got a pretty good record on referendums.'

'Odds are you're going to lose one of them.'

Nicholas picked up an open bottle of red wine. 'I've been letting it breathe.' He held the bottle up to Simon. 'Strictly speaking, young reds should be given a couple of hours. I opened this one about three-quarters of an hour ago. But what the hell. Will you join me?' Simon gave Nicholas a thumbs up.

'I was given it today.' Nicholas poured the wine into two glasses. 'One of the guys I had a meeting with owns his own vineyard.' Nicholas passed one of the glasses to Simon. He then picked up the bottle and inspected the label. 'You don't normally associate Germany with decent reds. What do you think?'

Simon took a sip and inexpertly swilled it around his mouth. 'It's lovely,' he said unconvincingly. He put his glass down on the table and asked Nicholas if he had heard about what happened at the Crossleys'.

'Yes, Jennifer filled me in,' Nicholas said. 'It all sounds quite disgusting. Thank God we haven't experienced anything as traumatic as Max and Emma. Make no mistake, we can smell it; there's a distinctly unpleasant aroma hanging around our basement. But luckily, that's as far as it goes.'

'Have you had anyone look at it yet?'

'We've got someone coming first thing tomorrow. But I presume it will improve once the weather gets better.'

'The Crossleys' plumber thinks the problem is a broken pipe.'

'How would that have happened?'

'I'm not sure. Possibly some sort of soil cave-in?'

'Has anyone else been affected?'

'Kitty.'

Nicholas made a face at the mention of Kitty. 'Of course she has,' he said.

'She's had some water in her basement. No sewage, thankfully. But apparently she can smell it too. You do know she's blaming you?'

'Well, she would, wouldn't she? The sewers back up after heavy rainfall, and it's my fault. She probably blames me for the weather too.'

'Kitty thinks the ground around this part of the park has always been unstable. She believes the combination of water from the Fleet and all the other excavations in the area has further weakened the soil.'

'That's rubbish. If the soil was compromised, my structural engineer would have said something. The woman's got a screw loose.' Nicholas tapped his finger against his temple.

'I must say,' Simon said, 'she was acting quite strange when I went around there earlier.'

'Strange, in what way?'

'Well, for a while I think she thought I was the plumber.'

Nicholas laughed. 'You don't look much like a plumber.'

'Even when I told her I wasn't the plumber, she carried on talking to me as if I was. It was quite odd. What's the latest with her insurers?'

'I've been granted permission to appeal. I'm going to take it to the Supreme Court.'

Simon puffed out his cheeks; he looked like some weird self-inflating fish.

'The hearing will probably be later this year,' Nicholas continued. 'I mean, for God's sake. I've already paid her one hundred and thirty thousand pounds out of court. The last thing I need now is anyone accusing me of being responsible for flood damage. She'll probably try and sue me again. Honestly, that woman. She's in a permanent state of indignation. You've known her a long time; tell me, was she always so objectionable?'

'She was a lot more tolerable when Hugh was still alive. He was a good bloke. Don't get me wrong, she's always seen herself as some kind of class crusader, champion of the less fortunate and all that. But she never used to be quite so self-righteous. I would say it's got worse with age.'

'No doubt the older she gets, the more guilty she feels. She probably thinks she hasn't earned the right to be sitting on all that equity. Her politics are a shield from accusations of privilege. People who inherit as much as she supposedly did often suffer from money guilt.'

Simon shifted uncomfortably in his seat.

'Have they decided to cancel the party?' Nicholas asked.

'Unfortunately not. It's all systems go. They're going to move the marquee from the Crossleys' garden to the Frasers'. Laurie says the chefs can prepare most of the food at Max's restaurant. I just wanted to ask if we could store some drinks in your basement. I seem to remember Jennifer mentioning that you had a fire escape with access to your garden.'

'Yes, that's right. Have you not been down there?'

'Not since it was finished.'

'Come with me. I want to show you something.'

'Wow, that really is something,' Simon said, trying his best to appear enthusiastic but failing to hide a grimace.

'If you look closely,' Nicholas said, 'you can see tiny little crystals inlaid into the surface.'

The two men were in the basement looking at Nicholas' most recent acquisition. Simon leaned forward and read a tag still attached to the painting: '*The Haywain* by La Futura'.

The painting had arrived the day Nicholas left for Germany. He was hoping Georgi would help him hang it after the weekend. But for the moment it remained on the floor, leaning against the wall.

'It's based on a panel painting by Hieronymus Bosch. It's the most I've ever spent on a work of art.'

Simon looked around the room at the various pieces. 'It's quite a collection you're amassing here.'

'I love it,' Nicholas said. 'I can't afford to get in the game with the real heavy hitters, but to be honest, I'm not interested in the big names. I go long on these young and emerging artists and hopefully watch their prices soar. I've built a rapport with Melt and a couple of other artists whose work I've bought. But it's La Futura who I'm most excited about. I think right now he's the most exciting artist in the world.'

The painting was in three parts and mirrored the narrative of the original triptych. But instead of showing Flemish peasants helping themselves to the contents of a large hay wagon, the centrepiece of the painting depicted

Bloomingdale's being assailed by a rampaging crowd of looters. Judges, businessmen, religious leaders, policemen, politicians, all sections of society could be seen filling bags with stolen goods and money. Meanwhile, all-around pleasure-seekers indulged in acts of excess. All kinds of sexual acts, illicit drug-taking, violence, gluttony and greed had been represented. In Bosch's original, the left-hand panel depicts scenes from the Old Testament, including the casting out of renegade angels from heaven, while the right-hand panel reveals Bosch's vision of hell, where humans hang from the rooftops of burning buildings and grotesque monsters feast on human flesh.

In La Futura's version Mickey and Minnie Mouse, having taken a bite out of the Apple logo, have been expelled from Silicon Valley. To the far right of the painting, hell is represented by a raging environmental disaster engulfing the city of Los Angeles. The catastrophe is overlooked by a Googleland logo which has replaced the iconic Hollywood sign.

'I don't understand why so many artists still feel the need to include Mickey Mouse in their work,' Simon observed.

'I think for many,' Nicholas said, still studying the artwork, 'Mickey Mouse represents the American dream. He's the symbol of capitalism. Do you not like it?' he asked disbelievingly.

'No, no. It was simply an observation. I think it's... well, you know, it's, erm... it's really... great. Very ambitious.'

'In the original painting,' Nicholas said, turning back towards the picture, 'everyone has turned their back on God. He's looking down from above as all manner of sins are committed. Now there's just a void, an absence of moral guidance. In the place of a divine being there is nothing. It really makes you think.'

'It looks like we're damned.' Simon wafted his hand in

front of his face. 'I must say, it smells a bit hellish down here too.'

'Yes, it comes in waves,' Nicholas said. 'I don't think it's anything to worry about. Follow me. I'll show you where we can put the drinks.'

Chapter 24

Owen had spent much of the party trying to avoid Nicholas Rijkens and drinking champagne cocktails when no one was looking. There wasn't even that much work to do. Most of the heavy lifting had been done earlier that day. The venue had been moved from the Crossleys' to the Frasers' house. Although the rain had stopped, the gardens were severely waterlogged. Owen and Georgi had spent most of the morning laying down pathways of rubber treads that connected the Frasers' garden to the various marquees and yurts dotted around the park. In the afternoon he made sure the PA was working and all the bars were well stocked. He and Georgi had also been tasked with decorating the second marquee. The two of them had draped the ceiling in fairy lights and hundreds of paper lanterns. Owen had quite enjoyed doing the work. Apart from Simon Landes, who occasionally checked up on them, mostly they had been left to get on with it.

But now the park was full of guests, Owen felt self-conscious and worried someone might spot him. When two members of the bar staff failed to turn up, Simon had asked Owen if he could help behind the bar. Even though he knew he would probably be booted out the moment Nicholas Rijkens set eyes on him, the extra one hundred and fifty quid was enough to convince him that it was worth a try.

Owen had been told to wear a white shirt, black trousers and shoes. Although the outfit wasn't far off from what he might wear to a party, the other waiters and waitresses in similar clothes was a bit of a giveaway. In the absence of a pair of black shoes, Owen had decided to wear his customised Converse, a decision he now regretted. His shoes were damp, and the distinctive white rubber sole was covered in mud. As well as several champagne cocktails, Owen had also knocked back two large Dark and Stormy's. And a bottle of beer. Having eaten nothing since breakfast, he felt unsteady on his feet. It was his turn to take over at the rose garden bar. Owen asked the girl he was supposed to replace if she minded hanging in there for ten minutes while he went to get some food.

The buffet was courtesy of one of Max Crossley's restaurants. A queue of people eager to try his food had formed at the far end of the tent. Owen joined the line. He began to roll a cigarette while he waited. Struggling to focus on the task at hand, he held the fag close to his face and swayed from side to side as he tried to roll it. Eventually, he placed the finished cigarette in his mouth and searched for a lighter. The cigarette had been rolled with the sticky strip on the outside. The moment it was lit, it began to unravel. A compressed tube of tobacco fell to the floor. He bent over and picked up the contents of the ineptly rolled cigarette. As he stood back up, he spotted Kitty standing next to a woman with questionably bronzed skin and tightly pulled-back hair. The woman looked over towards Owen and then said something to Kitty. Hoping perhaps he could pretend not to have seen her, Owen was about to look away, but Kitty caught his eye and gestured for him to come over.

'What are you doing here?' Kitty asked.

'Don't sound too pleased to see me,' Owen said. 'I could

ask you the same thing. I thought you said you wouldn't be seen dead at one of these things.'

'I never said that.' A man holding a tray of hors d'oeuvres and dressed the same as Owen walked towards them. 'Have you tried these,' Kitty said, grabbing some food from the tray. 'Hollowed-out cucumbers filled with vichyssoise. They're delicious. You should try one.'

'I thought you were allergic to cucumber?'

'No.' Kitty pursed her lips with annoyance. 'Ed, this is Tanya. Apparently, you two know each other?'

Ignoring that Kitty had just called him Ed, Owen looked at Tanya and made a face suggesting he didn't recognise her. 'I'm sorry, I don't remember meeting you before.'

'I used to come to this park a lot when I was younger. I had a friend who used to live in the flats. I remember you. You haven't changed…' Tanya looked Owen up and down. '… much.' She smiled at Owen and sucked on a cocktail straw.

'Isn't that funny?' Kitty said, looking at Owen. 'Tanya and her husband have bought one of the houses in the new development.'

'Who was your friend?'

'Gail McDonald.'

Only a couple of days before, Owen had sat on a bench in the park and recalled a moment of intimacy with Tanya's old friend. Initially, through the layers of nips, tucks, lifts and alterations it had been hard to detect any semblance of a girl he perhaps once knew. The moment Gail's name was mentioned, though, like an apparition, Tanya's younger face emerged from the unfamiliarity of her new one. Suddenly he remembered the gleaming sheen of Tanya's long blonde hair. He recalled the heart-shaped gold studs she used to wear in her ears and the deep crescent-like dimples which framed a broad toothy smile. Owen remembered how he would find any excuse just to touch her skin. If he was sitting next to her in the park, he would constantly scratch at his own leg just so his hand could touch the bare skin of her thigh. When masturbating, it was Tanya he used to think about. Gail was easy; most of the boys from around the park got a hand-job from her. It was a rite of passage. But Tanya was different; everyone was crazy about her.

Owen found it hard to look at her face. She looked so different. Over the years, he had occasionally wondered what happened to her. He even once googled her name and searched for signs of her among other people's social media posts. But he never found anything. Someone once told him that she had a successful property business somewhere in Africa. But he had afforded that rumour little credence.

'You don't remember Gail?' A mischievous smile appeared on Tanya's face. 'That surprises me. You two used to get on quite well.'

At the far end of the tent, Owen noticed Nicholas Rijkens coming towards them.

'I'm really sorry,' he said, 'I need to go to the bathroom. Would you excuse me for a minute?'

A number of guests had gathered in the tent where Lada Orloff and a group of friends were standing. Although many of them pretended to be oblivious to her being there, Lada's presence had infused the atmosphere with a purr of excitement.

'What an absolute stunner.'

Gary was leaning against the bar talking to Mark Delaney and Simon Landes.

'Really?' Delaney said. 'I don't see what all the fuss is about. I think she looks a bit odd. Her eyebrows are too bushy.'

'Too bushy?' Simon said. 'Rubbish. She looks like a Hollywood starlet. She reminds me of Lauren Bacall.'

'Lauren Bacall?' Delaney said. 'No, she doesn't.'

'That's her dad over there.' Simon motioned towards Yevgeny, who was standing nearby.

'That explains the eyebrows,' Delaney said.

Simon had calmed down since the previous day when he had tried to convince the Crossleys to cancel the party. The bad weather had meant that guests were unable to explore the park without getting their shoes muddy. But the various marquees, yurts and the Frasers' generosity ensured everyone was still able to enjoy themselves.

'What do you do, Gary?' Delaney asked.

'Not much these days. You could say I'm semi-retired.'

'You seem very young to be retired. You must have done well for yourself?'

'I did OK.'

Delaney made a face, suggesting he expected a bit more information.

'I used to own a chain of shops,' Gary went on. 'I sold the business a few years back.'

'What was the brand?'

'The Discount Shop.'

It was evident from their blank expressions that neither Simon nor Delaney had heard of The Discount Shop.

'And what are you doing now?' Simon asked.

'I've got a property portfolio which I manage. But most of the time, I take it pretty—'

The three men were interrupted by Tanya, who excitedly announced to the group that Pat Mayes, the ex-Arsenal and England defender, was at the party.

'You're joking?' Gary said.

'Look, he's over there.' Tanya pointed to a nearby table where the ex-footballer was talking to Max Crossley.

'I take it you're a Gooner?' Delaney said.

'I've been a season ticket holder most of my life. Pat Mayes was my hero back in the day. He's old school. Fucking legend.'

'I think he might be Emma's brother-in-law's cousin,' Simon said. 'Or something like that. He comes every year.'

'Go over there,' Tanya said.

'Nah, don't be silly.'

'Go on. Max will introduce you; he won't mind. I'll get a photo.'

While Gary and Tanya made their way over to the table where Pat Mayes was sitting, Simon and Delaney stayed by the bar discussing the new development.

'I understand there are quotas to fulfil,' Simon said, 'but it all seems like a bit of a missed opportunity if you ask me.'

'How do you mean?'

'Well... look at this place. Who wouldn't want to live around here? I fail to understand why every new home you build isn't put on the market. You should pull out all the stops. Maximise the profits like they did with the new houses. Install gyms, pools, concierge services, landscaped gardens. I'm sure the properties would sell.'

'I'm sure they would too. But it doesn't work like that,' Delaney said. 'The villas were an entirely different situation. For starters, they weren't built on council land. There were no tenants to rehouse.'

'How many people would you say are on the housing list in this borough?' Simon asked.

'I'm not exactly sure... a lot.'

'Roughly. Three thousand, five thousand?'

'More than that,' Delaney said. 'I would say more like... sixteen thousand.'

'Sixteen thousand?' Simon's eyes widened. 'Are you sure? That's a horrendous number.'

'It might be more.'

'And are the council managing to make inroads into that figure?'

Delaney shook his head.

'See. My point exactly. Imagine the number of homes that could be built elsewhere in the borough with the profits generated from this place.'

'After they've paid their bills, that's probably where the council's share of the money will go,' Delaney said. 'If they could afford to fund the project themselves, they would be allowed to keep all of the profits. They could put the whole lot into social rented property.'

'I just can't see this mixed-tenure model working here. No one will be happy. Leaseholders will be priced out. Private tenants will resent paying all that money and having to share amenities with council tenants. Not to mention the impact social housing will have on the attractiveness of the development. Exploit the prime real estate. That's what I say. Sell it to the wealthy and build more houses elsewhere in the borough.'

'London will end up like Paris,' Delaney said. 'The rich will occupy zones one and two, while the poor will be shoved to the outer rings and beyond. There will be no place for middle earners, let alone the young. Instead, it will be a city populated by millionaires, tourists and immigrants.'

'It already is,' Simon said.

The tent was now filling up with guests eager to be in the vicinity of a supermodel. The music had been turned up, and a group of people were dancing in the centre of the tent. Apart from the occasional clash of beats from an overexcited DJ and an abundance of embarrassing dance moves, everything appeared to be going well. Simon looked on proudly at the revellers.

Still reeling from the hard-to-fathom sight of Tanya Parker standing alongside Kitty, Owen returned to the rose garden bar. On his way back, he had helped himself to a mini burger from a waiter's platter. A jet of cheese and marinara sauce squirted out as he squeezed the brioche buns together in an attempt to jam the whole thing into his mouth. The sauce splattered down the front of his white shirt. When he got back to the bar, he tried to remove the mark with a damp cloth, but this only increased the surface area of the stain.

'Excuse me, I asked for a Cosmopolitan. This tastes like a Sea Breeze.' A horsey-looking woman with a square jaw and dorsal hump on her nose clicked her fingers at Owen. 'Excuse me. Excuse me.' Owen continued to serve another guest, who had asked for three mojitos. Although a committed drinker, Owen had never done any bar work before. He was unaware his remit for the evening would involve making cocktails. While a group of impatient guests gathered before him, Owen continued to consult a list of classic cocktail recipes before making each drink.

'Why are you even working here if you don't know how to make a proper cocktail?'

The woman with the hump on her nose turned to a friend and gave a snorting bray. 'I thought everyone knew how to make a Cosmopolitan.' When Owen continued to ignore her, she eventually suggested to her friend they try the marquee bar, where 'at least the barman looks like he knows the difference between a lime and a grapefruit'.

While other guests hurled drink requests at him, Owen blocked out the noise and concentrated on finishing the three mojitos. When these were returned after the guest questioned whether they actually contained any rum, Owen picked up a bottle of Kraken and angrily emptied the contents into the three glasses. Most of the rum missed its target and splashed over the counter.

'What the hell are you doing?' Outraged, the man grabbed a tea towel from the bar and wiped the rum from his hands and shirt. Owen continued to serve the other guests, ignoring the protests.

'Right, who's next?' he said.

Evidently deterred by the barman's manner, the number of people waiting for drinks had thinned out considerably.

'Yo, can I get a beer, please?'

Owen looked up to see Danny Diamond standing in front of the bar. With his bleached blonde hair, backwards baseball cap and BAPE hoodie, he stood out from the plethora of men in linen jackets. He obviously hadn't recognised Owen. Why would he? The only time they had ever spoken to each other was from a distance and via FaceTime. Owen had immediately recognised Danny, though. After the amount of time enviously spent poring over every biog, review and online interview, Danny's image was indelibly printed on his memory. His head looked even smaller at close range; his neck was bulging with fibrous tissue, while his shoulders were freakishly broad. Owen could feel a surge of stress hormones flood his nervous system. Danny's presence at the party could only mean one thing.

'What the actual fuck?' Daisy clasped her hand over her mouth. 'Oh, my days…' She squeezed her eyes shut as if hoping Owen would no longer be there when she finally opened them. 'This is too frickin' weird,' she said, turning away. With one hand on her hip and another clasping her forehead, Daisy shook her head and laughed to herself before turning around and facing Owen again. She opened her mouth to say something, shut it again and then placed her index finger over her lips. After a moment's thought, she opened her mouth again to speak, then decided against it and walked off. Danny looked at Owen, shrugged his shoulders and followed Daisy.

Pretending nothing had happened, Owen served the two remaining guests who were still loitering by the bar. Once they were gone, he grabbed a bottle of spirits and poured himself a large drink. There was no one left at the bar now. Owen's performance had scared everyone off. He went out to the back of the tent with his drink and rolled himself a cigarette.

The way Daisy had looked at him. It reminded Owen of how his friends had reacted when he was made to perform ballet at a school assembly. Their jeers, whistles and blown kisses had put him off his performance. Owen never performed classical dance again. So much of his life had been spent flailing around, trying to find a version of himself that fitted. His dad used to criticise him for being too white. His mum, although claiming colour blindness, undoubtedly stifled his blackness. She said he was English; his mate Gavin's mum said he wasn't. His pals on the estate called him posh for spending time at Kitty's. But at Kitty's he was dogged by an inferiority complex because he came from the estate. His school friends thought his dance friends were gay, while his dance friends were scared of the kids he played football with. As clichéd as it sounds, music really was his salvation. It was the only part of his life where his desire to feel like he belonged was assuaged. Race, background, even class, none of this was an issue for the people he met through music. The Rubber Band had three black members and two white members. The drummer had been to private school, and the keyboard player was classically trained. Points of reference were the only thing that mattered. If you liked Talking Heads, ESG, Can and King Tubby, that was enough. No one cared about any of the other stuff. For Owen, music was a way of understanding how he felt about the world around him.

'Where are the people?'

Owen had smelled Georgi's body odour before he even heard him speak.

'Search me.' Owen flicked his cigarette away. 'They've probably gone to the marquee.'

'Yes, very busy there. They need more boozes. Can you help me?'

Owen wobbled as he got up.

'Are you OK?' Georgi asked. 'Maybe have too much?' He mimed someone drinking from a glass.

'I'm fine. I've only had a couple.'

Georgi looked Owen up and down. 'You look like mess. After we get drink, maybe change shirt.'

'What about the bar?' Owen asked. 'I can't just leave it.'

'It's OK. Come, follow me.'

Georgi and Owen stood at the entrance to the Rijkens' garden.

'You didn't tell me the drink was here.'

Georgi looked at Owen with a deadpan expression. 'What difference makes?'

'Rijkens will shit if he finds out I've been in his house.'

'He's at party, dancing like fool.'

A series of floodlights were activated when Owen and Georgi crossed the threshold from the park into the garden. Like convicts under a searchlight the two men were lit up by the blaze of light.

'There's water everywhere,' Owen said.

'Yes, the pond overflow. Is bad.'

In the middle of the lawn, two walk-on roof lights shimmered under a build-up of water. Owen followed Georgi down a shingle path that led away from the flooded area. Georgi could hear Owen muttering to himself as he gazed through the downstairs windows.

'Come back, door is here…' As if hypnotised by the lights, Owen continued to slowly walk towards the house. Georgi called out again. 'Owen…'

Georgi was standing at the top of a staircase that provided side access to a basement which, judging by the roof lights embedded in the lawn, ran the length of the garden. Owen followed Georgi down the stone stairs.

'This place is insane,' Owen said. 'I've never seen anything like it. You can't see it properly from the park.'

'London is city for rich,' Georgi said. He held up a Bluetooth fob and tapped a code into the keypad. '4321. These people may be rich. But still very stupid.'

'Is that all there is?' Owen hiccoughed as he spoke. 'A single code?'

'No, they turn this off.' Georgi pointed to a face recognition screening terminal. 'And this,' he said tapping a fingerprint sensor.

The door to the basement was reinforced with steel deadlocks. Its thickness appeared to be that of two regular doors. A volley of bleeps and alarms turning off and resetting pinged around the foyer they were now standing in. Stacked in the corner were dozens of crates of alcohol.

'Jesus.' Owen vigorously wafted his hand in front of his face. 'What is that smell?'

'It's bad sewage from drain.'

'It's disgusting.' Owen's face jerked and twitched in response to the smell.

Georgi rolled up his sleeves. 'Come. We take these.'

'Hold on a moment.' Owen tried to open another heavy-set door. 'What's in here?' Georgi shook his head. 'Pass me those keys,' Owen said.

'We don't have time. Let's get back to party. I have to help carry food for Max.'

Owen reached forward and grabbed the keys from Georgi. 'I just want to see what's behind this door.'

'No, Owen. Let's go.'

Owen stopped and pressed his ear against the door. 'Can you hear that?'

'I don't care.' Georgi grabbed Owen by the shoulder and pointed to the crates of drink.

'At least let me open a bottle of champagne.'

'No.' Georgi looked at Owen impassively. 'You drunk already.'

Georgi picked up two crates and asked Owen to place another one on top. 'Do you have keys?' Owen nodded his head and picked up two more crates.

Chapter 25

Georgi placed his hand on Owen's shoulder. 'I think you take rest of night home.'

'Don't you need me behind the bar?'

Georgi's thick eyebrows lowered over his eyes.

'Don't look at me like that. I'm fine. Look.' With his arms outstretched like a tightrope walker, Owen tried to prove his critical faculties had been unaffected by the alcohol he had consumed.

'You wobble much.'

Owen stood on one foot but immediately lost his balance and fell into the side of the marquee. Georgi's eyes sparkled as he laughed at Owen's antics. His whole demeanour changed. Owen wasn't even sure if he had ever seen Georgi smile before.

'Are you sure you don't need me?' Owen said, hiccoughing in mid-sentence.

'It's OK… really.'

A woman in a long, draped evening gown with a plunging neck walked towards the two men. A baguette diamond pendant drew Owen's attention to her chest. Georgi noticed Owen's ardent glance. 'You should go home,' he said.

Owen laughed and offered Georgi a fist bump. 'Don't worry about me.'

As he followed a path towards the marquee, Owen could feel a tingling sensation in his legs. They felt unreliable, as if he didn't have proper control over them. His booze-saturated cortex was struggling to manage his processes. Aware that he was weaving as he walked, Owen tried to concentrate on maintaining a straight line.

The music coming from the marquee was loud. A crowd of guests had congregated near the entrance. At the far end of the tent, a small dance floor was crowded with bobbing heads. Owen noticed a group of girls dancing in front of a bald, overweight DJ, dressed in a sequin jacket and with glitter sprayed across his face. He walked over to where the girls were dancing and positioned himself at the edge of the dance floor. One of the girls was particularly beautiful. She had silvery hair, vertiginous cheekbones and a long slender neck. Her eyebrows were thick and dark. They rested languorously on top of heavy-lidded eyes, which made her look stoned. Largely ignoring the gaggle of guests who had gathered near them, the girls were dancing with each other. Owen could tell by the way they exchanged amused glances that they were enjoying the attention.

A young guy in a pink suit jacket and skinny black trousers started dancing next to them. Although encroaching upon their space, he was favourably received. One of the girls was soon dancing with the boy. Emboldened by her reaction, he began to dance more vigorously, paying little heed to the timing of the music. It looked as if he was dancing to a song with a different tempo and time signature. Discouraged by the boy's lack of rhythm, the girl soon returned to her friends.

Owen perceived the rebuff as an opportune moment to join the revellers. He stood next to the girls on the dance floor. Slowly, but with a certainty in his moves, he began to click his fingers and sway rhythmically from side to side.

Even with such economic movement, Owen's musicality was evident just from how he rocked within the music. He may have been drinking solidly for the last five hours and struggled to walk in a straight line when asked but, remarkably, his dancing did not betray the amount of booze he had consumed. When the DJ played 'No Diggity', Owen began to roll his forearms and increase the movement in his shoulders and neck. One of the girls moved towards him and started dancing with her back to him. With her hands on her knees, she pushed her arse into Owen's groin. Her friends laughed and themselves began dancing in a more overtly sexual manner. Owen was only interested in the girl with the silvery hair. He repeatedly tried to secure her attention, but she seemed more interested in fooling around with her mates.

Although the years were starting to reveal themselves, Owen was still a good-looking man. For much of his life, he had enjoyed the attention of both women and men. This had instilled a belief that he could probably get any girl he wanted. Although rare, he found knock-backs hard to accept. When they did occur, he was often bad at reading the signs. When he stumbled and toppled backwards into a couple dancing behind him, the girls decided to vacate the dance floor. Owen, however, did not interpret their departure as an attempt to get away from him. After about a minute of dancing on his own, he followed them to the bar.

'Do you know that man?' Nicholas tapped Nat on the shoulder and gestured towards Owen.

'Who?' Nat said.

'The guy standing behind Lada Orloff.'

'Yes, he's a friend of Kitty's. He lives over in the flats. He's been around the park forever. He's harmless.'

Nat returned to the conversation he had been having with Tambah and Dino. A pattern cutter who used to work for Tambah had recently made allegations about him on Twitter. These had been followed by a separate set of claims made by a former male model on a popular fashion blog. Dino had been hoping that Nat might offer some advice on how best to deal with the allegations.

'So, the first claimant is alleging that you exposed yourself to him. Is that right?'

Tambah nodded his head sheepishly.

'And this other man is claiming…'

'That I behaved inappropriately.'

'In what way?'

Nicholas tapped Nat urgently on the shoulder. 'Look,' he said, 'It looks like he's thrown a drink over someone.' Although Lada Orloff remained seated, there were now three people from her table remonstrating with Owen. 'That guy's a bloody troublemaker,' Nicholas said, craning his neck to see what was going on. 'I'm going over there.'

'It's all lies,' Dino said. 'They are trying to damage Tambah's career.'

'Are you expecting any further allegations?'

'Maybe.'

'It's a campaign of harassment,' Dino said.

Many of the guests were now distracted by events on the other side of the marquee.

'It does look like something's going on over there,' Nat said.

Owen was now embroiled in a disagreement with Yevgeny Orloff and one of Lada's friends. After the girls left the dance floor, Owen had attempted to initiate a conversation with Lada at the bar. Patently uninterested, she had turned her back on him and continued chatting with her friends. Vexed by her now frosty demeanour, Owen tapped Lada on the shoulder. This had prompted the three girls to move over to one of the tables where Lada's father was sitting. Detached from his actions and struggling to successfully communicate with his body, Owen had ventured over to the table. As he approached Lada and her friends, he had lost his balance. The drink he was holding slipped from his hands, the contents spilling all over one of the girls.

'I think you should leave,' Nicholas said. He was standing in-between Owen and Lada's father, who had got up from his seat and confronted Owen after he had spilt the drink. 'You're upsetting the guests. Please leave quietly, or I'll call security.'

Ignoring Nicholas' plea, Owen leaned over towards the table and attempted to apologise to the girls. However, he was immediately pushed away by Yevgeny, whose face had reddened and was sweating heavily. Nat Fraser, who had come over to placate the situation, placed a hand on Owen's shoulder. 'Come on, old chap. I think you should probably leave.'

Owen shoved Nat's arm away. 'I'm going, I'm going...'

'Go on, fuck off,' Nicholas said. 'No one wants you round here.'

After the incident with Lada Orloff and her friends, Owen had hurried from the marquee before the security guards arrived. He wandered around the park, drinking a cocktail swiped from the bar on his way out. Eventually he sat down on a bench next to the tennis court. Looking down at his feet, he noticed marinara sauce on his trouser leg. He licked his finger, hoping he might be able to rub the stain off his jeans. A large rat scurried out from underneath the bench and ran across his foot. Owen shrieked and pulled both feet up onto the bench. The rat was soon followed by two others. One of them turned around and headed back towards him. It stopped about three feet away from the bench. For a moment Owen and the rat locked stares, before it turned around and ran off again. It was a strange moment of connection. The rat's look had been empathetic, as if, like humans, it had evolved to feel the pain of others. Owen tried to think whether any other mammal was so loathed by the people it lived amongst. If anything, Owen thought, rats should be applauded for their resourcefulness. For centuries humans have tried to annihilate them. But somehow, they have managed to survive. Even the most egregious offence they had been accused of, namely wiping out a third of medieval Europe's population, might have been unfairly attributed to them. Worldwide they were abominated for something they may not even have done.

Owen's phone pinged. It was a message from Daisy

where r u?

Owen stared at the screen for a while before eventually replying

bye the tennis country bring drinks

Within eight minutes, Daisy arrived carrying a bottle of red wine.

'Where's your mate?' Owen asked as he took a swig from the bottle.

'Who, Danny?'

'Yeah, the boy wonder.'

'He's back at the house playing *Bloodborne* with Hector.'

Daisy sat down next to Owen. 'Look, I'm sorry for walking off earlier. It was just a bit mad. Why were you working behind the bar? I don't get it.'

Owen leaned forward, his elbows resting on his thighs, his hands clasped in front of him. 'Do you want to know something? You've got no idea how the real world works.'

'Huh?' Daisy scrunched up her face.

'You and your mate, Muscle Mary... clueless.' Owen's head wobbled as if it might fall from his neck.

'Are you going to have a go at me now because you feel bad about yourself?'

'You live in a fantasy world.'

'*I* live in a fantasy world? Ha!'

'Big house in London... house in LA. Holidays whenever you want. You don't even have to work.'

'I think maybe my real world is your fantasy. Or what if everything is an illusion and nothing is real?' Daisy laughed and made a spooky ghost noise.

'What's that supposed to mean?'

'Look, I'm sorry that you're pissed off because you had to work behind the bar.' Daisy put her hand over her mouth and suppressed a snigger. 'But... you know, it's not exactly my fault.'

'What's so funny?'

'Nothing.' Daisy rolled her eyes. 'Look, you're drunk. Maybe we shouldn't talk about this right now.'

'Don't fucking patronise me!' Owen shouted.

Two women dressed in similar vintage summer gowns and a middle-aged man wearing a striped collegiate blazer with matching trousers walked past the bench where Owen and Daisy were sitting.

'Daisy, is that you?' Daisy looked up. 'It's me, Alister.'

Looking like a child who had unexpectedly bumped into one of their teachers outside of school, Daisy stood up and smiled nervously.

Alister took a sideways look at Owen. 'Is everything OK?'

'Yes, everything's fine. Lovely to see you.'

'Look how grown-up you are.' Alister grabbed Daisy's hands. I think the last time I saw you you'd just had your braces taken out.' Alister stepped backwards and looked at

Daisy admiringly. 'You look fabulous,' he said. 'Your dad must be so proud of you.'

Alister turned to the two women he was with and introduced Daisy. 'Me and her old man go way back. We were at school together.' One of the women feigned interest with an impatient nod of her head while the other looked at Owen quizzically. 'How is your pa?' Alister continued. 'I've not managed to catch up with him yet. No doubt he's doing the rounds.'

'Just look for the TV crew,' Daisy said. 'He won't be far away from them.'

'He's not filming tonight, is he? Christ, he never stops.' Alister glanced over at Owen again. 'Is your friend feeling OK?' Owen looked up and gave Alister a dead-eyed stare. 'Well, I'm going to go and look for him.' Finally, he let go of Daisy's hands. 'It's so good to see you. Promise you'll come and find me later. I want to hear about everything you've been up to.'

'Who was that creep?' Owen said.

'He's OK.'

'He was totally checking you out.'

'No, he wasn't. I've known him like… forever. He's one of Daddy's, I mean my dad's best friends.'

'*Daddy*?' Owen adopted a plummy accent. 'Daddy. Daddy… How old are you?'

'Why are you being like this?'

'*I fucking hate my parents. My Daddy is so mean to me.*'

'God, you're such a dickhead.' Daisy's expression was one of pity mixed with disgust. 'You know what? I feel sorry for you.'

Owen turned his head towards Daisy and narrowed his eyes. 'You're just a fucking child pretending to be a grown-up.'

'It's better than being an old man who can't grow up.'

Daisy grabbed a straggle of her hair and put it into the corner of her mouth.

Owen took a drag of his cigarette, but it had already gone out. He threw it to the floor. 'What's it like to know that however badly you screw up, you'll never end up on your arse? You don't even know how lucky you are. That's what makes me angry. Or perhaps you do... maybe that's why you pretend to hate your parents.'

'You're not even making sense.'

'You hate them because they've given you everything. And you don't deserve it. You've manufactured a cross to bear. You've been desperate to suffer a little bit.'

'What, you don't think anything bad has ever happened to me?'

'Maybe it has...' Owen said. 'But still, that doesn't cancel out your privilege. No matter what happens to you or how many setbacks you suffer, you'll still have more opportunities, more advantages than everyone else. Do you get what I'm saying?'

'No, I don't.' Daisy got up from the bench.

'Daddy will always make sure you're OK. You can go on about how hard life is. But it's not. It never has been, and it never will be. You have no idea.'

'What do you want me to do? Shall I apologise? Would that make a difference? I'm sorry. OK? There you go. I'm sorry that my dad's successful and that he wants the best for his kids. What an arsehole.'

Owen shook his head and kissed his teeth.

'Should I also apologise for being younger than you? That obviously makes you angry. How about Danny, shall I get him to come and apologise for being more successful than you?'

'More successful than me, are you joking? I've done more than he ever will.'

'Yeah, you looked like a real high-flyer working behind the bar tonight.'

'Spoilt little rich bitch, that's what you are. Daddy's ungrateful little girl.'

Daisy's lip curled as she looked at Owen. 'I don't even know who you are.' she said. 'You're not the person I thought you were, that's for sure.'

'Who did you think I was, Daisy? A potential boyfriend?' Owen smirked. 'The guitarist from your favourite band? Or am I the black man you slept with to get back at your dad?'

'Do you know what? I don't need to listen to this.' Daisy tried to walk off, but Owen stood up and grabbed her wrist.

'Get your hands off me.' Daisy pulled her arm away, the muscles in her neck strained and tightened. 'You make me fucking sick!' she screamed.

Emma and Max always managed to put on a show of unity at these sorts of things. 'Remember,' Max had said as the guests started to arrive earlier that evening, 'appearances are everything.'

The previous day had ended with a hateful argument between the two of them. While Emma had been downstairs, ankle-deep in shit, Max had carried on filming with the crew. The smell coming from the basement had been horrendous, but Max had insisted that they got all the necessary shots and cutaways of him preparing a bouillabaisse. The intention was for the family and film crew to all eat together once the filming was done. Unsurprisingly, no one really felt like eating mussels and monkfish while the whiff of excrement still lingered. When Emma eventually came back up from the basement, Max had suggested that the failure of the backwater valve had been her fault.

'When was the last time we had it serviced?' he asked.

Emma replied that she wasn't even sure if it had been serviced since they had it installed. Max had gone ballistic.

'Are you fucking kidding me?' he shouted. 'Why do you think we had it installed in the first place? It's the only thing that's preventing our basement from filling up with other people's shit. And you can't be bothered to maintain it? Do I have to do everything around here?'

Emma had picked up one of Max's copper saucier pans and hurled it at him. Although Max had seen it coming and managed to turn around in time, the pan still hit him on the back of the head, drawing blood in the process.

'If you had been here instead of nuts deep in some LA bimbo, then maybe you could have made sure it got serviced. This house needs the attention of a proper man. Not some narcissistic nellie who refuses to get his hands dirty.' Emma had stormed out of the house while Laurie ran to the freezer to get a cold compress for Max's head.

Alerted by the noise, Daisy had come downstairs to see what was going on. She was greeted by the sight of Max leaning over the table with a bloody bag of frozen peas held to the back of his head. 'Ha!' she said as soon as she saw Max. 'I hope it hurts.'

That night Emma stayed with a friend but returned first thing the following morning to help with preparations for the party. She and Max didn't say a word to each other all day. But the moment guests started to arrive, Max took Emma's hand, and like young lovers they remained by each other's side for much of the evening.

'Oh my God,' Daisy said as she spotted Max and Emma greeting guests together. 'You two make me sick. You are so completely fake.'

'Max, Emma. How are you guys doing? Bit of a different vibe this year, isn't it? Shame about the mud. But once

374

you've necked a couple of grand royals, you quickly forget about the condition of your loafers.'

'Alister, darling. I was wondering when you'd turn up.' Kisses on both cheeks were exchanged. 'So good to see you. You're looking very snazzy in your blazer.'

'Italian, would you believe.' Alister opened his jacket and looked down at himself admiringly. 'It looks very English, don't you think? It reminds me of the school's First Eight's jacket. Do you remember that, Max?' Max shook his head and laughed.

'Of course you don't. Silly me.' Alister did an impersonation of someone sucking hard on a joint. 'You'd been booted out by then, hadn't you?'

Alister opened his arms and beckoned for Max to give him a hug. The two men embraced before Max asked Alister if he was going to introduce his friends.

'What must you think of me? Please forgive my appalling manners.'

Alister introduced the two women he was with to Max and Emma.

'The first time Max and I ever met, I tried to steal a sausage off his plate. The vicious git fended me off by sticking a fork in my hand. Not the most auspicious of starts. For a while, we were rather wary of each other. And then, one day, Max heard me blasting "Too Drunk to Fuck" in my study. We bonded over a shared love of Dead Kennedys, The Cramps... and what was the name of that other band we used to listen to all the time? The ones with the haircuts.'

'The Meteors.'

'The Meteors, that's it. Fantastic wedge hairdos. The amount of crap we used to put in our hair trying to emulate their style.' Alister rubbed his hand over his head. 'It's probably why mine has fallen out.'

'It was "Viva Las Vegas".' Max said. 'You would have

been too scared to play "Too Drunk to Fuck" in the house. Doc Edwards would have had you out quick as a flash.'

'Doc Edwards, don't remind me. That man was a total sadist. Remember the time he threw one of those wooden board rubbers at Jonty?' Alister turned to his friends. 'He punctured the poor boy's eardrum. It was horrific. I doubt if the bastard was even reprimanded. That kind of thing was a daily occurrence at our school.'

'Where have you guys been all night?' Max asked.

'I've just been showing these two the delights of your fabulous park. Hence the condition of our shoes. Funnily enough, we bumped into Daisy. I almost didn't recognise her.'

'I bet she was pleased to see you,' Emma said.

'Hmmm. I think I turned up at a bad moment. She seemed to be in the middle of a rather heated discussion.'

'Who with?' Max said.

'I asked her if she was OK. She told me not to worry. She obviously knew the guy. I presumed he was her boyfriend.'

'What did he look like?'

'Black chap. Looked to be a fair bit older than Daisy. To be honest, he seemed pretty out of it. They were down by the tennis court.'

Chapter 26

Owen had no idea how he had ended up lying face down in the mud. One minute he had been trying to prevent Daisy from running off. The next minute he was lying prostrate on the ground while someone stood over him, urging him to get up. The left side of his head throbbed with a fierce pain. He could taste the iron-tinged flavour of blood swirling around his mouth.

Owen had no intention of hurting Daisy. He had wanted to say sorry for behaving badly. Although he was too drunk to articulate his outermost thoughts, let alone his innermost, Owen had wanted to tell Daisy that she was right. His behaviour was about self-loathing. He was punishing her for the things he no longer had and for the things he never had. He had wanted to soothe his own pain by watching Daisy suffer.

'Get up, get up.'

'Daddy. What the fuck are you doing? Stop.'

For a moment, Owen considered staying where he was. As voices raged around him, he wished he could just go to sleep. Instead, he rolled onto his back. A faint splash of light was spread across the sky. He wondered how scientists had managed to locate our planet's position within a galaxy of hundreds of billions of stars. If we were a part of the Milky

Way, why did its glow only exist within a narrow strip and not dominate the whole sky?

'God help you if I ever see you so much as look at my daughter again.'

Owen could see Max Crossley leaning over him. His hair was ruffled and unkempt, his eyes crazed and unblinking. Owen tentatively touched his jaw. Had he just been floored by the competitive chef?

'Put that down now!' a woman's voice shrieked. 'You cannot film this.'

Max was still raging; Owen could hear him saying something about his shoes. He had no idea what he was ranting about.

'Mum, will you please calm him down.'

Owen sat up. The glare from a camera light made him squint. Someone next to Max was holding a shotgun microphone. Owen raised his forearm in front of his eyes and attempted to focus on the faces leering at him.

'Turn that off now.' Owen could see Daisy's mother trying to wrest a camera from a man standing next to Max.

'I think you might have broken my jaw.' Owen spoke as if his mouth had been clamped together. It felt like his teeth weren't aligning properly. He could barely move his mouth. 'You fat fucking prick.'

'Oh yeah?' Max clenched his fist and moved towards Owen. 'Do you want some more?'

Owen looked up to see Nicholas Rijkens staring at him, an expression of smug pleasure smeared across his face. 'Not so tough now, are you?'

Daisy grabbed her dad's arm as he stood over Owen. Max swung around. He looked deranged.

'Who are you calling a narcissistic nellie now? Huh?'

'What is he going on about?' Daisy looked beseechingly

at her mum. She couldn't believe what she was witnessing. Nothing was more important to her parents than others' perceptions of them. Everything in their life revolved around maintaining their precious image, which had been so carefully constructed. In a moment of madness, Max had exposed the dysfunction behind the happy family facade. The whole thing had been caught on camera, and now guests were filming the drama on their phones. Although witnessing Owen's humiliation had provided Daisy with an alloyed sense of catharsis, she felt repulsed by the look of pride on her father's face. He resembled a teenage boy emboldened by the gaggle of hangers-on that surrounded him.

Even though he was drunk, Daisy was surprised at how submissive Owen had been. She thought he would have fought back. She would have put money on Owen being able to overcome her father. Max wasn't a fighter; he was a coward. Daisy recalled an incident outside a restaurant in New York when a man loudly commented on the size of Emma's breasts. Realising her husband had no intention of defending her honour, Emma decided to upbraid the man herself. When she told him that obsession with breast size suggested alienation from one's mother, the man reacted badly. An onslaught of invective was unleashed, and still Max did nothing. When the man threatened Emma for deriding his relationship with his mother, Max went back into the restaurant to get security, leaving Emma and the kids alone on the pavement.

In one way, Daisy should have felt pleased that Max had rushed to her defence. Was he not doing what any father would do? He obviously knew about Owen because he had shouted something about recognising his shoes from a photo on Instagram. But there was nothing brave or admirable about her father's actions. Owen had been a sitting duck; her dad had watched him drunkenly stumble before hitting him. He was surrounded by people on his payroll. No harm was going to come to him.

Daisy felt sorry for Owen. Splatters of mud patterned his face. Slowly he got to his feet. His jaw was swollen; he looked unsteady and confused.

'I'm going to kill you.' Owen's empty threat provoked a condescending howl of laughter from Nicholas Rijkens. 'Motherfucker.'

Max flinched extravagantly as Owen lunged towards him. With a cowering sidestep, he managed to avoid Owen's swinging arm. The missed target ensured Newtonian laws of motion exerted their principles. Owen careered forward towards a nearby table. Unable to prevent the inevitable, he bashed into the aluminium bistro table and fell once more to the floor. Max looked at Nicholas and began to laugh.

'Oh my God, you're just a bully,' Daisy shouted. She ran over to where Owen now lay crumpled on the floor. A cut had appeared on the side of his head. Stripes of blood rendered his appearance even more pathetic.

'Georgi, take care of it, will you?' Nicholas motioned towards Owen, who was still lying on the floor. Daisy was crouched next to him, cleaning the cut with a napkin. Georgi stared defiantly at Nicholas. For a moment, he thought how enjoyable it would be to rub his face in the mud. He and Max evidently revelled in degrading Owen; Georgi would receive huge satisfaction meting out a similar punishment. If ever there was a moment to unburden himself of resentments and deliver retribution, it was now. Georgi could feel every received insult and perceived slight gathering as potential justification for his actions.

'Just get him out of here,' Nicholas said.

Since coming to live in England, Mariya had tried to

disabuse Georgi of the notion that degrees of masculinity were measured by physical strength. But Georgi liked this type of appraisal. Everything was clear cut. Men like Nicholas and Max didn't understand. Georgi could make them cry if he wanted to. He possessed the power to do so. Yet still, they spoke to him like he was shit on their shoe.

Georgi walked over to where Owen was sitting. Having shooed Daisy away, Owen had pulled himself up onto a chair.

'Come, I take you home.'

'I need a drink.'

'You need shower.'

Georgi bent over and draped Owen's arm over his shoulder. The two men lumbered back through the park towards Kitty's house.

'How you let that man punch you down?' Georgi said. 'You should win fight easy.'

'Sucker punch,' Owen said. 'I had my back to him. I didn't see it coming.' Owen cupped his jaw and tried to open his mouth fully. 'I need painkillers.'

'Mariya has some. You want me to get?'

'It's OK. I've got some at home.' Owen touched his face. 'My jaw is killing me.'

'In Bulgaria, we have saying – is no heroes with no wound.'

'You calling me a hero? He punched me for schtupping his daughter. I'm nearly twice her age. You would have done the same.'

Back at the flat, Owen slumped onto the sofa. His arms were splayed out over the sofa back. Streaks of blood and red wine stains were splashed across his shirt. His hair was spiky and matted.

'Owen, I made you coffee. Here…drink.'

'I need a proper drink.' Owen got up from the sofa

and went to the kitchen. There was nothing in the fridge apart from a pint of milk, some butter and some eggs. He slammed the fridge door shut and stomped out of the flat to the storerooms. Kitty had locked the doors. The pain in his jaw was getting worse. He went to the bathroom and swallowed two 100mg capsules of tramadol.

'Georgi, would you go back to the party and get me something to drink?'

Georgi closed his eyes and shook his head slowly. 'Already you have too much. Go to sleep. You need more drink not.'

Owen held his jaw and winced. 'It's just to help with the pain.'

'The pills have work soon. Go to bed.'

Owen sat down on the sofa and rolled himself a cigarette. His head was pounding. It would only get worse as the effects of the alcohol wore off. He didn't want to feel the pain and didn't want to reflect on the events of that night. He reached into his trousers for a lighter. Owen felt an unfamiliar object amongst the coins, packets of cigarette papers and keys. While Georgi went to the kitchen to get a glass of water, Owen pulled a tanned leather pouch from his pocket. He held it up in front of his face and gazed at it. It took several seconds before he realised that he still had the keys for Nicholas Rijkens' basement in his possession. Owen thought about all the crates of booze residing in the house next door. When Georgi returned from the kitchen, Owen placed the key holder back in his pocket. Finally, he lit the cigarette.

'Georgi, go back to the party. I'll be fine.'

'You are sure?'

'Yeah, I'm sure.'

'You go to bed?'

'Yes. I'll have a shower and go to bed. I promise. Thanks for your help.'

Seemingly oblivious to whatever had occurred earlier, the party was still in full swing. A group of women dressed as flappers, all wearing rhinestone-beaded headbands, feather hair clips and wellies, passed Owen as he skulked along the path which connected the houses. One of the girls grimaced as she looked at him. The rest sashayed past, paying him no attention.

Unsure of the garden gate lock combination, Owen hoisted himself up onto the wall. A flood of light illuminated his crouching body. Unconcerned, he jumped down on the other side. There wasn't anyone else in the garden. Owen ran across the shingle path and hurried down the stairwell to the basement.

The penetrating malodour of sewage gas was even more potent than it had been earlier that evening. It seeped out from between the gaps of the reinforced door. Owen's muddled mind managed to recall the backward sequence of numbers which would enable him to enter the basement. He didn't care if he got caught. The effects of the tramadol had kicked in. He felt spacey and numb. A hazy opiated tingle had enveloped him in its glow.

Undisturbed by the chorus of alerts announcing his arrival and undeterred by the smell, once inside, Owen immediately picked up a bottle of champagne from one of the crates. He shook it up and popped the cork, hoping the velocity of its release might leave its mark on the wall. A spray of liquid erupted from the bottle. Owen spun around and vigorously shook the bottle even more. Eager-to-escape gases exploded over the walls. He slumped onto the floor and held the bottle inches away from his mouth. A gush of fizzing liquid poured over his face. He enjoyed the carelessness and feeling of abandon as it cascaded down his chin onto his chest, dripped down his stomach and gathered in a loathsome pool around his belly button. When the bottle was empty, Owen threw it against the wall. He reached for another one. Instead of releasing the cork, he smashed the bottle against the poured concrete floor. It felt good breaking things, to wallow in nihilism and pretend he didn't care. He proceeded to smash more bottles of red wine and overturn a crate of beer. Thick shards of glass were scattered across the floor; occasionally, they floated off as eddies of alcohol swirled around them.

Owen opened another bottle of booze and guzzled the contents. Although his vision was blurred and he felt encumbered by the drug interactions circulating in his bloodstream, the pain in his jaw had dissipated. He kicked at the internal door which he had wanted to open earlier. The mud from the sole of his shoe left a dirty footprint on the paintwork. Leaning against the door frame, he pulled the key pouch out of his pocket. Several fobs and four other keys were attached. It didn't take long to try every permutation. After a minute or so, the door slowly opened.

A set of stairs led down from the door to the gallery. Like a reed shaken by the wind, Owen stood in the entrance, swaying from side to side. Beneath him, dirty water was flooding into the gallery. Even with his senses dulled, the smell was heavy and stomach-turning. Lurching forward, he stabilised himself by holding on to the doorframe. A large crack had appeared in one of the walls. Water had penetrated the rupture and was also coming in from the walk-on roof lights.

Owen sat down on the stairs and rested his head against the doorframe. Most of the artworks in the gallery were hung or standing on plinths. The few pieces which remained leaning against walls were being ruined by the dramatic rush of incoming water. Owen watched as the paper on La Futura's *Haywain* started to wick and curl. The simplistic cautionary tale warning a spiritually bankrupt society of imminent destruction was being destroyed by its very own environmental disaster.

Owen's temples were perspiring. His eyes felt heavy as he stared at the water rising behind the picture frame. His intoxicated mind was playing tricks on him. For a moment, he imagined himself sitting on a patchwork quilt beside a river. Janet was next to him. She was wearing a green 1950s-style swimming costume with daisies on it. She turned towards her son. A radiant disc, like a glowing aura, bleached out the details of her face. Janet held out her hand. The thick blue veins, which as a child Owen used to enjoy pressing down with his finger, snaked beneath her skin. Chicago's 'If You Leave Me Now' weaved in and out of his hallucination.

Like a puppet, his head lolled forward and flopped to one side. A hint of a smile emerged on his face as water from the river gently lapped against his feet. It felt soft and serene. Capable of recognising his thoughts and emotions, Owen knew he was dreaming. He knew that he had drifted off and would soon have to confront the chaos unfolding around him. But while his mother still sat next to him, he wanted to sit by the river a little while longer.

A loud crack, like a clap of thunder, startled him from his semi-conscious state. The side wall of the room was pulling away from the rest of the building. A chunk of masonry fell from the ceiling. It smashed down onto a large bronze sculpture of an astronaut being crucified. The piece fell from its plinth and crashed to the floor. More rubble descended from the ceiling, destroying other items from Nicholas' collection. Owen squinted as a sculpture of a foetus holding a Big Mac rolled onto its back and stared up at him. Managing to scramble to his feet, he tried to escape from the gallery. He staggered to the top of the stairs, a cluster of falling bricks narrowly missing his head. As he dodged out of the way, Owen stepped on an empty champagne bottle. Everything then seemed to happen in slow motion. Events took place in a time and space completely different from his own. It was as if he had stepped out of his own body and was now watching disaster befall someone else. While his body flipped into the air, Owen checked the ground to see where he would land. Broken bottles and empty crates guaranteed his landing would be an unpleasant one. Meanwhile, debris continued to fall from above. A large chunk of timber fell to the floor while a billowing cloud of dust rushed through the room. As the basement was being torn asunder, Owen fell to the ground, his head smashing against the cold grey concrete floor.

Nicholas was sitting at a table enjoying a drink with Yevgeny Orloff and Dino Sarti when Agrippina appeared in front of him. Her hair was dishevelled and white with dust. Tears were streaming down her face. She was agitated and incoherent.

'Agrippina, take a breath. I can't understand what you're saying.'

'The house… the house.'

'What about the house?'

Agrippina buried her face in her hands and started to sob.

'Nicky, your *telefono*.' Dino picked up the phone, which was flashing on the table, and handed it to Nicholas.

'Jen. What's wrong?'

As Jennifer implored Nicholas to hurry back to the house, Simon arrived at the table. He was out of breath and looked pale and frantic.

'Nick, you need to come. Quick.'

Nicholas could see the floodlights in his garden as he made his way up the path. The fierce glow wrapped the evening in an inauspicious light. He sensed that he was walking towards something awful. He had felt a similar sensation on that late afternoon when the ambulance and police car had pulled up outside his parents' house. It was a through the looking glass moment. Up to that point, Nicholas' life of privilege had been sheltered from the caprices of the world. He had no conception that, at any moment, everything could suddenly change. Forever.

The day was hot and still, and Nicholas had gone to the sweet shop while his sister stayed at the house with their brother. But instead of keeping an eye on Thomas, Chloé had gone inside the house and turned on the TV. Wondering where his big brother had gone, Thomas walked out of the gate, into the road, straight into the path of an oncoming car. With his pockets full of mint-covered liquorice and polka pastilles, Nicholas spotted the flashing lights of the ambulance from the bottom of the road. A crowd had congregated outside his house. That moment signalled the end of his childhood as he knew it. Up until that day, he had been a happy and carefree boy, secure in the protection his family provided. His brother's accident heralded the arrival of all the terrible feelings that would reside in his psyche for the rest of his life.

'Get out of my way.' Nicholas pushed past the horde of guests who had gathered at his garden gate. Christine Pritzker was standing in the doorway, her hands cupped over her mouth, her eyes wide and fearful. He walked down the shingle path; the water lapped around his ankles and spilt into his shoes. More people had gathered near the entrance to the basement. They were looking down into the ground. Nicholas thought they resembled mourners at a funeral staring into an unfilled grave. As he approached the group Jennifer turned around and threw herself at her husband. Nicholas looked over her shoulder. Where previously there had been walk-on lights and a grassed-over roof there was now a hole. A massive, gaping hole. Nicholas moved away from Jennifer and peered down over the edge. His gallery was submerged in rubble and shitty water. The scene was one of utter devastation. It looked like the aftermath of an earthquake.

'Where are the kids?' Nicholas asked.

Jennifer moved towards Nicholas and held his hand. 'They're with Lovely. She's taken them to Tanya's house.'

'Are they OK?'

'They're fine. They were in the annexe.'

Nicholas looked up at the house. It looked like the bottom part of the rear section was coming away from the rest of the building. He squeezed Jennifer's hand and closed his eyes. Sometimes when his eyes were shut, a malevolent whisper would emerge from the noise inside his head. Like tinnitus, the voice was always there, but mostly he had learned to mask it.

Look. Look what you've done. This is your fault.

An image of his little brother in the hospital bed, an array of tubes, cylinders and braces holding him together always accompanied the poisoned phrase. Next to the bed, Nicholas' mum was sitting in a chair holding her baby's hand. She stared at Nicholas. Her expression was loveless and devoid of maternal instinct. He knew his mother had wished it was him lying in the hospital bed rather than Thomas.

Nicholas opened his eyes. Jennifer was crying. He wanted to cry too. He could taste the bitter flavour of bile in his mouth. Peering into the hole, he briefly considered jumping in. It was no more than he deserved; to drown in a super-prime cesspit.

'It's all my fault,' he said, banging his head with the palm of his hands.

'No, it's not.'

'It is. You know it is. I never listen.'

It was his fault. The first contractor Nicholas hired to investigate the possibility of installing a two-storey basement extension had warned him that the expansive clay soil was too unstable. Any excavation, he said, would structurally undermine the existing foundations. The following contractor echoed this opinion. He told Nicholas there would be a real risk of cave-ins if he tried to go too far down.

'Are you telling me', Nicholas had argued, 'that we have the engineering capability to build a twenty-mile tunnel under the Thames, but you can't excavate two storeys under a house because of shifting soil and a high water table?'

Nicholas' determination, stubbornness and non-aversion to risk in many ways had been the key to his success. But in this instance his refusal to heed the warnings of those who knew better than him had proved to be catastrophic. After a second expert expressed similar concerns, instead of modifying his plans Nicholas continued to consult engineers and contractors until eventually he found a company prepared to follow his instructions.

A final section of timber, glass and plaster crashed into the hole. Nicholas and Jennifer both turned their heads to avoid the debris which erupted from the pit. More people arrived from the party eager to witness the calamity. One of the guests began filming, while another took a selfie in front of the crater. Nicholas couldn't even be bothered to rebuke them for their insensitivity. When Max's film crew arrived with their cameras and recording equipment, Nicholas didn't have the energy to throw them out.

'What's the point?' he said, turning to his wife. 'What's the point in anything?'

Chapter 27

May 2017

'It seems like the whole of North London is awash with red placards. Even the Frasers have got an "Only Labour Will Save Our NHS" sticker in their window. There are signs of support for the Greens and the Lib Dems, but I don't think anyone beyond Wandsworth or Westminster would dare show their support for the Tories.' Ed took a drag of his cigarette, a plume of thick blueish grey smoke drifted towards Kitty, which she batted away with a waft of her hand.

'While I was walking here,' Ed continued, 'I couldn't help thinking what historians of the future will make of this city's obsession with money and status.' He took off his felt fedora and wiped a film of sweat from his brow with a handkerchief. 'How is it that one of the richest cities in the world became a left-wing heartland? It was only five years ago we voted in that desperate bleach-blonde buffoon back in as mayor. And now the citizens of this city are about to vote for a radical socialist as prime minister. Honestly, I can't keep up.'

'Chipping Barnet,' Kitty said.

'Huh?'

'Chipping Barnet. That's always been a safe seat for the Tories.'

Ed looked surprised. 'That's right,' he said. 'But maybe not for much longer. Villiers is a Leaver. Hopefully they'll boot her out. There's even talk of Kensington falling. Can you imagine? Again, I don't understand how that's happened. It's the wealthiest borough in the country.'

'I doubt if many of the homos can vote in this country.'

Ed raised his hands to his face and laughed loudly. 'I think you're mistaking the UK for Poland,' he said, once he had finally stopped laughing.

'What are you talking about?'

'You said that you doubted if the Kensington homos would be allowed to vote.'

'I meant homeowners.' Kitty scratched at her arm furiously. The inside of her forearm was raw and livid. 'Don't laugh at me.'

'I'm sorry,' Ed said. 'But yes, that makes sense in a borough like Kensington. But how do you explain all the support around here? Rich, eligible to vote. It can't just be about Brexit.'

'It's all for show. Most of my neighbours would probably describe their politics as being on the left...' Kitty stopped for a moment. Virtually every other word these days was preceded by a word-searching pause. 'They'll be outraged by the treatment of refugees... or vote to appoint a trans local councillor. But would they lift a finger for anyone from their own community?'

'Nimbys one and all,' Ed said.

Kitty tipped her head back and looked up at the canopy of slender branches, which intertwined with one another like grabbing hands. She could feel the replenishing rays of the early summer sun on her face. A blue-crowned jackdaw swooped down from a nearby chimney and landed on a branch. It was soon joined by a friend; together, they cast a lordly gaze over the park. Another bird with highly coloured markings and a red face had the temerity to embark on a flypast, only to be chased away by the two jackdaws. The birds spiralled higher and higher until they disappeared into the flowers of a lime tree, only to reappear seconds later out of the dense foliage of a neighbouring ash.

'Do you know what I have always loved about this place? Although it's so much more manicured than it ever used to be, more or less it still looks the same as it always has. At least I think it does.' Kitty straightened her neck; the slack worry creases that hung around the corners of her mouth embellished a frown. 'Who knows any more?' She looked at Ed and half-smiled. 'While my memories evaporate like water molecules, the trees and the park remain...' Kitty stopped in mid-sentence and closed her eyes. There was a long pause before she opened them again. 'Immutable.' A look of relief appeared on her face as she successfully retrieved the word she had been looking for. 'There's something so reassuring about it.'

'If you ignore the sirens, you could almost be in the country.'

Kitty smiled. 'And got rid of the CCTV cameras and searchlights. I don't know why I never moved to the country. I always liked the idea of it. Too late now.'

'I always remember you saying you would go out of your mind if you had to live in the country. Don't you remember that time we stayed at my mum's old house?'

Kitty looked at Ed with an unfocused stare. Sometimes it looked as if no thoughts were going on beneath the surface. 'Where was that again?'

'Near Glastonbury... where I grew up. We took a walk up to the Tor and went to the Abbey. You did a painting of the Oaks of Avalon? I still have it on the wall in my study. You named your dogs after them.'

'Which dogs?'

'Gog and Magog.'

'See.' Kitty scratched at her arm again. 'This illness is a thief, stealing away my memories.'

'Who needs memories? They're overrated, I say. It's just history.'

'That's easy to say when you don't have a diseased brain.' There was a break in the conversation while Kitty prepared the following sentence. 'The ones that have vanished, I fear, are gone forever. Never to come back.'

'But it's being here, now, that's important. Who cares about the past? It's all made up anyway. Everything that has ever been, and ever will be, is here right now. The present is the only thing that matters.'

'The future doesn't matter?' Kitty shut her eyes and clenched her jaw; the muscular tension suppressed her emotions. Thoughts of the future terrified her. Having witnessed Hugh's aunt nursing his uncle through the end stages of a similar illness, she knew what awaited her. Alzheimer's rendered him depressed, incontinent, unable to swallow and incapable of recognising his own family. Immobility left him plagued by bedsores, while a diminished brain ensured the most straightforward tasks became an ordeal. The end of his life had been tyrannised by pain and confusion. There was no way Kitty could contemplate enduring a similar fate.

'Somerset,' Kitty suddenly said. 'We should go there again one day.'

'Sadly, my ma's house is no longer there. But my sister has a place in the Quantock Hills. Near where Coleridge once lived. On a clear day, you can see across the Bristol Channel as far as Wales.'

'That sounds lovely.'

A break in the conversation was punctured by the compressed snap of a sweetly timed forehand. This was followed by a grunt of exertion and what sounded like a racket being hurled across the court.

'You do know I'll always be here for you, don't you?' Ed took Kitty's hand and rubbed the back of it with his thumb.

'That's sweet of you,' Kitty said, 'and I know you mean it. But I have no intention of burgeoning anyone with my illness. I don't want to ruin the life of someone I love. It won't be me any more. You know, for the first time in my life… I'm glad that I don't have children. I'm glad Owen is dead.'

'Owen? Do you mean Hugh?'

'What did I say?'

Ed stubbed his cigarette out on the arm of the bench he was sitting on and smiled tenderly. 'You said Owen.'

With her hands resting on her lap, Kitty closed her eyes and took deep diaphragmatic breaths. Slowly she breathed in through her nose, counted to four and exhaled through pursed lips. The process of concentrating on the journey of each breath calmed her down. It eased her anxiety.

'Have you seen him recently?'

A stray tennis ball landed on the lawn about ten feet from where Ed and Kitty were sitting. A smiling young man all in white emerged from behind one of the trees. Ed pointed to where the yellow ball lay. He watched as the man bent over to pick it up with his back towards the bench. His shorts looked like they might rip as his buttocks stretched the fabric.

'Owen? I haven't seen him for a while. I think the meetings I introduced him to were perhaps a bit too… uncompromising. He prefers those touchy-feely West End get-togethers, where everyone loves the sound of their own voice.' Ed shuffled in his seat. 'I think you should tell him what's going on. You can't keep avoiding him.'

Kitty had chosen not to tell Ed about the end of Hugh's uncle's life. She had decided not to tell him how, towards the end, he had begged for someone to release him from the hell he was living in. She had never described the effect all of this had on Hugh's family. Or how quickly his uncle's Alzheimer's progressed from moderate to severe.

'There's no way I can even contemplate enduring a similar fate. Why should I?' she said.

'A similar fate to what? I don't understand.'

'I can't allow my brain to deteriorate to the point where I'm no longer in control of my... my...' Kitty snapped her fingers as she tried to grab the word which hung in front of her. That was the thing that frustrated her most. She knew what the word was but somehow couldn't pluck it from the blizzard of other words swirling around her brain. 'Oh, you know what I mean.'

Ed continued to look puzzled.

'I want to arrange my own death.' Kitty blurted the words out. 'Hugh's involvement will just make things harder. He's done so well to get sober and start again. I don't want to hold him back.'

Ed squeezed the bridge of his nose and heaved a shuddering sigh.

'Please don't get upset,' Kitty said.

'Talk of death... well, it all feels so premature. You're still full of life.'

'Look, I'm not saying I want to die tomorrow. But... it's a procession I must make while I'm still of mind sound. I still have some control over my future. But not for long. I know it all feels a bit...' Kitty gave up trying to hold onto the word as it slipped from her grasp like wet soap. 'But I'm OK with that,' she said. 'The alternative is so much worse. Can you imagine me in a care home?'

Although many of her memories were disappearing by the day, Kitty still remembered her and Ed's promise to each other. It would have been unfair to bring it up, though.

Surely everyone at some time or another has promised a loved one that they would never let them suffer, that they would be the one to administer the fatal dose if life ever became intolerable? One says these things without ever really believing it will happen. Ed probably hoped that this was one of those memories which now eluded his friend.

'How will you… you know?'

Kitty smiled and shrugged her shoulders. 'Like everything in life, you only have a choice if you can afford it. I would kill myself. But suicide is too risky, don't you think? So much can go wrong.'

Ed lit another cigarette; his fingers were trembling.

'If I knew it would never get worse than this,' Kitty continued. 'If I knew I could stay connected to the person I once was… I wouldn't be thinking about a way out. But it's going to get worse. So much worse. This disease chips away at you until there is nothing left. No dignity, no semblance of the person you once were.' Kitty sighed and looked up at the trees again. 'Once the hope has gone, there's not much point getting up in the morning.'

'There is always hope. Who knows? They might find a cure.'

'Maybe… one day. But we're years away from that.' Kitty looked at Ed and smiled serenely. 'Please don't try and change my mind, Ed. It feels like my brain is dying… like I'm dying. But I've accepted it. You must too.'

'We're all dying, Kitty. That's what life's about.'

'Well, let's just say I'm dying a bit faster than everyone else.'

'I still think you should tell Owen what's going on.'

'No. I don't want anyone else to know. Promise me you won't tell him.'

'How will you know when you're ready?'

'I can't let it get to a point where I can't make that decision for myself… I want to finish this book first. The girl from the publishing company is going to help me.'

After the success of recent exhibitions, a small publishing imprint had asked Kitty to compile a book of her work. Ed had agreed to write a piece for the introduction. The book, Kitty had decided, would be a document of her time in Albion Park. She believed the park was a microcosm of the city at large. Both ruled by money. Both plundered by profiteers and parasites who cared little for its rich creative past.

'Do you have a title yet?' Ed asked.

'I did… typically, I've forgotten what it was.' Kitty closed her eyes and used her breathing technique. Ed watched as she placed one hand on her upper chest and the other just below her ribcage, her tummy expanding with each intake of breath. 'I might have written it into my phone.' Kitty picked up her phone and scrolled through pages of reminders. 'Here we go,' she said. 'I have a couple. The first is *Journey Through the Past*. The other is *Epilogue*. What do you think?'

'Sorry to bother you.'

Kitty looked up with a jolt of surprise to see Simon Landes standing in front of her. She sighed.

'Is this a bad moment?'

'What can I do for you…' Kitty's expression froze until she remembered Simon's name.

'You missed Tuesday's meeting.'

'Meeting?'

'The committee meeting. Are there any other meetings planned?'

'I'm sorry, it must have slipped my mind.'

Simon looked confused. 'Kitty, I saw you on Sunday. You promised you'd be there.'

'She's been busy,' Ed said.

'Well, I'm afraid we had to vote without you. I'm sorry,

but I did tell you it was an important meeting.' Simon's voice sounded more triumphant than apologetic. 'The motion was carried, anyway. We should be able to cover the costs with the money we eventually receive from the developers for access to the park.'

Ever since the refurbishment of the tennis courts, it had become increasingly difficult for residents to reserve time at weekends. The booking schedule had become a point of contention between some of the neighbours. Dino Sarti and Seth Pritzker had fallen out over what each perceived as the other's domination of weekend slots. To satisfy demand, it had been suggested residents pay for the construction of another court.

Kitty blankly gazed straight ahead. Seemingly disappointed by her reaction, Simon looked as if he had been expecting fireworks instead of a vacant expression of indifference.

'Cosmo proposed a motion for the next meeting to have a cricket net installed in the park. Nicholas suggested we could dig up the lawn next to the sundial.'

Simon looked at Ed and then back at Kitty. It was as if he couldn't believe the blows he was landing without retaliation.

'Are you feeling OK?' Simon asked.

'Who wants to build a tennis court?' Kitty asked.

'That's a done deal, I'm afraid. If you'd been there last night, your vote might have made a difference. But, unfortunately, it's too late now.'

'You said someone wants to...' Kitty's voice trailed off.

'Cosmo Thwaites. He wants to install a cricket net.'

'Who is Cosmo...?'

'Thwaites.' Simon rolled his eyes. 'He bought the Hardmans' place. I'm sure you've met him already... pleasant enough chap. He's another hedgie. Part of that Business for Britain group, which is a bit of a shame.'

'I don't even know what that is,' Kitty said.

'He's a Leaver,' Simon hissed. 'Tabitha won't even talk to him. His boss was one of that lot who shorted the pound on referendum night. God knows how they got away with it.' Simon looked over his shoulder to make sure no one else was within earshot. 'He was reported to have made over two hundred million pounds. Can you believe it?'

'Nothing surprises me any more,' Ed said. 'This country has been ruined by cretins and crooks.'

Kitty yawned and stretched her arms. 'I'm hungry,' she said.

'Sorry, am I boring you?' Simon asked.

'Yes, a bit.'

Ed stifled a laugh with a pretend cough. Kitty got up from the bench. Ed noticed that she was wearing two shirts underneath her jacket.

'Before you go,' Simon said. 'I was hoping we could have a chat about the front of your house.'

'What about it?'

'This is rather awkward... but someone at the meeting mentioned that it could really do with a lick of—'

'Bye then, Simon.'

An array of expressions ranging from puzzled to amused to offended appeared on Simon's face. He stared open-mouthed as Kitty and Ed turned around and walked off through the park.

'You're so naughty,' Ed said.

'He deserves it.'

The two of them walked silently arm in arm until they got to Kitty's gate.

'I meant what I said back there,' Ed said. 'I could move in with you. We could see our days out together.' Ed bent down and kissed the top of Kitty's head as she rested it on his shoulder. 'It would be an honour to look after you.'

'I would only cramp your style,' Kitty said. 'I saw the way you looked at that young man just now. You're still an old horn dog. I don't think an incontinent housemate dribbling into her cornflakes would be a very good look. Do you?'

'Oh, don't say that.'

'I have plans in place,' Kitty said. 'Let's go and make a pot of... of...' Kitty tapped at her forehead with her fingers.

'Tea?'

'Yes. Let's go and make a pot of tea, and I can tell you more.'

'I just want you to know that, whatever you decide to do' – Ed put his hand on his chest and took a deep breath – 'I'll always be there for you. I do love you, Kitty.'

With one hand, Ed pinched the skin between his thumb and forefinger. Kitty noticed that his face had turned red, and his bottom lip was quivering.

'Oh, you soppy git. Please don't get upset. You know, I've really had the most wonderful life.' Ed dragged his nose across the back of his hand and sniffed loudly. 'There is still more living to do,' Kitty continued. 'I want to enjoy the time I've got left. And then... well, we'll see.'

Chapter 28

'Have you seen the *Standard* today?' Mark Delaney repeatedly tapped his finger on an article in the newspaper, which lay open on his desk. 'That's the flipping guy from your party, isn't it?' The pitch of his voice steadily rose until it became little more than a squeak. Delaney took a deep breath before reading the article to Nicholas, who had just walked into his office.

A businessman who made millions selling legal high drugs has been jailed for 15 years after police seized over £10 million of drugs and 700 kilos of raw materials. Gary Hardman, 44, from Albion Park in North London, made more than £25m from a crime operation with 175,000 customers and sold drugs as far afield as Taiwan and Australia. Police also seized 15 firearms, including an AK-47 and a sub-machine gun, £575,00 in cash, 10 million etizolam tablets and 12kg of cocaine worth more than £1 million.

'J-e-s-u-s C-h-r-i-s-t.' Delaney's mouth hung wide open. Nicholas could see the gaps in his gums where his wisdom teeth had been removed. 'Did you know about this?'

Nicholas turned the newspaper towards himself. 'Yes. Well, we knew that he had been arrested on a drugs charge.

I'm surprised you didn't already know about it. The story was all over the tabloids a few months ago.'

'What is it with you lot in Albion Park?' Delaney said, laughing. 'You can't stay out of the news. First, there was that film of your basement collapse and now this.'

'Don't remind me,' Nicholas said.

'How come you didn't say anything?'

'I didn't know you knew them.'

'I don't. I didn't. I mean… I briefly talked to him at your party, but…' Delaney inclined his head and wagged his finger. 'I knew there was something dodgy about him. He was so shifty when I asked him what he did.'

'Did he mention pound shops and property portfolios?'

'Something like that. Considering what the man had to hide, you would have expected him to be a bit more convincing. What about his wife? She was quite sweet. What was her name again?'

'Tanya. She was implicated too.' Nicholas passed the newspaper back to Delaney. He pointed to a section at the bottom of the piece, which Delaney read aloud.

During a series of raids, police arrested nearly thirty people at an industrial unit in Loughton, where the substances were prepared and packaged before being sent to customers. Hardman and his wife Tanya were arrested at Heathrow Airport after returning from Kenya, where police said the couple owned several properties'

'Wow!' Delaney had a look of thrilled incredulity on his face. 'It doesn't surprise me. He looked like a gangster.'

Gary and Tanya's arrest had inevitably caused uproar around the park. Simon Landes, in particular, had been distraught that the story made it into the newspapers. After the evident glee with which reputable news agencies had reported on the collapse of Nicholas' basement, Simon had been dismayed to see bottom feeders from the tabloids descend upon the area. He couldn't bear to see his beloved Albion Park traduced by red-top journalists. Pictures of Gary and Tanya's house had featured in many of the articles. The New Park Villas were described as *hyper-gentrified*, *chic* and *exclusive*.

Meanwhile, a journalist wrote that Albion Park was the domain of bankers, celebs and criminals. One of the tabloids had managed to obtain the photograph Tanya had taken of Gary with his arms around Max Crossley and the ex-Arsenal and England footballer Pat Mayes. This inevitably led to speculation that Max was somehow caught up in the Hardmans' world of crime. The following day pictures of Lada Orloff appeared in the same paper. A *close friend* of Gary and Tanya's, who *wished to remain anonymous*, told of a debauched summer party where guests were openly seen taking drugs. It was also reported that several residents had attended a *gathering* at Gary and Tanya's house. There was no mention anywhere of it being a residents' committee meeting.

After Gary and Tanya's profile on a website for *adventurous couples and non-monogamists* was published, one newspaper alleged that Gary and Tanya had hosted swinging parties for the *wealthy residents of upmarket Albion Park*. Utterly distraught at the amount of negative press their arrest had generated, Simon sought the advice of a PR expert. He was told that the residents of Albion Park had become exemplars of an out-of-touch rich elite. A bit of wealth bashing was a fun distraction from the political turmoil that had been dominating the news over recent months. 'You're just unlucky,' the PR exec told Simon. 'Ever since they aired that documentary about the effect bad news is having on society, the press has been waiting for another story like this. They couldn't believe their luck when they discovered the couple lived in Albion Park. They're going to rinse it for all they can. It provides a bit of respite.'

Although Jennifer had tried her best to appear unfazed by the stories, Nicholas knew she was hurting. Especially from the revelation that Gary and Tanya were serial swingers. She told Nicholas that she had never believed the story about the pound shops. Jennifer claimed that she had suspected all along that Gary was probably involved in criminality.

'They did own a chain of pound shops,' Nicholas said to Jennifer. 'I just don't think they made much money from them. More than likely, they were a front.'

After two weeks of disparaging press, a clip of Max shouting threats at Owen was leaked online. Although Owen's face was pixelated, there was no doubt over Max's identity. Fortunately, no footage of him physically assaulting Owen materialised. Even so, Max's publicist and marketing team embarked on what Emma described as a brand damage limitation offensive. Having hired a Reputation Management Expert, Max was advised to do an interview with a friendly newspaper. In a candid chat, Max described how the pressures of celebrity had got to him. Following advice not to talk about Daisy's relationship with an older man, Max spoke of an unrelenting work schedule, anger issues due to a father who never spoke to him, and how being overweight had affected his mental health. He apologised profusely for his behaviour and even managed to coax out a tear or two. Max's team couldn't do anything about the bad press that had already landed, but his confessional seemed to stem the flow of negative stories.

'That has made my day.' Delaney folded up the newspaper and put it in the bin underneath his desk. 'I bet Max Crossley wasn't too pleased about that snap appearing in the papers?'

'That was the least of his worries,' Nicholas said. 'Emma thinks the whole affair cost him an OBE. And if that wasn't enough, his UK show got cancelled.'

Delaney made a face as if he had just touched something hot. 'That's got to hurt.' He began unfolding a large piece of paper on his desk.

'What's this?' Nicholas asked.

'This, my friend, will hopefully be our next project. It will make all of those millions you made in beaten-up health stocks look like chump change.'

Nicholas moved around to Delaney's side of the table and began studying the plans. 'Enfield?

'Trust me,' Delaney said, his eyes sparkling with excitement. 'This is going to be huge. It will be one of London's biggest-ever housing regeneration projects. Eight sites consisting of fifteen estates to be regenerated over the next twelve years or so. Four hundred hectares, fifteen thousand jobs, over ten thousand homes. It doesn't get much bigger than this.'

'How much will we be expected to invest?'

'Fifty per cent of the capital. The council will get their share from housing revenue. The GLA has also confirmed that seventy million will be available in grants.'

Nicholas looked at the map laid out on the table. The boundaries of the areas to be regenerated had been highlighted in neon marker pen. 'All of this is going to be regenerated?'

'Yup.' Delaney nodded his head as if he couldn't believe it himself. 'There are also additional local authority-owned sites that can be developed too. And we'll be acquiring other sites along the way.' He pointed to a large green area on the map between two of the highlighted estates. 'All of these playing fields are local authority owned,' he said. 'They've not announced it yet – and believe me, there will be a hell of a lot of opposition – but I reckon we'll be able to build another twelve hundred properties on there.'

'What are our chances like?'

'Good. Out of the initial ten bidders who responded, we've made it down to the last three.' Delaney picked up a document and passed it to Nicholas. 'This is our invitation to submit final tenders.'

'When will they announce the winning bid?'

'September,' Delaney said. 'Then we'll have to wait for a bit while council funding is confirmed and legals are sorted.'

'Sounds exciting.' Nicholas sat down in Delaney's chair while he continued to pore over the plans. 'What's the latest with the Bevan Estate? It looks like there are still people living there.'

'Eviction notices have been served,' Delaney said. 'One or two stragglers are refusing to leave. But once we've got rid of them, we can start demolishing the place.'

Introductions were barely over before Jennifer, in no uncertain terms, explained to Ivor the particular problems she and Nicholas were experiencing. 'We never have sex,' she said. 'He refuses to fuck me.'

Ivor tried to explain that issues around sex were often a manifestation of built-up resentments. He told Jennifer and Nicholas that there is rarely a single issue that can be identified as the source of the problem. 'Admittedly,' he said, 'some problems can simply be due to physical changes, like decreased hormone levels. But more often than not, a sexless marriage is symptomatic of accumulated resentments.'

'I didn't resent him before,' Jennifer said. 'But I do now.'

'We want to peel away all of these rotten layers of rancour,' Ivor said, 'and basically start again. You obviously care about each other, or else you wouldn't be here.'

Ivor's assertion that Jennifer and Nicholas obviously

cared for one another instigated the first of Jennifer's many tirades. She claimed Nicholas was more concerned about his wine and art collections than he was about their relationship.

'I honestly thought he might kill himself after the basement collapse. I've never seen anyone so depressed. He was catatonic. Don't get me wrong, it was a bad scene. But it's just stuff, you know? No one died.'

When Jennifer suggested the two of them try couples counselling, Nicholas had consented on condition they see his therapist. Although they rarely spoke about what happened during Nicholas' sessions, she was suspicious of Ivor's effectiveness. 'You don't seem like someone who has done much work on themselves,' she once said to Nicholas. After all this time Jennifer sometimes wondered whether Ivor could possibly be any good at his job. Impartiality had also been a concern. She was worried Ivor would take Nicholas' side. Ivor had been clear to Nicholas that although he had done some marriage guidance related stuff in the past, it was not his speciality. This declaration heaped more doubt on Jennifer's misgivings. But Nicholas was adamant. It had taken such a long time for him to feel comfortable with Ivor; he couldn't face going through that process with someone else. It was Ivor or no one.

'Why did you tell Nicholas about your affair?' Ivor asked.

For Nicholas, Gary and Tanya's arrest had ruined everything. Up until that point, it had felt like he and Jennifer had reached a tacit agreement which enabled them to happily co-exist. Jennifer had given up trying to coerce her reluctant husband into having sex. Meanwhile, Nicholas willingly turned a blind eye to whatever his wife was getting up to.

'He already knew,' Jennifer said. 'I was so hurt that he didn't seem to care. I wanted to shock him into a reaction.'

'But this didn't have the desired effect.'

'No, it didn't.'

'How did that make you feel?' Ivor took off his glasses and wiped them with a green optical cloth.

'It made me realise he was willing to risk everything. If he loved me, he wouldn't want to share me with anyone else.'

Jennifer explained how she wanted Nicholas to feel like their marriage was in jeopardy. She told Ivor that she wanted Nicholas to fight for her. 'Everything in his life', she continued, 'is about conquering, consuming, owning… but apparently not when it comes to his marriage.'

Ivor picked up a glass of water and took a sip. He leaned back in his chair and crossed his legs. One of his trouser legs lifted slightly, revealing the bottom of a taut and defined calf muscle. He looked sinewy and over-exercised.

Ivor turned to Nicholas. 'Jennifer is right. You are a competitive man. Why do you think you didn't, as Jennifer describes it, compete for her?'

'I knew it was something she wanted to do,' Nicholas said. 'I didn't want to deny her. She's always had a higher sex—'

'You didn't want to deny me?' Jennifer interrupted. 'It was an act of munificence? So you're a sexual altruist, is that it?'

'Did the two of you have a conversation where this was discussed?' Ivor asked.

'There was no conversation,' Jennifer continued. 'But he encouraged me to spend time with them.' Jennifer leaned forward in her chair. 'I think Nicholas believes that if I'm receiving pleasure from elsewhere, it relieves him of responsibility.' Nicholas looked up at the clock. 'It's one less thing for him to worry about,' Jennifer continued. 'It lightens his load. It enables him to focus on what's important.'

'Which is?' Ivor asked.

'His work, of course. What else? It's the only thing that matters. It's the only thing that has ever mattered. Look at him now,' Jennifer said, gesturing towards her husband. 'He's clock watching. Nicholas wants to get out of here as quickly as possible. He's got a meeting at three, and he's worried he'll be late. That's all he's focusing on.'

'Nicholas,' Ivor said. 'Any thoughts?'

'My work is important,' Nicholas said. 'Of course it is. That's no great revelation.' He turned and looked at Jennifer. 'But... just because my work is important to me, it doesn't mean your happiness isn't.' Nicholas turned back to look at Ivor. 'She seemed happier. More fulfilled. We argued less.'

'And would you say this made your life easier?' Ivor asked.

'Yes.'

'See!' Jennifer shouted. 'That's my point exactly. It's not about what makes me happy. It's about expedience. By encouraging me to have an affair, he hopes I will make fewer demands on him. Yes, I'm happier when sexually fulfilled. Who isn't? But I would prefer it if the source of fulfilment was my marriage.'

A moment of silence followed while Ivor jotted something down on his notepad. Jennifer looked at Nicholas but was unable to catch his eye.

'Earlier on, you said that you believed Nicholas was willing to risk everything. Would you say, perhaps, Jennifer, that you were the first to risk everything?' Ivor looked up from his notepad. 'After all, it was you who initiated proceedings with... sorry, what were their names again?'

'Tanya and Gary.'

'I'm interested to know what it was you saw in them.'

'You're not the only one,' Nicholas said.

'They were interested in me,' Jennifer said. 'They made that abundantly clear. I liked their forthrightness. They were uncomplicated... straightforward. They clearly loved each other, yet they were secure enough in their relationship to include someone else. When I was with them, it was like… it was like I was finally part of a happy relationship.'

'Did you feel fulfilled?' Ivor said.

'I got a glimpse of what that could feel like.'

'And you were aware of this?' Ivor turned to Nicholas.

Nicholas offered a casual shrug of his shoulders. 'She seemed happy.'

'It's clear', Ivor said, 'that Jennifer was seeking out the very qualities she felt were missing from your relationship. Openness, attentiveness—'

'Sex,' Jennifer added. 'Lots of sex.'

'Yes, sex as well.' Ivor said. 'But what strikes me most of all is that this isn't just about sex. It's about an emotional connection. An intimacy.' Ivor looked at Nicholas. 'It's about letting go of painful experiences and trying to focus on what's really important.'

Letting go. Nicholas knew what Ivor was alluding to when he mentioned this phrase. It had become a recurring theme of their sessions together. Ivor believed Nicholas equated letting go with helplessness and thus a sense of being out of control. He thought everything stemmed from his brother's accident. The feelings of helplessness Nicholas felt at the time had resulted in a constant attempt to protect his emotions. According to Ivor, intimacy was his biggest challenge.

'I don't understand what he's so afraid of,' Jennifer said. 'Deep down, he knows I don't want to be with anyone else. But being with Nicholas is exhausting. It's impossible to know where you stand. I try and read his moods. But too often it ends in rejection.'

'And does that make you feel like your needs will never be met within this relationship?'

'Well, yes,' Jennifer said. 'There's only so much a person

can take. I wish more than anything that he could just tell me what he wants. But he won't talk to me.'

When Ivor asked Jennifer how it was at the beginning of their relationship, Nicholas couldn't help releasing a groan of despair. The primary reason for seeking out a therapist was to discuss the aftermath of his brother's accident and its effect on him and his family. But, beyond talking about superficial problems within his marriage, there were some subjects he couldn't bring himself to discuss with Ivor.

'I think maybe at first I found his wealth to be such a turn-on that I didn't focus on whether I was sexually satisfied or not. Who was it who said that power is the ultimate aphrodisiac?'

'Napoleon?'

'I don't think so. Maybe. In the beginning we had lots of sex, but… it's just never been as important to Nicholas as it is to me.'

'I've been stressed out about work, that's all.'

Jennifer emitted a disparaging gasp. 'For four years?'

Jennifer looked at Ivor. 'He never even touches me.'

Nicholas buried his face in his hands.

'When one partner has a higher libido than the other, it can place a huge strain on the relationship. It often leaves one person feeling rejected and undesired. Meanwhile, the other can be left with feelings of inadequacy and guilt.' Ivor explained how these types of problems can lead to anxiety about any kind of physical contact. 'If there is an imbalance in sexual appetites, the one with the diminished libido may even avoid cuddling for fear that it will lead to a demand for sex, which they have become fearful of. There's a risk that person might find it easier to disconnect, thus creating an even greater chasm.' Ivor took a sip of water and turned to Nicholas. 'Do you recognise any of this in yourself.'

Nichols hesitated before replying. 'I don't know, really. I've not thought about it in those terms before.'

'Hold on a minute.' Jennifer slapped her hand against her forehead. 'Do you two not speak about this stuff?'

'You know I'm not at liberty to reveal anything of the private conversations I have with Nick.'

'If you don't discuss the problems within our marriage… what exactly do you talk about?'

'We have covered a lot of ground during our sessions together.'

'Do you speak about anything other than his childhood?' Jennifer looked despairingly at Nicholas and then at Ivor. 'Surely it's the here and now that's important? I've done therapy before, I know that by addressing the past one can better understand the present. But it just doesn't seem to be working. How has analysis of Nicholas' past helped the present?'

'That's a question only he can answer.'

'So?' Jennifer said.

Nicholas remained silent for a moment as if assessing how much he could say without compromising himself too much.

Once again, Jennifer asked, 'How have these sessions helped you understand what is happening to us?'

'I think…' Nicholas continued to stare at the floor as he spoke. 'The way my parents reacted to me after my brother's accident… I think it has left me…' He turned his head to one side and coughed as he finished the sentence. The words were almost unintelligible. '… with a fear of rejection.'

Jennifer gave Nicholas a narrow look as she contemplated what had been said. Meanwhile, Ivor allowed a break in the conversation before adding: 'Fear of rejection is a potent emotion. It can be at the root of issues around—'

Jennifer held her hand up in a halting gesture. 'Why didn't you tell me this before?' she said.

'Why do you think?'

'I don't know… you were scared of being rejected?'

'Ivor has made me realise that my way of coping with emotions is not to feel them. After my brother's accident, my feelings were ignored. If I tried to speak about them, my mother just got angry.'

'We are ruled by our childhood experiences,' Ivor said. 'They are the foundation upon which the rest of our lives are—'

'Hang on, hang on,' Jennifer said, interrupting Ivor once more. 'How does this fear of rejection explain a lack of desire?'

'I think…. well. Perhaps… I've…' Nicholas scratched at the side of his neck. He looked pleadingly towards Ivor, who was watching his laboured attempts at an explanation with unconcealed fascination.

'Instead of speaking to you about his problems,' Ivor helpfully intervened, 'Nicholas threw himself into his work.'

'But why couldn't he talk to me?'

'Do I have permission to tell Jennifer what we discussed last week?'

Nicholas encouraged Ivor with a vigorous nod of his head.

'Just tell me already,' Jennifer snapped.

'Nicholas is afraid of being intimate. He's scared of revealing too much. When he was younger, he learned to manage his mother's feelings by hiding how he felt. When you are governed by these types of behaviour, it can be hard to unlearn them. His core beliefs dictate that vulnerability will be met with hostility. And, as you know, intimacy requires vulnerability.'

In a rush of realisation, Jennifer stared at her husband. She covered her open mouth with her hand. 'Oh, my poor baby,' she whispered. 'I'm so sorry you felt you couldn't discuss this with me.' Jennifer looked at Ivor. 'I feel so bad,' she said.

A gentle flute melody accompanied by the sound of crashing waves signalled the end of the session. Jennifer looked up at the clock on the wall.

'Surely we have another ten minutes or so?'

'It's the fifty-minute hour, I'm afraid. You can thank Sigmund Freud for that. We can pick up where we left off next week.'

Chapter 29

September 2017

'You don't have to do this, you know,' Jacquie said. 'You might find it upsetting.'

'I'll be fine,' Owen said. 'I want to come and see the place one last time.'

Jacquie was one of the last secure tenants to leave the flats. Most of the other residents had been moved to an estate at the further reaches of the borough. She was supposed to have moved out three weeks before, but the only available flat on the estate was a tiny one-bedroom. It was going to be a while before the new development was finished. They hadn't started demolition yet. If Jacquie and the kids were going to be in temporary accommodation for that whole time, they couldn't all be expected to share one bedroom. After she complained about the size of the flat, Oak Grove Housing had offered her a temporary two-bedroom flat in an old Arts and Crafts-style block not far from Albion Park.

The flat was packed and ready to go. Jacquie's brother, had already done a lot of the heavy lifting. There were just a few more boxes and bits of furniture which still needed moving. Owen parked the hired van in the small car park at the front of the flats. He got out of the vehicle and stared up at the block. It was strange how quickly the absence of any internal activity had affected the outward appearance. Like a corpse, the departed soul had rendered the physical unrecognisable. He made his way to the entrance and walked up the stairwell. The silence was loud, like the sound of air resonating within the cavity of a seashell. The doors and windows on every landing were boarded up. Apart from Val and Randall, who refused to leave, and a couple from the Keynes flats, all the other tenants had left. It was only a matter of time until the council got rid of them, though. They had already announced that both the electricity and the water would be shut off the following week. The council were going to make it as unpleasant as possible for those who insisted on staying put.

Owen got to the top of the stairwell and walked down the corridor towards his flat. The building felt utterly abandoned. He had never seen it look so wretched. A child's toy, a couple of bits of clothing and some paper plates which had been dropped when others moved out were scattered on the floor. For the last couple of years, Owen had been sanguine at the prospect of the flats disappearing. It was happening everywhere; London was being redeveloped. He had accepted it as part of the evolution of a city. While he was still living in Albion Park, the flat had assumed the role of an existential burden which he couldn't escape. The sense of atrophy and decay around the buildings mirrored his own mental state. Over the last year or so, he had only been back a few times. Jacquie would either meet him halfway or come to his place whenever the kids came to stay at his new flat in Latimer Road.

At one point, he had even been looking forward to the flats being demolished. But the fire on the Lancaster West Estate, which was only half a mile from where he was now living, changed everything. The burnt-out husk which towered over the surrounding area stood as a tragic monument to everything that had gone wrong with attitudes towards social housing. The brazen disregard displayed by landlords, developers and politicians from both left and right had resulted in the death of seventy-two people. It later transpired that residents of Grenfell Tower had repeatedly voiced their concerns about the risk of fire. In a horribly prophetic blog from the previous year, a member of the local action group predicted that it would take a catastrophic event to expose the incompetence of their landlords, who they later described as an evil, unprincipled mini mafia. It was still too early to know what the impact of the disaster would be. Would policies that had seen public housing, hospitals and schools torn down to make way for investment opportunities be re-evaluated? Or would normal service be resumed once the requisite amount of soul searching and hand wringing had been completed? The demolition of the Bevan Estate felt like a continuation of a market-driven strategy that required the maximum amount of profit to be squeezed from any available assets. The same strategy that had overseen London becoming one of the world's wealthiest cities, yet paradoxically one that couldn't find the money to provide for those most in need. The market knew no morality; therefore, it was up to the politicians to inject some morality into the market. But they had failed miserably.

As he stood in the doorway of his old flat, Owen felt like an astronaut watching his safety tethers fray and unravel. Soon he would float off according to whatever forces were acting on him. No resistance or flailing could change his fate. Would he fall back into the atmosphere and burn up? Or would he be spinning forever, untethered and lost?

'Hello?' Owen's voice bounced off the empty walls.

'I'm up here,' Jacquie said.

Spared of its contents, the flat looked miserable. Sun-bleached paint rendered it colourless. Without anything on the walls to distract the eye, Owen couldn't help but focus on the multitude of cracks, patches of mould and peeling strips of paint. It looked like it could have been empty for months. Jacquie came bouncing breezily down the stairs. She was wearing a black vest top, and her hair was tied up in a floral silk bandana. Like someone whistling at a funeral, her ebullience seemed out of place.

'It's a bit weird, isn't it?' Jacquie said. 'Are you going to be alright?'

'Yeah, yeah. It's just taken me a bit by surprise. A little overwhelming. There's a lot of shitty memories attached to this place. But it's always been full of life. It feels completely lifeless now.'

Jacquie didn't seem to be listening; she had already turned around and was taping up a large box. 'Right.' She stood up straight and wiped her brow with her forearm. 'Shall we start loading up the van?' She was radiant with excitement. Owen, conversely, felt discombobulated.

He picked up one of the large cardboard boxes and began taking it down to the van. There were ten of them altogether. He also had to move his and Jacquie's old bed and a chest of drawers. He was able to take the bed apart, but the drawers were too heavy and unwieldy.

'I don't know how we're going to move this,' Owen said, staring at the solid pine chest.

'We'll be able to manage it, won't we?'

Owen's knuckles cracked as he stretched out his fingers. He leaned into the chest of drawers and lifted one end. 'I don't think so… we could do with some help. Randall is still here, isn't he?'

'He won't help,' Jacquie snorted dismissively. 'He took sides with Val a long time ago.'

'Is she still pissed off with you?'

'Are you kidding? I thought she was going to kill me when she found out I had been offered a place in the new development. She went nuts.'

'What has she been offered?'

'Apparently, she was told the only way to get a new flat was if she handed over her tenancy. That's why she's refusing to move out.'

'What about Randall?'

'There's no way he'll be able to afford a place in the new development. Shared ownership is an option, but Val reckons his bills will go up by something like seven hundred quid a month.'

'And you've got the same tenancy as here?' Owen gave a breathy half-formed whistle of astonishment.

'It's not my fault,' Jacquie said. 'Val has probably got low band ratings. She's always in arrears on her rent. All of that will affect the council's decision. She and Randall are convinced I've been acting as some kind of double agent.'

Owen hesitated before replying. 'You can kind of see why people might think that.'

Jacquie curled her lip and frowned.

'Not only have you got a place in the new development. But while every other poor sod has been moved out to another estate, you get rehoused around the corner in a choice mansion flat. Anyway, how does Val even know what kind of tenancy you've been offered?'

'I don't know. Estelle probably told her. Val called me a Judas slag the other day. Jack even had a pop at Harley. He told him that I was a grass.'

'Why didn't you tell me about this before?'

'It's not worth it. I just want to get out of this place...' Jacquie walked over to the chest of drawers. 'Come on,' she said. 'I reckon we can move this thing together.'

Once they had finished filling up the van, Jacquie asked Owen if he would like a minute to himself in the flat. His initial response was to say no. Like her, he was keen to leave. Jacquie reminded him, though, that he would never have another opportunity. 'In a few weeks,' she said, 'this will all be rubble and dust.'

Owen dragged his hand across the walls as he walked through the flat for the last time. He could hear the tap-tap of water dripping in the kitchen. He was supposed to have replaced that washer years ago. The noise never really bothered him while he was living there. Jacquie had never complained either. But now, the sound of water dripping on the steel sink was laden with an ominous reverb. Everything seemed unnaturally louder. It was as if the absence of lives being lived amplified the silence. Starved of everyday sounds, his brain zoomed in on any available noise. Where he usually wouldn't have even noticed them, the creaks and clicks of his footsteps became loud and intrusive.

Standing in the front room, Owen tried his best to recover happy memories. It was virtually impossible to associate somewhere which more resembled the scene of abduction and incarceration in a gritty BBC drama with anything joyous that might once have happened. Any semblance of a place he once called home had vanished. Deciding not to go upstairs, Owen made his way to the front door. He didn't want to see the kids' rooms. No doubt they would look as grim as the rest of the flat. He had seen enough. Nothing was to be gained by hanging around there any longer.

Owen rejoined Jacquie on the landing outside the front door.

'Are you OK?'

'Yeah, fine.' Owen's bottom lip jutted out as he tried to appear unmoved. He leaned on the wall and looked towards

Kitty's house. The windows of her studio were shut. Usually, at this time of year, they would be wide open.

'Have you still not spoken to her?' Jacquie asked.

'I rang the doorbell earlier, but there was no answer. She left a weird message on my phone a couple of weeks ago. I couldn't understand what she was saying. I tried to call her back, but she didn't pick up. When was the last time you saw her?'

'The other day. She was sitting on that bench outside the flats.'

'Really?'

'Yeah, I thought it was strange too. I've never seen her sitting there before.'

'Did you speak to her?'

Jacquie had been trying to avoid Kitty. She hadn't wanted to get embroiled in a conversation where she would have to justify the decisions she had made. She knew Kitty had disapproved of her involvement with the steering committee. Equally, Jacquie believed Kitty should never have got involved with the campaign to save the Bevan Estate. Her bourgeois guilt meant she was forever embarking on ideological crusades. Ultimately none of it would ever make any difference to her life. No one was about to take her house away from her.

'We chatted for a bit,' Jacquie said. 'It was weird she didn't even mention anything about the flats. I was expecting her to have a go at me.'

'What did you talk about?'

'Not a lot. She asked me if I wanted a recipe for home-made bread. And then she called me Rachel.'

'Rachel? That's odd. She didn't mention me?'

'No.'

Owen laughed, as if nothing surprised him any more. He was used to the cornerstones of his life crumbling. It felt strange not having any contact with Kitty, though. She obviously wanted to be left alone. His sponsor had advised him not to push it and to be respectful of her wishes.

Owen could only assume Kitty's refusal to see him was something to do with what happened that night in the Rijkens' basement. In the immediate aftermath, Kitty had just been relieved that both Georgi and Owen had got out of the house unscathed. But after Georgi lost his job and eventually went back to Bulgaria, Owen detected a shift in her attitude. Even though Georgi's dismissal was nothing to do with the collapse of the house (Owen's antics in the basement that night remained unknown to anyone but Georgi and Kitty) and everything to do with Nicholas Rijkens lashing out at anyone who had worked at the party that night, Owen still sensed Kitty blamed him for the sacking. After saving Owen's life, Kitty felt Georgi deserved better. She was right, of course. But Owen felt powerless to help.

December 2017

That evening's meeting was a busy one. The room was full of semi-familiar faces, most of them belonging to people Owen had got to know over the last ten months or so. Everyone was sitting behind a series of tables which had been arranged in a big square. As he sat waiting for his turn to share, Owen began to regret having come in the first place. The prospect of speaking in front of all these people, the expectation to be candid, made him squirm. Usually, he would try to avoid meetings where he was expected to share. But it had been a rough day at work.

Although he had been teaching at the London Institute of Music Production for nearly a year, Owen still felt like an imposter. Initially hired as the guitar and songwriting teacher, his remit had gradually broadened. After the tutor who was supposed to be teaching the Introduction to Sound Engineering course unexpectedly resigned, Tomer, the course director, convinced Owen that he would be more than capable of filling in. Owen had made it clear that he wasn't an engineer, but Tomer assured him that he would only be expected to teach the basics. 'Besides,' he said, 'the students like you. Unlike the other tutors here, you've worked with artists they've actually heard of.'

Typically, one of the students in Owen's class was an ex-physics undergraduate who had recently packed in uni to become a sound engineer. The boy kept on catching Owen out and evidently took great pleasure in doing so. Earlier that day, while Owen had been trying to teach the class about microphone placement, Robbie kept asking him about comb filtering. At one point, he interrupted the lesson to ask Owen if he knew of an equation that could calculate the position of comb filter notches. Owen wasn't even sure what comb filtering was. Was it the same as phasing? He thought it was but wasn't certain. He felt like a fraud.

On his way home from work, he phoned Fitz, his sponsor, and told him that this kid was driving him mad. 'He brings up all these old feelings of doubt and self-loathing. All the stuff that used to make me drink.'

Fitz instructed Owen to get to a meeting. 'You need to release these feelings. Things become clearer when they're spoken out loud.'

Owen had turned over responsibility for major decision making to Fitz. If Fitz told him to do something, he did it. It was an incredible amount of power for an ex-con with no professional medical or psychotherapy qualifications. When Owen's doctor suggested that maybe he should try a low dose of antidepressants, Fitz had vetoed the decision. He believed a person in recovery should not take any mood-altering substances, whether prescribed or not. 'No matter how bad you feel', Fitz had told him, 'you need to feel it.'

Owen felt increasingly nervous as his time to share loomed nearer. When he was a newcomer, he had felt obliged to speak at meetings. It seemed to be an integral part of the experience. He reasoned that if everyone else was doing it, well, then so should he. In alcoholic parlance, Owen hit his rock bottom that night in Nicholas Rijkens' basement. Acute powers of perception were not needed to conclude his way of doing things was not working. Owen was prepared to try anything that might lift him from the misery which enshrouded him. If occasionally that meant spilling his guts in front of a roomful of strangers, then so be it. But now, having been around the rooms for a while, he believed that, for many, the process of sharing was an opportunity to perform.

During the first few months of his sobriety, when he was attending meetings virtually every day, Owen would frequent a meeting in Kilburn, which Ed had recommended. The meeting was full of chronic alcoholics. Owen would often hear truly hair-raising stories of people attempting murder during blackout or embarking on binges which wouldn't stop until a liver was ruptured or financial ruin achieved. He regarded these meetings as a type of penance. He had messed up badly and deserved to be sitting in a dank church basement drinking lukewarm tea with a bunch of hardcore alcoholics. After a while, though, as he began to reap the mental benefits of abstinence, he found these meetings too depressing, too gruelling. It was hard to relate to so many of the stories he heard and the people he sat amongst.

Eventually, Owen bumped into an acquaintance at a meeting in Camden. After telling her how he struggled with the meetings he was attending, she introduced him to some gentler ones in Soho and Chelsea. Comparatively, these get-togethers were more akin to a social club. Many of those in attendance were of a similar age or younger than Owen. He recognised several people from the time he had spent hanging out in the pubs and clubs of London. Sobering up in AA and NA seemed to be a rite of passage. It was what London's Generation X did once they got bored of humiliating themselves. The camaraderie available at these meetings plugged the hole which often appeared once drink and drugs had been kicked into touch. After listening to the stories in the Kilburn meeting, Owen believed some attendees, possibly himself included, maybe never even had that much of a problem in the first place. Perhaps they relished the opportunity to unload or were lonely and simply enjoyed talking to an attentive and non-judgemental audience? Everybody wants to be heard. Sometimes it's hard to find someone who will listen. If all of that wasn't enough, where else could you get a ringside seat while an A-list actor regaled everyone with their war stories? And perhaps even go for a coffee with them afterwards.

Owen wriggled uncomfortably in his chair as he thought about what to say. Although sharing wasn't compulsory, so far everyone at the meeting had highlighted what aspect of the guest speaker's share they identified with. Fitz had advised him that his reluctance to talk at meetings was part of his 'ism'. Owen, however, had become increasingly cynical about many aspects of the format, particularly the religious overtones, the shared jargon and the tyranny of niceness.

Fitz told Owen that he would never properly get better until he could shed his ego and present his true self at these meetings.

'Hi. My name is Owen, and I'm an alcoholic.' A chorus of compassionate voices welcomed his presence. 'To say that I don't enjoy this aspect of the fellowship would be an understatement.' A ripple of amused acknowledgement filtered around the room. 'I'm fifteen months without a drink or drug…'

Owen contemplated sitting back down. Sometimes, in meetings, he would find himself having to stifle an exasperated sigh or squash the urge to heckle. There was nothing he hated more than a sharer who ignored the basic tenet of sticking to addiction-related topics and bleated on about the minutiae of their daily lives. The thought of being one of those people terrified him.

Owen glanced around the room. He spotted Marie staring at him. Together they had discussed Owen's aversion to sharing at meetings. 'It's part of the process,' she once told him. 'It's not all about you. You need to get over yourself. By sharing, you're helping others with their recovery too. That's what it's all about.'

And now Marie was looking at him expectantly, her arms folded on the desk in front of her. Through her thin black cashmere jumper, Owen could detect the weight of her breasts pressing down on her forearms. Sobriety had sent his libido through the roof. So much of his time in meetings was spent checking out other women. It was like being back in the classroom at school. He would miss so much of what was being said because he was staring at some girl, trying to work out whether she had big tits or not.

'… but today, the urge to pick up has been strong. All my life, I've suffered from imposter syndrome. I always feel like someone is about to expose me as a fraud or call me out for not being good enough… even here. Wherever I am, whatever I'm doing, I always feel like a fish out of water… like I don't belong.'

He hoped Marie was impressed by all of this. He had noticed, at other meetings, how she responded to other men when they opened up. Marie was a devoted attendee of several fellowships which catered for the addict of every variety. As well as Alcoholics Anonymous, she frequented Narcotics Anonymous and Cocaine Anonymous too. Sometimes she went to Debtors Anonymous and occasionally Sex Addicts Anonymous as well. Anyone would have thought a résumé like that would have belonged to someone damaged beyond repair. But Owen enjoyed her company. She was so mild-mannered and gentle. He found it hard to imagine her participating in a lifestyle that would ultimately result in her attending the full deck of fellowships. With her thin, mousey-coloured hair and pale complexion, she wasn't the sort of person Owen was typically attracted to. But he found the dichotomy between her present serene self and her probable past exciting.

'I would bury negative thoughts with drink and drugs,' Owen continued. 'Alcohol provided me with the courage I needed to function. You see, for someone like me, feeling like you don't belong... it's not just voices in your head.'

Although he struggled with these public outpourings of honesty, Owen discovered that one's fallibilities could be worn as a badge of honour in the fellowship. Past misdemeanours could be excused as part of one's illness. To admit one was an alcoholic was almost to absolve oneself from previous bad behaviour. Owen still wasn't sure whether his 'ism' was at fault, or he had simply lacked the strength of character to prevent bad things from happening. He was more inclined to think that he was driven by choice rather than the victim of a disease. This school of thought did not go down well amongst other alcoholics. Most people at meetings welcomed having their condition described as an illness. It made self-analysis less traumatic. But the idea that you could recover from a medical condition by accepting a power greater than yourself, saying sorry to people you'd hurt and asking God to remove your shortcomings seemed not only paradoxical but also far-fetched.

Although he enjoyed the new lease of life sobriety had offered him, Owen sometimes wondered whether all this concentrated introspection was just another form of self-indulgence. Unlike the characters who populated the grittier meetings, Owen didn't see his drink or drug-taking as a matter of life or death. He got fed up with hearing people say *If I pick up another drink, I'll die.* While undoubtedly true for some, for most it was hyperbole. Some people who enjoyed reeling off this often-used quote would give up the programme and be drinking normally within a few weeks. And yet, attending meetings and being around other people pursuing a similar goal of sobriety worked. There was a lot Owen hated about the fellowship, but if he did what he was told and kept going back, he believed that he could stay sober.

'… I've realised, though, since coming here, that the drink and drugs were fixing something that was broken inside me. That thing is still broken… but working the programme provides me with the tools to tackle it without picking up. I'm just grateful for being here today.'

Owen sat down in his chair and stared at his feet. While the chairperson thanked him for his share, Owen was wondering whether he was too old to be wearing Nike Airs.

At the end of the meeting, as the group stood up, held hands and recited the serenity prayer, Owen noticed Ed standing at the back of the room, his hands deep in the pockets of his suit jacket. Ed never attended any of the meetings which Owen frequented these days. He much preferred hanging out with the old-timers and hardcore ex-junkies. Owen had known nothing about Ed's past until he heard him share at the first meeting he ever went to. It was the only time he ever heard him speak at a meeting.

Looking back, Owen realised it had been done for his benefit. Ed had just wanted him to know that, whatever advice he offered, it came from a place of deep experience. If the path of excess really did lead to the palace of wisdom, then Ed was the recovery equivalent of a Buddhist Satori.

'Wow, you've come a long way, baby,' Ed smiled.

'Oh God,' Owen cringed. 'Did you hear all of that?'

'Don't be ridiculous, you silly man. You should be proud of yourself.' Ed raised his arm and patted Owen's shoulder. 'Have you got time for a coffee?' Owen looked around to see where Marie was. She was probably waiting outside. 'Just the two of us, if that's OK?'

'Is everything alright?' Owen asked.

'I need to talk to you about something.'

Chapter 30

January 2018

'**Papa, watch this.**' Nicholas peered out over the top of his laptop and watched Luc as he hurled himself into the swimming pool. The two-hundred-and-seventy-degree spin followed by an ungainly entrance had been Luc's party trick ever since they first had a pool installed in their basement. And now, nearly three years later, as they sat around the pool in a rented house while they waited for their property in Albion Park to be rebuilt, Luc performed the same lame trick. Nicholas had been moderately impressed when he first saw Luc leap and spin into the water. Happy to see his ordinarily unadventurous son throwing himself about, he had called Jennifer down to the pool to watch him do it again. At the time, Nicholas presumed Luc would graduate to more daring manoeuvres. Maybe front flips, or even a backflip. He had never really managed to progress, though. And still, he demanded his father's attention every time he enacted it.

'Papa, are you coming in?' Camille sat on the edge of the pool, swishing her legs in the water.

'I will do soon,' Nicholas said, without looking up from his laptop screen.

'Where's Mama?'

'She's having a workout, sweetie. She'll be with us soon.'

'She's taking forever.'

At that moment, Jennifer appeared wearing a hooded Missoni bathrobe. Her hair was up. Her skin glowed and glistened under a sheen of sweat beneath the overhead lights. Nicholas almost choked on his latte as Thiago, Jennifer's new personal trainer, emerged from behind her, dressed only in a pair of bright green swimming trunks. The outline of his penis was clearly visible through the fabric of his trunks. It looked like a felled tree. Thiago was a thirty-two-year-old Yoga Asana World Championship finalist from Belo Horizonte. With his Phelpsian physique and Hellenic profile, he reminded Nicholas of the athletes and warriors who adorned the sides of prized painted amphoras. Nicholas watched with wonder as Thiago sashayed across the room and lowered himself into the swimming pool. He looked like a mythical sea creature as his sublime frame glided through the water. Neither Jennifer nor Nicholas had been able to take their eyes off him. Nicholas wasn't sure whether his wife was fucking him or not. At least she hadn't said anything which suggested she was. He presumed she wasn't. Jennifer wasn't nearly celestial enough for someone as godly as Thiago.

'That was a long session,' Nicholas said as Jennifer sat down on the sun lounger next to him.

'Thiago is very meditation focused. He likes to do twenty minutes or so before we start exercising.' Jennifer picked a towel up off the lounger and patted her face. 'Have I got time for a swim?'

'You'll have to be quick. The meeting starts at twelve.'

'What could possibly be so important that it can't wait until the next committee meeting?' Jennifer stood up and undid her bathrobe.

'I've no idea.' Nicholas watched intently as Thiago climbed up the steps of the pool. 'I've not managed to speak to Simon yet. But we should go soon.'

Do you guys know what this meeting is about?'

As they got out of the car, Nicholas and Jennifer bumped into the Frasers.

'Did Simon not tell you?' Nat said, sounding surprised.

'I've not seen much of him recently.'

'The executor of Kitty's will asked Simon to arrange it,' Tabitha said. 'There must be a special instruction of some sort.'

'Why couldn't they just send out an email?' Nicholas said. 'Why do we all have to be there? It's ridiculous. Who is the executor anyway?'

'No idea,' Nat said.

'She must have left some money, or something, to the committee,' Jennifer added.

'It wouldn't surprise me,' Tabitha said. 'She had no dependants. And she really did love this place.'

When the group arrived at Simon's, Bruno and Tambah were standing at the top of the stone stairs which led up to the house. Simon greeted all the men with a handshake and the women with a light kiss on both cheeks. Nicholas was the last person through the front door.

'Any idea what's in this will?' Nicholas asked as the two men shook hands.

'I know as much as you do.'

Nicholas and Simon walked into the sitting room where the others had gathered. It wasn't a full meeting, but the usual faces were there.

The bell-like chimes of the doorbell rang out. 'That will probably be Kitty's guy'.

While Simon answered the door, residents speculated about what Kitty might have bequeathed to the park.

'Do you think she had much money?' Tambah asked.

'I know there was a lot of family money,' Nat said. 'Her father, or maybe grandfather, founded one of those huge construction companies. Not Balfour Beatty, but someone like that.'

Tambah gasped. 'I never knew,' he said regretfully.

'Does anyone know what's happening with the house?' Dino asked.

Christine Pritzker looked over her shoulder, making sure no one else was listening before leaning towards Jennifer and Nicholas. 'Whoever the new owner is,' she said, 'I'm sure they'll take a lot more pride in its appearance than Kitty ever did.'

Jennifer gave Nicholas a conspiratorial smile. The two of them had already decided they would put in an offer as soon as the house appeared on the market. Jennifer had fizzed with excitement as she and Nicholas discussed joining the two houses together. Nicholas reasoned that he was technically already a stakeholder in the property after the amount of money he had paid out to Kitty and the insurance company.

The excited whispers of conjecture stopped the moment Simon walked back into the room. 'Everyone, this is Edward Revel. He was a very old and dear friend of Kitty's. I'm sure many of you recognise him from around the park. His connection with Albion Park goes way back. I think maybe even before my time?'

'Definitely before your time,' Ed said, smiling. 'In fact, I used to squat in this house. We put on Circle of Shame events in this very room.'

Simon emitted an uncomfortable laugh, while Christine Pritzker's inverted smile conveyed her disapproval at the idea of squats and squatters.

'Before we start,' Simon said, 'I would like to say just say how incredibly sad we all were to hear of Kitty's passing. She was a… she was a real character and will be sorely missed.'

'Absolutely,' Nat said. 'Kitty was a one-off. They broke the mould when they made her. Tabitha and I will miss her terribly.'

Apart from Nicholas, whose expression remained wooden, everyone in the room adopted a far-off look of sombre reflection. Dino folded his arms and placed a single finger over his pursed lips as he contemplated his non-existent relationship with Kitty. Meanwhile, Emma Crossley, evidently stirred by talk of Kitty's unexpected demise, dragged a finger across her eye as if wiping away a tear.

Ed acknowledged the pseudo sentiments of the group. 'Thank you all for coming today,' he said. 'I know she would have appreciated it.' He took an envelope from his inside pocket. 'Kitty left some very specific instructions in her will. These included a stipulation that all beneficiaries, wherever possible, should be informed of their entitlement in person. As shareholders of the park, you are all considered beneficiaries. Kitty thought that a short park committee meeting would be the most effective way of implementing her wishes.'

Looking very serious, Simon slowly nodded his head as if successfully executing Kitty's estate was of paramount importance to him too.

'So…' Ed took a piece of paper out of the envelope and unfolded it. 'As you may or may not know, Kitty was responsible for planting many of the trees in the park. In particular, the oaks, red maples, ash and beech trees which she planted after the storm of '87. Kitty has bequeathed forty thousand pounds to be used for the maintenance and upkeep of these trees. I will oversee the fund and will pay for an arborist to regularly attend them.'

'Wow,' Tabitha said. 'That is so generous of her.'

Nat and Emma both nodded in earnest agreement. 'Typical Kitty,' Nat said.

Ed then proceeded to run through several other minor park-related bequests, the most significant being Kitty's wish for her share of the developer's money (in exchange for access to the park) to be given to the charity Trees for Cities.

Nicholas looked at Jennifer and rolled his eyes. 'It's all so bloody worthy,' he said.

'Lastly,' Ed said, 'Kitty wanted you all to know she will be getting both the front and the back of the house painted very soon. She left some money specifically for this to be done.'

'She's painting the house?' Simon said.

'Yes,' Ed said, a mischievous smile breaking across his face.

There was a moment before Simon continued. 'I'm afraid I don't understand. Will the house not be sold?'

Like a cat ready to pounce, Jennifer performed a little arse wriggle in her seat.

'No, the house will not be sold… Kitty has left it to the Bowen Trust.'

Silence ensued as everyone present processed the information. Jennifer was the first to interject. 'The Bowen Trust?' she said. 'Who the hell are they?'

'They're a charity. Over the years, Kitty did a lot of work for them.'

'And what do they do this… this trust?' Simon said, blinking several times.

'The Bowen Trust helps people who have offended, or might be at risk of offending, to reintegrate into society.'

Nat bolted forwards in his seat. 'What?'

'Ex-cons?' Christine Pritzker exclaimed. 'Over my dead body.'

Simon now looked like he was having a blinking spasm.

His eyes were opening and closing at an increasingly rapid rate. He looked at Nat, the only legal professional in the room. 'Can she do this?'

Dino got up from his seat with his hands locked as if in prayer. '*Ti prego*,' he said. 'Calm down. Charities have no money. I'm sure they will sell the house to raise funds. Don't worry.'

'No,' Ed said. 'That will definitely not be happening. Kitty and the charity's CEO have put a strict covenant on the property. This stipulates that the charity must use the house for resettlement of clients.'

'We're going to have a fucking halfway house on our doorstep,' Emma yelled. 'You can't do that. We're about to put our place on the market.'

All around the room, previously solemn looks of funereal deference had morphed into fearful expressions of panic. Simon Landes fell back in his seat, while Christine Pritzker warned Ed that he wouldn't get away with it and that they would contest the will.

'Good luck with that,' Ed said.

'What a bitch,' Jennifer said, shaking her head in disbelief. 'What a complete bitch.'

Emma immediately phoned Max. Meanwhile, Nicholas and Nat were huddled together, discussing legal implications. 'Could we contest it?' Nicholas said. 'I mean, she had dementia, for fuck's sake.'

'Maybe...' Nat furiously scratched at his head. 'Perhaps we'll be able to challenge on the grounds that she lacked the necessary mental capacity. It's not really a good look, though, is it?'

'What do you mean?' Nicholas replied sternly.

'Imagine the headlines when the papers hear about it,' Nat said. 'Wealthy residents of Albion Park challenge charitable legacy because of the effect on house prices.'

Ed surveyed the tumult of the room with the contented

grin of one who knew his aims had been accomplished. This was the scene he and Kitty had envisaged when they first discussed the possibility of transferring ownership to the Bowen Trust. It was perfect. Not only had she provided the charity with their biggest ever single donation, but she had also struck a palpable hit for those she felt were powerless to redress the balance.

Owen sat on a bench opposite the marketing suite and looked over at the site where the Keynes, Attlee and Beveridge blocks once stood. He couldn't believe the size of the hole demolition had left behind. It was vast. So much bigger than he would ever have imagined. It was now possible to see right the way through to the park and beyond. Trees, distant houses and a newly revealed expanse of sky had replaced the three buildings. The effect was disorientating. Bizarrely Owen almost struggled to remember what it had looked like before. It was a feeling every Londoner was familiar with. All over the city, new landscapes would appear almost overnight. Beloved landmarks, sprawling estates, public institutions: all had been targeted by indiscriminate wrecking balls and replaced with bland housing developments and poorly designed high-rises.

Owen had recently heard someone describe London as a city of holes. All over the place, developments had rendered the familiar unfamiliar. Gaping holes resembled wounds. Each one representing another organ ripped from the body. It was as if those in charge had forgotten what the purpose of a city was. Cities are places for people to live and work in. A place where its citizens can access a culturally rich existence. Somewhere where people can cultivate social and civic relationships within like-minded communities. What they are not, or at least shouldn't be, is a place to provide capital for investors to exploit.

Owen checked his phone. Ed had said that he would message him once the meeting with the residents was over. The two of them had arranged to meet at Kitty's house when he was done. Although Ed had stayed at the house while he organised probate, Owen hadn't been around there since he learned of Kitty's death. While it had been a relief to find out Kitty had been protecting rather than reject-ing him, Owen was still struggling to absorb everything that had happened. Obviously he was upset about Kitty's death. But he was also angry at the way she had handled things. Ed had been her only companion on her death trip to Switzerland.

After he found out what had happened, Owen watched a documentary online about assisted dying. The film fol-lowed a woman ending her life at the same place Kitty had gone to. Surrounded by factories and workshops, the clinic was located on a dreary industrial estate. It was functional and lacking in humanity. Owen couldn't stop thinking about Kitty waking up on the morning of her appointment, armed with the knowledge of what the day had in store for her. Her last ever journey would be through dreary Swiss suburbs. He understood her reasons. It was just upsetting that such an interesting life should be snuffed out in such drab settings.

The letter Kitty wrote for Owen left him in no doubt of her feelings. But still, it was hard to comprehend her actions. She should have allowed him to say goodbye. He wouldn't have tried to dissuade her. It was her choice, no one else's. Her concern that Owen's knowledge of her condition would make already impossibly hard decisions even harder wasn't a good enough reason for shutting him out completely. Ed said that impaired judgement was one of the hallmarks of the disease. Inevitably this presented challenges around all kinds of decision making.

'She was suffering from a serious neurocognitive disorder,' Ed said. 'She wasn't thinking straight. Besides, I think she liked the idea of choosing her time of death. It was a way of taking back control of her own fate. And as you know, Kitty was nothing if not a control freak.'

While waiting for Ed to contact him, Owen crossed the road and walked over to the new development site. Placards on the builder's hoardings promised spacious suites, duplexes and penthouses. Young professionals were targeted with promises of a fitness centre, proximity to the city, twenty-four-hour concierge service and a Wi-Fi lounge. A modular office in the car park was being used as a sales and marketing suite. Above the automatic doors, a billboard announced the name of the new development: Albion Way #A Vision for A New Way of Life.

Inside the office, the clumsy play on words continued to be exhausted with wall stencils proclaiming #Our Way of Life, #An Easy Way of Life, #Live Life Your Way, #The Right Way of Life. Owen walked around the office, looking at the prints of architects' drawings that lined the walls. Apart from him, no one else was there. He walked over to the main desk and rang a bell. Eventually, a young woman emerged. She smiled at Owen and asked if he was interested in buying a property in the new development.

'All of the top-tier and premium properties have been bought off-plan,' she said. 'But there are still some one, two and three-bedroom properties available.'

'How much for a one-bedroom?' Owen asked.

'Prices range from £590,000 for a one-bedroom, £680,000 for a two-bedroom and up to £1.75 million for a three-bedroom apartment with views of the park.'

'And all of this stuff that's advertised,' Owen asked. 'The gym, the concierge service… Wi-Fi lounge. Is that for everyone?'

'No. Only private residents have access to these amenities. If you would like to register your interest, we can email you a brochure. You'll also receive our newsletters which will keep you up to date regarding availability.'

The woman handed Owen an iPad. He typed in his details and began answering questions in a section titled 'What are you looking for?' Once he had registered his interest in a two-bedroom apartment with an available budget of £650,001–£750,000, he handed the iPad back to the woman. He didn't know why he was bothering with this charade; except he enjoyed the woman thinking that he could afford to buy one of these places.

Only someone who had never been skint could suggest money can't buy happiness. It's well established that the primary source of stress for most people is a lack of money. And even though the funds Kitty had left Owen were tied up in shareholdings and other assets, the prospect of their arrival had changed everything. It's not like he would never have to work again. But knowing he could now afford the deposit on a flat – and therefore provide security for the boys – had lifted a heaviness that had been pressing down on him for as long as he could remember. Suddenly his head felt less constricted. A grave mass of pressure had been released. It was like a hole had been bored into the part of his skull which suppressed his worries.

The night Ed unexpectedly turned up at the AA meeting was one of the strangest moments of his life. In the space of ten minutes he not only discovered Kitty was dead but that she had also left him a considerable sum of money. How does one process that sort of information? Especially when you're sitting in a sushi bar, surrounded by strangers, and you've just eaten a prawn cracker with too much wasabi on it. Owen was shocked. But, at the same time, elated. No sooner had Ed told him what had happened, though, he immediately began to feel guilty for even thinking about the money. The sense of relief, however, had been overwhelming. Kitty was dead. But it felt like he had won the lottery. While Ed described their final day in Zurich, Owen wondered whether his reaction was proof that he was devoid of emotional empathy. On balance, he wasn't even sure if he was receiving good news or bad news.

A message from Ed popped up on his home screen. The meeting was taking longer than anticipated. He would message again once he was back at the house. As Owen left the marketing suite, Max Crossley drove past. Owen turned his head, hoping not to be spotted. He hadn't spoken to Daisy since the party. She had tried to contact him a few times in the immediate aftermath, but after a while had given up. Owen had recently been looking at her social media accounts. The intention was to send her a message and ask if he could see her. Inevitably Daisy featured high on the list of people he wanted to make amends to. From the pictures she had posted online, it looked like she was living permanently in LA now. Gone were the semi-naked photos and tirades against online stalkers. She looked fantastic. In many of the pictures, Daisy was standing outside glitzy events holding a microphone. It looked like she had a job in TV. Fitz had told him that although the preferred option was to make amends in person, a letter would suffice if this was not possible. Owen was currently on the fourth draft. He couldn't locate the appropriate tone. Everything he wrote sounded too creepy, too contrite. He could imagine Daisy and her mates laughing at the self-pitying confessions of some older bloke she once shagged.

'Just write the letter,' Fitz had said. 'As long as you feel shame and guilt, you're never going to get better. Park your ego and think about the misery your behaviour caused others.'

Owen was dubious as to the wisdom of this advice. Apart from alleviating his burden, what good could come from it? Daisy was evidently thriving. Their affair no doubt consigned to an ever-growing list of life experiences. He didn't doubt for a second that he thought about her a lot more than she did about him. She probably didn't think about him at all. For Owen, their relationship had been symptomatic of a collapse. It had presaged a prolonged period of epic degeneration. The ramifications had been far-reaching and the source of endless bouts of self-recrimination. He wondered if that was what a midlife crisis was. A phase characterised by intense introspection that's as routine as puberty. The objective, presumably, is to come to terms with where you've landed. To reconcile yourself with your achievements, or lack of. To finally shed the layers of idealism and ambition which have kept you warm for so many years. In this way, you ready yourself for the harsh reality of life. Life is death. It may always reach for the sun, but its end is inevitable. Once you've accepted that, though, what is there to look forward to? How can you move forward without being dragged back by the burden of regret? And how do you live with those feelings without being derailed by them?

A bus drove up next to him. Emblazoned on the side was a giant poster advertising the new Run for the Shadows album. The record had been nominated for the Mercury prize, topped the album charts and was a hit all over Europe. Although the album had been out for a while, the band's label had embarked on a second run of promotion. Owen looked up at Stuart's supercilious sneer. Arrogance of that magnitude was hard to hide. He stared down from the bus like a feudal lord surveying his vassals.

Remarkably Owen was OK with it all. The band's success was not the source of perturbation it might have been had he not been sober. And at least Harley and Dexter were able to tell their mates that their dad used to play with RFTS. Most of his achievements were in the past tense now. Like the flickering light of a distant and dying star, they emitted a fading glow. But at least they once existed. It was good to know that, once upon a time, they had burned brightly.

Owen checked his phone. Ed hadn't messaged him again. He wasn't really in the mood for going to Kitty's house now. He and Ed were supposed to be going through those possessions which hadn't been allocated in the will. Owen couldn't imagine any of Kitty's belongings residing anywhere else but in her house. So much emotion, so many memories were invested in those objects, each item a personification of her outward self.

Deciding that he had enough for one day, Owen got on the bus. He made his way to the top deck and sat down on the back seat. As the bus pulled away, he turned around and watched Albion Park as it began to recede from view. He could just about still see Kitty's house. It was the only house without a high surrounding fence and automated doors. The only house which didn't gleam and glisten from a distance. No doubt the neighbours were thrilled at the prospect of Kitty no longer living there. For years they had been complaining that her house lowered the tone of the area. The more everyone complained, though, the more obstinate she became. If they had just let her be, no doubt Kitty would have pruned the trees and painted the outside of the house of her own volition.

Soon, Jacquie, Harley and Dexter would move into their flat in the new development. It was strange to think they would be living in Albion Park, but neither he nor Kitty would. He would much rather not have to go back there again. At least not for a while anyway. Similar conflicts would rage on. The residents would find other issues to stoke the flames of discord. Only Kitty would no longer be there to provide a voice of reason, to act as a bulwark against the inward-looking tendencies of her neighbours.

Owen squinted his eyes as he looked at the street. From that distance, it almost looked the same as it always had. The sky was the same, the same houses were there, the trees were in the same places. Like the rest of the city, it was superficially similar but profoundly different. Owen continued to stare at Kitty's house until the bus turned a corner and Albion Park finally disappeared from view.

Rattles & Rosettes

STEVE GODDARD
Rattles & Rosettes

ship of fools

First published in Great Britain by Ship of Fools Ltd 2014

www.shipoffools.com

ISBN 978-0-9928618-0-3

A CIP catalogue record for this book is available from the British
Library

Cover design: GS Design Partnership
Typeset in Minion Pro Regular
Printed and bound by Hiskey Ltd, Unit d3, 9 Ferguson Drive,
Knockmore Hill Industrial Park, BT28 2EX

For ancient football

'What is a club in any case? Not the buildings or the directors or the people who are paid to represent it. It's not the television contracts, get-out clauses, marketing departments or executive boxes.

'It's the noise, the passion, the feeling of belonging, the pride in your city.

'It's a small boy clambering up stadium steps for the very first time, gripping his father's hand, gawping at that hallowed stretch of turf beneath him and, without being able to do a thing about it, falling in love.'

Sir Bobby Robson

Prologue

Today I lined up behind the lads, ready to go over the top. I stood my stretcher upright and did what the corporal said I should do. I didn't think.

I didn't think about the smell of human excrement, rotting flesh and chloride of lime that is all around us, all the time. I didn't think about the burst of German machine gun bullets about to go phut, phut, phut into the mud, or the soothing hum of others, whistling inches over our heads. As we waited and waited, I didn't think about the lad second from the front, sickly pale, who clenched and unclenched his fists before heaving up all over his boots. I didn't think about losing my footing in knee-high mud, trying to stretcher a man with his leg blown off; or how he may die of shock from a sudden jolt. I didn't give a passing thought about getting tangled up in barbed wire near Fritz's trench, or dwell on the way the wire clings to you like a desperate lover, satisfied only when a sniper's bullet whispers you into sweet nothing.

'Penny for your thoughts,' said the lad in front.

'Don't have any,' I said.

He looked at me and my stretcher.

'Blimey, it's the Grim Reaper's cousin.' He smiled and took a long, nervous drag on his cigarette. I smiled back but my legs were like lead weights holding down a body about to float away.

'Our Father, which art in heaven...' began Padre Brooks. I wanted to run. Like the wind. Anywhere. Even if I did, the end would be the same. I would be shot at dawn by our own guns. But I swear it was only because my legs wouldn't obey me that I stayed put.

7

Don't think, the corporal had said. Don't think. Don't think. In a distant dream I heard the whistle blow. The first men went over. One slipped. At least, I thought he had. He slid back down the trench wall, head split clean in two, from the crown to the top of the nose. An axe blade couldn't have done a better job than that German bullet. He quivered in front of me. Our first fatality and I wasn't even out of the trench. Now I had no time to think. There were calls for bearers to help the injured. We had to leave the poor bugger, still twitching and jerking.

The last few words, scrawled at the bottom of a page in a battered old exercise book, are barely legible. The old lady puts down her magnifying glass and takes another sip of Cragganmore. It's a fine whisky. It needs to be. Dipping into the journal, towards the end, hadn't been such a good idea. She'll ask her grandson to read from the beginning. My, their handwriting was beautiful in those days. She turns back to the first page of the first journal. It is still the same young, disciplined hand but neater here, more leisurely - all curves and loops and old-fashioned innocence. She shakes her head in wonder. Such sweet, sweet innocence...

CHAPTER 1

Five months earlier

Dan Howard escapes the clutches of a clogged-up M25 for the faster-moving M40. He is at the wheel of a mustard-coloured Morris Ital, first registered in 1980 to one Rhoslyn Cadogan. The vehicle is even older than him. Seven years older. He is puzzled how a set of wheels with such primitive technology was ever deemed roadworthy. Life before built-in i-pod docks must have been unbearable. Essence of motor oil and grease seep from the upholstery like incontinence. Three scent sticks of sickly coconut fail to overcome it. He's the first to admit, though, that, as rust buckets go, this one is reliable and workmanlike – the Shaun Derry of saloon cars. Like Crystal Palace's greying midfielder, it does the simple things efficiently. Every successful team needs reliable, no-nonsense players like Derry. Dan sighs. That babe magnet of a motor will have to wait until his band gets a break.

Being fair, there are only 39,763 careful miles on the clock. That's how Nanna Neath drove it. Carefully. Considerately. And not very far. He can't remember his 94-year-old grandmother ever driving from the Welsh valleys to Croydon. Whenever she ventured across the border for the occasional family bash, it had always been by train or coach.

'Merging is dangerous,' was her excuse. She wanted to drive gently down the slip road to the motorway, stop, look right, left, right again

9

and pull out in her own good time when the coast was clear. No chance, Nanna. For 15 years the car had been sitting in a lock-up: until two weeks ago when Dan took the train to Neath to pick up his grandmother, the car and half her belongings. Now she was a reluctant resident of South Croydon. A month's loan from Neath – with an immediate recall clause – would be almost bearable. It's a permanent transfer, though, until the end of her playing days.

All the family bar Dan agreed that his room was the only one big enough for the paraphernalia needed to look after a Very Old Lady. Sister Becky's bedroom was of similar dimensions but she's female, so it was different. It was only different in that, unlike Dan, she hadn't invested far too much of her student loan in some of the best technology available: specifically a 50" plasma TV with built-in 2D to 3D converter, allowing Dan to watch any programme with added depth of 3D. Ironically, the TV is too big to fit into the large cupboard (box room is too grand a description) that's Dan's new abode.

Still, he now has a car, of sorts: and a job. Not the kind he had in mind before graduating from the Liverpool Institute for Performing Arts but, in the middle of the biggest recession in decades, it's a job. At Waste Solutions 2010, a three-day trade show which opens tomorrow at the National Exhibition Centre near Birmingham, he will have a chance to prove he can shift a few units. He hasn't told friends exactly *what* he will be shifting. Too embarrassing, what with those unfulfilled dreams of making it big in the music business. Sally knows what he's selling, of course. Well, she has to. She'll be taking a day out of her own studies to help him on the second day of the show. Men are drawn to Sally like… perhaps not. A waste solutions analogy gives entirely the wrong impression. Moths to a mesmerising flame: that's more like it. Sally's presence can only help. Waste disposal is an industry about which he knows next to nothing. It will be difficult to strike up conversations with hard-nosed practitioners. They'll want to talk to Sally, though. Who wouldn't?

His i-phone rings. Oddly enough, the 1980 Ital doesn't offer a hands-free mobile solution as standard. It reminds him of that recent journey back to Croydon from Neath.

'So you've got bluetongue,' Nanna had said as he fiddled with his earpiece.

'Blue*tooth*, Nanna.'

'Same thing.'

'Not exactly.'

'Well, you know what I mean.'

He did know what she meant. In fact, he was astonished she had even heard of bluetooth but that's Nanna Neath: far too aware for her years. Dangerously knowledgeable. It's high time she showed some respect and faked a little dementia.

Dan's ringtone is the riff to the Beatles' *Hey Bulldog*. That means it's Sally. The opening line of the song is loaded with significance – *'Sheepdog, standing in the rain'* – her first and lasting impression of him when they met on an outward bound weekend a year ago. Their initial attempts at conversation, stuck in deep mud halfway up the boggy Rhinogs in North Wales, hadn't been promising. She said how the hole in her shoe was letting in water and started humming the Traffic song. He said he was surprised she knew it. She said she was surprised he could be so patronising. He said he was surprised Steve Winwood had never liked the song even though he wrote it. She said she was surprised he didn't know that Winwood didn't write it, Dave Mason did. And that he sang it, too. Annoyingly, when they managed to get a signal between mountain ranges, Wikipedia proved her correct. An hour of conversational jousting followed before he returned to that Traffic song. Black clouds were rolling in over the mountains. Given a chance, he said, he would summon a giant albatross, climb on its back and fly with her, through a crack in the cloud, to a place where happiness reigned all year round and they could play music together, ever so loudly. She giggled. He fell in love.

'Hi babes.' Dan mutes BBC Radio 5 Live on the car's primitive radio.

'Where are you?' asks Sally.

'In bluenose country... hate it. Can't wait to get back.'

'You've only just left.'

'Pathetic, isn't it?'

11

'Big day on Wednesday.'

'How so?'

'It'll be 27 January 2010, which means we're a whole year old.'

'Yep, 12 months and we're no further on.'

'What do you mean?'

'Palace. Still no buyer.'

'*Typ*-ical.'

'Gotta say you really nailed *I'd Rather Go Blind* last night.' And she had sung it brilliantly, with no encouragement from an apathetic pub crowd that can't have numbered more than 30 tops. The band had made a collective agreement never to return to the pubs of Balham any time in the next decade.

'Awww, thanks,' says Sally. 'It's a great song.'

'You make a perfect Christine Perfect.'

'Don't you mean Christine McVie?'

'Not on that song. She was still with Chicken Shack and hadn't yet shacked up with John McVie.'

'Pedant. We could do some of her Fleetwood Mac songs. *Go Your Own Way* is great.'

'Nah. FM went downhill after Peter Green freaked out. And anyway Stevie Nicks sings that one.'

'*Rumours* is a classic album.'

'West Coast 70s sell-out.'

'In your not-so-humble opinion! Before I forget, the manager at the Birds and Bees in Battersea has offered us a gig next Tuesday. Kula Faker and Phoney M have dropped out.'

'Nice – but we've got Wolves in the FA Cup.'

'*You've* got Wolves.'

'Did you remind him we don't do Oasis covers after last time?'

'You didn't have to slag off Gallagher *and* Man City.'

'Fake band. Fake club.'

'And finishing with *Glad All Over*?'

'Couldn't resist. Tell him we'll take the gig. Wolves will thrash us if Victor goes.'

'OK. Laters.'

'See you, babes.'

Hmmm. Battersea. The Birds and Bees. It's a good venue. Better than Balham, at least. It will help to get a bad gig out of the system. It will also mean missing a cup tie under lights, against a Premiership team. Ah well. The league is what counts. Palace still have a good chance of reaching the play-offs, in spite of money worries and the imminent transfer of star player Victor Moses. A win tomorrow night in Newcastle will send a serious message to the rest of the league that we mean business.

Dan takes the M42. The NEC is a matter of a few miles away. He hits the rush hour, sighs and returns to BBC Radio Five Live.

'Sport – and we can confirm that in the past hour Crystal Palace have gone into administration and face an immediate 10-point deduction.'

'Oh for...'

'The Selhurst Park outfit have been struggling financially for some time with chairman Simon Jordan actively seeking new investment. Their 10-point deduction will see them plunge from ninth in the table and on the fringes of the play-off race to 20th, just four points above the drop zone.'

CHAPTER 2

The Journal of Tom Daws

Sunday 15 Jan 1914. St Helens, Lancashire - They say Tommy Boyle, our centre half, is quiet and shy off the pitch but he's a snorting bull on it, I can tell you. A bit like Reverend Whitehead. Speak to him in the churchyard and he's decent enough. Fetch him into the pulpit and he gives a right good rant, like this morning.

Being Daws and not a posh family, we sit near the back at St Cuthbert's. Every man knows his place, if you know what I mean. No-one says anything but I would get some strange looks if I sat at the front, in one of *their* pews. I wouldn't want to, what with the fancy clothes they turn up in. Any road, Reverend Whitehead was on about Zacchaeus, the tax collector. Big crowds were coming out to see Jesus but Zacchaeus was such a shrimp he had to shin up a tree to see him. I love being in a big crowd, me. I blame Uncle Albert for that. He took me to my first game at Turf Moor. Needless to say we didn't sit in the grandstand, though I would have had a better view from the seats. The grandstand's for posh folk. I was perched on Uncle Albert's shoulders most of the game.

'Keep thine eyes peeled and ears covered,' he said. Covering my ears was on account of the bad language all around. If Ma had known how bad it was, she wouldn't have let me go. Uncle Albert never let on, of course.

As I was saying, while Reverend Whitehead blethered on and on in his sermon, I remembered I had some cigarette cards, spares of Taylor, Dawson and Mayson. Jack Crawshaw was sat behind. He had three I needed to complete my set: Lindley, Bamford and Harris. His weren't in such good nick as mine and we started arguing, quietly like. Not quietly enough. By now Whitehead had gone on to the story of the prodigal son, the one who ran away from his family.

'Talking of which!' Whitehead raised his voice and looked straight down at me. He must have noticed the cards. 'I cannot but be appalled at the way these so-called professional footballers have left hearth and home to ply their dubious trade in football clubs up and down our land.' Grandpa had nodded off but suddenly came back to life, a bit like Lazarus. He slapped his thigh in agreement. It seemed to encourage the Reverend who took off like a wild stallion. He moaned at the way such a great game, created by honourable men, to improve the character of the 'local uncouth', had fallen into the hands of barbarians, thieves and cheats.

'Playing sport for money,' he said, 'is an abomination.' He chunnered on about being at university with Lord somebody, Kinnard I think but I'd never heard of him. 'Arthur (that was his first name) is a gentleman. A leader, a tough tackler, a man of distinction who would never lower himself to be paid for playing sport.' I can't help thinking he's wanted to sound off like that for a good long time and finally came out with it this morning. Of course, I didn't argue with him in the churchyard afterwards. Ma would clip me one if I did. On the way home, out of sight of other folk, she gave me both barrels.

'How old are you?' she said.

'Sixteen,' I replied.

'Exactly. At your age you should know better than to start an argument in church. We'll get a bad reputation.' Sometimes I think that's all people worry about at St Cuthbert's, their reputation.

Well now, all that happened this morning. I've stayed out of harm's way for the rest of the day, making a start on this here journal. It's made Ma curious.

'Scribbling again?' she said.

'Yes, a letter of apology to Reverend Whitehead,' I lied.

'That'll be the day.'

'Here, read it if you like.' I handed her this journal. I knew she wouldn't read it. That's because she can't read. She doesn't know I know she can't read, mind. She says her eyes aren't what they used to be. Ever since I was a nipper she's said that but she sews and knits for the Bettridges without any problem. Most days she goes up the road to that lazy bunch. They have her doing all sorts, cooking and cleaning, for next to nothing. Once a week I take their dog for a walk. I only do it for Ma. For tuppence, I'd kick it round Taylor Park.

Ma just asked me to read the headlines on yesterday's newspaper. Being Sunday we don't get one today.

'Not the back page,' she says, every time – but who wants to read the rest? There was a gob fire in a mine down Nottingham way on Thursday but I didn't read that out. I never do. It would only make Ma fret. It isn't just accidents she worries about. Grandpa has never been right since he finished at the pit years ago. Something is growing on the inside of his lungs like moss on a sea wall. He can't walk far before his lungs fill up and he can hardly breathe.

Ma wishes I hadn't started down the pit but there's no other employment around here. At least I've got a pal in Billy. He's quite old. 30 maybe. The others laugh at him. His knees knock, he's got bandy legs and veins that stick out but they're just jealous. None of them has ever played inside right for Accrington. Billy did. At one time he was earning £3 a week. He's even played at Turf Moor, has Billy. Three times. Once against Boyle's Brigade! Billy's been on at me about writing a journal. He says I have a way with words but he's the one for words, believe me.

Mostly it's cold and dark when you go down at six in the morning. In the winter it's just the same when you come back up. I walk to the colliery two miles away and it's a mile and half to the face. That's when my shift begins. Whatever the weather up top, it's roasting hot down there. We throw everything off to just a pair of short drawers. Often I'm on my knees at the face but sometimes crawl on my belly for hours at a time.

For lunch we sit where the roof is blown about five foot high. We have 20 minutes. Most days I pester Billy to tell me about another match. He writes a report for each game he goes to and can recite them by heart. Down there in the dark it makes for a right good atmosphere. He remembers where each match took place, what the crowd was like. The way he describes it, it's more like poetry than a report. If it's a big game, like an FA Cup tie, he can even recall which songs were struck up by the brass band. I play them on my harmonica. I take it down in my Tommy tin.

This is my first go at writing a journal. It doesn't read too bad, that. Billy says none of his friends back in Scotland can hold a pen, never mind write with one. He says he was lucky to play football for a living, even though it didn't last long, what with the injuries.

'What are you writing about?' Grandpa just asked me.

'Whatever comes into my head,' I said.

'Well, that won't take long.'

He's always tut-tutting when I read out match reports from the papers. I've lost count how many times he's asked me how one player can be worth a thousand pounds. When I remind him that Alf Common saved Middlesbrough from certain relegation he rolls another cigarette and says the world's gone daft.

'Your Grandpa loves rugby,' says Billy. 'What do you expect from an egg chaser?' Hardly anyone plays rugby in Burnley but they love it in these parts.

Now Grandpa is down the yard, banging and rattling on the privy door. He's got his hobnail boots on and is giving it a right good kick or two. When it's dark you need to be sure you've frightened away the rats. He can be a crotchety old beggar but Ma is kind to him. On cold nights like this she warms a brick by the fire, wraps it in a blanket and gives it to him on his way to bed. The Bettridges bought a chihuahua to do the same thing. Dear it was. Ma says that little monster turns his snub nose up at some of the best beef you'll ever smell or taste, the likes of which we might have once a year at ours.

It's late now and I'm in bed. Grandpa is at the other end. He's hung his cap on the bedpost, as normal. It's the last thing he takes off at night and the first thing he puts on in the morning. I sleep head to tail with him. The room isn't big enough for a double bed. It's been this way since I can remember being able to remember. Grandpa taught me how to play musical instruments, mind, and I'll always be grateful to him for that. He's one for pipes and whistles. I can play those but I prefer the harmonica. He's just asked me to strike up *Abide With Me*.

'It'll wake the neighbours,' I said.

'Bugger next door. Their latest has us up all hours.'

He'll drop off to sleep now, once I've turned down the wick. There are two things I can still see through the gloom. They loom up from beneath the blanket, like icebergs waiting for the next unsinkable liner. Grandpa's feet. They're next to me, on my pillow, as they have been all my life, inches from my face. At least tonight they've scrubbed up well. Yesterday Grandpa had his usual Saturday evening bath by the fire. Ma heats up the water in the copper and insists he gets first use. Then it's Pa, then me. If the water gets cold Ma scoops some out and puts in another bucket of hot. Grandpa's feet get dirtier and dirtier through the week. I reckon I could tell you what day it is by the muck between his toes.

When I was young I was for ever getting tonsillitis and lay in bed with a fever for hour after hour. At night, with nothing better to do, I would plot great adventures across Grandpa's bunions and corns. I scaled his toes one by one, like a mountaineer, planting my flag on top of his big toe. Then I would slide down the toes on the other foot. Round and round, time after time after time again. Things have changed, mind. Until last year my legs weren't long enough to reach Grandpa's pillow. Since I've been down the pit, it's his turn to moan.

I can't imagine what it would be like to have my own bed in my own room, like the Bettridges. Their house is so big they hardly know whether each other is in or not. I've never been inside but Ma says they have two staircases – one for 'them' (that's what the servants call the family) and one for the staff. 'Their' staircase curves its way up to the first floor landing that overlooks the front hall. She says it's wide, so wide you could walk four abreast, with a lush, deep burgundy carpet right across it. The only time Ma dare walk on that carpet is to clean it. She's proud of it, too. She treats it like her own. We don't have any carpet on our stairs, perhaps that's why. The servants' stairs are at the back of the house, well out of sight. They're really narrow, she says and there's a tiny piece of linoleum in the middle of each stair. When the servants run up and down from floor to floor Ma says it makes a real racket but they can't hear anything so it doesn't matter.

I've just read this back and it sounds like I'm jealous. Maybe I am but I'm not complaining. In the house next to us there's four and five to a bedroom.

CHAPTER 3

Dan arranges the spotlights at four corners of the Bintastic exhibition stand and positions himself in the centre circle, ready for the whistle. He tucks some unfashionably long hair behind his ears. Splashed aftershave lingers leisurely. He stands awkwardly in a new, unfamiliar suit – his first for several years. Black with a thin pinstripe, it's a cheap cut but all he can afford. He doesn't dare think about that student loan he has yet to begin paying off. At least this whistle gives him a chance to show off that Christmas present from Sally, a red-and-blue tie, knotted perfectly.

It's almost opening time at Waste Solutions 2010. He looks around at this strange new world of all-singing, all-dancing, all waste-disposing companies. They offer products and services he knew nothing about this time yesterday. Who would have thought there would be worldwide demand for filter overpressure systems for earthmovers and vehicles that work in soil remediation, recycling or demolition? Then, of course, there's the ultra-lightweight, fold-flat cardboard alternative to your average plastic clinical waste container. He tries to marvel at rotating paddles, vibrating forks, plumb bob systems, shredders, trommels, ballistic separators, eddy currents and air density separators. For the first time he, Daniel James Howard, is rubbing shoulders with the very people behind iodine and solvent recycling, thermal treatment of composite materials and new ways to incinerate wastewater that cannot be handled by treatment plants.

The doors to Hall 10 open. Here they come. He smiles. Here come the punters. Pouring in. He makes eye contact. He smiles again. He makes eye contact again. He is appearing accessible, approachable. He is remembering his brief sales training. But behind the engaging smiles Dan's mind wanders all too easily from waste gasification and melting technology solutions to potential offers for the club. What would the administrator accept? Loads of figures bandied about in the media. Say, club plus ground. £10m? If the club is liquidated the ground will be re-developed for housing. Whichever bunch of vultures buy it will have to secure change of use. But they've got the money. They're hovering. Waiting for the final twitches of life. Please God. Surely there must be someone...

A sallow-faced, intense man in his late 30s stops to take a look at Bintastic.

'Yes, it's a brand new idea that secures your wheelie bin to the wall,' says Dan. 'One borough council alone is currently spending £200,000 every year replacing stolen and vandalised bins.' Of course, none of this trauma at the club would have been necessary if Agilo, the investment group owed £4m by the club, hadn't called in the administrator. 'You can't believe no-one has made one of these before, can you?' Now some club will steal Victor, our most valuable asset, for a song. He's been superb all season. The administrator won't care. 'Fire services across the UK have their work cut out with wheelie bin fires. On average, most regional fire services respond to six to eight incidents every day.'

The sallow-faced man takes a leaflet. He's showing all the right buying signs but wants to talk to his people back at the office. He's managing agent for a housing association and thanks Dan. He'll be in touch again in a few days. A housing association, eh? They've got serious money, these associations. Enough to buy up failed football grounds and re-develop them for housing. People like him are hovering.

OK, say £10m for the whole bang shoot. The Bintastic lock retails at £32. So, let's just suppose. He pulls out his smart phone and calls up its calculator. £10m divided by...

'Yes, it's a brand new device that secures your wheelie bin to the wall.' A grey-haired, bespectacled punter disturbs the calculations. He gives the Bintastic lock a good going over. 'One hundred per cent galvanised steel. It's strong, durable. As you can see it requires considerable force to get a wheelie bin out of its grip once it's locked in.' The punter looks interested, so interested that Dan's calculator times out and powers down. 'The back plate here fits easily onto any wall using the supplied concrete screws. The locking bar has these two steel hooks that fit round the handle of any standard wheelie bin.'

First sale of the day! Nice bloke, too. No fuss. No hassle. If only every sale was like this. Dan verifies the pin. As he does so, the man quietly hums Tony Christie's hit *Amarillo*.

'Hate that song,' says Dan. 'Brings back painful memories.'

'Thought it might.' The man smirks and points to Dan's tie. Charlton fans sang *Amarillo* to celebrate Palace's last relegation.

'At the end of the day it's only a game,' says the man.

'Yeah, only a game,' returns Dan. Is it hell. 'And now you lot are a league below us. Who's laughing now?'

Sale and bragging rights sorted, it's time to forget that match and finish those calculations. £10m divided by 32. If he could sell, let's see, 312500 units the club could be his – lock, stock and two smoking wheelie bins.

'How's it going?' A text from Sally. It's going well, he replies. In truth he's finding it almost impossible to concentrate. Nothing wrong with the product, lots of interest: the Bintastic lock sells itself. But this isn't the kind of job he had in mind the day he met Sally in Snowdonia. She had arrived, mentally knee deep in *Reflection in Practice: Maximising Pupils' Progress in the Foundation Stage* (her first year of teacher training). He had arrived mulling over *Back to Mono: Re-discovering the Superior Sound of the 60s* – his final dissertation at the Liverpool Institute for Performing Arts – the college founded by Sir Paul McCartney. Macca himself had handed him his degree. All that and now he's a sales executive at Bintastic. What a waste.

'Poor turn-out,' says his neighbour on the Dutton and Mather Recycling stand. Dan doesn't know him, knows nothing about last year's show, or how busy it ought to be so he nods in agreement. Dan has never exhibited at an exhibition before. It's the first trade show he has ever been to, let alone exhibited at but he is not going to give that away. A coffee trolley rumbles past.

'Three pounds for an Americano!' says Mr Dutton. Or Mr Mather. Or maybe neither.

'Scandalous,' agrees Dan.

'Dehydrating, too. Make sure you have some bottled water.'

'Thanks, I will.'

'The air conditioning doesn't help. Causes chronic rhinitis and pharyngitis, throat irritation and hoarseness.'

'Can't say I've ever...'

'Colonies of microscopic organic dusts grow in large air conditioners. When you inhale the air it causes asthmatic problems. Do you suffer from asthma?'

'Not as far as I know.'

'Count yourself lucky.'

'I do.'

'Done many shows?'

'A few.'

In some detail Dan discovers which exhibition venues offer the best value coffee, Danish pastries and most reliable barcode zappers. Thankfully, another punter disturbs them and takes a real interest in Bintastic. He places an order for 40 locks, any chance of some discount? More enquiries follow. Lunch comes and goes. Dan checks the bulletin boards on his iPhone. Neil Warnock, manager of Crystal Palace, has called on loyal fans to rally round the club and players in these difficult days. He is determined to see the job through while new owners are found. Nice one, Neil. And surely the least he, Daniel James Howard, should do is roar on the lads at as many games as is humanly possible – home and away – beginning tonight in Newcastle.

No, that would be foolish. Sally would go utterly ape if she found out. His devotion to the club is already causing tension in their relationship. Yet, yet... Birmingham International Airport is literally within walking distance. Eastern Airways have a flight to Newcastle leaving just after four o'clock. He can get a taxi from the airport and be in the away end half an hour before kick off. If the cost has to go on a credit card already close to the limit, so be it. It's a question of priorities. All being well he'll cadge a lift to the Birmingham area after the game and be back well before Sally arrives to help him on the stand tomorrow morning.

Right, that does it. He needs an excuse to close the stand early. No current deaths in the family, sadly, but he could use Nanna Neath as an excuse.

'STAND CLOSED EARLY DUE TO ILLNESS IN FAMILY'

Dan hangs up the sign, locks and puts away the cashbox and dons his coat. These are difficult days for everyone in SE25. Oh, it's easy to turn up for home games in August with the summer sun on your back, a batch of fresh signings and all the bubbling optimism of a new season. The real test is when the club's in trouble in deepest mid-winter with a difficult mid-week game in the freezing north-east. Now is the true test. Now is the time for all good men to come to the aid of the Palace.

'Sorry to see your sign,' says Mr Dutton. Or Mr Mather. Or neither. 'Hope it's nothing too serious. Anything I can do?'

But Dan is already out of earshot. He does a sharp right at the glass bottle crushers, ghosts past the drum magnets and barely glances at the rotating paddles and vibrating forks. Daniel is travelling tonight on a plane.

24

CHAPTER 4

Saturday 21 February 1914

Now then, about this here dog. This chihuahua. He's looking at me as I write. He thinks we're going for a walk does Brutus. Not today. I've walked him to Taylor Park, that's true, but I've found this handy bench near some bushes and Lady Emily's dog will just have to sit while I scribble. That's who owns him, Lady Emily. Her Ladyship of Bettridge I call her. I doubt she's much of a lady. Like this isn't much of a dog. Hey, give over! I'll take you when I'm ready. Brutus is small, ugly and spoiled, much like his owner though I haven't seen Her for a few years. They wouldn't put Lady Emily in a school round here. She might start to talk and behave like us lot. That wouldn't do.

Brutus has given up any hope of a walk and jumped on my lap. I can see why they have these daft dogs, well-off folk. They keep you warm on a cold day like this. I don't want to be here, in this park. Not today. There's nothing wrong with the park, you understand. It has a lovely, wide lake where you can take out rowing boats in the summer. I've done that many a time. The place is teeming with people then. Today it isn't. In February it's deserted. Anyone with any sense will be at Turf Moor this afternoon. It's the third round of the FA Cup and we're playing Bolton Wanderers. The match kicked off about 30 minutes ago. We beat Derby County 3-2 in the last round. Teddy Hodgson got a hat-trick. The paper said it was a great game with a fine crowd, almost 30,000. The reporter mentioned a dog, come to think of it. Derby's mascot was a black-and-white terrier who howled at the brass band. He was howling in the last few minutes I shouldn't wonder when Teddy got the winner. Even if we still lived in Burnley I couldn't have gone today. They doubled the ticket prices. Up from sixpence in the second round to a shilling. That's why people like Grandpa say football has lost its soul. It's becoming a dear do for the likes of us, the ordinary working man.

It's darker now, must be near enough half-time. I'll not know who won until Monday morning at work. I'm not allowed to buy a newspaper tomorrow, being Sunday. So that means waiting until early Monday when Billy, or one of the other lads, tells me the score. If we get to the final I'm going to London to watch it. No-one's stopping me. They say the Crystal Palace sparkles up on a hill in the afternoon sun. They say the magnolia and cherry trees are in full blossom there at the end of April. Not that I'll spend too much time admiring flowers. If I can find the money I'll be off to London for the first time for one reason only, to watch Boyle's Brigade lift the cup.

Lads like me don't write journals. Reading this one back I'm sure it isn't worth the paper it's written on. So why do I keep on with it? Mrs Knapp, that's why. She's a tiny hunchback who smells of rosewater and has a right temper on her. Lads are feared half to death when she gets going. Other teachers dish out the beatings, that's true. Mr Hartley keeps a slipper on the harmonium, chalks an 'x' on the sole and gives some backsides an almighty spanking. Funny thing is we never worried about him. But when Mrs Knapp sees a sentence start with a conjunction, like this one, you're in for it. It's the way she looks at you. The way she says things. Sticks and stones can hurt my bones, they say, but names can never harm me. Rubbish, that.

I must have been nine or ten when she called me out to the front of class.

'Let me tell you what this boy has done.' She was holding up my exercise book and I was about to be humiliated. I was expecting her to say 'You are a lemon, Tom Daws. What are you?' And I would have to reply 'I am a lemon, Mrs Knapp.' The rest of the class would laugh but more out of relief that they weren't standing where I was standing.

'This boy has done something shocking,' she said. Terrified, I was. 'In my hand is the finest description of a day out at the seaside I have ever read from one so young. How you had such a good time at New Brighton, young Tom, with only thrupence to spend amazes me. Every boy in this class should read it.'

You could have knocked me over with a feather. From that day on I began scribbling, scribbling and scribbling some more. Maybe I could become one of these journalist types, I thought, writing for the sports pages of the Burnley Post. The next year I even won a place at grammar school. Me. A Daws: at grammar school. But Ma and Pa couldn't afford to send me. The books and uniform were too dear. Mrs Knapp even called round to ours.

'On no account must this lad be sent down the pit,' she said. She were very upset. I mean she WAS very upset. That's the problem. Sometimes I write how I speak and when I do I can feel Mrs Knapp looking over my shoulder, shaking her head.

'If you want to write for the papers you'd better get used to writing properly, not proper,' she said, many times. She also said writing is like football – if you don't keep at it, you lose the skill. That's the reason I started this journal.

When Pa lost his job we moved from Burnley to St Helens. I ended up down the pit with him two years ago. I was 14. My first job was oiling and greasing the coal tubs on the pit top and then I went on the belts picking stones out of the coal. Six months later they got me drawing for the colliers, pushing coal in wagons from the coalface to nearer the pit bottom. I couldn't believe how hard it was. The coal tubs are big 'uns ('big ones' sounds too posh by half) and if yours is full and you're going downhill you have to put two steel bars through the wheels to act as a brake. It's only four feet high in parts so if you're going uphill you'd best be wearing a beret with a bag inside full of sawdust, to stop your head banging on the top of the tunnel. You have to pull on the rails with your hands using all your strength.

The empty space left behind when the coal has been taken out is called the gob. Don't ask me why. Last year we were working at the face and everything seemed normal. The gob had held fine for several days. Then we heard a slow rumble.

'Run for it, lads,' shouted the captain on the face. We got out with 30 seconds to spare. We went back to look at what had dropped. Not even a mouse could get through. The manager made sure the horses came up before us. He's told to do that. The mine owners reckon the horses are more valuable than us. We were shaken, I can tell you. Most of the older lads got good and drunk that night but we were all back next morning, opening up another face.

Some haven't been so lucky. If you have an accident you have to prove it was the fault of the owners to have any hope of compensation. Only a few get anything. Some lads have to come back to work with a limp, trying to do their old job no matter what. They have no choice. Jimmy Pember, a friendly sort is Jimmy, lost a leg. What with him not being able to get another job, Jimmy and his family had no money to pay the rent. When they tried to fetch him out of his house, he bolted all the doors and locked the windows. So they put sacks over the chimney and smoked him out, his wife and kids too.

I don't know why I started writing about school and the mines but it gets it off your chest, I suppose. Maybe one day I'll write football reports. Mrs Knapp thought I could be good enough to work for the newspapers. Billy said that, if I keep at it, I'll play football for England one day. He's sure of it. Grandpa says my head's full of jolly robins and I should be happy I've got a job, any job at all. He's probably right.

CHAPTER 5

Dan is assisting an ailing grandmother in South Croydon. He is taking it easy after a long day in his hotel room. He is roaring on his beloved club at St James Park, Newcastle. It just depends.

The plane landed on schedule. He has even had time to drop in at O'Neills. The usual crew are there – the lads he has met through an unofficial Palace bulletin board with monikers like Wretched Car Crook, Comet and Tadworth Terry. They had pretty much forced him to down a swift pint or two (ostensibly to offset but in fact to compound the debilitating effects of dehydration he wasn't suffering from). Now he's in the away end at St James' Park, high up in Nosebleed City.

'Hope you got to your grandmother in time.' It's a text from Dan's next door neighbour at Waste Solutions 2010. Mr Whatever.

'She should pull through, thanks,' texts Dan in return.

Out come the teams to Mark Knopfler's theme from the film Local Hero. Never mind these jokers from Geordieland. Look at our lads. Heroes all. Look at them, walking tall. Never mind what they're saying about a cash-strapped club in crisis. It's not their fault, not these lads. So what if we've got a makeshift side – only to be expected, given everything that's going on. And here's the living legend, Julian Speroni, clapping the away fans, taking his place in front of our goal: player of the year, best goalie in the Championship by a country mile. Forget that cheating little git Maradona. This Argie has the hands of God. 'Ju-ju-ju Julian Speroni...' He'll keep us up. He may even take us up. Stuff the deduction. Ten points lost but we can still make the play-offs. Anything is possible with this club and these fans. Look around. At least 2000 have pulled sickies and trekked 300 miles for this match. That's commitment. That's what it's about. Look around you, you Geordie boys. Listen. That's us. Loud and proud.

'My mother is causing us problems.' It's him again.

'Sorry to hear that.'

'Vascular dementia. Nasty business.' He's a walking medical reference book.

'Sounds it.'

'Will you be back tomorrow?'

'All being well.' All being if Dan can cadge a lift from a friendly fan tonight, to somewhere near the NEC. He's put out the feelers. The match gets underway. Newcastle's Jose Enrique beats full-back Nathaniel Clyne (Wolves can go and do one if they think they're getting him on the cheap) and puts over an inviting cross. Peter Lovenkrands stretches but toes it just wide. Close. Too close. The phone vibrates. Surely not his new 'friend' again.

'I've tried to call you but I'm getting voicemail.' A text from Sally.

'Sorry, babes. Been asleep. Dehydrated from being in the hall. Not taking calls.'

'I phoned your hotel room but there was no reply.'

'Switched that off too.'

'How are you feeling?'

'Rough ☹ xxx.'

At least this game gives Nick Carle a chance to prove himself. Much was expected from the Aussie midfielder when he first signed but this is only his second start of the season. He whips in a dangerous cross. Get in there, Danny. Oh… close. Makeshift forward Danny Butterfield shows why he usually plays at full back, nodding wide from five yards.

'You say that you love me,' bellows a lone voice, two rows up from Dan.

'Say you love me,' returns Dan and several hundred round him. Once more the hardcore, the true remnant beckon the team to even greater efforts.

'Drinking plenty of water?' Sally again.

'Trying to.'

'Listening to the match?'

'No, just trying to chill. Text me if there's a goal.'

The Geordies get a corner on their right. The ball is fired to the forehead of Andy Carroll, Newcastle's latest world dominating, Bertie Big Bollocks of a centre forward and current holder of the 'iconic' Newcastle No. 9 shirt. They love their No. 9's up here, so they say. Legends like Malcolm MacDonald, Micky Quinn, Andy Cole, Les Ferdinand, Alan Shearer – all of whom won bugger all in the shirt. Carroll, a pony-tailed predator, rises like a salmon on stilts and thumps a header goalwards. Shaun Derry fails to clear the danger and slices the ball into his own net. Oh, at last. Noise. Noise from the home fans. Well done. That's worthy of an ironic clap.

'We forgot that you were here,' chant the Palace fans in Nosebleed City.

'0-1 ☹ xxx.' Sally's as good as her word.

*'****. Who scored?'* It has to sound authentic.

'Own goal. Derry.'

'☹'

Going a goal down only inspires Dan, Wretched Car Crook, Comet and Tadworth Terry – and realistically 1200 others – to greater efforts. And it's paying off. The lads can hear us and are refusing to lie down. They know we're fighting for them – for all our lives; for all our Saturdays. Lovenkrands breaks through the Palace defence again and puts the ball in the net. The linesman flags for off-side. A good decision followed by bad vibrations. A text from Eric Kelly, Dan's boss (aka Captain Bintastic to his employees).

'How did it go today?'

'Decent sales. Excellent prospects.'

'Good crowd?' Just for a moment the guilt kicks in. He's been rumbled. Of course! Mr Kelly means at the NEC.

'OK but died off at the end of the day.'

Twenty minutes left. We've got to get something from this game. Carle swings over another good cross from the left. Top scorer

Darren Ambrose gets to the ball first but their goalkeeper tips the midfielder's volley onto the foot of the post. Neil Danns follows up but his shot is blocked. We can do this. We can DO this. On comes Alan Lee. Built like an ox, not quite as fast: a bustling bully boy of a striker who never scores but we love him to death for trying. Dan gets another text from his boss.

'Good news. Meeting in Bath off. I can give you a hand tomorrow J.'
Oh, God. No. The adrenalin races.
'Don't worry. I'll be OK on my own.' It's worth a try.
'I want to see the show. Could be useful.'
'Don't come just for me.'
'I'm not.'

Damn. Palace throw men forward in a desperate search for an equaliser but Newcastle's Nile Ranger races clear to slot calmly past Jules.

'I see you're losing.'
'☹'
'Bet you're glad you're not in Newcastle.'
'☺'
'See you tomorrow.'
'OK. What time are you arriving?'

'I'll be there for 8am…' There is something else at the end of the text but it is indecipherable.

Defeated but defiant, the Palace players stay on the pitch longer than usual, acknowledging the applause of the away fans. And there is some good news for Dan. A friend of a friend, one Silent 'n' Dudley – so called because he was born in the eponymous Midlands town and travels to most away games on his own – will drop Dan off at Birmingham New Street station. He can get a train to Birmingham International early in the morning and, a tad worse for wear admittedly, be all present and correct at the Bintastic stand by 8am.

One snag. Silent 'n' Dudley is 'dropping in' at the Mood nightclub in Newcastle before driving back to Birmingham.

CHAPTER 6

Monday 23 February 1914

When I got to the pithead this morning several of the older men were looking out for me. They've never done that before. George Goldthorpe handed me the Daily Mail.

'This is what tha'll be needing, young feller,' he said. I must have looked puzzled. Being a bunch of egg chasers, they don't care much for football but this morning was different.

'Aye, go on. Take a good long look,' said George. 'It'll do thee good.' (Mrs Knapp says I can write it the way they say it, as long as it's in speechmarks). I feared the worst. It could only mean Burnley had lost. They were out of the FA Cup. Maybe Tommy Boyce had been sent off. I turned to the back page. In place of the football reports they'd put the picture of a girl wearing a sleeveless woollen swimsuit and laced footwear.

'Now then, this football lark is all well and good but it's high time tha turned thy attention to t' finer things of life.' The other lads egged him on. 'There's many a young lass out there waiting to be swept off her feet.' All of this was because I chose to go to football training last week instead of a trade union dance. And what kind of fair lady would I have found there? Not one I would dare bring home. Ma has her own designs, mind. She keeps dropping hints about the Williams' youngest. Nellie will become somebody's ideal daughter-in-law, a perfect companion for Ma. She can sew and cook and do all the things expected of a young lady. She is right pretty but if we have ever had a conversation that lasts more than a minute I cannot remember it. The Williams family, all eight of them, called round to ours the other day. An hour after they left Nellie came back on her own. By then I was the only one in. She said she had left her scarf by mistake, did I know where it was? I had already found it and left it ready by the door.

'Here,' I said.

'Oh.' She looked disappointed and mentioned something about a church outing, was I going? I shook my head. Then she mumbled something else and left. As I closed the door I wondered why Ma and Pa and Grandpa had gone out all of a sudden. Of course I might be imagining things but it all seemed too convenient, to my mind.

Reverend Whitehead thinks everything is planned from the beginning of time, that there is a perfect partner, a 'helpmeet' for everyone. Beryl, his wife, is much bigger, stronger and louder than him. No wonder he preaches like that. 'It is a dreadful thing to fall into the hands of the living God,' says the Bible but Beryl Whitehead would stand in well if the Almighty got fetched away.

I almost forgot! We won. 3-0. Goals by Freeman, Hodgson and Halley, who, says the Daily Mail, 'dribbled around a defender and shot hard and low past the Bolton keeper. Burnley's forwards ran around the Bolton defence as they pleased – on that play the team must be a strong tip for the Palace.' I hope we draw Liverpool in the quarter-final. It's not so far to Anfield and if they don't put up the prices I may be able to go.

CHAPTER 7

Dan's finger trembles over the send button on his iPhone. One touch and the world will know of this intoxicating turn of events. One touch, that's all. One touch. He hesitates. He must think rationally. He should keep the news to himself but it's oh so painful. He is reminded of the only two executives in the world who know the secret mix of Kentucky Fried Chicken's eleven herbs and spices. Just as well he isn't one of them. Put under pressure, he would crack, no finger-lickin' question. And what about that book he read recently – *I Was Monty's Double* – in which the author impersonates General Montgomery during World War II, to fool the Germans before D-Day? Not even his closest relatives could know what he was doing. How could they keep their secrets for so long? He wants to tell the world what happened just a few moments ago. One touch of the send button and, potentially, more than 400 million users of Facebook could know. It's that simple. The power. The pain.

A visit to Newcastle's celebrated Mood nightclub would never have been Dan's choice to get over the bitter pill of defeat, particularly as he is due back at the exhibition in a matter of hours. It's going to be a close run thing. But Silent 'n' Dudley was decent enough to offer him the lift so he could hardly refuse to drop in at Mood. He had never figured out the attraction of club culture. This DJ-orchestrated oomph-oomph-oomph-oomph-techno-trance-hip-hop-whatever left him stone cold. Then there were the punters: blokes dancing like idiots and female flesh shoe-horned into tight skirts and low-cut blouses – two quarts in a pint pot. Call him a walking anachronism at 23 but he'd sooner settle for the boozer, a game of pool and a quality jukebox offering serious music.

Disorientated by the pulsing lights and incessant beat, he glances endlessly at his iPhone, checking early morning timetables from Birmingham New Street to Birmingham International. Fatigue is setting in.

'Jumpin', ain't it?' shouts Silent 'n' Dudley, three inches from his ear. 'You all right?'

'A bit of fog on the Tyne.' He points to his head.

Silent laughs. He has, it seems, got over the pain of defeat in time-honoured fashion. She's got a half-sleeve tattoo and her name is Jade.

'Can I get you anything, pet?' shouts another female voice. It's Jade's friend. This one has a little gold handbag, big hair and is playing two up front.

'I'm fine,' says Dan.

'How do you do, Fine? I'm Charlie.' She giggles at her own joke and leans revealingly forward. 'Your pal tells me you've come a long way.' She pecks him on the cheek and, Ronaldo-like, half collapses, half dives into his lap. 'I like a man in a nice suit.' He is still in the suit he put on what seems, oh, at least a week ago. It has seen better hours.

'I like women who aren't going to throw up any minute,' says Dan.

Charlie cackles drunkenly. 'And I like a man with a GSOH.'

'Who makes it?'

'Makes what?'

'That kind of car.'

Charlie cackles again. 'It means a good sense of humour.'

'Oh.' Dan acts dumb.

'You obviously don't read the personal ads.'

'Only when I'm looking for a girl with a BPOT.'

'What does that stand for?'

'Basic Probation Officer Training,' he lies.

'What?'

To pass the time, he recounts how a recent report suggests men can laugh women into bed, because a sense of humour makes them seem more intelligent. Women have evolved to find intelligence an attractive quality because it suggests that a man will be a good provider for her and her children. He thinks better of explaining how psychologists say studies have also shown the same does not hold true when the sexes are reversed – men are not more attracted to funny girls. It does the trick. Charlie loses concentration and looks around for her friend. Jade is all over Silent 'n' Dudley, like the rash he may get in a few hours' time. The DJ raps out more unintelligible nonsense – something about a special guest being in the house – and starts up C+C Music's *Gonna Make You Sweat (Everybody Dance Now)*.

'It's Dannzy,' shouts Silent. 'Dannzy's here. *Here!*' Palace midfielder Neil Danns has also dropped into Mood after the game. From nowhere, two dozen fans crowd round the dreadlocked Scouser.

'Everybody Danns Now,' they sing, drink clutched in one hand, air punched with the other. Out of pockets fly pens and bits of paper. Silent 'n' Dudley gets an autograph on the back of a petrol receipt - it's better than nothing. Dan has a matchday programme. The amiable athlete signs it for him. Both bag a pic or two with him. Moments later the DJ puts on White Stripes' *Seven Nation Army*.

'We're the red and blue army,' sing the delirious fans. Minutes later Neil Danns has gone – leaving Dan poised over his iPhone, desperate to tell the world what's just happened, with pics to prove it, but of course he cannot. Dare not.

'Hey Dan. We're in here, my son,' says Silent. 'I've told Jade and Charlie they can come back to mine.'

'Yours? In… *Dudley*?' says Dan.

'No problem.'

'But, I'm not… I've got, you know, a girlfriend.'

'Chill. I'll take 'em both on. Double bubble. The wife's at her mother's.'

'The *wife?*'

'Yeah, well... you know.'

'But…'

'Charlie and you in the back.'

'The thing is…' Dan notices a rising panic in his own voice. 'I *have* to get back to the NEC before 8am.'

'No worries. Four hours to New Street. Early train from there. Job's a good 'un.'

Minutes later a battered X registered Nissan saloon pulls out of Low Friar Street into Fenkle Street, then Westgate Road, through Neville Street onto Blenheim Street – heading for the A1. All the roads are new to Dan. So are his companions. Uninvited, Charlie snuggles in.

'What a bit of luck, bumping into you,' she slurs.

'I'm not here,' murmurs Dan. He wipes the window, heavy with condensation and looks up at orange streetlamps rhythmically flashing by against a dark, dark sky. 'If I close my eyes I will wake up in my hotel room. This is just a dream.'

'You must be dead beat,' says Charlie. Any minute, without warning, she'll throw up and there'll be no escape. 'Ah, never mind, pet. We'll soon be tucked up in bed.' Oh dear God.

Why did he trust Silent 'n' Dudley? Of course, Dan knows he has been lucky to get any kind of lift. But on what basis has he put his trust in a total stranger? Silent is Palace – and that is good enough. He's a philandering Jack the Lad with two very full lips that look like two slugs making love. He dances like David Brent. He drives a beat-up Primera that shudders in fifth. But he is Palace – and that is good enough. Without knowing each other until tonight, Silent and Dan have stood on the same rain-swept terraces (at wonderfully-unimproved grounds), inhaled the same second-hand smoke, held their breath above the same overflowing urinals, disputed the same referees' parentage and hero-worshipped some of the worst professional players known to mankind. They've celebrated an insignificant 4-3 win at the Bescot Stadium, Walsall with more euphoric passion than most Man U fans muster winning three major trophies. Dan doesn't know Silent's surname. They aren't bound by the ethical standards of a professional association. There have been no letters of reference exchanged, no third knuckle, freemason

38

handshake. They share no religious ideals. But they had both been at the Wembley play-off final in 1997 ('Hopkin... looking to curl one... absolutely amazing') and Stockport in 2001, cacking it before Freedman's last-gasp winner saved the club from relegation. Silent is Palace – and that is good enough.

The car is slowing and turning through tighter bends. Now it is stopping at traffic lights and pulling away again. Dan is hauled back into consciousness from a shallow, uneven sleep. For some reason he notices a shop called Castle and Crystal. There is an unfamiliar body lolling on him in the cramped darkness. So it wasn't a nightmare. The car pulls to a halt. The engine dies.

'Told you,' he hears Silent say. 'All tickety-boo. Let the fun begin.' He hears him get out of the car. Charlie stirs, murmurs something incomprehensible, goes back to sleep. There is silence. Still half asleep, Dan glances at his watch. After alcohol-induced stops on the way, it is much later than Silent had promised, gone 6am and still very dark. And this isn't New Street station or the NEC or the Metropole Hotel. It must be Silent's house. Moments later, a rear door of the Primera is snatched open. Cruel, icy air rushes in.

'The wife's back,' hisses Silent. It's his turn to panic. 'Quick.' He opens the front passenger door and drags the still drunk, sleeping Jade into the back seat. 'Make room for your sister-in-law.'

'My *what?*' says Dan.

'Ooh, I like the sound of that,' says Charlie, dreamily. 'That makes me Mrs Howard.'

'I don't believe this,' says Dan.

'You're all on the way to Magaluf,' says Silent. 'I'm giving you all a lift to Birmingham International, OK?' He sounds like Basil Fawlty.

Mrs Silent 'n' Dudley arrives on the pavement.

'These are the people I was telling you about, love,' says Silent. 'This is Dan, his wife Charlie and her sister Jade.'

Mrs Silent doesn't look convinced. Silent must have form.

'They don't look much like sisters,' she says.

'Adopted,' says Silent. 'Their plane was cancelled, so I said I'd take them to the airport.' It's almost convincing.

'So why bring them here?'

'Your husband said he had a guidebook of Magaluf we could borrow,' says Dan, quickly. Not bad for the time of night. Or is it day?

'Yes, almost forgot.' Silent scuttles into the house.

'So… you're Palace fans.' Mrs Silent peers further into the car. 'Garry hasn't told me about you.'

'Garry?'

'That's who he really is. He calls himself that daft name on those bulletin board thingies to protect his real identity. He's for ever on the internet. If it was porn I could understand but it just isn't healthy. At the last count, he'd posted 78,000 comments on one board alone.'

'Impressive.'

'They weren't so impressed in court. It was cited as a major reason for his divorce.'

'My Baz is like that,' chirps Charlie. 'Ruins a relationship. My Baz can't go more than…'

'It's good of Garry to bring us all this way,' interrupts Dan in the nick of time. He is aware Mrs Silent is staring at Charlie's 'Shag me, Shearer' tattoo at the top of her thigh.

'When did *he* play for Palace?' says Mrs Silent.

'Oh that,' says Dan. 'Oh *that!* We put in a big offer for Shearer when he was at Southampton but it was rejected.' Unconvincing but the best he can do. 'And Charlie's a big England fan.' Better.

'Found it.' Silent returns with a book in his hand and jumps into the driver's seat. 'See you later, love. I promised these good people I would get them to the airport on time.' He starts up the car. 'And I'm always as good as my word.' Dan is aware the book Silent is holding is called *Bravo Bulgaria* but isn't going to let on.

'For God's sake, Silent,' he says. 'You've got to get me to the NEC in the next hour. My job and relationship depend on it.'

'No problem.' The car shudders into fifth.

Charlie suddenly shrieks with laughter. 'BPOT. A big pair of… the penny's dropped.'

CHAPTER 8

Friday 6 March 1914

So much for Liverpool at home. We've got Sunderland away, the worst possible draw. The match is tomorrow and I'm already a bag of nerves just thinking about it. Sunderland beat us in the semi-final last year, thanks to a foul on Tommy Boyle by their Charlie Thomson. One game away from the final, we were. Ninety minutes from the Palace. Dirty and clever is that Thomson. He made sure the referee didn't see him nobble Tommy below the kneecap. The injury slowed Tommy down and he wasn't the same player after that.

Perhaps it was just one of those matches we were destined to lose. The tie went to a replay. Two days after the first game, eight of our players caught a train to Blackpool. As the train reached Kirkham station, steaming at full speed, the players and passengers heard a loud crash and saw huge pieces of iron fly past their carriage windows. A crankshaft had broken. The passengers were lucky the train hadn't come off the rails and that no-one was hurt.

There's a saying round here that these things come in twos and threes. The replay was held at St Andrews, Birmingham City's ground. Our lads set off for the game on another train out of Burnley. There were very few seats available so they had to stand. The train was delayed and got into Birmingham less than two hours before kick-off. There were no taxis left at the station, either. Anyway, the game began on time but it wasn't the best way to prepare. What's more our winger, Eddie 'Mossy' Mosscrop couldn't play. Runs like a red-haired whippet, does Eddie. He's a teacher in Southport. 'Aye, and he looks as much when he puts on them spectacles,' says Billy. I'm told Mossy wasn't let into one ground because the gatekeeper didn't believe he could be a footballer, looking a bit nesh like he does. He even has to doff his cap to the school board to be released for mid-week games. He was taking a class on the afternoon of the Sunderland game so the board refused to let him play. The odds were stacked against us and that's not even mentioning a soft penalty awarded to Sunderland, who won 3-2.

So I'm pacing the floor tonight. Tommy Boyle wants revenge. I want revenge. The whole of Burnley (and this small corner of St Helens) wants revenge. The truth is, we're in poor form. Since the last round against Bolton, we've lost 0-2 to Tottenham Hotspurs and 3-4 to Preston North End and those two teams are at the foot of the First Division. Not that we care much about the league. Ask anyone, the FA Cup is what really counts.

I'm fretting, even more than before my first day at work. I'll never forget that morning. The cage dropped down the shaft as if the steel rope had broken. It's hundreds and hundreds of feet to the bottom. The wet, slimy sides of the shaft rushed past you in a blur. Believe me, you drop like a stone. I just smiled and swallowed hard as my stomach hit my jaw. Of course, I tried to look like I didn't care. As the cage got near the pit bottom it suddenly slowed up until it almost came to a stop. I don't know how my breakfast stayed down.

We cut a five-foot seam last week and there was dirt in the middle. We had to cut that out as well and put it in packs. To hold the weight of the coalface we put in square wood chocks about two-foot long and six inches square at the end. We shoved these sprags about every two yards under the coal where the dirt had been cut out. After that one of the lads drilled holes all the way down the coalface. The shotlighter fired explosives in them to break up the coal. Then we took out the sprags and the coal dropped to the floor in pieces.

What I'm trying to say is that I should feel a bag of nerves down there, what with all the gunpowder, the heat and the dark. You get used to it though. I know lads who died just yards from where I've been working. They didn't have time to get out when the gas leaked. It could happen again, at any time, and I might not be so lucky. But here's the funny thing: my stomach's churning more about tomorrow, about something I cannot control, a game I cannot even watch, in a town where I've never been, involving players I have never met.

It doesn't make any sense.

CHAPTER 9

Almost there. Dan hot foots it past the glass bottle crushers and vibrating forks, dives left at the drum magnets, hangs a sharp right at the rotating paddles. He's made it. No sign of Captain Bintastic. Sweet relief. Out of breath and drowning in sweat he takes down that hastily-erected 'closed early' notice and nods a relieved greeting to the sales lady on sustainable corrugated packaging. He does not venture across the aisle, for social reasons. Then it's straight to the Gents where, taking no notice of bemused people around him, he strips to the waist and dowses himself in refreshing cold water. He studies the mirror. The deepening five o'clock shadow must remain, there's been no time to go back to the hotel room across the road and grab a razor.

He buys a coffee and a muffin and walks back to the Bintastic stand at a leisurely pace. All's well that ends well. On reflection it would have been wise to give Newcastle a miss but he is still proud to have got there and back, against the odds. What a night! OK, the team lost and he's knackered but that goes with the territory of being an away fan, more particularly of being a *midweek* away fan in the middle of winter. Several of the travelling hardcore had noted his presence and congratulated him on making the effort. That made it all worthwhile.

Now, with each gulp of latte, Silent 'n' Dudley, Jade and Charlie are becoming a distant dream. Fair dos to Silent. He made it to the NEC on time. The man isn't to be trusted but there was something endearing about him. Exactly where he was going with Jade and Charlie, and what he was going to do with them, was anybody's guess. At least it is no longer Dan's problem. If he has any commonsense he'll apologise and put them on the first train back to Newcastle.

'*Hey Bulldog*' sounds on his iPhone.

'Where are you, babes?' he says.

'About 10 miles away.'

'Any hold-ups?'

'I set off early so hopefully I've missed the worst... your voice, it sounds hoarse, like it does after you've been shouting at a game.'

'It's the air conditioning in these buildings. It causes chronic rhinitis and pharyngitis.'

'Oh, well, last night, when I couldn't get hold of you, I thought you might have lost it completely and gone to Newcastle.'

'I'm devoted but not mad.' Time to change the subject. 'You're best parking at the Metropole.'

'Can I dump some stuff in your room?'

'Number 249. I've left the keycard with reception.'

Another close-run thing. He'd been singing and chanting at the game as normal but shouting to be heard above the din at Mood had really strained those vocal chords. And he needs them in shape for the Battersea gig. He glances at his watch. It's gone nine o'clock. Captain Bintastic is already an hour late. It's unlike him. Dan checks his texts. Yes, he definitely said 8am. Of course, he didn't have to be in the hall that early, the show only opens at 10am, but that's how he is, committed to building a successful business and a stickler for punctuality. Dan decides to call him but just as he starts dialling, the Captain himself appears, sporting a wry smile. It is very unlike him. He playfully punches Dan in the arm.

'Well, I under-estimated you, Danny boy.' Danny boy? That's a new one. They say people look like their pets. Dan's boss owns two Cheshire cats and his well-fed, oval face looks like it has just polished off a saucer of cream. 'I didn't think you had it in you.' Dan waits for an explanation that doesn't come. Instead his boss turns and starts checking the cash box and stock.

45

'I'm not sure… exactly what…' Dan has to be careful, respectful.

'Playing it cool. Admire your style.'

'Really. I don't know what you're talking about, Mr Kelly.'

'I won't say anything to the little lady.' The *what?*

'Sally, you mean?'

'They just don't seem your type.'

'They? Who?'

'You might have sent them their breakfast, like you said you would, *Dudley*…' A little dig in the ribs.

'I… don't…' That name. 'I think you'd better tell me what you know.' Dan's attempt at a casual smile fails. The Captain winks – a sickly, knowing wink.

'I arrived at the hotel just before 8am as I said I would on the text.' The end of the text that didn't appear. Damn. 'I waited in the restaurant, expecting to see you for breakfast. After half an hour I thought you must have overslept so I knocked on your door, 294. A woman with a Geordie accent called out "Come on in, the door's open… *Dudley*."'

'Oh dear God.'

'There were two of them in your bed. When they realised I wasn't Dudley, they asked me if I worked at the hotel. They wanted their breakfast delivered, as *Dudley* had promised.'

'Bloody hell.'

'I would never have imagined…'

'I… what can I say?'

'They didn't seem your type. Sally, well…' Kelly's eyes glaze over. 'Sally is different class.'

'He dumped them in my room.'

'Who dumped who?'

'It's… a practical joke, played on me last night by a friend of mine.'

'Where did you pick them up?'

'I didn't pick them up, I… my *friend* picked them up.'

'But they're in *your* room.'

'It's a long story. Sally. *Sally!* Oh God! I'll explain everything, Mr Kelly. It's just that I need to go to my room. Now.'

'But these figures.'

'What figures?' Dan feels himself floating outside his body. Maybe that albatross has returned to carry him off. His heart beats ever so loudly.

'I can't make sense of the cash box and orders from yesterday.'

'But...'

'The details don't tie up. It's going to take a while to sort it all out.'

'But, I have to...'

'We can't open the stand until it's done. It's as if you weren't really concentrating yesterday, as if you threw it all into a heap and walked out.' Dan's heart is beating out of his chest. If he goes to the hotel, he may lose his job. If he stays he may lose his girlfriend. He may lose both, whatever he does. Perhaps he can sort these figures out quickly. Perhaps he can get Sally to come straight to the stand before going to the hotel.

'Mr Kelly, let me make a quick call.' It cuts to voicemail. Unbelievable.

'You've got an order here for 40 units and something about discount,' Eric Kelly is saying somewhere in the distance. 'What did you offer him?'

'Er...' The combined effect of lack of sleep and panic are making Dan's mind a fuzzy blur. 'I'm not sure.'

'The divine as well as the devil is in the detail,' intones Kelly. 'Looking after customers is all about seeing the sale through to successful completion. Forty good sales could mean 400 more through recommendations and referrals. Let me explain...'

For the next 10 minutes Eric Kelly explains. It seems interminable, longer than 10 minutes, much longer. With every slow second that elapses, the situation is becoming irredeemable. But finally. Finally. Dan says he will only be a few minutes, the hotel is only over the road. He will be back before the show opens, no problem. He runs. A large Italian mother is blocking the entrance to the hotel with half-a-dozen suitcases and too many children. He pushes past them, apologising. He asks for the keycard from the receptionist who tells him a young lady took it a few minutes ago. Damn. He waits by the lift. Come on. Come on. His mobile rings. '*Sheepdog... standing in the rain.*'

'Hi,' says Sally. 'Where are you?' She doesn't sound angry.

'I'm coming up to the room,' he says.

'Only, I can't get in with the key card. It keeps showing red.'

'Oh...'

'You said room 249, didn't you?'

There have been few times in Dan's short life when he has thanked whoever-it-is-up-there for mild, numeric dyslexia. But this morning, it is a gift from the Almighty.

'Yes, 249. I'll be there in a minute,' he says.

Head down and taking three stairs at a time he gives up on the lift and rushes up the stairs, almost colliding with a heavily-pregnant woman who gasps and swears in surprise. He shouts back another apology. He reaches Room 249 and Sally.

'You look awful,' she says.

'Thanks.'

'Here, you try with yours.'

He tries, just once.

'It won't work. Must be a technical problem,' says Dan.

'Give it another try.'

'No point, let's go back to the exhibition.'

'But, what about my stuff?'

'We'll put it back in the car.'

'I need to get myself together. I can't go on the stand looking like this.'

'You look great, as always.'

'But I...'

'No buts. We need you on the stand.'

'But...'

Eric Kelly wears a furrowed brow. Not even the sight of Sally walking towards the stand, and he adores her, is enough to dispel the gloom. It is five minutes before the exhibition is due to open. He is staring into the mid-distance.

'Just had our very helpful bank manager on the phone.' He is trying to disguise a trembling rage. 'The banks got us into this economic mess and are doing bugger all to get us out of it. He's threatening to foreclose on Bintastic unless we pull in some serious cash – and quickly.'

'But it's a great product,' says Dan. 'People like it. You saw the orders I took yesterday.'

'These days, that's irrelevant,' says Kelly. 'The government wants the private sector to lead us out of recession but the banks are letting perfectly good businesses go to the wall – the very ones that could help them do it. It's madness. We'll have to step things up a few gears, take some firm orders and convert the leads. No pressure, Dan but if you want to keep your job we need some sales – and fast.'

CHAPTER 10

Saturday 7 March 1914

On no account must Ma find out what happened today. It is probably foolish writing about it here (she has no idea where I hide this journal) but it might help me get over the incident.

This being Saturday, we came back up at 12. If Burnley had been playing at home I would have tried to knock off early and get the train to see us take on Sunderland at the Moor. As my bad luck would have it, we were playing away. After lunch, Grandpa and Pa argued about politics yet again. Pa thinks Lloyd George is right to 'sort out thems what's running things once and for all.' Grandpa says he's as bad as the rest and that power goes to all their heads sooner or later. He started going on about the shares Lloyd George bought in Marconi, something about insider dealing. I couldn't tell you what went on because I never take much notice of politics. Pa weighed into Grandpa, saying it was only through Lloyd George that he got an old age pension and that giving us all pensions could bankrupt the country. Grandpa said the Germans brought them in nigh on 30 years ago and they're all the better for it. And so it went on. Ma just shook her head. I got out of the house before things got really heated. In any case, I was due to walk Brutus. At least it would keep my mind off the FA Cup.

They keep the dog in a kennel outside the house. He is only allowed inside when it suits them, to keep them warm on cold nights and suchlike. As usual he went mad when he saw me, licked me half to death, rolled over on the ground, tail wagging. Does he have no idea how much I despise him? I suppose he looks forward to seeing me because none of them can be bothered with him. The grounds of their house are so big they could wear him out walking round just once but they never do. I had to use up a bit of time so I took him past the vegetable pitch. Well, that's what I call it because it's near enough the size of a football field. One of their three gardeners, Sydney Crouch, was working on it today. In the summer they grow all sorts – tomatoes, pole beans, lettuce, beetroot, peas, potatoes and marrows. I asked Syd if any of them were around. He said they were all in Manchester for some posh do or other and wouldn't be back until gone midnight.

I took Brutus over a large lawn, past the summer house (I've never seen anyone in it whatever the season) and into the orchard. I go scrumping there in the summer. After that there's a short brew to a natural pond with mallards, moorhens and the like. At the very end are woods where Brutus sniffs and digs around, marking his territory. Then we crossed over the road to the park and took our usual route by the boating lake. While we were at the side of the lake the little feller was set upon by a snarling Alsatian. He asked for it, mind, standing right in front of the ugly beast, yap-yap-yapping. He scampered back to me, tail between his stubby little legs. I picked him up and the daft thing was all of a quiver, bleeding from a nasty wound. Then he started growling at the Alsatian, looking up at me with his big round eyes, too big for his body, as if to say 'let's see him off together.'

I kept the silly beggar inside my coat on the way back to the house. It was dark by the time we got there and Syd had left. I put Brutus back in his kennel but his wound needed washing. I didn't have any water so I had to find the kitchen. The thing is I had never been inside the house, what with Ma being just a skivvy. There were no lights on but I was in luck. The back door was unlocked. I cleaned Brutus' wound, filled his bowl and became nosey, like you do. The kitchen is a cavern, at least twice the length of our house. Even in the gloom I could make out a long row of copper saucepans along the wall. The tiniest can't hold more than a teacup full of anything, the most enormous could take three footballs, side by side. Hanging down from the ceiling were half a dozen pheasants. I'm sure they were ready for the pan because they were beginning to turn, if you know what I mean. Pa says that's the best time to cook them.

On the other side of the kitchen was the range with ovens each side of it, one big, one small. Opposite was a dresser with big cupboards in the lower half and six shelves on the upper half. It makes the one in our back kitchen look like it belongs in a doll's house. I'd say more than 100 pieces of china were on those shelves. On the flat part of the dresser were vegetable dishes, a sauceboat and, luckily for me, some candles with a box of matches. I couldn't resist. Now I could see just how big the room was. On the long table, in the centre of the kitchen, were knives of all shapes and sizes, big long carvers and small ones with strange curves. I saw half a dozen metal spoons, the largest ones had measures on them, from ounces right up to desert-spoonfuls. There was a flour sifter, egg whisk, three graters, two chopping boards - one big, one small. It was just as Ma said, many times.

By now I couldn't help myself. I went out of the kitchen along a passage. On the wall was a box with a large bell and two rows of indicators above it to show which room wanted attention. There was the blue room, pink room, drawing room and seven bedrooms. I crept upstairs to the main reception hall. It was like entering another world. On one wall was a huge mirror in a gilt frame. On the other side was a mahogany hallstand and a grandfather clock that ticktocked, tick-tocked. Ma was right about the carpets and staircase that leads up to the bedrooms. I had never walked on anything so deep and soft. And that smell! Beeswax polish, the same stuff Ma uses at home.

I should have turned round and scarpered but something caught my eye. I had never seen one in a private house before. Doctors have them but it goes with their jobs. The Bettridges have one for their own personal use, that's how much brass they have. In the corner of the hall was a telephone. Their very own. It gave me an idea but there was one snag. I had never used a telephone before though I had seen important people using them.

I must have been there more than 10 minutes, with the clock tick-tocking then striking on the half hour, wondering whether I should or shouldn't. In the end I plucked up the courage, picked up the earpiece and put it to my ear. Nothing happened. 'Hello,' I said. 'Is there anybody there?' Still nothing. I put the earpiece back, picked it up again, pressed a button this time, and again said 'Hello… hello… is there anybody there?'

'Yes, there's somebody here,' said a voice. 'Who in heaven's name are you?' At the same moment the electric light went on in the hall. I felt sick and began to panic. I wanted to run, anywhere.

'Wait a minute. I know who you are,' said the voice. 'You're… you're *Daws'* boy, aren't you?' A girl, about my age, maybe a little older, looked down from the balcony. The Bettridges always refer to Ma by her surname. Never Mrs Daws. Whether anyone's a Miss or a Mrs means nothing to them. What follows is the conversation between myself and this girl, as much as I can remember anyway. I may have missed bits out because I was in a state of shock. I still am.

'What are you doing in our house?' she said.

'I, I… came to walk Brutus…' I don't usually stammer like that.

'Why are you using our telephone? Good grief. Is anything wrong?'

'No, there's nothing wrong. I… well, I needed to find out… something.'

'What?'

'It doesn't matter.'

'Who were you telephoning?'

'A newspaper.'

'A *newspaper*? Which one?'

'It's not important.'

'Yes, it is. You should have asked.'

'I'm sorry. I didn't think… anyone was in.'

The girl came downstairs. Well, almost floated. She was wearing a long blue velvet dress and a fancy blouse with billowing sleeves.

Round her neck was a fine-looking silver necklace. Her long auburn hair was tied up in a bun held in place by a sparkling jewelled butterfly clip. She had to be one of the Bettridges, all right. I had been down the pit a few hours before and looked like it, too. Not that I have anything dear enough to wear in that house. I scuttled towards the kitchen.

'Where on earth do you think you are going?' she said. That's the way they speak. They say things like 'in heaven's name', 'good grief' and 'where on earth?'

'I think I've caused enough trouble,' I said.

'But… you can't just walk out like that,' she said. 'You… you scared me.'

'I'm sorry, er, Miss, er…'

'Emily.' She held out her hand. I was shocked she introduced herself to me and especially with her first name. She looked nothing like the way I remembered her from years ago. Her hand was as white as snow, delicate and soft.

'I'm… Daws,' I said.

'That's your first name as well as your surname?'

'No, that is… my first name's Thomas but you can call me Daws.'
She giggled.

'Well, Thomas Daws, this place is old and haunted. It's scarey when you're on your own. And anyway, I'm bored. I've been here all week without friends, just a pair of awful brothers.'

'I'm sorry, er, Miss Emily. I didn't mean…'

'It's just Emily.'

'Well, I…'

'You were trying to make a call to a newspaper. It all sounds terribly exciting.' Terribly. That's another one of their words.

'It wasn't.'

'Oh, come now. Do tell.' She disappeared into one of the lounges. 'Brandy?' I had never tasted the stuff. Ma doesn't approve.

'It's not my place to be in your house drinking alcohol.' I hung around the door. 'If your parents come back…'

'Nonsense, you're my guest.' She gave me a full glass.

'I didn't break in,' I said. 'I needed water for Brutus and the back door was open. Sydney said no-one was in.'

'My family are at some do in Manchester. And I shouldn't be at home at all.' By now she had re-awoken the fire. It was blazing. She offered me an armchair – three times wider, deeper and comfier than anything I had ever sat in before. I asked for an old newspaper to put on it before sitting down, like I have to in the parlour at home.

'The school sent me home again. I'm a boarder,' said Emily. 'They've lost patience with me. I can't go back until I've *changed my ways*.' She said the last three words like a headmaster, telling someone off in his study.

'What had you done that was so bad?'

'Not studying.'

'What, *all* the subjects?'

'Yes but especially Latin.'

'They didn't teach that at my school.'

'Count yourself fortunate.'

'I'd like to learn another language.'

'Believe me, you wouldn't.'

'My English teacher said many of our words come from Latin and studying it helps you master your own language.'

'Well you wouldn't want to study anything at my school.'

'I would gladly be stuck at a desk learning Latin, Ancient Greek, Egyptian hieroglyphics, anything is better than spending the rest of my life down the pit.' I was shocked how deeply I felt. It was the first time I had admitted it to myself, let alone someone else – and a girl at that.

'I should imagine your work is great fun,' she said. 'I've seen miners like you. You seem a rather jolly gang, going off together each morning with those Davey Lamps and a packed lunch in little tins.'

I stared at her. 'You… you make it sound like a picnic.'

'I'm sure you work very hard but you get paid for it. Studying is tedious, apart from games and, at my school, football is deemed unladylike.'

I could not imagine such a delicate thing as Lady Emily donning a pair of leather boots and throwing herself into a goal-saving tackle. Very few girls I know like football. I told her about Saturday afternoons at Turf Moor, about Tommy Boyle, Bert Freeman, Eddie Mosscrop and Teddy Hodgson. She poured another brandy and even wanted to know what positions they played, whether they were left or right-footed, if they could head a ball well, who they played for before transferring to Burnley and the rest. Maybe the brandy got to me but I stood up and started to show her how Eddie would beat his man and centre for Bert to score, how Tommy tackled men six inches bigger and broader than him.

'I should like to see your team play,' she said. 'Will you take me?'

'Well, I… I, that is… of course.' Not for the first time today I was shocked. 'But your parents…'

'They need never know.'

'It wouldn't be right for me to…'

'Nonsense.'

'I'm sure they wouldn't take kindly to someone like me taking their daughter to…'

'I dare say we can meet any opposition head on, like your Tommy Doyle.' I saw a delicious defiance in her deep brown eyes.

'It's Boyle, actually.' I said actually! God help me, I sounded like one of them. They'd never forgive me at work. 'I would like to have been at the match today. That was why I was using your telephone. I was trying to make a call to the Burnley Post to find out the score.'

'Oh, well, let's do it now,' she said and disappeared into the hall. Five minutes later she was talking to a reporter.

'A crowd of 34,581… first half dull… Tommy Boyle outstanding… goal by Dick Lindley ruled offside… Halley hits the crossbar… Freeman fouled in the box but no penalty… lots of good chances, none finished off… final score 0-0… replay Wednesday afternoon.'

'So we're still in the cup,' I said. 'It might still be our year. Well, er, Emily… you've been very kind but I've got to go. Ma will wonder where I am and…'

She spun round and stood in front of the door, blocking my way. 'Let's go.'

56

'Go… where?'

'To the match. On Wednesday.'

'But… that's impossible.'

'Nonsense. We'll go on our bicycles.'

And that was that. Miss Bettridge seems used to getting what she wants. I dare not tell Ma what happened and why I was so long walking Brutus. I would like to go to the match with her ladyship but, in heaven's name, if anyone finds out what on earth will they say?

CHAPTER 11

After rasping joyously through the Small Faces' *All or Nothing* on guitar, Dan moves over to the stage piano in the shabby, upstairs function room at the Birds and Bees. It's not his favourite Beatles cover but *Hey Jude* always goes down well. As Macca himself said, the song doesn't really need the big na-na-na, na-na-na-na finale but that's the bit we're still singing and swaying to more than 40 years later.

'How many of you were around when this song came out?' says Dan. A couple of dozen hands go up among the 70 or so punters. 'And how many of you saw the Fab Four live?' No takers. 'It's the same everywhere we go. You had the chance we never had and didn't take it.' He shakes his head. 'Well I suppose some of their gigs *did* cost 25p to get in.'

'Hey, five bob was a lot of money then, you cheeky git,' shouts a man from the back.

'Yeah and too many screaming girls,' says his mate.

'I *was* only *four*.' This time it's a woman at the front. Her friends laugh.

'Well, whatever… we're going into a break but before we do I'd like to introduce the band,' says Dan. 'On sticks, please give a big hand to Mark 'Ginger' Sumner… behind the bass, Kev Yates… showing me up on guitars, Graham Hall… on keyboards and vocals, and much too good for the rest of us, Sally Cavender…'

The Birds and Bees is one of the better pubs on the circuit. While he banters with the audience, Dan is only too aware of similar pubs disappearing week by week. Venues that once played an integral part in shaping the UK's musical heritage are becoming extinct, replaced by more profitable, soulless theme bars.

Before launching into a pop classic that will last more than seven minutes, Dan checks the iPhone hooked to the belt round his waist. It is on the highest vibration setting, one short of pneumatic drill.

'Hey Jude, don't make it bad...'

Tadworth Terry has promised to text him the moment a goal goes in at Selhurst Park where Palace are playing Wolves in that FA Cup replay. All the pre-match yatter has been about the financial lifeline afforded 'cash-strapped' Palace by securing a bonus match at home against Premiership opposition. Even better, national TV are broadcasting the whole game live. It's all about the money, of course – so much for the romance of the FA Cup. Dan can only imagine that time, before the coming of 'modern football' and the gulf between mega-rich and minnow, when the playing field, if never actually even, only tilted gently.

'Take a sad song song and make it better...'

He has read the history books. Good management, careful investment and hard graft meant unfancied teams often made it to the final. Some even won it, Sunderland and Wimbledon to name but two. But as the saying doesn't go: if it ain't broke, fix it. The elite got together in smoke-filled rooms and, when we weren't watching, shagged the rest of us senseless. Their bastard offspring: the Premiership and Champions (joke name) League. Might as well tot up how much the owners of each club are personally worth and the amount each club pays players in wages. You'll pretty much see the final Premier League table before the season begins.

'Remember to let her into your heart...'

Dan's uncle has wound on, endlessly, about the FA Cup Final, how it used to be the pinnacle of the footballing year, the only club game televised live. Now it's a snoozefest, nearly always featuring at least one of the top four Premiership clubs. The early rounds are worth watching, though. Thank God for tin-pot clubs like Hinkley,

Burscough and Totton. Dan has no idea where they are but that's half the fun. Real football on tight little grounds where you get close enough for the players to hear your best insults and, on a helpful breeze, still whiff the Bovril and liniment.

'Then you can start to make it better...'

It's 15 minutes into the second half and there is no score at Selhurst but Dan fears the worst. Mid-song, his mind wanders. Administration has meant the squad is down to the bare bones and weakened even further by the enforced sale of Victor Moses to Wigan for a rubbish fee. Never mind. Taking his place upfront is a player who will have Wolves quaking in their day-glow boots – full back (yes, full back) Danny Butterfield, scorer of one goal in six years and, ironically, sporting an early Beatle mop top.

'Hey Jude, don't be afraid...'

Dink. Dink. Bzzzzzzzzzzzzzzzzzz. Dan doesn't hear his phone but gets the hippy, hippy shake. And now he can't sit still. While he sings of fears calmed, his own are aroused. Looking at the screen of his phone in the middle of a song would be pushing it too far (though he is tempted) but to his mind there is no doubt what has just happened. We are one down and going out of the Cup.

'Better, better, better, better, better, better, ohhhhhhh...'

Dink. Dink. Bzzzzzzzzzzzzzzzzzz. More bad vibrations. Now we're getting thrashed, made even more painful by Wolves' manager Mick McCarthy's failed attempts to steal one of our best young prospects, Nathaniel Clyne, before the transfer deadline. Get off our cloud, Mick. Clyne is on our side, yes he is.

'Na-na-na, na-na-na-na...'

Standing next to the bar, a group of men, Finchcock's Original in hand, sing 'n' sway. Five women wave mobile phones above their heads.

'Na-na-na, na-na-na-na...'

Desperate to be put out of his misery, Dan is tempted to end the song prematurely but the punters won't let him. Hushing the band, he calls for the women in the audience to sing the refrain on their own. They oblige. Now he calls on the men. They oblige. Now the band crash back in.

'Na-na-na, na-na-na-na... Hey Jude.'

Dink. Dink. Bzzzzzzzzzzzzzzzzzz. Not again, surely. Dan lurches into the final bar to a smattering of applause. He grabs his phone to check three new text messages.

Butts!!!!!

Butts again!!!!!!!

Butts hat-trick!!!!!!!!!

Tadworth Terry, who sells bespoke zimmer frames to the elderly, should know better. Practical jokes by way of ridiculous texts are not cricket. Dan checks the BBC Football page. He can scarcely believe it. Danny Butterfield, of all people, has scored not just any old hat-trick but a *perfect* one (left foot, right foot, header) in six minutes 48 seconds – the quickest by any player in the club's 105-year history.

Dan punches the air and, buoyed and jubilant, considers Andy Warhol and the hapless mayfly. For it was the American artist who, understanding the ephemeral nature of celebrity in an age of mass media, said everyone will be world-famous for 15 minutes. Danny Butterfield doesn't even need a quarter of an hour. After years as a quiet, model professional, less than seven incredible minutes will do. It's long enough to put him in the history books, possibly for the next 100 years. Danny Butterfield! A perfect hat-trick! Where did that come from? Perhaps he has studied the mayfly which starts life as an egg on a riverbed before hatching into a nymph. Hidden from view, it feeds on algae for two years before finally emerging as an adult with one obsessive thing on its mind. In a matter of minutes it must find a mate – no courtship ritual, no foreplay, just full-on copulation – before dropping down dead. Consider Wolves, shafted thrice in 408 pulsating seconds. Whatever befalls him during the twilight of his career, Danny Butterfield can retire a legend in South London, a big fat, satisfied smile on his face.

By the end of their second and final set, Born Too Late have given the audience a guided tour of their favourite decade, covering everything from the Kinks' *Waterloo Sunset* to the Mamas and Papas' *Dedicated to the One I Love*. A good response from the punters has almost made up for missing those moments of history a few miles down the road. Plugs are pulled, leads wound up, expensive guitars laid gently to rest in flight cases.

'I don't remember seeing Keith Moon pack away his own drums,' quips Mark 'Ginger' Sumner.

'Nothing left to pack away,' says Kev the bass.

'True.'

'Thanks everyone.' Dan is packing up even faster than normal. A hat-trick awaits.

'I'm Hank,' says Graham, as usual.

'Me too,' says Mark.

'Where shall we go?'

'Dunno…'

'Indian suit you all?' It's an unfamiliar voice. They turn to see a tall, slim man, probably in his early 30s, dressed casually with a thin shadow of a beard, sporting square-rimmed Ray-bans. 'We've not met…' He offers Dan a business card. 'Stuart's the name. Stuart Bensham. Pouring In Productions.'

'Oh… hi.' Dan looks at the card quizzically and shakes the man's hand.

'You might have heard of us,' says Bensham.

'It rings a faint bell.'

'We specialise in tribute acts. When someone famous dies, the newspapers always talk about tributes pouring in?' He goes up at the end of the sentence, turning a statement into a question: annoyingly Aussie-style.

'Yeah, that's right. You handle Kula Faker…'

'Among others. I thought they were playing tonight but I'm glad I saw you instead. I'd like to propose something over a curry… at my expense?' Another half-question.

Few things prevent Dan from busting a gut to see highlights of a Palace victory but he can already smell a lamb bhuna, peshwari naan, onion bhaji and a hat-trick of poppadoms consumed in a lot less than seven minutes. And it's free.

'We're intrigued,' says Dan. 'What's it all about?'

'A new TV music series. We're looking for bands like yours.'

'A competition.'
'Yes.'
'Called?'
'*Britain's Got Tribute.*'

CHAPTER 12

Thursday 12 March 1914

The entire town of Burnley shut up shop yesterday. Mills, foundries and factories closed after lunch. 49,737 squeezed into Turf Moor including 3000 from Sunderland. Even Mossy was able to put away his mortar board for this one. Everyone was there. Everyone, except me.

The day started well enough, what with Billy doing my shift. Her Ladyship had suggested we go to Turf Moor on our bicycles, even though it's more than 40 miles. Keen cyclist, she is. I told her that would be a grand idea. There was only one problem. I'd never ridden a bicycle in my life, though I wasn't going to tell her that. If I could afford one, that might be a different matter. Guess who came to the rescue! I spent the best part of this week learning how to ride Billy's boneshaker. I was still a bit unsteady by yesterday morning but it would have to do. I thought a good place to meet up would be on the road out of St Helens at Billinge, away from wagging tongues. If I were seen with the Bettridges' daughter, especially on the way to a football match, Ma would get the sack. 'Nonsense,' said her Ladyship but that's because she has no idea what it's like to be anything other than one of them, if you know what I mean.

The match was due to kick off at 2pm so we agreed to meet at 8am and try to get there before most of the crowd arrived. Billinge is at the top of a long brew. I got there way too early. It was still only half light and very cold. Waiting up at the crossroads I was full of nerves and here's a funny thing, not about the match. That's what surprised me. I was worried sick about Ma losing her job. I should never have gone into that house on Saturday. Like as not I'd be in for a fearful beating if anyone finds out. It's not too late to go home, I told myself and had finally decided to do just that when I saw her Ladyship toiling up the brew on one of these fancy new tricycles. She was wearing a brown coat with big, padded shoulders and a fur bonnet. Expensive leather gloves, too. I tell you, her cheeks were glowing pink all right.

'Made it,' she said, out of breath and all of a do. Her eyes sparkled. So I hadn't been wrong for the past few days because, you know, your mind can play tricks on you and all that. I have to admit it. A right lovely looking thing is our Lady Em.

'Do you like it?' She pointed to the rosette pinned to the front of her bonnet. It was claret and blue. I said something like 'Oh, it will do, I suppose.' Then I noticed a wicker basket strapped behind the saddle.

'Lunch. Come on.' Before I knew it we were peddling at full tilt towards Wigan. 'Nice bicycle.' She glanced my way. I wondered if she was joking but didn't want to find out.

'Yours is useful, what with the basket and everything,' I said.

'It's mother's, though she has no idea I've taken it today. She's promised me a new two-wheeler if I return to that awful school.'

'And?' I found myself hoping she wasn't going back.

'It will take more than a bribe.'

'What are you going to do?'

She shrugged her shoulders. 'Today I don't care. I'm off to see a game of football.' We rode and talked about all sorts – the match of course, the Kaiser, the white rabbit of Crank (a ghost I'm told), Isobel Robey, the famous witch and growing turnips. I found out her two brothers, Walter and Freddie, both work for 'father' at the local sand works run by Pilkington. They make glass and own most of the town.

'When I say they work I mean they do the least they can,' she said. 'And they do even less at home. Yesterday Freddie actually took Brutus for a walk. Mother just wanted him out of the house. She had special guests. Freddie came back without Brutus. He still can't find him.'

I slammed on the anchors so hard I almost went over the top of the bicycle. We pulled up next to a pub on the other side of Wigan.

'What do you mean?' I said. 'Where… where was he going? Where did he lose him?'

'He's not sure,' said Emily. 'Somewhere in the park. A big dog chased him away. Maybe the same one that went for him on Saturday. It was Freddie's fault. He has to find him.'

'You mean Brutus was out all last night?'

'Well… yes.'

I felt sick. For one thing Brutus should never have been taken for a walk so soon after being attacked. As for losing him… we cycled on for another mile or so but I couldn't get that wretched little scrap out of my head.

'How far has your brother looked?' I said.

'He says all over,' said Emily. 'He was out for at least an hour yesterday.'

'An hour? One hour? Is that all?' I braked again. 'Brutus won't last another night in this weather. I'm going back.'

'But, what about the match?'

'If we win 6-0 I won't enjoy it, thinking of that little feller whimpering somewhere.'

'I… I didn't realise he meant so much to you.'

'He doesn't. At least I didn't think he did.'

The hills we had come down seemed much longer and steeper on the way back, the wind gustier. It bit into our faces. We hit a stretch that was flatter, got our breath back and rode along, quiet like.

'You must think me heartless,' she said, at last. I didn't reply. She glanced over to me. 'You do, don't you?'

'No, well, yes I did but that was, like, before…'

'Before… what?'

'Before I talked to you, the other day.'

'You think I'm proper posh, me. Stuck up, like.' She spoke in our accent, perfectly. I was still mad angry about Brutus but couldn't help grinning. She grinned, too. 'You do, don't you? I know you do.'

'Absolutely not,' I said, mocking her back. 'I just think you belong to a different world. You don't understand mine and I don't understand yours.'

We cycled on for another mile or so – in those different worlds, I suppose. By now we were near Billinge again and if it wasn't yet lunchtime no-one had told my stomach. Maybe she read my mind.

'I didn't pack this basket for nothing,' she said. We found a sheltered spot and out came a picnic fit for a king. She had to tell me what most of the food was called. I hadn't ever had oysters in my life, never even heard of potted pâté (she told me about those marks over the letters, too). Then there was broiled chicken, devilled eggs, potato salad, layered sponge cake and beer brewed by Sydney, the gardener. Like I said – another world. I started on the chicken and then remembered Brutus.

'This is some spread,' I said, 'but I won't enjoy it until we've found the little beggar. Sorry.' So we packed it all away again and rode straight to Taylor Park. For more than an hour we called out for that dog, around the lake, in the trees and bushes.

'Perhaps he's gone much further away,' said Emily.

'I don't think so,' I said. 'He wasn't one for running off. He must have been scared by that other dog and hidden somewhere, a safe place he knew already.'

That was when I remembered an incident in the summer. Brutus had chased a rabbit, a good bit bigger than him it was, towards trees at the far end of the park. We went over there and I put my hand down rabbit hole after muddy rabbit hole. I had just about given up when I heard the faintest whimper coming from one I had already searched. I stretched even further down and felt a piece of warm fur. I suppose it could have been a rat, that's always a risk. I yanked hard, heard a pathetic little yelp and out he came, more dead than alive. He gave me a weak, snuffly lick. What happened next shocked me. In the wide open space of Taylor Park, in public view, Her Ladyship of Bettridge threw her arms round me. It wasn't just a little hug, mind. She wouldn't let go. I kept looking to make sure her brothers weren't anywhere to be seen, worse still 'mother'.

'Careful,' I said. 'We don't want to crush the little feller.' I had put Brutus inside my shirt. He was shivering like mad. 'We need to find him some water.' Needless to say it was that daft rat of a dog who had most of the broiled chicken but that didn't bother me. He was safe. Now I can happily go back to despising the little runt.

The match? The reports say that, five minutes into the game, with our boys kicking toward the Bee Hole end, Billy Nesbitt centred to Bert Freeman whose header shook the crossbar. The ball fell to Teddy Hodgson who thumped it against the Sunderland post. It bounced around the area before Teddy got on the end of it again. 1-0. Sunderland went on the attack but our half-backs Halley, Boyle and Watson and goalkeeper Jerry Dawson, were too good for them. Thank the Almighty they let Mossy off school this afternoon. Twenty minutes into the second half he gave their full-back Hobson a lesson instead, dazzling past him before sending over the perfect cross. Dick Lindley glanced a header into the far corner. 2-0.

Sunderland changed formation. Connor moved to outside-right and Mordue to inside-right with Buchan in the middle. Jerry had to make another good save and David Taylor and Tom Bamford did some last-ditch defending on the goal-line. We were surely on our way to the semi-final but, just when it seemed all over, with two minutes left Connor scored for Sunderland. 2-1. I can only imagine the atmosphere with almost 47,000 of us wishing the moments away, especially with only 10 men left on the pitch. For the final moments we struggled to hold on but hold on we did. Next up are Sheffield United at Old Trafford.

I had to copy most of that from the paper. I don't usually read the rest of it but I noticed a big story on the front page about one of these suffragettes who went into the National Gallery in London on Tuesday and slashed a famous painting with a wood chopper. Emily will have an opinion or two about that. She has about most things.

Reading back this journal I've noticed something. Her Ladyship of Bettridge has become Emily. I had better watch my step.

CHAPTER 13

Denis Law's apologetic, back-heeled flick for Manchester City that sent neighbours United plunging into the Second Division in 1974 is probably the most famous example but there have been hundreds of others down the decades – players coming back to haunt their former clubs. The vast majority have left Crystal Palace and returned to wreak havoc on the beleaguered Eagles. That's the conclusion reached by Dan and 12,000 others as they shuffle disconsolately out of a freezing Selhurst Park on a dark, February night. Palace's ridiculously expensive panic buy of 2006, £2.5m Shefki Kuqi, now of Swansea City, has just joined a seemingly endless list of players returning to score against their former club. The list includes Dave Swindlehurst, Clive Allen, Stan Collymore, Chris Armstrong, Matt Jansen, Leon McKenzie, Ricardo Fuller, Neil Shipperley and Steve Claridge's shin. Ade Akinbiyi doesn't count. He haunted the club from the day he joined.

Perhaps most painfully recalled of all is Ian Wright. As an Arsenal player, he celebrated like a bell end after scoring one of the goals that relegated Palace, the club that gave him his big break in professional football. True, the red and blue end of Highbury had thrown dog's abuse at him all game but he deserved that.

Now it's one thing to score a winner against your old club, quite another to do a Wrightie and be a complete twat against the very fans that once sang themselves hoarse to your name. Kuqi, who received his own share of abuse from the Palace faithful *before* he left the club, could have been forgiven for doing his trademark dying swan dive this evening. Instead the big Finn simply acknowledged the Swansea fans while his teammates joined him to hug it out. Class.

'I had £5 on the Kuqi monster scoring first,' says Wretched as they jostle their way through the crowd. It is cold comfort on a disappointing night but a pay-out of £60 eases the pain of a 1-0 home defeat. Betting against your own team – the disappointment hedge – is often perceived as an act of betrayal. There is a logic, though. Win the match and you don't care about the lost fiver. Lose the match and there's beer money to ease the pain. On the dull, icy trudge to Norwood Junction station, Terry and Wretched count at least 20 former players who have come back to haunt Palace over the years. Of course, like every true fan, they fail to consider the other side of the same coin. 'Famous' academy products like John Bostock, Ashley-Paul Robinson, Rory Ginty, Steve Kabba, Sagi Burton – all were sold off cheaply, refused to sign a contract or were released on a free. An army of armchair managers freely tipped them to return and wreak mystic mischief in SE25. Touching goalposts, none of them has.

'What about the Villa side on Sunday?' asks Terry. After their heroics against Wolves, Palace have drawn the Birmingham outfit in the next round of the FA Cup. And it's on TV again.

'We haven't sold any players to them recently,' says Wretched. 'No-one will be coming back to haunt us.'

Coming back to haunt us: five words that resonate with Dan. Nanna Neath is haunting *chez Howard* even though she isn't yet a ghost. If only she was. Every day she consumes a never-ending diet of low-budget game shows on his 50" plasma screen, unaware it has the added depth of 3D.

Tadworth Terry finds the right spot on the platform. The 'right spot' depends on the number of carriages that form the train. Terry knows exactly how many carriages to expect on which train and therefore knows exactly where the doors will open – a skill appreciated by Dan, Wretched and friends when thousands of supporters flood platforms.

'Chin up,' says Wretched. 'We could still make the play-offs.'

'No chance,' says Dan.

'Warnock is a miracle worker.'

'He's off to QPR.'

'He's mates with Jordan. He won't drop us like that. Anyway...' Wretched conspires with Dan. 'I hear you seriously hooked up in Newcastle. Three Geordies.'

'It was only two...'

'And Sally is *so* perfect...'

'In fact, I didn't hook up at all. Who told you, anyway?'

'Most of the Holmesdale knows. You're a bit of a ledge.'

'Well, the truth hasn't been told. And if Sally hears the lies...'

'I'd dine out on it if I were you.'

'I'd dine out every night if I could. I am going home to a room the size of the box my TV came in.'

'Ah! Nanna has finally landed,' says Tadworth Terry.

'Here to stay,' says Dan. 'We have one thing in common. Our first and last hero is Gascoigne. Trouble is mine is Paul, hers is Bamber.'

'It will all end in tears,' says Terry but Dan doesn't make the connection.

'I don't mind *University Challenge* now and then,' he says. 'It's just that she knows too much. Always has. She still gets half the answers right. She's *94*.'

'Here's your starter for 10.'

'Please no...'

'What subfield of physics deals with plasmas, such as those in fusion reactors and interplanetary space...'

'Not funny.'

'...and more generally with the interactions between a conducting fluid and a magnetic field?'

'Wasting your time.'

'I'll have to hurry you...'

'Ah, now that's what Bamber would say but not Paxman.'

There is a moment's silence.

'Never got used to Paxman presenting,' says Terry. 'I'm not sure what he would say.'

'Oh *do* come on.'

'Hang on, I'm still thinking.'

'No, that's what Paxman would say. Oh *do* come on.'

'You're right,' says Terry. 'He's so tetchy.'

'It really annoys the old girl. She met Bamber at Cambridge back in the 50s, before he was famous. As far as she is concerned, Bamber is a true gentleman. Paxman, a conceited bully.'

'Well, the answer is magnetohydrodynamics.'

'It was on the tip of my tongue.'

'I would have accepted hydromagnetics.'

The train to East Croydon pulls in and, sure enough, they are right in front of the sliding door.

'Fingers on buzzers.' Wretched presses the illuminated button. They bag the last three seats.

'Forgetting administrations, relations, quiz shows and whatever,' says Terry. 'How's the wonderful world of waste?'

Dan takes a deep breath. 'The bank could foreclose any day. Eric, the owner, reckons we need more effective marketing. He's looking to me for inspiration. There's a campaign scheduled but no great ideas from the ad agency.'

'Marketing a bin lock. Hmmm... tricky,' says Terry. 'You could always bring your band into the picture. You're auditioning for some TV show or other, I hear...'

'*Britain's Got Tribute*,' says Dan. 'We're playing at the 4000 Holes in Blackburn.' Terry looks puzzled. 'You know, the Beatles' *A Day in the Life*. Lennon sings *"4000 Holes in Blackburn, Lancashire..."* It's now the premier tribute venue up north. They're auditioning dozens of acts there.'

The train rattles towards East Croydon. Dan's phone rings. 'Hi babes.'

'Stuart just called,' says Sally. 'The auditions are on the 20th and 21st March.'

Dan checks the match programme. He notices Palace are playing at Blackpool on the Saturday. A slot on Sunday afternoon would be ideal.

'I'll ask Stu,' says Sally. 'He says we've got a really good chance of going all the way.'

'Great.'

'I meant to tell you. I can't make it on Friday. I *must* get this dissertation finished.'

'Shame.'

'Sorry.'

'I'll ring you tomorrow.'

'Till then...'

Dan relates the conversation to Wretched and Terry.

'I could see you as Dylan. Friz your hair, dangle a cigarette out of your mouth with a pair of shades,' says Terry.

'Not sure what we would call ourselves,' says Dan.

Minds whirr.

'Everybody Must Get Cloned,' offers Wretched.

'What about Highway 61 Re-revisited?' says Terry.

'Another option could be Elton. You know a lot of his songs,' says Wretched.

'Yeah. Go as Beltin' John,' says Terry.

Dan shakes his head. 'Already being done and he's a bit good.'

'OK, Nanna. What's occurring?' It's a poor attempt at a Welsh accent but Dan cannot resist. The old girl is propped up in front of his TV, the one with added depth of 3D.

'I'll tell you what's *re*-occurring, young Daniel,' says Nanna Neath. 'Your old strikers scoring against you, that's what.' Nothing gets past her. Nothing. 'Another tonight for that shifty feller and he was playing for one of our teams, Swansea...'

'Shefki,' says Dan. 'It's pronounced Sheft...'

'...and no-one in Wales ever said "What's occurring?" until that wretched sit com. And they still don't, except people taking the mick.'

Her thin, boney fingers are wrapped round the remote control. *His* remote control.

'If you don't mind,' says Nanna. 'I'd like you to tape a couple of programmes for me.'

She will never assume final mastery of the remote, of course, not while she cannot work out what the majority of buttons are for.

'*Eggheads* has got to be the dullest show on the planet.' Dan hits the necessary buttons to record an entire series.

'Pure grey matter.' Nanna taps her head. 'No gimmicks.'

'Cheap and not so cheerful.'

'Well if you want contestants appearing through dry ice to tell us they know which US president was shot dead in 1963, you're welcome.'

'But you watch those shows, too – *Who Wants To Be a Millionaire?* and *The Price Is Right*.'

'It's that or *Cash in the Attic*.' Nanna looks out of the window into the distance. 'And I don't have an attic anymore…'

CHAPTER 14

Sunday 15 March 1914

If you've read this far you will notice there are two different colours of ink on this page. My penmanship is different, too. The reason is… let me go back to the beginning.

I will have to watch my step. That's what I said last time. I'm taking my own advice. I told Emily she'd best be taking Brutus home on her own, same as if she had been the one to find him. She said that wasn't fair and that I deserved the credit but thinking it through, she realised I was right. How would I know Brutus had escaped without someone (Emily) telling me? Why would she tell me unless we had been talking? And if anyone found out we had been talking, well… she is a Bettridge. I am a Daws. It doesn't feel like we are that much different, though. Not really. Not when you end up talking like we did today, for hours. We disagree about things. In fact, we disagree about a lot of things. Perhaps the reason we disagree makes it interesting, if you know what I mean. I'm sure I'd never disagree with Nellie from church but that's because I'd never speak to her.

I told Ma I was taking Brutus for a walk but he didn't get much of one. I had arranged to meet Emily at her summerhouse. I was careful not to be seen. Thanks to Brutus I know those gardens like the back of my hand. I hopped over a wall and kept behind a row of cherry trees before bolting for it across the lawn. The summerhouse has eight sides (I think), is made of wood and painted light blue with white panels. A few slates are missing from the roof but other than that it's in good nick. Emily was waiting. She ushered me in and we started giggling because it all seemed so childish, as if we were playing a game of hide and seek at a birthday party.

The summerhouse smells damp and stale but has two old armchairs and a settee. There's no heating but Emily brought 'all the b's' as she put it - blankets, brandy and Brutus. Lying around the floor were large, coloured balls and the strangest looking hammers I had ever seen.

'It's a croquet set,' said Emily.

'What's croaky?' I said.

'Cro-*quet*. It's French. You hit the balls through hoops, *comme ça*.' She swung one of the hammers dangerously close to me. 'The king plays it with his mistresses, so they say. We'll have a game on the lawn if you like… well, one day anyway.'

'Doubt it,' I said. 'I'll never be important enough to be here, officially.'

'You sound bitter.'

'No I'm not.'

She was right, though. I was discovering things about myself I didn't want to know. Emily poured us both a very large brandy, the size of a croquet ball.

'And I've something else here, too,' she said, 'to thank you for finding Brutus and also… for finding me, if you know what I mean.' I didn't really know what she meant but her eyes were trying to tell me something. She gave me three boxes, one oblong and two square, all wrapped carefully in expensive paper.

'You shouldn't have…'

She shusshed away my protests. The two square boxes contained ink – claret and blue! Inside the oblong box was a brand new black fountain pen. A Waterman. I've never owned anything as expensive. It has taken a bit of getting used to, I can tell you. There's some lettering on the pen, too, in Latin: *Sine timore, vei favore sed semper in amore.*

'For some extraordinary reason you want to learn a dead language,' said Emily. 'So here's your chance. I had it done especially.'

Getting it engraved must have been a dear do. I have no idea what the words mean.

'Give me a clue,' I said.

'No.'

'But I won't be able to show this to anyone at ours. They'll think I've pinched it. The only thing we've got as smart as this is Grandpa's watch. After 45 years down the pit he got that and a fatal disease.'

'Well, like it or not, the next four decades are mapped out for me,' said Emily. 'Father is determined I won't struggle like he did. That's why I'm still at a school I hate. Apparently it's best for me in the long run.'

'You still haven't told me what you want to do.'

'Well, I'm female…' she began. Yes, I had noticed. I hadn't stopped noticing from the moment she turned on that electric light. 'It seems we are to do what men decide we should do. It makes me mad. Give me a wood chopper and I'll finish off that painting.'

'You could always do an Emily Davison.'

'I have no intention of falling in front of the king's horse.'

'Impale yourself on his croquet hammer, then.'

'Mallet. They're called mallets.'

'Mallets? These?' I picked one up. 'Don't make me laugh. Come down the pit and I'll show thee a mallet.'

'All right.' I thought she was joking.

'Women don't work at the face these days,' I said. To my mind that was the end of it but she is feisty, Lady Em. When she gets something in her head you can't shift it for love nor money. For the next half hour we argued whether it was better to be born male or female. Then we veered off onto Sir Edward Carson and the Ulster Volunteers, gramophones and whether planes should be used in wars. I thought I had thrown her off the trail but she started mythering me again.

'I need to know what it's like at work. Real work,' she said.

'Oh, I can just see you as a pit brow lass,' I said, 'going off to Weaver Green in your shawl and clogs.'

'I'd like that.'

I just looked at her.

'I'm being serious,' she said.

'But you have all this.' I pointed to the lawn. 'Why would you…?'

'Because it's not me. It's not mine.'

'Have you any idea what those women have to do?'

'No but I've seen them coming back together, laughing and joking. It can't be all bad.'

'They won't allow it.' I pointed towards the house.

'No need for anyone to find out. I'm not planning on making a career of it. I just need to know what it's like, even for a day.' She wore me down, of course. I promised to find out whether they were taking on staff at Weaver Green, on one condition. I held up my new pen. 'I want to read about it. In your own words.'

'But you're the writer.'

'You're not at that school for nothing.'

'Right now I'm not at that school.'

We talked more. Lots more, until it got dark and their dinner gong sounded. We never heard it, mind. We're going to the FA Cup semi-final at Old Trafford. Nothing will stop us getting there this time.

I write most of this journal at night and I had just written that sentence when Grandpa, who had dozed off, sat up and looked straight at me from the end of the bed.

'Fancy pen, that, lad,' he said. It's funny how easily he can see when he wants to, even in the grim light of a dying candle. 'Where'd tha gerrit?' I didn't answer. 'Hmmm, well tha can't have paid for it, not on thy wage. Tha might have pinched it but then tha'll not be showin' it off. Someone's give it thee, I'll be bound.' I thought he had gone back to sleep but he turned suddenly. His right foot crashed onto this page, smudging the lines above. 'Whoe'er the lass is, if she's got a bit of cash behind 'er, I'd stick in there. If she's got a *lot* of cash behind 'er…' He shook his head '…tha don't stand a bloody chance.'

CHAPTER 15

Dan and Sally tip-toe past her door but the landing floorboard creaks. Too late.

'That you, Daniel?' comes a voice.

'That's me, Nanna.'

'Five down. *The greatest hit Dylan never had, man.* Six and five.'

Dan shrugs his shoulders at Sally. 'I did warn you.'

'Warn me?' says Nanna.

'Not you, Nanna. I was talking to Sally.'

Propped in her chair, Nanna looks round. Sally enters what was once Dan's bedroom and bends down to kiss the little, white-haired lady who has a pen in one hand and a folded newspaper in the other.

'Hello,' she says. 'I'm Sally. I've heard a lot about you.'

'Twelve minutes.' Nanna shakes her head.

'Twelve minutes?'

'That's all it used to take me. Less, usually.'

'I'm... sorry, I don't know what...'

'The crossword.'

'Oh.'

'Now *Heir Hunters* and half of *Build a New Life in the Country* is over before I complete it.'

Sally smiles. 'If it's any consolation it would take me all morning to do three or four clues and then I'd give up.'

'Well, if you heard me sing for 30 seconds you'd give up on me.' Nanna studies her guest. 'Daniel tells me you are very talented.'

'I enjoy singing but you must, too. *Bread of Heaven* at the Millennium Stadium…'

Nanna sighs. 'A wonderful hymn desecrated by drunks.' She dons her spectacles and taps the newspaper, impatiently. 'I can solve cryptic clues about Bach and Beethoven in seconds but when it comes to pop stars…'

'You're pre-supposing the clue is about Bob Dylan,' says Dan from the landing. 'It could be about Dylan Thomas.'

'Or that rabbit from *The Magic Roundabout*,' says Sally. 'He's always saying "man" at the end of sentences.'

'Yeah, the word "man" is a definite clue,' says Dan.

'Like penis rhyming with Venus, there must be a reason,' says Nanna, distantly.

'Like… *what?*'

'Oh, nothing. It was something Dylan Thomas said.'

'I hear you like quiz shows,' says Sally, brightly. 'We've been studying the genre at uni.'

'*Studying* it?'

'It's part of our course on the media.'

'Well, I never. The word "media" didn't even exist when I was doing my degree. Mind you, that was before the war.'

'The TV quiz show is a bastion of British culture,' says Sally, 'dominated by white male presenters.'

'I hadn't thought of it like that,' says Nanna. 'Mind you, *The Weakest Link* is presented by a woman.'

'Debatable,' chips in Dan. 'What's with Anne Robinson and those long, black dresses and steel-rimmed glasses?'

'Proves my point,' says Sally. 'They masculinised her to fit the role.'

'She's half Mary Poppins, half dominatrix.'

Sally frowns. 'A typical male reaction to any female authority figure.'

Nanna studies Sally again. 'So… you're one of these feminists.'

'Not really. I'm just interested in popular culture.'

'You've got her going now,' says Dan. 'Sally eats text books for breakfast.'

'While you're on your smart phone, hopping from one football bulletin board to another,' says Sally. 'That's *so* much more productive.'

Nanna raises a gnarled hand. 'When did you two get married?' Dan and Sally exchange a rueful smile. 'The clue.' Nanna taps the paper again. 'I'm counting on you.'

'It sounds like a song Dylan wrote but didn't make a hit,' says Dan.

'Hendrix recorded *All Along the Watchtower*,' says Sally.

Dan shakes his head. 'Four words.'

'Wait a minute.' Sally holds up her hand. 'Rage Against the Machine… they covered *Maggie's Farm*. That's two words.'

'Nope… wrong number of letters.'

Dan disappears downstairs.

'I'm sorry about, you know… the bickering,' says Sally.

'Oh, no need to apologise,' says Nanna.

'We seem to be doing it a lot recently.'

'Arguing proves you care. Dan's grandfather and I rarely quarrelled. The worst thing is two people living together in silence. People on Earth don't argue with people on Mars.'

Sally sits next to Nanna. 'Your husband died a while back, Dan tells me.'

'More than 20 years ago.'

'Giving up your home must be traumatic.'

'My daughter insisted I should come here rather than go into a nursing home. They keep us alive too long these days.'

'Oh, don't say that.'

'It's true.' Nanna points to a plastic box on the sideboard. 'I have to take those coloured pills every day but I'm tempted to throw them in the bin.'

'But you're doing really well.'

'Because of the orange one, the yellow one, the green one – twice a day. If it wasn't for those I could do the decent thing and expire gracefully.'

'I'm sure there's a good reason for all the medication.'

'But it's got to the point where we feel guilty if someone dies from a treatable illness.'

Sally grasps Nanna's hand. 'Surely we should do anything to help people live longer?'

'But what if the treatment means we suffer more? The green pill prevents one thing, the yellow another but I'm slowly declining and eventually I've got to die from *something*. Very few people end up dying in their sleep of natural causes.'

'Come on without,' sings a voice from the landing. 'Come on within. You'll not hear nothing like the...'

'Mighty Quinn,' answers Sally.

'By Manfred Mann. They heard the demo...'

'Is Quinn spelled with two n's?' Nanna is uninterested in the song's history. 'I knew we'd get there in the end.' She completes the crossword in a spidery scrawl.

'When you've finished, can I use that pencil?' says Dan. Nanna and Sally talk female stuff while he scribbles. 'What about this as a promotional song for Bintastic?' he says.

'*Lock up, without.*
'*Lock up, within.*
'*You'll not let no-one*
'*Steal your wheelie bin.*'

CHAPTER 16

Friday 20 March 1914

Well, I did what Emily asked me to do and found out they were taking on lasses at Weaver Green. She has done nothing like it before. I warned her it isn't going to be easy but that hasn't put her off.

She's had to find the right clothes to wear. After searching around, I must say she looked the part in a pair of knee-length breeches and a long skirt, with an apron wrapped round. She got hold of a cotton waistcoat, too, a cast-off from brother Freddie. I found her one of Ma's old shawls and a padded cotton bonnet to keep coal dust out her hair. She already had a pair of clogs but they looked brand new as she's never worn them. So I took Brutus for a walk and threw them for him to catch and chew. It did the trick.

After that I helped her practice our local accent. She's already good at it, mind, but if she comes over all posh and uses long words, they'll have her out of there soon enough. And by 'they' I mean the other girls. It's like us lads down the pit. We don't have much but what we do have is each other. If anyone gets above himself, he soon hears about it. It's the same with the lasses on the pit brow. All for one and one for all. Emily's parents have no idea about all this. She's walking over to Weaver Green tomorrow morning and has to be there for six. She's promised she'll write about her days at work. I want to include them here. There again, she has no idea about this journal either.

What happened today for me? It was too dull to report.

Dear Tom

Well, you asked for it so here it is!!! I hate this sort of thing! Too much like a school essay but you've kept your side of the bargain so I suppose I must keep mine. Please do not mark it and send it back with a grade!!

Day 1

Where do I begin???? Well, I couldn't let anyone at home see me in my new working clothes so after changing in the summer house, I set off for Weaver Green. It was dark and cold. Halfway there the heavens opened! I was absolutely (you'll be pleased to know I remembered not to use that word all day!) soaked to the skin within a minute or two. It was so bad I decided to go home and try again tomorrow but, turning round, I saw a girl behind me. She was so tiny I thought she must be going to school but, as she came closer to me, I noticed she was wearing clothes like mine!!! She said she was heading for the pit, was I new? Her name is Eliza, she's 15 and quite lovely. She said it was just as well I was in good time because if I had been a minute late on my first morning I would have been in trouble.

We stood at the entrance to the pit with several other girls. The manager, Mr Borst, nodded us all in. Moments later another girl turned up. It was her first day as well. She was dripping wet and all flustered. Borst glanced at his pocket watch.

'Tha's late,' he said.

'I'm dreadful sorry, sir,' said the girl, 'but I had for t' take long way round on account of t' rain' (well, you told me to write it exactly as they say it!!!)

'Too bad,' said Borst. 'Off 'om with 'ee.' I couldn't believe it!

'But, but, me Ma'll beat me.' Tears rolled down the girl's cheeks. 'Please...' But Borst wouldn't listen. I felt so sorry for her. I noticed how none of the girls ever looks that odious man in the eye. They huddle together, hunch-shouldered, staring at the floor, just saying yes sir, no sir. Do they think *so* little of themselves?

84

I asked if there was anywhere to dry out. Borst stared at me like I was Oliver Twist.

'What's thy name?' he said.

'Dorothy.' I looked him straight in the eye. He didn't like that.

'Thy *sur*name,' he said. I was tempted to say Bettridge, just to put the wind up him but thought better of it. For some reason, your Eddie Mosscrop, the Burnley winger came to mind.

'Mosscrop,' I said.

'It's Mosscrop, *sir*,' he said. 'Aye, and I'll be marking thee.' Then he shooed me away like I was Brutus!

The pit brow has no heating. We laboured all day in damp clothes. As for the work itself: well, the coal comes clattering down a chute and onto moving belts. I suppose the best way to describe them is like venetian blinds, undulating up and down. Five of us stand either side of the belts at intervals and separate the dirt from the coal. If the lumps of coal are too big you split them with a hammer (not a mallet!), picking off the dirt with your fingers. For a reason I cannot fathom, you're not allowed to wear gloves. It wasn't long before my hands were covered in blisters. Eliza said I should soak my hands in cold tea when I get home, to soothe the cracks in my skin. I took her advice but didn't dare let mother see my hands so I wore some fancy gloves round the house.

You have to be careful near those belts!! They can pull a finger out. Eliza lost a thumbnail the other day and it is still septic. One of her friend's arms got caught in the belt. She says it was cut clean off. Only a little stump is left. The poor girl was only 15 and couldn't work any more. They told me how, a few years ago, someone got caught up in the machinery and was scalped.

It was cold, very cold but, I'm telling you, those girls work like lightning. It's the only way to get warm. They are so strong and work as a team. I have to admit, they quite put me to shame. I did my best and they said I would soon get the hang of it but I was pathetic and weak by comparison.

No-one is allowed to talk until breakfast. Lunch lasts all of 30 minutes. Eliza told me she earns 8s 4d a week. She has to hand it all over to her mother who gives her back 3d to spend. 3d!!!!! She can't wait until tomorrow because she will be 16. Hopefully her wage will increase, depending what Borst says. Her pocket money will double to the princely sum of 6d. I told her she earns less than a quarter of the men at the coalface. She just shrugged her shoulders. She told me her grandmother worked underground and this is a better job than the one she had. She was curious as to why I was curious, of course. I felt a fraud as I told her about my hard-up family in Burnley and how I just needed a job, any job.

It was difficult trying to remember what words not to use!!! I did slip occasionally. I said 'that's appalling' and 'how frightful' but then made it sound as if I was mimicking someone well-to-do.

'Is Burnley a posher town than St Helens then?' asked one of the girls. That question made me realise I hadn't been entirely convincing but, at the end of the day, Eliza and her little gang insisted on walking most of the way home with me (I couldn't let them walk *all* the way!) They were so funny and friendly. I felt I had known them for years. I managed to wash out the coal dust from my face in the summerhouse and then changed for dinner. I told mother and father I had been in Manchester for the day. I'm sure they weren't bothered one way or the other. In spite of my lack of muscle, Borst said I could have a job and that he'd pay me 1s 2d a day. He made it sound as if he was being *so very* generous. I thanked him and said I will be there again in the morning. And I will but right now I'm heading for bed!!!!

Day 2

Something I forgot to mention yesterday: there's a glass ceiling over the belts and Borst lies on the glass, for minutes at a time, watching us all. It made me shudder, seeing his horrid face distorted against the glass. You are allowed to go down to the toilet twice a day but this afternoon one girl had to go for a third time. It was an emergency.

''Ome. Go on,' he shouted. She had worked most of the day but she'll not see a penny for it.

We all wished Eliza a happy birthday, of course. At lunch I asked her if she had thought about doing any other kind of work.

'I'd rather be here than in service, running up and down stairs for Lord and Lady Snooty or shut up inside a mill all day,' she said. 'You'd not recognise us when we're on t' town on Saturday night.' I have to say, under the grime, Eliza has a fresh complexion, the sweetest smile and is very slim. She also has limitless energy. I asked her where she got her lovely, coloured shawl – nicer than any other I had seen.

'I made it myself,' she said, proudly. I told her she has real talent and should consider making more. 'Oh, I couldn't do that,' she said, blushing. 'The materials are too dear. Besides, who'd buy 'em?' I told her she could sell them to rich folk. She said she wouldn't know where to start and I was just about to tell her I could help when Borst called out: 'Roberts – up 'ere'. Roberts is her surname.

When she came down, twenty minutes later, she was clutching half-a-crown, an unexpected birthday present, I imagine. I hoped she had news of a wage rise, too. Well, maybe Borst isn't so mean after all. I smiled across the belts at her but she barely looked at me. Instead, she took hold of a huge spade – almost as big as her – and crashed it down on a large piece of coal. She gave it a really good whack. And again.

I wanted to speak to her when we finished work but she disappeared in another direction. 'Her Grandma lives that way,' said a girl called Lottie.

This evening at dinner I told the family I had been shopping in Liverpool where I am having special beauty treatment on my hands and that's why I've bought these new gloves, do you like them? They weren't convinced and are becoming suspicious.

Day 3

How could I have been so very naïve??!?? You're right. I have lived a sheltered life. Today was my last day at the pit brow. It wasn't supposed to be. I walked to work with Eliza and said how pleased I was she had got more money out of Borst. She was reluctant to talk about it. All a bit strange. I asked her if I had offended her. No, she said, it was nothing to do with me. In fact I had made her happy because I liked her shawl. In spite of that she seemed quite upset, almost tearful, but, try as I may to open her up, she wouldn't talk. I soon found out why.

Just after lunch Borst shouted 'Mosscrop – up 'ere now'. At first I didn't think he was calling me. I had forgotten my new name. It was only when a girl nudged me that I went up to Borst's office. No-one else was around and he shut the door quietly behind me. I asked if I had done anything wrong. He waved away my question. 'ave a seat,' he said. He wanted to know how old I was and how long I had lived in the town. What did my father do? Did I have any brothers and sisters? He was surprisingly pleasant and seemed really interested in me. I told him my father had died when I was young and my mother was in service to a family near Taylor Park. Sorry, but it was the best I could do under pressure. He sat down and told me that he, too, had come from a poor family with more than its share of problems. At times he looked like a little boy lost. I felt quite sorry for him.

'Most of t' lasses down there don't 'ave much about 'em.' He pointed through the glass. 'But I'm keen to help the brighter ones. I make it my job to pick t' best from t' rest and give 'em a chance. Tha's got a way about thee, young Dorothy. I think tha'll go far, given the right steer. I've a good many friends in high places.' He got up from his chair and perched on the desk in front of me. Then he wrapped both hands round my right hand and slipped a half-crown into it. His hands were all clammy. He wouldn't let my hand go.

'Aye, and you're a fine-looking lass,' he said. 'I'm sure there are ways we can help each other, like.' What he wanted me to do then I cannot put down on paper. Suffice to say I threw his miserable money on the floor. 'When you find out who I *really* am,' I said, 'it's not *me* who'll be kneeling but *you*, to say your prayers.'

I ran outside the pit and burst into tears. I think it was the shock. Eliza followed me. Thinking about it now, that was a very risky thing to do. She put her arm round me and I noticed she was crying as well. I didn't need to ask why.

'I'm going right back in there to tell him to leave you alone,' I said.

'Please don't,' she said.

'But we can't let him get away with it.'

'You don't understand. I've no choice.'

'Of course you have a choice. People like Borst have to be brought to account.'

'Not by people like me. Who am I against him? No-one would believe me. 'e'd sack me on t' spot. I need the work for my family's sake. Please don't.' By the end she was pleading with me, tugging on my waistcoat.

'In which case, that's me done and dusted.' I hugged Eliza and said I would stay in touch. She hugged me back and said she hoped I would. I think she meant it. I'm not sure if I will see her again. I doubt she will trust me if she finds out about my family and that I have been pretending to be Dorothy Mosscrop.

What else can I tell you? I feel really angry about what happened in Borst's office but it is as if it had to happen, to wake me up. I've learned a lot in just three days. I didn't expect to be at the pit brow for very long but ending like that, well... I am doing some serious thinking about everything and maybe that is good. It's like a light has gone on. Everything is loaded against girls like Eliza. Have I written enough? It's far more than I ever expected!!!!!!

Your loving Emily

Your *loving* Emily? What does this mean? Has she just written those words because she always finishes letters like that? Her account of those three days is really good (except she uses too many exclamation marks for my liking) but, your *loving* Emily? Suddenly, I don't want to watch my step any more and because of that it's probably exactly the time I should.

CHAPTER 17

Stretched full length on the settee, Dan dozes. He has been out and about all day, following up leads made at the show in Birmingham. He also offered his *'Lock up, without...'* song to Mr Kelly who said he would ask Bintastic's advertising agents what they think.

'Welcome to *Eggheads*.' The voice of Jeremy Vine drifts in and out of Dan's addled brain. 'The show where a team of five quiz challengers pit their wits against possibly the greatest quiz team in Britain.' Cut-and-paste intro. Again. 'You might recognise them as they've won some of the country's toughest quiz shows. They are the *Eggheads*.'

'And I am the walrus,' Dan mutters.

'You're what?' says Nanna.

'Nothing.' Dan drifts off again with Lennon's semitonal seesaw of a song, inspired by a police siren, swirling round his head. He finds himself on the set of the *Magical Mystery Tour*. Macca won't tell him where he got the psychedelic, puff-sleeved jacket he wears for that song. It is Dan's all-time favourite piece of 60s clobber. Now he's one of those four pretty little policemen in a row, tottering on that wall. He falls and wakes to Jeremy Vine's final, decisive question.

'What was significant about the match between Blackpool and Blackburn in December 1965?' asks Vine.

Dan clicks his fingers and points to the screen. 'I know that one.'

'Oh, you startled me,' says Nanna. 'Thought you were well away.' The *Eggheads* confer. Thanks to Sally, Dan notices the challengers this week are all as white as the driven snow. No, he's wrong. One of them is only three-quarters Caucasian. She would regard that as subtle tokenism.

'Taking a guess,' says a full-on Caucasian *Egghead*. 'We think it was the highest-scoring draw ever between two teams in the First Division.'

'No' says Vine. 'Bad luck.'

'It was the last-ever, First Division fixture to be played on Christmas Day,' say Dan and Jeremy Vine in unison.

'Gracious, what a good idea,' says Nanna.

'Playing on Christmas Day?' says Dan. 'I'd have thought you'd disapprove, what with your father being in the church and all that.'

'And living in a cave in Wales.' Nanna peers reprovingly over her glasses.

'Well, I didn't mean…'

'But you're right. There's nothing like taking something imaginative – peace on earth, goodwill to all men – and ritualistically squeezing the very life out of it every week. The church is good at that.'

'Like *Eggheads*,' jibes Dan, 'except that was never imaginative.'

Nanna nods away the comment. 'I mean, what better way for a family to celebrate Christmas Day than to watch two teams kick merry hell out of each other. Fresh air, passion, profanity. It beats dozing off during the Queen's Speech.'

'Never thought of you as an insurgent.'

'I'm telling you…' Nanna looks hard at Dan. 'Rebellion is at the heart of anything worth believing in.'

'Well, it would help if the players rebelled against matches scheduled for Valentine's Day.' Dan yawns and sits up straight.

'Yes, your game against Aston Villa. It's an afternoon kick off.' Nanna points to the back page of her newspaper. 'You've still got all evening to wine and dine that young lady of yours.'

'True, but there's just one small snag for mankind…'

It's more than just a small snag, of course. It's a potential relationship breaker. Several days before Butterfield hit that ridiculous hat-trick, Dan had booked two tickets for a matinee performance of *The Lion King* at the Lyceum in London – on Sunday 14th February. At the time there was little chance of Palace going through to the next round of the FA Cup. Even if they did, the game was likely to be scheduled for the Saturday. The best-laid plans… up steps Butts. Palace land Villa at Selhurst Park. Up step ITV, scheduling live coverage of the match on (well, they would, wouldn't they?) the afternoon of Sunday 14th February.

'Ah, I see,' says Nanna. 'Even if you go to the Lyceum, your mind will be somewhere else.'

'Pathetic, isn't it? Especially as it's quite a show. *Nants ingonyama bagithi Baba…*' he sings, imitating Rafiki's opening wail from the wings of the theatre. He tells Nanna how the huge, papier-mâché sun rises slowly, majestically from the stage and rhythmic African harmonies greet two giraffes (men angled perfectly on stilts) ambling across the sun, followed by leopards and zebras, even an elephant. Then a hippo lollops its way down the aisles and onto stage before the lion cub Simba is presented dramatically on Pride Rock, at the climax of Elton John's *Circle of Life*. Each time Sally has seen it, she has welled up. Dan cannot, dare not have his phone with him, even on silent.

'It's great theatre but when you've seen it three times…' says Dan.

'Hmmm. Mind you, I had already seen *Gone With the Wind* six times,' murmurs Nanna, distantly.

'I… I'm not with you.'

'The movie.'

'I know, Clark Gable and the woman that cracked up big-time.'

'Vivien Leigh. I'd seen it six times but didn't tell Dafydd that.'

'Dav… what?'

'Dafydd. Pronounced Davith.'

'Who was this Davros then?'

Nanna obviously doesn't watch TV sci-fi or chooses to pretend she doesn't. Instead, she sighs deeply and shakes her head. 'Ah, Dafydd…' Her eyes glisten. She has very intense eyes, something Dan had not really noticed before. 'Now we're both being pathetic.'

'He sounds… *Welsh*.' Dan states the bleeding obvious but cannot think of anything else to say. Handling the reverie of an emotional grandmother is well beyond his experience and skill set.

'A boy from the valleys,' says Nanna, slowly. 'When I said I was going to England he was devastated.'

'You came to England…'

'During the war.'

'Whereabouts?'

'Oh, they moved us around. It was the war.'

'So you stood him up?'

'Well, not exactly. *Gone With the Wind* is a long film. I told him during the interval.'

'That you were going to England?'

'Yes.'

'So you liked this, this… boyo.'

'Oh, I didn't like him, no… I was hopelessly in love with him.' This was getting heavy. This was his grandmother. This was Nanna Neath. Matriarch. Tough as old German jackboots. He wished Sally was here. Sally would know what to say. Sally would do the female bit – warm, sympathetic, understanding – while he disappeared and made the tea. 'I never saw him again.'

'Never?'

'Never.'

'How long were you here, in England?'

'Three years.'

'Three years!'

'The best part.'

'Were you in the forces?'

'Goodness me, no.'

'So what were you doing?'

'Oh, it's too long ago to remember much now. It was the war. It was disruptive.'

'What happened to Davros?'

'As I said, I never saw him again.'

'Well, he can't have meant *that* much to you.'

Nanna fixes her grandson with a steely stare that could buckle an Iron Cross. 'Oh, he meant everything to me. But there was a war on.

93

We did as we were told.'

'So… when it was over, I mean the war.' Dan chooses his words carefully. 'What did you do about the relationship?'

'A friend said he had given up on me and married a girl from Llanelli. I was heartbroken.'

'I see. Well, I don't see but, you know…'

'I met your grandfather and we lived happily ever after. Often in separate rooms, mind, but there you are.'

Jeremy Vine is wrapping up *Eggheads*. The credits roll but Nanna has, to Dan's amazement, found the mute button on the remote control.

'You must go to the theatre with Sally,' she says, 'and if you simply cannot trust yourself…' She puts out a boney hand. 'I'll confiscate your mobile phone.'

Dan smiles, ruefully. 'It's a deal.' The torment is over. The right decision has been reached. He can relax in the sure and certain knowledge that, if he wavers, Nanna Neath will frogmarch him back to the straight and narrow. The house telephone rings. Dan answers.

'If it's that BBC Wales researcher again, tell her I'm not interested, whatever it's about,' says Nanna. It *is* that BBC Wales researcher again. Dan tells her his grandmother is not interested, whatever it's about and hangs up. But now he's interested, whatever it's about.

'It's nothing,' says Nanna. 'Some documentary or other they're putting together.'

'What about?'

'Oh,' Nanna hesitates. 'The, er… something about the local history of Neath.'

'And they tracked you down here? They must be keen.' He is just about to push his grandmother a little further on the matter when *Hey Bulldog* sounds.

'Hi,' says Dan.

'Hi. How'd it go today?' says Sally.

'OK. Closed a few sales. Kelly's considering my idea. And you?'

'Mad busy. Seems there's an extra assignment we should have been given before Christmas. It's got to be handed in by the end of March.'

'When we're up in Blackburn, you mean?'

'Seems so.'

'I don't believe it. What's the subject?'

'Er, I'm not sure. Maybe I've got it here. Hang on…'

Dan points to the phone. 'It's Sally,' he mouths.

'Never,' smirks Nanna.

'Here it is,' says Sally. '*The popularly-claimed notion that new technologies are re-wiring society and driving social and political change is a media myth. Discuss.*'

'Nice.'

'What do you mean nice?'

'Well, up your street.'

'Hmmm… the thing is… don't be offended…'

'By what?'

'If we're going to make it up north I'm going to have to put in some extra study. I'll have to work all day Sunday.'

'*This* Sunday?'

''Fraid so.'

'Valentine's Day?'

'Sorry.'

'Oh…'

If the call had come a few minutes earlier, before the conversation with Nanna, Dan would have punched the air discreetly in celebration. Now he genuinely feels flat. Of course, he has found salvation. He is free to anticipate the match without guilt but it is a strange anti-climax. The decision has been taken away from him. He is no longer in control. Talking of controls…

'Which one do I press to play back *15 to 1*?' says Nanna.

'Here, give it to me.'

CHAPTER 18

Thursday 26 March 1914

I've just been reading Emily's account of her three days at Weaver Green again. Borst is well known for being cratchy and sending girls home when they're a couple of minutes late. Mind you, some of the lads arrive at the pithead, all of a do, saying the bobber never called and suchlike. Me, I'm never late. Mr Reliable they call me. I'm not saying I'm wide awake when I get to the pithead but at least I'm there on time.

My secret is to have a clock as certain as sunrise itself and which never needs winding up. Sharing a bed with Grandpa has had its advantages. The clock downstairs in the hall no longer chimes. It hasn't for years and would cost too much to fix. But Grandpa has always known exactly when I need to get up. And those feet have done their job every morning, first a nudge and if I don't respond, I get a mouthful of toes. The nudge usually does the trick. I don't know how he's done it all these years. Maybe it's because he was a miner himself and his body has never lost the daily rhythm. Whatever it is, I've cursed and blessed him every morning, in the same breath.

That is why I was surprised to wake up at six o'clock this morning, to the sound of next door's new baby skriking. Straight through the wall it came.

'Grandpa, I'm late,' I said and gave him a good kick. I looked down the bed to see him peaceful and unconcerned. Not surprising, really.

He was dead. His legs were still warm but he was definitely dead. We all tried to bring him back, of course, but he was having none of it.

We are all shocked. Ma is very tearful. The funeral has been arranged for next Wednesday. Needless to say I won't be going to the semi-final tomorrow, not when we're all in mourning. Part of me wants to go just to take my mind off it all. The other part says I won't be able to enjoy the game after what happened today. I can't imagine life without Grandpa. He's always been there and now he isn't. The bed will be too big without him. That's all I can write today.

CHAPTER 19

Perhaps it was the mention of Valentine's Day that unleashed those closely-guarded memories of Dafydd Broderick but she must never allow a slip like that again. Not even her daughter knows about Dafydd, or the circumstances surrounding their relationship. She chides herself for an uncharacteristic lapse. Daniel had caught her off guard. She must also be lenient on herself. It's going to take some time to get used to this cramped, south London suburb.

It would have been so much easier for everyone if she had just fallen off the perch before young Daniel came to collect her. Back home in Neath many of her friends had had the good sense to do so. For years, Olwen had sworn she would sooner watch an uncut DVD of the Queen investing Charles as Prince of Wales than end up in Golden Sands. Coming from Olwen Parry that was quite something. Olwen collapsed and died days before they came to take her to that most dismal of nursing homes. All those poor old souls sitting round a room in a long line. 'Dr God's waiting room', Olwen used to call it. She misses her dearest, oldest friend. Back in primary school they became inseparable –impersonating teachers when their backs were turned, passing silly, scribbled notes to each other under desks, camping out in tents in each other's gardens in the summer. The war and husbands separated them but only for a while. Widowed, they came back together, drinking coffee, drawing pensions, linking arms on blustery coastal walks, avoiding any route that took them past Golden Sands. Now even Olwen has abandoned her.

As for these phone calls: they had better understand, these journalist types. It is her past. Hers and no-else's. The powers-that-be had made it quite clear. No-one else must know or there would be Official Consequences. She had solemnly put pen to paper and signed the document, a long time ago but no matter. No-one had ever returned to sign her off. And from that day to this she had had the dreams, waking up startled some nights, certain she heard the creak of a footstep on the landing. Someone was listening on the other side of the door. She prayed she had not disclosed anything in her sleep. Careless talk and all that. Occasionally, she still crept out of bed to make sure they had gone.

The BBC had no business poking around, putting her under pressure. Oh, the producer, Bronwen, was pleasant enough, a young thing with a warm and friendly voice. She spoke good Welsh, too. Perfect, in fact. Mind you, that's all in the softening-up process. 'Na gyd I ni eisiau neud…..' 'All we want to do…' That was her opening line. In fact, it was how she started every sentence. That's how they lure you into a false sense of security, these media types, telling you they are making nothing of it. If they are making nothing of it why are they making something of it?

Of course there are plenty of people who love to be in front of the microphones and cameras and what not. Let them get on with it. Take this Neil Warnock who's on the TV now, for example, barking out instructions to Daniel's team in the FA Cup. He can't get enough of it. And the cameramen can't get enough of him, zooming in on his face as he strides up and down the touchline. It's no use the commentators talking loudly, trying to cover the stream of profanities pouring out of that big mouth of his. We can still hear you, loud and clear, and it's live on daytime TV. Serves them right for putting a microphone so close. That's what the media does. Sets you up, knocks you down. He had better take note, though, this Warnock fellow: those that live by the soundbite (oh, she's heard these fancy terms, don't you worry), die by the soundbite. Daniel has shown her the newspaper reports. A week ago Warnock was spouting off to reporters, how everyone must pull together and ride out the bad times until new owners can be found for the club. Now it looks as if he is going to 'sod off' (Daniel's words) to Queens Park Rangers. As for the club's current owner, the blond and orange one, Simon Jordan – his first job should have been to make sure the club stayed solvent, not offer his opinion on everything and everyone. She may not get out much these days but that doesn't stop her watching TV and reading the papers. These larger-than-life characters were welcome to give their opinion. She wants no part of it.

The young thing from the BBC will phone back. Once again she will say she just wants to find out what happened all those years ago. Then she will start digging and digging some more and then everything might come out. Everything. Do they think she's stupid? Do they think she doesn't know that old adage about the elephant who wanted shelter in the hunter's tent? If he could only cover his trunk from the rain, he'd be really thankful. Then, if the hunter didn't mind, his head. Then the top half of his body. Then… she's not going to get dumped out in the squelching mud. It's her past and if they think… oh, but the commentator is right, that is a truly stunning free kick. Where did that come from? Darren Ambrose. He's been good for Palace all season, Daniel says. 'And that's the midfielder's 16th goal of the campaign,' says the commentator. It's put them 2-1 ahead. Somewhere in the crowd her grandson is going potty, no doubt. Here's that Ambrose again, hitting the bar. Unlucky! That would have put them through to the next round for sure. Yes, she's beginning to warm to Daniel's club. The commentator calls them 'plucky Palace'. Like it or not, they're her local team now. She will celebrate by taking the blue pill followed by the red. It's turning into an FA Cup tie of the old kind… oh, but someone should have picked up that Villa player running into the box. It's a late equaliser. She is surprised how disappointed she is for Warnock and his team.

Still, the draw means more money from the replay and the club badly needs every penny. That will please her grandson. Now the TV pundits are having their say at the end of the game. They reckon the replay will net Palace £400,000, if it gets shown on TV. 'There's every chance,' says one of them, 'after that blood and thunder display this afternoon.' It's all about money at the end of the day. Everything is all about money at the end of the day. And this is the end of her day. She had hoped to leave something behind for her daughter and grandchildren, at the end of the day. Going into Golden Sands would mean what cash she has left from the sale of her home would be burned up just keeping her alive. At least this way, by living with her daughter, she'll be able to pass on what little is left.

Of course, Golden Sands may still beckon if she cannot climb the stairs. It would help if her daughter had a downstairs toilet. Reaching the landing in time can be a monumental effort, though she's not telling the family. She's steady enough until the turn. That's the bit she dreads: the turn and the last four stairs. She has learned two tricks. Drink as little as possible and set off in good time. The doctor warned her about dehydration but, well, he'll understand when he gets to her age.

The phone rings and her daughter answers. Thank goodness, it's a personal call. At least it's not them. They'll be back, though, the BBC. Maybe she should take advice from Daniel's young lady. She said she was studying the media or something. Daniel's a lucky lad. Maybe *she* can give the producer short shrift. She seems an intelligent, friendly sort. What was her name, now? She can remember the names of so many obscure people she hasn't seen for the best part of 70 years but as for people she met a few days ago... She remembers that she worked out a way to remember her name. The trouble is, she can't remember how she was going to remember it. It was something to do with the war and Daniel's girlfriend being a singer and his sweetheart. That was it: the Forces' Sweetheart – Vera Lynn. 'Sally, Sally, pride of our alley...'

When Sally comes again she will have a quiet word.

CHAPTER 20

Wed 1 April 1914

I didn't realise how many people knew Grandpa and would respond to the bidding. Our house was packed to the gunnels before the funeral. A couple of dozen were out in the street at any one time because there was no room inside. Old workmates, cousins, uncles, aunts, they all turned up, along with distant relatives I hadn't seen since the last family funeral but that always happens. Most of them said a few quiet words to Grandpa in the parlour. The coffin was open and he looked likely in his Sunday best. What is it with people these days who keep the coffin lid shut? Who wants to say goodbye to a wooden box? Grandpa insisted the top should be off at the front of church, too. 'Me, I spent too many bloody years in t' dark,' he used to say to Ma. 'When I've woven me piece, 'fore they send me below for good, lemme take one last good look at t' sky.'

Talking of the sky, it's been a breezy day with scudding clouds. Only clouds scud it seems. I don't know what the word means but I've always liked it. In the end I was glad the funeral was today because it took my mind off the semi-final replay against Sheffield United. The first game on Saturday finished 0-0 so the replay was scheduled for this afternoon. Just my luck to miss both games. I bought two tickets for the first game at Old Trafford, for Emily and me. I was lucky to get them. The club sold out of its 14,000 allocation. In the end, more than 55,000 turned up. The papers say it's a record for an

FA Cup semi-final. I gave my tickets to Billy and a friend. What with borrowing his bike, I owe Billy a favour or two. I could have sold them for twice face value, mind. Round here they say that would have brought bad luck. Who 'they' are, I have no idea. I don't usually take notice of all that stuff but, being so close to the final, I'm not taking any risks. I was surprised to find out how many of our players are superstitious. The train carrying the team to Manchester had a coffin on board (not Grandpa) and several of the players believe it was a bad omen. They blamed the corpse for not winning the game. Well, that's what the papers say, anyway.

Billy said there were street vendors everywhere selling pictures of Tommy Boyle and the Sheffield United captain. I can't remember his name and I'm not looking it up. Billy said you've never seen so many buttonholes, rosettes and coloured umbrellas. One Sheffield United fan was carrying a huge penknife, shaped like a scythe with the blade on one end. Others had red-and-white quartered suits and painted faces. As usual, the Irwell Springs band played hymns and anthems before the teams came onto the pitch. I wish I had been there but, with Grandpa hardly cold, it was the right thing not to go. The other semi-final at White Hart Lane, between Liverpool and Aston Villa, pulled a crowd only half the size of ours. So much for people saying we're a small club. Compare the population of our town against the city of Liverpool and ask yourself which club has the real fans?

Reading this back I feel guilty. Today we buried Grandpa and here I am talking about my team again. Forgive me, Grandpa. For years 'th' eld feller' (I can't write 'the old fellow', it looks wrong) had given the Death Man a little each week to pay for his funeral so it was quite a do, one way and another. Grandpa didn't make much in his life but he was determined people would enjoy him dead, so to speak. All along our street the neighbours pulled down their venetian blinds, a mark of respect round our way. The hearse turned up with a horse-drawn carriage that took Ma, Pa and me to the church. As the hearse left ours, the undertaker and his men carried their top hats and walked behind the carriages until the end of our road. Then they took their seats on the carriage. The horses had black velvet covers on their backs and black plumes over their ears that bobbed up and down when they broke into a trot. Quite a sight, it was.

I helped carry the coffin to the front of the church. The place was nigh on full. Reverend Whitehead welcomed everyone and after a hymn and a prayer, talked about Grandpa and his life. The coffin lid was open as Grandpa had insisted. I felt mixed up inside. I still do. It was hard to believe I would never see him again. He was lying there just like he did in bed. The only thing missing was his cap on the bedknob and me at the other end.

The trouble was my mind kept wandering to the replay down the road at Goodison Park. So near and yet so far. I couldn't help wondering how big the crowd would be. Far fewer than Saturday, what with it being a replay and a midweek afternoon. Maybe 25,000? With Burnley being nearer to Everton than Sheffield, we would probably have more fans. That would help the atmosphere and maybe turn it into a home tie. I was worried because Tommy Boyle had never won a game at Goodison and they say he hadn't been fully fit on Saturday. Then I felt guilty and thought about Ma and Pa, how they were feeling. I also hoped Emily might be somewhere in the church, though she hadn't been in the building for years. There are only a certain number of times you can look round without people wondering who you are looking for. Nellie Williams was sitting a couple of rows back, sweet as ever. I didn't look her in the eye. I don't want to give the wrong impression. I haven't seen Emily or heard from her for a few days. I was surprised how much I wanted to talk to her. What with this being a Daws funeral I wouldn't have expected the Bettridges to come as a family but you never know. Even if she had been there, I couldn't be seen talking to her, not with everyone around. Wagging tongues and all that.

'Now Tom is going to lead us in the next hymn,' said Reverend Whitehead. It was Ma who asked me to start *Abide With Me* on my harmonica. I stood at the coffin, by his head, and played the melody through on my own. Any noise at all, just a footstep, echoes round the church but the notes of the harmonica sounded especially rich. Second time round everyone joined in.

'Shine through the gloom and point me to the skies
'Heaven's morning breaks, and earth's vain shadows flee
'In life, in death, O Lord, abide with me.'

You'd have to have a heart of stone not to find that hymn emotional. A fair few of those funeral handkerchiefs with black edging came out, right enough. At the end of the hymn the congregation sat down. I was supposed to as well but I wanted to bid Grandpa my own farewell. I stood at the other end of the coffin, put the harmonica to my mouth and played the first verse of 'Jerusalem'.

'And did those feet in ancient times...'

I doubt many people understood why I did it. Ma did, though. When I finished, she came up and hugged me. It isn't like her to do that, either. Playing at the front meant I could have a good look round to see if Emily was there. No sign.

After the burial we all went back to ours. Ma and the neighbours laid on quite a spread. As we say round here ''e were buried 'wi' ham.' Everyone shared their favourite Grandpa stories and chatted on about anything and everything. Grandpa would have liked the laughter. He wasn't one for standing on ceremony. There were still plenty left in the house when I heard the ring of a bicycle bell. It was Billy. He had been to the replay at Goodison Park.

'Put me out of my misery,' I said, as he walked in.

'Aye, well I'll be needing a wee drop of something good and strong before doing that,' he said. He can be infuriating, can Billy. There's no point in trying to read his face. He would look the same whether we had won or lost 5-0. Inscrutable, that's the word I was looking for. Another nice word. I poured him a good-sized Scotch.

'Now then,' I said. 'If you have any heart at all... are we through to the final?' He didn't reply. Instead he stood in the corner of the room, coughed for attention, coughed a little louder, raised a hand and waited until everyone had stopped talking. Stoney-faced, but with glassy eye (the whisky had done its work), he said a few pleasant words about Grandpa (though they never got on, if truth be told) then took out of his pocket three sheets of paper and began to read. This is what he said, word for word.

Dear friends, we hardly dare read our newspapers in these most turbulent of times. Suffragettes torch and terrify. Pillarboxes burn. Houses blaze. But today 22 gladiators good and true set the green grass of Goodison on fire. The red rose of Lancashire, the white rose of Yorkshire. Burnley's brightest and best against the sharpest blades in Sheffield's mighty cabinet.

They sent forth the trains: hissing, snorting, steaming. From their snaking bellies the faithful poured. Claret and blue, red and white, was there ever such a colourful duel of umbrella, rattle and rosette?

It is 2pm: time to let slip the northern dogs of war! Battered and bruised, out step the teams, aching from their Stretford stalemate but sure in the knowledge that only one titan can book a date with destiny, under glass that glints and gleams o'er London town. George Utley in red and white. Two thousand pounds for a half back. Two thousand! What lunatic price then a full back? And what of 'Professor' Eddie Mosscrop, the bandy-legged boffin. Will he pass with distinction or wear a dunce's hat?

The whistle blows. The game ebbs and flows like the Mersey: the action at times deft and balletic, at others agricultural. No place for faint hearts, this: too much at stake, too highly-charged the crowd. Sturgess lunges. Mosscrop falls. Utley's nose bursts and bleeds. Let slip the sponge of magic: balm for troubled brow. Freeman shoots. Just past a post. Gillespie shoots. Sewell saves.

Half-time. Burnley huddle. 'Play up lads… it's do or die.' Mosscrop responds and rattles the bar. Brelsford hacks Freeman. Penalty! Referee Taylor wafts away the claim like a tiresome wasp. And finally, as God Himself has surely seen enough and beckons dusk descend, it falls to the youngest son of a Barnsley miner, one Thomas William Boyle of this parish. Did Moses ever lead the chosen people with such purpose and passion? Can Captain Courage inspire the Burnley faithful, through the winding wilderness of broken dreams, to the promised land of Sydenham Hill?

Mere minutes remain. Watson's free kick rebounds to Freeman. Gough clears. Mosscrop shoots. Cook clears again but straight to the crouching tiger that is… Tommy Boyle. This is the moment of his short *life. History will ever recall that, had he lifted a staff to the heavens, the Sheffield defence could not have parted wider. His shot rips past Gough like a bullet from a machine-gun. The net shivers and shakes as if the Lord Almighty, thinking of one more capricious plague for Pharaoh, did send forth a mighty whirlwind. 1-0.*

Back come the brave lads from o'er the Pennines, wave after wave of red and white, caution thrown to the prevailing westerly. But it's too little, too late. Referee Taylor raises his arm and blows his whistle. Delirium and despair descend in equal measure. 10,000 Burnley caps are hurled into the air. 10,000 caps now have different owners. Who cares? Lift that man Boyle high. On April 25th Burnley will shut shop and move more than 200 miles south. And when your grandson sits on your knee and asks where you were on that day, what will be your reply? It was too far to go? The queue for tickets was too long? I couldn't spare the cash?

Pawn your pianos. Pawn your sideboards. Pawn your beds. Pawn your sheets. Pawn your wives. The trains on platforms 1, 2, 3, 4, 5 and 6 are bound for London town and this is your invitation to a royal party at the Palace.

With that Billy handed me the paper as if it really was an invitation from the King himself. He then walked straight out of the house and rode away on his bicycle. I told you he could write! He says I have a way with words but I could never put together something like that. So, we're bound for the Crystal Palace at last, where we'll play Liverpool for the FA Cup. And I'm taking Billy's words as a warning. I'll not be one of those left behind, humiliated by my grandchildren.

It is strange to be here in the bedroom, on my own, though. I need to talk to someone and she isn't anywhere to be found. I overheard Ma say that the Bettridges aren't sure where she is, either. Any road, today was Grandpa's day. He is at peace in his own bed for eternity. I feel he is here with me, though. Perhaps that's because his flat cap is still on the bed knob as I write. I'm not letting that go in a hurry.

CHAPTER 21

They say you shouldn't shop for groceries when you're hungry. By the same token Dan should definitely not be on the internet when he's angry. Or ill. He is both. He sneezes. On the phone earlier, Sally told him it was just man-flu and wasn't the least bit sympathetic. She doesn't appreciate that man-flu is more painful than childbirth, a scientific fact. Of course, when her Auntie Flo calls each month, he is not as disrespectful. He is understanding, compassionate and has the depth of character to bear and forbear.

It is Saturday afternoon. He is propped up in bed in a room not much bigger than the ipad in his hands. Between life-threatening sniffles, he hammers away on the keyboard. He sneezes again, violently. Some of the mucus hits the wall at the end of his bed. No surprise, this. The wall is literally at the end of his bed. The four walls round him are one of the reasons for his distracted state of mind: this bloody, bloody box of a room. How long does he have to suffer such indignity? Then, of course, there's the sick man of SE25. More rumours all over the media today that Warnock is jumping ship and taking the best players with him. In fact, there is even talk that Brendan Guilfoyle, the administrator, is happy to see him go and will use the compensation from QPR to help pay this month's wage bill. Dan's message to Warnock is simple: shit or get off the pot.

Palace are warming up on the pitch as Dan types. He would be at Selhurst (of course) for the match against Coventry but for this energy-sapping ailment. Instead, he is about to listen to commentary on the match, broadcast over the internet. He will also add comments to chat rooms and bulletin boards devoted to the game. The usual suspects from round the world log on, pre-match. He marvels at the devotion of the Palace diaspora. Take Auckland Eagle who, depending on the UK kick-off time, comes in from a day's work late in the evening, local time. He goes to bed for an hour or so, gets up at 2am, listens to live commentary from some of the most depressing, forgettable games in history, tries to go back to sleep at some time after 4am before getting up again for work at 7am – 'and wouldn't miss it for the world'.

Dan reaches for another paper tissue. This kind of flu is terminal. And there are other reasons not to be cheerful, too. After dispensing such loving care over the phone, Sally has pretty much gone to ground. OK, it's her final year and all that but there's a limit – and the band has to rehearse for the *Britain's Got Tribute* audition in Blackburn.

Then there's the situation at Bintastic. On Thursday, Eric Kelly called him in to say that the company's advertising agents turned down his suggested re-work of *Mighty Quinn*. Too derivative, they said. So their better ideas include what? Mealy-mouthed Kelly said the ad agents were 'drafting alternatives'. Well, we'll see, won't we? What they've come up with so far has been piss poor.

While Dan was getting the bad news from Kelly, he got the even worse news: a reduction in his working hours. From now on, because of the recession and the credit crunch and the state of the world economy generally (yeah, yeah, cut the flannel) he will be on a three-day week, until sales pick up. At the same time, Kelly is hiring more sales staff. Clearly, he is making life difficult. Dan hates the job but it's a job and there isn't much else out there. So now, whether he likes it or not, he needs to prove his worth by closing sales from prospects at the Waste Solutions exhibition. As the match against Coventry is about to get underway, he listens to the wonderful and utterly pro-Palace commentators and composes an attention-grabbing, hard-sell e-shot on his ipad.

Wheelie bin vandalised or stolen? Replacing it again? What a waste of your time and money. Lock it or lose it.

Yes, that's a good subject line. Straight to the point. He labels the file 'What a waste'.

Dear _____ <call in name here>

It was great to meet you personally (in fact, he can't even remember who is who from the leads in front of him) *at Waste Solutions 2010. I can honestly* (may he be forgiven) *say I was honoured to be Bintastic's representative at the show and was delighted to discover you and hundreds of others love our product* (a few dozen expressed an interest might be more accurate but never mind).

I write with good news! I have twisted the arm of Bintastic's dynamic (he'll like that) *boss Eric Kelly to let you, a valued contact at Waste Solutions 2010, enjoy an EXCLUSIVE deal on the Bintastic wheelie bin lock* (in fact, if anyone walked into Bintastic's showrooms from the street that very morning they would have got the same deal).

Dan pauses, awaiting further inspiration. He hears slow, laboured footsteps on the landing, a loose, watery fart, and another, followed by the flush of a toilet.

A frail voice comes through a crack in the door. 'No Danns, then.'

''Fraid not. We're down to the bare bones.'

'Mind you Butterworth could do some damage if that loudmouth manager of yours brings him on as a sub.'

'Lightning, twice and not are among the words that spring to mind,' says Dan. You have to give the old bat credit. Days ago she hardly knew where Selhurst Park was. Now she knows who's warming the bench, even if she gets the names wrong sometimes. Whoever Warnock brings on, we have to win this game. The cup run is one thing, relegation to League One (if that's what they all it now) is unthinkable. We are hardly an attractive proposition to prospective owners in the Championship, let alone the 'third tier of English football'. Two successive losses at home have sent us careering down the table. A month ago we had a real chance of making the play-offs. Another loss today could see us in the relegation zone. But we can do it today. We must do it today. Coventry? Nothing special.

Demand has been so great for the Bintastic lock that we are expanding the range (in truth, there might possibly be more products in three or four years' time 'when things improve') *which means that you can now save up to 40 per cent on the fantastic Bintastic lock you saw at our stand.'*

The match gets underway. 'Good morning from New York,' posts bulletin board member Acky the Eagle. 'Very drunk once again.' Zach 82, from Stockholm, comforts fellow fans by confirming that his lucky underpants are on, outside his trousers. Well, it worked against Wolves. Similarly, Doc Tor has promised not to take a leak before half-time, though the tension is already taking its toll. He is encouraged to brush up on the knots he learned at Scouts.

The first half proves a turgid affair, lacking in any real drama. Dan finds himself humming Ian Dury's song *What a Waste*. It has been on his mind since he put the words in the subject line of the e-shot.

'I could have been a writer with a growing reputation
'I could have been a ticket man at Fulham Broadway Station
'What a waste…'

With the football commentary still on in the background, he watches a YouTube clip of Ian Dury and the Blockheads performing the song. Tight as a crab's arse, that rhythm section. Dury may not have belonged to the 1960s but Dan has a grudging admiration for the little feller's infectious ditties – part jazz, part punk, part music hall. He's Johnny Rotten, George Formby and Duke Ellington rolled into one. And that unmistakable grunt and growl of a voice, like loose gravel sliding off the back of a tip-up truck.

'I could be the catalyst that sparks the revolution
'I could be an inmate in a long-term institution
'What a waste…'

Oh, close! In the 24th minute a free kick from Darren Ambrose goes just wide. Dan is finishing his e-shot with a PS. He has read somewhere that a PS is one of the most read things in any letter, as it's underneath the signature. *PS This offer MUST end by 28 Feb. Act now. Lock it or lose it!*

Yes, that's good. He's good. He's very good. In fact he's a lot better than Bintastic, or Eric Kelly, or anything to do with the wonderful world of waste disposal. If Dury could have been 'a doctor with poultices and bruises' he could have been, wait a minute, there's another version of the song brewing in his head...

'Someone wake me up at half time, please,' posts Hedgehog in California. As he does so, Coventry clear a shot off the line, creating a brief murmur of excitement on the bulletin boards and chat rooms. Half-time. 0-0. We've been much the better side, according to the wonderfully and utterly pro-Palace commentators and, more significantly, the voice of Sky Sports News. Dan has that on as well in the background. Who said men can't multi-task?

'Coventry are very much a first half team, trust me,' posts jobiinthelastmi.

Mrgin: 'Well, jobi, that's us doomed then.'

Sirdougie: 'Would be happy to scrape a 1-0 with an own goal or deflected shot.'

JamTheEagle: 'I'd take that any day.'

'Think I'll hit the pillow,' says Men At Work, from God-only-knows-where. 'The commentary will keep running in the background so if a moment of excitement does make a rare appearance it may wake me. Night all.' No-one blames him for hitting the sack but the remnant will watch and pray. Dan goes downstairs to make a cup of tea. Dury-esque words and phrases buzz through his brain. Laughing, he jots them down on a sheet of paper. Kev will love this. He's always raving about the Blockheads and their bass player in particular.

'Here you go, Nanna,' he says, passing her a cup of tea.

'Thanks, Daniel love,' she says. 'I won't drink most of it, mind.'

'No worries.'

'Reading are one down to Blackpool. That's good for you.' Now she's even keeping tabs on other teams fighting the drop. Respect.

'We shouldn't be in this position,' says Dan. 'We shouldn't be wondering how the Scunthorpes and Plymouths are doing. It's embarrassing.'

'Not after the way you played against Aston Villa,' says Nanna. 'Are you seeing your, er, young lady at all?'

'Sally?'

'That's right, of course, Sally, Sally…'

'Yes, but not sure when.'

'Only…'

'The BBC again?'

Nanna nods. 'But I don't want to bother her if she's up to her neck.'

'I'll mention it to her.'

'That's good of you.'

The second half commentary gets underway but Dan has it on low. He is having too much fun re-writing Dury. It's more entertaining than the match. Every now and then he glances up at the bulletin boards. Desperation is growing. Fortunately, former Palace hero Clinton Morrison doesn't manage to haunt his old club, firing weakly at Speroni who saves comfortably. A distracting conversation develops over where and how you inflate a football. It's that kind of game. It's that kind of bulletin board.

Seaside Eagle: 'It's slowly starting to sink in; we're in trouble.'

SpikeyMatt: 'Those missed chances are going to come back and haunt us, you just know it.' Ah, if it wasn't a former player…

JamThe Eagle: 'I washed my lucky pants today, might stick them on even though they're ringing wet.' Selfless devotion.

Ten minutes to go and the sides are still locked at 0-0. Dan listens to Dury again. Never mind the waste, what a rhythm section. He writes another verse for his version of the song and chuckles. He catches another report from the game on Sky Sports News. He glances at the bulletin board. He finishes the e-shot and loads up several dozen addresses. It's ready to go. It's do or die. Like Palace, he really needs a result. Meanwhile, he's also finished re-writing *What a Waste*. He'll send them to Kev when the e-shot has gone. He writes a short note to his bass player and loads the verse as an attachment but as he does so, the inevitable happens. Coventry's Bell lobbs Speroni. It's a sky blue smash and grab.

Mrgins: 'oh **** **** ****. Typical.'

Joshuah: 'FFS'

AJ: '**** When will we learn to defend?'

Less than five minutes left. There's no way back. Dan hits the keyboard in anger, sending the email to dozens of exhibition leads. He then sends the email to Kev with his 'new' song. The whistle blows. Sky Sports confirm Palace, after suffering three home defeats in a row, have dropped into the relegation zone.

'Brighton next year, lads,' sighs The Stig.

Meanwhile, delighting in the result, Brighton fan wellquickwoody posts: 'La La La-La La! See you next season!' The south coast club are languishing in League One and want to see their dearest rivals grovelling down there with them. It doesn't get much more depressing than this.

'I'm going for walk,' he tells Nanna, 'to calm down.'

'Is that wise?' she says. 'You're not feeling so well.'

Dan is already through the front door before the end of the sentence. He knows he is being petulant and childish but there are times when it's much better to stride around the local park after a bad result and insult a few mallards, than say things he will regret to his family. It isn't their fault. A rush of cold air hits his lungs. He wraps his scarf tightly round his mouth. So what is the worst that can happen? The club going out of business all together: that would be a tragedy. If it has to re-form and work its way up the football league, so be it. At least there will be a club bearing the name Crystal Palace directly connected to the one formed in 1905. And, it has to be said, there would be plenty of new grounds to discover – smaller, tighter grounds full of genuine atmosphere where you can stand on the terracing. Like the old days he had never known.

Half an hour later, and calmer, he walks back through the front door of the house, thinking positively about the midweek cup replay at Aston Villa. We could still spring a few surprises up there in Birmingham. He goes straight upstairs to his computer and checks to see if there has been any response to his e-shot. Six already!

'Brilliant,' says Oli McKay from Princes Risborough. 'I loved your new Ian Dury lyric. I'll take six locks.'

What is he on about?

'A risky strategy,' says Alistair Plowman from Cirencester. 'But I've ordered a dozen for my flats.'

Oh God! Oh no.

'Not all the Catholic priests I know are child molesters,' says Linda Batey from Kings Lynn. 'Take me off your mailing list. I shall be writing to your managing director.'

It cannot be true. He surely hadn't.

'Eric Kelly is a personal friend of mine and I can assure you he's put a difficult past behind him,' says Joanna Grimstone of Swindon.

The Dury re-work has gone out with the e-shot. His prospects received the hard sell e-shot OK but they also received *What a Waste 2010.*

I could be a footballer with a sod off silver Merc
I could be a stuntman doubling up as Captain Kirk
I could sell my body, what a good life on the game
I could be a banker or a wanker, they're the same
What a waste!

But I'm selling bloody locks on a wheelie bin
For a poncy little git with a double chin
Too much of what he does has made him almost blind
What a waste! What a waste! Of course I mind

I could be a heart throb in a trashy all-boy band
I could write a sitcom full of characters so bland
I could be in parliament and fiddle my expenses
I could be a Catholic priest and bugger young boys senseless
What a waste!

There's another email, too. It's from Kev. 'No attachment. Where's this funny lyric, then?'

CHAPTER 22

Sunday 5 April 1914

Went to church as usual this morning. Well, not quite as usual. Grandpa had always sat next to me at the end of the pew. I put his flat cap where he should have been. I suppose I'll get used to him not being around but for now it seemed the right thing to do. All the way through the service I could only think about two things – 'where on earth' is Emily (now I'm even thinking in the way she speaks) and how am I going to get down to London for the match?

I had plenty of time to think, too. The choir chanted another one of those psalms that makes no sense, something about Moab being a wash-pot and throwing shoes over Eden. No, Edom, throwing shoes over Edom. We sang *Guide Me O Thou Great Jehovah*, a fine hymn, that. Then Reverend Whitehead preached for almost an hour, I reckon. This time he went on about Mary and Martha, two women in the Bible who 'knew their place'. One of them sat at Jesus' feet, listening to him attentively, while the other went and prepared food. He said all women should follow the example of Mary and Martha and be content looking after their home, children and husbands. The story shows there's no need for women to have the vote. He said the vote carries with it 'serious responsibilities' (that was the phrase he used, I jotted it down). God didn't give women the character to deal with big issues. He made them caring and compassionate but while these virtues are very important, women also suffer from hysteria.

He explained that the word came from the Greek word meaning a uterus. It means women cannot think straight. Worst of all they may vote for the pacifists. If we ever go to war, he said, we can't allow them to make us more liable to the threat of invasion.

He read out something from a medical journal, I think it was, where some doctor or other claims that women are becoming more like men through things like cycling and playing football. These activities are increasing their muscles while their pelvises are getting smaller. This will reduce their ability to have children.

'If we are not careful,' he thundered, 'women who have been well educated won't want to have children or, even if they do, will be unfit for motherhood.' He said that too many married school mistresses (I thought of Mrs Knapp who is about 35) are working for too long and avoiding their 'biological and social duties'.

I wish Emily had been there. I couldn't imagine her quietly listening, not after what happened at Weaver Green.

After the service we filed out of church. Lots of people came up and said how sorry they were to hear about Grandpa. They were very kind and all that but I noticed Freddie Bettridge take Reverend Whitehead to one side. I wanted to ask Freddie where Emily was. Of course I couldn't. I had no business knowing. At first I wondered if Freddie was talking about the sermon but he's never been bothered by any of the sermons before. They both looked very serious and I became more and more curious. I started talking to Nellie Williams and used her to edge within a few yards of Freddie, so it didn't look as if I was listening in. I asked Nellie what kind of week she had had but didn't really listen to the reply. It was mean of me but I'm not perfect. I couldn't make out all of what Freddie was saying but they were talking about Emily, no doubt about that. It seems she has definitely gone missing. The police are on the look out for her now. Reverend Whitehead asked Freddie if she was in trouble at school and he nodded. Nellie asked me what kind of a week it had been for me. If I talked I couldn't listen to Freddie so I avoided answering her question and asked Nellie how her mum was. I walked a little closer to Freddie, not really listening to Nellie's reply. Maybe Freddie thought I was getting too close because it was his turn to edge Reverend Whitehead away. The pair of them went into the vestry and shut the door behind them.

After that there was no point in talking to Nellie. She looked disappointed when I said I had to look after Ma as it had been a difficult week for her. When we got home Ma opened the door, bent down and picked up a letter that had been posted through our front door while we were at church. She handed it to me as normal. It's just as well she can't read.

'Who's it from?' she asked.

'Oh, Mrs Beecroft, a teacher from school,' I lied. The letter was for me, from Emily. 'She says she was sorry to hear about Grandpa and to pass on her love to all the family.'

'That's nice of her,' said Ma. 'Folk have been kind.'

'Yes. They've been very kind.' I took the letter upstairs.

Dear Tom

I am sorry I haven't been in touch. There are lots of reasons why and I will explain. Can you be on your bicycle at the top of Crank Hill at 10pm tomorrow (Monday) without anyone knowing? We need a look-out!

Your loving Emily x

PS I was very sorry to hear about Grandpa but delighted to hear Burnley reached the final.

At the top of Crank Hill? At 10pm? It will be pitch black. On a bike I don't own? And who are 'we'? A look-out? For what? And, for the first time, an 'x'.

CHAPTER 23

'Because of Boxing Day...' Sally stands with her arm raised, fist closed, head back, ready to do bloody battle with a non-existent enemy. Then she flops untidily into an armchair. 'It's just... just *pathetic*.'

'I don't know the significance of the verse.' Nanna sits with a knitted quilt over her knees, the family cat curled in her lap. The FA Cup fifth round replay is live on TV but, as unchallenged master of the remote control, Nanna has hit the mute button.

'It's one of *their* songs, Dan and his friends,' says Sally huffily, 'about something that happened at a match against Brighton, decades ago. But the foe is never there.'

Nanna smiles ruefully. 'I doubt that matters.'

'Palace haven't played Brighton for years. While they're all up there in Birmingham,' Sally points to the TV, 'the foe is 150 miles due south, not the least bit interested. But they'll still sing those songs and the Aston Villa fans won't know what they're going on about.'

'Lest we forget,' murmurs Nanna.

Sally looks at her in surprise. 'Soldiers making the ultimate sacrifice isn't a fair comparison.'

'I didn't say it was.'

'Dan hadn't even been born on the Boxing Day they sing about.'

'The story bonds the community – passed down from dad to lad.'

'Well, he should know better.'

It is Wednesday evening. Dan has been unemployed since first thing Monday morning – sacked on the spot by a quivering double chin. He is now at Villa Park, watching the lads put Saturday's depressing defeat behind them and continue a glorious cup run. What better way to forget the whole sorry business of still being alive. Sally, meanwhile, has gone round to see Nanna, at the old lady's request. However, it is Sally who is setting the agenda.

'I just don't get it,' she says.

'Get what exactly?'

Sally nods at the TV screen. 'The intensity.'

'You feel excluded.'

'Baffled, more like. Football is a soap opera without an ending – another game, another storyline. Elation one week, rage the next. Dan feels every kick, every tackle. The match is going on in his body, in his veins, in his gut. I might just as well not be there.'

'Everything that happens to the team is happening to *him*, and to the tribe.'

'Except that it's not a tribe, there's no war... it's just *sport*.'

'And a cause.'

'But it's a cause without a purpose.'

'It doesn't matter what the cause represents.' Nanna sits up, disturbing the cat who lets her hurt feelings be known. 'What matters is that those who follow the cause become absorbed into something bigger – a kind of corporate hope.'

Sally looks curiously at Dan's grandmother. 'That is it, exactly.'

'You must understand, I grew up in the Welsh valleys,' says Nanna. 'It might have been a dull Sunday morning outside but within an hour my father's church would be a sea of emotion. He didn't so much preach as transport people, right out of themselves.'

'I hadn't looked at it like that,' says Sally. 'Your father's faith, the fairy story it's based on, at least it has an ethic. This is just football. The rituals, their history – it's all based on a kind of distorted nostalgia. I mean, *"We scored five, they scored none. Brighton take it up the bum..."*'

Nanna grins. 'It lacks subtlety, I'll grant you.'

'There's no ultimate destiny, no salvation. And the only personal demand is to love the club.'

'And the fans can be demanding if things aren't going well. They can lose faith.' Nanna looks intently at her guest. 'Like any lover.'

'I mean, take the match against, I think it was Scunthorpe.' Sally steams on, missing the inference. 'I listened to it on the radio with Dan and his friends. They were singing,

"I'm Palace 'til I die, I'm Palace 'til I die,

"I know I am, I'm sure I am,

"I'm Palace 'til I die".

They went 1-0 down. They sang the song again. 2-0. They sang the song again. At 4-0 down they sang, and pardon my French,

"I'm Palace 'til I die, I'm Palace 'til I die,

"I know I am, I'm sure I am,

"I'm Palace fuck knows why."'

Nanna smiles. 'A modern psalm.'

Sally looks puzzled.

'In spite of everything, he has no choice but to keep the faith,' says Nanna, 'to keep believing.' She glances up to see Aston Villa take the lead. 'Oh, that's a pity. I'm beginning to like Dan's team.'

Sally shakes her head but not because of the goal. She bends down to hug the shrivelled old lady in front of her. 'You're almost making sense of it.'

'Well, I don't know about that.'

'Trying to cope with an addictive personality is a nightmare.'

'You think Daniel's addicted.'

'He can't live without football.'

'Interesting.'

'He's like one of those gamblers in Las Vegas, where the slot machines are programmed to deliver rewards at regular intervals – just enough to keep the gambler believing he is going to win big-time.'

'I see what you mean.' Nanna muses on the idea. 'The team win just enough games to keep supporters loyal.'

'Exactly. Dan knows he will be rewarded now and again, if he carries on going to games. The team is unlikely to win promotion and some top players have been sold for a pittance, but, against the odds, they knock Wolves out of the FA Cup. It's enough – for now.'

'That makes sense.' Nanna encourages the cat back onto her lap. 'The odd win ensures he keeps shovelling coins into the fruit machine.'

'He's addicted.'

'Hmmm, I don't think so. From my experience, addicts tend to be self-destructive. They sell all their possessions and steal from friends and family. And they're usually solitary and secretive.'

'And football is a shared thing…'

Nanna nods. 'Fans may fear losing their clubs through liquidation but most of all they fear losing each other as a result.'

'But Dan doesn't fear losing me.'

'Oh, now that's… a different issue.' Nanna reaches out for the hand of her young visitor. 'Is that a possibility? I think he loves you, a lot.'

Sally wells up. 'You're appallingly perceptive and I hate you for it. I shall divert the conversation by pointing out that Aston Villa are now 2-1 up, I'm glad to say and there isn't long to go, although I really don't care. I will also make us a drink.'

Minutes later she is back holding a tray with tea brewing underneath a tartan cosey.

'Oh,' says Nanna. 'So they do have a pot!'

'You need to know where to look.'

'They usually just throw a teabag in a cup.'

'The old ways are the best. I bought some custard creams on the way here.'

'You spoil me.'

'Now then, Nanna… can I call you that, too, by the way?'

'Of course.'

'What's all this about the BBC chasing you… something to do with a documentary on Neath?'

'Well, it's not *strictly* about Neath. That was just to throw people off the trail.' Nanna grasps her visitor's hand again. 'If I tell you what it's really all about I need to have your absolute assurance that you won't say anything to anyone.'

CHAPTER 24

Tuesday 7 April 1914

When I started this journal it was to sharpen up the way I write, in case I get the chance to become one of those reporter types, that's all. But if I put down what happened last night, and someone reads it, I could be hauled up before a judge. The most sensible thing to do is pretend it was just another dull day but you can't always do what you are supposed to do.

At about nine o'clock I yawned, told Ma I needed a good night's sleep but instead of going to bed, crept out of the house. On Billy's bicycle (again) I headed for the top of Crank Hill, in the pitch black. I passed the place where that witch Isabel Robey lived 300 years ago. Creatures scurried around in the woods on either side. Owls warned me I was trespassing on their hunting grounds. It's a country lane and clarty with it. I fell off a couple of times and had to push the bike a lot of the way. One thing I dare not write down is the language I used. Ma would be shocked I even know the words. Crank Station was deserted. I was relieved no-one saw me as I pushed Billy's bike over the level crossing. I already felt guilty and hadn't done anything wrong.

I reached the top of the brew. Only a tiny village is Crank, a few scattered houses, a chapel, a public house – that way on. I heard some girls' voices by the wall of the village school. Muffled they were, in the darkness. The talking stopped as I got close.

One of them said: 'Are you Tom?' I couldn't see her at all.

'Who wants to know?' I said.

'We're Emily's friends,' said another voice. It sounded posh.

'Oh, so you're the "we"'.

'The what?'

'Emily said she'd not be alone.'

'She was right. We're the "we"'. They giggled. One of them lit a small lantern and held it up. All I could see were her eyes. Their faces were covered in coal dust.

'I didn't expect you to look like that.' I almost said I might as well have come straight from work but thought better of it.

'I'm Lily and much prettier like this,' said the taller one.

'And I'm Felicity but most people call me Fliss.' They sounded so much like Emily I thought they must go to her school.

'Come far?' I said. They looked at each other.

'Best if we don't say,' said Lily.

'Like that, is it?' I said. 'What's going on?' They glanced at each other again, waiting for each other to speak.

'We're very grateful you're here,' said Fliss.

'Is this legal?' I said.

'Is what legal?' said Lily.

'What Emily has planned.'

'We don't know what she has planned.'

'Well, if *you* don't know…'

'Emily just told us to be here.'

'Same as me,' I said. 'I hope she's not playing a joke on us.'

'Oh no, it's not a joke. We just don't know the address.'

'Address? Of what?'

'The place.'

'What place?'

'The place which…' I think Fliss kicked Lily to stop her talking but I can't be sure. It was dark.

'Have *you* come far?' she said.

'Not as far as you, by the sounds,' I said.

'We don't normally have somebody with us of the opposite… you know…' They both giggled.

'Well, I don't normally act as a look-out,' I said.

'Is this your first sortie?' said Fliss.

'Sortie? What do you mean?'

'You know, mission.'

'No, I don't know,' I said.

'Only they keep a watch on us.'

'They?' I seemed to be asking an endless list of questions.

'You know... the Cat and Mouse Act,' said Lily. I said I'd read something in the papers. Lily explained how two of her friends had been caught on a sortie in Manchester and were due up in court again next week.

'Oh, so you're suffragettes.' I wanted to take it back as soon as I'd said it. I felt stupid. The penny hadn't dropped until that moment.

'Of course,' said Fliss. 'What did you think we were, thieves?'

'Emily didn't explain,' I said, weakly.

'That's because we make sure as few people know who we are as possible,' said Fliss.

'I didn't know Emily was one of them... I mean, one of you,' I began. 'All she said...'

At that point we heard another bike coming up the hill. It was Emily. I expected her to be blacked up as well but she wasn't.

'Hello, everyone. Thanks for coming,' she said. 'The paint and brushes are under those bushes over there. The house is 400 yards away in that direction. You can't see the lawn from the house so as long as we're quiet no-one will see or hear us.' That was exactly how she was. I hadn't seen her for what seemed weeks and weeks but that didn't matter. She was in 'sortie' mood. 'Tom, you keep guard at the end of the drive. If you see anyone approaching, run down to the lawn and tell us. Or if there's no time for that, blow this whistle and scatter. All set?'

'I don't know what's going on,' I said. 'Whose house is it? What are you going to do?'

'After we've finished, I'll explain. I promise,' said Emily.

For the next half hour I found myself crouching down, hiding by the iron gates of a long drive. I had no idea whose house it was but it had large grounds. One or two people walked by the end of the drive but they were just locals, not police. It was very quiet until I heard the sound of a motor car spluttering its way up the hill. I had no idea whether it would come down the drive but I wasn't waiting to find out. I blew the whistle and ran towards the girls. By the time I got to them it was too late. The car came towards the house with its headlights on. I saw who was driving the car: Borst from Weaver Green. So this was his house. As the car turned a bend in the drive, the headlights shone on the lawn. Emily and her friends had painted 'Votes For Women' in huge white letters on the grass. I crept along, hidden by the bush, to get a closer view.

All three girls had had plenty of time to get away. Fliss and Lily were nowhere to be seen but Emily just stood in the middle of the lawn, in full view of the headlights, paintbrush in hand. Borst got out of his car and walked up to her.

'I thought I might si' thee again,' he said.

'I had no desire to see *you* again,' said Emily.

'Why that's Bettridge's daughter,' said Borst's wife from the car window.

'I don't think so,' said Borst. 'The little flibbertigibbet's from Burnley.'

'No, it's definitely Bettridge's daughter,' said Mrs Borst. 'Her photo was in the paper this week. The police are after her.'

Emily just stood there.

'Oh, so tha's a liar *and* a criminal,' said Borst. 'Well, we can help the coppers in their search, can't we?'

'Go ahead,' said Emily. 'And I'll tell them what you ask girls to do on their knees, in your office, for half-a-crown. Your wife would like to know, I'm sure.' She walked over to the car. 'The girls need the money and have to do what your husband demands. He calls the police at his own peril.'

There was silence for a few seconds.

'Off 'om wi' thee,' said Borst.

'Aren't you going to call the police, darling?' Mrs Borst sounded shocked.

'They've better things for t' do than waste time on a limb o' t' devil, like her,' he replied.

'But…'

'No buts.' Borst got into his car and drove to the house. They both went inside.

'Quick,' I said to Emily from the bush. 'Let's get away while we can.'

'You go, don't worry about me,' she said and started painting on the lawn again.

'But the police will be here any minute. Look.' I pointed to the overhead wire. 'They have a telephone.'

'Oh I don't think they'll be making any calls,' she said. 'And if the police come, I'll happily testify in court.'

To be honest, I didn't know what to do. Fliss and Lily came out of hiding.

'What's she playing at?' I said.

'She's quite mad and we love her,' said Fliss.

'But… she *wants* to get caught.'

'I think this sortie is personal. We don't normally do residential gardens.'

'What do you mean?'

'Didn't she have an incident with the man or something?'

'Yes, but…'

'She wants to humiliate him.'

By now Emily had finished painting. She held the lantern over the whole scene. It now read 'Votes for Women. We're not for sale.' With that she threw half-a-crown on the lawn and walked over to us. Her eyes were on fire.

'You see, I told you so,' she said. 'No police to be seen. I bet there's an almighty row going on in that house.'

We got on our bikes and took the back roads into St Helens. Fliss and Lily left us before we got to town. They were staying overnight with a local family who support suffragettes. Emily hugged them both, got on her bike and beckoned me to follow.

'Where are we going?' I said.

'The summer house. They'll never guess I'm there. And I'll be gone before they get up.'

'Gone? Where?'

'I can't say.'

'What's happened to you?'

'I've… woken up.' Her eyes shone brighter than Borst's headlights. By now it was well gone midnight and I had a shift beginning at six. I was in a dream, as if the incident up on Crank Hill had never happened. We crept into the summerhouse and sat together on the old settee, a blanket over our knees, just talking and talking and talking. She had been so angry at Weaver Green that she went to a meeting of one of these suffragette groups in Manchester, at the Free Trade Hall. A leading light of the movement was speaking. She told me her name but I can't remember it.

'I could have listened for hours. It was like a light going on,' said Emily. That's how she put it. She said that phrase several times. With Emily, it's owt or nowt. Within a few days she had moved into a secret address with a family committed to the cause. That's another word she used a lot. The cause.

'Ever realised how few women are tried for serious criminal offences?' she said. I said I hadn't really thought it. 'That's the trouble, most men haven't really thought about it because they haven't had to,' she said. 'Until we get the vote, you will go on ignoring us.'

'Plenty of men believe women should get the vote,' I said.

'Why aren't they protesting then?' I couldn't answer that. 'Men like Borst are slave owners. They degrade women. I feel sorry for his wife. She's just an instrument for the production of children.'

'Wait a minute…' I said but she wasn't going to stop for me.

'Surely mankind is capable of a higher purpose.' It was like listening to one of those street preachers. 'Carnality belongs to the animals. Spirituality is what distinguishes us from animals. In the earliest period of human history, women ruled over men but since then men have held them in slavery through the institution of marriage.'

She said a lot more but after a while I went quiet. I was tired but it wasn't because of that.

'Anything wrong?' said Emily.

'I'm not sure,' I said. 'It all seems so far away from what I know.'

'I don't understand.'

'I opened your eyes to my world of dynamite and mallets. Now you're opening me up to fire bombs, bricks and, worst of all, text books.'

She laughed.

'You've become a dangerous person to know, Miss Bettridge.'

'Do you think so? That's rather fun.'

'I might get a stone through my window if I cross you.'

'The last sortie was the ninth hole of a golf club in Rochdale,' she said. 'I used up the rest of the paint tonight. I'm sworn to secrecy about next week's activities.'

'Aye, well the police know you're up to something,' I said. 'That's why they've put your picture in the paper.'

'The photograph wasn't very flattering, was it? Trust Freddie to give them one that looks as if I've been on hunger strike.'

'I thought you looked lovely,' I said.

She opened her bag and took out an envelope. 'Well, here's something to say thank you for tonight.' Inside was a ticket for the FA Cup Final, including rail fare, drives, three good meals, admission to the Crystal Palace and a seat in the grandstand. A seat! I've never sat down at a game in my life. The ticket cost 26/-. That's two weeks' wages. I couldn't believe it. I just stared and stared at the ticket. I was in dreamland.

'And,' she said, 'if you don't mind…' She put her hand into her bag and pulled out another one. 'I'm coming with you. And this time *nothing* will stop us.'

Usually when I arrive at the pithead first thing I've had a good night's rest and I'm half asleep. This morning I arrived, not having slept a wink and wide awake. Floating, I was.

CHAPTER 25

'So… at last.' The voice comes from behind Dan. He turns to see a man in his early 30's, medium height, dark-haired, sporting Palace's 'team of the 80s' classic white strip with red-and-blue sash. There are early signs of a beer gut playing an advanced full-back role, overlapping between shirt and trouser belt.

'Sorry, I can't hear you properly.' Pint in hand, Dan is trying to communicate over the pre-match hubbub in The Cherry Trees. Normally full of quiet and considerate locals, the pub becomes a seething mass of hyped-up humanity before each home game.

'S'cuse.' Another fan squeezes past them both with four full pint glasses lifted above his head. 'Ta.'

Today, with a match soon to begin against Sheffield United, all the talk is of Neil Warnock's acrimonious defection to Queen's Park Rangers. But smoke ascended almost immediately from the jerk chicken shop on Whitehorse Lane, confirming the appointment of the dour and dependable Paul Hart as his replacement. Hart will be assisted by a Palace legend and fans' favourite, the ever-loyal Dougie Freedman.

'A legend in our midst.' The man bows before Dan. 'Front man of a top, top band.'

'Well, we do our best.' For a moment all the legend talk leads Dan to fear the worst, that this stranger knows about Newcastle.

'Name's Gav.' He puts out his hand. Dan shakes it. 'I'm launching a new Palace website called andthisiswhathesaid.com. I'll be interviewing fans with interesting stories to tell. I hear your band is in a TV competition or something...'

Dan is keen to talk. Searching for a new job is frustrating and you never know who might read the interview or book the band. It can't do any harm. 'What kind of things do you want to cover?'

'Everything. Music, the club, administration, modern football.'

'Oh, now don't start me on modern football.'

'You have strong views...' Gav clicks a pocket-sized recorder.

'We've been betrayed by sharks in suits. Give me the ancient football I never knew – anytime.'

'But football's safer now.'

'It wasn't dangerous.'

'What about Hillsborough?'

'Don't start me on that, either.'

'All-seater stadia are family friendly.'

'For the few who can afford to go. In any case, kids soon tire of libraries.'

'So you prefer terracing?'

'We stand all through the game, anyway. Seating is dangerous.'

'You have a romantic view of the past.'

'I'm not just talking about the stadia, I'm talking about the players. You must have seen film of Joe Jordan.' Dan bares his teeth.

'I'm not with you.'

'Joe Jordan's publicity agent wouldn't let him out of the dressing room without dentures if he were playing today. The way he celebrated after scoring a goal, threatening to give opposing fans a nasty suck – that's class, that's our heritage. Not some Carlos Fandango wearing day-glo orange boots, gloves, tights and God help us, a snood.'

'Well, they say the Premiership is the best league in the world.'

'Yeah, I toss and turn at night wondering who'll finish fourth.'

'Matches are beamed live around the world to dozens of countries.'

'And to create a bit of atmosphere in the grounds, clubs are giving out free flags and clappers to plastic fans, funding card displays and piping in drum beats through the PA. It's just shocking.'

It is seven minutes to three before Gav and Dan finish their conversation. By that time they've covered everything from the bourgeoning Ultra movement at Selhurst Park to the ghost of Billy Callender, a Palace goalie who hung himself from a crossbar at Selhurst Park in 1932. Gav heads for the door as Dan looks for Wretched and the others.

'Oh, by the way,' calls Dan, 'do you want some pictures?'

'I've already got some.' Gav is halfway through the door. 'Looks like you were having a great time. I'll let you know when the article goes online, probably just before your gig at the 4000 Holes.' He melts into the crowd with a wave.

He's already got pictures? Where did he get those from? Who's in them? When were they taken? What did he mean it looked as if he was having a great time? Oh well, it can't do any harm. Surely.

CHAPTER 26

Thursday 23 April 1914

There's nowt so queer as folk, they say. We reach the FA Cup Final for the first time and our so-called supporters get a right cob on, firing off letters complaining about our poor league form. In the Burnley Express, 'Disgusted Member' – he didn't even have the courage to use his real name – wrote 'the directors and players of the club seem to think because they are in the Cup they can put anything they like on.' Now I know we only picked up two points from seven league games recently but who cares about the First Division when you're in with a fine chance of lifting the FA Cup? Everyone knows they only dreamed up league football because there were too many meaningless friendlies between FA Cup games. I'd sooner get relegated and win the cup than stay in the First Division and lose the final. Any true fan thinks the same way. League football will never be bigger than the FA Cup.

Tomorrow I'll be meeting Emily at Burnley station and we'll get the midnight train to London. I'm writing now to try and pass the time. Every long hour seems like a week. They say there's over 150 specials going down to Euston and St Pancras from all over Lancashire. All the talk is how this will be the first royal final. King George himself will be sitting just a few rows away from me and Emily. Or is it Emily and I? I'm never sure about that. Emily and I sounds too posh but I need to get it right because I will be near King George himself.

It will be the first time any King or Queen has been to an FA Cup Final. Horse racing and egg chasing is more their style. Football, on the other hand, is our game with all the best teams coming from the north. Apart from us there's Barnsley, Newcastle, Everton and Bradford to name just a few. Hardly any team south of Birmingham is much good. No matter what Reverend Whitehead says, football has become what it is today through ordinary people in the likes of Sheffield and Glasgow, Billy's neck of the woods. It makes you wonder why the FA Cup Final is played down in London where, by and large, they'd rather watch the Boat Race. Down there they think we're all cloth caps and whippets. They see tens of thousands of us at games, hunched-shouldered and chain smoking. They reckon we're all like that. Some of the teams down south, full of amateur 'gentlemen' so-called, take pride in the fact that no-one turns up to watch them. They're puddled.

Mind you, it's changing and about time, too. I cut out the following report from a paper this week.

'Professional football of the best kind is no longer regarded as a spectacle suitable only for the proletariat. The King's presence at the Cup Final, let us hope, will put an end to the old snobbish notion that true blue sportsmen ought to ignore games played by those who cannot afford to play without being paid for their services.'

They say the King may not be able to stay for the whole game and present the trophy to the winners. They're worried some of Emily's new-fangled friends may use the final as another way to win publicity. Last year they planned to rent houses facing the grounds, a couple of minutes from the Crystal Palace pitch. Three of them were going to scale the fence and blow up the stand with explosives. Two others planned to dig up the turf and make it unplayable while the last member of the gang was to give a false fire alarm, drawing the nearest fire engine away from the scene. They gave up in the end because the place was too well guarded.

All of which makes me wonder if I've got myself in too deep with Emily, what with all this protesting and the like. Shop windows have been smashed in Preston. It wouldn't surprise me if Emily had something to do with it. They are on the watch for anyone who even looks like a suffragette, especially in London. What's more her photograph is doing the rounds and we'll be sitting just a few rows from the King himself. Emily says I shouldn't worry because she'll get overlooked in such a big crowd. I'm not convinced, me. The thing is that she's changed. It's as if the suffragettes have become her family and that she no longer needs one of her own. They make her feel she belongs.

We had great conversations until all of this. The last time, in the summerhouse, after the prank in Crank (as I call it), we talked for hours but she was different. She kept bringing everything back to 'the cause'. She went on about women I have never heard of, foreign some of them. They believe there should be new forms of relationships, trial marriages, communes and wages for women doing housework. It all seemed a bit far-fetched to me.

Any road, tonight I am a bundle of jangling nerves. I've been working all hours to get time off for the trip. A lot of the lads down the pit are Scousers and tell me every day, and every hour of every day, that we have no chance against Liverpool. Ma hasn't any idea where I've got the money from to go to London (of all places) and I dare not tell her. I'm due to meet Emily tomorrow evening for my first-ever visit to our capital city but it's just as likely she'll be arrested before she gets there.

Then there is the small matter of the biggest game in Burnley's history.

CHAPTER 27

'So they don't know about the other matter?' says Nanna.

'No-one knows anything about the "other matter,"' says Sally, using air quotes.

'And I'm only going to be asked questions about what happened here during the war?'

'The producer has given her word.'

'The programme goes out…'

'…some time next week.'

The driver of the hired car pulls up at the end of the short drive. Sally helps Nanna out of the car.

'Oh my,' she says, steadying herself and looking round. 'Everything is just the same. The house, the woods, the lake. I'd forgotten about the Wellingtonia tree. It's grown so high. I can't believe I'm here again. It's been so long.'

A woman in a pair of smart jeans, sporting a coloured scarf over a green body warmer, pulls away from three men and walks quickly towards the car.

'Rhoslyn, lovely i gwrdd â chi o'r diwedd. Rwy'n Bronwen,' she says.

'Wnes ti ddod a mi erbyn y diwedd!' Nanna accepts a brief hug from the woman.

'Yn wir, ac rwy'n ddiolchgar iawn i chi,' says Bronwen. 'We should speak in English or we may confuse the camera crew.'

'Whatever you say. Mind you, too much talking of any kind was

136

banned here.' Nanna turns and looks to her left. 'The huts. They're still here. And the chimneys. The day I arrived they were coughing out thick, inky smoke. All the windows were covered for the blackout. That reminds me...'

'Whoah,' says Bronwen. 'I want to catch this on camera. Your first impressions are very important. Don't say another word for now, please.' She beckons to the cameramen.

'I've never done anything like this before,' says Nanna. 'I'm sure I'll be perfectly hopeless.'

'I'm sure you won't,' says Bronwen.

'There were plenty of others like me you could speak to.'

'No-one from Neath.'

Within three minutes Nanna is standing with her back to a rambling country house, a discreet microphone clipped to her coat.

'So, Rhoslyn, this is the first time you've been here for almost 70 years.' Bronwen stands behind the camera. 'You were just 25.'

'So you know how old I am.'

'Well, yes.'

'You've been checking up on me.'

'Well, only as far as we need to. We must aim to be as accurate as possible.'

'I'm not sure about this, you know...' Nanna searches for the microphone and attempts to unclip it.

'Really, that's all there is to it. Really...' Bronwen looks pleadingly at her interviewee and Sally.

'It's not a problem.' Sally gives Nanna an encouraging hug.

'Well... I've come this far, I suppose. If you say so...' Nanna gathers her thoughts. 'I must have stood about here when I first arrived. The thing I remember most of all was a train whistle in the distance. I wanted to get the first one back home.'

'So you weren't looking forward to the challenges ahead,' says a relieved Bronwen.

'No-one told me what I would be doing, so it was hard to get excited. Back in Neath a gentleman had noted I could complete the Daily Telegraph crossword in under 12 minutes and speak German, that sort of thing. They did some tests and the next thing I knew I was in a hut miles from home – for three years.'

'Do you remember who met you?'

Nanna smiles ruefully. 'I think an army captain was supposed to do the honours but there was no-one on the platform. The journey from Neath took all day. I was sitting on my suitcase in the train's corridor most of the way. I arrived late at night during the blackout. The red lights of the train disappeared in the distance and it all went quiet. I just stood there alone, with my suitcase. I was terrified.'

'And?'

'I remember climbing some iron steps which took me over a bridge. I virtually felt my way up to the house. A security guard heard me and took me inside.'

'That's lovely, thank you,' says Bronwen. She gestures to the camera crew. 'Right, we're going to go round the buildings, Rhoslyn. I need your comments as you see all the places again, so let's walk and talk as we film. When you woke up on that first morning what do you remember most of all?'

Nanna walks slowly up to the house.

'I was sent upstairs to sign an official piece of paper. Everything was very hush-hush. That same morning I started work in one of these huts. I'll show you the exact room.' Behind her back, Bronwen does a thumbs up to Sally. Nanna leads the party towards a dilapidated, single-storey wooden building. The paintwork is peeling, the windows are boarded up, frames rotten. A damp, musty smell hangs in the air.

'It could do with some tlc.' Nanna walks slowly down a corridor into a deserted room.

'I believe a lot of people worked here,' says Bronwen.

'Dozens of us, side by side. Chess masters, mathematicians, professors with wild hair and bad breath, queers - but I suppose you will have to edit that out. A strange bunch, really. It was suffocating in summer, freezing in winter. We wore mittens a lot of the time.'

'So what did you actually *do*?' Bronwen beckons the cameraman to pan around the room.

'Let's say it was a reading room.'

'What did you read?'

'German. It was boring, day after day. They chose women because we pay more attention to detail than men.'

'And there was a purpose to the reading…'

'Yes, but I can't say what it was. We were sworn to absolute secrecy. I was terrified in case I gave anything away. I talk in my sleep, you see. I changed lodgings because I thought my landlord was listening at the keyhole. It made me ill. We assumed that if we divulged anything we would be taken out and shot.'

'Seriously?'

'Seriously. We were at war.'

'But it's been 70 years. We aren't still fighting the Nazis.'

'I signed the form.' Nanna fixes Bronwen with a cold stare. 'No-one has told me it doesn't still hold. I haven't even told my family and now this will go out on television. I hope you know what you're doing.'

'What about the Prime Minister?'

'Oh, we saw Churchill once. We were all scribbling away in our huts as normal and somebody appeared out of a hole in the ground. We looked again and realised it was the PM. There's a secret tunnel underneath the building to the train station, so we found out.'

Bronwen smiles. 'I was thinking more of the current PM, Rhoslyn,' she says, reaching into a bag. 'I have a certificate signed personally by Gordon Brown and a commemorative badge, recognising your part in what many experts say shortened the Second World War by two years…'

CHAPTER 28

Monday 27 April 1914

I got to Burnley station way too early on Friday evening, I was that excited. I watched half a dozen trains leave before mine. That smell of smoke and steam and burning coal! Packed to the gunnels they were with supporters in Sunday best, waving flags and banners. The train taking the team to London left before I got there. As it pulled away, detonators along the track went off like giant firecrackers. I wish I'd seen that.

The 11.50pm to Euston pulled in at last. I wasn't sure what time it would get to London but it would be very early in the morning, or as Grandpa used to say, 'before the sparrow farts'. I found the carriage and the seats Emily booked, praying she wouldn't be late. I had just settled in when I saw a 'friend' from my old school in Burnley.

'Dawsie! 'Ow's tha doin'?' he said.

'Teddy Hughes…' I said.

'Might 'a known tha'd be on the way to t' Palace. On t' strap, like us?'

'Aye, I'll be down t' pop shop for t' best part of a year,' I lied. I found myself talking just like him. Funny how that happens. And the truth is that I really was weighing up a visit to the pawnbrokers before Emily produced those tickets. I can't abide Teddy. He is a right blether-yed, as we say down Burnley way. His ears stick out like jug handles and whatever went on between them curled up and died years ago.

'Goin' down by tha sel'?' he said.

'With a friend.'

'From Saint 'Elens?'

'Aye.' I wasn't telling him anything more.

'Some of t' other lads'll be 'ere in a tick.'

'Maybe I'll see you all in London.' I was trying to get rid of him.

''Ow's the pit?' He sat down in Emily's seat.

'Not so bad.'

'Wish you were back 'ome in Burnley?'

'Sometimes.' Even dull, one-word answers didn't put him off. He started telling me what happened to friends we knew at school. I kept looking along the carriage for Emily. Then all his pals got on. Well bevvied up they were, what with it being late at night. They sang new words to that Tipperary song.

'It's a long way to t' Crystal Palace

'It's a long way to go

'It's a long way to t' Crystal Palace

'For the greatest team I know...'

I knew a few of the lads and would have been pleased to see them if I had been travelling on my own. They all crowded round, acting on.

'I'm not goin' down for t' game,' said Harry Grabham. 'I'm after a chitty or two, me.'

'They'll not look twice at thee,' said Arthur Foster.

''Ark who's talkin'!'

'Ah've 'eard they're picky, London lassies.'

'Depends what type tha's after,' said Teddy. 'Plenty of time after t' match for a little tappin'.'

'Ne'er mind t' match,' said Harry. 'Before Tommy's lifted t' cup I'll 'ave lifted some skirt.'

That sparked off another, bawdier version of that song.

'That's the wrong way to tickle Mary

'That's the wrong way to kiss

''Cos I've heard that down in London

'They like it best like this...'

141

'Where are your seats?' I said. I hoped they would move away and quickly.

'Not bothered 'bout seats, us,' said one of them. 'No-one sits at a party.'

'Aye, we'll be up and down all t' way to t' smoke, looking for a nice filly or two,' said another.

'There's nowt in 'ere, more's t' pity,' said Harry.

'Oh, now then,' said Teddy. 'I don't know about *that*...' He was looking out of the window. The others crowded round and started wolf whistling and waving. 'Nice, *very* nice.'

'Too good for t' likes of thee,' said Harry.

'She's got a rosette in 'er bonnet,' said one of the lads. He wound down the window. They all leaned out. 'In 'ere, love.'

'Is this Coach F?' said a female voice.

'Certainly is,' said Teddy. 'It means we'd all like to give you a...' Someone kicked him hard. 'Friendly welcome. We're all very friendly in 'ere.'

'I'm looking for seat 24,' she said. I still couldn't see her but it was Emily, all right.

'That's 'ere,' said Harry, leaning right out of the window and pointing back to the seat next to him.

'No, no... it's this one,' said the lad on his right, pointing in the opposite direction. I got up to bring Emily onto the train but the mob had already bolted down the carriage to open the door. I could just about see her bonnet as they helped her into the carriage. Couldn't believe their luck, the lot of them.

'Ah'll take that.' One of them grabbed her suitcase. He began scuffling with another lad who had hold of the handle.

'Is Tom here?' I heard Emily say.

'Tom? Tom 'oo?' said a lad.

'Never 'eard of a Tom,' said another. 'If tha's been stood up, mind...'

'Over here,' I called. She was still obscured by at least six people.

'Ah.' She peered through the crowd of bodies. 'At last. Sorry I cut it so fine, Tom.' There was a stunned silence broken only by the shriek of the train's whistle and a mighty gasp from the engine. She looked wonderful, did Emily, that's the only word I can use. I was relieved she'd made it, proud she was with me and feared half to death these lads would show me up. Lifting his jaw from the floor, Teddy stood up and dusted the seat next to me. Emily sat down.

'Your friends?' she said.

'Well, I know a few of them…' I started.

'Name's Harold,' cut in Harry, wiping and then holding out a grubby hand. 'Me and Tom, I mean Thomas. We've been pals for years. Go back a long way, don't we, Thomas?'

'That's nice,' said Emily. She didn't take his hand.

'Ah've not seen thee at t' Moor. Ah'd 'ave remembered if ah 'ad,' said Teddy.

'I confess, I've never been to Burnley,' said Emily. 'Tried but failed.' She smiled at me.

'Best ground in t' land. Ah'll take thee, whenever,' said a voice. I couldn't see who it was.

'Hands off,' I said, slowly. 'The lady is with *me*.'

'Ooooooh,' they chorused.

'Take no notice, they're all drunk,' I said.

'No, just made giddy by a lady what's stepped into our dreams,' said Arthur Foster. They all cheered.

'Did tha 'urt tha sel'?' said another lad.

'Hurt myself?' said Emily.

'When tha fell outta heaven.'

'I'll find us another seat,' I said.

'No need,' said Emily.

'Hast tha ever been to a match?' asked Harry. 'Only, what with never 'aving been to Turf Moor an' all…'

I began to protest but it was Emily's turn to kick me quiet.

'Perhaps you can tell me how the game works,' she said. 'At the start…'

'The kick off,' said someone.

'Yes, the kick-off. The umpire blows the whistle and then all the…'

'Tha's thinkin' of cricket,' said Harry. 'We have referees.'

'Of course. Silly me. And the two clubs tomorrow, Burnley and Crystal Palace…'

'Crystal Palace? They're not even a proper team. We're playing Liverpool at *the* Crystal Palace. Dawsie, 'aven't tha told t' young lady owt?'

I shrugged my shoulders.

'What puzzles me is this, er, what do they call it? Offside rule,' said Emily. That set them off. In the cramped gangway five lads took up positions.

'Now then, stand 'ere, Miss Emily,' said Harry.

'I don't think she wants to…' I started but she was already on her feet.

'Ah can pass t' ball if there are at least two players 'twixt thee and t' goal.' Harry took out a small football from his pocket. 'If tha kicks this…' A whistle blew. Steam and smoke billowed along the platform. The train lurched forward, sending Emily tumbling into Arthur Foster's lap.

'And some say there's no God,' he said.

'Right, that does it. Get lost, the lot of you,' I said. Reluctantly, they moved down the carriage, still cracking jokes and singing songs.

'I'm a dreadful tease,' said Emily, when they had all gone. 'Do you think badly of me?'

'They deserved it,' I said. 'Knowing you, they got off lightly.' I squeezed her hand. 'You look lovely.'

'And you in your Sunday best. What more could a hopeless, ignorant girl ask for?'

I can't remember ever being on a train where there was so much noise and commotion. From all quarters came beer, whisky, pork pies, whole hams with loaves of bread and pickled onions in large jars. Knowing we needed to spend most of the next 24 hours on our feet, I had travelled light. I was surprised to see Emily carrying a suitcase. She saw me looking at it.

'Just a few necessities,' she said. 'Where shall we go before the game?'

'Up to you, it's all new to me,' I said. 'They say it's going to be a hot, sunny day.' I couldn't wait to see London. You grow up with ideas in your mind from pictures in books and newspapers. Now I was going to see it all for myself. I told her how my 'friends' were going to the waxworks, Madame Tussauds. They were offering free entry with a valid train ticket.

'Good idea,' she said. 'I can melt Lloyd George.' I hoped she was joking.

We were about 20 minutes into the journey when the ticket collector came along the carriage. He was some time getting tickets from a bunch of lads in high spirits. Drunkenly they fumbled around in their jackets. Eventually he reached us. Emily had pulled out a book from her suitcase.

'Your ticket please, sir,' he said. I showed him mine. 'And yours madam. That's a fine bonnet, if I may say so.'

'Thank you,' said Emily, buried in her book. There were very few women on the train, and even fewer attractive ones, so I wasn't surprised he took her in. He didn't say anything more, just stared at her. Then he walked quickly down the carriage without checking any other tickets. Emily watched him go and immediately put the book away. She stood up and said: 'See you later.'

'What? I don't…'

'He recognised me.'

'The ticket collector?'

She nodded.

'Don't come after me. Just say I've gone to find one of your friends.'

'What… what are you doing? Where are you going?'

'Trust me.' She squeezed my arm. 'See you later.'

With that she walked quickly along the carriage, in the opposite direction from the ticket collector. He returned a minute or two later with another official.

'The young lady,' he said. 'I wondered if I might have a word.'

'She's looking for a friend,' I said. 'One of those rowdy ones in the carriage down there. She'll be back in a minute.'

'That way?'

I nodded. It was the wrong direction, of course. By now we were slowing down for Crewe station. The train pulled up. I saw the ticket collector run over to an official who ran to a policeman. I looked up and down the platform for Emily. I expected her to jump off, hide on the platform and take the train behind. No sign, though and just as well. The platform was swarming with police.

We pulled out of Crewe and, as we got up speed again, I gazed through the window into the fields lit up by a full moon. All around me was celebration, laughter, song but I didn't feel part of it anymore. The ticket collector returned with a policeman. They asked me to accompany them to the guards van. They grilled me there. Where did I think she was? How long had I known her? Had we ever gone anywhere together before? I said she must have got off at Crewe. After half an hour they let me go back to my seat. There was still no sign of Emily. Back came Harry, staggering down the carriage, blind drunk.

'Ah did say.' He swayed with the motion of the train.

'Say what?' I said.

He pointed to the empty seat. 'Too good for t' likes of thee and me.'

'Speak for yourself.'

'Ah'd see if she's in First Class. She belongs with them posh types.'

'Get lost.'

'I'm warning thee as an old, old friend, Dawsie.' He leaned down and stared me in the face. He stank of beer. 'It'll all end in tears.'

God help me, I almost landed him with a right hook. He went back to the other lads and told them 'Dawsie's posh one' had done a runner, no doubt. I felt humiliated.

We drew into Euston at some early hour of the morning. The sun was coming up but dark thoughts swirled round my head. Had Emily jumped off the train and injured herself, fatally? I walked down the platform with hundreds of others. We were like a claret and blue army on the march but I couldn't share the excitement. I began thinking how I hadn't seen the team in action since I started this journal. Perhaps these pages were bringing me bad luck. Football makes you superstitious, if you're not already. You'll try anything to make sure the gods are on your side.

There were police at the end of the platform, lots of them. Teddy, Harry and the others said they would be in the queue for Madame

Tussauds at 9am. I waited at the station for the next two hours but there was no sign of Emily. Train after train arrived. Thousands of people poured through the station. Eventually I gave up, got myself something to eat and walked along Euston Road to the waxworks.

So this was London. It was eight o'clock on a Saturday morning and the cafes were already full. Londoners were walking far too fast from place to place. Why? I was trying to take it all in.

''Ey up, Dawsie,' said Teddy Hughes. He was standing near the head of the queue at the waxworks. 'T'others are 'aving sommat to eat. Any sign of your good lady?'

I shook my head.

'Nice looking girl, that. 'ave you, yet…?'

'That's got nothing to do with you.' I was angry he even asked.

'Ah'll take that as a no…'

'I told you, it's got…'

'All right, all right. Keep tha 'air on. Just tryin' to 'elp, like.' He leaned towards me so he couldn't be overheard. 'If she doesn't want to, you know, there may be a reason. 'Arry thinks she may be one of those women protestor types. 'E thinks 'er picture was in t' paper.'

'He's mistaken.'

'They're all spinsters, of course. Not right some of 'em.' He pointed to his chest. 'They like their own.'

'Their own what?'

'Their own kind. They'd rather not have…' This time he pointed to a woman's chest in front of us. 'Those.'

'I don't know what you mean.'

'They'd rather be one of us. Lads. They wish they'd been born lads. They dress like us and get up to, you know, funny stuff with each other.'

'I don't understand.'

'What I'm trying to say is… if she doesn't want to, you know, it may be for a reason.' He leaned towards me again. 'She may be queer.' I had no idea what he meant. I soon did. He insisted on telling me. A few minutes later, the others joined us in the queue.

''Ey, Dawsie didn't know what a queer was,' shouted Teddy. I was getting used to being laughed at. We went round the waxworks but my mind was in a whirl. I tried to forget what Teddy said but things kept coming back to me. The way she'd been so taken by the women she had met. Who were they, exactly? Why did she talk about them non-stop? By the time we came to Lloyd George I hoped he would be a pile of melted wax. At least Emily would still be alive. No such luck. We headed off to look at the sights of London, the Houses of Parliament, Big Ben, Tower Bridge and the River Thames before going further south to the Crystal Palace and the match itself.

It is now well past two o'clock in the morning and I don't have the energy in my bones or the oil in my lamp to finish writing about the strangest and longest day of my life. I shall finish the account tomorrow and the strangest is yet to come.

CHAPTER 29

'We need Channel 972.' Sally gives Dan the remote control. She holds
Nanna Neath's hand. Dan glances at both of them. They've bonded
since that excursion together for BBC Wales. What was all that
about? 'Wait and see' is all they've told him. The waiting is almost
over. Dan has never before tuned his 50" plasma TV with built-in 2D
to 3D converter, featuring added depth of 3D, to Sky Channel 972.
He keys in the three numbers. It doesn't sound like a babe channel
(not that he knows where to find them, of course).

'So this programme,' he says, 'they've interviewed you about your
childhood in Neath, then...'

Nanna looks at Sally, Sally at Nanna. 'Wait and see,' they say in
unison.

'I liked staying there when I was little. The click-click of knitting
needles always takes me back.'

'Have you still got that red and blue scarf I made?' asks Nanna.

'Somewhere.' He's never worn it. The red was too near West Ham
claret, the blue too near Chelsea royal.

'Here we go,' says Sally. Dan turns up the volume.

'And now on BBC Wales a special documentary that tracks an
unsung hero of the Second World War...' From voiceover straight
to Nanna Neath, standing in front of an old, stately home that looks
familiar to Dan.

'No-one told me what I would be doing, so it was hard to get
excited,' Nanna is saying to camera. 'I could complete the Daily

149

Telegraph crossword in under 12 minutes, that sort of thing. They interviewed me, did some tests and the next thing I knew I was in a hut miles from home.'

'Bloody hell,' says Dan. 'That's… that's Bletchley Park!' Sally smiles at Nanna.

'Hundreds of bright young things were plucked from families and friends and brought here, to try and crack the famous Enigma code.' It's the voice of Bronwen. 'This is the story of one of them.'

'Nanna, what the… why have you never…?' begins Dan.

'Shhhhhhh,' says Sally. A black and white portrait of a vibrant 25-year-old woman comes onto screen. All Dan's life that photo has been on the sideboard.

'This is… unbelievable,' he says.

'Shhhhhhh.'

'Little has been told of thousands of young people who worked tirelessly, month in, month out, playing a vital part in the war effort,' says Bronwen. 'Such was the need for total secrecy that even close family and friends had no idea what they were doing. And, seven decades later, it took us months to find one of them – Rhoslyn Cadogan from Neath.'

'I didn't cover my tracks well enough,' murmurs Nanna to Sally.

'Their work was critical,' continues Bronwen. 'One night, here in Hut 6, the code was cracked that led to the sinking of the formidable German battleship, Bismarck.'

'That was quite a night.' Nanna is standing in what is left of the hut.

'The *Bismarck*! 'kin hell, Nanna,' says Dan.

'Shhhhhhh.'

'We just did what we had to do,' Nanna is saying. 'Most nights it wasn't exciting. We got these messages. We translated them. We decoded them. That's all. Night watches could be hell. We'd sit wearing mittens, dog tired but too cold to nod off which was just as well. Every now and then we'd get an important message. The position of a U-boat, or in this case, the Bismarck – something really worth it. That woke us up!'

'So these were your digs.' Now Bronwen is standing with Nanna outside a small terraced house near Bletchley town centre.

'There was no lock in the bathroom,' Nanna is saying. 'I had to jam a chair against the door handle and hope it held.'

'Just to make life more difficult!'

'The debs struggled more.'

'The debs?'

'Glamorous girls with a bit of background.'

'They found it harder...'

'Well, they weren't used to little houses where people kept coal in the bath.'

'So did you get on with the family here?'

'They were friendly enough but I felt cut off from everybody back in Neath.'

'Did they write?'

'Yes and I wrote back but I couldn't say much. They didn't know, they couldn't know, what we were up to. I lost close friends who thought I didn't care.'

'That must have been tough.'

'It was devastating.'

Twenty minutes later, certificate from Prime Minister Gordon Brown duly presented, the credits roll. Dan is shaking his head in disbelief. Sally disappears into the kitchen.

'Well, that's over and done with,' says Nanna. 'Now I can sink back into obscurity.'

'I am so proud.' Dan hugs Nanna. 'And astonished. I don't understand why you never told us.'

'I signed the Official Secrets Act,' she says. 'And still no-one has signed me off. It's only because of your young lady that I went ahead with the film. Well, they've got what they wanted. Now they can leave me alone.'

Sally returns with a bottle of champagne and a tray of canapes.

'Time to celebrate,' she says. 'Not often we have a hero in our midst.'

'I make you right,' says Dan. 'A toast is in order. To Nanna Neath, aka Rhoslyn Cadogan, who spent three years eaves-dropping on

Adolf Hitler and…'

The telephone rings. It's Nanna's godson, saying how much he enjoyed the programme. How did she stay quiet for so long? While he and Nanna are in conversation, Mrs Denbridge, one of Dan's neighbours, calls round.

'I had no idea,' she says.

'Nor did we,' says Dan. 'Have some champagne.'

'Don't mind if I do…'

As soon as Nanna puts down the phone it rings again. This time it's Bronwen, thanking her (and Sally) for the interview.

'Texts and emails are flying into BBC Wales from all over,' she says. 'I'll pass on the most interesting.'

Dan's mobile rings. This time it's his estranged father, complaining that the BT line is permanently engaged. He chats briefly to his former mother-in-law. Then Nanna's neighbour from Neath calls.

'Never mind sex offenders,' she says. 'They should publish a list of war heroes living in the neighbourhood. A quarter of a century living next door and you never breathed a word, you sly old thing…'

Four more neighbours call round. Dan offers them champagne. Sally pops open another bottle. Just as well she had got it in. The room is a hubbub of celebration

'Well, I'm amazed.' Fifteen minutes later, and all talked out, Nanna finishes her champagne. 'I can't believe all these people bothered to tune in.'

'You see, there was no need to worry.' Sally sits on the arm of her chair. 'You deserve all the fuss in the world.'

'But I wasn't a hero. I never held a gun.'

'That's not the point.'

'I was never in danger.'

'You were taken away from all you had known.'

Dan reads out text messages from friends and family. The phone rings yet again.

'Who is it this time?' asks Nanna.

'Someone speaking Welsh,' says Sally. 'Here, you'd better take it. I can't understand a word…'

'Helo, pwy yw hwn?' says Nanna. She gestures for quiet in the room.

'Rwy'n flin, ond fydd rhaid I ti siarad yn uwch. Rwy braidd yn gallu dy glywed. Beth ddwedais ti o'dd dy enw? *Bloody hell!*'

If clattering knitting needles take Dan back to summer holidays at Nanna's, so does the curious sound of English exclamations punctuating unintelligible Welsh sentences.

'Mi af fi'n wyllt os yw rhywun yn chwarae da fi...fedrai byth credu'r peth. Ti'n swno'n wahanol ond eto year un peth, os ti'n fy neall I. Anhygoel...Rwy'n cofio, wrth gwrs, y waciau hir 'na ger llwybr Tonna. Ti'n cofio'r ddafad 'na wnaethon ni tynnu mas o'r ffens? Roedd ei ben yn stuck, poenus ofnadwy. Wy'n clywed dy fod wedi priodu merch hyfryd. Mae'n dda clywed oddi wrthyt...perffaith. Tri o blant? Ti wedi gweithio'n galed wrth gwrs, nid bod fi'n credu...O, wy'n flin I glywed hwnna on ti'n swno'n tip top. Rwy'n gobeithio dy fod yn deall pam na ddywedais unrhywbeth wrthyt. Cefais siom ofnadwy pan glywais dy fod wedi priodu...cwmpais I bisis. O paid dweud 'ni. Mae hwnna wneud I fi deimlo', waeth. Ti'n bod yn ddwl nawr. Wrth gwrs lice ni siarad a ti eto ond fydd rhaid I mi feddwl am y peth. Hyfryd clywed dy lais unwaith eto...ti hefyd. Pob hwyl.'

Nanna puts down the phone, slowly and says nothing. She stares at the dull reflection of herself in Dan's TV screen.

'So, who was that?' asks Sally.

'Who was who?' says Nanna distantly.

'The phone call.'

'Oh, somebody from the old days.'

'You seem distracted.'

'Call it a profound state of shock.'

'I hope no-one's upset you.'

'No.'

'So...'

'It was an old friend.'

'And a significant one by the looks of it.'

'You could say that.'

There is a moment's quiet. No-one knows what to say. Suddenly,

Dan wheels round. 'I know. It was… oh, what's his name?'

Sally throws him a warning stare.

'I'm not making this up,' he says. 'Nanna went to see *Gone With the Wind* with him. Six times. It was… Davros…'

'Dafydd,' says Nanna, quietly, reverently. 'Daniel is correct. The last time I saw him was April 23rd 1940.' A tear escapes from the corner of her eye and edges down a wrinkled cheek. 'Here's me being pathetic.'

'She was in love with him,' blurts Dan.

'God, you can be so crass,' says Sally.

'Oh, but he's right.' Nanna snuffles on a handkerchief. 'Dafydd thought I had found someone else. And by the time I could tell him I hadn't, *he* had.'

'I'm sorry,' says Sally. 'That must have been a difficult call.'

'I'll tell you tomorrow, when I've recovered from the shock.'

'He seemed very chatty.'

'Yes, he sounded much the same as 70 years ago. I thought he must be long dead.'

'Well, maybe this will bring closure, as the Americans say,' says Sally.

'Oh, I doubt it. He wants to meet up. He says he's never stopped loving me…'

CHAPTER 30

Tuesday 28 April 1914

It wasn't that I didn't want to see the dinosaurs. After all, they are one of the major attractions at the Crystal Palace, along with the magnificent glass house itself. When I was little I had seen pictures of the Ichthyosaurus and Iguanodon models. They were impressive close up, too. No, it's just that I didn't expect to see them in the company of those other monsters, Harry Grabham, Arthur Foster and Teddy Hughes.

After what happened on the train, I had no choice but to tag along with them. We got to the Palace at midday. Dozens of policemen were on the look-out for suffragettes. Even if she had made it this far, I doubt Emily would have got into the ground. There were very few women around and the turnstile operators would have had her picture to hand, I'm sure.

All over the park men were sleeping off last night's hangover or tucking into picnics on grassy banks. It was Cup Final weather all right, boiling hot, so queues to the beer tents were long and noisy. With kick-off four hours away we killed time by taking a look at those dinosaurs by the lake.

'That one there,' said Teddy.

'The Iguanodon,' I said.

'Aye, the Igu... whatever. 'E could come in 'andy this afternoon. We could park 'im across the goal-line in place of Dawson.'

'So Jerry's injured?'

'Yep, Sewell's in goal.'

'That's bad news.'

'He 'asn't played much recently. What a game to make your comeback!'

'Our Tommy'll scare 'em half to death. Beware the Boylasaurus.' I was trying to encourage myself. My nerves were shredded.

'It's hard to believe those big lads ruled the earth.' Teddy rolled a cigarette as he gazed at the life-sized models.

'A long time ago,' I said.

'Aye, they died out and no-one knows why. Some say a flood.'

'Why didn't it wipe out all the other animals? That's the problem.'

'Well...' Teddy drew deeply on his cigarette. 'I've got my own theory.' A gleam came into his eye. 'It's like... take your Emily, I mean.'

'She's not *my* Emily,' I said.

'Well, that's obvious.'

'No, what I mean is... Emily knows her own mind.'

'Like these 'ere dinosaurs.'

'You're talking in riddles.'

'What I'm saying is... what keeps creatures going, generation after generation?'

'I don't know. Having enough food to eat, water to drink?'

'Besides all that.'

'What do you mean?'

'Well, take that Iguasaurus, whatever it is, over there. She's not going to keep the species going on her own.'

'You mean she needs a mate.'

'Exactly. And what if lady dinosaurs suddenly went suffragist, if they all lost interest in male dinosaurs, preferring other ladies?'

This time I did hit him. Hard.

'Lay off, Tommy lad. I'm only joking,' he said.

'Well, the joke's wearing thin,' I said.

Looking back, it was only a bit of fun but I was on the edge, one way and another. With about an hour and a half to kick-off, thousands more flooded into the park. It's right, what they say. The place crackles with atmosphere with one of the best fairgrounds I've ever seen. All sorts of people were there, selling their wares. Army staff sergeants urged passers-by to become new recruits. The smell from thousands of flowers made us light-headed. Harry Grabham and the others found a grand place to watch the match, not easy in a crowd of 72,000. But I was one of the privileged few with a seat in the Pavilion, a few rows from the King (perhaps I mentioned that before) so I left them there. By the time I got to the Pavilion, dozens of people had already taken their seats. The Pavilion was decked out in flowing red velvet for the royal visit. You could still smell the freshly-painted gilt handrails.

I handed my ticket to the steward who gave me a long look. My seat was in the fourth row from the front, six in from the gangway. I counted along the row and noticed a young lad already sitting there. I checked again. It was definitely my seat. He was dressed like everybody else, in suit, tie and flat cap and reading the Cup Final souvenir programme very closely.

'Excuse me,' I said. 'I think you're sitting in my seat.'

He didn't look up.

'Sit down and don't look surprised,' said Emily from beneath the cap.

'What, what are you doing… how come…?'

'I said don't look surprised.'

I sat down in a state of shock, never mind surprise. Under that flat cap must have been the biggest knot of hair imaginable. I couldn't help noticing what a lovely neck she has.

'They think I'm you,' she said.

'What do you mean?'

'I told them I was Tom Daws.'

'And they believed you?'

She nodded. 'Now they're waiting for me to arrive.'

'But… but how did you get to London?'

'Answers later. Let's move. The steward behind me suspects something. We have to convince him I am Tom Daws.'

157

She headed straight for the men's toilets. Not for Emily the obvious option of getting lost in the grounds. With so much alcohol consumed by such a large crowd, a queue had formed, even in the exclusive Pavilion facilities. As I feared, the steward followed us and stood in line, two behind. I shook my head in disbelief. I wanted to make a run for it but that would have given the game away. To make matters worse, two posh lads behind us started to ridicule our supporters.

'Bunch of northern oiks again this year,' said one.

'All turned out in their one and only suit,' said the other.

'Which looks old enough to belong to their dads.' They both laughed, more of a guffaw, the way they must teach them at one of their schools.

'Ee oop, Ma, borrow us five bob for t' train to t' coop final.'

'Not 'til tha's taken t' whippet for a walk.'

They found themselves so amusing.

'Be fair,' said the first one. 'It's just as well there's so many of them.'

'How so?'

'If we go to war, they're fodder for the front line.'

It was all I could do to keep quiet and move slowly forward.

'What are you going to do when we reach the wall?' I whispered.

'Oh, I shall stand next to you and pretend,' said Emily. 'I rather like being a man.'

I didn't need to hear that last sentence. Until that moment, I considered Teddy Hughes a harmless trouble-maker who simply wanted to try his luck with Emily. Perhaps he was right, though. Perhaps I had mis-judged him. We approached the wall.

'Even at the best of times I can't... you know... under pressure,' I said.

'Don't mind me,' she said. 'I'll not look.'

'That's not the point.'

We reached the wall. She stood next to me. Right next to me. I couldn't even begin to do what I was supposed to do.

'Just think about the match,' she murmured, unbuttoning her fly.

'That makes it even worse.'

'The steward…'

'What about him?'

'Make sure he doesn't stand the other side of me.'

'I can't stop him.'

'Well, if he does, cause a diversion.'

'How am I going to…?' I didn't finish the sentence. The steward stood the other side of Emily and tilted his head her way. I took a deep breath.

'I say, it's a jolly, rotten shame that a southern team hasn't won the cup for 13 years,' I said, loudly. 'What do you say, chaps?' I turned my head to where the two lads were now standing, flies open, at the wall. 'Aye,' I went all northern. 'Praps it's 'cos their shooting is so bloody bad that when they have a piss they splash their shoes.'

It did the trick. All eyes, including the steward's, were on me. My back, that is.

'Well said!' came a northern voice. 'These southern softies should stick to their rugg-ah.'

As I'd hoped, it got feisty. One of the posh lads said: 'I'm surprised you've got enough *brass* (he used the northern pronounciation, of course) to be hanging out with the big nobs.'

'And I'd be surprised,' said the northern voice, 'if tha's got enough brains to 'ave a decent 'eadache.'

'Enough,' said the steward. 'We'll have no more of this.'

'He started it.' One of the posh lads pointed at me.

'I can't 'ave that,' said the northerner. 'Thems was talking all 'igh and mighty in t' queue.'

The argument got heated. Emily and I made for the exit and melted into the crowd. I use the word 'melted' deliberately. It was scorching hot in the full heat of the sun.

'That was a close shave,' I said.

'If I wear this suit long enough, I'll need one of those,' said Emily. 'I'm not used to men's clothes.'

'I'm glad about that,' I said to myself.

She told me how she had packed the suit in her suitcase and made the change in the ladies cubicle on the train, before we reached

Crewe. She stayed well away from me while the ticket collector, guard and police searched for her. The police followed me from a distance, all the way to Madam Taussauds, even to the Palace itself, thinking I would lead them to her. Instead I led them to a young lad, sitting in the wrong seat.

'I've no doubt they're still looking for me,' she said. 'However hot it is, I daren't take off this suit or cap. And we can't go back to our seats. I'm sorry to spoil the day. I know the King will be disappointed to miss us, too.' I supposed she was joking but with Emily you're never sure.

Now, as I have said in another entry, Miss Bettridge is not the tallest of God's creatures. Her lovely neck isn't as long as that of the Plesiosaurus, I'm pleased to say. But it did mean that, without a seat in the Pavilion, she wasn't going to see much of the match. Then I remembered that story about Zacchaeus.

'I think you may still get a good view of the game,' I said.

We passed a blind paper-seller, well-known at Turf Moor. They say he hasn't missed a match all season.

'Haven't seen you for a while, Ronnie,' I said.

'I've never seen you at all,' he said. 'Hold on. Is that… is that you, Dawsie?'

I shook his hand. He's one of the best, is Ronnie.

'The coppers are after me,' I joked. 'Keep an eye open, eh?'

'Will do.' If he could, he would have winked.

'There aren't many women here,' said Emily.

'What did you expect?' I said.

'Well, a few more at least and not just in the Pavilion.'

'It's a working man's game.'

'Lots of girls play.'

'But they don't watch.'

'Well they should.'

'Is that your next cause, once you've got the vote?'

She didn't answer. There's so much spinning round in that crazy little head of hers. I can't keep track of it all. A few moments later we were standing by one of the park's magnificent oak trees. It is all of 60 feet high with wide branches all the way up, though the higher you go, of course, the thinner they become. At the foot of the tree was Teddy, keeping guard. He and the others had got to the park early enough to secure the whole tree for themselves. Harry, Arthur and the rest were already perched on branches. It gave them a perfect view of the pitch.

'Ah thought tha'd buggered off with t' posh set,' said Teddy.

'It's a long story,' I replied.

'Tha'll not be findin' a perch 'ere, Dawsie, not after we weren't good enough.'

'It wasn't like that.'

'Looks that way to me, lad.' It was only then that he noticed a young, fresh-faced boy standing next to me.

'I'm sure you're not the kind to leave a girl in the lurch, Teddy,' said Emily. She stood close to Teddy and tilted her head so he could see her clearly.

'Bloody hell... it's... it's the girl on the train.' Making Teddy's jaw drop was becoming routine for Emily. 'Why are you...?' He waved his hand at her clothes. 'What's all this about?'

'I'd better explain. Harry was right,' I began, making sure no-one overheard. 'Emily is a suffragette.' A broad grin slowly spread across that smug face of his '...she changed on the train...' he lit another cigarette '...she doesn't usually dress like this...' he shook his head and smiled '...the police are after her...'

'Whoaahh. Hold your horses. A young damsel in distress?' Teddy looked up the tree. 'Harry! Another for t' grandstand.' He pulled again on his cigarette and flicked away the butt, still shaking his head and smiling. 'Find the best branch up top for t' little feller.' He began to help Emily to the first branch.

'It's all right, I'll do that,' I said.

'Told you,' he mouthed.

'What?'

'Not right.' He shook his head.

'What do you mean?'

'Who'd 'ave thought it?' Behind her back, he pointed to Emily's

161

clothes again. 'Bad luck, Dawsie. Couldn't 'appen to a nicer feller.' He smirked and slapped me on the back. I followed Emily onto the first branch.

'Hey, where's tha goin'?' he said.

'Up the tree,' I said.

'Tha's doin' no such thing.' The miserable sod blocked my way. 'If we weren't good enough for you then, lad, we're not good enough now.'

This time I put him flat on the deck. I had no option. I couldn't let those oiks (the term offended me in the Pavilion but here, well, it was a different matter) get their grubby paws on her ladyship. Needless to say, when all the other lads realised who was coming up their tree, they went out of their way to help her.

'Ah'll keep tight 'old,' said Arthur Foster, grasping her hand. 'Tha's fallen from above once already.'

'But unlike you, I didn't land on my head,' said Emily. You have to say, she gives back as good as she gets, does Miss Bettridge. The trouble is, lads like her all the more for it.

'Tha looks like my first wife,' said another of the gang.

'Really?' said Emily. 'How many times have you been married?'

'I'm a bachelor,' he said.

By now we were both near the top of the tree. Only Harry Grabham was above us. Funnily enough he didn't make any of the usual comments. He was polite but disinterested as Emily passed. As I reached him he said in my ear: 'Bloody 'ell, Tommy lad. She's gorgeous. What a waste.'

He pointed to her clothes.

'No, listen, that's because...' I couldn't finish the sentence. There was one almighty roar from the crowd. The King's car was pulling up outside the Pavilion and we had the best view of all.

Well, that's me all written out again. I am still finding it hard to believe what happened next. Then there is the small matter of the final itself to report. How could so much occur in less than 24 hours? Her name is Emily Bettridge.

CHAPTER 31

It is the afterwards of love. Just afterwards. No more than twelve short seconds afterwards. Sweet stillness has taken repose after the sensual storm. Limbs lie limp and disentangled. One frantic heart beats smoothly as two again. Twelve seconds after such absurd ecstasy, Dan considers re-working his CV. He needs a good reference from somewhere, too. His former employer is unlikely to be helpful. Then there are tomorrow's rehearsals for Sunday's audition at the 4000 Holes. Twelve short seconds and passion has given way to pragmatism, mystical to mundane. He envies smokers who light up afterwards. It must calm the nerves, soothe the troubled breast.

And, for no good reason, he thinks distantly about pro-creation and how it mirrors creation itself: life-force released in one explosive act. And, for no good reason, too, he thinks of God. Not Julian Speroni this time but the old feller up there, somewhere way beyond the red and blue. Perhaps he is still recovering from the shock of his own creation. Never mind the earth, the entire universe must have moved for him. And now, here we are, in the afterwards of it all. A long time afterwards. And maybe the old feller is still distracted. Maybe that is why he shows little concern over the ensuing turmoil. Perhaps, billions of years after the biggest of bangs, he is drawing long and hard on one he's rolled himself, thinking of other things.

'I hope we didn't wake Nanna,' says Sally.

'She's well away,' says Dan.

'I felt awkward, sneaking past her downstairs.'

163

'You sound guilty. Where's that come from?'

'I don't know.'

Dan turns to try and make himself comfortable. The single bed squeaks again. The bed in the box room has always squeaked. He shouldn't have to do it here.

'Nanna's old boyfriend...' says Sally.

'Davros.'

'What do you imagine is going through his head right now?'

Dan imagines. '*In-sem-in-ate...*'

Sally pulls a face.

'Well, I could have said wrinkly sex,' protests Dan.

'Oh God, you had to bring it right down, didn't you?' Sally pulls away in protest. 'The sort of love he must have felt for all those years, it's sweet.'

'More sad than sweet. There's only one thing worse than imagining your parents doing it...'

'Your grandparents,' they agree together.

Sally gazes at the ceiling.

'The older you get, though, the more meaningful it must become,' she says. 'I've told Nanna she really ought to meet up with Dafydd.'

'That's just the hopeless romantic in you,' says Dan. 'Biologically, sex is unnecessary by the time you're 40.'

'Well, I can't wait to know you in a few years' time.'

'I said biologically. Anyway, when did feminists go sentimental?'

'I'm not a feminist. How can I be? I'm a fool for black-and-white romcoms.'

'The cocked trilby, the double-breasted suit...'

'Just love 'em.'

'*Leave the dame alone, treat the lady like a lady.*'

'For all the machismo,' says Sally, 'it's the third reel before he gets up enough courage to touch her.'

'Well, we're into the eighth reel with Dafydd and there's no-one left in the cinema.'

Sally reaches for Dan's hand.

'What if we'd never done it?' she says. 'You know... what if I'd been like Nanna with Dafydd?'

164

'Frigid, you mean.'

'That's cheap. She's not like that.'

'Yeah… you two, you've got quite a thing going. You're becoming a bit of a unit.'

'She's so astute.'

'And formidable.' Dan looks straight at Sally. 'Do you think she likes me, Sals?'

'Who? Nanna? Why do you care?'

'Oh, I don't know. She's a sort of matriarch, I suppose. It was bad enough before this Bletchley Park stuff came out but that's put her on another level.'

'I do believe you're threatened.' Sally smiles wryly.

'I've always felt threatened. And now she likes you.'

'And you feel left out.'

'Perhaps. I've only ever visited her house before, as a kid. Now I live with her, as an adult. It's different.'

'You see?' Sally drops his hand. 'No reaction.'

'What do you mean?

'Like I said. Your hand. It's like a wet fish.'

'That's… that's just stupid. Of course you're going to remember the first time you hold someone's hand – the anticipation, the fear of rejection.'

'So you're not afraid I'll reject you?'

'I can't spend my life in a state of perpetual anxiety, no.'

Sally folds her arms.

'The real excitement is in the longing.' She stares again at the ceiling.

'Like anticipating your first match.'

'Oh God, no…' Sally pulls a pillow over her face. 'Everything comes back to football.'

'Hear me out.'

'Do I have to?'

'Some of my friends saw their first match in a hospitality suite, with the prawn sandwiches. They were too young to appreciate it. I had to beg dad to take me to a match. He just wasn't interested.'

'So who took you?'

'My uncle. I couldn't wait. Finally, that magical moment, clicking through the turnstiles, the rain hammering down, seeing the green grass under dazzling floodlights. Waiting so long made it all the more exciting.'

'Well, pity our Dafydd,' says Sally. 'Seventy years is a long time to be wishing and hoping.'

'…and thinking and praying.'

They begin humming the Dusty Springfield hit. A door opens downstairs. 'Shhhh…' Dan holds up his hand. 'Nanna's on her way up.'

The footsteps are slow, the breathing laboured. The steps get closer to the landing. Dan counts them.

'Just… about… here,' he whispers. They wait. It's three seconds later than he expected but he is not disappointed. Watery flatulence echoes round the landing during the final, monumental footstep.

'You're cruel and you're mean,' mouths Sally.

The footsteps stop outside the door of the box room. Sally disappears under the duvet.

'What's got into you?' whispers Dan.

'I don't want her to see me here.'

'Why not?'

'I wish I knew.'

A piece of paper appears underneath the box room door.

'See,' whispers Dan. 'She doesn't think we're here.' He creeps over to pick up the paper. The writing is spidery but legible.

Daniel, when you next see Sally, tell her I will meet Dafydd if she goes to a match with you. Deal? Love Nanna

'Now that's just unfair,' mouths Sally.

Dan looks at her, pleadingly.

Sally throws the pillow over her head again. 'You're right. She is formidable. But the meeting with Dafydd, it's written in the stars. I haven't any choice.'

166

'No corporate hospitality, I promise.'

'Oh, *thanks*.'

'It has to be an away game. It's more fun, more hardcore.'

'Nanna bloody Neath.' Sally shakes her head. 'No-one else would get me anywhere near all that testosterone.'

'The boys are playing at Blackpool on Saturday. And we're all in Blackburn on Sunday for the competition. It works brilliantly.'

'I was going straight to the 4000 Holes.'

'We'll go there from Blackpool.'

'Oh… bugger it.' Sally throws the pillow at Dan. 'If I must.'

'You won't regret it.'

They hear footsteps slowly descending to the lounge.

'When she's settled again I'll sneak out of the back door,' says Sally.

'You're acting strangely,' says Dan. 'Anyone would think we were doing something wrong.'

'There's no room in here,' says Sally. 'I'll get dressed in the bathroom.' She gathers her clothes and opens the door, knocking something over as she does so. 'Dan, what's a can of WD-40 doing outside the door?'

CHAPTER 32

Wednesday 29 April 1914

What with it being an all-Lancashire final, the King was sporting a red rose in his lapel. Lord Derby was with him, well-known up our way. He owns half the land. I was told afterwards that Lord Kinnaird was with them. He was the tough tackler Reverend Whitehead said 'would never lower himself to be paid for playing football.'

'Ah've 'eard the King likes the ladies,' said Harry from the branch below. 'Like you two, eh?' He looked up at Emily and I.

The other lads laughed.

'Your friends are making some strange comments,' said Emily.

'They're not my friends,' I said. 'I just know them. It's different.'

She pointed to Harry. 'And what did he mean by "what a waste"?'

'Oh, that.' I had to think quickly. 'He was admiring your figure.'

'Really?'

'Of course.'

There was another mighty roar as the King came out of the Pavilion and onto the pitch. The Irish Guards and Liverpool Regiment bands struck up 'God Save the King'. Everyone stood still and doffed their caps (except Emily) to sing the National Anthem.

'Three cheers for His Majesty,' said the two captains before introducing him to the teams. It was at this moment I found myself looking at myself, if that makes sense. I mean, how did all this happen? A few months ago I was walking a daft dog round the local park, cursing 'Lady' Emily Bettridge, dreaming of Boyle's Brigade reaching the FA Cup Final in far off London. Now I was halfway up an oak tree with the lady herself, in the presence of King George V! Every emotion it is possible to feel went through me as the two teams swapped ends, ready for the kick-off. I imagined Grandpa at the foot of the tree, looking up, shaking his head and saying 'Yer a puddled bugger, you.' I wished he had been there to see this incredible scene. Perhaps he was.

I looked over at the Pavilion. All those people sitting near the King had a 'bit of cash behind 'em' as Grandpa put it. I didn't fit in there, right enough, so perhaps it was just as well I was up this tree with ordinary folk. I thought of those two posh lads, how they consider us mere cannon fodder. On the other hand, I looked at some of the lads they were on about – Harry, Teddy, Arthur and the rest of them in the branches below – and realised how little I had in common with them, too. And I knew that, whatever the result of the match, on Monday morning I would be crawling on my belly again, deep underground – the sunshine, the crowd, the occasion a distant memory.

Then there was Emily. What had I got myself into here? We were pressed up close to each other on the bough of the tree. She may have been dressed like a young boy but her perfume was making my head swim. All the time I was thinking about what Teddy said. Not right.

'What's not right?' I heard Emily say. I must have said it out loud by mistake.

'Nothing.'

'There's something wrong, I can tell.'

'I'm just a bundle of nerves about the game.'

'It's more than that.' She turned towards me. She was very close.

'Well, you see…'

'Go on.'

'This lot.' I took a deep breath and pointed downwards. 'They think there's something… wrong.'

'I knew it. Wrong with what?'

'You.'

'Me? In what way?'

I looked her up and down.

'Oh, the suffragette movement,' she said. 'They don't agree with women getting the vote...'

The referee brought the two captains together on the centre circle. They shook hands. The noise from all four sides of the ground grew deafening.

'It's not that simple.' I had to get even closer to her and speak loudly in her ear. 'They think you... how can I say this? They think you wish you'd been born a man, not a woman.'

'You mean...' Emily put her hand to her mouth. 'They think... I'm a Lesbian.'

'No, they know you support Burnley.'

As I write it down it looks stupid but I thought it must be a nickname for a Liverpool supporter. I had no idea that a Lesbian is the correct term, how can I say it, for those kind of women. I don't think even Teddy knew the word. Emily explained.

'So what do *you* think I am?' she said.

'Bloody gorgeous.' I blurted it out before I could stop myself.

'That's all I need to know. Coom 'ere, Dawsie lad.' She held onto the trunk of the tree with one arm, and wrapped the other around me. At one point I was afraid she would slip. It was a long way down. The alternative words to that Tipperary song came into my head. *'That's the wrong way to tickle Mary. That's the wrong way to kiss...'* I've learned a lot of things from one Miss E. Bettridge, including the right way.

Teddy made the mistake of looking up at us. To be honest, I am worried for his jaw. There are only a certain number of times it can hit the floor before he'll need medical assistance. By now the match had begun. It was a good job it didn't go the way of the 1895 final. On that day Aston Villa scored their 'Crystal Palace thunderbolt' within 30 seconds of the start. We would have missed it, no question. It took a shot by our Dick Lindley, which soared over the Liverpool bar to a chorus of 'Oooooo's', to bring us back to the real world.

'So... other than bloody gorgeous what do you think I am now?' said Emily.

'Perhaps I should say not right, so that you do it all over again,' I said.

But enough of this. I need to tell you about the game. That's why I was there, after all. Tucked in my pocket was some paper and the pen Emily had given me. Before leaving for the final I decided to write a report and send it to the Burnley Post. Time I stopped thinking and started doing. As I wrote a few weeks ago, the purpose of this journal is to sharpen my writing skills. Maybe now is the time to show people what I can do.

My mind was on other things, though. Emily slipped her hand into my writing hand. She rested her head, flat cap and all, on my shoulder. And that perfume! As you can probably tell, I am new to all this. When our goalie, Ronnie Sewell, fumbled the ball, first at the feet of Miller and then Metcalf, I felt his nerves. I've said it before and I'll say it again. I am a Daws. She is a Bettridge. It's impossible. Like Sewell, I'm not first choice. There's bound to be someone more suitable waiting in the wings. Maybe I shouldn't be out on the park at all.

Then I looked at Tommy Boyle, fists clenched, arms waving, clapping, urging, dominating. 'Mossy, Mossy... Billy, Billy, c'maaan...' He wasn't going to let the occasion get the better of him. King or no King. Lord This, Lord That or Lord The Other. Ne'er mind. Today was his day. This was his moment. After being on the losing Barnsley side four years ago, he could have crawled away to lick his wounds. But here he was, taking them all on, more determined than ever. There was a lesson for me, down on the grass below.

And here's another thing. After a shaky start Sewell leaped like a cat to pull off two fine saves from the Scousers' Lacey and Nicholl. Mrs Knapp used to say that the world is full of good starters but there aren't so many good finishers. Our keeper was gaining in confidence. Maybe I could still end up on the winning side.

Half-time and the scores were locked at 0-0. The Irish Guards struck up *Land of Hope and Glory* and *When the Midnight Choo-Choo*. I'm sure that was played just for the fans. Below us, people headed to the tents for a beer. In spite of the intense heat we dared

171

not drink any. If we had come down, for a call of nature, our places would have been taken. I have to be honest, I was just happy to be sitting next to Emily.

'What do you think?' she said, squeezing my hand.

'I'm not sure,' I said. 'Your family won't approve.'

'I meant about the match.'

'Oh.'

'What did *you* mean?'

'Nothing.'

'You thought I meant about us.'

'Well, sort of.'

'You sweet thing.' She squeezed my hand again and kissed me.

The teams came out for the second half. Billy was at it again, cajoling his players to even greater effort. He never gives up, that lad. They say that a good time to get a goal is just before half-time. I've never agreed with that. For me, the best time is just after the break. A quick goal can wreck the half-time tactics set out by any manager.

The first 12 minutes of the second half panned out like the last dozen of the first. The width of cigarette paper divided the two teams. Then Tommy sent out a pass to Billy Nesbitt who hared off down the wing. Pursell tackled him but Billy won us a throw-in. From the throw Billy collected the ball again, jinked around a defender and put in a good cross to Teddy Hodgson on the edge of the Liverpool penalty area. Teddy back-headed it over a defender, Ferguson I think it was. The ball fell straight into the path of Bert Freeman, about 15 yards from Campbell in the Liverpool goal. As the ball bounced up Bert cracked it on the volley, cutting it across Campbell and into the right-hand corner of the net. Campbell was caught flat-footed and turned his head to see the ball fly over the line and into the front of the net. Please note, I said the front of the net. If it had hit the back of the net it wouldn't be a goal, would it?

Of course, I wasn't thinking of that detail the moment I saw the net bulge. Tommy and Bert hugged each other in the Liverpool penalty area and we went mad, all of us hanging out of that tree. Emily may never have been to Turf Moor but she celebrated like a true Claret, one arm round a tree trunk, the other punching the air. Her flat cap flew off and dropped thirty feet to the ground.

'Oh, who cares?' she said. Her luscious hair fell out, wild and free. We could have been Tarzan and Jane the way we swung on those branches. The tree next to us was packed tight with Liverpool supporters. A few words were exchanged, I admit but it was all good-natured. There's never any trouble at football matches, in spite of the huge crowds. A few people have too much to drink but that happens wherever you go. Which is why it was a surprise to see two policemen at the foot of our tree. I thought nothing of it until I looked closer at the person standing next to them: our friend the steward. He was pointing up at Emily.

'Here, put my cap on,' I said. 'Quick.'

'Too late,' she said. 'And anyway it's my time.'

'What do you mean?'

'I should have been arrested before. It was in the plan.'

'What plan?'

'Our plan.'

'Whose plan?'

'I wanted to hold it off until we'd seen the final, that's all.'

'I don't understand.'

To be fair to Teddy and the lads, they were shaking their heads, trying to persuade the police they had got the wrong person. All this while the FA Cup Final was going on in front of them. I couldn't hear what they were saying but later Harry told me one of the policemen said something like: 'We're looking for a female by the name of Miss Emily Bettridge.'

'Tha's wasting tha time. It's a feller oop there,' said Teddy. 'Look at 'is suit.'

'The suspect's hair is far too long for a male,' said the policeman.

'That's the way we grow it up our way. It'll catch on down 'ere, soon enough. And tha's plenty of room to 'ide it under that fine 'elmet of yours, sergeant.'

'I saw a kiss being exchanged.'

'Aye, well they're fond of each other, if tha knows warra mean.'

It's just as well HM Constabulary didn't believe a word of it. The laws of the land being what they are, both of us would have been in even more trouble if they had.

'Time to face the music.' Emily began clambering down.

'I'm coming,' I said.

'There's no need. Don't miss the match.'

'I've seen enough, we're going to win.'

I was right, of course, we did win. Bert Freeman's goal was the only one of the game. I wasn't there to see the final 30 minutes, or Tommy lift the trophy. But no matter. I had seen the winning goal and Emily Bettridge was not a Lesbian. I could rest easy in the far from comfortable hospitality afforded me in a London police station, for that was where we were bound.

CHAPTER 33

'He's a star.'

'And a gangster.'

'He's got money.'

'And form.'

'He's cool.'

'He's a crook.'

Banter and gossip occupy Dan, Wretched Car Crook and Tadworth Terry in the long drag to Blackpool. Top US rap artist P. Diddy has emerged as the latest person to consider buying Crystal Palace FC. To confuse matters P. Diddy was previously known as Puff Daddy, having originally been baptised Sean Combs. No wonder he changed his name. Sean Combs sounds nothing more than a promising left back at Cork City. If Colonel Gaddafi wasn't prepared to follow through and buy the club in 2004, P. Diddy will have to do. He fits the Palace model perfectly: another unsafe pair of hands.

'I could do with a P. Diddy,' murmurs Sally, half asleep in the back.

'Almost there,' says Dan at the wheel.

Blackpool on a chilly March afternoon: not the most glamorous place to experience your first-ever game but, as Dan has stressed time and again en route, this is the real deal. They may catch prawns in the nearby ocean but they won't serve them up in hospitality. For fans with any self-respect, it's battered cod, old-fashioned, greasy chips and a large dollop of mushy peas along the Golden Mile – followed by a slow rumble onboard Britain's oldest working trams.

And this club has history, no-nonsense footballing history: 1953 and the Matthews FA Cup Final. With 22 minutes remaining, and Blackpool 3-1 down to Bolton, Sir Stanley Matthews jigged his way down the right wing to set up two goals and inspire the Seasiders' 4-3 win with seconds remaining. The club named its west stand after the great man. But, in these harsher times, even heritage of the finest kind becomes a victim of commercial dictates. The home fans now reside in the Pricebusters Matthews Stand. Meanwhile Dan and gang will be ushered into temporary, uncovered seats reserved exclusively for the away contingent, known unofficially as the Gene Kelly Stand.

The gang of four's schedule is straightforward enough: match, pleasure beach, curry, stroll, drive to four-star Blackburn hotel (with Dan and Sally's room paid for by the producers of *Britain's Got Tribute*). Hold-ups on the motorway mean they've arrived too late to get in a drink or two before the match. Instead they head straight to the ground. Both sides need the points. With a 10-point deduction, Palace stare relegation in the face. Blackpool need a win to maintain a late push for the play-offs. Their fans have turned up in force, decked out in tangerine.

'You never told me we were going to a B&Q staff convention.' Drowsily, Sally wipes condensation off the car window.

With kick-off just 30 minutes away, all four click through the turnstiles at the away end.

'Why-aye, man,' calls out a fan in an unconvincing Geordie accent. 'I see you've brought her with you!' He nods towards Sally. The man is a friend of a friend and Dan can't remember his name.

'It's Sally's first game,' says Dan, proudly.

'At least she didn't have so far to come, eh?' The man winks, knowingly.

'We've travelled up the M6, like you.'

'Really? Oh…'

A middle-aged woman taps Dan on the shoulder.

'Good luck tomorrow,' she says.

'Hi Katie,' says Dan. 'You know about the gig?'

'Of course. In Blackburn, isn't it?'

The auditions have been advertised on TV so that must be how she knows. Dan stands in the queue for refreshments.

'Everybody seems friendly if a bit strange,' says Sally. Looking at the limited menu, she refuses anything more substantial than a cup of tea. The gang find four seats together. The players finish warming up and leave the pitch, to applause from both sets of fans. The tannoy belts out music in between announcements. Another fan spots the foursome and makes his way along the row.

'Dan, isn't it?' he says.

Dan nods.

'I'm Colin. I recognised you from the photo.'

'Photo?' Dan shakes Colin's hand.

'And I agree.'

'Agree? With what?'

'The article on andthisiswhathesaid.com. Modern football is shite.'

The penny drops. Of course. Gavin, editor of the site, said the interview would appear in time for the auditions.

'I haven't seen the feature yet,' says Dan.

'Best thing on the site,' says Colin. 'Is this one of your... *friends?*' He looks at Sally. 'Makes it worth going on these long away trips, eh?'

Dan smiles, humouring the stranger.

'I'm Sally,' says Sally. 'Pleased to meet you.'

'You don't sound like you're from oop north, pet,' says Colin.

'That may be 'cos I'm not.'

'Ah. OK. Anyway, let's hope we get a win today.' Colin slopes off.

'Are you sure we're in Blackpool and not Newcastle?' says Sally.

'The position of the sun and sea suggests this is definitely the west coast,' says Wretched.

'Then why does everybody keep talking in fake Geordie?' says Sally.

Surely not... nervously, Dan calls up that article on his iPhone without showing it to the others. The interview is there all right, a straight transcription from their meeting in the pub. It's the story alongside that makes his pulse race. 'Geordie jaunt for Dan the Man' is the headline. Underneath is a picture of him with Charlie and Jade in the Mood nightclub in Newcastle. How the hell? Who the hell?

Next to the photo it reads: 'Dan's trip to the 4000 Holes in Blackburn, Lancashire follows hard on the heels of the singing salesman's other intrepid venture north. A little bird informed us of Dan's late-night adventures with fellow Eagle Silent 'n' Dudley. Dan persuaded S 'n' D to drop in at the Mood nightclub in Newcastle after our undeserved 2-1 defeat to the boys in black and white. As the photo reveals, they were made more than welcome by two friendly Geordies, Charlie and Jade who bagged a lift all the way back to Dan's Birmingham hotel. That's the kind of 2-1 result we'd all settle for.'

Oh God. Oh God. Dan puts his head in his hands.

'Anything wrong?' says Sally.

'No, er... it's OK.' He puts the iPhone back in his pocket. 'Always get like this before a match.'

Moments later Dan senses a man's hand on his shoulder. The man has put his other hand on Sally's shoulder. They both turn round. It's the friend of a friend with a poor Geordie accent.

'Just wanted to apologise,' says the man. No trace of Geordie this time. 'I've just re-read the article. You must be Sally, the singer in Born Too Late. Good luck tomorrow.'

'Thanks,' says Sally. 'That's nice of you.'

'Only, I got you confused with one of the Geordie girls in the article. No offence taken, I hope.'

Sally throws Dan a quizzical look. Dan stands and glares at the man.

'I'm not sure what you're on about,' he says, 'but thanks anyway.'

'Oh... right... let's hope we win today, eh?' The man melts back into the crowd.

'What was he going on about? Who are these Geordies?' says Sally.

'The bloke who's put this new website together... he's got the wrong end of the stick.' Time to divert the conversation. 'What's our line-up, Terry?'

'You already know the line-up,' says Sally. She pulls out her smart phone. To Dan's dismay she remembers the name of the website.

'Look...' he begins. Sally starts to read the interview. 'He's picked up some gossip, that's all.'

Sally spots the photograph and the story underneath. Her face darkens.

'That's not how it happened.'

Sally says nothing, gathers her things together. 'Let me pass.' She stands to leave.

'I can explain.'

'You could at least deliver a better cliché than that.'

'No, I mean it. That is not the truth.'

'Let me pass.'

'I did not suggest going to the nightclub.'

'So you *were* in Newcastle?'

'Well, yes.'

'So you lied to me.'

'Yes, but I didn't...'

'Let me pass.'

'Eeeeeeaaaaaaagggglllles... Eeeeeeaaaaaaagggglllles,' bellow fans all round. The match gets underway.

'What's up?' says Terry.

'A misunderstanding,' says Dan.

'It's a bit more than that.' Sally pushes her way along the row, to indignant mutters from fans.

'You're all hooligans, anyway,' she says.

Dan follows, apologising. They reach the turnstiles. 'Sal babes, it's not what it seems.'

'No, it's probably worse. I knew I should never have come, you bastard.'

'I didn't touch those girls.'

'Even though they were in your hotel room?'

'Yes.'

'So they *were* in your room?'

'Yes, but I didn't...'

'Quit while you're behind, Dan.'

'I should have told you I went to Newcastle.'

'You're an idiot.'

'I know.'

'I wondered why you didn't want me to go into your room.'

'It's not like that. You need to let me explain. You're over-reacting.'

'I've been under-reacting, that's the problem.'

Sally marches past a couple of bemused stewards.

'Where are you going?' says Dan. 'What about tonight and tomorrow?'

Behind them the away fans let out a collective roar. Against the form guide, Palace have taken the lead. It's only the third minute of the match.

'You've much more important things to get excited about.' Sally points to the fans jumping around in celebration. 'Don't you dare follow me.'

'But, I can't just let you…'

'I'll look after myself. I'm a big girl. And an even bigger idiot.'

'Give me a chance to explain.'

'I mean it, Dan. Leave me alone.'

Dan throws up his hands in frustration but thinks twice about kicking the wall. The stewards are keeping a watchful eye. He sees Sally walk down an alleyway until she is out of sight. He wanders back to his seat, a jumble of conflicting emotions. In spite of the most traumatic of incidents he chides himself for wanting to know who scored. He wishes he didn't need to know. He turns to run after Sally and thinks better of it. Best if he lets her cool down. He can always give her a ring, or text her. He finds Wretched and Terry.

'Problems?' says Terry.

'You could say that,' says Dan.

'Nerves about tomorrow, I reckon,' says Wretched.

'If only. If only…'

The rest of the game passes in a misty blur. Defying the odds Palace go into a 2-0 lead before half-time. Dan tries phoning Sally. No reply. He texts. No response.

'Chin up,' says Terry. 'These things happen.'

'Nothing did happen, I've told you before. It's got to be Silent 'n' Dudley. He's behind this. For some reason he's put all the blame on me. Funny how he hasn't been at a game for weeks.'

The teams come out for the second half. Dan tries phoning Sally. No reply. He texts. No response. Blackpool are like a team re-born. As their manager Ian Holloway says after the game: 'In the first-half we were like the Dog and Duck, in the second-half we were like Real Madrid.' They grab a goal back early in the second half and an equaliser in the 89th minute. Only the injury-time heroics of Julian Speroni (again) prevent defeat.

The jubilant Blackpool fans mock the Palace faithful:

'Two-nil and you fucked it up
'Two-nil and you fucked it up
'Two-nil and you fucked it up
'Two-nil and you fucked it up…'

The words whirl round and round in Dan's head. Never mind his team, they're singing directly to him.

CHAPTER 34

Thursday 30 April 1914

Grandpa always said: 'If you get in a tight corner, flatter your foe.' I took his advice at the police station.

'They're like the handlebars on my friend Billy's bike,' I said.

The copper standing at the desk looked puzzled. 'Not with you, son.'

'The two ends of your moustache, superintendent. They curve over the strap of your helmet. Very fetching.' He was only a constable and the moustache was like Burnley's league form: very average. He lifted his chin, proudly.

'You sound like a bright lad.' It had worked. 'Take some advice. Stay away from these lunatics. Nothing but trouble.'

'The suffragettes, you mean?'

He nodded. 'We have enough problems with the riff-raff – prostitutes and the like – without having to deal with daddy's little darlings.'

His colleagues had taken one of those little darlings into a separate room for questioning. I was left alone in reception for what seemed hours. They brought in a few drunks after the game, both Burnley and Liverpool supporters. By now they were the best of pals, singing songs and cracking jokes at Londoners' expense. A night in the cells and they'd be packed off home. I wasn't sure I'd be that lucky.

'It strikes me you don't belong to the posh set.' The copper leaned over the counter and peered down at me. I was sitting on a wooden bench.

'You mean I'm riff-raff?'

'I wouldn't put it quite like that.'

'How would you put it?'

'I'm just saying you could be charged with aiding and abetting her ladyship.'

'To do what?'

'Resist arrest.'

'I went to a football match, that's all.'

'The judge may not see it like that.'

'The judge?'

'If charges are pressed.'

I hadn't thought about that. I must have looked shocked.

'Like this girl, do you?' he said.

I was about to say 'What's it to do with you?' but then remembered Grandpa's advice. Get them on your side. The only way to do that was to sound nesh.

'I'm head over heels,' I said.

'Well, we've all felt like that at some time,' he said. 'The day I met my Ivy I was a young whippersnapper like you. I was on a tram, heading over Kingston way when the conductor...'

I was spared the detail. They brought out Emily.

'About time,' I said. 'We can catch the last train.'

'The young lady's going nowhere,' said the copper escorting her.

'I did tell you I was happy to face the music,' said Emily. 'I'm sorry to spoil the day.'

'What are they keeping you for?' I said.

'You'd best know, for your own sake,' said the copper. He pulled out his notebook. He was determined to drive a wedge between us. 'Smashing plate-glass windows at a golf club in Preston, vandalising the golf club's greens, setting fire to pillar boxes in Bradford, Manchester and Wigan and burning down a refreshment pavilion in a park in Liverpool.'

'Is all this true?' I said.

Emily didn't answer the question. 'They're keeping me in but letting you go.'

'I'll stay, too,' I said.

'Oh, there's no room here for you, not with this lot.' The copper pointed to the noisy rabble along the corridor. 'Now scarper.'

'I'm not going anywhere until I know what's going on,' I said.

'I'll be up in court on Monday morning,' said Emily. 'It's all part of the plan.'

'I don't understand.'

'Peaceful protests don't work. We have to make them listen.'

'But where do you fit in?'

'I can't say right now.' She glanced at the policemen around her, looked me in the eye and kissed me. It was more like a peck. 'I'll write.'

'You'll *write*… how long do you expect to be here?'

'I can't say.' She hugged me as if she meant it. She may even have been crying a little but she's a tough one all right. I mumbled that I had had a great day but I'm not very good at that sort of thing. They took her away and I left the police station on my own.

I had no idea where I was. The copper with the moustache told me the way to the railway station but I couldn't take it in, I was in that much of a daze. A couple of our supporters came out of a public house opposite the police station and I tagged along with them until we reached Euston. I was lucky. The trains were still running, even though it was very late. I bought an early edition of Sunday's newspaper (I've hidden it under the floorboards, Ma would not approve) with a report of the match in it. There were still supporters of both clubs all over the station. And who should I bump into yet again but Arthur Foster? He was drunk, very drunk. He was still singing that Tipperary song but the words had changed yet again.

'It's a long way to t' Crystal Palace,
'It's a long way to go.
'But the greatest team in England
'For the King, put on a show (1-0)
'Goodbye, Piccadilly,

'Farewell, Leicester Square!
'The FA Cup has come to Burnley,
'And my heart's right there.'

'Where's Harry?' I said. 'Did he find what he was looking for?'

'Oh aye,' said Arthur. 'Like 'e said, after Tommy lifted t' cup 'e'd do some lifting of 'is own.' He gave me a look. 'Not the type 'e wanted, mind. 'E were nicked pinching stuff from 'Arrods.'

I shook my head. 'And where's Teddy?'

'In a right mood,' said Arthur. 'He gets like that sometimes. Feeling fine one minute, down in t' dumps next.'

I felt bad about laying Teddy out like I had. I mean, he can be a daft sod but he tried his best to stop the coppers arresting Emily. I found a corner of the station concourse and settled down to read the paper. The next train wouldn't be for half an hour, they said. The front page had pictures of the King at the final and Tommy lifting the cup. Inside were stories from overseas. People are getting nervous about the strength of the Kaiser's navy. The back page was all I wanted, mind. I was gazing at pictures of Bert Freeman's goal, re-living it all, when I felt a gentle kick. I looked up. It was Teddy.

'What's 'appened to that girl of yours?' He sat down next to me.

'Up in court on Monday,' I said. 'Thanks for trying to help, anyway.'

'Did my best. Women should 'ave the vote, by my way of thinking.'

'I shouldn't have laid into you.'

'Deserved it, me. Ah were just jealous.' He looked dejected. I changed the subject.

'What a day, eh? Bet you can't wait to get back.'

'Me? No. Nowt for t' look forward to.'

I was surprised how gloomy he'd become.

'It says here there'll be a parade in the town centre on Monday afternoon,' I said.

'Not even sure ah'll get on t' train,' he said.

'I thought you hated London.'

'Ah do.'

'So…'

'But anybody what's anybody is down in these parts. Every

bugger's got a chance.' He pulled on his cigarette. 'Next time you're a mile underground, Dawsie, lying on your side in six inches of filthy water, swinging a steel sledgehammer to knock another wooden pit prop into place and it cracks like a gunshot and you begin running on your bare knees as fast as you bloody well can, ask thaself if tha's ever been given a bleedin' chance.'

I knew what he was saying. I'd pushed thoughts like that to the back of mind, what with one thing and another.

'Me, ah'm just looking for a future,' he said. 'To make summat of meself.'

I'd never heard him talk like this before. I showed him a photograph of the King on the front page of the paper. He just pointed to other, depressing news.

'It's all boiling up, sad to say,' he said. 'Germany, Serbia, Russia. They're all getting on their 'igh 'orses. Ah were chattin' to a lad from th'army today. They're takin' more on. I'm throwing me 'at in and joinin' up.'

The whistle sounded from our train. I can't see Teddy Hughes in the army myself, but at least I got him back to Burnley. For the first 20 minutes of the journey we talked about the armed forces. There were plenty of songs being sung up and down the train but after half an hour we slept most of the way. It wasn't surprising when you think about it. The morning was well underway before I finally got home. No-one was in. I went straight to bed. I think it was after mid-day – I'd lost track of the time – when Ma came in from church.

'I hear they won,' she called up to me.

'Oh aye,' I said from my bed.

'Did you see the King?'

'Of course.'

'More's to the point, did he see you?'

I wanted to tell her everything about the day but couldn't. 'I bumped into Teddy Hughes.'

'He's puddled, that lad.' Ma came upstairs and sat on my bed. 'I hear someone else was there. You'll never guess who.'

I had a good idea who she meant but I went through all the people she might mean, friends of hers, people we had known back in Burnley. She was desperate to tell me her news.

'When I got to church this morning there was a rumour going round that the Bettridge girl was there.'

'Really?'

'Aye, and I've also heard she was arrested. All to do with these daft women campaigning for the vote or summat. I always said she'd come to no good, that one.'

'Well,' I said, 'there were a lot of police at the match, that's true.'

'I'm going up to the house later. I'll let you know if I hear any more.' She started back downstairs. 'That family think they can hide things from the staff but we know everything that's going on, I can tell you.'

I lay back on my bed. Not everything, I said quietly, not everything.

CHAPTER 35

Dan and band have arrived in Blackburn, without Sally. Dubbed the 'premier tribute venue in the north-west', the 4000 Holes doesn't look much on the outside but inside it's a different world. In the foyer is a 3D model of the Albert Hall: a perfect replica, from the Fareham Red brick to the terra cotta block decoration. Even the dome on top, originally made of wrought iron and glazed, looks authentic.

'I wouldn't like to admit how much it cost to make.' The venue's event manager meets the band at the door. 'But it's paid us back a few times over as a tourist attraction.'

'Tourists? In Blackburn?' Kev leans his bass guitar against the wall.

'Japanese, mainly. We're an optional bolt on to one of the Beatles tours in Liverpool.'

The band study the model.

'The detail is superb,' says Kev, 'but I'm not sure why people would travel to see it.'

'Think of the song.

'*A Day in the Life*?'

'Correct.'

Puzzled silence.

'I'll give you a clue,' says the manager. 'We worked out the number of cubic metres in the pub and created the model based on our measurements.'

'OK… I'm getting there,' ventures Dan. 'So the model is built to scale?'

'Yes.'

'And its exact size is significant?'

'Compared to the venue.'

Dan glances round at the bar, stage area and other function rooms. He looks back at the model. 'The cubic metres, you had to count them all...'

'Now you know how big the Albert Hall would be...' cuts in Kev.

'...to fit 4000 of them into the venue,' says Dan.

'Precisely.'

'Awesome,' says Kev.

'Bizarre,' says Dan. To a man, the band nod in appreciation.

'Some tourists think we were here before the song.' The manager takes them into the heart of the venue. 'I've even overheard people tell friends that the Beatles played here before they were famous and wrote the song because of it. I don't shatter the illusion.'

The walls are adorned with alternative 60s memorabilia. In one glass case hang a pair of black flares with split crotch, allegedly belonging to PJ Proby. Displayed on a velvet cushion is the fly button Mick Jagger lost on stage during the Rolling Stones' 1969 tour – Jagger famously saying to the crowd: 'You don't want my trousers to fall down, now do ya?' Next to that are the remains of a TV thrown from the 12th floor of a US hotel room by The Who. Reputedly.

'I've OD'd and gone to heaven,' murmurs Dan.

'Which band are you?' asks the manager.

'Truly Driscoll and the Brian Auger Trinity.'

'Ah, yes.' He consults his running order. 'Fourth on, after Canned Cheat and before Fleetwood Back Again.'

Dan shakes his head. 'I think you'll find we're last on.'

The manager double checks his list. 'There's been a change to the schedule.'

'Well, we haven't been told. Who made the changes?'

'The management, that's all I know.'

'Right, I need to contact Stuart Bensham.' Stu got them the gig. He has the band's best interests at heart.

'He was around earlier,' says the manager.

'Any idea where he is now?'

'Can't help, sorry. Your sound check is in two hours.'

The rest of the band take stock of the venue while Dan checks his phone again. No call from Sally since the match, just a text telling him to leave her alone. He has phoned her flatmates. No sign there. He even considered phoning Nanna, what with all that bonding and stuff. Better not. Too desperate. Without Sally they can't do the gig but it's more than that. She has never gone to ground before. She's had her moments but never walked away like this. The trouble is he can't blame her, after what she read yesterday.

'Depressing, isn't it?'

Dan turns round to see a tall, middle-aged man with dark hair and a sharp, long nose, sporting a grey trilby hat.

'I'm Leonard,' he says. 'Leonard Clone.'

Dan laughs. The look is almost perfect.

'Did Suzanne bring you down?' he says.

'If I had a pound...'

'Sorry.' He shakes Leonard's hand.

'Thought I'd give it a shot. My wife says I'm a boring old git so I should win comfortably.'

'It's our first go at this sort of thing.'

'Well, good luck. I came fourth in one competition.'

'As Leonard Clone?'

'No, Val Doonagain. Struggling for the last note of *Walk Tall* did for me.'

Dan has a vague idea who Val somebody-or-other was but that's all.

'I'll bet you've a lot of your own songs you'd rather do,' says Leonard.

'I've written a few, yes.'

'Like the rest of us. And here we all are, sad nobodies pretending to be somebody we aren't.'

'I don't know about that...'

'You will, when you've been round the block a few times. Everyone in this business would rather be doing his own stuff. We write decent

190

songs but are told they're "not what people are buying now", or we "haven't got the look" or some such bollocks. We end up doing the rounds, pretending to be someone famous who just got lucky.'

'I hadn't looked at it like that.'

'Mind you, there are tributes around these days that are pretty much as good as the originals. Ever heard Con Jovi?' Dan shakes his head. 'Great act. Decent lads, too. They'd clean up here. Who are you?'

Dan tells him.

'I had a big thing about Miss Driscoll when I was your age,' says Leonard. 'Her eyes, dear God. Brian Auger was a lucky man. I'll bet she put some delicious vibrato on his organ. If your singer is half as nice...'

Dan's mobile rings. It's Stu.

'I was about to call you,' says Dan.

'Great minds and all that.'

'We've a few problems.'

'Yeah. I had a call from Sally.'

'Is she OK?'

'She's fine. Look, it's not for me to get involved in personal matters but if I can be of any help.'

'Thanks. It's a huge misunderstanding.'

'These things happen. I just want the best for both of you.'

'I don't even know where she is.'

'Here in Blackburn...'

'Thank God for that.'

'...and I've suggested she does the gig, then the two of you sit down and sort things out.'

'Cool.'

'There's... one other thing...'

'Ye-es...' The pause between words unnerves Dan.

'I've talked to the powers that be and Truly Driscoll isn't what they're looking for,' says Stu. 'You'll stand a much better chance if you do a Dusty Springfield tribute.'

Dan takes a deep breath. 'But we haven't rehearsed anything by her.'

'If you do Dusty, they'll give you back the final spot. Believe me, it could make all the difference. I can get you a room to rehearse in and we've a team of make-up artists who can go to work on Sally. I've even thought of a tribute name.'

'Hmmm, well, I'll have to have a word.' Dan consults the band.

'We've come this far,' says Graham. 'Might as well give ourselves the best chance.' Heads nod. Dan sighs.

'OK. If Sally and the other lads are up for it, I'll play ball.'

The 4000 Holes is a great venue, no doubt about that. The packed crowd is well up for the event. Every band and soloist receives enthusiastic support as they perform before four judges. Al 'Most' Green has gone down particularly well. So, too, has My Sweet Fraud: the George Harrison Experience. Now it's Leonard Clone's turn.

'*So long, Marianne*
'*It's time that we began*
'*To laugh and cry*
'*And cry and laugh*
'*About it all again...*'

Leonard finishes with a flourish on his acoustic guitar. The audience applauds. Leonard doffs his trilby – to the left, to the right.

'Not an easy artist to cover,' says one of the judges. 'A good effort.'

'But not good enough?' says Leonard.

'Well, it was all a bit of a downer.'

A few boos from the audience.

'What do you expect?' says Leonard. 'I'm supposed to be Leonard Cohen. The man's a friggin' depressive.' Laughter. 'Tell you what, I'll change the lyrics.' He strums a chord on his guitar. 'How about "*Hello Marianne, it's time that we began to laugh and laugh and laugh and laugh (ha ha ha) about it all again*"?' Applause.

'OK,' says another judge. 'Nice try. Maybe you should put together a comic act. With your personality, you could send people up.'

'Starting with you lot,' says Leonard.

A sustained burst of applause.

'We're not just here to criticise,' says the third judge. 'We want to encourage and advise.'

'Bollocks. You've already decided who you want in the final. We're wasting our time.'

More applause.

'Not true.' The first judge puts up his hand to stop the clapping. 'Everyone stands an equal chance.'

'Only if they do what you want them to do. I've heard the conversations.'

'Say what you like,' says the fourth judge. 'If you've got it, we'll back it. Thanks for coming, anyway. So long…'

Below the belt, that. The audience boo.

'A big hand for Leonard Clone,' says the presenter. The audience gives him a very big hand as he marches off stage.

'Good luck,' he says to Dan, waiting in the wings. 'I'm out of here.' In less than a minute he has got his belongings together and disappeared.

'And now we come to the final act.' The presenter turns to check Dan is ready. 'Of course we all know the 60s were largely about groups dominated by men. There were some notable exceptions, however and we are privileged to have one of those stars with us tonight.'

Dan and band file onto stage. Dan sits at the piano. The band take up their instruments.

'Our guest formed a successful group with her brother then went solo and became one of the best-loved singers in the world. Ladies and gentlemen, tonight at the 4000 Holes, we only want to be with her. Please welcome the white queen of 60s soul… Mustbe Springfield!'

Dan crashes a big, D minor melodrama of a chord. Sally strides onto stage in a low-cut, ankle-length gold dress trimmed with fake fur. She sports a pair of false eyelashes (big and very black), a blond bobbed wig and daisy ear-rings. She throws her arms to the audience, palms outstretched.

'*When I said… I needed you…*' Dan glides up and down the keyboard in bittersweet arpeggio. Bass, drums and guitar kick in and Mary Isobel Catherine Bernadette O'Brien is born again in Blackburn.

'*You said you would always stay...*' It isn't just the husky, soaring vocals that bring conversations to a screeching halt. She must have studied those old black-and-white clips on YouTube: that dismissive flick of a wrist and those beseeching arms. She could be doing semaphore or out on an airport runway, guiding in a 707.

'*You don't have to say you love me*
'*Just be close at hand*
'*You don't have to stay for ever*
'*I will understand*
'*Believe me, believe me...*'

Channelling one of Britain's most celebrated pop divas takes some front. Dan and the boys are surprised how confidently she delivers the goods and at such short notice.

'*All that's left is loneliness, there's nothing left to feel*
'*You don't have to say you love me*
'*Just be close at hand...*
'*You don't have to stay for ever*
'*I will understand*
'*Believe me, believe me, oh believe me...*'

The punters give her the biggest applause of the night. Still playing the part, she blows kisses and disappears backstage. Now they stamp their feet and roar approval. 'More, more, more, more...'

The band join Sally off stage and huddle together in the wings.

'We're through,' says Sally, in Dan's ear.

'What do you mean?' says Dan.

'To the final.'

'Yes... of course.'

'Brilliant.' Stu joins them. 'Sally, what can I say? They love you out there.'

The band is called back to the stage for the judges' comments. It's a formality. All four agree that Mustbe Springfield has 'got what it takes to go all the way.'

'OK... OK... I'll ask.' Stu cups the phone and turns to Sally. 'Sky News. Tomorrow morning... Are you up for it?'

Following their victory, Dan and Sally have been inundated with requests for interviews from local newspapers, radio and regional TV. After a long, intoxicating evening, it's time for the long haul south. The call from national TV is late and unexpected.

'Are we up for it?' Dan asks Sally. Maybe they'll get a chance to be on their own in London. There's been no chance since the end of the auditions.

'No, I mean… sorry I didn't explain… Sky only want Sally,' says Stu.

'Oh.' Dan looks at Sally, Sally at Dan.

'It's a drag but I think you ought to do it, Sally,' says Stu. 'In this game you need to strike while the iron's hot and it doesn't stay hot for long.'

'I'm not happy doing it on my own,' says Sally. 'It's Dan's band, after all.'

'I think you should go,' says Dan. 'I'll come down and cheer you on.'

'That's the other complication,' says Stu. 'They want to fly Sally down immediately, to make sure she's there for the morning show. They're keen, all right.'

'And I've got to drive the car back,' says Dan, shaking his head. 'Life's a bitch.'

'Listen, it's been a long day and a hell of a weekend, right?' Stu looks sympathetically at Dan and Sally. 'The least I can do is put Sally on the plane at Manchester, Dan, so you can take your time getting home without worrying.'

Dan looks at Sally. Sally at Dan.

'Go for it, babes,' says Dan.

'Are you sure?'

'Of course.'

'OK…' Stu is back on the phone. 'Miss Springfield is as good as on the plane…' He walks away from Dan and Sally to conclude the arrangements, leaving the pair on their own.

'Half of me still wants to kill you,' she says.

'Half of me has already died,' he says.

CHAPTER 36

Friday 1 May 1914

The longed-for homecoming was on Monday afternoon. After such an eventful weekend, I couldn't wait. I tried to be as patient as possible but it was impossible to concentrate on anything else. I gazed down the road. The whole of Burnley was waiting for Tommy Boyle to return with the Cup but I wasn't there. I didn't want to be, either. Anytime now Ma would come back from the Bettridges, hopefully with news.

All day I had done everything I could think of to take my mind off Emily. Not knowing what's happening is bad enough but the worst thing is being unable to ask anyone who might know.

'What's tha doin' readin' t' front pages?' said a lad at work. 'The Cup Final's all over t' back.'

I was looking down every column for the name Bettridge. Nothing. I read it through three of four times. Still nothing.

'There's more to life than kicking a pig's bladder round a field,' I said.

'Well, that's rich coming from you.'

To be honest, it surprised me, too. Nothing has been more important than football until now. Until Emily. When I got home from work I found myself going over to my suit time and again. I'd hung it up on the back of the door. Her perfume was still on it. Ma got home late. There was a special do up at the house and she had to help out longer than normal. Even when she got back I didn't dare bring up the subject.

'He's a frumpy beggar, OMB (it stands for Old Man Bettridge, all the staff call him that), but he doesn't deserve sons like those two,' she said, hanging up her coat. 'Good for nothing, they are. They'll fritter the lot away, given half a chance. OMB built up the business. They'll let it all fall down again. Clogs back to clogs, mark my words.' Ma often walks in like that – half thinking, half talking.

'What have they done now?' I said.

'It's what they haven't done. They should be taking care of business while he tries to sort out that young daughter of his.'

'You said she was at the Cup Final.'

'With some lad or other, they say.'

I wasn't expecting that. I tried to hide my surprise. 'You've no idea who…'

Ma shook her head. 'Bad as her brothers, that girl.'

'Oh, I don't know about that.'

'Why, what have you heard?'

'Nothing much, just gossip, like you.'

'More money than sense, the lot of 'em.'

'What has she been charged with?'

'All sorts, to do with these suffragettes and the like but here's the funny thing.' Ma was bursting to pass on what she'd heard. 'She's refused bail.'

'You mean she been refused bail.'

'No, she's refused bail. They say she's staying in prison, even though she could come out until the case is heard. No-one knows why. That's what OMB was trying to sort out. He went down to London to bail her out.'

'She wouldn't want that.' I was thinking aloud.

'How do you know?'

'Oh, just a hunch. From what you've told me, they can be very single-minded, these suffragettes.'

'Well, she's in with them, all right. Can't see the point of it, me. Most women don't even want the vote.'

197

Now Ma can't read but she's not stupid, either. The trouble is she gets most of her views from Reverend Whitehead.

'The woman's place is here, in the home,' said Ma from the back kitchen. 'Oh, you can get all fancy if you've got cash like the Bettridges but men go out to work, women look after the home. That's how the world works and it will fall apart if we change it.'

'But you go out to work *and* look after a home,' I said but Ma wasn't listening.

'Besides, it's never a good thing when women are in charge,' she went on. 'Even Mrs Liddington (the Bettridge's cook) gets all of a do when things go wrong. I'd rather take orders from a man any day. They're less moody.'

The long and the short of it is that I'm still not sure what's happening to Emily and I shall have to wait until I see something in the paper.

'Any road, you haven't forgotten about Saturday afternoon, I hope,' called out Ma. I muttered a couple of words I shouldn't know. Reverend Whitehead has been at the church for 10 (long) years and they're holding a party for him. I promised Ma I would help her out by laying the tables in the church hall. Following Grandpa's funeral I've been asked to play a few tunes on the harmonica as well. At least the party was arranged for the week after the Cup Final. Billy had to go to a family wedding on Cup Final day itself. How can people be so inconsiderate?

'I saw Nellie Williams earlier,' said Ma.

'That's nice.'

'She doesn't have *her* father running up and down to London on a fool's errand.'

I didn't respond.

'She's a lovely girl,' continued Ma.

'I know.'

'She likes you.'

'I can't think why.'

'They're a fine family, the Williams.'

'And very dull.'

Ma came through from the back kitchen. 'That's unfair.'

'Nellie wouldn't say boo to a goose.'

'She's just shy.'

'And dull.'

'She doesn't cause her father grief like Miss Emily does.'

'That's what I mean, she's dull.'

'You're acting strange.' Ma folded her arms. 'If I didn't know how much you dislike the Bettridge girl, I'd think you'd taken a shine to her, right enough.' She narrowed her eyes. 'You didn't see her in London, did you?'

This was getting too close for comfort.

'Naturally,' I said, in a posh voice. 'The King, Lady Emily and I had tea. I introduced His Majesty to Lord Teddy Hughes... Come on, Ma. We know our place. I was with the riff-raff.'

This entry is longer than I expected because I can't sleep. For the first time since he left this world I have moved Grandpa's flat cap (forgive me again, Grandpa) to the foot of the bed and wrapped my suit round the bedpost. If I breathe in deeply...

CHAPTER 37

Nanna Neath grips Sally's arm. 'Going back to Bletchley was bad enough but Shearwater Gardens, God help us…'

'I bet that ivy over the front door looks sensational in the autumn,' says Sally, brightly. 'It's a lovely old manor house.'

'So is Golden Sands.'

'I'm not sure where…'

'It's in Neath.'

'Another nursing home?'

'Where I'll end up.'

'Nanna, you're shaking.' Sally links arms with Dan's grandmother. They walk slowly down the path to a grand front door of gnarled oak. 'Dafydd will be as nervous as you.'

'He remembers me as a young thing with luscious, give-a-damn hair like yours. Now I'm a shrivelled walnut. No good can come of this.'

Sally rings the bell. 'This will mean so much to Dafydd.'

'He knows… things.'

'You've nothing to be ashamed of.'

'Not a day has passed when I haven't worried someone will find out.'

'Times have changed, Nanna. People are more tolerant, more understanding.'

'And they've no pride, either.' She shakes her head. 'Anything goes and no-one bloody well cares.'

The doors of Shearwater Gardens open.

'How lovely to see you again.' A tall woman in her 70s, with an angular face and hair in a severe bun puts out both hands in greeting. Her vowels are long and educated. 'And you've brought your grand-daughter with you. My dear, how many years has it been?'

'I'm not sure who...' starts Sally. 'We're looking for...'

'Come in, come in,' beckons the woman. 'Albert flew in as soon as he heard. Mavis tootled up in her Traveller. The kettle's on. We'll have tea and scones with your favourite raspberry jam. I know how you love that.'

Nanna and Sally look at each other, then at the woman.

'Alice, these are *my* guests.' A young nurse arrives at the door. 'Alice thinks everyone has come to see her. Don't you, darling?' She puts an arm round Alice and guides her to a room along the corridor.

'Now do you understand why I'm shaking?' says Nanna. Sally grips her arm tightly.

'Sorry about that.' The nurse returns to the entrance foyer. 'Now then, it's Mrs Cadogan, isn't it?' Nanna nods. 'I saw the programme about Bletchley Park. It's an honour to meet you. Mr Broderick is very much looking forward to seeing you, I know.' She goes ahead of her visitors. Nanna points Sally to the chandelier and tropical fish aquarium. She shakes her head.

'Don't be fooled, they always have a nice entrance hall,' she says out of the side of her mouth. To the right is a lounge. In the corner, a large TV is broadcasting BBC News 24 with subtitles.

'A survey released today shows cyber-bullying among children is on the increase,' says the manicured presenter. Nine residents in armchairs, heads lolling at strange angles and in various states of slumber, show no immediate concern about threats posed by new technology.

'Oh dear God.' Nanna takes a deep breath and holds it.

'It isn't so bad,' whispers Sally. 'It's just very strong chlorine.'

'Masking incontinence,' mouths Nanna.

They reach Room 43. The nurse knocks on the door.

'Mr Broderick, your guests,' she says.

'Here we go.' Nanna takes another deep breath.

'That you, Rhoslyn?' comes a voice.

'It's me, young man.' Gingerly, Nanna puts her head round the door.

'I'd know those tones anywhere,' says the voice. 'Come here and let me touch you.'

'Oh, Dafydd!' Nanna grasps a quivering hand. 'You're… you're as blind as a bat. Thank God.'

'Typical. Only you.' Sitting back in a chair that reclines, Dafydd rocks with laughter.

'I really shouldn't say such things,' says Nanna.

'God knows, I've waited an eternity to be on the end of your wicked, wicked tongue again.' His breathing is laboured, his accent richly Welsh. 'At least I know they're not palming me off with a ringer.' He reaches out for Nanna's other hand and holds it to his cheek. 'Oh, my dear Rhoslyn, I cannot begin to find the words to say how much I've missed you… for all these years.'

The last four words are choked in tears that cascade from unseeing eyes.

'Ti'n swno mor dwp ag erioed,' says Nanna.

'Fe gymerodd amser on mae Duw wedi ateb fy ngweddi,' says Dafydd.

'I think that's our cue to beat it,' says the nurse. But Sally is already in the corridor, pulling a tissue from her handbag.

'Well?' says Nanna.

'Well what?' Sally pulls out of the visitors' car park at Shearwater Gardens.

'You and Dan.'

'There's nothing to say.'

'Nonsense.'

'Nanna, you've just met the love of your life.'

'And it was very pleasurable.'

'Well?' Sally glances at Nanna.

'Well what?' says Nanna.

'How did you leave it?'

'Oh, we'll probably stay in touch.'

Sally arrives at a t-junction, lets three cars go past, then joins a major A road that leads to the M4 motorway. 'I can't believe that's all there is to say.'

'Ditto. You storm off at a football match, the judges jump up and down about your lovely voice, you get rave reviews all over the media. Meanwhile my grandson mopes round the house like a bear with a sore thumb. Discuss.'

'That's the trouble. He's your grandson.'

'So?'

'There are sensibilities.'

'You're saying I can't be objective.'

'I'm saying it isn't fair to dump stuff on you of all people.'

'Because I'm too old and frail.'

'I didn't say that.'

'Or I'm being nosey?'

'Possibly.'

'Yet you want to know all about Dafydd.'

'Because I care.'

'And I don't?'

Sally smiles. She changes gear. 'You win. If you must know there is, how can I say this… a third party. In fact, there's a fourth party.'

'Oh, I see.'

'He went to a match in Newcastle when he said he was in Birmingham. He met two Geordies and took them back to his hotel.'

'And you discovered them?'

'No. He says it was a misunderstanding and somebody else dumped them there. Oddly enough, that person is nowhere to be found.'

'And you don't believe him.'

'Why should I?'

'What were these girls like?'

'From the photo – tarts.'

'Who took the photo?'

'A friend your grandson "can't locate"'. Sally air quotes with one hand.

'Show me the photo.'

'What... *now?*'

Nanna nods.

'It's on the website,' says Sally.

'You can call it up on your i-thingy.'

'Yes, but I'm driving.'

Nanna is silent. Sally shakes her head. 'Only you.' It is a passable impersonation of Dafydd. She pulls into a lay-by. 'Here it is.' She hands Nanna her iPhone. Nanna pulls a magnifying glass from her handbag.

'Well,' she says after a minute or so. 'I wouldn't jump to conclusions.'

'It's pretty damning.'

'Look at the body language.'

Sally studies the photo and shrugs her shoulders.

'He is not posing for the camera,' says Nanna. 'He seems unaware the photo is being taken, so he's not exactly revelling in the situation.'

'You're clutching at straws.'

'The girl is all over him but he seems to be ignoring her. Look at the way he is angled, as far from the girl as he can go.' Nanna taps the magnifying glass. 'In fact, I'd say he's more interested in his watch than the girl.'

'Well, he's an idiot.'

'There I cannot disagree with you.'

'He says this "friend" insisted on calling into the nightclub on the way back to Birmingham.'

'And Dan goes to nightclubs regularly?'

Sally makes a face. 'He hates them. In fact, he can be a complete bore.'

'Now that's *much* more like my grandson.'

Sally turns on the ignition grouchily. She jerks out of the lay-by, back onto the dual carriageway. 'The photo's one thing. Explain away two women in his hotel bed.'

'That is more of a problem. I'll have to think about that.' Nanna puts her head back and, within a minute or two, is dosing. She is at the door to Shearwater Gardens again. This time it isn't some batty woman greeting her but Dafydd. He beckons her in for tea and scones. This time he can see. She is naked and ashamed. He can see right through her. He's laughing. She says she thought he was blind. He is holding her by the arm. 'I hoped against hope that you'd call for me, but you didn't,' he is saying. She looks around. This isn't the nursing home. It's Tara. She's on the set of *Gone With the Wind*. She looks around again. Now she is in that cinema seat, watching the film, but this time old and shrivelled. Dafydd is young, vibrant, alive. 'I've loved you more than I've ever loved any woman,' he is saying, 'and I've waited for you longer than I've ever waited for any woman...'

'Nanna,' says Sally, gently, 'we're almost home.'

'We're... where?'

'Dan's house.'

'I must have dozed off.'

'For two hours.'

'That was the strangest dream.'

'You kept mumbling that you'll think of a way to get him back.'

'Did I?'

'I deserve an explanation.'

'It's been quite a day.'

'Nanna...' It's Sally's turn to reprove her passenger.

'Well, if you must know, Dafydd's wife died three years ago.'

'And?'

'He proposed to me this afternoon.'

'I knew it.' Sally crunches the clutch and misses a gear. 'I just knew it. What did you say?'

'Keep your eyes on the road,' chides Nanna.

'And I've seen a perfect hat for the wedding.'

'I told him to grow up. We'd pass for Mr and Mrs Floyd in *Under Milk Wood* – side by wrinkled side, like two old kippers in a box.'

'Oh, Nanna!'

'Things have moved on. We're different people now.'

'That's not important. Do you still love him?'

Nanna hesitates. 'He was too powerful. He still is.' Sally draws up outside Dan's house, turns off the engine and locks the car door.

'I see. No escape.' Nanna sighs. 'They say that if you dream you're naked, it is because you feel inferior to the people around you in the dream. Something you are concealing is in danger of being exposed. Dafydd saw right through me. He always could.'

Sally muses. 'Maybe, subconsciously... you were relieved to see the relationship whither.'

Nanna nods. 'It took the responsibility away from me. I had told him things no-one else knew. I feared he might use what he knew against me. It was easier to walk away.'

'And now?'

'Well, he still knows.'

'So what are you going to do?'

'He says I need to sort myself out, once and for all. He can't believe I haven't already done so.'

CHAPTER 38

Saturday 2 May 1914

REBELLION IS OBEDIENCE TO GOD, SAYS SUFFRAGETTE

Scenes of Wild Disorder in Sydenham as Industrialist's Daughter is Tried for Arson

Stormy scenes were witnessed in Sydenham yesterday when Miss Emily Bettridge of St Helens, Lancashire was tried for arson and willful damage to property.

Miss Bettridge immediately upon being put in the dock commenced a running fire of commentary on the Court procedure, which she kept up during the course of the trial, which lasted for an hour. Over a score of police were on duty in various parts of the Court, while a similar number of plain-clothes constables were also prepared for eventualities.

When Miss Bettridge entered the Court, loud applause from a large number of women greeted her and cheers were raised on her name being called.

When asked to answer the indictment, Miss Bettridge replied, "Trying voteless women with man-made laws is morally indefensible. I am not going to listen to you or anyone whatever. To be militant is a moral obligation. It is a duty that every woman owes to her own conscience. Rebellion against tyrants is obedience to God."

Women in the Court again applauded vociferously.

The Judge said, "I take this as a plea of not guilty." He then ordered the Court to be cleared. There was pandemonium as a number of women sternly resisted the efforts of the police and had to be forcibly ejected. A man was heard to shout, "Tie them all to the table leg."

Miss Bettridge was found guilty and sentenced to three months' hard labour. Even after she had left the Court her protests were still audible.

'Well, I never did,' said Ma when I'd finished reading the report. 'It sounds even worse than the rumours.' We were in the church hall kitchen. Ma was rolling out pastry, making apple pies for the vicar's tenth anniversary party later in the day. I began peeling the apples.

'A Bettridge in gaol,' I said. 'OMB must be spitting feathers.'

'Aye and we've all been on the end of it, I can tell you,' said Ma. 'Silly girl. She's always been a problem. Not right, that one.'

'Not you and all, Ma.' I shook my head.

'Right little hothead. OMB spends a fortune on a lah-de-dah school and she ends up an arsonist.'

'It's not that she just loves setting fire to things, Ma. She's trying to force the government into changing the law. It's a political act.'

Ma looked me up and down. 'You've changed your tune. Sounds like you'd have been happy enough defending her in court.'

'No, it's just that... how's Brutus?' Changing the subject seemed a good idea.

'Missing you. I told him you'd take him for a walk this week.'

'I've been busy.'

'Busy upstairs, right enough.' Ma pointed to her head. 'Can't make you out, presently.'

'What with Grandpa and the FA Cup, life's been full,' I said. 'Maybe after...'

I can't remember what I was going to say next because at that moment I heard the sound of a piano. It came from upstairs in the main hall. A lovely tune, it was. I recognised it but, for the life of me, couldn't name it. Nor could Ma. Now let me say that the church hall piano is German, a good make. With young children hammering it to death, it's not usually

208

in tune. The odd note is missing as well. Ma said it had been tuned and repaired especially for the party. The person playing had a lovely touch.

'Back in a moment,' I said, expecting to find the church organist. Mind you, he plays piano as if he's riding a boisterous stallion. His head rocks up and down and the pedals might just as well be stirrups. This was softer, almost apologetic. I listened outside the door. The melody lilted with melancholy. I put my head slowly round the door. To my astonishment it was Nellie Williams.

'Nellie, that's… that's beautiful,' I said. Without even looking at me, she broke off, closed the piano lid, grabbed the music and started stuffing it into her leather satchel.

'I'm sorry,' she said. 'I didn't know anyone else was in.'

'I didn't realise…'

'I can't do it if anyone's listening.'

'You play really well.'

'No I don't.'

'I've forgotten what that piece is called.'

'*To a Wild Rose.*'

'Please… play it again.'

'I can't. I'm, I'm… sorry.'

She was all of a do, as Ma says.

'Please,' I said.

'You scare me.' She was looking down at her feet.

'What have I done?'

'Just… I don't know.'

'Why don't you play in front of people?'

'Because there's always someone around better than me.' She wouldn't look up.

'No-one I know can play half as well.'

'Now you're just being polite. Anyway, what are you doing here on a Saturday?'

I explained that I was helping Ma prepare for the party.

'Oh, I see.' She was still looking at her feet. 'We can't afford a piano at home so they let me play here for two hours every Saturday afternoon.'

'I had no idea.'

'Good.'

'I'm sorry if I scared you.'

'I used the present tense, not past.'

'What do you mean?'

'If you don't understand, there's no point trying to explain.'

I've known Nellie a long time. Thinking about it, I can't remember a time when I didn't know her. This was the longest conversation we'd ever had. Maybe it's just the only one I remember.

'I think you should play tonight, at the party,' I said.

She laughed and shook her head. 'They only ask the talented ones like you.'

'But they won't ask you if they don't know you play.'

'You have to have self-confidence to do anything in front of a lot of people.' She paused. 'Like Emily Bettridge...'

For the first time she looked at me. She studied my reaction to her last comment. I may have given the game away in those few seconds, too.

'Ma thinks she's a hothead.' It was the first thing I could think of saying.

'And you agree?'

'It's not for me to say.'

'So you *do* like her.'

'I hardly know her.'

'I may look it but I'm not stupid.' I was discovering that at speed. 'They say she was with a lad at the Cup Final. I think it was you.'

Maybe I didn't conceal my surprise but I tried. 'Nellie, there were more than 70,000 men and boys at the Cup Final.'

'So you're not denying it.'

'I'm being interrogated for no good reason.'

At this point she put her hand to her lips.

'Listen,' she said. 'Can you hear it? The sound of a cock crowing.'

What I said next just slipped out. She was putting me under pressure and I did it to throw her off the trail.

'Anyway, they say she's a Lesbian.' I also wanted to find out if she knew what a Lesbian was. Childish, I admit.

'In case you're wondering, I *do* know what it means,' said Nellie. 'And anyway, who are "they"?' Neither of us knew what to say next. 'You caught me off guard,' she continued, at last. 'I didn't want you, of all people, to hear me playing.'

'Me of all people?'

'Yes, you... Thomas Daws.' She packed away all her music and walked towards the door.

'Will you be at the party?' I said.

'Are you asking me because someone else *won't* be there?'

With that, wouldn't-say-boo-to-a-goose Nellie fairly slammed the door behind her.

'A prodigal son is bad enough. Imagine how much more worry a prodigal daughter would bring to that ever-patient father...'

It was obvious who the guest speaker was talking about. Sitting next to him at the top table was the prodigal daughter's father, Old Man Bettridge, who stared humbly at the floor. It had been quite a party, one way and another. I imagine there were 400 people squeezed into the hall. The great and the good turned up to acknowledge the vicar's anniversary – local businessmen, councillors and headmasters. The food was prepared by Ma and friends: women who had never let even a prodigal thought escape between them. It was consumed at speed, mainly by men. After the choir sang, I played *The Lord Is My Shepherd* on the harmonica, Mrs Whitehead's favourite. There was no sign of Nellie. All evening I thought how good it would have been to hear her play again. She is brilliant.

'Let us hold in our thoughts and prayers those fathers who, like the one spoken of in this parable, have sacrificed much to ensure their children have the best start in life, only to see that love spurned...'

Now I may be speaking out of turn but as far as I know, we can't be sure whether the father in the Bible story, who was rich, made his money fairly or not. Nor do we know how he treated his son or servants. Maybe the prodigal son had every reason to leave. All the guilt is dumped on the young man. The speaker went on about young people getting 'carried away by the latest political fad and fashion,' a reference to the suffragettes, I'm sure.

However (that's a word I hadn't used much before I met Emily) I had no business arguing with the speaker. It would be considered impertinent coming from someone of my age. After all, Ernest Borst, manager of Weaver Green Colliery, is a pillar of the local community.

CHAPTER 39

Those familiar slow steps. The creak, creak, creak of the stairs. A grunt. A gasp. Sitting on his bed, Dan waits for the inevitable. This time it doesn't come. Instead, a timid knock. The box room door opens a few centimetres.

'Daniel, I've been thinking.'

'Dangerous.'

'This business in Newcastle.'

'Less said, the better.'

'I'm trying to make sense of it.'

'Nanna, it's my problem. You've more important things to concern you.'

'Such as?'

'Dafydd.' He's got his name right at last.

'Oh, that's neither here not there.' Nanna is still breathing heavily from climbing the stairs. 'You've your whole life ahead, the two of you.'

It has been ten days since Blackpool, that website article, the 4000 Holes and the outbreak of cold war with Sally. It seems like ten years. But Dan has read the history books. Cold wars are like that: harsh words exchanged, lines drawn, followed by a long, slow, disengaged stand-off. The band could get its first big break in the music business and disintegrate in the process. Dan considers another reading of history: clashing egos, artistic differences, the fights, the flouncing, the fury. It's so *rock 'n' roll*. The band must be a genuine force to be reckoned with. Cold comfort but right now he'll take it.

'It's my mess. I've got to live with it.'

'Sounds like you've given up.'

'I need a bit of luck, like we had tonight.'

'3-1. Good result.'

'Scarcely deserved. Watford hit the woodwork three times.'

Nanna grasps the door handle to steady herself. 'That photo.'

'The one in the nightclub.'

'I was talking to Sally about it.'

'Believe me, Nanna. I really *was* trying to get away from that, er...' he chooses his words carefully '...young lady.'

'And Sally won't wear it.'

Dan shakes his head. 'And the rest of the "evidence", the hotel room and all that...'

'It looks damning, until you think about it.' Nanna leans on the door handle. 'And these days I have far too much time to think.'

Dan suddenly appreciates his hunched, 94-year-old grandmother is standing in the doorway with nowhere to sit.

'Here...' He gets up from the bed. 'I'll make us some tea.'

By the time his grandmother has creaked downstairs, Dan has brewed up.

'Only half a cup.' Nanna eases slowly into an armchair.

'Firstly,' says Dan, tray in hand. 'Why you are so bothered?'

'You think I'm being nosey.'

'It could be just another puzzle to solve. You and Sally. You've hit it off, big-time.' There is disaffection in his voice.

'Well, I...'

'When you get together it's as if I'm not there. Together, you are formidable.'

Nanna smiles wistfully. 'I never thought I would ever meet someone like Olwen.'

'Everything's changed.'

'Since I arrived?'

'Maybe. I'm not sure.' Dan slumps in an armchair. 'That's the problem. I'm not sure... about anything.'

'I felt like that for 70 years,' says Nanna.

'Well, I've told Sally the truth. I can't do any more.'

'Nonsense.'

Dan laughs, nervously. 'Well, what would *you* do?' He folds his arms defensively.

Nanna taps her head. 'I've thought about nothing else for days. I mean, *really* think it through, logically. You say you talked to Sally on the phone, that morning in Birmingham.'

'Yes.'

'You told her to dump her gear in your hotel room.'

'Yes.'

'So you hadn't been back to the room after returning from Newcastle.'

'No. I mean… what is this, Nanna? I haven't *murdered* anyone.'

'So you had no idea the girls were in your room?'

'No. My boss told me about them. I panicked and tried to head off Sally.'

'So you didn't deliberately tell her the wrong room number?'

'Of course not.'

'No.' Nanna ponders. 'No, that would have been too risky. Logically, had you done so, Sally could have gone down to reception and found the correct number. Instead…'

'…when my boss told me about the Geordies, I found Sally at the door of the wrong room and steered her away to the exhibition hall.'

'And when you eventually went to your room…'

'The girls had gone.'

'So.' Nanna narrows her eyes in concentration. 'We now need to establish the motive.'

'Nanna, we don't have a library to assemble in. Motive? For what?'

'For the rumours.'

'I'm not with you.'

'Someone – presumably this Dudley fellow, whatever his name is – had left them in the room to ensure you picked up the pieces.'

'His wife returned home earlier than expected. That's why he drove us to the hotel.'

'Ah.' Nanna takes a sip of tea. The cup rattles in the saucer. Her aim isn't so true these days. She gazes at the curtains without seeing them. This is more engaging than the crossword in front of her, though it may take a little longer to solve. 'What happened after the Geordies left your room? That's what we need to know. Let's just suppose they wanted to make you pay for your actions.'

'But I hadn't done anything.'

'Exactly. They could have come looking for you at the exhibition but didn't. They may have wanted to expose this Dudley fellow. I would. Do you know where he lives?'

'Somewhere near Dudley town centre. I can't recall the name of the road but it was quite near a shop called something and Crystal. I can't remember the something.'

'Well, you know what you've got to do.' Nanna leans forward in her chair and points to the door. 'Go up to Dudley and track down the man who's dropped you in it. It's your only hope.'

CHAPTER 40

Saturday 23 May 1914

Being Saturday, what with my shift finishing at lunchtime, Ma might have steamed open the letter before I got home. If she had, there was no sign. She couldn't read it in any case but that wouldn't have stopped her getting May across the road to tell her what it said.

I don't get many letters and I've certainly never had one before with a London postmark. I'd been expecting it, mind, so at least I was ready when Ma handed me the envelope. She was trying hard not to appear curious.

'I know what this is,' I said but didn't open it there and then. I went upstairs, changed and came down with the opened envelope in my hand.

'They'd sold out at the ground,' I said to Ma, all casual. 'They've sent me one like they promised.' In my other hand was a copy of the FA Cup Final programme. It's only four pages long but I will treasure it for life. There's an excellent picture of Tommy Boyle on the cover and, for me, it's the best penny I've ever spent. 'You never know, Ma, one day it might be worth a lot of money.'

The truth is, I had bought one in London and kept it in my room. Ma seemed to believe me. I chatted on, then went upstairs and read the letter. It was from Emily.

Dear Tom

I promised I would write and I've finally got the chance!! I hope you got back safely from the match. I'm sorry the day didn't turn out as expected. I really had no idea what prison was like before I was sentenced. The whole system is set up to humiliate you.

First of all they take away your clothes, every last stitch, and search you for concealed weapons. Then they make you take a bath. Each bath is separated by a partition but the low doors mean the wardresses can keep a beady eye on you. Ugh!!! You dress yourself from a pile of clothes lying on the floor. None of the prison dresses fit me. They are all too big and shapeless. They say they've nothing smaller but I doubt that's true. It means I am constantly tripping over myself, especially as the shoes they've given me are a couple of sizes too big and aren't even a pair. We all have to wear white caps and blue and white check aprons. They give us stockings made of thick, coarse wool. I asked for some suspenders to keep them up and they just laughed. As for underclothes, I will spare you the detail. I still have some pride!!!

On the way to my cell, I was given sheets for the bed (a straw mattress on four planks), a toothbrush, Bible, prayer book and religious tract 'The Narrow Way'. Once in the cell, which is about nine feet high and maybe ten feet by six, I was given a yellow badge to wear. On it is the number of my cell. No-one calls you by your name. I'm now 512.

They wake you at 5.30am, two hours before breakfast which consists of a pint of sweet tea, a small brown loaf and two ounces of butter (which has to last all day). We empty our slops, scrub the floor, then go to chapel for half an hour. In chapel and during the daily hour of exercise in the yard, we are not allowed to talk. Lunch is at noon and supper consists of a pint of cocoa with thick grease on top plus a small brown loaf. The electric light in the cell is controlled from outside and turned off at 8pm.

The other girls told me what to expect. Some of them have been inside three or four times now. However, it isn't until you experience it for yourself that you realise what it's actually like. We're the lucky ones, too. A lot of women are, how can I say, of the fallen variety! Some of them aren't much older than me and have already had two children. They rarely see them, if they haven't already had them taken away completely. When I say we're campaigning to make life better for them, they just call us posh do-gooders who don't know they're born. It's demoralising.

I told you there was a plan behind getting arrested but didn't explain. I thought you would try and talk me out of it. After two days in prison I went on hunger strike. Of course, they tested my resolve. From nowhere appeared a piping hot roast dinner with thick gravy, potatoes, carrots, peas and the smell of sage and onion stuffing. Intoxicating!!!!!! The wardress insisted on leaving it in the cell. The worst thing was hearing the other girls plead with me to eat it so they could no longer smell it.

I dare not fully describe the wardresses' next plan. Suffice to say that after seven days they threatened to force feed me. This involves pushing a tube through your nostril and pouring liquid food into your stomach. They did this to me just once. It is painful and, like everything in this place, humiliating. Several sisters, Helen Liddle and Sylvia Pankhurst to name just two, have been through it several times. They have been held down by eight people at a time.

The next day three wardresses, big and powerful, marched into my cell and told me they would return within 24 hours to put the tube in, well, another place!?! I spent the night petrified. All day I waited but they didn't come. Finally, another wardress told me I was being released under licence. It's to do with this Cat and Mouse Act. They let you out for a certain number of days to recover and then re-arrest you.

I am currently with some supporters who have been kinder than I can say. The trouble is that they are well known. The police know I am here and have the house under surveillance day and night. In a few days' time they will re-arrest me and send me straight back to prison. I am not as strong or courageous as the other sisters. I am no hero, Tom. I realise that now. The thought of going back to that cell has made me ill. We have worked out a way to get me away from here without the police knowing, before my licence runs out. I shall write again in a few days when we have hatched the plan properly. We will need your help, if it's not too much to ask!

Your loving Emily xxx

I made some excuse to Ma and walked out of the house with the letter in my pocket. I walked and walked. I must have gone round the lake at Taylor Park four or five times. I didn't know what to think. I didn't know what to do. I still don't. I'm not sure what I've got myself into. I wandered up to the church. The door to the hall wasn't locked. Being Saturday afternoon, Nellie was at the piano, on her own. I hoped she would be. I crept in and sat down where she couldn't see me. I didn't recognise all the pieces she was playing: *Canon in D*, yes, but the rest were new to me. She hit the odd bad note, let out a curse or two and carried on. She really does have a lovely touch. There was something comforting in being there. I thought I would stay a few minutes and then leave without disturbing her. Instead I closed my eyes and drifted off. I have no idea how long I had been dozing when she hit a difficult section. She slammed down the piano lid. I was startled and coughed.

'Who's that?' she said, nervously.

'It's only me… Tom.' I walked into the hall.

'How long have you been there?'

'Just arrived.'

'You should have said.'

'I didn't want to disturb you.'

'Why are you here?'

'I was just passing.'

'You're such a liar.'

'I know.'

She smiled. 'I'd given up on you.'

'You said you didn't like anyone listening.'

'For someone so bright…' She shook her head.

'I don't understand.'

'That's obvious.'

'What do you mean?'

She got up from the piano stool and started putting away her music.

'Don't stop,' I said.

'Time I finished. I have to hand back the key.'

'I'll walk you home.'

'So it's safe to be seen with *me*.' She threw me another reproachful look. 'Yes, of course, it's all right because I come from your end of town.'

'Ah, so this about Miss Bettridge.'

'You're wrapped around her rich little finger.'

'I don't know what you mean.' My voice was too weak to be convincing.

'You've been discreet, I'll give you that.'

'We're… friends.' It was too careful, I suppose.

'What about the "just good" bit in the middle?'

'Look, I must have done something wrong,' I said. 'Whatever it is, I'm sorry.' My apology (I'm still not sure I've done anything wrong) seemed to change everything. She dropped off the key and we walked towards her house.

'This isn't enough for you, is it?' she said.

'What isn't?'

'This.' By now we were walking past overgrown chimneys that pumped dark, dirty clouds into defenceless blue skies.

'We all have dreams,' I said.

'Like playing Chopin's *Fantasy-Impromptu in C sharp minor*, faultlessly.'

'I doubt you're far off.' I meant it, too.

'She's your way out of this.' Nellie pointed to the curling smoke.

'Emily, you mean.'

She nodded.

'Well, we both like football,' I said, trying to be casual.

'Oh, it's much more than that. More than you even realise yourself.'

She was right. Again. In the same way that Teddy Hughes was right about the pit. I don't know how but she teased it all out of me: that first meeting with Emily; the bike ride to Burnley; the raid on Borst's house; the Cup Final; the arrest. I had to tell someone.

'I wasn't imagining things, then,' she said.

'About what?'

'This town. It's not enough.' She looked down at her feet. 'I'm not enough.'

'Nellie, you're lovely.'

'You don't have to be polite.'

'I mean it.'

'I could never be enough.'

'Of course you are.'

'Then why do you look straight through me?'

Reading this journal back, I see what she means. I have looked round her, above her, below her. For the first time I was looking at Nellie Williams. We arrived at the end of her road. Some lads were playing football along the full length of the street with jumpers for goalposts. It was just a kick about but they celebrated each goal as if they'd won a cup final. Their shouts rebounded off the walls of the terraced houses. Grandparents sat by their doorsteps in the late afternoon sun, chatting to each other across the street.

'Embarrassing, isn't it?' said Nellie.

'What's embarrassing?'

'This.' She pointed along the road.

'I don't know what you mean.'

'We've no hope.' Nellie's house was at the bottom of the street, a dead end. She began walking away, quickly.

'I'll come to your door.'

'No need.'

I started walking after her but she waved me away without looking back. When I got home I was even more confused than when I'd left. I expected Ma to ask me where I'd been. I was working out which bits to admit to when I opened the front door.

'That you, Tom?'

'Yes.'

'You'd best be getting to the pithead. They say there's been an accident and half a dozen are trapped, including Billy.'

CHAPTER 41

So this is Dudley on a Saturday afternoon. Or *Dood-lay* as the locals pronounce it. Dan is searching for a shop called something and Crystal. What's the something? If only he could remember. He has foregone the trip to Middlesbrough (where Palace are 1-1 with minutes left) to drive up and down the side streets of Dudley town centre looking for a shop called something and Crystal. When a man loves a woman...

He had been half asleep when he saw the fascia from the window of Silent 'n' Dudley's car. That was more than two months ago. The last word stuck in his mind but not the first. Funny, that. Find the shop and he may be able to locate Silent's house. It was just a couple of blocks away. It's all he's got to go on.

He knows nothing about Dudley. Without a major football club the town has no personality: it is the wallflower of the West Midlands. Leicester has crisps. Grimsby, fish. West Ham, jellied eels. Burnley, Hovis. He saw no cobblestones or cloth caps on a recent away day to Turf Moor, that's true, but the town has character and has punched above its weight for decades. He seems to recall the club even won the FA Cup, way back when.

'Burnley will have to play better than this if they want to stay in the Premier League,' says a reporter on the radio. 'It's been a long while since they were last in the top tier of English football.' Dan thumps the steering wheel in annoyance. Yet another journalist forced to use a generic term - 'the top tier of English football' - to reflect the true, magnificent history of English football, caring little for the full narrative.

'United recently pulled off one of the greatest Premier League comebacks of all time,' says another presenter. *Of all time* – as though the Premier League and the Big Bang happened simultaneously. Learn some respect. Football League Division One survived two world wars, the Great Depression, the Cuban Missile Crisis, the destruction of the Berlin Wall and six albums by the Partridge Family. In 1992, this magnificent creation was dumped into the bin of history, replaced by the Premier League. Ironically, within a few short years, like a troubled adolescent teenager called Darren, the Premier League decided it didn't like the name given to it by its parents and changed its name by deed poll to the Premiership. Then, like a troubled adolescent teenager no longer called Darren, it decided the new, new name sucked and reverted to the Premier League. As messed up as Prince, formerly known as the Artist formerly known as Prince.

'Football League Division One... Football League Division One'. Kerb crawling the retail backstreets of Dudley, eyeing up every fascia from Nails 4 U to Naik's Mini Market, Dan murmurs the four words like a mantra. A crazy idea begins to brew in his mind, too crazy for words...

'Good afternoon,' says a voice on the radio. 'It's five o'clock and this is Sports Report. First, the classified football results read for us today by James Alexander Gordon.' Back in the good old days James Alexander Gordon ('Alexander' gives his name a strong midfield) called it as it was and ever should be: 'Football League Division One...' Dan sighs. More evidence that he was born too late. He looks left and right along another minor street. Pet Pantry. BetFred. Caspian Pizza. Still no sign of something and Crystal.

The powers that be must think the longer the Premier League exists, the more we will accept it. Perhaps the next generation will presume that Football League Division One was an obsolete curiosity, like Saint and Greavsie, shirts without sponsors, Grandstand's vidiprinter. Grandstand itself, for God's sake, never mind the vidiprinter. But this isn't Orwell's 1984. You cannot become immune to hearing something you know is not true. We are not the dead.

'Doncaster Rovers 1, Plymouth Argyle 2

'Ipswich Town 2, Reading 1

'Middlesbrough 1, Crystal Palace 1'

Dan sighs in relief. It's another valuable point in the battle to stay up, to stay alive - thanks to a header by Frenchman Alassane N'Diaye.

'N'Diaye will always love you...' he sings, turning down New Street, a name with built-in obsolescence. Surely, the good residents of Dood-lay could have thought of something more than... at *last!* This must be it. *Castle* and Crystal. He pulls up outside the store. Yes, that's the one. Now, if his hazy memory serves him correctly, he should take the first on the right. The road he needs will probably be the second on the left after that. He eases along in third gear. This is the one. He recalls the petrol station on the corner. Now which house? An overgrown hedge. Yes, he remembers that hedge. This must be the house. He gets out of the car, walks to the front door and rings the bell. There is no reply. He rings again. He knocks hard. And again. He bangs on the window.

'You're wasting your time.' It's a woman's voice in the garden next door. Dan looks over the fence. 'They won't come back. Tell the landlord to give up. He'll not get his rent.'

'I'm not after any money,' says Dan. 'I need to contact Silent 'n'... er, Garry.'

'Not been here for six weeks or more,' says the woman. 'Jane left a week later.'

'You're joking.'

'Only been here a year or so, the pair of them. I knew they wouldn't last. When you've been here as long as I have, you soon get the measure of people.'

'Any idea where they are?'

'They wouldn't tell *me*. I might point people in their direction. People that's owed money, like.'

'It's not about money. I just need to see him,' says Dan. 'I've come a long way.'

'I'd help if I could.' The woman disappears inside her house.

Dan kicks the garden gate. Now what? Or, more to the point, what would Nanna do? He wonders, should he call her but he knows what she would say. He has no choice. He must find Jade and Charlie himself. 'All right, Nanna. I'll do it,' he sighs. She has already given him the petrol money to get to Dudley. He has just about enough to get to the north-east and back.

Three hours later he sees signs for the A66(M) for Middlesbrough. How ironic. All those Palace cars he's passed going the other way, southbound. He could have gone to the game at the Riverside, if only he'd known. An hour later he walks into Mood in Newcastle. The code is 'dressy'. He is in a t-shirt and jeans he'd only throw on to empty the loft. A bouncer looks him up and down but, eyebrows raised, lets him in. It's this place again. 'Oomph-oomph-oomph…' The music booms, spotlights dart hysterically from ceiling to floor, picking out revellers who throw down drinks and shout at each other over the music (so called). He walks round and round the club, checking out the girls, feeling like a perve. This is the last place on Earth he wants to be, especially dressed like this. No sign of Jade and Charlie. Perhaps someone, a regular, will recognise them from the photos on his phone. The DJ finishes hyping up another interminable dance mix. Dan shows him pictures of the two girls. He shakes his head and points to the bar staff. Dan shows them the photo. One after another they shake their heads. Try the door, they say. Dan goes back to the bouncer who let him in.

'I'm looking for two girls,' he says.

'Dressed for the part, too,' smirks the bouncer.

'Yeah, well. Long story.' Dan shows him the photo.

'Met her on the internet, then?'

'No, in this club.'

'Never look as good in real life.'

'The photo was taken here, a few weeks back.'

'A Cockney, eh? You've come a long way. You must be James.'

'James?'

226

'You don't know your rhyming slang, then?'

'I'm not a Cockney.'

'James Dean.'

'James *Dean?*'

'Keen.' The bouncer nods beyond Dan's head. 'She's over there.'

Dan spins round. 'Where?'

'And there.' The bouncer points in the opposite direction. 'And there. They all look the same. Take your pick.' He turns away.

'You don't understand.' Dan follows him. 'It's, it's… a personal matter.'

'A rash.'

'It's not like that.'

'Look, thousands of girls pass me every week.' The bouncer takes another glance at the photo. 'I don't recognise her.'

'Have a closer look.' Dan zooms in on Charlie's face.

'Nope.'

Dan attempts to call up Jade's face but scrolls down Charlie's body by mistake.

'I've got a job to do, so if you don't mind,' says the bouncer. 'Wait a minute. What's that at the top of her leg?'

Dan enlarges Charlie's thigh.

'*Shag me, Shearer,*' reads the bouncer. 'I'd know that tattoo anywhere.'

'So you recognise her thigh and not her face?'

'Well, you don't look at the mantlepiece when you're stoking the fire, do you? It's Laura.'

'Laura?'

'That's her real name. Her "professional" name is Chickpoint Charlie. She's in and out of here with clients. They're on the game, those two.'

'You're, you're… kidding.'

'I'd keep well clear. Unless, of course,' he grins smugly, 'you come to some arrangement. Sometimes it pays to have friends in low places.'

'I need a phone number.'

'Can't help you.'

'But, you know them.'

'Not like that. I'd never call them and wouldn't tell you if I did. Try above the payphones along the street.'

Shocked, relieved, confused, Dan heads outside. Silent had paid the pair to go to Birmingham. No wonder they went willingly. He finds the phones. Time for the final embarrassment: he's a Billy No Mates, dressed like an NFA, hanging round public payphones, trying to act as if he's not really straining to read the names and numbers scrawled on prostitutes' adverts.

'Letitia... Water Sports... One-hour visits'

'Mistress Evilyn. Categories: Domination, Ethnic'

'Candy's College of Correction. Renowned for caning'

'Saturday Night Beaver. Whips and wet knees'

Dear God, help us. But he's in luck. Tucked high above She-Male Latin TV and Assisted Bubblebath, he spots Chickpoint Charlie. She specialises in A Levels: an unexpected academic talent or is he missing something? He dials. Moments later he is through to Charlie, Laura, whatever her name is. It is a moment or two before the penny drops (again) but, yes, of course she remembers Dan.

'It's a long story,' he begins, 'but I really, really need your help.'

'Your friend, the Silent Type,' says Charlie.

'He's not my friend...'

'He owes us £350.'

'Three hundred and... I don't know anything about that.'

'Well, I can't help you.'

'No, wait. I mean...'

The phone goes dead. Three hundred and fifty quid! Never mind Palace, at this rate Daniel James Howard will soon be in administration. How the hell did he manage to get himself into this? Sally has no idea where he is. If she knew he was phoning whores at midnight in Newcastle, she would go utterly mental. Who would blame her? In fact, for that matter, he has no idea where she is, either. He wanted all this resolved before the finals of *Britain's Got Tribute*. Now it could drag on indefinitely. Three hundred and fifty quid! Thanks, Silent. He wanders slowly along Gallowgate towards

Chinatown. Gaggles of good-timers pass him as if he doesn't exist. What to do? He hasn't any choice. He takes a deep, resigned breath. When all else fails.

'Nanna, it's Dan...'

CHAPTER 42

Sunday 24 May 1914

Ask anyone. There's nothing worse than waiting around at the pithead after an accident, especially when you're not sure if the lads trapped are dead or alive. Minutes seem like hours. Those up top are in shreds about relatives and friends. It does you no good at all to be there, feeling useless.

The blast happened where 14 level and the 19's crossgate. Methane, they reckon, judging by those lucky enough not to get caught up in it. One faulty lamp can trigger an explosion. There were still half a dozen unaccounted for when I reached the pithead. Men from the local rescue station are trained for emergencies and work day and night to bring men up alive. If Billy hadn't been trapped I might have hesitated when an idea came to me. One of the rescuers needed a break. It's exhausting work. He took off his breathing equipment and went to the canteen for a bite to eat. When the next crew set off below I put on his gear and followed. In the chaos and confusion, no-one knew it was me. As the cage dropped, I was even more nervous than my first day down. There was a chance I may not get back up. Most of all I worried about Billy and what condition he was in, if he was still alive. Life without him wasn't worth thinking about.

The leader of the team swore at me when he realised I shouldn't be with them but they needed all the help they could get so he didn't send me back up. All six men were behind the fall. The rescue team had already spent hours trying to work their way through to them. You have to go at it carefully and quickly and those two things fight against each other. At one point I thought the whole thing would collapse and we'd all be crushed. Finally, after three or four hours, we worked a gap, underneath a fallen girder. One by one we squeezed through. Albert Stribley was unconscious when we got to him. A big, strapping lad is Albert. He plays centre half in the colliery Second XI. We pulled him through the gap and onto a stretcher. Three times he got off the stretcher, breaking the straps, even though he was still unconscious.

'Quick, lads,' he shouted. 'Come on…' and his legs went nineteen to the dozen. Eerie, it was. We went back behind the fall and found Jack Chambers. He was a goner. His boots stuck out from under tons of rock, pit props and girders.

'Jack did nae feel a thing.' Billy was just beyond him, weak and short of breath. At least he was alive. Both his legs were wedged under a fall.

'Billy,' I said. 'Thank God.' It took him a few seconds to recognise me.

'What the…' He tried to move. 'What the hell are you doing down here?'

'I'm part of the rescue team.'

'Are you… heck as like.' He struggled for breath. 'Get back up top with your Ma and Pa.'

'I'm staying here until we get you out.'

'Don't be soft.' He coughed weakly. 'I'll not see daylight again.' He lost consciousness. The leader of the rescue team called me away.

'We'll be at least a couple of hours lifting this lot,' he said. 'Do you know him well?'

'Billy? Ever since I began.'

'Well, keep him awake. Swear at him if you have to. Forget you ever went to Sunday School.'

'But he's unconscious.'

'No buts… he'll slip away for good if you don't.'

So, while everybody else was hard at it, moving a mountain of rock and rubbish that threatened to squeeze the flickering life out of Billy, I talked to him. At him, more like.

'You Jocks you're in for one hell of a hammering when you come down our way,' I said. 'You were lucky to beat us last time out. That Jimmy McMenemy of yours. The one you call Napoleon...'

'Get under his skin. Make him react,' said the team leader. I don't know if I should put down the words I used next but I was under strict orders, if you know what I mean.

'Next time he'll meet his fucking Waterloo.' I've never written down that word before. Thank goodness Ma can't read. But it's what I said.

The team leader nodded. 'Keep going.'

'You're nothing but a little Scottish bag of wind. Always bleating on about how you jocks made football what it is today, how the boys from "Glasgae toon" invented the beautiful game. Funny how you all have to come down here to earn a decent bloody wage.'

Billy lifted two feeble fingers at me. The team leader nodded again. And so it went on. I'd do a little shouting, as if I was on the terraces. I even sung a hymn or two and *It's a Long Way to Crystal Palace*... I didn't sing the only Scottish song I know, *The Bonnie Bonnie Banks o' Loch Lomond*. That's all about dying, so Billy had told me.

Bit by bit they wedged up the load crushing him. Finally, after more than three hours, we got him onto a stretcher. I walked with him to the cage, his face ghostly white. I thought we had lost him for good. Maybe it was the motion of the stretcher that brought him round but he reached out a weak hand and grasped mine.

'For God's sake.' It was barely a whisper.

'Save your strength,' I said.

'You're worth more... more than this.'

'I don't what you mean.'

'The pit...'

'Billy, this can wait.'

'Get the hell out.'

He lost consciousness again. We got him up and away to hospital. The colliery manager gave me a right ticking off. If I had been injured he would have got the blame, what did I think I was playing at? I doffed my cap and apologised. He's only doing his job, after all.

Jack Chambers and George Hully (I didn't know him at all) died. The other four are in hospital. As I write it's still touch and go whether Billy pulls through. It's certain he won't work down the pit again, not with those injuries. Being at the face without him is unthinkable.

CHAPTER 43

As she feared. Four £10 notes and two fivers. That's all she has. Daniel needs £350. Nanna puts the money back inside the cushion and zips up the cover. The hole-in-the-wall cash machine is at the top of a steep hill. She hasn't yet tackled the slope. To the rest of the family, it's five minutes: for her, a major expedition. She must plan the journey in detail but all the preparation in the world cannot guarantee success. These days her mind makes contracts her body can't keep.

She could ask her daughter to take £300 from the account but that would lead to awkward questions. Why does she need the money? She could give the cash to Daniel on the quiet, but then it would appear as if she hadn't spent it. In which case, why take it out? Besides, they say you should never tell anyone your four-digit, personal PIN number thingy. If she could, she would keep all her cash handy, like before. She had seen the queues outside Northern Rock when it went bust. Then there was that bank that crashed in the USA. The name escapes her. Terrible business. The best place to keep cash is right next to you. She adjusts her cushion. She would keep it all in there if she could. There is something comforting about sitting back on your money. Talking of which, Chris Tarrant is at it again, in a mid-day repeat of *Who Wants To Be A Millionaire?*

'In the chair today is Dennis Roberts, a yogurt factory worker from Carlisle,' says Tarrant. 'Dennis stares at 15,000 gallons of yogurt every day... so you're a factory worker, Dennis. Realistically, what would be a nice sum of money to win today?'

'Well, a thousand pounds would do,' says the amiable Dennis.

'Fingers crossed,' says Tarrant.

She's right, is young Sally. Contestants with low-paid, manual jobs (refuse collectors, window cleaners, shelf stackers) find their work identities highlighted on shows like these. The more mundane the job, the more the presenter can ride to their financial rescue. Dennis is a northerner, with a strong accent. That supports the stereotype, as well. Without too much trouble, he answers enough questions to bank £32,000.

'Now then, Dennis,' says Tarrant. 'I won't ask you exactly how long but I imagine you need to work for some time in a yogurt factory to earn £32,000.'

'Six years,' volunteers Dennis.

'As much as that,' says Tarrant. 'Well, here goes for £64,000.'

Sally is spot on when she says she can recall no such discussion when an accountant or a teacher is in the chair. Nanna notes that this episode was first broadcast in 2002. She switches off the TV and wonders where Dennis is now, whether he understood if he was being typecast, or whether he even cared.

Everyone has left the house. Aware of family routines, she has an hour and a half to get up the hill and back without anyone knowing. It's now or never. She pushes herself up from the armchair by installments. She steadies herself. Time for one last visit to the little room. Olwyn had it just about right. Her old friend was out shopping one day and finally accepted she was past it when she kept looking for the nearest toilet, not shop. It also depressed Olwyn when an all-nighter had become all about not getting up to use the bathroom. There is a chance she could get caught short today, so she has drunk even less than normal, as a precaution.

The success of a major trip like this is in meticulous planning. She searches for the right footwear. She has five pairs of slippers and only one pair of decent outdoor shoes. They look brand new, too, even though they're five years old. She puts on her coat and wraps up warm. It's pleasant enough outside but you can't trust the weather. Front door key, walking stick, bank card: is that everything? To jog her short-term memory, she has been using a pen and notepad. She jotted down her PIN thingy on the notepad but can't remember where she put it. No matter.

She closes the front door behind her. She walks slowly down the street, perhaps 100 yards. Did the door close properly? She returns to make sure. She sets off again. It's nice to be out, nice to feel the warm sun on your face. If anything, it's a little too warm. She undoes the top bottom of her coat and loosens her scarf. The first length of pavement, to the crossroads, is flat. Other than a dog jumping up at her (she is loathe to use her stick to push him away) the walk is uneventful, if slow. She promises herself she will get out more often, now the weather is improving. This area doesn't have the drama or atmosphere of Neath, though. And there is so much traffic. So many cars. So many fumes that hang in the air. This street would have looked nice when it was first built but that was before the tyranny of the motor car. She passes small front garden after small front garden, destroyed and paved over to provide parking spaces.

She walks as quickly as she can over the zebra crossing. Cars edge impatiently. All right. All right. She can go no faster. There is a tetchiness about this town. She nods a hello or two to people who pass her on the pavement but no-one stops to talk. There was always a friendly face or two in Neath. She might chat to a total stranger there for hours. No-one here can spare the time.

Now then. She steadies herself. Time for the hill. Everything hurts and what doesn't hurt, doesn't work. She hauls and rests. Hauls and rests. For the umpteenth time she wonders if she is right to do this. There is something reprehensible about prostitution but that really isn't the point. Daniel is naïve enough to get himself into this kind of situation. At his age she was naïve enough to think Dafydd would be waiting for her. He wasn't. There was no-one to help them when it counted. She doesn't want the same for her grandson. If his relationship with young Sally falls apart, let it be for the right reasons. It's really warm now. She holds onto some railings, takes off her scarf and stuffs it untidily in a pocket. She loosens all the buttons of her coat. Slowly, the cashpoint machine comes into sight, at the end of a long parade of small shops. A bunch of school children tumble out of a sweet shop and almost knock her over. They scarcely notice her, still less apologise. She presses on, past Ladbrokes, Top Teen Nails, Rapid IT Solutions and the smell of burning fat rushing out of Superfryer.

Almost there. She rests. A gang of young lads, six or seven of them with those hoody things over their heads, are a few yards from the machine. Two of them are on pushbikes. They are listening to loud music booming out of a big radio, or whatever it is. She waits, nervously, hoping they will move on. Some of them are coloured. Sally would chide her for using that term and presuming they are any more hostile than their white peers. They haven't noticed her. They're too busy talking to care about her. She edges towards the cashpoint machine. She mops her brow.

Here goes... she fumbles around for the bank card. Which pocket did she put it in? She couldn't have lost it, surely. Ah, that's right. She put it in the pocket-inside-the-pocket for safe keeping. Which way round does it go? She's been told many times but can never remember. The card is refused. She turns it the other way. Still not right. Third time lucky. The screen is hard to read with the sun blazing overhead. She bends over and can just about make out the words. It wants her Personal Identification Number: the four-digit thingy. She had chosen a number to do with... what was it to do with? Kings and queens. She can remember the reigns of kings and queens going way back. She wrote the number on the jotter. The jotter is back at the house. Which king or queen? Which year? What event? All that knowledge, all that useless information she has acquired over the years and she cannot remember four numbers in a row. Maybe it was the year Victoria became queen. Slowly, carefully she presses the numbers 1, 8, 3 and 7.

'*Personal Identification Number incorrect,*' says the screen. '*You have two more attempts.*'

She takes a deep breath. The sun seems a lot hotter all of a sudden. It was so much easier when you went into a bank and everyone knew you and called you by your name. Now you're just a four-digit number you can't even remember. Come on, think. It was definitely something to do with a monarch. Maybe it was the current queen. 1, 9, 5 and 2.

'*Personal Identification Number incorrect. You have one more attempt.*'

She becomes light-headed with anxiety. She steadies herself. If the machine gobbles up her card it could be several days before she can access her money. Daniel needs it today. Trembling, she drops her walking stick with a clatter. She struggles to pick it up. Oh dear God, no. One of the coloured teenagers is sauntering over to her. His trousers are hanging untidily off his hips. His peaked cap is on the wrong way round.

'Give it a break, Wills,' shouts one of his friends.

'Yeah, leave the daft old bitch alone,' shouts another.

Her heart races. Her head buzzes. She grasps the side of the cash dispenser. Her legs buckle under her. He's going to attack her. His hands are deep in his pockets. She can't see what kind of weapon he has in those pockets. He picks up her walking stick. He is going to hit her.

'Lie down,' he says.

'Don't… don't hit me,' she says, weakly.

'Lie down on the ground.'

'I haven't any money.'

'If you don't lie down you'll fall down.' He takes off his jacket and makes it into a pillow. He feels her hands. 'Sweaty, as I feared. If you don't lie down you'll faint.'

Against every better nature known to mankind, Nanna lies down on the pavement.

'Right, I'm going to lift your legs slightly.'

'Oh dear God.'

'When did you last have a drink?'

'I… I don't remember.'

'How far have you come?'

'Only up the hill.'

'Walking?'

238

'Yes.'

'No wonder you're dehydrated.'

A member of the gang shouts at him to join them. They are on their way somewhere. Leave the old bag alone.

'Shut the fuck up and get the lady some water,' he shouts back. He turns to Nanna. 'Excuse my language. They don't understand otherwise.'

'I'll… I'll be all right, I'm sure.'

'That's what all the old folk tell my mother.'

'Your mother?'

'She's a GP.'

'Oh, I see.'

'Is there anyone I can phone to pick you up?'

'No, no… that would spoil everything.'

A gang member returns with a bottle of cold water. Nanna takes a few sips.

'So you're… you're not going to pinch my purse.' She is aware, in her anxiety, that the pitch of her voice is sing-song Welsh. The boy smiles.

'You can't be too careful.' He gestures towards his friends. 'Especially with chavs hanging around. I'm Joel, by the way.'

Slowly, surely, Nanna comes back from the brink. 'I… I thought someone just called you Wills.'

'He did.'

'How come?'

'It's an epithet.'

'Explain.'

'A nickname.'

'I know what an *epithet* is,' says Nanna, haughtily.

Joel laughs. 'You must be feeling better.' He nods towards the gang. 'I'm too posh for this lot. My dad's a baby father.'

'A *what*?'

'I wouldn't know him if I passed him in the street. My mother brought me up. I can't do all this "blood" and "fam" stuff.'

'This what?'

239

'You know, Jafaican.'

'No, I don't know.'

'This brother stuff, bro slang.'

'Oh, I see. I think. And they call you Wills…'

'Because I sound like Prince William. To them, anyway. And I sometimes put my hands behind my back like Charles when I walk. I can't help it.'

Nanna steadies herself and fumbles around for her card. 'Now then… I think you've solved my problem.' Joel helps her to her feet. She slots her bank card into the machine. Joel steps back. 'My number is the year Charles was invested as Prince of Wales by the Queen. It was 19…'

'Nooooo… don't tell me.' Joel puts his hands to his ears. 'You should never tell anyone your PIN.'

Nanna keys in 1, 9, 6 and 9. It works. She puts the cash in her purse.

'Is there anyone I can phone to pick you up?' says Joel.

'No.'

'In which case I'll get the bus with you.'

Twenty minutes later, Nanna is back home. Dan is first to arrive.

'How did the job hunting go?' she says.

'Not so good,' he says from the landing. He leans into the room. 'Dare I ask?'

'Yes, I have the money.' Nanna leans back on her cushion. 'Thanks to an angel who wouldn't leave the old bag alone.'

CHAPTER 44

Monday 8 June 1914

Nellie's reaction was only to be expected. 'You want me to do *what?*'

'It will only take a couple of minutes,' I said.

'And the whole morning to get there and back...'

'Well, yes.'

'... if we get back at all. We could be thrown into gaol.'

I knew it was a lot to ask but I couldn't think of anyone else capable of pulling it off.

Yesterday I received another letter from Emily. She is waking up with nightmares about being sent back to gaol and being forced fed. She's been sick with a fever for the past week and decided her days as a suffragette are over. The police don't know this, mind. As far as they are concerned she is still at the top of their wanted list. They've got their beady eyes on the house day and night and her licence has almost run out. In a few days they will re-arrest her and make her serve out the remainder of her sentence in prison. The owners of the house can do nothing to stop the police seizing her. She has to try and escape before then, without the police knowing. That's where Nellie comes in.

For the past two Saturdays I've met Nellie at the church, after piano practice. It has become a bit of a habit. We don't arrange to meet. That would make it feel as if we're going out but it's just the same, really. I suppose you could say she fills the gap left by Emily but it's not that simple. I really like her. We know all the same people and seem to laugh at the same things. I can talk to her about anything and anybody. Well, anybody except Emily. So when I suggested Nellie might help me rescue Emily, in broad daylight, I wasn't surprised she thought I was mad.

Of course Emily could sneak out of the house in the dead of night but several suffragettes have tried that. They've been caught and sent back to prison. So the plan is to try and fool the police when they least expect it. On Tuesday a cart is due to deliver coal to the house, as usual. The suffragettes have hired another cart which will arrive half an hour before the real one. I will be the coal man and Nellie will be my assistant.

'Me? On a coal cart?' she said.

'All you've got to do is take a sack into the coal bunker where Emily is staying and Emily will come out with the empty sack. Anyone watching will think it's the same person.'

'But I'm not strong enough to carry a sack of coal.'

'There will be fluffy cushions in the middle of the sack.'

'And they're going to believe I am a coal man!'

'You will be dressed like a lad.' I couldn't believe we were back to this routine. 'Emily will be dressed exactly the same.'

Nellie shook her head. 'But I don't even look like Emily.'

'You'll both be wearing those leather hats worn by coal men, the ones with a long flap down the back. Your hair will be tied up in a bun underneath.'

'But they'll still see my face.'

'Not with your hands above your head, holding the sack.' I showed her how. 'Both elbows will cover your face as you walk, like so. Besides, we'll put coal dust on you as well. They'll do the same to Emily and she'll come out carrying an empty sack. The police will think the lad who goes in is the lad who comes out.'

'You're really stuck on her, aren't you?'

'She's got herself in a jam. I want to help.'

'Because you love her.'

'Well...'

'Of course you do.'

'She's restless.'

'And that's exciting because you're restless, too.'

Nellie puts into words what you're thinking before you've even thought it.

'I'd understand if you refused to help,' I said.

'Are you sure she's not just a bored little rich girl and these capers, well, *they're ever such fun*?' Her impersonation of Emily was cruelly accurate.

I told her how Emily had been treated in prison, the forced feeding and her fever.

'And she's tugged your heart-strings.'

'Maybe.'

'She's used to getting her way. That lot always are.'

'I know. I'm not stupid.'

And so it went on. The conversation drifted to other things. We talked about the accident. Billy is recovering slowly, I'm relieved to say. We swapped a few songs and Nellie impersonated a few more people we both know. She can do Mrs Whitehead perfectly. Close your eyes and you'd think it's the old battleaxe herself. I hadn't finished laughing when she said: 'All right, I'll do it.'

'Do what?'

'Deliver the coal.'

'What's made you decide?'

'It sounds *ever such fun*. Besides, I've always fancied being a boy.'

CHAPTER 45

Chickpoint Charlie hadn't even heard of BACS. She certainly didn't want to be paid by it, whatever it was. Thanks to Nanna, Dan had sent £350 in £20 and £10 notes by registered post to a dubious address in Newcastle. The world's oldest profession demanded an outdated method of payment. That's how he rationalised it, anyway. Cash to hand, Charlie phoned him straight back. She couldn't be more helpful. In fact, she will help him out again in any way she can, at any time.

'A kind thought but not necessary,' Dan had replied. 'I just need you to talk to my girlfriend and tell her what *really* happened that night.'

'No problem, pet, but if you're ever up this way...'

'I'll bear it in mind.'

He won't, of course. He pulls up outside the rehearsal studio. He is early. Nice place, this. Much better than the garages and cramped living rooms in which the band usually rehearses. It's all been paid for by the producers of *Britain's Got Tribute*. And that's all thanks to Stu.

He checks in with the studio manager. She's a 20-something with long, frizzed hair pulled violently to one side, probably blown there and abandoned by a prevailing westerly. The other side of her head is shaved. A nit infestation, maybe? Very strange.

'Hi, I'm Dan. Dan Howard,' he says.

'OK, let me just see...' She checks her list but draws a blank.

'I'm part of the band.'

'The backing band, you mean?'

'Well, no. The band is called Born Too Late.'

'Hmmm.' She looks up and down her lists again. 'No, I don't have that here. I've got several other names. Sally Cavender…'

'Yes, Sally is one of us.'

'Phillip Worth. Is he in the band?'

'No.'

'Martin Price?'

'No.'

'I've got a Craig Clarkson. He's already in the studio.'

'No, he's not connected. How about Mark Sumner, our drummer?' says Dan.

'Can't see his name.'

'Kevin Yates?'

'Nothing here… I may not have an up-to-date list.'

The double doors of the studio entrance swing open. Born Too Late's guitarist walks in, clutching a couple of instruments.

'This is Graham, Graham Hall,' says Dan.

The receptionist leans to one side, the hair side. It seems to be pulling her over. She scratches the shaved side. 'Sorry, I haven't got him on the list.'

'OK, well I'll wait until Sally and Stu arrive.'

'Just as well we got here early,' says Graham.

They dump themselves on easy chairs in the studio's reception area and grab a coffee from the dispenser. A few minutes later Sally arrives. She waves a greeting to Dan and Graham and walks quickly to the reception.

'Hi babes.' Dan comes up behind her and attempts a hug. Sally murmurs a greeting as she signs her name at the counter.

'I need to have word,' says Dan.

'What about?'

'Us.'

'Now's not the time.'

'Now's *always* the time.'

'Stu will be here any minute.'

'This is important.'

Sally glances at her watch impatiently. 'It will have to be quick. Time is money in these places.'

'Hah! You're beginning to sound like him now.' Dan finds a quiet corner and explains the lengths he has gone to in tracking down Charlie. 'I want you to talk to her on the phone.'

'What – *now!*'

'Yes.'

'But, it's all in the past.'

'No it's not. You've never believed me. That means it's firmly in the present. I can prove I was telling you the truth.'

'Dan, this can wait.'

'No it can't.' He hands her his phone. She refuses to take it.

'I'm not talking to some two-bit whore.' She begins walking down the corridor as Stu comes into the reception. 'Sorry Dan but it isn't going to happen.'

'Yeah, we're both really sorry it's come to this,' says Stu. 'I wanted to tell you myself.'

Dan looks quizzically at Stu, then at Sally. 'Tell me? Tell me what?' Sally turns away. Stu looks at Sally.

'He doesn't know, then,' he says. Sally shakes her head and looks at the floor.

'Look, there's no easy way to say this, Dan,' says Stu. '*Britain's Got Tribute* have dropped the band.'

'Dropped the band?' Dan looks wildly at Sally then back at Stu. 'What do you mean, dropped the band?'

'They've decided Born Too Late doesn't work.'

'I don't get it. What are we all doing here then?'

'It's a last-minute decision. They want Sally as Mustbe Springfield, backed by session musicians. I'm sorry.'

Dan looks at Sally again, then at Stu, then Sally. 'How long have you known about this, Sals?' She offers no response. Instead, she looks at Stu for support. 'I can't believe it. Tell me you're both joking.'

'I'm afraid not,' says Stu. 'It's their show at the end of the day.'

246

'But… but the contract. We've signed a contract.'

'The contract is for a performance of Sally Cavender as Mustbe Springfield.'

'They can't change the rules.'

'They haven't changed the rules.'

'But… I don't get it. We come as a unit. They knew that. That's how we performed in Blackburn.'

'I know. It's disappointing. There's nothing more I can do.'

Something in his body language doesn't ring true. He is hardly looking at Dan. He seems anxious to get away. And why is Sally so sheepish all of a sudden? Normally she would be fighting for their rights, her above anyone.

'Hang on, hang on,' he says. 'None of this makes any sense. I don't think you've argued on our behalf at all. You've known about this all along. You agree with them. In fact, it's probably your idea.'

'Believe me, I've done my best,' says Stu.

'Bollocks.' Dan stares at Sally. 'And you. Why are you so quiet all of a sudden? If you knew about this before, why didn't you say anything?'

'You're not making it any easier,' she says.

'Making it… *what?* Oh, I get it. You've hatched this up together. That's why you've been so elusive. Anyone would think…' A cold cramp grips Dan's stomach. Ice runs through his veins. He suddenly feels detached from his body. He could be sick. 'Oh God. The pair of you. You are, aren't you? You, you… bastards.'

'That's quite enough,' says Stu.

'So you're not denying it. Sals?'

'You blew it.' She is still not looking at him.

'What do you mean I blew it?'

'You know full well.'

'Newcastle?'

She nods.

'How many more times? It was all lies. I've told you over and over.'

'This isn't getting us anywhere,' says Stu.

'Us? Who's us? This is all about you and her. It's not getting *you*

247

two anywhere. We've been stitched up.' Dan lunges at Stu. Caught off balance, Stu topples backwards. The pair of them land in a heap on the floor. Graham and Sally restrain Dan. The receptionist phones a studio and two engineers race out to the reception. Together, they pull Dan away. Stu brushes himself down.

'When you've cooled off we'll talk about this like grown-ups,' he says. 'Sally?' He gestures to her to follow him.

'No, Dan and I need a few minutes,' she says.

'OK, but there's work to be done.' He strides into one of the studios.

'Studio 4 is free for the next half hour, if the two of you need it,' says the receptionist, sympathetically. Dan and Sally nod their appreciation. Dan shuts the studio door behind them.

'I need to know, Sals. Is it true?'

Sally nods. Dan pounds the Steinway grand piano in anger then buries his head in his hands.

'I should have told you before,' says Sally.

'Too right.'

'You didn't tell me about going to Newcastle.'

'Because nothing happened.'

'You said you were in Birmingham.'

'I never touched those Geordies.'

'Why should I believe you?'

'Because it's the truth. I've spent the last week getting evidence to prove it.'

'Dan, I've had enough competing with your obsession. Every few days, for 90 minutes, the world stops turning. Take the other week – you squeezed me in during half-time. It's pathetic. And when the radio commentator said they're coming out early for the second half, so did you.'

Dan sits at the piano stool and stares at the floor. 'When did it all begin?'

'It doesn't matter.'

'Of course it matters. He's worked on you behind my back.'

'It wasn't like that.'

'I don't believe it.'

'If you must know, I asked him to pick me up outside Blackpool's ground. Seeing that website was the last straw.'

Dan walks round the studio. The piano lid is down. Still standing, he rests his arms on it, trying to avoid his pathetic reflection in the polished wood.

'No,' he says. 'No, he must have worked on you before that. It has to be more than anger and revenge. That's not your style. It goes back further. All those excuses about essays that needed to be handed in… bloody hell.' He points at Sally. 'Valentine's Day. He took you out on *Valentine's Day!* That's why you turned down the Lion King. He took you out on *friggin' Valentine's Day.*'

'You wanted to go to the match. Besides, there was nothing in it.'

'On *Valentine's Day?*'

'He just wanted to talk. It was the only time he had.'

Dan looks at her, incredulously. 'I thought you were better than that.'

'Better than picking up a couple of whores?'

'Is that it? Is that your only defence? Something you can't prove and which I have denied repeatedly?'

'Look, I'm sorry it had to come out like this. I was going to talk to you.'

'So…' Dan takes a shallow, anxious breath. 'This is a permanent thing. You're an item.'

'Yes.'

'And you're cool about it.'

'Dan, this isn't helping. Being with you, it's… it's like Princess Diana said about Charles and Camilla. The marriage was crowded. This football thing. It's like coping with a mistress.'

'It's nothing like that.'

'It is to me.'

Briefly, they fall silent.

'I'm sorry about the band,' she says, at last. 'I would rather have you and the lads supporting me.'

Dan starts clapping, slowly. 'Oh, that's brilliant. Supporting you. That sums it up. That sod has worked on you, all right. Got it into your pretty little head that you're already a star.'

'It's not like that. It's just that… this is an incredible opportunity. I'd be mad to turn it down.'

'For God's sake, Sals, listen to yourself. Next you'll be telling me it's something you've wanted all your life and it's a dream come true. The usual *X Factor* crap. You were beginning to sound like that when they interviewed you on Sky News. Bloody *hell*!' Dan spins round. 'That's why he put you on the plane to London. You went down together from Blackburn.' Again, Sally offers no denial. 'That does it.' He strides to the door.

'Dan… I didn't want it to end like this.'

'Enjoy your "personal journey", Sals. Look how far you've come in such a short space of time and all that bollocks.'

'Dan, I…'

'Make sure you soak it up, like they tell you to. Live the dream, babes. You'll be like every other over-hyped winner in six months' time, wondering what the hell *that* was all about.'

CHAPTER 46

Thursday 2 July 1914

For the second time in a month I found myself sitting next to a girl dressed as a lad. This one was decked out in a dirty old suit, her face covered in soot. It was the first time we had gone out together, too!

'You certainly know how to spoil a girl,' said Nellie. We were rattling along together, driving a cart pulled by a handsome carthorse named Dandy.

'It's good of you to do this, considering what you think of Emily,' I said.

'Oh, I don't dislike her.' Nellie threw me a sideways glance. 'I'm just envious – of what she has and how much you like her.'

'We're not… going out.'

'You don't need to be.'

What do you say to that? We reached the road where Emily was staying. I dare not say in which town. I am sworn to secrecy. Suffice to say (another Emily phrase) it's less than an hour from St Helens. The road is full of big houses where posh people live. We headed straight for the end of the road and passed a dozen properties on the way. The clattering of Dandy's huge hooves brought people out of their houses. I hadn't allowed for that. We pulled up outside the house where Emily was staying. At least, I hoped it was. A man followed us up the road.

'You're early this week,' he said. 'Why didn't you stop at mine?'

'I'm new to the round,' I said.

'What's happened to Eddie?'

Eddie is the regular coal man, so I was told.

'He's ill. We're standing in,' I said.

'Well, I need two more than usual.'

'All right,' I doffed my cap. 'I'll bring them in on the way back.'

That probably would have been the only drama if a well-dressed woman, probably in her sixties, hadn't called out at the top of her voice: 'Who are you? What are you doing down our street? Where's our regular man?'

'He's ill. We're standing in,' I repeated.

She looked at the name plate on the cart.

'You're a completely different firm,' she said. 'You're not coal merchants at all. Are you trying to pinch Eddie's round?'

'No, Eddie's cart is in for repair. I've had to borrow a different horse and wagon.' The woman came out of her garden and started arguing with me, loudly. All the commotion alerted more people. Within a minute there were four or five round the cart.

'That's the house,' I said to Nellie. 'Quick as you can.' She loaded the sack on her back and took it down a long path to the tradesman's entrance.

'Delivering to them first, eh?' said the woman. 'Didn't Eddie tell you to do the street in strict order?'

There was quite a crowd by now. Out of nowhere, three coppers appeared. They must have been the ones keeping an eye on the house. My heart sank.

'What's going on here?' said one of them.

'I'm standing in for Eddie, the regular coal man,' I said.

'What's the name and address of the company?' That threw me. I told him I was new, that I'd picked up the cart from a friend and that I was just doing what I had been told.

'Who's that working with you?' He pointed to Nellie. Out of the corner of my eye I could see Emily coming up the long path towards us with her empty sack.

'Oh, he's new too,' I said.

'Hmmm, looks like another swap to me,' he said. 'It isn't going to work this time.' Suddenly Emily cut across the front garden and ran full pelt down the street.

'After her,' said the copper, blowing his whistle. 'And you, stay right here, my lad.'

I have to say, Emily ran like the wind! Not bad for someone who has been so unwell. She reached the end of the street and disappeared to the right.

'They'll catch her soon enough,' said the copper. 'You'd better follow me.'

'I'm just doing what I was told,' I said.

'That's what they all say.'

'I've no idea what's going on.'

'Well, you can tell us everything you don't know, then.'

For the second time in a month I found myself sitting in a police station, wondering if I would be kept in overnight. Ma would have gone mad had she known where I was. I got to the police station well before Emily. They asked me all the usual questions. How long had I known her? Who hired me? I kept telling them I was just doing a job for someone without knowing what it was all about. They didn't believe me but I didn't care. The questions were becoming so tiresome (I must stop using Emily's favourite words). After an hour, the desk sergeant received a telephone call.

'They've got her,' he said. 'She was hiding in a coalbunker. Silly girl.'

Minutes later there was a right old commotion outside the station as the police brought in their catch.

'What are *you* doing here?' I said.

Nellie put a finger to her lips.

'So you *do* know the young lady,' said the copper. I couldn't deny it after my last comment. 'Are you aware she is one of the most dangerous suffragettes in the country?'

I laughed.

'But that's not...' I said. Nellie beckoned to me to say nothing. 'That's not... *fair*.'

It took them a while to accept they had the wrong person. We were small fry. The big fish had slipped out of the net. They let us both go with a stern warning. It could have been a lot worse. We were well away from the police station before Nellie explained what happened. Emily and her friends realised the noise at the front of the house would attract the police.

'I said I would run away as a decoy,' said Nellie. 'They said that wasn't fair on me but I started to run down the path before they had a chance to stop me. It worked. Emily will be a long way away by now.'

'You didn't have to do all that.' I gave her a hug and a kiss. It was our first. It lasted longer than I expected. I don't think it will be our last.

CHAPTER 47

'Bright lights, big city
'They've gone to my baby's head...'
The Animals' version, with Eric Burdon's Geordie growl, is darker, more brooding than the Stones' suburban cover. Head swimming in anger and Cragganmore, Dan digs out Jimmy Reed's original: a lolloping, lazy lament and, in his very humble and inebriated opinion, the best.
'Bright lights, big city
'They've gone to my baby's head
'I tried to tell the woman,
'But she don't believe a word that I said...'
Old bluesers like Reed were born too early and froze to death in gutters, clutching cheaper whisky. Jimmy sounds like Dan feels: slurred and smashed. Jimmy's wife, Mary 'Mama' Reed is on backing vocals. Yoko sang with Lennon. Linda with Macca. At least they knew their place: in the background. Well, apart from Yoko. Gawd help us when she starts wailing. Dan drains and re-fills his glass. He lies spread-eagled on his bed. Like Lennon, he's been duped. Sally saw him coming, too. Where is she now? Right now. He closes his eyes. He counts to ten. He can't believe it. She's still not here. The minutes crawl by like hours. Those incidents, so innocuous at the time, go round and round and round his head. He remembers her call on the train home from the Swansea match. Stu had phoned *her* about dates for the auditions. Born Too Late isn't *her* band. When

did she give him her number, anyway? That 'busy on my dissertation' bollocks. And Valentine's Day – the 'only time he had and he just wanted to talk'! Sod that. The smarmy git was quick to pick her up from Blackpool's ground. It must have been planned. All she needed was an excuse. And what about doing Dusty Springfield, when it was too late for any other option? The flight to London. The hotel room. Round and round and round go his thoughts, insanely, like the fairground waltzer on Lennon's *Being for the Benefit of Mr Kite*: an endless loop of rage and regret.

The only thing that dulls the pain is different pain. Wedged into the loop is a goal-line clearance by Marek Cech of West Bromwich Albion, earlier that evening. His brilliantly-timed lunge denied Darren Ambrose a certain winner for Palace in the last minute of injury time. Three points would have ensured the club avoided relegation to the 'third tier of English football' for the first time in 33 years.

But there are even bigger issues at stake than pride. Many fans, Tadworth Terry among them, gazed at the green, green grass of home that evening and feared they had seen the very last game *ever* at Selhurst Park. A win would have made the club more financially viable for prospective purchasers. Instead, the team needs to get at least a point from the last match of the season, at a tension-wracked Sheffield Wednesday on Sunday, to stay in the 'second tier of English football'. If Wednesday win, they stay up and Palace go down. Liquidation could follow. The stakes could hardly be higher.

'*Go ahead, pretty baby*
'*Honey, knock yourself out*
'*Oh go ahead, pretty baby*
'*Honey, knock yourself out*
'*I still love ya baby*
'*'Cause you don't know what it's all about.*'

Sally and English football: both getting shagged, big-time. Neither of them knows what it's all about. They don't want to know. There are still Palace fans hoping an oil-rich sheik will jet in and spray petro-dollars around SE25. Brendan Guilfoyle, the administrator trying to find a buyer for the club, had better be listening. No matter how perilous things are, we don't want to go the way of Chelsea, Manchester City and the rest. We don't want to become some plutocrat's fuck buddy. Dan tunes into a late-night, radio phone-in. Some of the punters' calls are pitiful.

'I've been a Chelsea season ticket holder for 25 years,' says one. 'I've been through the bad times...' Yeah, yeah, usual defence – proving you're no Johnny-Come-Lately glory seeker. Though happily basking in winning a trophy or two (at last), we know you're embarrassed at what's really happening at Stamford Bridge. But it isn't the punter's fault. The blokes at the top of the game, they're the ones pulling the strings. And we're allowing them to shaft us all. Time was that football was the working man's sport. Now there's very little change from £200 if you take a family of four to a match in what used to be the First Division.

A couple of callers have their heads screwed on, at least. Summing up the state of British football, one of them says: 'Drop a frog in cold water and heat it very slowly. It has no idea it's dying until it's too late.'

'We'll be right back with more of your calls after the break,' says the presenter.

'Gavin, 30, technician for Autoglass. One of my customers got a chip on her windscreen and didn't do anything about it until she went over a pothole – and crack!'

The ads are mind-numbingly dull and repetitive.

'Two or more cars? Don't pay a penny more for insurance than you need to! Make sure you save with Admiral's multi-car policy. Two cars, two discounts, one policy.'

Two or more cars? That'll be the day.

'Lock up, without. Lock up, within. You'll not let no-one steal your wheelie bin – with the fabulous new bin lock from Bintastic...'

CHAPTER 48

Tuesday 28 July 1914

The football season seems a long time ago. We've had cricket weather all summer. Some days you could fry an egg on the bonnet of a motor car, it's been that hot. I've scanned the newspaper every day for news of a suffragette on the run. The police want to put Emily back inside, what with her having four months still to serve. I have no idea where she is but no news is good news, I suppose.

'So?' said Ma.

'So what?' I said.

'Are we going to war?'

'Oh, that... I doubt it.'

'What does it say?

'About what?'

'About the crisis.'

'What crisis?

'The crisis in Europe.'

'I don't know.' And I didn't. For once, I wasn't even reading the back pages, either.

'Only this feller they shot.'

'The archduke.'

'Aye, that's the one.'

'What about him?'

'They say it's all boiling over because of that.'

'Who are they?'

'Well, *people...*'

It must be terrible not to be able to read. It means Ma can only pick up bits and pieces from everyone else. She's bright enough but when you're a girl and the eldest of eight, your first job is to help your mother bring up the family. She had no time left to go to school. I turned to the front pages of today's newspaper.

'The situation in Europe is grave,' I read. 'Austria has broken off diplomatic relations with Serbia and Russia has threatened to come to the support of Serbia. Germany and France would in all probability enter the conflict.'

'There you are, I told you.'

'Nellie thinks the royals will get round a table and sort it out. They're related, after all.'

'So, you and Nellie. You seem to have become... *friends.*'

I knew that mentioning Nellie would take her mind off politics.

'It's not serious.'

'Is she saying that, or just you?'

'Both of us.'

Ma just smiled. 'I saw Nellie's mum yesterday. We're making plans.'

That's the problem. Get attached to anyone a few streets away and your life is as good as over. It's all mapped out. I could end up like our Walter. He lives three doors down from my aunt in Burnley. On his wage, he'll be there for the rest of his life, I shouldn't wonder. He delivers milk for a living but he's a right Mr Fix It in his spare time. Mends anything, he does. He could use his skills if someone pointed him in the right direction. No-one will. That's exactly how I could end up. Billy's right. I need to do something more than dig up dead trees. It's all very well Mrs Knapp saying I should carry on writing but I posted my report of the FA Cup Final to the Burnley Post and haven't heard a dickie bird. I'd like to have written about what *really* happened, with Emily and the police and what have you, but I doubt anyone would believe me.

Eddie Mosscrop has got it sorted. When his football career at Burnley is over he can carry on teaching. He's got the best of both worlds. Mind you, he was the only one who couldn't go on the team's summer tour of Europe. The School Board wouldn't give him permission. He had to report back for the exam period. Imagine sitting in a classroom in this heat, wearing one of those long black gowns. All the time you'd be thinking about your pals, going to places you can only dream about, playing some of the best teams in the world.

That reminds me. I took Nellie to Burnley the other day. She had never been before. It was boiling hot in Scott Park. There's a huge flowerbed celebrating our victory at the Crystal Palace. They've used more than 2000 plants, someone said. All the players' names, and the cup, are in claret, blue and gold flowers. What a sight and smell. After a cool drink or two we called in at Walter's. Well, we had to really. They were all over Nellie, of course. As Hilda, Walter's wife, said: 'You're one of us, aren't you, love?' Walter brought out his piano accordion. He isn't much good and he struggled through *Lily of Laguna* and a couple of other tunes before Nellie took over. I had no idea she could play the accordion, too. She had them all up and dancing to the *Can Can* and *Sailors' Hornpipe*. So much for that shy little thing I once knew. Or didn't. I kept wondering what they would have made of Emily. Nellie must have read my thoughts.

'When Hilda said "You're one of us", I saw your face,' said Nellie. We were walking back to Burnley station.

'I was pleased,' I said.

'No you weren't. It's the last thing you want, someone who fits in.'

'That's not true.'

'You want to fly the nest and Emily can fix it.'

I didn't even try to answer. We were right back where we started. We hardly said a word to each other on the way home. She marched off down her street before I had a chance to say goodbye. I've never felt so mixed up inside as I do tonight.

CHAPTER 49

It is Sunday 2nd May 2010. Scarves flutter from Tadworth Terry's Audi as it zips up the M1 to Sheffield Wednesday's Hillsborough ground. After 105 years of league football, Palace may be about to play their last game. Ever. That's why Terry, Wretched Car Crook and Dan are taut, tense and queasy like Sunday morning.

'Crank up the Beach Boys, baby. Don't let the music stop.' Dan instructs Tadworth Denise (Terry's wife) from the back seat. Denise is unaware that the instruction is, in itself, a song lyric. She dutifully obeys. Brian Wilson's umpteen-part harmonies spiral and dive, swoop and fall, bringing a measure of west coast calm to a car wracked with nervous tension.

'Ooh, this is my favourite. Ba-ba-ba, Ba-ba-ra Ann,' sings Denise. Dan groans.

'I thought you liked the Beach Boys,' she says.

'Wilson was more inventive than this.'

'He went a bit weird, didn't he?'

'Genius and madness, it's a thin line.'

'I like their surfing songs best.'

'Most punters do.'

'What's that supposed to mean?'

'It's formula pop.'

'Well, I like it.'

'You can't compare it to *Pet Sounds*. That was ground-breaking.'

'Pet what?'

'And *Smile*.'

'Never heard of it.'

'That figures.'

'Hey…' Terry fixes Dan in the rear-view mirror. 'Whatever's happened between you and Sally, don't take it out on the rest of us.'

Dan grunts half an apology. He knows he is being smug and superior but he just can't help himself. He avoided *Britain's Got Tribute* on TV last night. It was too painful, too close. Nanna knocked on his door to tell him Sally was 'through to the next round'. Yes, Sally had gushed a bit but she didn't do the 'dream come true' routine. Thank God. In fact, Nanna said she looked decidedly uneasy but maybe that was just a grandmother sweetening a bitter pill.

'Who's going to win it for us today?' Diplomatically, Wretched switches the conversation from *Help Me, Rhonda* to Hillsborough.

'The big match players, like Ambrose. This is their stage,' offers Terry.

'We'll need some of the unsung brigade to come to the party, too,' says Wretched.

'Let's just hope there are more heroes than villains,' says Dan. No-one gets the song reference and he feels too chastened to push the point. To kill time, he sketches his own dream team on a piece of paper. A draw is all Palace need and he has the perfect line-up.

'I've gone a tad defensive,' he says. 'It's important not to concede. In goal, no question. The hands of God: Julian Speroni. I'm plumping for a flat back four. On the right, an Olympic-sized swimming pool of starving Piranha fish with a centre back pairing of the number 468 London bus and an unexploded World War II bomb. At left back, Muslim cleric Abu Qatada. Protecting the back four, Anne Widdecombe. She's all we need across midfield. If the odd flukey goal is required, I'd put Steve Claridge's shin up front…'

'Steve who's *what*?' says Denise. Hard to believe but this most desperate of affairs is her first football match. Ever.

'Claridge scored a winner against us in the last minute of injury time. It hit his shin and went in. Leicester were promoted in our place,' explains Terry.

'Oh...'

The exercise has burned up some long minutes and eased the tension. Dan taps the top pocket of his jacket for luck. In it is a small plastic bag with nothing inside but crumbling dust. But what dust! A square inch of the Edgeley Park pitch, dug up after Palace grabbed that 87th-minute Freedman winner against Stockport County: a goal which maintained the club's status in League Division One (or whatever it was called then).

The foursome arrives in Sheffield, to a sea of blue and white and red and blue. Fans of both sides stride towards Hillsborough, decked out in replica shirts, draped in flags, daubed in paint.

'I just want it all over and done with,' says Wretched, parking in a side street above the ground. He could do with some of that paint. His face is an insipid grey. There is, of course, no essential pleasure in this fixture. It is not a triumphant Wembley final where both clubs bask in early summer sunshine and celebrate a fine cup run. This match is about avoiding a trap door to that depressing underworld of Hartlepool United on a bitterly-cold Tuesday night in February. It has to be said, though, that for thousands of Palace fans milling around Hillsborough, a trip to the north-east coast on a bitterly-cold Tuesday night in February is preferable to *no trip at all.*

With Steve Claridge's shin unavailable (a season-long loan to BBC Radio Five Live), Alan Lee plays up front for Palace. And it is Lee who gets up to a corner swung over by Darren Ambrose to thump an unstoppable header into the Wednesday net: a training ground routine delivered to perfection. 1-0 after 24 minutes. Now Wednesday need two to stay up. The 5,700-strong red and blue faction, already out-singing more than 30,000 home fans, bounces with joy. Dan hugs a startled Denise. He has never hugged Denise before. He has never wanted to. He has often wondered why Terry wants to. She would do well not to take Dan's overtures personally. Had she been a giant porcupine with halitosis, he would hug her just the same.

The goal takes the stuffing out of the home team. They create little by way of real chances until two minutes before the interval.

Wednesday's Leon Clarke pickpockets Danny Butterfield (from the away end, it looks a clear foul) and unfurls a delicious, rising drive. A despairing Speroni gets a glove to the ball but cannot stop it nestling in the right-hand corner of the net. 1-1. The Wednesday fans wake up at last. Leon Clarke, however, hasn't studied the American Journal of Sports Medicine. According to a report published in the journal, six per cent of injuries are caused by goal celebrations. Injuries range from ligament and muscle strains (knee sliding) to rib and clavicle fractures (players piling on top of each other). Real Salt Lake's Fabian Espindola was one such casualty. During a match against LA Galaxy, Espindola headed the ball into the net. In front of adoring fans, he back-flipped in celebration, breaking an ankle in the process. It kept him out for two months. In a cruel twist of fate, Espindola's goal was ruled offside. Worse still, Paolo Diogo of Portugal leaped into the crowd to celebrate a goal for Swiss club Servette, catching his wedding ring on perimeter fencing. The top of his finger was ripped off. The finger was found but surgeons were unable to reattach it.

Unaware of these mishaps, a pumped-up Leon Clarke celebrates his equaliser by kicking the advertising hoarding in unfettered joy. Solid, no-nonsense football boots are a thing of the long-gone past. Clarke dislocates a toe and has to sit out the rest of the match. Something approaching justice has been meted out, as far as the away fans are concerned.

Half-time. The game is on a knife-edge. Dan's sphincter muscle has played a disciplined, holding role for more than an hour. He heads to the Gents. With almost 6000 bladders stretched to crisis point by warm lager, he fears joining the end of a very long queue. He'll be lucky to get back before the start of another angst-ridden half. He enters the toilet and steps back in astonishment. The back of the wardrobe leading to Narnia could not deliver a greater surprise. Facing him is the longest row of urinals he has ever seen, stretching off in the distance, left and right. Uretha! No need to stand three or four deep, flies down at the ready, shuffling forward, shoulder to shoulder. Simply pick your spot and point Percy. Mind you, being at the top of the stand it's a miracle the whole lot hasn't come crashing down to pitch level through sheer weight of porcelain. In spite of a huge number of hyped-up fans, the toilet is virtually silent. Everyone stares forward, breathing deeply (though not through the nose), dealing with the torment of that equaliser in his own private way. Even the urine itself seems to sympathise, tinkling against the Armitage Shanks with more solemnity than usual.

Bouyed by their goal, Wednesday come out for the second half on the front foot. They dictate play for more than 15 minutes with Palace unable to mount a serious attack. The Owls' Luke Varney wriggles clear but shoots straight at Speroni. For all their dominance, Wednesday fail to score. In the 62nd minute, Palace starlet Sean Scannell works his way to the by-line and pulls the ball back to Ambrose, lurking on the edge of the penalty area. Head down, eyes locked on the ball, he drills the ball low past Lee Grant. 2-1. The Palace midfielder cannot be a subscriber to the American Journal of Sports Medicine, either. He knee slides in front of the ecstatic away fans. Sean Derry knee slides towards him. The rest of the team jump on top, risking rib and clavicle fractures.

Now Palace defend deeply. While every minute passes all-too-slowly, Speroni is scarcely troubled. Both managers begin tactical substitutions. On such decisions are reputations made or lost. Memorably, Sir Alex Ferguson pulled off strikers Andy Cole and Dwight Yorke in the 1999 European Champions League Final against Bayern Munich. Their replacements, Sheringham and Solksjaer, scored twice in injury time to snatch the trophy in a frenzied finale. Conversely, with England winning 2-0 against West Germany in a 1970 World Cup quarter-final, Sir Alf Ramsay called off Bobby Charlton with some 20 minutes left, ostensibly to save the 32-year-old's legs for the semi-final. There are those who argue that, as a footballing nation, we have still to recover from that decision. West Germany won 3-2.

Now it is these two gaffers' turn to prove their worth by weaving a little tactical magic. Wednesday's Alan Irvine brings on former Palace junior Tom Soares. Surely Tom won't come back to haunt us. Dan banishes the notion by touching the holy relic of Stockport dust. Palace manager Paul Hart takes off Sean Scannell and brings on Stern John.

John may well have scored 70 times for Trinidad and Tobago. He may well be the fifth-highest goal scorer in the history of international football. He may well have bagged a vital point for Palace at Derby County with a sweet turn and finish. But that is all in the past. It is what you do now in the emotional cauldron that is *Hellsborough*. Stern John must play his part for the team and those 5,700 desperate fans.

Three minutes are left on the clock and the away end begins to celebrate. Surely the work is as good as done. Wednesday still need two goals. They win a throw-in deep in the Palace half. Centre back Darren Purse chugs up to the Palace penalty area.

He's your player, Stern John! You need to follow Darren Purse!

But for Stern, read Elton. And we all know how *that* Mr John would rather follow roads made of sunshine-coloured brick. Unmarked, and less than two yards from goal, Purse gets to Beevers' deft flick-on and slides the ball into the bottom right-hand corner of the net. 2-2. Thirty-one thousand home fans believe again. Stern John is still standing, yards from his opponent.

Dan sinks into his seat, head in hands. Denise checks her watch.

'Will there be extra time?' she says.

'No,' says Terry. 'It's a league game.'

'What's the difference?'

'Well… you see… I'll explain afterwards, love.'

Now it's the Alamo. Wednesday pour forward. Palace defend desperately. Mattie Lawrence makes a last-ditch tackle. Speroni falls on the ball. Halfway through five eternal minutes of added time, the ball is cleared to Darren Ambrose, just short of halfway. With Wednesday committed to all-out attack, it is suddenly two versus one. Ambrose passes to Stern John. He has already proved to be a villain but the languid West Indian can still become a hero. He is given an undeserved shot at redemption. He advances unchallenged into the penalty area. All he has to do is look up and pass back to an unmarked Ambrose in front of goal.

All you have to do is look up...

They burned effigies of David Beckham when his sending off cost England the match against Argentina in the 1998 World Cup. The Daily Mirror even published a dartboard with his face on.

All you have to do is look up...

Conversely, they are still campaigning for a town centre statue of on-loan goalkeeper Jimmy Glass, who scored that astonishing injury-time goal to keep Carlisle in the Football League. Stern John can still be a hero or a villain.

All you have to do is look up...

Stern John doesn't look up. Someone who's scored 70 times for Trinidad and Tobago doesn't need to look up. He's at the Palace now and just can't wait to be king. With goalkeeper Lee Grant advancing to narrow the angle, John goes for glory. Grant gets a big hand to it and the ball bounces behind him towards the goal – once, twice, three times. Each bounce takes at least one full rotation of the Earth. The ball kisses the post – a brief peck, no tongues – and takes a 90 degree deviation along the goal-line. It *must* cross the line. It *has* to cross the line. Ambrose accelerates goalwards to make sure but Grant scrambles back and drops on the ball. It hasn't crossed the line.

The course of the next two minutes will decide whether Stern John dare set foot in SE25 ever again. He will either slink away, forgotten in the euphoria of survival or, 60 years on, still be remembered and reviled. Two minutes is going to be a long, long time. Now he must pray the defence holds on. Wednesday get another throw in. A flicked header. Speroni gathers. Now they get a free kick in their own half. Grant launches it long. McCarthy heads it out for a Wednesday corner. But there's no time to take it. The referee blows his whistle once, twice, three times.

'Are there penalties now?' says Denise. 'They're the best bit.'

No-one's listening.

'We are staying up, say, we are staying up,' sing the 5,700. Several Palace players run to the away end to celebrate with the fans. Meanwhile, Julian Speroni, God in a green jersey, ministers consolation to the Wednesday players who lie distraught on the ground. Dan is too busy singing at a small bunch of Wednesday fans on the pitch, to take any notice of his phone. It buzzes with incoming texts. More than 20 minutes after the final whistle, the away end doors are finally opened. Dan checks those messages. The first one had arrived a mere 20 seconds after the final whistle.

'Really pleased you've stayed up. Never been so nervous watching anything in my life. Sally x'.

CHAPTER 50

Wednesday 9 September 1914

We looked a rum bunch, hanging around outside Baxter Street Sunday School this morning. There were mill hands, office clerks, school boys (who never go). Some of the lads were leaning on the wall, cracking jokes and rolling their own. It's hard to believe Lord Kitchener is going to make an army out of us. Arthur Foster and Harry Grabham were in the queue. They think we'll send Fritz packing before Christmas. They can't wait to get stuck in before it's all over. Both of them were laid off two months ago, so this little skirmish has come at a good time for them. By joining one of these lads' battalions, we all get to be with our mates (well, better the devil you know and all that). The pay is decent, too. £1 1s a week.

One by one they called us in.

'Sit in the chair, son,' said the doctor. I suppose he was a doctor. He never said he wasn't.

'Nine stone six pounds,' said someone behind me. I didn't realise I was sitting in a weighing chair. I don't remember ever being weighed before. A clerk at a desk in the corner wrote down the figures.

'Stand up,' said the doctor. 'Take off your shirt and expand your chest... thirty-seven inches,' he called. The clerk scribbled. 'Now stand here.' I stood under a height scale. 'Five foot nine.' The clerk scribbled again. The doctor got out a stethoscope and tapped around for a bit. 'Open your mouth.' He looked at my teeth and seemed satisfied. 'Now tell me what those letters are on the wall.' The letters are in rows and get smaller and smaller the further down you go. I couldn't help thinking of Ma. She'd never let on, of course. She'd probably just guess and fail rather than admit the truth.

'Hmmm... well, you're in good shape,' he said.

'Thank you,' I said.

'You're a miner?'

'Yes sir.'

'And you play a bit of sport, by the looks of it.'

'Football, whenever I can.'

'We'll put together a battalion team.'

'I'd like that, sir.'

'How old are you?'

'16.'

'Hmmm... are you sure?'

'I could fetch my birth certificate.'

'No, no. That won't be necessary.' He put a finger to his ear and waggled it around a bit. 'My hearing isn't what it used to be, I'm afraid. What age did you say you were?'

'16, sir.'

He stood up and looked straight at me. 'No, sorry. I didn't quite catch that. Come back this afternoon when you're a bit older.'

'I'll see what I can do.'

'Good lad... *next!*'

I went back after lunch. He acted as if he'd never seen me before. This time the examination lasted all of a minute.

'By the way, how old are you?' he said. 'And speak up, son, because I'm a little deaf.'

'18, sir.'

'Ah, that will do very nicely.'

He sent me to another room with half a dozen others. A man told us he was the Recruiting Officer and gave us each a copy of the New Testament.

'Kiss the book then take it in your right hand and say after me "I swear"...'

'I swear,' we all said.

'To serve His Majesty the King…'

'To serve his Majesty the King…'

There were more words, something about being obedient to the officers put over us. We all shook hands and I went with Arthur and Harry to collect our first day's pay from the town hall.

'So, you've decided to come back 'ome to Burnley. Very wise,' said Arthur, pocketing a handful of coppers. 'That posh girl of yours, what's she got to say about it?'

'She's not my girl,' I said. One stolen kiss halfway up an oak tree, that's all it amounts to. I've come to accept that Emily Bettridge isn't anybody's but her own. It's been weeks since Nellie and I helped her escape. She's still on the run and I've no idea where she is. They know I am connected with her and, because of that, I think I am being watched. They could be reading letters sent to our house, as well. Envelopes arrive, looking as if they've been opened and re-sealed. Whatever the case I've decided to make the break. That's why I've answered Kitchener's call. I might as well enjoy the ride. I doubt we'll see any action. They say the regular army will be back home by the time the carol singers are out and about.

'She's a fine-looking one, that Emily.' By now Harry had bevvied away most of his pay.

'Plenty more fish in the sea,' I said. 'Anyway, I've met another lass.'

'I'll bet she's posh, too,' said Arthur.

'No, she's one of us.'

One of us. I don't even know what I mean by that. I'm not sure who 'we' are or if I belong anywhere. Until I've got Lady Bettridge out of my system I'm no good to anyone, least of all Nellie. Being part of the Burnley Pals Battalion will give me some breathing space. Our Walter's also joined up so I'll be billeted in Burnley with him. It means I'll get a chance to see a few games at Turf Moor as well. Harry had a map of Belgium spread open on the table.

'I can't even say some of these places,' he said. 'You're the one for words, Dawsie. What town's this?' He pointed to Beauvois.

'I think it's pronounced Bove-*wah*,' I said.

'Ooh, Bove-*wah*,' they said. 'Maybe we should stop for cocktails at La Carrie… Carri-ere, is it?'

He and Arthur are treating it all like a bit of a Sunday School outing. Whether there's a picnic at the end of it, well, we'll have to wait and see.

CHAPTER 51

Nanna abandons The Times' crossword after only two minutes and five completed clues: a sacrilegious and unprecedented act that may require absolution. Distracted and preoccupied, she tosses the paper onto the occasional table in front of her. Word conundrums are easy to solve. Human ones are more complicated. Dan and Sally. Dan and Sally. She shakes her head and chides herself for not acting sooner. Sally had confided in her about the relationship. With the depressing benefit of hindsight, she should have listened more. What to do now? Should she do anything? Maybe it's none of her business. Maybe she's just another meddling old woman with nothing better to do with her time. Or is that an excuse to duck responsibility? Conundrums. Dilemmas. She glances at her watch. Dan will be back soon. At least the result in Sheffield today will have lifted his spirits.

Dan arrives, surprisingly subdued.

'Quite a game,' offers Nanna.

'More like a torture session.'

Nanna nods. 'I'd have been hiding behind my chair if I could still bend down that far. As for your Stan John...'

'*Stern* John.'

'... he nearly cost you the game.'

'Shocking. Just shocking. Thank God we had some heroes, too.'

'Well, you're safe for another season in Division Two.'

'That's what it *used* to be called.'

'What is it now, then?'

'The Championship.'

'I thought that was the new name for the European Cup.'

'No, that's the Champions' *League*.'

'I thought it was a cup competition.'

'It replaced the European Cup.'

'But it's a league.'

'And a cup.'

'The teams that play in it, they're not all champions.'

'Don't start me.'

'I don't get it.'

'You're not supposed to, Nanna. It's all decided in smoke-filled rooms by the rich elite.'

'So?'

'So what?'

'So what are you going to do about it?'

Dan shrugs his shoulders. 'Nothing I can do.'

'Nonsense.'

'Nanna, I'm just another mug punter.'

'Exactly.'

'…like millions of others.'

'…letting the powerful few dictate and control. They're counting on you to moan but carry on going to games, spending your money.'

The house telephone rings.

'Whoever it is has tried several times today,' says Nanna. 'I haven't picked it up. It won't be for me.'

Grandmother and grandson throw a knowing glance at each other. But it isn't her. Dan picks up the receiver.

'I'm trying to contact a Rhoslyn Cadogan.' It's a female voice.

'And this is…' says Dan, carefully.

'Elen, a reporter on the South Wales Express. I'd like to follow up a lead given to us by a Dafydd Broderick. He was re-united with Rhoslyn after seeing her on a TV programme. We thought it would be great to interview both Dafydd and Rhoslyn together, 70 years on. Quite a story!'

'Ah, well… she's not here right now,' says Dan. 'I'll let her know you called.'

'We won't be intrusive.'

'No, I understand.'

'Our readers love these happy reunions.'

'I'm sure.'

'You *will* pass on my message…'

'Of course.'

'My number is 02920 574093.'

Dan jots down the number and relates the call to Nanna.

'Well, I never,' she says. 'You could learn a lesson or two from young Dafydd.'

'What do you mean?'

'He knows how to work the media.'

'I don't understand.'

'Dear, dear me. Use your noddle. You're the one born into this world of 24-hour TV and the like. Dafydd knows I'm not going to pursue the relationship so he's using a newspaper to bring us together again. I've got to give him credit. For years I've avoided these reporter types but now I realise how much you can use them to your advantage. I've learned a lot from that young lady of yours.' Nanna looks at Dan apologetically. 'I know… I'm sorry. I can't believe you are not… it doesn't seem right.'

Dan acknowledges her faux pas graciously. 'I see what you mean. An old, blind man discovers his first love is still alive after 70 years, the original relationship severed by the war. Like the woman said, it's a great story.'

'And it puts me on the back foot. Now I've got to respond. I was afraid of something like this when the TV first called me about the war. They'll go digging around.'

'But what is there left to find?'

Nanna is silent.

'Nanna?'

'Well, you can never be quite sure.'

'They already know about Bletchley Park.'

'Yes, but one thing leads to another.'

'What other?'

'They may start looking into our family history – distant relatives, that sort of thing. You've seen these TV programmes. When they start, they never stop.'

'But your father and mother were pillars of the community. What is there to dig up?'

'Well, you never know.' Nanna pauses. 'I've left the rest of my belongings in storage. Would you go back to Neath for me and pick them up?'

Dan nods. 'Of course. I'll make a day of it. Are you going to return the reporter's call?'

'Maybe. I need to think about it. As for you…'

'Me?'

'Your club is saved from relegation by the skin of its teeth. New local owners, genuine Palace fans they say, are waiting in the wings and all you can do is moan about the powerful elite who control modern football.'

'Nanna, there's nothing I can do.'

'My father always used to say it's better to light one small candle than complain about the dark. It just depends how much you *really* care about the situation. There again, maybe you're just like the rest, happy to be a victim.'

Half an hour later, Nanna climbs the stairs. Every day it seems they are adding another stair at the top. Bringing all her belongings here makes sense. She's glad she's finally decided to let Neath go, however hard it is to do. Sally had said she would help her sort things out, once and for all. That was before the break-up. It's sad and disappointing what happened between her and Dan. She pauses at the turn to catch her breath. Her grandson has had an eccentric, bizarre idea. She likes it. She has often wondered what inspires her to be so rebellious, even now, after all these years. Curiously, her parents were so very well behaved. She really ought to know better.

CHAPTER 52

Wednesday 14 October 1914

A dream came true last week. I'd wanted to do it for years but never had the chance, until last Tuesday.

The Blackburn Pals challenged us to a game of football and I got picked to play inside right. I tell you, it was the next best thing to turning out for the Clarets themselves. We were taken to a pitch near Rishton. The regular army plays there. Tucked away it is, well off the beaten track. Now, I've played games of football all my life. Mostly they've been kickabouts with an old pair of boots for goalposts, that way on. I've turned out for the colliery team, too, on decent-sized pitches, all marked out with white lines, corner flags and proper goalposts. Yet, here's the funny thing. It took Germany invading Belgium before I played my first game *with nets behind the goals!*

If you don't play football you won't understand why I was so excited. The professional clubs brought nets in years ago to stop arguments over whether the ball went over or under the bar and suchlike. That's what they say, anyway. To my mind, they make the game more dramatic, and that's a much more important reason. I've played in hundreds of games and scored loads of goals but, without a net behind the goal, there isn't the same drama. Someone has to scamper over and pick up the ball. For years I've dreamed of sending a pile driver past a diving, despairing goalkeeper. A spilt second later the net billows and bulges and the ball drops dead in the corner of the goal. The trouble is nets are dear, so you'll not find many around. Only professional clubs have them. And the British Army, it seems.

For most of the first half, the Blackburn Pals were all over us. They'd played a couple of matches before. This was our first. They only scored one goal in the first 45 minutes, mind, so we were still in it at half time. Ten minutes into the second half, Arthur Foster squared the ball to me on the edge of the penalty area. I met it with a sweet volley. I'd like to say it flew straight into the net. The honest truth is it took a wicked deflection off one of the Blackburn Pals, leaving their goalkeeper stranded. The ball ran along the ground like a putt on a golf green and trickled into the goal. It just about reached the net with two Blackburn defenders tumbling after it. No matter. Even if the ball didn't hit the net, it touched it. That was good enough for me.

We drew 2-2 in the end. Not bad for a bunch of lads who hardly know each other. Not bad, too, considering we looked a right shambles at our first drill last week. A few lads had just stumbled out of the pub that afternoon. Turning up in old suits and clogs won't scare Fritz. Most of us have never done any marching and the like. The drill instructor, Sgt Whittaker, walked up and down the line and gave us a dose of what we can expect for the next few weeks. He stopped in front of me. Why me, I've no idea. I did what someone had told me to do. I looked straight ahead, didn't make eye contact and agreed with everything he said.

'Is that your body, boy?' he said.

'Sir!'

'Well I wouldn't have your body as a gift.'

'Sir!'

'I wouldn't give your body to my dog for its dinner.'

'Sir!'

'And when you have a shave…" He can't have been more than an inch from my ear '…*stand a pace nearer the razor!*'

'Sir!' I was pleased he thought I had to shave, to be honest.

Hundreds of people came out to watch. They jeered when half of us 'about turned' and the other half kept going. One person told the

Burnley Express we looked like 'Fred Karno's Army' and that it was all 'a farce and a humiliating public exhibition of poverty.' At least we'll all get uniforms in a few weeks.

So we were made up when we got that draw against the Blackburn Pals. We all went to the pub afterwards. Being 18 now, I feel free to drink as much as I like! Some of the lads got well bevvied up and when I played three or four songs on my harmonica, everyone joined in. You should have heard them sing *Hold your Hand Out, Naughty Boy* and *Hello, Hello, who's your Ladyfriend? Who's the Little Girlie by your Side?* By the end of the evening we were all warming to this army lark. I was about to go back to our Walter's when Sgt Whittaker came over and bought me a pint. I was surprised after what he said to me earlier.

'Took your chance well this afternoon,' he said. 'Good man.'

'Thank you sir,' I said.

'Been playing the mouth organ long?'

'All my life. My grandfather taught me.'

'You did him proud.'

'He was the best.'

'Play anything else?'

'Whistles and pipes.'

'Excellent. We're marching through town a week on Saturday. We need more pipers.'

'Well, I've never…'

'Band practice is Tuesday. Eight o'clock sharp. Sheldon Village Hall.'

'The thing is…'

'Good man.'

And that was that. He just marched out of the pub. It means I'll not be available to go on all the route marches they've planned for us and there are a fair few, I can tell you. On Monday we went to Blackburn and back. That's 22 miles in all, in our ordinary clothes. On Tuesday, we had two drill parades. On Wednesday we did another seven-miler. On Thursday we marched to Hebden Bridge and back. That's another 20 miles or so. On Friday, it was more drilling and a five-miler.

Anyway, I turned up at Sheldon Village Hall, not knowing what to expect. I've never had a proper music teacher. Grandpa taught me his way. I play mostly by ear and I'm not that good at reading music. Nellie's much better than me. I struggled a bit so I took the music back to Walter's and haven't stopped playing since. We'll be knocking out marching tunes like *Whiter than the Whitewash on the Wall* and *They Were Only Playing Leapfrog*.

Ma is in two minds about me joining the Pals. She's proud that I'm doing my bit for the country and all that. On the other hand, things aren't going as well as expected in France and Belgium. Fritz has pushed our boys back and it's a stalemate. Ma's worried I might end up like some of the regulars who are returning with missing arms and legs. As for Emily, I've no way of contacting her. She doesn't know where I am or what I am doing. Nellie says Emily was my way out, my 'wings' as she put it. Maybe I don't need them after all. This war may have come at just the right time.

CHAPTER 53

Dan channel hops on the rental van radio. He is clattering west on the M4 to pick up Nanna's things from Neath. He hopes for more news from SE25 but the sports bulletins are only concerned with transfer speculation at Premiership clubs and the upcoming World Cup in South Africa. He tries the music stations.

'Imagine no possessions
'I wonder if you can...'

Dan shakes his head. Dream on, Johnnie boy. Great melody but that lyric: written on a stretch Steinway in your rolling Surrey mansion? Yeah, well. Not possessing the ground we play on has been the bane of our lives since Uncle Ron (Noades) separated ground and club.

P. Diddy notwithstanding, rumours of new suitors abound, though. In the red corner, former boxer Winston McKenzie, who fought to become Mayor of London under the slogan: 'I float like a butterfly and sting like a bee; I've got the policies they can't see'. So hidden, indeed, that McKenzie came in last of 10 candidates. For a rank outsider, what about businessman Steve Bisciotti, owner of the Baltimore Ravens and listed in the Top 400 richest Americans? Let us consider his fellow Yanks' record in the UK: the Glazers at Manchester United and Hicks and Gillett at Liverpool. Very politely – thanks, buddy, but please don't spare us a dime.

Preferred by the administrator is a consortium of four local (that word warms the heart) businessmen and Palace fans, under the title

CPFC2010. Let's hope this comes off. No matter what Lennon says, someone has to imagine Palace as a possession and make it so, in a matter of days. If not, the club will be liquidated and the players sold off in a fire sale no less dramatic and depressing than the inferno that roared out of control on Sydenham Hill in November 1936.

Dan rattles the van up to 55mph. It's good just to be on the open road, doing something practical. It beats moping around the house, avoiding *Britain's Got Tribute* and applying for job after demoralising job. Nanna has given him strict instructions about *her* possessions, in a spidery scrawl. Most of all, he must guard the case marked RC with his life. He sings along to an Abba track, changing the words to eulogise about a long-gone Palace player.

'If we ever make the Prem again
'I'd sign my friend, Sorondo.'

Well, no-one can hear him, though he wins a curious look or two from passengers in passing cars. His phone buzzes. It's a text alert. He is driving. He ignores it. Another buzz. He travels five more miles and pulls in at Chieveley service station near Newbury. It's from Sally. He kills the radio. He wasn't expecting this. Still too hurt and downright fucking angry, he had ignored her text after the Sheffield Wednesday game. This is the first communication since.

'Dan, I hope you're OK. Can we talk?' says the first message.
'Dan, I'd quite understand if you ignored me' says the second.

Dan's heart races, his stomach lurches, his breathing becomes shallow. What do you say when you've said it over and over and over again in your head, yet haven't said it at all? He stares out of the window at a family of four, mum and dad with two children under five, heading for the food court. They seem happy enough. For no good reason, he wonders if that couple, so chilled now, ever fell out, big-style. Why is she making contact now? What does she want? She must want something. Sod her. He starts up the engine. He'll make her wait. He pulls out of the parking area. There again, what if it's serious? He pulls up suddenly. The driver in the car behind brakes just in time, sounds his horn and gesticulates. Dan mouths an apology. Best to get it over and done with.

'Thanks for calling me back,' says Sally. 'I really appreciate it.'

'Yeah, well...' says Dan.

'I... I haven't been... I didn't mean it to happen like that.'

'Yadda, yadda, yadda.'

'I should have told you how I was feeling about everything, before it all blew up. I *did* try...'

'So it's my fault.'

'No, I mean... I'm not sure what I mean. Look, I want us to be friends.'

'I can do without friends who humiliate me.'

'Yes, I know.'

Silence.

'Sounds like you're doing well on the show.' Dan changes tack.

'Have... have you watched any of it?'

'No.'

'No, well... I understand. I can't blame you.'

'Nanna tells me they seem to like you.'

'It's been strange. It's as if it's someone else up there. I'm just watching her. I didn't plan it like that.'

'No, but we know who did.'

'Look, it wasn't Stu's fault. I'm the one to blame.'

'He saw us coming.'

'No, he just reacted to my... situation.'

'He made you feel like the star you're about to become...'

'It's not as simple as that.'

'... and I'm in the way.'

'No, it really isn't like that. I was angry and hurt. I didn't even know I could *feel* that angry.'

'Oh God, we're back to the Geordies.'

'I phoned her.'

'Who?'

'Charlie.'

'When?'

'Just now. That's why I've called you.'

'And?'

283

'She told me what happened. I owe you an apology.'

Dan takes a deep breath. 'At *long friggin' last*.'

'I wish you had told me at the time.'

'Told you what?'

'About the girls.'

'When?'

'At the exhibition.'

'You've got to be joking... Hi Sally. Come on in, babes. Meet Charlie and Jade, two tarts I was forced to meet in a nightclub in Newcastle. Oh, didn't I tell you I was going to the match up there? Sorry, it must have slipped my memory. Of course I haven't had my wicked way with them, even though they're propped up in my hotel bed, waiting for breakfast.'

'You could have told me about Silent 'n' Dudley.'

'Who has gone missing, never to be found again? *That* would convince you.'

'Well, I'm sorry. That's all.'

Dan puts his feet up on the dashboard of the hired van. Cars drone past on the motorway.

'It's the next round on Saturday,' he says. 'How do you think you'll get on?'

'I'm not sure. Whatever will be and all that.'

'What are they saying at uni?'

'They've allowed me more time to get my work in. They say it's all good PR for them. I'm not sure I can sustain it, mind. I've been feeling sick some days.'

'Pure nerves. Lennon always puked up before gigs.'

'Is that right? Well, I'm in good company.'

They both laugh.

'I'm on the way to Neath,' says Dan.

'For Nanna?'

'Yeah, and I really need to get a move on. I'm picking up her stuff.'

'I encouraged her to sort things out, once and for all.'

'What do you mean?'

Sally hesitates. 'She confided in me. All I can say is that you are doing the right thing.'

'Another newspaper are on the chase. They want the exclusive on her and that Welsh boyo.'

'Really?' Sally laughs. 'Move over Posh 'n' Becks.

'They're so yesterday. So *noughties*.'

'Here come Dafydd and Rhoslyn.'

'So *nineties!*'

'Hah, yeah.'

They both laugh.

Awkward end-of-call courtesies conducted, Dan heads out for the motorway again. Nothing can be resolved while that bastard Bensham is still around but at least he has been vindicated over the Geordies. He will thank Nanna when he gets home. She really is one formidable little lady. Funny how both she and Sally have become so beloved of TV producers. He's beginning to figure out how it all works, this media business. Much to his chagrin, they had used his idea for the Bintastic advert. There are more ideas where that came from. Perhaps he can make some waves of his own, if he's got the inclination. If he's got the balls.

He arrives at the storage depot in Neath and is shown a room full of boxes and familiar furniture.

'I spent entire summers bouncing on that settee,' he tells the depot manager. 'During long rainy days, I made tents out of blankets between those two armchairs.'

In one box he finds an ornate vase, teapot, caddy and cosy (Nanna still insists tea is so much better made in a warmed pot), poached egg maker and black-and-white photos of the family in old silver frames. In another box, a few musty clothes, cardigans mainly, tacky holiday souvenirs from Palma Nova, dated paperback novels, a set of Readers' Digests from the 50s and 60s, a butterfly-shaped mirror – and a padlocked case marked RC. So this is the prized possession. He is under strict instructions to bring it back, unopened. No need to worry on that count. Without a hacksaw, he has no chance of discovering what's inside.

It's an hour or two before he's put everything into the van. He secures the furniture with rope. Most of it will go straight into an auction or to the dump. No wonder Nanna wants a day or two to go through everything before saying her final goodbyes. He trundles back along the M4, kept company by more radio talk about the World Cup.

'It's been 20 years since England reached the semi-finals of a major football tournament,' bewails a presenter.

'There's a reason,' murmurs Dan.

'Two long decades.'

'Make the connection, someone.'

'It's disappointing when you consider the Premier League is full of great players.'

'Yeah, mainly from abroad. How many foreign players were in the old First Division?' yells Dan. 'Make the connection, someone…'

No-one makes the connection. Irritated, he switches over to the music stations again. Nanna's right. It's time to take a few bigwigs to task. She's always rabbiting on about true prophets being rebels, challenging the system, making a nuisance of themselves. Maybe he can cause a little mischief. Maybe, just maybe they will listen to an average football fan's lament. Maybe he can be that fan – the voice of one chanting in the wilderness.

CHAPTER 54

Saturday 24 October 1914

As Grandpa used to say, people who know what they're doing make anything look easy. Try it for yourself, mind, and it's another matter. Marching and playing at the same time: it's harder than it looks. I had to learn quickly. You have to keep your body straight and your head held high. You musn't look at the ground and your legs must never bend, even when you're marching fast. There are different step sizes, such as 8-5 (eight steps to five yards) and 6-5 (six steps to five yards). Tall lads with long legs take smaller steps, of course.

If you are off stride, there are ways to get back. You can do a slight skip on one step and switch your legs quickly but that will make you jump up. You can slow down for a second but you look awkward getting back in step. What I'm trying to say is that I've spent the last 10 days at it, almost non-stop. Most of the lads have been at it for months, years even. Most days I've been staying behind in the hall well after they've gone. I had some catching up to do.

They gave me a spare bandsman's uniform for today's parade. The legs were on the long side but it was better than nothing. I was nervous as we set off from the parade ground towards the centre of town. I felt like an imposter. Arthur Foster, Harry Grabham and some 600 lads marched behind us, wearing a right hodgepodge of old suits. Some sported straw boaters and trilbies, others flat caps. They haven't got their uniforms yet. We headed down Brunshaw Road, past Turf Moor, before heading for the town centre. The atmosphere was electric, like being at a match except this time *we* were on the pitch, so to speak. The crowds along Trafalgar Street were six deep, so they told me. I could hear them shouting and clapping but I daren't look round. I was too busy trying to look ahead and march in time.

We played *Whitewash on The Wall, Ragtime Soldier Man, Keep the Homes Fires Burning, It's a Long Way to Tipperary* and *Goodbye Dolly Gray*. I wasn't note perfect and the other lads helped me out when I missed a march or two. Our route took us in a large circle and we ended up back at the parade ground. The Pals were dismissed but, as part of the band, I had to report to Sheldon Village Hall. We all got there and congratulated each other on a good day's work, as you do. A matter of a couple of weeks before some of us had been working down the pit or running errands. Now here we were, ready to give Fritz a bloody nose. Sgt Whittaker arrived at the hall and told us to line up. I am still getting used to how quickly everyone gets into position.

'Well done, chaps,' he said. 'Couldn't have asked for a better display. As you know we've a few new recruits among us as well as some old hands. Proud of the whole lot of you. Unfortunately I have some bad news. With great regret I must let some of you go.'

As he read out the names, my heart sank.

'McGregor, Tilling...' I knew I would be on the list. All that work, too. '...Sangster and Daws.' Ah well, it had been a great experience. I had felt part of something much bigger, something special.

'The men whose names I called out, see me in my office immediately,' barked Sgt Whittaker. 'Band dis-missed.'

'It's like being summoned by the headmaster,' said Sangster from the corner of his mouth. 'Put a newspaper down the back of your trousers.'

'You're going *where?*' Ma collapsed in her chair with shock. I thought I had better tell her as soon as possible so I got the last train home. It's been hard enough for Ma already, what with Pa being poorly and her only son billeted miles away.

'Ypres,' I repeated. 'Some of the lads call it Wipers but it's pronounced Ee-per.'

'Where the hell is that?'

'Belgium.'

'*Belgium?* But… but you've only just joined up.'

'The regimental band out there needs replacements. Some of the regulars have been injured.'

'But you're… you're no age… you're not even trained to fight.'

'I'll not be fighting.'

'So you'll be playing *Goodbye Dolly Gray* while the bullets whistle over your head? Don't talk daft.'

'We're stretcher bearers when we're not playing in the band.'

'But… but that's even worse. You'll not even be able defend yourself.'

Pa had been sitting in the corner of the room, quiet as usual.

'Give the lad credit,' he said. 'We should be proud of him.'

'Of course I'm proud. I'm right proud.' Ma was fighting back the tears. 'That's not the point.'

'I'll be fine.' I put my arm round her. 'This gives me a chance to see what the war's about before it's all over.'

'What if… it's all too sudden,' said Ma. 'I'm going to tell them you're only 16.'

'You'll do no such thing,' said Pa. 'I'd have gone out there myself at his age. I've spent my whole working life down one bloody hole or another. What use am I now? I can hardly breathe. You go, lad and make something of yourself.'

So I'm in my room again, writing this entry. It's good to be back. Grandpa's flat cap is still on the bedpost. It's down to him, of course. I would never have had a chance like this if he hadn't had the patience to teach me how to play. It looks like I'll only be back here once more before I go to 'Wipers'. I can't believe it's all happened so quickly. We're likely to be there over Christmas, if the war lasts that long. I hope it does. I'd hate to go out and come straight back home. I'm glad to say Billy is going to recover but, like him, I'm never going down the pit again. Not now.

CHAPTER 55

They're a faceless bunch, the bankers. We know they like money. We know they like to gamble, though not with their personal cash. We know they like their bonuses. Oh yes, we know all about those bonuses, those obscene rewards for failure. But apart from the shamed few – Fred the Shred and a handful of other suits – we don't know who they are, or what they *look* like. That's because they look just like us. Boring. They don't have the personality to be personalities. They crunch numbers in the city, umpteen floors up. They melt into the evening rush hour, crushed up against us on the tubes, with a fatter wallet and thinner conscience.

It is June 1 2010. Quantitative easing is in full swing but billions in newly-printed banknotes are going where, exactly? Back to the faceless few, of course. We, the taxpaying many, pick up a debt the bankers will be unable to repay. It is unprecedented and bizarre. Never in the field of human commerce was so much owed to so many by so few. Our anger simmers but, because we don't know who they are and where they work, we do not unite and protest.

Rain hammers down from leaden skies. Defying the weather, a baying mob gathers at the headquarters of Lloyds TSB, one of those bailed-out banks. Is this the start of a movement for change? Is this the defining moment when the bankers get that bloody nose? Hundreds swarm into the entrance foyer, railing at the faceless ones in the offices above. TV crews jostle among the throng. The mob is passionate and determined but you'll not hear a single cry for fiscal revolution. They're only here because those number-crunching suits upstairs could seriously damage something much closer to their hearts: Saturday afternoon. Put simply, D Day has arrived. The potential new owners of Crystal Palace FC are deep inside the building, trying to do a deal to buy club and ground out of administration. Negotiations are intense and tortuous. There is a real chance no agreement will be reached. If so, the liquidation of the club will begin at 3pm. First out of the door will be prized assets like Darren Ambrose and Julian Speroni, at give-away prices. It's more than the loyal fans milling round Gresham Street can handle. That's why they're here. The suits must get their act together. Time to encourage them with a song or two.

'Oh south London
'Oh south London
'Is wonderful
'Is wonderful
'Oh south London is wonderful
'It's full of tits, fanny and Palace
'Oh south London is wonderful...'

There. That's driven home the message. Now they know we mean business. Now they've got to listen. Someone kicks a football at a window on the first floor.

'Let's go fuckin' mental
'Let's go fuckin' mental
'La-la-la-la
'La-la-la-la...'

Dan wanders around at the back of the crowd. It has edged past 3.30pm. There is still no sign of a sale. The mood is tense and volatile.

'Think it'll turn violent?' says a voice. He glances round to see a sharply-dressed blond, probably in her early 30s. Next to her, a TV cameraman pans the crowd.

'So that's why you're here,' he replies.

'We're covering the story whichever way it goes.'

'But a scuffle or two would make better TV.'

She smiles. 'It's nice to see fans from a small club caring so much.'

'A *small* club…'

'It's been a while since you were in the Premier League.'

'So that makes Wigan a *big* club.'

'Well, I wasn't saying…'

'Tell you what,' says Dan. 'Go back to your studio and update us on that really important story – the one about the England team not being allowed to see their wives and girlfriends between World Cup matches.'

The woman smiles again. 'You're very articulate.'

Dan shrugs off the compliment. 'It's down to you lot that we're here.'

'How so?'

'Because of all the silly money you throw at the game. We sold our soul to you. All those atmospheric old grounds, swept away for over-policed, all-seater libraries. We're paying through the nose to make hundreds of footballers millionaires, most of them foreigners. And the England team just gets worse and worse at every tournament…'

'Whoah, this is great.'

'What do you mean?'

'We've scheduled a special programme on the state of the game. Can I interview you about that?'

Dan points to the top floor of Lloyds TSB. 'Well, I'm not going anywhere until we get some news.' He vents off for a further ten minutes, this time to camera. He is disturbed only by that rogue football. He punts it back to the chanting mob.

'That'll do nicely,' says the reporter, winding up the interview. 'I'm Frankie, by the way.' She holds out her hand. 'You're…?'

Dan pauses. Why not? In for a penny and all that. He shakes her hand and gives her a name. It isn't Daniel James Howard. It is nothing like Daniel James Howard.

'No… your proper name.' The reporter stands with her arms folded.

'You don't believe me.'

'I need a real name.'

'That *is* my real name.'

'I can't put it to my editor.'

'Here's proof.' Dan pulls a sheet of paper from his pocket. 'Granted, it wasn't my name until a few days ago.'

'I... I don't believe it,' says the reporter. 'This is one of those internet jokes.'

Dan shakes his head. 'It's for real and perfectly legal.'

'You're barking.'

'Of course. I've just taken the next bizarre step. I was going to send out one of those press release thingies but I've bumped into you instead.'

'I'm not sure what to make of it but I like your intensity. Can I give you a call?'

'Up to you.' Dan shrugs his shoulders again. He gives her his number.

'I'll have a word with my editor and...' Her mobile rings. 'Talk of the devil.' She points to the phone. 'Yes... yes... right. OK.' She puts a thumbs up to Dan. 'The deal's done. They're coming down with a statement.'

The news spreads. Hundreds surge towards the entrance to the bank. The TV reporter, Frankie, or whatever her name is, disappears into the crowd, cameraman in tow.

'And I'm feeling...' bellows an hysterical fan.

'Glad all over...' sing back the 300.

'Go on, Tarrant.' Nanna raises an agitated hand at a celebrity edition of *Who Wants To Be A Millionaire?* 'Ask him.'

It is later the same day. Dan has just arrived home. 'Ask him what, Nanna?'

'Ask him how much he earns.'

'He's never going to ask a top actor that question.'

'Exactly.'

'What do you mean?'

'He'll pry into a factory worker's wages but not a celebrity. It's deeply patronising. Sally's right.' There is a moment's awkward silence. 'How are things between you?'

Dan shrugs his shoulders, yet again. To change the subject he tells Nanna of his exploits in London and the encounter with a TV producer.

'I doubt she'll call back,' he says. 'They're only interested in which big money player is signing for what club.'

'I wouldn't be so sure,' says Nanna. 'These stations have hours to kill over the summer and we're still 10 days away from the World Cup. The good news is that your club is saved.' She reaches for a bottle beside her chair. 'I think we should celebrate.'

Half an hour later, Dan's phone rings. It is Frankie. She is on the phone for more than 20 minutes, asking Dan even more questions.

'Well, you were right, Nanna. Again.' Dan puts his phone back on charge. 'They've asked me to join a panel discussion on modern football, wearing my Gazza World Cup 90 shirt. What's more they'll introduce me under my new name…'

CHAPTER 56

Sunday 8 November 1914

News has got around town that I am heading for Ypres tomorrow. Everyone has wished me well. The trouble is Reverend Whitehead wanted to make a fuss of me at church this morning and asked that hypocrite Borst to 'say a few words' before my departure. I'm not having any of that. Ma was all of a do, I can tell you. She pleaded with me to go. Pa told her to give over, it was my choice. Couldn't win, could I? By my reckoning, staying at home was the lesser of two evils. I went upstairs and watched Pa hold Ma as they walked down the road to church. She was sobbing. A few minutes later I decided I should do the decent thing by her after all. I changed into my suit and was about to run to church when I heard a footstep on the fourth stair. It doesn't matter how lightly you tread on it, that stair will always creak.

'Who's there?' I said.

'Me,' came the reply, followed by a giggle. I looked downstairs from the landing.

'Emily! What are you doing here?'

She was wearing a long, dark blue velvet coat and a hat with spiky hussar plumes and ostrich feathers in a strange fan shape. It looked almost military. She floated upstairs, though I'm sure her perfume entered the room several seconds ahead of her.

'How did you get in?' I began.

'Shhhhh….' She took off her hat. Her hair tumbled out, just like it did up that tree at the cup final.

'Ma and Pa… they could come back at any time.'

'So?' She threw her arms round me and kissed me.

'They'd never forgive me.'

'We'll just have to take that risk.'

'Where have you been?'

'Later.'

'Why are you here?'

'*Later!*'

'I don't understand.'

She took off her velvet coat and suddenly I understood. Being on the run for months, she might simply have run out of clothes, of course. A cosy, velvet coat may be all she had left to wear. Not a likely explanation. There again, we've had a bit of an Indian summer and she may have been making allowances: even less convincing. I kept thinking of Ma and Pa in their pew at the back of the church, praying for the safe return of their innocent young boy from the evil clutches of the Kaiser. I don't know how but we eventually ended up at Grandpa's end of the bed. His flat cap went flying onto the floor.

'Emily… oh God, Emily.' My heart was still thumping through my chest like an overheated steam engine. 'What… what have we just done?'

'Do you still love me, Tom?'

'Of… of course I do...'

'That's all that counts.'

'…but it's hard to be friends with a shooting star.'

'The war has changed everything,' she said. 'They want me to serve out my time in a munitions factory. It means I can come home. When I heard you were going to Belgium I could hardly believe our bad luck.'

'Who told you?'

'Cook.'

'Everybody seems to know I'm going.'

'She told me your mother was upset.'

'Right enough, she is.'

'I waited outside the church and saw her arrive with your father. I hoped you would be here.' Her eyes burned into mine. I was elated and guilt-ridden, excited and scared.

'I'll be gone by this time tomorrow,' I said.

'I'll still be here when you get back.'

'Really?'

'Of course.'

I sat up and shook my head. 'You and me. It's hopeless.'

'I'll make it work.'

'How can you say that?'

'Because I will.'

'Your father will sack Ma when he finds out.'

'With her son fighting for king and country? It would spread like wildfire and wouldn't do him any good.'

'Why should he care?'

'You're a piper in a military band.'

'From the wrong side of town.'

'He'll have to get used to it.'

And so it went on for half an hour or so. Neither of us could get our words out fast enough, there was so much catching up to do. We knew the church service would only last so long. As I wrote earlier, Whitehead's sermons go on a bit. The short ones last about 25 minutes. Others can be close on an hour. That's a long time when you're sitting on a hard, wooden pew and the warm sun is streaming through the Parable of the Ten Virgins. I remember yawning several times in one sermon. I wasn't tired. I just wanted to find out if it really does make other people do the same thing. This morning, for the first time, I hoped against hope Whitehead was preaching one of those hour-long, eyelid-droopers.

In the end we couldn't risk it any longer. Reluctantly, I eased every delicious piece of Emily back inside her coat. She positioned her hat carefully in the mirror.

'You'll be back home in England before the carol services begin,' she said.

I kissed her. I had her at last. I didn't want to let her go. I began to unbutton her coat again. At that moment I heard a door open. I held up my hand and pointed downstairs. Moments later the fourth stair creaked again. I ushered Emily behind the door and walked to the landing.

'Nellie!' I said.

'She's here, isn't she?' Nellie was halfway up the stairs.

'Who's here?'

Before I could say anything more, Emily (her coat buttoned up tightly again) walked onto the landing with me.

'Nellie, how nice to see you,' she said. 'I've been meaning to thank you for helping me like you did and...' Before she could finish the sentence, Nellie had turned and run back downstairs.

'I don't believe it,' I said. I ran after her and grabbed her arm in the back yard.

'I knew it.' She wouldn't look at me. 'No wonder you weren't in church. I knew she'd come back sooner or later and you wouldn't be able to resist.'

'That's not fair.'

'You're right. Nothing's fair. I've been saying that for weeks. At least I know the truth.'

'I didn't plan this. She just turned up, like you.'

'And you sent her away...'

'Nellie, I'm going to war tomorrow.'

'Which is why...' Tears flooded her cheeks. 'I've come round to give you something. There's no point now.'

'Oh, Nellie.' I pulled her towards me. She resisted.

'Believe it or not I've still got a little bit of pride left,' she said. 'I need to keep it. Go back to the love of your life.'

'She only came round to wish me well.'

'And you simply couldn't turn her down.'

I didn't know what to say.

'I've been a fool for too long,' she said. 'I thought if I was patient, maybe, just maybe – but that spoiled little brat was always going to steal you back.'

'Nellie, I'm confused. I don't want to lose you.'

'Goodbye, Tom. I'm angry with you. I'm proud of you. All at the same stupid time.'

Not for the first time she strode away from me without turning round. Emily came into the yard.

'I'm sorry,' she said. 'I had no idea you were close. If I'd known...'

'The only person to blame is me,' I said.

'I'm going after her,' said Emily. 'The least I can do is thank her properly for what she did.' With that she ran after Nellie. I haven't heard from either of them since.

What a day. As I write this, Pa is still comforting Ma downstairs. I keep telling her I'll be back before you can say Lord Kitchener. All she talks about are the casualties returning from the front every day. I'm just one big jumble of emotions tonight. I have no idea know what to do with them all. I'll never sleep.

CHAPTER 57

Dan sits in Gazza's World Cup 90 shirt – not the tear-stained original from that famous semi-final against Germany but an exact replica. The colours are washed out and it's fraying at the edges, adding credibility.

'Going live in ten seconds… good luck, everybody,' says the studio manager. 'Five… four…' He silently counts in presenter Rob Donnison who sports a dark blue suit and an almost full head of speckled grey hair.

'Hello and welcome to a new series of *State of Play*, where you rant about everything on planet sport,' says Donnison. 'Want to get something off your chest? Do it here. Reckon the media are biased against your team? This is your chance to answer back.'

More music and snatches of bygone World Cup games follow. The producer takes a close up of Donnison.

'South Africa play Mexico in the opening match of the World Cup on Thursday. But what do you, the fans, think of England's chances?' he says. 'Do you *really* care about our national team these days? And which would you prefer to succeed – your club or country? Our guests tonight have three contrasting views. Brian Barker is a chartered surveyor from High Wycombe. A Manchester United fan, Brian has never been to Old Trafford but has followed the Red Devils since they won the Premiership for the first time in 1993. In his opinion, international football is over-rated but he *may* watch England if they reach the quarter-finals.

'Our second guest is Zoe Halsall, a Rochdale season-ticket holder. Zoe flies out to South Africa tomorrow to see England's group matches and will drape her Union Jack on "whatever wall she can find".

'Our final guest is a Crystal Palace fan who won't watch *any* of England's upcoming games on TV. We'll find out his name and why he's turned his back on our national team later... but firstly Brian, who thinks international football is over-rated...'

'It's a damp squib at the end of a long season,' says Brian. 'The players would rather be on the beach.'

'So, given a straight choice,' says Donnison, 'you'd rather United won the Champions League than England won the World Cup.

'Any day. We watch our clubs week in, week out. And let's face it, our national side is never going to win anything.'

'Some argue we have too many foreign players in the Premier League,' says Donnison, 'and our own lads don't get a chance to compete at the highest level.'

'Maybe, but ask any fan if they'd rather be in the Premier League with foreign players or in the Championship with English players,' says Brian. 'They'll choose the foreign option every day of the week.'

The camera catches Zoe Halsall shaking her head furiously.

'OK, well that's clearly irritated you, Zoe,' says Donnison. 'Your club, Rochdale, has just been promoted from what was the old Fourth Division into League One, the third tier.'

'Great, eh?' Zoe is a bubbly, 20-something with a wide-open face and infectious smile. 'If we'd won the Champions League, Premiership and FA Cup in one go, we couldn't be happier.'

'I believe the club spent 36 consecutive seasons in the bottom division.'

Zoe nods. 'It just makes promotion all the sweeter. We may be a small club but it's like an extended family. We sometimes chat to our players on the bus.'

'You've a reputation for spotting talent, too.'

'Yeah – Grant Holt, Glenn Murray and Adam Le Fondre, they've made a name for themselves at Spotland.'

'All English, as well.'

'To be honest, we're glad the Premier League is full of overseas players,' says Zoe. 'Our own lads are overlooked, so family clubs like Rochdale snap them up.'

'And you'll be flying the flag in South Africa.'

'Too right. A lot of fans from fashionable clubs don't bother. For us, it's a chance to be part of something bigger and what's bigger than your national team?'

'Well, according to Brian, Manchester United.'

Brian shifts uneasily in his seat. 'Of course I want England to win,' he says, 'but not at the expense of the club. We pay the players' wages.'

'Which leads me neatly to our last guest.' Donnison turns to Dan. 'Thousands of people have supported Crystal Palace over the years and, in spite of this, gone on to lead normal lives. Not this one, though. Disenchanted and disillusioned by modern football, he's *changed his name* as an act of protest. Last week I would have introduced you to Dan Howard. Now, believe it or not, please welcome to *State of Play* – Mr Football League Division-One.'

'To avoid confusion, I'd like to point out,' says Dan, as the applause dies down, 'that my surname, Division-One, is double-barrelled.'

'So… Mr Division-One, can I call you Football?'

'I'm not embarrassed by my middle name. League is fine, as well.'

'Perhaps FL?'

Dan nods. 'If you like.'

'So, FL…' Donnison scratches his head. 'Let me get my head round it all. You've done this because…?'

'Football League Division One was a perfectly good brand that had stood the test of time. But the rich elite wanted to separate themselves from the also-rans. So they dumped it, like a husband dumping a faithful wife for a young floozie. There are many, many fans like me who think Football League Divisions 1 to 4 still makes more sense.'

'And your protest is being noticed…'

'I was interviewed yesterday on the Light Programme.'

'The *Light* Programme? Now that really *is* going back. It's been called BBC Radio 2 since the 1960s.'

'The Light Programme and the Home Service were confusing, weren't they? It made sense to have several expressions, under the BBC brand. So they called them Radios 1, 2, 3 and 4.'

'OK, I see what you've done there.'

'Football League Divisions 1, 2, 3 and 4 worked perfectly well. What the hell were they thinking when they messed it up? They keep fiddling with the names, still. We have unending confusion as to what the different leagues are called and which one is above and below the other. Like Gazza at the World Cup, it's all ended in tiers.'

'Yes, that shirt you're wearing...'

'He might as well have wept for the future of English football.'

'You're going to wear it throughout this tournament?'

Dan nods. 'Italia 90 was the last World Cup before they brought in the Premier League. We almost won it, too. All my conscious life, the England team has been in slow decline. It's time the authorities woke up and smelt the Bovril.'

'So, you won't be watching this World Cup.'

Dan shakes his head. 'I'll be standing all the way through England's games – in protest against all-seater stadiums. And I'll be re-playing videos of our matches at Italia 1990 and writing new verses to *Football's Coming Home,* a revised version of the Euro 96 song.'

Brian shifts uneasily again.

'Cheap criticism of modern football is just fashionable,' he says. 'The Premiership is the biggest league in the world and we should be proud of it. Football was dying before it was brought in. Crowds were shrinking, stadiums were decaying, hooligans had scared off families. The knockers are usually fans of clubs like Palace who want what we've got. If they ever get back into the big league, they'll change their tune.'

'I doubt it,' says Dan. 'Real fans of Man U, not the plastic ones but those who actually *go* to games, formed FC United as a reaction against what was happening at the club and modern football in general.'

'You calling me a plastic?' says Brian.

'He's not calling you anything,' cuts in Zoe, 'but if the cap fits...'

'OK,' says Donnison. 'That's got us off to a flier.' He looks to camera. 'You can join in the debate by texting us on…'

Football League Division-One (the football fan formally known as Daniel James Howard) settles back in his seat on the train home, still pumped up from his appearance on TV. Several congratulatory texts have arrived. The contributor's fee will come in handy, too. Like most football clubs in the lower leagues, he is teetering on the edge of skint. Again. The train rattles out of London's Victoria Station and is crossing the Thames when his mobile rings.

'Is that Mr Football League Division-One?' says an unfamiliar male voice.

'This is he,' laughs Dan.

'I enjoyed watching you on TV earlier.'

'Thanks.'

'Frankie gave me your number. I'm Phil Croft. I work for the BBC, in the fifth tier of British radio broadcasting.'

Dan laughs loudly, disturbing a commuter nodding off to sleep in front of him. 'Ah, Five Live.'

'Yeah, we're putting together a new programme called *The Onion Bag* and wondered if you might like to be a special guest. You mentioned re-working the song *Football's Coming Home*. Are you making a recording? If so, we'd like to feature it on the show.'

CHAPTER 58

Saturday 21 November 1914

I think the first few pages of this exercise book are in Flemish. That's because it used to belong to a Belgian girl called Florinda. Her name is in green and yellow crayon on the front cover (look carefully among the flowers). I found the book at the school we are using here in Belgium. It was in one of a dozen desks piled up in the corner of a classroom. I wonder what Florinda looks like and where she is now.

The school is in a small village a few miles from Ypres. I dare not say where. If anyone found this journal I would be in for it. Most of the people who live here have moved away to safer areas. I feel as if I am in a strange dream, marching up and down a school playground in a foreign land. Then the guns rumble in the distance and men limp back from the front on crutches. No need to pinch myself.

We're billeted in the barn of an abandoned farm. It has rough-looking timber beams and a very low roof. The straw on the floor has already been slept on by too many lads before us. We've been handed blankets that are old and torn but we make do. I've discovered a good way to make a pillow. Lay out your boots on their sides with the soles facing out and the uppers almost meeting. Then place your folded trousers in between. It's almost comfortable.

You would think the best place to leave shaving tackle and soap would be on the barn's low walls. Trouble is, we share the place with some regular tenants. Rats. Big 'uns, they are. They run along the wall and scoff anything they fancy, knocking off what's left. They jump down on top of you, just to let you know you're not welcome. Even half asleep, you can send them flying and squealing with a well-timed kick but if you leave your face uncovered, they'll run right over it and even lick off the sweat. I've learned how to nod off with my head under the blanket. I've not suffocated yet.

Every morning we cross the only street in the village and queue up in the open yard of another farm for breakfast. We are given a daily ration of half a loaf. Mess tin at the ready, they serve us tea (already milked and sugared). There's an open trench fire where they fry bacon in a large deep pan of fat. We dip our loaves into this if we want. Some days we're given an egg as well. If the weather's good enough we stay in the yard to eat. Otherwise we go back to our billet and use the folded blankets for a seat. It seems like years since I sat in a chair at a table.

After sweeping away rat droppings and polishing our boots, we assemble for square bashing, stretcher drill and band practice. Today, we were challenged to a game of football by the barn next door.

'We're bound to win,' said Sangster. He's billeted in the other barn. 'We've God on our side.' What with having one man less than us, they called in the chaplain as their goalkeeper. The chaplain! Padre Brooks wasn't another Whitehead, mind. He must be in his late 30s or that way on. He isn't tall but he's wirey with the agility of a wild cat. Needless to say, he blocked a couple of my shots with no effort. We were changing ends at half-time when two local boys called out to me in Flemish. I didn't understand a word.

'You want to play?' I said. I thought the other lads wouldn't mind if we put one on each side. The boys shook their heads and pointed to a young girl behind them. Now I know girls can play football and all that but she was far too young. I turned away. One of the lads pushed her onto the pitch.

'You… have…' he said.

'Only boys can play,' I said.

'No, you… have…' He pushed her again.

Padre Brooks came over and talked to them in their own language.

306

They slunk off.

'Thanks,' I said. 'We can't have girls playing.'

The Padre smiled. 'You're new,' he said.

'I've been here just over a week.'

'Thought so. In the band?'

'Yes.'

'You're playing at the service tonight, then.'

I nodded. Throughout the second half he fair threw himself round that goal as if his life depended on it. We lost 3-0.

To be honest, I didn't expect many lads to turn up to the service but the hall was packed. When we struck up *What a Friend We Have in Jesus* you could tell they wanted to sing their version: *When This Lousy War is Over*. They behaved themselves, though. After two more hymns and a few notices, Padre Brooks got up to speak. I expected the kind of lecture Whitehead gives. Instead, Padre Brooks sat on the edge of the platform, legs dangling and asked how many of us had a younger sister. Plenty put up their hands.

'Any photographs?' he said.

'Here,' said one lad. 'Her name's Ada.' He stood up and showed us a picture, though it was too small for most of us to see.

'How old is she?' asked the Padre.

'15,' he said.

'I've got two, 12 and 14,' said another lad. 'They're blond and beautiful.'

'Got a letter here from mine,' said someone from the back of the hall. He held it high. 'She says God's told her I'll be home by Christmas.'

'Aye, a heavenly home,' someone said.

'How old is she?' asked the Padre.

'14,' said the lad.

'Funnily enough, I saw your sister this afternoon.' Padre Brooks got up and began walking round. 'And yours… and yours… and yours.' He pointed all around the hall. 'She was by the football pitch with two lads, probably her brothers. She was no more than 15, I'd say. I'll bet none of you would let your mates touch your sister but

307

you'd turn a blind eye if they touched that girl.' He glanced at me. 'Her brothers were trying to sell her body.'

And there was I thinking… I looked away.

'As if this bloody war wasn't enough already,' he went on. 'She may be just another local girl but she's somebody's daughter and somebody's sister, too. And if she was *your* sister…'

They're a rum bunch of lads, these, the sort that don't take too kindly to being told off. But he's clever, is this Padre. He changed the mood by telling a few jokes about his own sister, who's married to an army officer. We played a final hymn, *The Church's One Foundation*. I'm sure he chose it, knowing we would think of the alternative version – *We are Fred Karno's Army*. Then he did something that would appal Whitehead. After the closing prayer he handed out cigarettes. Perhaps that's why everyone comes to his services. He offered me a packet.

'I don't smoke but I'll take them anyway,' I said. 'I collect the cards inside.'

He laughed. 'So do I. Who do you support?'

'The FA Cup winners.'

'Ah, Burnley. A good team. When I was growing up my local club was Wrexham. Not quite as famous.'

We started talking about the game, as you do. I told him about my trip to the Crystal Palace. He told me how all professional footballers will have to get some kind of military training from now on. The top players, the ones that earn more than £5 a week, will have their pay reduced while the war is on. Some of the players have even found white feathers in their changing rooms. He kept on asking me questions, though a lot of the other lads wanted to talk to him. I even told him about Emily and Nellie. I'm not sure that was a good idea, looking back, but it all just came out.

'So, who are you missing?' he said, finally.

'Emily and Nellie – and Ma, of course,' I said.

He laughed again. 'I meant which cigarette cards?'

'Lindley, Bamford and Harris. I've had offers but they're not in good enough condition.'

He smiled. 'I'll see what I can do.'

Later, back in our barn, I got out my harmonica and the lads taught me some more songs – not for singing during the Padre's services. One of them was *Three German Officers Crossed the Line, Parlez-Vous*. Fritz doesn't come over too well in it, I can tell you. I dare not write down the words. Never mind Ma, they make *me* blush. Going to war has already been an education and not the kind I expected.

CHAPTER 59

'If you'd like to come through, Mr, er...' The young BBC research assistant hesitates. 'I've got Mr *One* written down here. Should that be Juan, as in the Spanish?'

'Exacto.' Dan follows the assistant along the corridor. 'My family came over from Spain in the 1930s, during the Spanish Civil War.'

'Only you don't have Latin looks.'

'Mum is English. Her genes made a bigger splash in the pool.' Well, why not pull the odd leg or two? This media lark is fun. He had caught a bad cold from that website interview but this is different. Besides, it's taking his mind off other things – Sally, looking for a new job, a lengthening overdraft. Time to forget all that. The campaign is gathering momentum. A news agency photographer took shots of him watching England's match against Cameroon in Italy. Of course, England weren't actually playing Cameroon in Italy. They were playing Slovenia in South Africa. However, as he vowed to do, Dan stood throughout the 90 minutes watching a DVD of the World Cup 1990 quarter-final. He's the first to admit England were a tad lucky to win 3-2. Cameroon were the better side. However, slack defending by the Africans resulted in two penalties, duly dispatched by Gary Lineker. England will play West Germany in the semi-final. As for their no. 19: it was 20 years ago today, Sergeant Gazza taught the band to play. What a star. Oh, to go back and be there when we were good. Where's a beat-up DeLorean and flux capacitor when you need them most?

Enterprisingly, the photographer had brought with him a pair of outlandish spectacles with palm-tree frames, beloved of Timmy Mallett. A clever move, this, with the TV presenter's *Wacaday* programme a huge hit in 1990. He had also brought a replica of Mallett's foam-rubber mallet. So there was Dan, in his Gazza shirt, banging the TV with the mallet, moaning about the 1990 price of fuel (41p a litre) and sounding off about That Bloody Woman – Prime Minister Margaret Thatcher. The pictures featured in the next day's Daily Mail and Express.

'They gave me a good idea,' says the researcher. She takes him into the studio's control room. A few minutes later, he enters the holy of holies, the studio itself.

Presenter Joe Newton reminds listeners of Dan's one-man protest during the World Cup, notably his debut as a retro Timmy Mallett.

'And, to get you in the mood,' he says, 'how about a few "oh yeahs" from the redoubtable Mr Mallett in a band called Bombalurina. Remember this?'

'She was afraid to come out of the locker
'She was as nervous as she could be
'She was afraid to come out of the locker
'She was afraid that somebody would see
'(Two, three, four, tell the people what she wore)
'It was an itsy bitsy teenie weenie yellow polka-dot bikini
'That she wore for the first time today (oh yeah)...'

'So....' Joe Newton spares his audience by talking over the track. '1990. Quite a year. The destruction of the Berlin Wall. Nelson Mandela walks free at last. 200,000 people protest against the Poll Tax. Channel Tunnel workers from the UK and France meet 40 metres beneath the English Channel. And, as far as today's guest is concerned, 4th July 1990, when England lost to West Germany on penalties, was the day the music – and football – died...'

'No, I'll have to correct you on that,' says Dan. 'The day the *music* died was 30th January 1969 in Savile Row.'

'Now then... don't tell me.' Joe puts up his hand. 'That... was... hang on... the day of the Beatles' rooftop concert.'

Dan nods.

'For one so young you seem obsessed by the past,' says Joe.

'Respectful not obsessed.'

'It's easy to look back through rose-tinted spectacles.'

'It's even easier to just accept what's placed in front of you. I struggle to find anyone of my own age who doesn't wish he'd been alive during the 60s.'

'And you run a covers band to prove the point.'

Dan nods.

'I'm told your lead singer is in the final of *Britain's Got Tribute*,' says Joe.

'Yeah… Sally.'

'Your girlfriend…'

Dan is wrong-footed. He wasn't expecting that. 'Well, no. That is… it's a long story.'

'*Right*. Well, we won't go into that.'

'I think she'll win.'

'Let's hope so. Meanwhile, you've been working on something of your own…'

Dan had been up for most of the night, recording and mixing his own version of the Euro 96 theme. All that training at the Liverpool Institute for the Performing Arts is about to pay off - at last.

'So, this is Football League Division One,' says Joe, 'and *Football's Going Wrong*.'

'*Sponsors on the shirt*

'*Where's their money going?*

'*Millions pouring in*

'*But the debts keep growing*

'*It's going wrong*

'*It's going wrong*

'*It's going…*

'*Football's going wrong.*'

The track fades.

'That was Football League Division-One and *Football's Going Wrong*,' says Joe. 'Ok, so, then Mr Division-One – if I gave you a magic wand, what would you most like to see happen to our national game?'

'Well, most of all, clubs run by their fans,' says Dan. 'There are strict qualifications for anyone who wants to play for a national team, be it football, cricket or whatever. If you've not been born here, you have to have lived here for a number of years. The fit and proper person test for club ownership should include whether the people buying a club actually support it. They should have to prove they've personally bought a season ticket for the past five seasons and produce the stubs to prove they've attended a minimum number of games – home and away.'

'That's unrealistic.'

'Not at all. Genuine supporter-owned clubs are what the majority of fans want to see. Winning trophies is of secondary importance. And I'm not just on about smaller clubs. Talk to fans of big clubs with silverware cabinets bursting at the seams. They're just as disillusioned. We can't change our loyalties in the way we choose supermarkets. The long-distance owners see us as mug punters: in the same way drug dealers consider their regulars to be junkies. They exploit us. Each club needs to be owned by its fans. That way, rich or poor, owner or occasional walk up, we are all hooked together.'

The interview plays out with another snatch of *Football's Going Wrong*. Dan leaves the studio. Already his phone is buzzing. And there's more to come. Next week's real match, England against Germany in South Africa, will be an excellent platform for the alternative match he and his friends will watch on video, from start to finish – *that* match: England v West Germany, July 4th 1990.

CHAPTER 60

Friday 11 December 1914

So much for being home by Christmas. Instead they've sent us in the opposite direction. They must have some raid planned against Fritz but they're not telling us what it's all about. As we got near the front we were met by an endless stream of horses, wagons, guns, limbers and ambulances. Dozens more were bogged and being dug out. I saw at least half a dozen dead horses, most of their bodies submerged. The ones still living were up to their bellies in mud, their wagon wheels to the hub. We branched off the road and walked along miles of duckboard. I say walked but much of the duckboard had sunk a foot or so beneath the mud. We slushed through what must have been, a matter of weeks ago, a large, quiet forest. Now it's just a mass of ragged stumps. There are many crude graves, too. The body has usually been carried to a shell hole and earth tossed over it. A few have a rough, wooden cross carrying the man's name and unit with 'KIA' and the date. One had a Liverpool rosette on the cross. He may have been at the cup final, up that tree next to us lot from Burnley. Who knows? Others have an old rifle stuck in the ground for a headstone. One had an old, upturned military boot, nothing more.

We heard the shrieking whistle and rushing air of a shell coming straight for us. We cowered to make ourselves as small as we could. I wanted to jump into a shell hole and take cover but the old soldiers moved on, head bowed, as if in a trance. The rest of us hid our fear by following them. Maybe the corporal could see my jaw quivering.

'First time?' he said.

I nodded.

'Give up thinking,' he said. 'If you don't, lad, your head will beat you, without any help from Fritz. The man who thinks is done for. You'll end up a jabbering wreck. Try to see the funny side of it all. You may not live any longer but you'll live a damn sight happier.'

We reached the trenches late in the evening. It was hard to believe hundreds of Fritz was just 70 yards away, over No Man's Land. We were told to find ourselves an empty dug-out. Each one is just a hole about five feet square cut into the wall of the trench. The roof is two sheets of old, rusty iron over which someone has shovelled an inch or two of mud. I went along the trench with Sangster and Tilling, pulling back the blankets that act as the dug-outs' doors. The dug-outs were full of sleeping men. We'd just about given up when we drew back yet another blanket and saw a man curled up in the corner. It is unusual to see a soldier on his own.

'This'll do,' said Tilling. 'If this lad budges up.' We started unloading our gear. Sangster lit a match.

'Bloody hell.' He held the match over the soldier's face. 'It's... it's only the bleedin' Padre. Pardon my language, sir, only I didn't expect... you know...'

Padre Brooks peered at us through the gloom, groggy with sleep.

'This is as close to hell as it gets,' he murmured. 'Don't apologise.'

'What are you doing here, sir?' said Sangster.

'I'm your Padre,' he said. 'What do you think I'm doing here?'

'No, sir, only... why are you... in this dug-out?'

'I repeat. I'm your Padre.'

What Sangster meant was that this wasn't the place for a Padre, not as far we understood it anyway.

'We'll leave you in peace,' said Tilling.

'Why?' he said. 'I haven't got a disease. Not yet, anyway. And more men mean less room for rats.'

Embarrassed, Tilling and Sangster apologised again and walked along the trench, looking for another dug-out. Maybe I felt it was my duty to stay with him. After all, we had had that conversation a few days earlier. Maybe I was just too tired to look for anywhere else. I loosened my boots and socks. They were sopping wet and thick with mud. I took off my uniform and folded it for a pillow. I didn't have any other boots or socks so I put them under the uniform. It's another important tip I've picked up: the heat of your head dries things while you're sleeping. Another trick is to turn your underpants inside out. It fools the body lice.

'I thought you'd be billeted further back, sir,' I said.

'I am, but unless I know what's going on here I can't be much good back there.' He rummaged around in a bag. 'Have a mince pie, with the compliments of the season and my wife, wherever she may be.'

A mince pie! I had chosen the right dug-out.

'I need...' I stuffed my mouth and attempted to talk at the same time, 'I need... to... befriend your wife.'

'So do I,' he said, quietly. It was an odd thing to say. 'Any news from Emily or Nellie?'

I was amazed he remembered their names. For another hour we talked or, at least, I talked and he just listened. It was embarrassing, come to think about it. I told him things I'd never told anyone. I know Catholics like confessing but it's never been my way. I wouldn't dream of telling Whitehead anything about my life. Padre Brooks pretty much knows the whole of mine.

'By the way, what's your wife's name?' I said.

'Clemmie,' he replied.

'Do you have any children?'

'No.' There was a difficult silence. 'It hasn't been for the want of trying. Clemmie would make a wonderful mother.'

'She can certainly bake.' I wasn't sure what to say next.

'You would think,' he said, 'that a stupid war like this would put pressure on a relationship. For us, Clemmie not conceiving is a far bigger problem. Coming out here has actually eased the tension.'

'Ma always hoped I'd have a brother or sister,' I said. 'She lost a few before and after me. I was the only one who made it across No Man's Land.'

316

He grinned. 'Before I forget, I have something for you.' As he rummaged around again, a German sniper had a go at someone along the trench. There was a sharp ping as a bullet ricocheted off the blade of a spade, maybe 10 or 15 yards away. 'Here's Harris.'

Believe it or not, he had located one of the three cigarette cards I was after.

'It's too dark to see it in here but it's in very good nick, straight out of the packet,' he said. 'I've put the feelers out for Bamford and Lindley.'

I was made up. Not about the card itself, that wasn't the point. I was dead chuffed he had remembered me and what I had told him about Emily and Nellie. He snores, too. Loudly. Enough, I reckon, to make the odd rat think twice about joining us.

CHAPTER 61

'Hi, I'm Colin, photographer from The Sun.'

'Yeah, we were expecting you.' Dan invites him into Tadworth Terry's hall.

'I believe you're running some sort of campaign against the current England team,' says Colin.

'No, no, no.' Dan closes the front door and shakes his head. He had made it clear enough to the paper's reporter on the phone. 'The campaign is against modern football and the decline of the England team. They coincide.'

'Oh, right.'

Dan leads Colin into Terry's dedicated TV room. It's more like a cinema, with a data projector in the ceiling and drop-down white screen that takes up an entire wall. There are no armchairs. In the middle of the room is a horizontal wooden pole, supported at both ends by two more upright poles tied firmly together. Terry and Wretched lean on the horizontal pole, beers in hand.

'Fancy a pint?' says Terry.

Colin shakes his head. 'Nice offer but I've got another job down the road after this. So... you've turned the room into a football terrace?'

'Like the good old days,' says Wretched. 'It takes you right back.' Dan has his Gazza shirt on, of course. Wretched is sporting a yellow, Peter Shilton goalkeeper jersey from the same era. Terry is in a surprisingly dapper grey suit and striped red and blue tie.

'It's the nearest I could get to what Bobby Robson was wearing in

Turin,' he tells Colin. 'Robson was a real gentleman, one of the old school.'

'And you'll be standing throughout the game?' says Colin. They all nod.

'Until West Germany win on penalties,' says Dan. He studies his beer: British Bulldog, a local heady brew. 'A few more of these and we may be able to adjust history, of course.'

'They're all barmy,' shouts Terry's wife Denise from the hall.

'And that's why we want them in the paper.' Colin checks the settings on his camera. 'Loved the Timmy Mallett angle, by the way.'

'Thanks,' says Dan.

'The Mail and the Express did you proud.'

Dan nods.

'So this is the first time you've done a photo call with your own terracing?' Colin takes a test photo.

'We're campaigning for safe standing areas at football grounds,' says Dan. 'All-seaters are lifeless...'

'...and, ironically, more dangerous,' says Terry.

'The way you've set up the terracing is great,' says Colin. 'They'll love it on the desk.' His mobile rings. 'Hi... I'm at the house now... Oh... Right... OK... I'll see what I can do.' He finishes the call. 'Just received more instructions.' He glances at his watch. 'I'll need to get on with it because they're very keen. In fact, the story may go up on the web within a couple of hours.'

After taking a few group shots from all angles, Colin asks Dan to put an image on the screen. It is that iconic moment when Paul Gascoigne breaks down in tears after being booked.

'Right,' he says. 'Can I have one of you on your own Dan, holding your pint and sobbing into your shirt, like Gazza? The picture desk want you looking really fed up, like you've just been booked and will miss the final... yeah... that's good.' He changes the angle and takes several more. 'OK, really depressed now... hold that... great... OK...' He checks the images. 'That will do nicely. I have to get these over pronto.'

'Do I need to talk to anyone at the paper?' says Dan.

319

Colin shakes his head. 'They've got all they want.' He gathers up his equipment. 'Good luck with your campaign. You've certainly got the knack when it comes to getting coverage. Ever thought of going into PR?' He shakes three hands and leaves for his next job. Terry and Wretched toast Dan. It's another national paper in the bag. He's getting good at this.

'Right,' says Wretched. 'They're about to kick off in Bloemfontein. Time to go to Turin.'

'Would you want you to be Chris Waddle now?' says John Motson.

Those fateful words.

Up steps Waddle, another World Cup Geordie. He fires the ball goalwards. Japanese scientists have since confirmed that the football found inside the Hayabusa probe after its seven-year space trip was his penalty attempt.

'And that, my friends, was that.' Dan hits the standby button and takes a final swig of British Bulldog. In spite of his disaffection with the football authorities, he is desperate to know how England got on in Bloemfontein. Maybe, just maybe, they've pulled off a shock victory.

'Lost 4-1,' calls out Denise in that disinterested, give-a-damn way of hers. Dan slumps into an armchair. 4-1. Against Germany. Nothing short of a national humiliation. He turns on the TV and is still mystified at why everyone in the stadium, except the referee and linesmen, saw Frank Lampard's shot cross the line. His phone buzzes. It's an out-of-the-blue text from Eric Kelly (aka Captain Bintastic).

'*Sorry to read about your problems. You two had a good thing going. Trust you will sort things out.*'

What is he on about? Probably meant to send the text to someone else. Dan shrugs his shoulders. Another text arrives almost immediately, this time from his father. He rarely phones and *never* sends texts.

'*Bastards, the lot of them. I'd keep well clear of the media.*'

Something is going on. Something he doesn't know about. The last time he got this sinking feeling was up in Blackpool. It can't have anything to with the campaign, surely. He opens up The Sun online.

Oh dear God...

I only want to be with Stu

SINGING sensation Mustbe Springfield, tipped to win next week's final of *Britain's Got Tribute*, has DUMPED her long-time boyfriend for the top TV producer who discovered her.

The 22-year-old from Godstone, Surrey, who has wowed the judges with Dusty's greatest hits, like 'I Just Don't Know What To Do With Myself', seemed to know EXACTLY what she wanted to do with 32-year-old Stuart Bensham at an elite London nightclub earlier this week.

It's a dream come true for the student teacher who, just a few weeks ago, was plain Sally Cavender, fronting an obscure 60s tribute band.

'All Sally needed was a break,' said a close friend of the couple. 'She got it when Stu spotted her in a Battersea pub, singing to a crowd of less than 50. All that has changed. Stu has some great plans for her. If she wins the final, she'll have the world at her feet.'

A recording contract is guaranteed for the winner and a promotional tour of the UK in prestigious venues.

Meanwhile, it was jilted boyfriend Dan Howell's turn to be in the middle of nowhere, drowning his sorrows during England's 4-1 humiliation at the hands of Germany. Looking tired and emotional, Howell, 23, sported a no.19 shirt – a replica of the one worn by Paul Gascoigne when he famously broke down in tears during England's defeat to Germany at Italia 90.

There are two pictures with the story. At the top of the page is Sally, arm outstretched in classic Dusty pose, looking magnificent under stage spotlights. The other, further down the page and much smaller, is of him – pint of beer in hand, downbeat and depressed. In fact, he looks a complete fucking loser. It is all he can do to stop himself hurling his expensive, uninsured iPhone at the wall.

'They couldn't even get my surname right,' he says.

'Shocking.' Terry shakes his head.

'There's no mention of the campaign against modern football or my new name...'

'Terrible,' says Wretched.

'...or the real reason why I'm standing in front of Gazza.'

'Have to say, Sally looks damn hot, though,' says Terry. Wretched leans over his ipad and nods.

'And that's a clever headline – I only want to be with Stu,' he says.

'In the middle of nowhere,' says Terry. 'Brilliant.' They both laugh.

'Oh, thanks,' says Dan. 'That is *really* helping.'

Terry and Wretched look at each other ruefully and murmur a half-hearted apology.

'I'm not running a tribute band,' says Dan. 'We do covers. There's a big difference.'

Terry and Wretched aren't aware of the big difference but are sure their friend is right.

'I mean... you'd think that this "obscure" little band was Sally's,' says Dan, 'and that it's folded now the "big star" has left.'

'Are you still doing gigs?' says Wretched.

'That's not the friggin' point, is it?' Dan stares at his friend.

'Only asking,' says Wretched, sheepishly.

'It's all very disappointing,' says Terry. 'We went to a lot of trouble, setting everything up and they didn't even use a pic of the three of us.'

Dan looks at him, incredulously. 'Tell me you're joking.'

'Well, I've never been in a national paper,' says Terry. 'It would have been fun, that's all.'

'You're totally missing the point,' says Dan. 'This is shocking journalism. It makes me look a complete dickhead.' Terry and Wretched stare at the floor. 'I mean, who is this "close friend of the couple" exactly?'

His phone rings. It's his mother.

'You've seen it, too, then,' he says.

'Seen what?' she says.

'The story in The Sun.'

'I've no idea what you're on about. I'm phoning about your Nanna. I think you should come home. She's had some bad news.'

CHAPTER 62

Tuesday 15 December 1914

Today I lined up behind the lads, ready to go over the top. I stood my stretcher upright and did what the corporal said I should do. I didn't think.

I didn't think about the smell of human excrement, rotting flesh and chloride of lime that is all around us, all the time. I didn't think about the burst of German machine gun bullets about to go phut, phut, phut into the mud, or the soothing hum of others, whistling inches over our heads. As we waited and waited, I didn't think about the lad second from the front, sickly pale, who clenched and unclenched his fists before heaving up all over his boots. I didn't think about losing my footing in knee-high mud, trying to stretcher a man with his leg blown off; or how he may die of shock from a sudden jolt. I didn't give a passing thought about getting tangled up in barbed wire near Fritz's trench, or dwell on the way the wire clings to you like a desperate lover, satisfied only when a sniper's bullet whispers you into sweet nothing.

'Penny for your thoughts,' said the lad in front.

'Don't have any,' I said.

He looked at me and my stretcher.

'Blimey, it's the Grim Reaper's cousin.' He smiled and took a long, nervous drag on his cigarette. I smiled back but my legs were like lead weights holding down a body about to float away.

'Our father, who art in heaven…' began Padre Brooks. I wanted to run. Like the wind. Anywhere. Even if I did, the end would be the same. I would be shot at dawn by our own guns. But I swear it was only because my legs wouldn't obey me that I stayed put.

Don't think, the corporal had said. Don't think. Don't think. In a distant dream I heard the whistle blow. The first men went over. One slipped. At least, I thought he had. He slid back down the trench wall, head split clean in two, from the crown to the top of the nose. An axe blade couldn't have done a better job than that German bullet. He quivered in front of me. Our first fatality and I wasn't even out of the trench. Now I had no time to think. There were calls for bearers to help the injured. We had to leave the poor bugger, still twitching and jerking.

We climbed out of the trench to the chut-chut of an enemy machine gun. Thirty yards ahead, a soldier flopped into a kneeling position, as if receiving bread and wine at church, then slowly rolled over. A second man reeled sideways and took a few staggering steps before toppling, face first, into the mud.

We reached another with a knee smashed and shattered by a bullet. Like all the lads he carried his own dressing and was busy trying to stem the bleeding. Blood gushed through his fingers. He grimaced with pain but nodded towards another soldier a few yards away.

'Never mind me,' he said. 'I haven't finished an argument with that cockney bastard over there. Go on.' He waved us angrily towards his pal. All we could see was a pair of boots, sticking out of a shell hole. I'm learning. When it really counts, in the white heat of battle, it's always pals before self. The cockney was unconscious when we reached him. He had a massive chest wound. The pool of water in the shell hole was only a few inches deep but he was slipping down slowly and would have drowned in minutes. We took him on the stretcher, past the soldier with a shattered knee.

'Typical,' he said. 'The lucky git's bagged a Blighty. Watch 'em patch me up and send me out here again next week.'

We carried the cockney over the rump of a half-buried body.

It gave a little to the heavy pressure of our boots. Whoever it was had probably been there for weeks. Chances are it won't be his final resting place, either. The poor sod will be thrown up and reburied by shellfire several times.

We brought back a number of men to the dressing station but no-one is sure whether the attack was successful or not. If you measure it by the number of good men lost, it was a failure. But, as they keep on telling us, we're in a war. This was just one battle along the way. It was the last for a few of us, though. After the shelling died down, we dug a row of shallow graves. Next to each grave was a dead soldier, sometimes only pieces of him. A few were sewn up in blankets. Others lay in muddy uniforms, waiting for a shallow tomb. Padre Brooks arrived and we stood to attention. The first body was lowered into a grave, if that's what you could call it. The Padre read a few Bible verses and said a short prayer. Then, before the first shovel of earth, the dead soldier's best pal chucked a cigarette on the body and hung his head in grief. One or two others did the same. That choked me up, good and proper.

After the last man was laid to rest, we trooped slowly back to our dugouts, all of us thinking the same thing. Who'll be next? Someone tapped me on the shoulder.

'Daws, isn't it?' I'd not spoken to the lad before though I'd seen him at the far end of the trench. 'Only, I was chatting to the Padre earlier about your collection of cigarette cards. You just got lucky, pal.'

He gave me Lindley, straight out of the packet, in perfect nick. You know what? Christmas must be just round the corner.

CHAPTER 63

'Suddenly and peacefully... last night... you were to be told first, then his two sons and his daughter... he stressed that many times.'

Nanna puts down the phone. Dafydd had given staff at the nursing home strict instructions, it seems. Typical of him: organised and efficient. He remained in control, even beyond his last breath. Perhaps, without knowing it himself, he had hung on for years for that reunion. Another meeting may have been a bridge too far. Now he could depart in peace. She is not sure whether to feel sad or relieved. She weeps silently – for Dafydd and for herself. Why couldn't he take her with him? What good can she do, sitting here day after day? She can only be a burden. She looks again at the envelope. Without Dafydd Broderick coming back into her life she would never have had the courage to go through with this. She thanks him through tears that fall like besetting Welsh rain. He was right – as always. It's time she knew the truth.

A couple of hours later, Dan is on a train to London. He is in the Quiet Zone (no mobile phones allowed) and stands cheek by jowl with dozens of frazzled commuters. They are always in their own quiet zone, to the point of comatose. Though the weather is dull and overcast he sports a brand new pair of Ray-bans, just in case. *Are you that jilted Dan feller from The Sun? Nah, some mistake.* In his breast pocket is a key in an envelope. Nanna has given him details of a safe deposit box. She has no idea what is inside. Wads of used notes?

Stolen jewellery? Brink's-Mat gold bullion? Class A drugs? Well, you never know.

The crowded train jerks out of Clapham Junction. His phone vibrates. He is pressed up close to a young Australian back-packer wearing a skimpy pair of frayed shorts and an Arlo Guthrie t-shirt. Arlo Guthrie! What does she know about that folk-singing genius? She feels the vibration, too. She giggles. He apologises. She says there's no need. He is about to ask her about that t-shirt when he checks the screen. It's Sally. *Now? Here?* The Quiet Zone of a crowded train is not the place. He gets off at Victoria and, while commuters and attractive backpacker swarm into London, walks to the deserted end of the platform.

'Jilted fucking Dan returning your call,' he says.

'I didn't phone for a fight,' says Sally.

'Of course not, you'd lose.'

'I don't blame you for being angry. I had no idea they were going to run that story.'

'Oh, come on. You told them you only want to be with dickhead.'

'It's a headline.'

'But you said it.'

'Of course I didn't. Where am I quoted? It's just a play on words.'

'Who's the "close friend" then?'

'Dan, you *know* that's the bit they make up. Look, I'm sorry about the article. I was so angry that I phoned the reporter. He told me they cut his story down. The bit about your protest got dropped.'

'Bollocks. The photographer got instructions to take that pic of me looking depressed. They knew *exactly* what they were doing.'

There is a brief silence.

'Well… all I can say is I wish it hadn't happened,' says Sally. 'I would never set you up like that. You still mean a lot to me, Dan.'

'Yeah, well… not enough it seems.'

A pigeon flutters down from the station's rafters and lands a yard away. Dan resists the urge to kick it halfway back to Clapham Junction.

'Nanna phoned,' says Sally. 'She told me about Dafydd.'

'Yeah, that was a bit of a shock. She's very emotional.'

'You've gone up to London for her?'

'I'm on my way to the bank now.'

'You're doing the right thing. She needs to know.'

'Know what?'

'What's in that box.'

'I have no idea what this is all about.'

'I think we all need to know... and Dan...' There is a long pause, so long that, at one point, Dan thinks he's lost connection. 'Dan... there's... there's something else I need to talk to you about...'

A train draws into Platform 18. It is several seconds before Dan can find a spot away from the noise.

'What's that, Sals?' But she has gone.

'Howard? Is your name Dan Howard?' says the bank clerk. 'And you've come to open Box 728?'

Dan nods. He removes his Ray-bans and puts them on the desk. He should be safe enough here. The clerk seems strangely excited when he pulls out proof of his old identity (the new one would be too confusing).

'Great Scott!' His accent has turned mid-Atlantic. 'Actually a bunch of us guys here were kind of hoping maybe you could shed some light on what's in that box. You see, we've had it in our possession for almost a hundred years.'

'OK, OK, I get it. Very good.' Dan laughs. '*Back to the Future II*... virtually the final scene.'

'Marty is marooned in 1955.'

'And the De Lorean has been struck by lightning in mid-air.'

'Correct. Transporting the Doc to 1885.'

'Car headlights appear in the pouring rain.'

'And... and out steps the man from, what was it now?'

'Western something.'

'Western Union.'

'That's right. He says: "We had a little bet as to whether this Marty would actually be here..."'

329

'Looks like I lost!' they say together.

'Man, I love those films,' says the clerk.

'Me too,' says Dan. 'Watch 'em over and over.'

'And box 728, in the name of Rhoslyn Cadogan, is a Marty. That's what we call one that hasn't been opened for so long, anyone connected with it must be dead.'

'Or in 1885, by mistake.'

'Or yet to be born. No, that's more Star Trek.'

'Well, you've been very patient all these years.' Dan takes the key from the envelope. 'But I'm here at last, on behalf of my dear old Welsh grandmother.'

'OK, that's great,' says the clerk. 'It's nice to meet you.' They shake hands. 'The boxes are kept in the basement of another of our banks, a couple of blocks away. I'll take you there.'

'Which road is it in?' says Dan.

'Road?' The clerk picks up Dan's Ray-bans. 'Where we're going, we don't need...' He dons the shades '...roads.'

CHAPTER 64

Christmas Eve 1914

What with the rain we've had, the trenches are knee-high in mud and water. One way of dealing with it is to wrap your legs in sandbags up to your thighs. It keeps out the damp but makes your legs heavy, as one lad found out the other day. He got both feet stuck solid in sludge. He was due to cook for an officer and already late. To move himself, he had to get on all fours but then his arms disappeared below the mud, too. He was trapped like a fly on flypaper.

'For Gawd's sake, shoot me,' he said. 'Put me out of my misery.' I'm telling you now, it made our day. We laughed till we ached. That's how it is here. In between raids, shells and snipers, you have to find things to laugh at, or you'd go mad. Keeping this journal helps me cope. I never thought a war could be boring but we're stuck here, in more ways than one. So is Fritz. With Christmas in the air, you can't help wondering what he's doing over there. The same wind freezes his skin. The same rain pours on his head. After a heavy shower you can hear him sloshing around, cussing and coughing as he bales out the trench, just like us.

The other night, someone must have left an empty bottle on top of our trench, by mistake. After breakfast next day, we came under fire from a sniper (we don't shoot at each other while the bacon's frying, that's how it works). Fritz wasn't interested in any of us, mind, only the bottle. His pals cheered when he hit it. They even rang a bell and shouted 'again', in English! That night we put out another bottle. Fritz put one up for us. At least they can see the funny side of things. Before the war I was told every German soldier was hell-bent on spiking babies on the end of bayonets, cutting out women's tongues and hanging priests as clappers for bells. Me, I'm not of the mind Fritz is a monster. Both of us wanted to come in, do a job and get out again, that's the army way. Trouble is, neither of us will budge and we've ended up as noisy neighbours.

Had a delivery of letters and parcels today. If Father Christmas himself had dropped them off, we couldn't have been happier. Inside were things like Oxo, Horlicks, Bovril, sweets, cakes, mufflers, socks, scarves, tobacco - simple stuff which make all the difference when you're living in a field. The food and clothing came from Ma and her friends who clubbed together to pay for it all. Nellie sent me a parcel. 'Inside is what I was going to give you before you went away,' said a note that came with it. Inside was a brand new harmonica, the very latest type. It's a beauty. I got a Christmas card from Emily and a bottle of rum. It makes me feel even worse about what happened on that Sunday.

The mood round here has changed for the better. The mud has hardened and the pools frozen. Snow fell this morning and turned the copses into Christmas trees. Then the sun came out and we put some holly along the trenches. Mind you, this festive mood has irked the top brass. 'You're here to defend democracy not polish off plum puddings,' we've been told. They reckon Fritz will catch us off guard if we relax, even for a second. To be fair, you can see why they're worried. There's been a lot of laughter along the trenches on both sides, what with so much beer being put away. If Fritz had raided us today, we might have been in trouble but hardly a shot has been fired by either side. No-one can be bothered. It makes you wonder what would happen if they ever declared a war and no-one turned up.

I'm still sharing a dug-out with Padre Brooks. I offered him some of Emily's rum and we got through the bottle soon enough. I told him how bad I was feeling about Emily and Nellie.

'Tomorrow's untouched,' he said. 'And the day after that. And the day after that. You've a long life stretched out in front of you, full of twists and turns.'

'I'd like to meet your Clemmie,' I said.

He smiled. 'You two would have a lot in common. She's for ever writing, as well. Children's bedtime stories, mainly.' He went quiet. I didn't know what to say, either.

I have no idea if anyone will ever read what I am about to write next. I am sure no-one will believe it if they do...

At about eight o'clock this evening, not long after I finished writing the entry above, I heard a harmonica in the distance. Someone really knew how to play it, too. Someone shouted: 'Look at what old Fritz is up to.' We peered through our letterboxes, as we call them (observation slits is the proper name). We could hardly believe what we saw: dozens and dozens of Christmas trees with lights, lanterns and torches on the German parapets, left and right, as far as the eye could see. In a matter of minutes, this churned up Belgian field had become a theatrical stage with footlights. The harmonica was coming from their side and they were singing *O Tannenbaum*, a German carol. Well, we cheered and clapped, I can tell you.

'Quick, Dawsie,' said Tilling. 'Fetch yours. Let's give 'em one in return.' So, thanks to Nellie, we sang:

'The first Noel, the angels did say

'Was to certain poor soldiers in fields as they lay...'

Fritz cheered when we'd finished. 'Komradd Tommy, Merry Christmas,' they shouted.

Padre Brooks was conducting a service for our troops several miles away and as no-one else knew any German, we just shouted back: 'Komradd Fritz, Merry Christmas to you too.' They clapped. We sang *Christians, Awake* and they sang *Adeste Fidelis*. Then their harmonica player started *Silent Night*. It's my favourite carol. I began dueting with him, adding harmonies.

A 'Sshhhhhh....' travelled along the German line. Everyone on both sides stopped singing and listened to us play. You could have heard the safety pin of a hand grenade drop in the mud.

'Komradd Tommy,' came a single voice. 'Together! Play!' And with that the German harmonica player stood up and, still playing *Silent Night*, walked towards us over No Man's Land. On any other day he would have been shot dead instantly but our lads, shocked at first, cheered and clapped him every step of the way.

It was at this moment that the corporal's advice kicked in at last. I didn't think. Before anyone could pull me back I was up and over the top like a jack-in-a-box. Of course, it could have been a trap. The moon was bright and I was an easy target but I didn't care. I felt outside myself, as if it wasn't really me on the field playing that harmonica. You should have heard Fritz cheer when they saw me. We met in the middle of No Man's Land, by the humps of two dead soldiers. Considering we didn't know each other and had never played together before, it wasn't a bad effort. Then everyone joined in again, from both sides, singing their hearts out.

'Silent night, Holy night
'All is calm, all is bright
'Round yon Virgin Mother and Child
'Holy Infant so tender and mild
'Sleep in Heavenly peace
'Sleep in Heavenly peace...'

At the end of the carol, Fritz held up his harmonica and shook my hand. 'Komradd Tommy, Merry Christmas. You play good.'

'Komradd Fritz, Merry Christmas,' I said. 'You play better than me.' I have no idea if he understood but we slapped each other on the back and hugged each other. Then the dam burst. Soldiers from both sides poured onto the field, holding lanterns and candles, laughing and singing. It was like being in a football crowd when a last-minute winner goes in. Our lads gave out bully beef, Tickler's jams, chocolate, rum and cigarettes. Fritz offered us sweets, nuts, sausages, coffee, cognac, wine and cigars. You could see those cigars and cigarettes being lit all over. Fritz struck a match for Tommy, Tommy for Fritz. German cigars smell good, too. Quite a few Fritz speak English, enough to get by anyway. Soon enough, out came photographs of wives, girlfriends and children. In spite of what we've been told, not one Fritz I saw has six fingers or an extra head. They look like us, very ordinary.

At times like these you want something to take back home, to prove it really happened. One of our lads went for some wire-clippers and we snipped the badges and buttons off our uniforms and did a swap. Another of our lads gave away his jack-knife for one of Fritz's spiked helmets. Chuffed, they were, both lads.

We must have been out there for well over an hour. One by one we drifted back, still laughing and singing. Three lads were so drunk they went the wrong way and wandered close to the German line. Some decent Fritz piggy-backed them to within yards of our trenches. Our lads, so drunk they couldn't stand up, were singing *Three German Officers Crossed the Line*. To be honest, we held our breath. The words are so nasty they could start a war on their own. The truce may have been over as soon as it had begun. As they got closer we realised they had changed the words.

'*Three German officers carried us yon, parlez vous*
'*Three German officers carried us yon, parlez vous*
'*Three German officers carried us yon*
'*We'll shoot to miss them from now on*
'*Inky pinky parlez vous.*'

It picks up exactly how we all felt and we joined in with them. Mind you, if our lads had seen the German trenches, they would have been taken prisoner, I'm told. Some rules can't be bent, no matter what time of year it may be.

As we settled in for the night, a message came round, from the top. It had taken a while to get through. '*On no account must there be any fraternising with the enemy.*' We all laughed. An old man with a white beard has spread a little magic round a torn-up turnip field tonight. I can't wait for tomorrow. I think he might have another gift or two left in his sack.

CHAPTER 65

Nanna quiz hops – *15 to 1, Countdown, Weakest Link* – all repeats of repeats. She's seen the whole lot before. In between shows, a succession of glitzy trailers for tonight's final of *Britain's Got Tribute*. Sally is up against some strange-sounding acts: 50 Years After, Real 69, Repeater Frampton and Crosby, Stills, Nash and Not-So-Young. Nanna has no idea of the original acts, let alone the tributes. She sighs. Sally had become a friend, an unexpected one, before this wretched competition. They have hardly talked since she reached the final.

'Lines of longitude on a map are called meridians,' says the quiz show presenter. 'What term is used for lines of latitude?'

'Parallels,' says Nanna, half asleep. They didn't get it last time. Or the time before that.

'In English law, what is deemed to be the first priority for payment from the estate of the deceased person?'

'Funeral expenses,' murmurs Nanna. This seemingly innocuous question will be followed in the break by an advert for Co-Operative Funeral Services. Nanna shakes her head. Daytime TV is a none-too-subtle exploitation of the old and vulnerable. She remembers Dafydd and hopes he left enough in the pot for a good send-off. She bemoans her frailty. How can you feel like the morning after when you've done nothing the night before?

The doorbell rings. Dan is due back from London but has a front door key so it can't be him. She doesn't attempt to get up. She never opens the door to strangers. In any case, visitors usually give up before she reaches the hall. Another ring, followed by an insistent knock. Perhaps Dan had forgotten his key. Whoever it is seems determined. Now the telephone rings.

'Nanna,' says a familiar voice. 'I'm outside your house.'

'Sally? Here? Oh, well... of course... give me a minute or two...' Nanna hauls herself upright, steadies herself and shuffles slowly to the front door. Sally is the last person she expected to see. It's the final tonight. Surely she should be warming up, or whatever they do.

'This a nice surprise, I...' Nanna opens the door but Sally's head is bowed. She is crying. 'Now then...'

'I... I didn't know where else to go.'

'My dear.' Nanna shuts the door behind her.

'I'm sorry to just turn up like this.'

'Don't apologise.' She hugs her guest in the hall.

'I quit the competition.'

'You've... *quit?*'

'A couple of hours ago, during final rehearsals. It's a long story.'

'Well, I'm not going anywhere.'

'I need to tell someone what's going on. And it really has to be you, Nanna. Can I make you some tea?'

Twenty minutes later, Nanna squeezes half a cup more from the teapot and reflects. Most of what Sally has said makes sense. Being in Dan's band had been a bit of fun and a good way of earning a few bob to supplement her student loan, that's all. Dan, though, had always seen the band as a personal mission to save music from itself. She had no plans to be a serious singer until that night in Battersea when this Stuart (whatever she said his surname was) heard her perform. She was flattered by his interest. That was all it was, honestly. But Dan's 'other obsession' (the air quotes said it all) and revelations about the two Geordies (how was she to know they weren't true at the time?) had tipped her over the edge. She was hurt. She was angry. She's not a tart. The thing with Stuart, it just happened. It was a reaction. Can Nanna see her point? Can she understand?

'I'm not sure why it matters what I think,' says Nanna.

'Because… I need you to affirm me.'

'I don't know why.'

'Nor do I. It's bloody annoying.'

'And I'm struggling to understand why you walked out of the competition.'

'It got too much.' Sally shakes her head. 'I was being sick. Dan thinks it's like John Lennon.'

'Lennon?'

'He used to get stage fright.'

'You seemed to be having a ball.'

'Believe me, behind the scenes it's Three Dog Night eats Three Dog Night.'

'It's *what?*'

'I'm being obtuse.'

'Oh, well, this Stuart…'

'He begged me not to give up.'

'Of course he would.'

'He says it's blown any chance of having a career in music.'

'And any chance he had of making money from it.'

'You think he's exploiting me?'

'It's one possibility.'

'Dan thinks so.'

'He would. He's hurt and angry.'

'Well, I'm not *so* naïve as to think Stu might not have an ulterior motive. That's why I didn't respond when he first came on to me.'

Nanna studies her visitor. 'But you relented.'

'He wore me down and… and then I found out about those whores in Newcastle.'

'And this Stuart, he made you feel a star.'

Sally nods. 'And then you start to notice things. Music consumes him, like football consumes Dan. If I couldn't sing, I'm not sure he would give me a second look. To cap it all, I caught him messing about with one of the dancers.'

'Oh, I see. That complicates matters.'

'It would be a little *less* complicated if the dancer had been female.'

'Ah...'

'You would think that settles it but... it's not that simple.' Sally puts her head in her hands. 'You see...'

A front door key rattles in the lock.

'I've got the package, Nanna,' calls Dan from downstairs. 'It doesn't *feel* very interesting.' He climbs the stairs and walks into Nanna's room. '*Sally!* What the hell are you doing here?'

Nanna sips from a glass. It's one of her own, made of top quality cut glass – the kind that, when empty, rings like a bell when you flick it with a finger. She's getting quite attached to what's inside: Cragganmore. There again, she's earned it. That was a difficult piece of emotional navigation. Dan and Sally are downstairs. Maybe hostilities have eased, if not entirely ceased. They certainly don't need any further interference from a batty old nonagenarian (she had lost count how many times that word had been an answer on quiz shows). She shakes the parcel. It had been professionally sealed and clearly marked 'Only to be opened by Rhoslyn'. Immense and deep hardly do justice to both the gulp of whisky and the breath she takes before breaking the seal. Dan will be disappointed. No drugs. No money. No jewellery. Instead she discovers an old journal, child's school exercise book, a few old letters, a fountain pen, a football programme and a harmonica.

'Thought there was something weird about him.' Dan finds it impossible to conceal his delight.

'I can hardly expect you to be sympathetic,' says Sally.

'Actually, I'm offended.'

'By what?'

'That he fancied you and not me.'

'I think he did have something going for you, looking back. He was probably lining up a three-way.'

Dan grimaces. 'You must have had your suspicions.'

'Not for a minute.'

'So what did he say when you found the two of them?'

'He was ice cool, completely unfazed. It was as if *I* was the one with the problem, *I* needed enlightening. He said we should discuss it after the show, like adults.'

'His favourite phrase.'

'I almost puked up on the spot. Of course, when he realised I was walking out of the show he came over all contrite. He said he was under pressure and was acting out of character. He begged me to stay.'

'And the first person you wanted to see was an aging grandmother from the Welsh valleys who doesn't know Procol Harum from Percy Sledge.'

'And that's her genius.' Sally shakes her head. 'She's coming from somewhere else. Somewhere I need to be.'

Dan sits back in his armchair and puts his hands behind his head, failing to disguise his anxiety. 'Where does this leave you and me?'

'I don't know,' says Sally. 'It's complicated because... look, the thing is...'

They both hear slow footsteps descending the stairs. The door edges open.

'Dan... Sally,' says a frail but excited voice. 'I think you'll want to see this...'

CHAPTER 66

Christmas Day 1914

Well, so much for a festive truce. So much for last night's back-slapping. And you can forget Christmas Day being 'the season of peace and goodwill to all men'. It was blood and thunder out there this afternoon, a real war with no quarter asked for or given. The battle went our way, then theirs and the result was in doubt until the very last minute. Fraternising with the enemy? That was the last thing on our minds. The generals, probably tucking into their turkey at the time, would have been proud of us.

After what happened last night the day started peacefully enough. A layer of frost made everything look seasonal and for once we didn't have to put up with squelching mud. An early fog meant we could only just make out the German trenches, though they're a few dozen yards away at most. Then the sun came out. For once there were no planes overhead, observation balloons, bombs, rifle fire. For once you could hear the birds sing. I fed a few crumbs to some sparrows. A couple of our officers agreed with Fritz that we should 'suspend hostilities' (the official phrase) and bury our dead. Some of the men had been lying in No Man's Land for more than six weeks. It may sound hard to believe but we held the service together with the enemy. Side by side, we were. Padre Brooks did the prayers and readings and even spoke in German. I can't begin to tell you how strange we all felt. It didn't matter which body was laid to rest, Fritz or Tommy, we all knew this war was a waste of lives and for what, exactly? We'd all like to know.

After the service we did some more swaps in No Man's Land. Out came the rum and chocolate, sausages and cigarettes. I played more tunes on the harmonica. As I played *The Bells of Hell Go Ting-a-Ling-a-Ling*, Fritz pulled out 10 balls from his trench coat pockets. Then someone found him a football and he did more tricks with that. His friend told us he was a professional juggler and, before the war, performed all over Europe. He's the best I've ever seen. Padre Brooks watched him, too and started chatting to several Fritz. They shook his hand, nodded and went back to their trenches. A couple of minutes later one of them returned with four pointed helmets. I thought he was about to swap them for a penknife or two. Not this time. He dropped one on the ground, measured six strides and put down the other. He then gave the other two helmets to Padre Brooks.

'Here,' said the Padre, throwing me a helmet. 'Help me measure out our goal. It isn't much of a pitch, with the shell holes and what have you, but who cares?'

'You don't really think…' I began.

'Why not? You'll play, won't you?'

'Of course, but all that stuff about fraternising with Fritz. If this gets back…'

'It will.'

'And?'

'I'll take the rap.' He did some stretching exercises between the helmets, the kind you see goalkeepers do all the time. A group of our lads saw what was going on and demanded to join in. We had a full team in no time. So did Fritz.

'Your friend Billy was a bit of a prophet,' said the Padre. I must have looked puzzled. 'You are about to play for England.'

I laughed.

'You said you want to be a reporter, too,' he went on. 'Why not write up the match and send it to one of the Burnley papers? Unless, of course, they already have someone at the game.'

So here it is, my own summary of England versus Germany, with a little help from Padre Brooks who found out the names of the German players for me. I've tried to write it like they do back home. I don't know if it's any good. A copy is already on its way to the papers. Well, you never know.

For King and for Kaiser! That was the cry from a small but vocal crowd as an England XI took on a Germany XI in a hastily-arranged fixture on Christmas Day.

Decaying turnips, rutted mud and half a dozen shell holes failed to deter the two sides, though regulation army boots meant pretty footwork wasn't on display. In spite of this, both sides were determined give their supporters something to cheer about.

The first to advance were Germany but the England team repelled the attack with great determination. Then it was England's turn to go on the offensive. From a lofted cross on the right, centre forward Selby headed them into the lead.

By now several players had warmed up enough to dispense with their overcoats. A pass from Germany's right half Eisenberg found centre forward Bergmann. Still in full army clothes, Garwood, England's centre half, failed to catch up with the speedy Bergmann who slotted the ball past goal-keeper Brooks. Within two minutes Germany had gone into the lead, Schulze heading powerfully home from a corner.

The game was held up for ten minutes while players from both sides chased several hares that had come to see what all the fuss was about. Four were caught and the spoils shared. It seemed the right point at which to declare half-time. The usual cup of strong tea was replaced by festive cognac and rum, something the keener players weren't too happy about.

As the second half got underway, England pressed hard, only to be met by keen resistance from the German defence, notably goal-keeper Werner. He made fine saves from Anderson, Harvey and May but could do nothing to prevent a goal from Greenfield. It followed a pass from Daws that split open the German defence. It was now 2-2 and there was everything to play for.

With two minutes left, Germany won a corner on the left. Maher floated over a cross that Brooks failed to hold. In the resulting melee, with army boots flying in all directions, the ball squirted up and fell towards goal. Brooks palmed it away. Had the ball already crossed the line? No-one was sure. Without a linesman to decide, the question was put to the crowd. After heated debate the goal was awarded: 3-2 to Germany.

England threw men forward but failed to trouble Werner in the German goal before time was called. Several players on both sides remain unconvinced that Germany's third goal was legitimate so it has been decided a return match will be played in due course.

Padre Brooks insisted I mention his mistake. He also said I should include my pass for our second goal. After the match, the Germans' right back tapped me on the shoulder.

'A grand pass, that. Got time for a quick bevvy?' The accent was pure Burnley. 'Your goalie said I should make myself known.' He put out his hand. 'Wolfgang Bauer.'

'But… how come…?' I began.

'My mum's from Nelson.'

'That's just up the road.'

'Aye.'

'And you're fighting for the Hun?'

'My dad's from Cologne. I had to spin a coin.'

'And tomorrow we'll try and shoot each other dead.'

'Pointless, eh? Especially when we both watched our team win the FA Cup.'

'You mean…'

'I was there. I hadn't missed a home game in three years until this daft war. I hear you collect cigarette cards…'

We shared our memories of that day at the Palace and swapped addresses. We even had our Christmas dinner together in No Man's Land. We've promised to meet up after the war and go to a game or two at Turf Moor. I am looking forward to that.

I'm still finding it hard to believe all this happened. As I write, there's still a party mood up and down the trenches. The songs have only just begun to die down on both sides. What a day! I wouldn't have missed Christmas in Belgium for all the plum puddings in England. I will remember it for the rest of my life. I can't wait to tell Ma and Pa, Emily, Nellie, Billy, in fact anyone who'll listen. I just can't wait.

CHAPTER 67

'I can't wait to tell Ma and Pa, Emily, Nellie, Billy, in fact anyone who'll listen. I just can't wait.'

Dan has been reading extracts from Tom's two journals to Nanna and Sally for more than an hour, during which the final of *Britain's Got Tribute* has gone out live across the nation. The 50" plasma TV with built-in 2D to 3D converter with added depth of 3D, lies silent.

'Nanna, I'm... I'm amazed.' Dan shakes his head. 'You never told us your father kept goal in that match, of *all* matches. He's a total ledge. This football thing. It goes back a long way, then. Never fancied myself as a keeper, mind. Why have you never mentioned this before?'

'I didn't know anything about it.'

'So who told you about the deposit box?'

'My father.'

'And he didn't tell you about the match.'

Nanna shakes her head. 'Most of the people who survived the war tried to forget it completely. They wanted to get on with their lives, as if it had never happened.'

'I still don't understand,' says Dan. 'I mean, what did this Tom feller do after the war? How come your father kept his journal?'

'He didn't. Here.' Nanna hands him three letters, hand-written in pen and ink.

26 December 1914

Dear Tom

I thought I would drop a line or two to my new friend, just a few turnips away. Somehow I'll have to find a way to smuggle the letter out as it is addressed to 'the enemy'. It is hard to believe you are the enemy after the fun of yesterday! There will be arguments for years to come, as to whether the ball crossed the line for our winning goal. There'll be plenty of time to talk about it when we meet for a beer before the first game of next season.

I am writing now because, in all the swapping of presents, we got many a packet of Woodbines over here. I am the only Fritz this side of the fußballplatz (it means football pitch, that's what we're all calling No Man's Land now) who collects cigarette cards of English players! Anyway, it wasn't long before I was given the one enclosed. I think Bamford completes your Burnley set.

Until next season at Turf Moor!
Your friendly Fritz
Wolfgang

3 January 1915

Dear Private Daws

Thank you for your report of the extraordinary football match between the British and German armies on Christmas Day. It is extremely well written and I am delighted you thought to send it to the Post for publication.

I should mention that accounts of this remarkable event have begun to appear in several newspapers, though there is no consistency to the information. Some suggest the match was a free-for-all, with up to 30 on each side. In others, an old tin, even a tied up sandbag, were apparently used for a ball. I trust you will appreciate that, until we verify the information you sent us, we cannot publish your report.

However, your account is so well written that, without hesitation, I would like to harness your undoubted skills here at the Post. When you are next on home leave, please make an appointment to meet me. If you are interested and available, we would like you to train as a member of our team of sports writers.

Believe me to be
Yours most sincerely
Alfred Miller
Editor
Burnley Post

4 January 1914

Dear Mr Daws

It is my painful duty to inform you that a report has been received from the War Office notifying the death of Pte Thomas Daws. His death was that of a soldier and a brave man, but fortunately it was painless as he was killed instantly. Unfortunately it was impossible to get his remains away and he lies in a soldier's grave where he fell. I and the C.O. and all the Company deeply sympathise with you in your loss.

Your son did his duty and now has given his life for his country. We all honour him and I trust you will feel some consolation in remembering this.

I am, Sir, your obedient servant
Robert M. Armstrong
Officer in charge of records

Dan gropes for the right words.

'That's just so... so *sad.*' They are nowhere near adequate enough to express his emotions.

Sally grasps Nanna's hand. It is trembling.

'I'm sorry it ended like that,' she says. 'Tom had so much to look forward to.'

'So what happened to Emily and Nellie?' says Dan.

'I had no idea about any of this until a few minutes ago,' says Nanna. 'My father said there was something about our family history in a safe deposit box in London. That's all. I was free to go and get it at any time. It was up to me.' She pauses. 'I just didn't want to know what was in the box.'

'You thought it must be scandalous…'

Nanna hesitates. 'Sometimes there are things you're best not knowing.'

'But why did your father put them in a safe?'

'He didn't. Emily did.'

'Emily? I don't understand.'

Dan's mobile phone bursts into life. Against the subdued mood of the room, the tune is crass and insistent.

'Is that, er, Football league Division-One aka Dan Howard?' says a man's voice.

'Who wants him?'

'I work on the news desk of the Daily Mail. Your one-man campaign against modern football, we're all very impressed here. Who does your PR?'

'The clue is in the one-man campaign.'

'That's even more impressive. Got a couple of minutes?'

'I'm busy right now.'

'Rumours are flying around. We need to get our facts right.'

Dan laughs. 'You lot never let facts get in the way of a good story.'

'I understand you and Sally Cavender were an item.'

'That's got nothing to do with you.'

'Her manager is putting it around that she pulled out of tonight's final on medical advice.'

'Medical advice? What did he say is wrong with her?' Dan glances at Sally.

'It was precautionary, owing to her pregnancy.'

'Her *what?*' Dan laughs. 'Oh, that's good. I've heard it all now. When will you ever give it a rest?'

'It's what her manager said.'

Dan shakes his head. 'You're being stitched up, mate. Sally's decision to quit humiliated Bensham. He'll try anything to save face.'

'Then you'll appreciate why we need to get hold of Sally. Her mobile is switched off.'

Dan mutes the phone. 'You won't believe this, Sals. It's the Mail. Apparently Stu is putting it about that you're knocked up. Shall I tell him to get lost?'

Sally looks at the floor. 'I've... been trying to tell you both for several days,' she says, weakly. 'I never had the courage to come out with it. I'm sorry.'

'Oh, my dear.' Nanna clasps Sally's hand.

'Oh my God,' says Dan. 'How long have you known?'

'A few weeks.'

'Why didn't you...?'

'Get rid?' Sally looks up sharply.

'You really want to have that bastard's offspring?'

'I can't believe you said that.' It is barely a whisper. 'It's my child, too.'

'Daniel... Daniel...' Nanna holds up a hand. 'Don't let your shock do the talking.' She squeezes Sally's hand. 'No wonder you were feeling under the weather. Have you seen your doctor?'

Sally nods. 'She told me my stress levels are way over the limit. I may lose the baby.'

Dan prowls. 'But... but you were on the pill.'

'So it's all my fault?'

'I wouldn't say that.'

'You'd think it, though.'

'Sals, this need never have happened.'

'That's how you see it?'

'Bensham has screwed it up for all of us.'

'It's that simple...'

'There's no other way of looking at it.'

Sally shakes her head. 'As usual, Dan, you've pole vaulted to conclusions. At least I know how you feel. I'd better level with the Mail.' She takes Dan's phone and leaves the room.

'Recriminations aren't going to help,' says Nanna. 'Sally has to be your first priority.'

'Try telling Bensham that.'

'Ah, forget him.'

'I hate the swine. I've hit him once. Next time, he's going down for good.'

'And that will solve everything.'

'I don't understand. Why didn't she…?'

'That's how you all think, isn't it?'

'She had everything going for her.'

'Nothing must stand in your way.'

'A career opportunity like this, it doesn't come round too often.'

'Conceiving a child, it's neither here nor there in the grand scheme of important things.'

'Nanna, she had plenty of time to do that later.'

'So get rid and order another when you're ready.'

'But… she's not in the right frame of mind to have a child.'

'Few are, even if they've waited 20 years.'

'You think I'm heartless.'

'I think you're a child of your time. You've been given the right to choose. You don't need to accept the consequences of your actions.'

'But I didn't have anything to do with it.' Dan prowls round the room, unable to settle. 'And there was me thinking she was channelling Lennon.' He looks around the house but Sally has left.

'I… I haven't been entirely fair with you myself,' says Nanna, slowly. 'I need to explain what this is all about.'

'I'm not with you, Nanna.'

She points to the journal. 'There is more.'

CHAPTER 68

The Journal of Emily Bettridge

Saturday 21 November 1914 – Well, it's hard to believe but now *I've* started a journal!!! Me!! Expelled a few months ago for refusing to pick up a pen in class!! I blame Daws' boy and, no matter what he thinks, I will liberally spread exclamation marks around these pages, thank you!! Tom (he's been in Belgium for two weeks now) thinks they should be used 'sparingly'. Not me! Anyway, Tom says, if things aren't going your way, writing it down makes you feel better. There's only one way to find out. I've mentioned Tom three times already. That's four!!! Heavens, this is my diary, not his!

It seemed like we were at the factory for ever today. They're stepping up production. There's a rush order for some nasty-looking equipment and we're working round the clock to meet the deadline. Oh, and Walter found a white feather in an anonymous letter. Serves him right!

Friday 27 November 1914 – Tom can't write to me as everyone would ask who the letter is from. So, as I left for work today, I asked Daws if she had heard from him. It was the first time I had approached her. Any earlier may have given the game away. She was polishing furniture in the hall.

'Good morning, ma'am,' she said.

'Good morning, Daws,' I replied. Written down like that it looks disrespectful, calling her by her surname. Yet that's who she is and always has been to me. I would get some very strange looks if I called her Mrs Daws. As for her Christian name: I haven't a clue what it is! 'Any news of your, er, son?' I asked nonchalantly. She stopped polishing and looked at me closely.

'He's in Belgium. That's about all we know, ma'am.' She carried on with her work. It was as much as she was going to tell me.

'You must be very proud,' I said.

'Aye, we are that but we want him home safe and sound.'

'Of course. When's his next leave?' I was risking it but I couldn't help myself. She gave me a long look.

'We hoped he would be back before Christmas but it will be January now,' she said. 'It seems the two armies are digging in for the long haul. Beats me what it's all about.'

'If you're writing, send him my regards.'

'I will, ma'am.'

I'm sure she won't. Perhaps she knows more than I think. I changed the subject. 'Walter has found another white feather in his Bible.'

'Oh dear.'

'He'll keep on getting them until he joins up.'

'That's unfortunate.'

'Well, I think it would do him good!' I think it would, too. In fact, if we win this war it will be down to women in the factories as much as men at the front. For the first time we're working on building sites, cleaning windows, driving vans, unloading coal wagons, stoking furnaces and building ships – unthinkable six months ago. Everyone, man or woman, rich or poor, is expected to pull their weight, including indolent brothers!!!

Sunday 29 November 1914 – Went to the park with Nellie and Brutus this afternoon. It may sound strange but Nellie and I really need each other. She is the only person I can talk to about you-know-who. When he comes back I am sure the two of them will pick up wherever they left off. They would be perfect together, though it pains me to admit it. Everyone reckons they will be married within the year.

'I really should be hating you, Emily, but I can't,' she said today. 'You're the only one who understands.' I have tried hard to dislike Nellie, too, but it's impossible. She's quite lovely. Autumn leaves were piled high on the path round the lake. We gathered them up in huge handfuls and threw them over each other, like confetti.

'Tom adores you. I haven't a chance,' she said. I told her not to be silly and that she and Tom were made for each other. She just shook her head.

'I envy you,' I said.

'*You* envy *me*?' She stopped dead in her tracks.

'People approve of you. I'm the spoiled little rich girl with a bee in her bonnet. They like to tut-tut about me.'

'We'll swap, if you like.'

'Oh, I know I'm ruined but sometimes I'd like to fit in, like you do.'

Nellie shook her head. 'I am exactly what Tom doesn't want. I have clogs. You have wings. I don't have your kind of confidence, taking on the law like that.'

'You did pretty well impersonating me!'

'True. That was fun.' She put her arm in mine. 'Perhaps we'll both lose out. Perhaps he'll meet a Belgian farmer's daughter!'

'And never see Tommy Boyle play again? Hardly!!!'

'That's who he ought to marry.'

'Tommy Boyle? Mr Daws is definitely not that way inclined,' I said. 'Mind you, at one time he thought I wasn't… *normal*… if you know what I mean.'

She nodded. 'I hoped he was right.'

'What… you mean…?'

'No, I don't like you that much.'

We both giggled.

'Look, Nellie.' I stopped us both on the path. 'Why don't you two just live happily ever after?' I offered her my hand in surrender.

'Now *you're* being silly.' She refused to take it and walked on.

'But you're so right,' I said, catching her up. 'I'm liable to fly off somewhere at less than a moment's notice. Tom needs someone he can depend on. I'm not ready. I can't even depend on myself.'

Nellie said I was confused and anxious and would soon change my mind. She may be right but I'm sure the kindest thing I can do is let Tom go.

Thursday 3 December 1914 – There are many ways to rid yourself of an unwanted pregnancy, so they say. Swigging a large glass of gin and taking a hot bath is one. There again, riding a horse may shake the baby loose. You can always throw yourself down the stairs but you may get rid of more than the baby. If you want to take the superstitious route, walking over the grave of someone who committed suicide works too, I'm told.

I've never been late before. This month I'm more than ten days over. I never imagined for a minute I would find myself in this position. I'm scared. I haven't slept properly for more than a week. At the factory they've been asking me if anything's wrong. The worst thing is not being able to tell anyone the truth.

Saturday 5 December 1914 – I told Nellie today. I thought long and hard about whether it was fair but there's no-one else I can trust.

She stared at the ground in shock. 'You're really sure?'

I nodded. We were sitting on a park bench. Nellie was quiet for an eternity.

'Was it that Sunday morning?' she whispered, at last. I nodded again. 'I can't say it doesn't hurt.'

'I hadn't seen Tom for so long and…'

'You don't have to explain.' She was sobbing, gently.

'But I want to.'

'I'd rather you didn't.'

'I'm to blame, not Tom.'

'It takes two to tango.'

'He was going to war. It just happened.'

She shot a reproachful glance at me. 'It *never* just *happens.*'

'No, no… you're right. I caught him at a weak moment. I'm not proud.'

Brutus tugged on my leg, growled and barked impatiently. We

began walking home, as slowly as possible.

'Do your parents know?' said Nellie.

I shook my head. 'They'll arrange for some shady character to get rid of it. A bastard under the Bettridges' roof would be far too humiliating.'

I explained to Nellie that, if they find out Tom is the father, they'll sack Daws and send me far away, before anything shows and anyone knows.

'Are you going to tell Tom?' she asked.

'Not until he gets home,' I replied. 'He has enough to worry about without news like this.'

I watched Nellie trudge home, hands buried deep in her coat pockets, head bowed. I have never felt so wretched. And, sorry Tom, but writing it all down hasn't helped one little bit.

Wednesday 9 December 1914 – I've made up my mind. I'm going to deal with this myself. I'm leaving tomorrow morning, before light. My bags are packed under the bed. It's not exactly out of character and I'm sure I won't be missed. Some suffragettes in Huddersfield are taking me in. Dozens of young girls have been left unexpected gifts by departing soldiers, so I'm told! They've even found me work. I'll do that until Tom returns. I'm not sure how he will react. He might disown me. I can't prove it's his baby, after all. What a mess.

Thursday 10 December 1914 – It was still dark when I came downstairs this morning. Daws had just arrived. No-one else was awake. We stumbled into each other in the kitchen.

'Off somewhere nice, ma'am?' She lit a lamp and took off her coat.

'Shhhh,' I said, pointing upstairs.

'Oh, I see. Mum's the word!'

'Yes, yes… you're right. Mum's the word!' The phrase caught me off guard. I hugged her. I've never done that before. It really isn't the done thing, embracing a cleaner like that! She was shocked but hugged me back. There was something so familiar about her. To my surprise, I started to cry.

'Whatever's the matter, ma'am?' she said. Of course I couldn't say, though I wanted to tell her everything. I wanted tell her that she'll soon have a grandson to be proud of as well as her soldier son. I wanted to tell her that, unlike his mother, he will be ridiculously gifted and hate exclamation marks. I wanted to tell her that his mother is foolish and headstrong but, in spite of this, she will try to be a good one. Her eyes were warm and compassionate like her son's. She tilted her head in just the same way. It was uncanny and comforting. Given the chance, I knew she would look after my son with all the strength in her stout little body. I wanted to tell her that Tom shouldn't be so selfish, that I needed her to be my mother as well. I wanted her to hold me, for ever.

'I'm sorry,' I said. 'I can't explain.'

'You could always try,' she said, softly.

I shook my head. 'Take no notice of me. I'm highly strung. That's what they all say.'

'Never mind what they all say,' she said. 'I think we both know someone who would love you even if all your strings snapped in half.'

Well, that did it. I was inconsolable. She wrapped her arms round me as if I were her very own.

'Can I ask you something?' I grabbed a handkerchief and tried to pull myself together.

'Of course, ma'am.'

'What is your first name?'

'My... *first name?*'

'Yes.'

'Well, most people call me Rose,' she said. 'Though I was christened...'

I heard a movement upstairs and couldn't wait for the full answer. I gave her a final hug, grabbed my bags and walked quickly through the back door without looking back. I didn't dare.

Monday 14 December 1914 – Started work at a bank in Huddersfield today. Most of the staff are women and new at the job like me. I've always been quite good with numbers so this suits me. The authorities will probably discover where I am but it won't be for some time. All that matters to them right now is winning this war!

Decorations are going up in town, though news from the front means the mood is sombre. Nellie has promised to write and tell me if she hears anything from Tom. I've sent him a card and some best rum. It will be a very strange Christmas.

Christmas Day 1914 – Went to the usual Christmas Eve service last night. It doesn't matter where you are, it is always nine carols and nine readings. A pregnant, unmarried girl in a strange town: that rings some bells!!! It may sound blasphemous but I wonder if, like me, Mary seriously considered walking over the grave of someone who had lost all hope.

Friday 8 January 1915 – I was surprised to see a man in a clerical collar walk up the garden path this afternoon. I was shocked when he asked for me.

'My name is Brooks, Ernest Brooks.' He offered his hand in greeting. 'I've heard a lot about you, Miss Bettridge.'

'How did you know where…?'

'Nellie Williams.'

'I don't understand.'

'I'm afraid I have some bad news.'

He explained he was a Padre in Tom's regiment and read me a letter sent to Tom's father. *'It is my painful duty to inform you…'* They were the eight words I dreaded. My head began to spin. I thought I was going to be sick. *'Death was instantaneous and Pte. Daws did not suffer.'*

'I wanted to tell you that he truly and honestly died instantly,' said the Padre. 'I was a matter of yards away.' The letter continued: *'Unfortunately it was impossible to get his remains away and he lies in a soldier's grave where he fell.'*

'You mean… he's still out there, in pieces?' I said. It was more of a whisper.

'I'm afraid so.'

'Oh God, no.'

'I'm sorry to bring you this news but I didn't want you to hear by letter. I made it my personal mission to tell you in person. I had great affection for young Tom. He was a special person and I know he loved you. His death doesn't make sense.' He folded the letter. 'This whole war doesn't make sense.'

Maybe it was the shock but something snapped inside me.

'Next time you have a cosy little goodnight chat with the Almighty,' I said, 'ask him what sense there is in allowing one perfectly decent human to be blown to kingdom come while another comes into the world who wasn't even asked for. It's so utterly, completely... *pointless!*'

What happened next I will always regret. I hit him. I hit him hard, maybe four or five times. He took each blow without retaliation.

'I could tell you a tale or two about you and your lot.' I kicked him, too, I'm ashamed to say. 'Hypocrites, all of you. You set yourselves up as guardians of our moral well-being and then prey on young girls. You're monsters. You can go to hell, for all I care.' I ripped off his clerical collar and threw it on the floor.

'If only Clemmie had done that.' He said it more to himself than anything.

'Clemmie? Who's Clemmie?'

'You are not the only one to have committed an indiscretion, Miss Bettridge,' he said, quietly. 'A young lady I had loved and lost before I met my wife, came back into my life. Clemmie and I had been married several years but had drifted apart when she couldn't conceive. She had been suspicious for months before I finally told her of the affair. She should have done what you just did. I wish she had. I deserved it. Instead, she just wept.'

We were still in the porch. He looked a pitiful sight.

'I... I think you ought to come in,' I said. 'I've behaved dreadfully. I'm so sorry.' He waved away my apology. 'You say you knew Tom.' I closed the door behind us. 'I need to know everything.'

Shirt ripped and collar in pieces, Padre Brooks stayed for the rest of the day. It seems he met Tom at a football match and shared a dug-out with him at the front. He explained how a truce had been called over Christmas and that Tom played a duet on the harmonica with the enemy!!! He showed me a letter to Tom from a German soldier. He had another, from the editor of the Burnley Post, inviting Tom to train as a sports reporter.

'This is just too sad.' I'm not ashamed to say I wept and wept. 'It's all he ever wanted.'

'Please keep the letters.'

'But they're addressed to Tom and his father.'

'They wanted me to keep them.'

He asked me how I had met Tom. I told him that I discovered a shy lad in our hall one afternoon. I told him I had been pitifully rude and arrogant to Daws' boy who had only come into the house to help a distressed dog. I told him I had made the poor lad stay, plying him with brandy. I told him about our meetings in the summerhouse, the train ride to London, climbing the tree at the Crystal Palace, getting arrested, going on the run and that last Sunday morning together.

He sat and listened. That's all. Eventually, when I had exhausted myself, he told me more about his own 'indiscretion', how Clemmie is only just beginning to trust him again. I have never known a man of the cloth admit failings. I'm not sure what to make of it all. Just before he left, he dug deep into his travelling bag and pulled out two journals.

'Tom asked me to give you these if something happened to him,' he said. 'The first one was hidden below the floorboards in his bedroom. I asked his mother if I could be alone up there, to pay my last respects.'

'So she hasn't seen it? Oh.' I began flicking through the pages. 'I don't believe it. It's all here... everything that happened between us. It's all here.'

I want to sleep but I can't. When I close my eyes all I can see is Tom's remains, shattered and scattered round a Belgian turnip field. The painful truth has risen with the sun. I do not have the means to bring up a child on my own. After Padre Brooks left I hovered at the top of the stairs, wondering if I had the guts to do it. I could ride bareback on a thousand wild stallions, jump up and down on a thousand graves and still end up giving birth to a child. Maybe I should simply go home and be sent to some shifty little back street. It will all be over in a few short hours...

Friday 20 August 1915 – 'You're sure this is the place you want, love?' said the cabbie, helping me down.

'It's the only address I have.'

'Are they expecting you?'

'No.'

'Well, good luck.'

I stood at the end of a long drive that led to a large and foreboding detached house. Next to the house was a chapel and beside that, a graveyard. In one corner, earth was piled high from a freshly-dug grave. I had never been anywhere near this place before. Quaking in my boots, I walked up the drive and knocked hard on the door. A face appeared, fleetingly, at an upstairs window. Moments later, the door opened a few, hesitant inches. Behind it, a woman said something in Welsh.

'I'm sorry, I don't know the language,' I said. 'Am I talking to Mrs Brooks?' She nodded. 'I know your husband, Padre Brooks.'

'He's not here, I'm afraid.' Her Welsh accent lilted softly. She began closing the door.

'I know.' I stepped forward. 'I've come to see you, Clemmie.'

She was surprised I knew her name. 'Well, I'm not sure who...' She looked at the little bundle I was holding. 'If you need help, there's a club for young mothers on Tuesday afternoons.'

'Your husband was kind enough to visit me after the baby's father died in Belgium. My name is Emily. Emily Bettridge.'

Clemmie looked me up and down. She was just as Padre Brooks had described with skin like marble and penetrating brown eyes. She's also much too thin. A puff of wind would blow her away. 'You're the one who ripped his shirt and collar in Huddersfield.'

I nodded. She opened the door a little wider.

'I understand how you must have felt, hearing such awful news and, besides, I hate clerical collars.' She invited me into the hall. The smell, perhaps aroma would be a better word, was instantly familiar. She uses the same beeswax polish as Daws.

'You've not travelled all the way from Huddersfield, surely?' She led me into a large drawing room.

'I stayed overnight in Bristol.'

'Why ever didn't you say you were coming?'

'I didn't know myself, until the last minute.' And I really, really didn't!

'What about the little one?'

'She's fast asleep.'

'Not surprisingly, after that journey! She looks delightful. May I hold her?'

'Of course.' I handed her my baby.

'How old is she?'

'Seventeen days.'

'Is that all? My! What's her name?'

I hesitated. 'She doesn't have one.'

'Oh, I see. You can't decide?'

'No. It's just that... it's not up to me.'

'Oh.'

'It's up to you.'

'Me?'

I nodded. I tried hard not to show that I was trembling from head to foot.

'I don't understand.' Clemmie gave me back the baby and grasped my hand. 'Are you sure you're all right?'

'I'm fine.' I hoped she couldn't see my jaw quivering.

'I don't think you are. Perhaps you should begin at the beginning and tell me why you're here.'

'... but it was when I read Tom's Belgium journal that I realised what I had to do.' By this time I had taken Clemmie through the whole story. She had listened patiently. I showed her Tom's entry about the way she wrote children's stories but was not able to have a child of her own. It was at this point I knew my baby was to be hers.

She welled up. 'But... I can't just take her from you.'

'Why not?'

'She's yours.'

'I cannot raise her. She needs a loving family. I cannot give her that.'

'Your parents are wealthy.'

'And when they find out the name of the father, this little girl's grandmother will get sacked. And *she* isn't wealthy. I can't let that happen, not when she's just lost her only son in the war.'

'But, but... Ernest and I. We're not ready for this.'

'Clemmie, you've been ready for years and years.'

She wept. When I say wept I mean she simply sobbed her heart out. It was my turn to comfort her.

'How can you be so brave?' she kept saying, over and over.

I held her hand tightly. 'Knowing my baby would be safe with you is the only thing that has kept me going.'

'But... you'll want me to return her. I would find that impossible.'

'Of course I'll want her back, every day, but she will be yours. I will stay out of her life until she chooses to find out how she came into being, if she ever does. That must be a decision left only to Rose.' I hadn't meant to call her that. It just slipped out.

'Rose?' said Clemmie. 'So you *have* given her a name!'

'That's what I've called until now. It's an abbreviation of her grandmother's name. You must be free to choose your own. She is your daughter now.'

'Then Rose she shall be.'

'I never found out her grandmother's full name.'

'Ernest did,' said Clemmie. 'He mentioned it to me because it is also his sister's name.' Her face a river of warm tears, Clemmie picked up my baby again, carefully, reverently. Those tears splashed onto the baby's head like water at a baptism. 'Welcome to the family, Rhoslyn.'

CHAPTER 69

Dan closes Emily's journal. He grasps his grandmother's frail hand. She is too choked to speak. Her shrivelled body shudders with emotion.

'I don't know what to say, Nanna,' he says, at last. It is more of a whisper. 'I'm struggling to understand why you waited all this time to find out who brought you into this world.'

'Children call each other bastards in the playground,' says Nanna, slowly. 'I pretended I wasn't one.'

'And you kept the secret all these years.'

Nanna nods. 'I was lucky. My father's job meant we moved home regularly. Wherever we went, people assumed I was Ernest and Clemmie's daughter by birth. Only Dafydd knew the truth.'

Dan stands, sighs and walks to the window. 'And he told you that you would never be at peace until you found out where – and who – you had come from.'

Nanna nods again.

Dan watches the young woman who lives next door get out of her car, slowly, awkwardly. She is heavily pregnant. 'I couldn't spend my life wondering who my real parents were,' he says.

Nanna mutters something unintelligible in Welsh. 'You really don't get it, do you? Ernest *was* my father. Clemmie *was* my mother.'

'It depends how…'

'You've read the journal. If I had made contact with Emily it would have broken Clemmie's heart.' Nanna hesitates. 'Besides… I was unsure what I would find. Some stones are best left unturned.'

'So... my great grandparents weren't Welsh after all. Well, that's a relief.' Dan risks a grin. 'Mind you, Palace play a lot of teams up north. I'll have to think twice about the songs we sing at their fans.' He hands back the journals to Nanna who receives them with careful reverence. 'Poor Nellie, I wonder what she did after the war. I'd like to have met her, as well as Tom and Emily.'

'I think we have met them,' says Nanna. 'In those few months, they lived more passionately than most of us do in a lifetime.'

Dan nods. 'Emily must have longed for you to contact her.'

'Yes... yes, I'm sure she did.' Nanna bows her head. 'I'm sorry for her sake but it wasn't the right time to discover the truth – until now. Maybe I was brought into this world to re-unite two people who loved each other. Perhaps, before I leave it, I am to do the same again.' She looks up at her grandson. 'I can't help thinking these journals are for your benefit.'

'Mine?'

'God knows, Daniel, I hope Sally keeps her baby but I fear she may have, well... other plans.'

'Now you're just being melodramatic.'

'Am I? When you found out she was expecting a baby you were as good as telling her to jump up and down on a grave or two.'

'I... I didn't mean it like that. I was angry. She's made her bed with Bensham.' He throws an arm in the air, dismissively. 'She'll have to lie on it.'

Nanna glances at the green and yellow flowers on the cover of Tom's Belgian journal. The crayon, though faded, is still visible. Not for the first time she wonders what happened to Florinda, the journal's first author. 'Sally is right, you really do jump to conclusions. I watched her during that phone call. She was trying to gauge whether you were still there for her.'

'Nanna, she's having that bast... that, that... swine Bensham's kid. Anyone else and it would be different.'

'But you weren't reading between the lines.'

'Lines? What lines? You're talking in riddles.'

'Put yourself in Sally's shoes. She's been humiliated and is also very, very scared. She was trying to find out if you would stick with her, in spite of what's happened.'

'You mean… and raise someone else's child?'

Nanna says nothing. Instead, she runs a gnarled hand over the cover of Emily's journal.

'Oh no. I'm not having that.' Dan folds his arms in protest. 'This is a completely different situation. It's all Bensham's doing.'

'You're certain of that…'

'Of course.' Dan slumps into a chair and nods in the direction of the bottle next to his grandmother.

'A good idea. I'll join you, after I've…' Nanna points upstairs and hauls herself from the chair. Reeling from a succession of revelations, Dan, for once, takes no notice of the slow creak of the stairs, flatulence that resounds on cue and those careful, cautious steps descending to the living room. Clutching a small bag, Nanna drops into her chair like a lead weight.

'Figured it out yet?' She is breathless from exertion.

'Figured out what?'

'I have very little energy left in this body from one day to the next, Daniel. I am an imposition…'

'That's not true…'

'Of course it is. I should have done the decent thing and checked in at Golden Sands months ago. But while my body is decaying, my mind just won't ease up. You young things think nothing of travelling to the other end of the earth and back, sometimes between weekends. You talk endlessly to each other on these mobile phones and computer screens and what not. But you don't give yourselves enough time to reflect. There's always another voicemail to check, another message to respond to.' She reaches for the journals again. 'All Tom and Emily had were pen and paper but what they've left behind is worth more than a million text messages. Thinking things through is the one thing left I *can* do.' She pauses. 'And I've come to a conclusion about Sally.'

Dan looks quizzically at his grandmother.

'First…' She lifts an empty glass. Dan obeys. Of course, after her transfer from Neath, he simply humoured his ailing grandmother. She had, after all, been knocking on heaven's door even longer than Robert Zimmerman. Not now. When she speaks, he listens.

'Well?'

'This… Ben Sherman,' says Nanna.

'Bensham.'

'You seem convinced he's the baby's father.'

Dan looks hard at his grandmother. 'What are you trying to say? Sally wouldn't…'

'You're sure of that?'

'Of course.'

'And if someone else is the father?'

'Nanna, this is wild speculation.'

'Indulge me.'

Dan shrugs dismissively. 'It would depend who.'

'Should it, *really*?' Nanna studies her grandson. 'Do you still love Sally?'

Wrong-footed, Dan looks at the floor. He takes a deep, anxious breath. 'That's a huge question.'

'And a simple one.'

Dan clenches his fist. 'God knows, most of the time I wish I didn't… but when I first met Sally, in those boggy mountains of yours in North Wales, it was like I'd found my soul mate. Only it wasn't just soul, she's my rock 'n' roll, rhythm 'n' blues, big ballad mate – you name it, she delivers. She's too damn good, to be honest. I've always known someone like Bensham would come along and steal her.'

Nanna nods sympathetically. 'It reminds me of that entry in Tom's journal you read out earlier where Nellie says he scares her because her feelings for him are so deep…'

'That's it. That's exactly how I feel. Sometimes you're so terrified it will all go wrong that you have a kind of death wish on the relationship, that you might as well get the break up over and done with because it's going to happen sooner or later. And football is a kind of relief from that reality. It forces important issues to the back of your mind. Nothing else matters for 90 minutes.'

'But your fears are unfounded. I know Sally loves you.'

Dan shakes his head. 'It doesn't feel like that where I'm standing.'

'Well, take it from me as a woman. We sense these things. I'd put this whole, sorry Bensham business behind you and move on.'

'It's not that easy.'

'She made a mistake.'

'A big one.'

'And you're blameless…'

'No, but…'

'Then forget who was right or wrong. Someone you love is out there, all alone, making the biggest decision of her short life – whether to keep her unborn child or not. Does that remind you of anyone?'

Dan glances at the journals and smiles wryly. 'I have to say, she was quite a lady was our Emily. Once she got a bee in her bonnet… does that remind *you* of anyone?'

Nanna smiles. 'I've always used exclamation marks liberally, that's true.'

'Ha!' Dan stands and prowls round the room. 'You're asking an awful lot. This has come as an almighty shock.'

'I know, I know… it's been quite a day.' A short silence is punctuated by the cap of a bottle being unscrewed yet again, followed by the splash of sherried, 12-year-old single malt with a delicate, peppery spice in the finish. 'You may be shocked by what I am about to say but I'll take the risk.'

'I'm pretty much shocked out,' says Dan. 'You'll have to go some.'

Nanna drains her glass. She studies it, carefully. 'I honestly don't think Sally is sure *who* the father of her baby is.'

Dan stares at her. 'You're… you're joking, of course.' Nanna looks back at him, unflinchingly. 'You're not, are you?'

'I haven't finished…'

'How can you say that? You know Sally well enough. She's no tart.' Dan strides to the door. 'Honestly, you of all people, I'm surprised you'd suggest such a thing.'

'Another of your giant leaps for mankind.'

'It has to be Bensham.'

'Unless, of course…'

'Unless what?'

Nanna beckons her grandson to sit down again. He momentarily recalls the last time she admonished him like this. Aged seven, he polished off four helpings of chocolate gateaux, including his cousin Simon's, before escaping to the top of a sycamore tree in his grandmother's garden. He refused to come down all afternoon.

'You're right, this Benchmark fellow has to be the father,' says Nanna, quietly. 'Unless… I think we must consider an alternative.'

'Which is?'

'That the child is yours.'

Dan laughs incredulously. He points to her glass. 'What do they put in this stuff? Sally walked out on me before the match in Blackpool. There's no chance I'm…'

'You're sure of that? Here.' Nanna pulls a can of WD-40 from the bag in her hand. She tosses it to her grandson. 'Do the maths.'

Dan is the first to admit he has never quite mastered the difference between mean, mode and median; and percentile rank and platonic solids are concepts he struggles to penetrate. But simple addition? That kind of mathematics isn't beyond even him. He stares at the can.

'But… but why didn't she say so?'

'Because she was hoping against hope it wouldn't make any difference.'

CHAPTER 70

It is Wednesday 24 December 2014. A 45-seater coach rumbles to a halt in genial Belgian countryside. Through its rain-splattered windows are very few reminders of those four desperate, tragic years, when armies fought tooth and nail for every square inch of an unremarkable terrain. Tour guide Peter Ridley, for 25 years an army sergeant until taking early retirement, stands at the front of the coach and 'one-twos' into the microphone.

'Ladies and gentlemen and citizens of the free world.' He addresses every party in this way. He said it once, as a bit of fun and it just stuck. 'As you can see, the roads are particularly busy. I hardly need tell you why. Let's thank our lucky stars we weren't here a hundred years ago. Back then it took them four years to move half a mile.'

He's used the same script on every group for the past eight years. As he has explained to countless trainees, it's like being a singer with hits that are decades old. You've got to put feeling into them, even though you've performed them a million times before. A paying audience expects nothing less.

'In a few minutes we'll enter the walled city of Ypres, or Wipers as our boys used to call it,' says Peter. 'They even made up a song:

'Far, far from Wipers I long to be
'Where German snipers can't get at me
'Dark is my dugout, cold are my feet
'Waiting for whizz bangs to send me to sleep.'

The microphone is turned up high. Too high. His voice distorts.

Two elderly ladies in sensible cardigans, are startled awake. He turns down the microphone. 'Better?' The ladies thank him with a polite wave. 'The towers and spires ahead of us were reconstructed exactly as they had been before October 1914. I don't know what you think but, from a distance, we might be looking at a scene from the Middle Ages.' The odd head nods in agreement. The coach draws nearer Ypres. Roadside memorials and military cemetries sprawl in every direction. 'To our left and to our right are unmistakable signs of that long-gone conflict. I know there are several of you whose relatives fought in this area. We'll stop for a few moments to collect our thoughts and pay our respects.'

Several minutes later, the coach heads south. Well-tilled fields slope smoothly down to a shallow valley then lift gently to the modest ridge on which sit the quiet, uninspiring villages of Wytschaete and Messines.

'The Germans seized this ridge at the beginning of November 1914, after some intense fighting,' says Peter. 'So much for being home by Christmas!' Soon the grey-green mass of Ploegsteert Wood comes into sight. 'Our boys called it Plugstreet Wood. Many of you have read about the astonishing events exactly 100 years ago today. It was here where those truces took place.' The coach pulls to a halt. The driver turns off the ignition.

'We're going to take a brief walk,' says Peter, 'during which we'll see signs of old trench lines, most deep in leaf mould. It's been a long time. Look out, too, for an old concrete first aid post, too, with 'Blighty Hall' scratched on the lintel.'

More than 40 people step off the coach. An attractive woman in her 20s, holding a young boy of three maybe four, apologises that her partner or husband (Peter is never sure what to call them these days) is taking a phone call at the back of the coach. She looks vaguely familiar.

'An emergency at work,' she says.

'Serious?' asks Peter.

'One of his clients is all over the media. No-one else at the company is up to speed on the project. He's in PR.' She shrugs her shoulders.

A minute or two later the young man runs down the steps of the coach and rejoins the party. 'Sorry about that,' he says. 'I've turned off the phone. They can sort it out for themselves from now on.'

Peter gathers the party together. 'Many of you will have read stories of football matches on Christmas Day between the two armies. No-one really knows what happened but this is where one of those matches is said to have taken place. The score was 3-2 to Germany. As far as we know, it didn't go to penalties.' That one always makes them laugh.

The young man pulls out a football from his rucksack and kicks it in the direction of the small boy, standing on the grass. The boy catches the ball and holds it up triumphantly, to applause from the coach party.

'Good save,' says the boy's mother. 'Ernest Brooks would be proud of you.'

'Who?' asks Peter.

'Our little boy's great grandfather,' says the boy's mother. 'He was a goalkeeper.'

'Oh.'

The boy drops the ball and kicks it back.

'Good pass,' says the boy's father. 'A touch of Tom Daws.'

Peter turns his head, enquiringly.

'The boy's other great grandfather,' says his father. 'We were told by my grandmother that both of them played in the match here in 1914.'

'Well, I never...'

'Had she lived long enough, she would be here with us. We are paying her respects as well as ours. It was her last request.'

Egged on by the attention of so many adults, the young boy begins running with the ball. He falls, face first, into deep, gooey mud.

'Now *that* wasn't so good. Very Stuart Bensham.' The boy's father throws a look at his partner.

'Bensham. Now then, that name rings a bell,' says Peter.

'I doubt it.'

'Didn't he play inside right for one of the Midlands teams, back in the 60s? Not that the name will mean anything to you. It was well before your time.'

THE END

Acknowledgements

In 1914, like other lads of 16, my grandfather told the authorities he was two years older, so he could join up 'to teach Fritz a lesson or two'. In his breast pocket on the Western Front, Grandad kept tobacco, a New Testament and a love letter from my grandmother. It was just as well, or I wouldn't be here to have told this tale. Together, they took the impact of a German bullet, diverting the lead just enough to miss his heart by a quarter of an inch.

As a cheerful 70-year-old, he would recline in an armchair at his Sunbury-on-Thames prefab, singing snatches of obscure songs – songs I'd never heard before or since. When I asked him where they came from, he would throw another sweet-smelling line of Woodbine into a Rizla wrapper, lick the gum, and misty-eyed, say: 'They kept us going in the trenches'.

Grandad's recollections were a starting point for this story but there are many other people who provided inspiration. I should acknowledge seven books in particular: *To the Palace for the Cup* by Ian Bevan, Stuart Hibberd and Michael Gilbert (Replay Publishing); *Therapy* by David Lodge (Secker & Warburg); *Beastly Fury – the Strange Birth of British Football* by Richard Sanders (Bantam Books); *Juliet, Naked* by Nick Hornby (Penguin); *Rebel Girls – Their Fight for the Vote* by Jill Liddington (Virago); *Christmas Truce* by Malcolm Brown and Shirley Seaton (Pan Grand Strategy Series) and *Tommy Boyle Broken Hero* by Mike Smith (Grosvenor House Publishing). Mike's painstaking research into one of Burnley FC's greatest players provided vital, historical information for which I am greatly indebted.

While studying in London in the 70s, I will always be grateful to have met Rev Jonathan Woodhouse, QHC, Chaplain General of the armed forces; Dr Iwan Russell-Jones, Eugene and Jan Peterson Associate Professor of Theology and the Arts at Regent College, Vancouver and writer and designer Simon Jenkins, redoubtable captain of shipoffools. com, publisher of this title. Three friends, old and true, who steadied my hand on the tiller. Splice the mainbrace, me hearties. There is enough wind in our sails for still more voyages together.

Thanks must also go to a number of other good people extant: Paul Savoie for helping me dream up some fine tribute bands and surviving a sodden Glastonbudget; Kristy Thomson for not merging; Debbie Isitt for telling me to get on with it; Michael May, for ensuring I was Palace before I knew what football was; Bill Allen for talking adoption; Heather Savoie for talking addiction; Ali Hull for pointing me to Sol Stein; Ray Horowitz for reading and believing; Sam Goddard and Andy Nicholson for being Dan when I need them to be; Jog for getting it first time; Sarah Goddard for remaining devotedly red and blue whilst selling replica shirts at Everton FC; Geoff Sims for a great cover design; my father, Arthur, for giving in and taking me to my first football match (27/3/1963, Crystal Palace 0 Colchester Utd 1) and my wife Allison, for putting up with the ratter-tat-tat of a keyboard in the early hours. I must learn to go gentle into that good night.

Then there are those expired, who breathed life into my characters: Father Geoffrey Anketell Studdert Kennedy – better known as Woodbine Willie – the most influential British chaplain of WWI; Mair Russell-Jones, whose closest family had no idea about her key role during WWII until she was into her 90s (documented in Lion Publishing's *My Secret Life in Hut Six* by son Gethin) and Hugh Thomas, my father-in-law who, as a young lad in St Helens, really did walk 'Brutus' for a rich family up the road, slept in the same bed as his grandfather, went down the mines at 14 and was an official street messenger during WWII – though he was never given a message.

And then there's my late and loving mother. Grace was top of the class at English and won a place at grammar school but never got there because my grandparents couldn't afford to let her go. She believed I could write a lick or two – even when I didn't believe it myself. Mum, this book is for you.